DJINN

Max Overton

DJINN

DOUBLE DRAGON

A DOUBLE DRAGON PAPERBACK

ISBN 978-1-78695-599-9

Double Dragon
is an imprint of
Fiction4All

Published 2021
Fiction4All
www.fiction4all.com

Cover Art by Julie Napier

Prologue

I began with the rushing hydrocarbon wind that ascends through the rock from the shale beds far below, blasting through the sand and erupting in a vast conflagration of fire. I do not remember the act of creation that engendered me and my brothers and sisters of flame, but I have seen it many times since and believe it was the same for me. The ground trembles and a distant thunder draws ever closer; the rocks dancing and the sand thrown upward with the approach of the underground wind. Then the surface of the land lifts into the air, and the rocks and sand grains strike together so violently great currents of electricity form in the dry air. Lightning rips through the swirling mass. The explosion that envelops the desert sands is red, orange and yellow, concentrating into white brilliance in the centre with small pockets of the deepest blue here and there. When the flames that consume the uprushing gas die away, when the intense heat fades and the fused sand glimmers like glass; these cold smokeless blue flames remain and sentience stirs within them.

I have gone by many names over the countless years of my existence, but in the desert lands of my creation, I and my brothers and sisters of the smokeless fire are called djinn and are generally feared by members of that other creation – mankind. In those early days, of course, I had no knowledge of man or of anything else in the world about me, being little more than a blue flame tinged with green that burned in the lonely places. I was aware of self and a vast outer not self, but being new, I was concerned solely with self and for long ages gave little thought to what lay around me. What need had I of what was not me? After a long time, time measured not in days or even years but rather in the slow oscillation of the bright points of light that wheeled slowly in the sky above me. I turned my attention outward. Curiosity drove me, and I wondered that anything could truly exist that was not me.

I saw much and understood little, but gradually I was able to piece together facts, assimilate them into groups and start to make sense of the world. I wandered the land, mountain and valley, desert and plain, venturing into forests and caves and even the rushing streams and restless seas, observing and growing in knowledge. Not mean feats for a smokeless blue flame that can see without eyes, hear without ears and understand without a brain. How was I able to do these things? As well you might ask a man how he stands upright on two legs and walks around. He cannot describe it – he just does it. So it was with me. I could not say how I did such things; I just accepted them as natural and did them. Now, after thousands of years, I have grown in knowledge and understanding. I have my theories of magnetic fields and patterned plasma, but I will not bore you with them. If you are of the djinn, you will know; if you are not, you probably cannot know.

In the early days, I saw the creation of my own kind and saw how I must have come about. I often approached these little dancing flames in the scorched aftermath of the act of genesis, but they never responded to my inquiries. I could feel their introspective sentience, dim and flickering, but nothing more. I have seen this act of creation many times, though less in recent years. I do not know if this is because the creative force has lessened with time, or if it is because the vast pockets of gas that form above the oil-rich shale beds deep underground are now all but exhausted. No doubt many djinn exist, but I seldom see another one now. I think we are solitary beings, having little in common with each other beyond the hot fire of our creation and the cold fire of our being, and even less with the coarse material creation that preceded us.

For a long time, I wandered the earth, crossing continents and seas, watching the pulse of glaciers and the rise and fall of the oceans, but I always found myself drawn back to the place I was created. Each time I returned, I found things had changed – the land grew dryer, animals moved away or died out, the scattered tribes of men fought and died or managed to live in harmony with their neighbours but still died. Man is short-lived, gone almost in the blink of his eye, and I remain for I am something greater than man. How much greater? I did not find out for some time. Some things I found out quickly by observing my surroundings and the creatures that inhabit it. For instance, I live but I do not grow. I sprung fully formed from the earth fires, whereas man grows from an infant to a child to an adult. I do not eat or drink but feed instead from energy. Not just the raw energies of the white light that flashes from the storm-clad heavens to the earth, but also from the energy that binds the life force of man and animal. I can feed on the electrical currents that keep men alive and drain them of life and soul, strengthening my own.

I do not produce others of my kind; djinn arise only from the smokeless fires and have no need of sex. I think, though not with a fleshy brain, and because I have no distractions of the flesh, my intellect is greater than a man's, my purpose stronger and my will indomitable. Men are governed by their appetites, and I often use their lusts to achieve my own ends. Humans are so easy to control; a word here, a promise there, and they fall over themselves to do my will. There are some, I admit, with greater control of their own intellect. They can govern their own minds, being fixated on higher goals: love, family, the service of a god or goddess; yet even these can be governed and directed, if I just take the time to appear not as I am but rather how they wish to see me.

I have mentioned gods and goddesses, and for a long time in the days after I came to be, I wondered about these beings. No doubt you want to know if they exist. Before I can answer that I suppose I must ask what is a god? I have asked this question of many people down the ages, for you must not suppose that I always exist as a still, blue flame. Sometimes I put on the guise of a man or woman and walk the earth. When I am in the guise of a man, I think and feel more as a man does. I experience lust, anger and pain, but also curiosity and a hunger for knowledge. I seek out the learned men, the priests and scribes, and draw out the contents of their minds, before I shatter the bonds that hold their brains together, feasting on the rich, dark energy of their being as their life force gutters and dies.

I have learned men see god as many things: all-powerful, all-knowing, capricious, loving, merciful, cruel, able to be placated or bribed but also quick to seek vengeance, jealous, proud and beautiful, having the attributes of creator, preserver and destroyer. They have all the worst faults of men but also the best attributes. I know; how can a god be all these things? In short, he cannot. Have I ever met a god? Yes, and he or she was some of these things but never all. I have seen the still blue flames riding the thunderclouds, dancing in the molten rock that spews from the belly of the earth or lifted aloft in the whirlwind. I have conversed with the flames that often sit atop hills, wrapped up in their own existence, thinking their own hill shrine is the centre of creation. These little Baals, as they are called, have a tribe of men to worship them and make the blood offering, burning the flesh of beasts that the god may feed. It is not the burnt meat of an animal's thigh, the fat that drips and sputters in the consuming flames or the blood pumping from a slit throat that is important to these little gods, but the life force they desire. I should know, for I am a flame myself. That is all a god is, believe me. Every god I have come across, every being happy to take what men offer so freely of their neighbour's livestock or of their own, is a flame – one of the djinn.

Many flames take names, for men do not like to worship a nameless god. Djinn may take the name of a hill, an attribute or one of the forces of nature. There are thunder gods, rain gods, sea gods, sky gods, and gods of war, of love, of soldiers, of shepherds, of the sun, moon and planets – a deity for any and every purpose. And as long as men need them, you can be sure there will be a flame ready to exploit these gullible creatures. Not all gods are strong, many being limited to a single hill or spring or grove of trees. Others wander the earth and walk about in it, taking life where they will. I have done both in my long existence. For a while, I wandered, and then for an age, I sat in a high place and was content. Then a man came and named me in fear and wonder, and I thought, *Why not? I too will become a god.*

Yes, a man first named me. Or rather, he thought of my name, and I plucked it from his mind, for the minds of men are open to the djinn. You look uncomfortable. Do you fear that I can see the thoughts in your mind? Why would I bother? Most men think of little beyond their immediate needs and desires. Of course, should I desire to, you probably will not even know I am doing it. You would feel nothing beyond a mild ringing in the ears or a feeling you are being watched. Have you ever felt eyes watching you and turned only to find no one was there? That was me, or one like me, delving into the soft matter of your brain, chasing your thoughts and tapping into your life force. You might have felt tired later, but if the djinn did not drink too deeply you recovered. Despite what the legends say, we are not necessarily ravening monsters, killing indiscriminately. It is much better to taste and move on, returning to sip again from an ever-renewing resource.

Do I taste all life? Do I sip from the wellsprings of animal and human alike? I have done so, but I prefer the taste of men. Their thoughts and emotions are raw and savage, as they exercise choice; whereas animals are largely governed by instinct. I can leave an animal untouched, but sooner or later I will feast on any human I get close to. It is in my nature, perhaps. I am a djinni, after all ... unless I aspire to be more.

I aspired to be more. I took a name and godhead. A name should be more than just an empty sound though; it should mean something. The name I took was a fitting name, for it reflected my nature, my position in creation and the place that was then my favoured abode. It meant high, lofty, sublime, in the tongue of the human inhabitants of the place of my being. Though I was created in the sandy wasteland and am at home in that hot, dry desolation, it is the mountains that call to me, where the air is clear and the rock clean and unspoiled. The wind sweeps between the peaks, and the only sound is the harsh cry of the raptor circling high above in the pale blue dome of the sky. There I sit, the flame of my being motionless in the gale that blows about me, and I contemplate the empty land stretched out before me. I was named Aali of the High Places. I may have stayed Aali of the High Places and been no more than a spirit alone on a mountain, but something changed within me when that first man made an act of worship and I became a god in his eyes. Once I was a god, of course, a simple name like Aali was not enough. I decided to leave my lofty domain and venture into the world again. I found the world much changed with men burgeoning upon the land, but I had ambition. I was no longer content to be a small baal, a nameless djinni. I would become a god, maybe even the God. Yes, I am laughing as I say that, but why not? Who is to stop me? Men cannot and only very powerful djinn could do so, but I do not know of any strong enough.

And so, on a day like countless thousands that had gone before, a man came to me. He was not looking for me, but his coming changed everything.

Chapter One

Ab'rim sat on a rock in the low foothills in the southern part of the mountain chain that ran along the western side of the Arabian Peninsula and regarded his charges gloomily. This was unusual for him as he was known among his neighbours as a cheerful person, but he thought he had good reason. The past two seasons had been hard ones; the monsoon rains that swept in from the southwest lighter than usual and the grazing had suffered. He looked up at the clear blue sky and muttered a prayer to his many gods for rain, especially Hubal, god of shepherds. Ab'rim waited hopefully, but no sign appeared to show his pleas had been answered. He shrugged and turned back to his contemplation of his small herd of goats.

The animals were healthy but starting to show the effects of poor nutrition. Months of grazing on the sparse vegetation had all but denuded the rocky slopes, and now the beasts spread out over the hillside, scraping at the stony ground in the hopes of uncovering a morsel of edibility. Most ignored their herder, intent on finding food, but one old ewe, the leader of the flock, lifted her head from her foraging from time to time to make sure the man was still there. Eventually she bleated, alerting the man to the straying of the flock.

Ab'rim picked up a handful of stones and worked his way across the hillside, judicious placement of the missiles herding the animals together again. He squatted and caressed the old female goat, calling her his Bahiyya, his beautiful one, and she responded by butting her head gently against him. He rose and started slowly up the slope, picking his way between the boulders. She followed, and the other goats fell into line behind her, dutifully climbing the faint track worn into the loose rock and soil. They crossed the hill and dipped down into a small valley on the other side where a tiny bit of moisture had collected, stimulating coarse grasses which had now run to seed and were turning brown. The goats hurried forward, bleating with excitement, and soon consumed every scrap of plant material down to its roots.

At noon or as near as Ab'rim could judge the hour by the position of the sun, he found what shelter he could under a towering rock and consumed a small meal of bread and two dried dates. He washed it down with tepid water from a skin flask and sat back, picking at tiny fragments of food caught in his chipped but otherwise healthy teeth with a broken fingernail. The goats sought scraps of shade beside the larger boulders and lay down. For an hour or more, the only movement in the valley was the occasional flicking of ears or waving of hands to dislodge the persistent flies.

By midafternoon, the goats were on the move again and Ab'rim and Bahiyya led the flock over the valley rim and angled across the next slope, working up toward the mountains. Ab'rim knew water flowed downward and vegetation was usually found on the lower slopes and the plains beneath the hills, but the years of drought had stripped the land of life. He reasoned the water had to come from somewhere and the gullies that dissected the steep-sided mountains may yet harbour moisture and fodder. The alternative was to go over ground already covered. His goats would find no food below, so he must chance everything on the high places.

Reasoning may have led to Ab'rim's decision, but the logic did not ease his mind. Other herders told stories of the wild places far from human habitation, and he had heard tales of strange beasts and even stranger things that walked the night. He did not look forward to the coming night, but he knew he must brave it or let his little flock starve. The look of reproach on his wife's face would be more than he could bear if he returned with a hungry herd just because he feared the darkness.

The night came swiftly as the sun vanished behind the mountains and the long cold shadows swept down from the heights. Ab'rim gathered his goats into a small area of the gully and rolled a few rocks across the most obvious gaps. Rocks alone would not pen his beasts as goats delight in climbing, but the presence of apparent boundaries often sufficed to keep them close. As darkness closed in, they huddled close, deriving security from the presence of the man.

Ab'rim made a small fire from a pinch of sawdust, a wisp of dried grass and dehydrated dung, twirling his firestick with a short length of cord from his pouch. The point rested in a hollow in a flat piece of wood, and as the stick spun and whirred, tiny wisps of smoke curled upward. In the silence of the evening, even this faint sound was loud in his ears, and it worried him as there was no telling what might be drawn to the steady noise. At last the sawdust caught fire, and he nursed the wisp of grass with the dry undigested plant fibres from the dung and a few brittle twigs. The resultant fire was small and produced almost no heat, but it threw back the darkness for a time and gave him a measure of comfort. Later the moon rose over the low plain, flooding the mountainside with a pale light and throwing inky shadows across the rock-strewn landscape. Things moved in the shadows, small things admittedly, but Ab'rim was nervous of the rustlings, squeaking and hissing and gabbled many prayers to his gods for their protection. Hubal he petitioned – god of shepherds, dominant in this season of the waxing moon; Manaf the sun god, who, though absent from the sky, had the power to banish all shadows; and of course, Al-Lat, the mother goddess. Ab'rim felt uncomfortable praying for help to a female god, but his wife, Hajar, had assured him of the Mother's power. He prayed too that the gods could hear his whispers as he feared raising his voice and attracting attention from other things. After a while, a near silence descended over the hillside, and he fell asleep warmed by the bodies of the nearest goats.

The dawn came, the sun rising over the plains and spreading a golden blanket over the high mountains, while the valleys yet remained in shadow. Ab'rim gave thanks to his gods again, especially Manaf now, and roused the animals, opening up the pen and ushering them further up the rocky gully. He had nothing with which to break his fast, so he took out his leather sling and hunted around for smooth water-worn pebbles. The goats moved slowly, and he was able to keep an eye on their wanderings and still scan the rocks and sky for prey. Despite the apparent lack of vegetation, there was considerable life on the mountain. By the time he stopped at noon, he had two songbirds, a mouse and several locusts in his pouch. He consumed the locusts raw but skinned and gutted the birds and mouse for his evening meal, putting the feathers and skin as well as the tiny corpses back in his pouch together with a few scraps of wood and dried dung.

His second night on the mountain was more comfortable than the first, and because no threat had eventuated the first night, Ab'rim felt considerably more relaxed. The goats found grazing in a small shallow basin where a pool of water still existed, dampening the soil sufficiently to stimulate grasses. He made his camp with his back to an overhanging rock wall and cooked his meat on a tiny fire. Bahiyya stood and stared disapprovingly with her yellow eyes, while the man devoured the half-cooked morsels, crunching the bones between his teeth and licking his fingers to absorb every hint of delicious juice. Ab'rim settled back, ready for sleep, his belly nearly full and wrapped himself in his robe against the chill night air. After watching the stars for a time, he drifted into sleep.

A scream ripped the night apart, a long wailing cry that guttered into despairing sobs before dying away. Ab'rim jerked awake and sat bolt upright, his back to the rock wall. Visible only as vague shapes, the goats were on their feet, staring off up the invisible gully, motionless and silent. The moon hid behind clouds, and the darkness pressed around, hiding whatever it was screaming on the mountain top. The night was very quiet now, as if waiting and watching for the thing to scream again.

A demon. An Ifrit or djinni ... O Al-Lat, Holy Mother, preserve me. Ab'rim gabbled prayers under his breath to every god he could think of, then he pulled his sling out with shaking hands and fitted a pebble into it. *What good is that going to do*? He remembered tales told around campfires when he was a boy and fumbled in his pouch. He drew out a handful of small feathers and pushed them one by one into the smouldering embers of his tiny fire. The stink of charring feathers curled up and around him in the still air making him cough. *Burning feathers repel demons ... I hope*. The scream was not repeated, and after a while, the goats settled down again. *My prayers or the feathers worked*. Ab'rim prayed again, offering up thanks for his deliverance, and many hours later toward dawn, he even slept.

The next morning, Ab'rim debated whether to stay high in the mountains or to descend to the plains once more. The scream of the demon had scared him, but the burning feathers and prayers had evidently seen it off. *If it even was a demon* ... The bright sunshine made him feel much braver, and he scanned the slopes confidently. He knew there was little chance of finding forage on the plains, but there was still vegetation to be found in the isolated gullies of the mountain. Fear warred against pride and the needs of his herd. The morning sun tipped the scale, the warmth and brightness of the day strengthening his resolve, banishing his fears. His small herd looked to him for guidance, alternately cropping the last of the grasses in the basin or looking silently at him as he made his decision.

"We go up," he told Bahiyya.

The old she-goat bleated mournfully but followed him willingly enough as he set off up the gully, the rest of the herd trailing after them. The bed of the dried stream steepened almost immediately, and Ab'rim found himself having to use both hands to scramble upward. The goats had little trouble negotiating the rocky incline, leaping nimbly from rock to boulder, step to ledge and calling encouragingly to each other. By early afternoon, he was higher up the mountain than he had ever been. He found a level space where a few stunted and wind-gnarled shrubs clung to the thin soil. The animals spread out, nipping at buds and even stripping the bark from the woody plants. Ab'rim looked out at the plain that lay far below him, trying to make out his route up the mountain or where his tents lay nestled by the foothills. The distance and the haze foiled his efforts, but he stood at the brink of the little plateau for a long time, drinking in the frightening expanse.

"I didn't know there was so much land," he murmured. Ab'rim turned away eventually, shaking his head. He became aware the day had slipped away from him and he was very hungry. While the goats stripped the plateau of vegetation, he took out his sling and started hunting among the rocks. An hour later, he gave up. The plateau was devoid of any form of animal life save for himself and his goats. “We'd better go back down,” he muttered. “At least there were birds and mice in the gully.” It was then Ab'rim discovered he had a problem. One of the young goats was missing.

He carefully counted his flock, ticking off their names against the joints and tips of his fingers – Fidda, Inas, Rabi'a, Bahiyya, 'Abla – fifteen. He counted again – fifteen. Little Nadra was missing, and her mother, Rabi'a, was now running back and forth bleating wildly. Ab'rim caught the mother goat and secured her to the chewed-down remains of a shrub and started searching the rocks along the rim of the plateau where the land rose up again toward the peak.

He found evidence at once that a goat had been there – small droppings still moist when squeezed gently between forefinger and thumb. Which goat was another matter. Any of the herd could have climbed this far. He kept searching, calling out at intervals. His goats would not answer to their names – except Bahiyya, the beautiful – but they knew the sound of his voice. There was a good chance if the kid heard him, she would cry out. The mountain was silent except for the sighing of the wind, the muted bleating of the herd on the plateau below and the cry of a hawk stretched out on the air high above. Ab’rim continued climbing, calling as he went.

The shadow of the plain swept over him, and Ab’rim saw with some alarm nightfall had overtaken him. Already he faced a difficult climb down to the plateau in failing light. If he delayed, it would become impossible. He scanned the rocks, desperately hoping the lost goat would suddenly appear, but nothing moved. Dejectedly, he turned to start back down, knowing the goat would be unlikely to survive the night alone.

Come.

Ab'rim stopped in his tracks and looked around, too surprised to be fearful. He saw only jumbled rocks and deepening shadows. *I'm imagining things*. Shaking his head, he started to lower himself over a large rock.

Come.

Ab'rim froze. *I heard that, I really did.* He looked round carefully but saw nothing that should not be on a rocky mountain slope in the gathering dusk. "Wh … who's there?" he called.

Come to me.

The hair on the back of his neck stirred. "Wh … where are you? Who are you?"

Here.

Ab'rim saw, far up the slope, a tiny glimmer of blue-tinged light. Even as he watched, the rocks darkened as the light faded from the sky and the blue flame surged brighter in contrast. The urge to approach became insistent, and he started climbing. It was easier going up than scrambling down in darkness, and only half an hour found him panting on a narrow ledge at the back of which, raised on a roughly shaped block of stone, sat a still blue flame. He stood and stared at it, curiosity replacing fear.

What is it? he asked himself, and then, *Is it dangerous*?

A soothing touch, reminiscent of a mother's gentle hand, calmed him.

No, it's no bigger than my hand ... and beautiful. How could it harm me, this ... this thing in the high places, lofty and sublime? Nothing evil could live up here in the pure air. It's pure, sublime, exalted. I ... I will call it Aali, for that means high and lofty ... Aali of the High Places ...

A feeling of amusement crept over Ab'rim, and he found himself smiling in response. "Wh ... what are you? Are … are you a god, or … or… ?"

I am ... Aali. Aali of the High Places. I called you.

Ab'rim fell to his knees in awe. *How did I know His name*? He remembered from fireside stories when he was a boy that demons never told you their names. They just ripped you apart, whereas a god … a god might … "H ... how may I serve thee, Aali of the High Places?"

The young she-goat is over there.

Ab'rim looked to his left without stopping to think how he knew there meant in that direction. On the edge of his vision he saw a small brown bundle and recognised the still form of Nadra. He rose to his feet and took a step or two toward the goat before realising he had got up without asking permission of the god. He turned hurriedly back and felt amusement sweep over him again.

Go to your ... Nadra. Bring her here.

Ab'rim laid the trembling animal in front of the blue flame. He gasped when the flame flowed down from the rock and hovered over the goat. The animal's trembling ceased, and she turned her head toward the flame, uttering a soft bleat.

She fell. Her leg was broken. I have healed her.

The blue flame moved back onto the stone block. Nadra got up; hind legs first, then her forefeet, and stood unconcernedly in no obvious pain.

Ab'rim knelt and put his head on the ground. "Lord Aali, thank you. I am in your debt."

Arise Ab'rim and depart my presence.

"How may I serve thee, Aali of the High Places?"

Silence reigned on the mountain side, and Ab'rim rocked back on his heels. The blue flame on the rock had vanished. He stood and looked around, but the ledge lay in darkness. Picking up Nadra, he started back down the rocky slope. Half way to the plateau where his herd waited, Ab'rim suddenly realised despite it being pitch dark, he was negotiating the treacherous slope with ease. "The Lord guides my footsteps," he murmured in astonishment.

Once on the plateau, he reunited Nadra with her mother and sat with his feet dangling over the drop, looking toward the east. He cast his mind back over his encounter with the flame. It was the first time he, or anyone he knew, had actual face to face contact with a supernatural being. *Well, face to flame*. That Aali was a god was now more than likely. A demon would have torn him limb from limb rather than healing the broken leg of a young she-goat. Ab'rim had never heard of Aali before.

He must be a new god. Can you have a new god? Or is he an existing god using a different name? Why would he do that? Wouldn't that be like lying – pretending you were someone else? A god's word is truth, the shamans say. Only demons lie. He must therefore be a new god, he decided. *Why would he reveal himself to me? Have I ... have I been chosen for some purpose?* Ab'rim felt excitement grip him, and he eagerly awaited the dawn, not feeling at all tired or hungry.

When the new light of day flooded the plateau and the lower reaches of the mountain, Ab'rim gathered his flock together and with Bahiyya in the lead, ushered them down. They traveled as fast as Ab'rim could push them for he greatly desired to bring news of the new god to his tent and his neighbours. The goats were used to eating on the move, so fanned out on the lower slopes and grabbed mouthfuls of vegetation where they could. Because Ab'rim was no longer looking for fresh pastures, he reached the plain by late afternoon and was within sight of his tent as night fell.

His wife, Hajar, was outside tending a small fire and preparing the evening meal. She looked up quickly when Bahiyya bleated and stared out at the unexpected sight of her husband. She blinked and looked again for his face almost shone in the darkness at the edge of the fire's glow.

"Husband, why are you home so soon? Is anything amiss?"

Ab'rim grinned and for a moment his face seemed to flare with light, and then he became serious, just the plain, ordinary man she had married. “I’ve seen God,” he whispered.

Hajar frowned and searched her husband's face for the jest, though humour was not one of Ab'rim's usual attributes. “Which god did you see? Are you sure, husband?” She restrained herself from casting further doubt on his words and instead searched for an acceptable alternative. “The mountains are lonely places. The wind can sound like voices ... the cry of an eagle ... the fall of a rock.”

“I didnt just hear Him, Hajar. I saw Him. Aali of the High Places.”

“Who? I haven’t heard of this god.”

“Nor I, but ... but I thought His name, and then He spoke, confirming it.”

“How could you think a name you hadn’t heard before? That doesn’t make sense.”

Ab'rim shook his head. “Well, Aali means lofty, and I was right up there near the top of the mountain. I ... I just thought it, and the god said it was his name.” He looked past Hajar to where his son, Isma'il, lay on a goatskin by the fire. The smells from the cooking pot awoke his suppressed appetite, and he started salivating. “You have food? I haven’t eaten in two days.”

Hajar immediately shook off all thoughts of deities and hurried to do what she liked best, caring for her family. Cushions were brought out, and Ab'rim sat by the fire. He washed his hands in a bowl of water she held and dried them on a clean linen cloth. She ladeled out a bowl of the barley soup and ripped off a crust of freshly baked bread, handing it to her husband.

Ab'rim fell on the soup and bread and was half way through the bowl before he looked up. “You aren’t eating with me?”

“I only made enough for one, husband, as I wasn’t expecting you home. I’ll eat something later.” She picked up Isma'il and held the two-year-old to her breast. He started sucking immediately, and she sat back with a look of contentment on her face. Desert folk suckle their children until the age of five.

“It would please me if you’d eat too, Hajar.” Ab'rim dipped a piece of the bread in the soup and reached across, putting it in his wife's mouth.

She smiled, swallowed the bread and kissed his fingers. “I love you, husband.”

“And I you, my beautiful one.” Ab'rim finished his meal and after Isma'il had been put to bed, went into the tent and embraced his wife lovingly.

The next morning, while Ab'rim sat at the fire sipping on hot water and herbs, Hajar busied herself with her morning chores, sweeping out the tent and feeding and cleaning their son. When she finished, she joined her husband and sat down alongside him.

“This god you saw on the mountain, what did he look like?”

“I was looking for the goat, Nadra. First, I heard his voice inside my head. Then, I saw this light high up on the mountain and climbed to see what it was. The god ... the god himself looks like fire. Like a cold, blue, unmoving flame that consumes nothing and gave me no heat.”

Hajar shivered. "Fire. A blue flame. I've never heard of a god like that. Are you sure it wasn't a djinni or even an ifrit?"

"I'm still alive." Ab'rim shook his head. "I felt safe. I even found myself laughing at one point. I cannot imagine a demon would make me feel like that. Besides, Nadra had broken her leg, and Aali healed her."

Hajar watched the goats and saw the young goat in question moved freely and without pain. She pondered this fact for a few minutes. "Are you sure it was broken?"

"Yes." Ab'rim hesitated and then admitted, "Aali said it had been broken. A god wouldn't lie."

Hajar frowned. "No, I suppose not, but ..."

"But what, wife?"

"I'm not sure. I just thought that ..." Hajar shook her head. "What are you going to do?"

"I don't know. He told me to depart, and I did. I'd like to go back, but I'm not sure if He would welcome me."

"Did he tell you not to return?"

"No."

"Then I think perhaps you should. To thank him for healing your goat, if for no other reason. You could take him a sacrifice, an offering. It never hurts to have a god – any god – friendly."

"What could I possibly offer a god as a sacrifice? One of my goats? They're all I have of value."

"If he wanted a goat, he would have taken Nadra. Give him honeycakes. I'll make some this morning."

Once the honeycakes were made, Ab'rim got ready to leave. Hajar urged him to wait until the next day, but he would not be dissuaded.

“I can travel fast without the goats, and I’ll be half way there by nightfall. I’ll take fuel for a fire and have a honeycake for my supper.”

That night alone on the mountain was not as pleasant as Ab'rim had made out. He camped late, being more concerned with pushing on as long as he could, only stopping when he missed his footing on the loose rocks, falling and bruising himself. He camped not far from where he had three nights before when he had heard the demon scream in the darkness. The thought made him shiver with fear, and he made his fire bigger to banish the shadows. As a result, the fuel ran out faster, and the night closed in around him before he fell asleep. He lay awake staring fearfully into the shadows cast by the moonlight, praying to all the gods. Now he added Aali to his list, but he knew so little about this new god he found it hard to praise him properly. All he could do was ask him for protection.

The demon did not scream that night, but an owl flew overhead and sat on a rock not far away, hooting softly. Ab'rim kept very still, hoping the owl had not seen him. He knew owls were birds of ill omen and had no doubt it had been sent as an emissary of the demon to find his master's prey. The night passed slowly, and after a while, the owl stopped its calling, but Ab'rim knew it was still there lurking in the darkness, waiting for him to give himself away. Though he was determined to remain awake, he fell asleep sometime in the early morning hours and awoke late with the sun already streaming down on him.

Ab'rim nibbled on a honeycake and drank from his waterskin. He looked up at the mountain, working out the fastest route to the top. The gully he had climbed before proved to be the most direct route, especially as he was not hampered by the presence of his flock. He made good time, arriving at the plateau mid-morning and the ledge where he had seen Aali shortly after noon. There was no sign of a blue flame, and Ab'rim felt thoroughly dejected.

Did I come all this way for nothing? He sat and stared out across the plains until his mood passed. *It doesn't matter. I wanted to come. Aali made no promise he'd be here*.

I am here.

Ab'rim jumped up and turned toward the stone block on which Aali had sat before. Once more the flame sat before him, only faint in the bright sunshine, hardly visible unless you knew where to look – or heard its summons. "Lord Aali." Ab'rim knelt and touched his forehead to the ground. "I've brought ... Lord Aali, please accept my offering." He undid the cloth bundle and showed the crumbly honeycake. The flame said nothing, did nothing. "Lord Aali, I bring you a honeycake my wife, Hajar, made." Still nothing. "We're poor, my Lord Aali, we've nothing else to offer ... unless ... unless you want a goat."

Thank you, Ab'rim. The barely seen flame descended onto the honeycake, dancing over its surface and then withdrew to the rock again. *I have no need of it, Ab'rim, but you have done well to offer it. Place your offering on the rock for this shall be my altar.*

Ab'rim rose on shaking legs and placed the honeycake carefully onto the stone block. He stepped back and knelt again. *What does he want? I've nothing of value except my goats and my family. He ... he wouldn't want my ... my wife or son, would he*? "What would you have me do, Lord Aali?" No reply came from the still, blue flame. Ab'rim waited as patiently as he could, despite the turmoil in his mind. One did not hurry a god.

After a long time, words formed in his mind again. *Return in seven days with your son. Offer him on my altar, and I will make your name great among men. Your descendants will be without number.*

Ab'rim felt his heart clench within his body. "M ... my son, Lord Aali?" No further words sounded in his head, and he saw the almost invisible flame had faded from sight entirely. With tears on his face, Ab'rim got up and stumbled away from the altar and down the rocky side of the mountain.

Hajar stared at him as if he had lost his mind when he told her what had happened. "He wants our son? Little Isma'il? Well, he's not going to get him. That's no god up there on the mountain but a demon. What god would demand you sacrifice your son? I hope you refused outright and denounced him. Well, did you?"

"My love, one doesn't refuse a god ..."

“You didn't say you would? By Al-Lat, Manet and Uzza, what sort of fool do I have for a husband?”

“You weren’t there. Aali is a god ... besides, he said he’d give me many descendants.”

“And how will he do that if you offer our son up as sacrifice?”

“I don't know ... He’ll give us other children?” Ab'rim added hopefully.

“I’m not going to allow my son, Isma’il ...”

“But Aali is a god, my beloved. If he wants ...”

“A fine god who wants us to sacrifice our son. I think he’s a demon ...”

“He cannot be a demon. A demon cannot heal goats and neither would it refrain from killing me.”

“You’re a fool if you believe that. Demons are powerful. Well, it doesn’t matter. It’s not going to happen.” Hajar clutched Isma'il to her protectively and stared her husband down.

Ab'rim looked down, thoroughly abashed, mumbled something indistinctly and left the tent for the more reasonable company of the goats. “What can I do, Bihayya?” he asked.

Bihayya fixed him with her yellow eyes and uttered a soft bleat.

“How can I refuse my god? He said he’d make me great.”

Bihayya vouchsafed no opinion on the matter. Ab'rim sighed and gathered the herd together, leading them off into the foothills again. He stayed out for four days but kept away from the mountain slopes, though he found himself glancing up at the high peaks from time to time. Once at night, he thought he saw a tiny blue light unwinking near the peak, but when he looked again it was gone. He thought of his wife, Hajar, and of his son, Isma'il, remembering the joy his birth had brought to them. There would be other children in time, he knew, but for now, the boy meant everything to him. Aali meant for him to sacrifice his beloved son on the altar. *What sort of a god is this Aali, of whom I've never heard? Maybe my wife is right, and he's really a demon. Yet the flame acts like no demon I've ever heard of. What am I to do*?

Does Aali have power beyond the mountain peak? If he's angry, could he seek us out on the plains in our tent and destroy us? He said he was Aali of the High Places – perhaps he was limited to the high peaks. But he was a god wasn't he? Could you put a limit on the power of a god? And if he said he'd make my name great, how could he do that from his mountain top? What then? Could I appease his anger with some other sacrifice? What else would be acceptable? A goat is all I have. It'll have to do.

Ab'rim returned to his tent on the fifth day and knelt before his wife. "Forgive me, Hajar. You're right. I'll offer up a goat instead."

"Why offer up anything? Stay away from the demon, husband. Never go to the peak again."

"If I ignore Aali, he may come looking for us. Perhaps a goat will keep him satisfied."

Hajar shrugged. "As you see fit." She set about preparing the evening meal.

The next day, the sixth, Ab'rim spent at the tent, mending equipment and carving a small piece of wood into a toy for Isma'il. The boy played at his feet for most of the day or slept close by in the shade. Ab'rim found himself looking at his son often, smiling at his antics or explaining in simple words what he was doing. *My son is my most precious possession, worth far more than any goat.* The day passed quickly, and they all shared a meal together under the stars before putting Isma'il to bed. Ab'rim made love to his wife tenderly but with passion, and when she fell asleep, he arose and crossed to Isma'il's bed.

"Come, my son," he whispered and gently picked up the sleeping child.

Outside the tent, Isma'il whimpered in his sleep as the chill night air touched him, so Ab'rim wrapped him in a woolen blanket and put him in a leather sling he sometimes used to carry injured goats. He stood still in the darkness for a few minutes, staring up at the night sky, praying to the other gods for guidance. A streak of light flashed from east to west in the direction he was heading, and he knew the sky gods had spoken. A rumble of sound followed the streak, and he thought for a moment he felt the ground quiver beneath his feet. He picked up a leather pouch containing food and water he had prepared earlier and set off for the mountain at a brisk walk, trying to keep his pace even so as not to rouse his sleeping son.

Isma'il woke with the dawn as Ab'rim negotiated the first difficult stretch of rocks. The child immediately cried for his mother, but Ab'rim was able to soothe him, pacifying him temporarily with a honeycake and a drink of tepid goat's milk.

As it was his father carrying him, his wails were half-hearted and he soon stopped, contenting himself with an occasional sob and a sniffle. Ab'rim climbed on, warmed by the rising sun, intent on completing the climb to the god's ledge by dusk.

The boy slept, awoke and cried, then slept again. Ab'rim talked to his son, sang him songs and after repeating these a few times, told him stories of his own childhood, embellishing them shamelessly. The sun slipped behind the mountain by the time they reached the plateau, and the first stars were showing as he staggered exhausted onto the ledge and sank to his knees.

The altar was dark with no presence of the god showing, so Ab'rim gently took his son out of the sling and stroked his head, kissing him tenderly. He wondered what Hajar would say to him when he returned and for a few minutes considered not going back to his tent but continuing on into the wilderness, becoming an outcast. Ab'rim shook his head. *No, though Hajar hates me for it, I'll face her, for I've only obeyed my god. Still, it's hard, for I love both my wife and my son and I've lost both.*

You have come.

Ab'rim looked up to see the blue flame once more sitting on the altar stone. He knelt and bowed his head to the ground, his heart beating faster. "Lord Aali, I've obeyed your command."

You brought your son to lie upon my altar as a sacrifice?

"I have, Lord Aali."

You are a man of great faith, Ab'rim son of Azar.

Ab'rim was not sure whether he was supposed to respond to this praise, so he kept silent.

Lay your son on my altar.

Ab'rim kissed his son's forehead again and then rose to his feet, carrying the now crying child. He advanced toward the stone altar and laid the child on the cold surface. Isma'il's protests became louder, and he held out his hands to his father.

Take out your knife and make your offering.

Ab'rim started to tremble, but he kept one hand on his son and fumbled in his pouch for the stone knife. The blue glow of Aali's flame reflected off the sharp scalloped edges of the flint as he brought it out. *Oh, my son, forgive me. I love you so.*

Sacrifice your son.

Isma'il wailed and cried out for his mother. As Ab'rim started to bring the flint blade towards his son's throat, stones rattled behind him at the cliff edge.

Hold your hand, Ab'rim.

Ab'rim halted the downward motion and sobbed, turning away. He saw Hajar standing behind him with a young goat in her arms. She said nothing, uttered no word of reproach, but held out the animal.

Remove your son from the altar, Ab'rim son of Azar. Offer the animal instead.

With trembling hands, he lifted Isma'il from the stone and placed him on the ground next to Hajar where he curled up and went to sleep as if he was at home in bed. He started to speak to his wife, but she appeared to stare right through him. The words died unspoken. Hajar handed Ab'rim the unprotesting goat, and he turned and laid it on the altar. Quickly, before it could start to cry out, he slit its throat with the sharp flint blade. It fell back, its blood spurting over the rock. Ab'rim withdrew a pace and knelt.

The blue flame flared over the altar, blinding Ab'rim as if a lightning bolt had struck the mountain. When the glare died away and the afterimages faded, Ab'rim saw there was nothing on the altar but the motionless blue flame again. He glanced round for his wife, ready to chastise her for standing in the presence of the god, but she was no longer there.

"Hajar? Where are you?"

She is not here, Ab'rim.

"But ..."

She was never here.

"But the goat ..."

There was no goat.

"I ... I don't understand, Lord Aali."

Your faith is strong, Ab'rim son of Azar. So strong you would sacrifice your only son because I commanded you to do so. Such faith will not go unrewarded. Your name is henceforth Ibrahim, for you are Khalil Ullah, Friend of God, and all men will know and praise your name. Your son, whom you have offered to your God will be a people chosen for his purpose. His children will be as the sands of the plain below.

Ibrahim groveled before the altar, overcome with emotion in the aftermath of the sacrifice. "Let your will be done, Lord Aali." After a few moments, he twisted his head and looked up at the flame with one eye. "If ... if it pleases you, my Lord, I ... I would rename y ... you also."

Speak, Ibrahim.

"Y ... you are m ... more than just a god, Aali – more than just'lofty or sublime. O ... O Great One, you are surely al-Ilah, The Supreme God."

Amusement swept over the man, and he knew his presumption was forgiven. *Let it be so.*

"What would you have me do, al-Ilah?"

A pause. *Return to your tent. Comfort your wife. Raise your son to know me. Worship me.*

"Yes, al-Ilah. Am … am I to bring sacrifices to your altar on this mountain every seven days then?"

A longer pause. *No, for I shall not be here. Al-Ilah is not found just in one place. You will raise up my altar where others may come to know me and worship me. Offer sacrifices there.*

Ibrahim looked dubiously at the rock altar. "I don't have the strength to carry this stone, al-Ilah."

This time the pause was so long Ibrahim wondered if the god was going to answer him. *Then I will give you another. Descend to the plateau below us and search to the south. You will find the place where the star descended. Take the star and raise up my altar where all men may see it.*

The flame of al-Ilah vanished, and Ibrahim sighed deeply. In the faint light of the stars, he could just make out the form of his son sleeping in his woolen blanket. He picked up the child and carried him back to the altar, but this time, instead of laying him on it, he sat with his back to the rock and cradled Isma'il in his arms.

Ibrahim awoke with the dawn. Isma'il had soiled his clothing and started bawling with discomfort and hunger. He cleaned him up as best he could and fed him the remains of the honeycake in his pouch. When the boy quietened down, Ibrahim fitted the sling around him securely and began to pick his way down the steep slope, thinking about the star al-Ilah had said was on the mountain. *How large is a star? They don't look very big but they're a long way away – until one falls.*

The southern end of the plateau slowly narrowed and became a thin trail winding around the side of the mountain. He followed it, picking his way cautiously over the loose stones, until he came to a place where the trail vanished. The side of the mountain looked as if it had been cut with a flint axe, a great gouge removed and an apron of loose rock spread out below. The upper edge of the gouge lay a short distance above him, and Ibrahim could detect the stink of crushed rock. He laid Isma'il down carefully away from the crumbling edge of the gouge and climbed up the slope to investigate.

A hollow lay at the upper margin of the scar on the mountain, and Ibrahim could see something black gleaming in its depths. It stood out against the greys and browns of the raw and weathered rock, and he remembered al-Ilah's words. *The place where the star descended.*

"Is that a star?" he muttered. "A star is bright, not black ... yet it gleams. Is this a star that has gone out perhaps?" *A fire when it goes out leaves ashes and blackened wood. Why shouldn't a star be the same*?

Ibrahim climbed gingerly into the crater left by the fallen star and picked his way down to the black object gleaming in its depths. He looked at it a long time before he dared to touch it. He reached out one hand, his fingers hovering over the shiny surface, admiring the reflection of his hand, and then dipped a finger to touch the black stone. It was warm. He withdrew his hand and studied it a bit longer, trying to work out how large it was, how heavy and whether he dared try and pick it up. *Al-Ilah wouldn't have sent me here if he didn't mean me to take it.* He squatted beside the stone and gripped it with his hands, tugging upward, more to test its weight than with any hope of moving it. To his surprise, it came up easily, and he overbalanced, sitting down hard on a sharp rock. Ibrahim started to mutter a curse then thought better of it as he was still holding the holy stone of al-Ilah. He got to his feet and awkwardly climbed out of the crater, holding tight to the black stone.

Isma'il was awake and watching him when he reached the path again. The boy stretched out a hand toward the rock cradled in his father's arms, and Ibrahim knelt in the dirt to let him touch it.

"This is the stone that al-Ilah has blessed, my son. Together we'll find the best place to set it up as an altar to our god."

Ibrahim shouldered the burden of his child once more on one side and the black stone carefully cradled on the other and started for home. It took him a long time, and he was staggering with exhaustion by the time he reached the lower slopes. Dusk overtook him here, so he stopped to let Isma'il down. The boy was crying again from hunger and thirst. Ibrahim turned over rocks and dug with his fingers at the base of leafless shrubs and found a handful of grubs. He pinched the heads off and fed the fat juicy bodies to his son. They provided a little filler for his stomach, and after a bit as the goddess Astarte rose in the sky as the evening star, they set off for home at the pace of a toddling child.

They heard the wailing of women as they approached the tent and saw considerable activity around it, donkeys tied up and men standing around talking. A man saw Ibrahim and Isma'il and let out a startled yell. The wailing ceased, and Hajar ran out. She saw Ibrahim and ran at him screaming abuse, hitting him with her fists and tearing at his clothes. He could not defend himself because of the black stone he carried so resorted to yelling at her to desist.

"Isma'il is alive, woman. You're frightening him. Stop hitting ... ow!"

Hajar caught sight of her son cowering behind his father and snatched him up, running off with him and disappearing into the tent. The men gathered round, neighbours from as far away as half a day's travel, asking where he had been and laughing about the trouble he was now in with his wife.

"What's that you're hanging onto?" Mahir asked.

"Bring it into the light so we can see it," Hasim added.

Ibrahim did so, holding the stone close to his body but allowing the light of a torch to fall on it.

He grimaced slightly but did not pull away when the other men stretched out their hands to touch its glossy blackness.

"Where did you find that?" Sakhr asked. "I've never seen anything like it."

"On the mountain."

"Where on the mountain?" Sakhr persisted. "I've been up there, and there's no rock like that."

"A star fell last night. Al-Ilah led me to it and bade me bring the stone down."

"Al-Ilah?" Hasim queried. "The God? Who do you mean? Which god?"

"Do you mean Hubal?" Mahir asked. "He's god of shepherds and you're a shepherd …"

"Not Hubal. Al-Ilah. He used to be Aali of the High Places."

Hasim shook his head. "Never heard of him."

"Neither had I," Ibrahim confessed, "But he exists. I saw him – there on the mountain top."

The men looked at him in astonishment. "You saw a god? A real god? Not just a statue, a likeness?"

Ibrahim nodded. "I heard a voice calling me – a voice in my head. It bade me approach his altar and on it I saw a flame – a flame that burned on the rock yet didn't consume the rock, nor wither for lack of fuel."

"Wh … what did this flame, this god, want of you?" Mahir asked shakily.

"A sacrifice." Ibrahim hesitated. "He wanted me to sacrifice my only son, Isma'il."

The men gaped. "And you did?" Mahir laughed uncertainly. "I mean, of course you didn't, but that was where you took the boy?"

Sakhr whistled. "No wonder Hajar is so angry with you. I don't suppose you discussed it with her first?"

"What happened?" Hasim asked. "You took your son to this Aali or al-Ilah and then you refused him? You defied a god?"

"No, I offered my son on the altar, but al-Ilah stayed my hand. He provided a goat in place of my son, and I sacrificed that."

"That doesn't make sense," Mahir observed. "He tells you to sacrifice your son and then stops you. What kind of a god can't make up his mind?"

"It was a test," Sakhr said excitedly. "The god was testing your resolve, your faith."

"Yes. The god changed my name from Ab'rim to Ibrahim and named me Khalil Ullah – Friend of God. He said my name would become great and that my son, Isma'il, would have more sons than the grains of sand in the desert."

Mahir laughed. "Isma'il's going to be a busy lad. Did this god say how many wives he's going to have?"

"Curb your tongue, Mahir," Hasim growled. "This is serious. We have a new god in our midst. We must learn all we can of him. Ab'rim …"

"Ibrahim," Sakhr said softly.

"Indeed, Ibrahim," Hasim continued. "Did al-Ilah say what he wanted generally? What's his ... er, sphere of influence, so to speak?"

Ibrahim shook his head. "If he's truly al-Ilah – The Supreme God – then he controls everything."

Sakhr whistled again. "One god to control everything? How is it possible? There's too much in the world."

"Who are men to know the ways of the gods?" Hasim said.

"Alright," Mahir said. "We have a new god that Ab'rim says is al-Ilah, but could just be another god. Why do you say he's The Supreme God, Ab'rim?"

"Ibrahim," he corrected absently. He stood in thought a moment. "He's of the High Places, yet he bade me bring his holy stone down to the plains, so he might be worshipped here too. He healed my goat of a broken leg …"

"Hubal," Mahir whispered.

"And he commanded a star fall from the heaven. And … and … I almost forgot. When the sacrificial goat was produced, a woman in the likeness of Hajar appeared. Yet she wasn't there – it was an apparition or … or a goddess doing his bidding."

Hasim nodded sagely. "A demon can take the form of an apparition, I've heard, but only for evil purposes. From what you say, nothing evil happened, so it must've been a god. If not a demon, then only a god can command an apparition, and only a great god – al-Ilah – can command a goddess. It's enough for me."

"Who was the goddess?" Mahir asked.

"I don't know. She looked like Hajar."

"Not Uzza then," murmured Mahir so that Ibrahim could not hear. "Hajar's no great beauty. Al-Lat perhaps?"

"It doesn't matter who the goddess was," Hasim observed. "Only the god." He looked quizzically at Ibrahim and the black stone. "What are you going to do?"

"What the god told me to do. Take the black stone and raise up an altar to al-Ilah at a place where all the faithful may worship him."

"Where's that?"

"I don't know," Ibrahim confessed. "The god didn't say. I'll have to think on it."

Ibrahim had ample opportunity to consider the matter. It was three days before Hajar let him into the tent and another two before she deigned to speak to him. Then it was only to berate him. Ibrahim stood her scolding for a whole day before he asserted himself.

"Enough, woman," he growled. "Isma'il is alive and none the worse for being on the mountain. Now make me some supper. I'm hungry."

Hajar glared at her husband. "No thanks to you. I cannot believe you meant to sacrifice my son to this new god of yours."

"Our son, and I've told you Al-Ilah was testing me. Isma'il was in no real danger."

"But you didn't know that, did you? You offered him in the belief he'd die."

"You prayed to the gods to give us a son. Do you not think that gives the gods the right to ask him back from us? As it happens, al-Ilah was merciful. Shouldn't you be thankful instead of complaining and making my life a misery?"

Hajar said nothing, but she busied herself with the evening meal and even served her husband. She did not allow him into her bed that night, or the next, but then relented and welcomed him lovingly.

"What will you do with the black stone, husband?" she asked later. Hajar had not fully accepted his new name and tended to avoid it.

"I'm to set it up as an altar, so that all men may worship al-Ilah, but I don't know where that should be."

"How about the rich farming land to the south and east? Your brothers would surely welcome you home, and we could take our ease there with fertile pastures."

Ibrahim snorted. "You forget I am the youngest son and have no inheritance from my father save these tents and the herd. My brothers would see my return as a threat to their prosperity. No, I must look elsewhere for the future of our son and our god. Remember al-Ilah said his sons would be as the grains of sand in the desert? That must surely mean his destiny lies far from the moist farmlands of the south."

Hajar yawned and settled herself for sleep. "Well, the god appeared to you, so you must decide where our future lies. In the meantime, the pasture has all but vanished from here and we're low on barley, wheat, salt ..." She yawned again. "... and a dozen other things. We need to move somewhere."

Ibrahim considered his options over the next few days and announced his intention to journey north. “There are trading routes along the foothills of the western mountains, so we’ll not be alone.”

Hajar nodded her acceptance. “As you will, husband.”

“No, as al-Ilah wills.”

“Either way, we still need grain, salt, honey, herbs ...”

“Tell me all that you need, and I’ll go south first, trading goats. When I return, we’ll go north.”

Ibrahim was back within the month, having traded several of his goats for what they needed in the markets that flourished in the ports of the great southern sea. The provisions were packed onto the back of his donkey, and he led the unprotesting beast back from the moist lands of the south-eastern coast into the drier interior. He had traded well and secured all they needed and a little beside. Ibrahim put this down to the intervention of al-Ilah, for he prayed to him before every transaction. Naturally, he had not risked taking the black stone with him, but he had buried it beneath the rug in their tent before he left, with strict instructions it was not to be disturbed. He looked forward not only to the company of his wife and child but also to looking on the holy object once more.

The tent was no longer where he had left it a month before. Ibrahim stood in the spot where he judged their encampment had been and scanned the land, turning slowly in a full circle, anxiety slowly gripping him. He saw nothing that indicated what had happened. He made camp, gathering up dried dung as fuel, and while he sat by the fire that night, he considered what must have happened.

There's no forage here. Hajar has shifted the camp and herd to find new pasture – but in which direction? Not south, for I would've seen her, or east into the desert. West are the mountains ... it's possible, but I think she went north, following the trade route. She knew of my intention to go north. He debated whether to seek out his neighbours and ask them for news of her. But if the forage was gone here, it would be gone there too, and they would have moved on. It might be more fruitful to seek his family out in the only direction they could have gone.

Ibrahim prayed to al-Ilah and then went to sleep, confident his god would facilitate matters. He set out at dawn, heading northeast to intersect the main caravan route. He followed this with his donkey for a day, before he met travellers from the north. They confirmed the presence of a woman and child with a flock of goats barely half a day's walk away. Ibrahim thanked them and moved on, finding his wife camped near a shallow dry stream bed. Tough scrubby vegetation offered feed for the goats, and after a cursory glance at the dispersed flock, he hurried toward the tent.

"Ibrahim!" Hajar came running to greet him and Isma'il was not far behind, toddling as fast as he could go. "You're safe and well, my husband?"

Ibrahim embraced his family. "I was worried when I saw the tent gone. There was no trouble?" he asked anxiously.

"No, but there was no feed for the flock either. I couldn't take them out foraging with Isma'il, so ten days ago I asked our neighbour Hasim to help me move everything. Was that the right thing to do, husband?"

"Indeed, you've done well, dear Hajar." He picked his son up and embraced him, tickling him until he laughed. Isma'il pulled at his beard, and Ibrahim roared with feigned pain, making the little boy laugh harder. At last he kissed the boy and handed him to his mother. He patted the rug and asked, "And the black stone? It's still safely buried under here?"

Hajar nodded. "It's safely buried, but not under here."

"What do you mean?"

"You gave me strict instructions that it wasn't to be disturbed, so when I moved the tent I left it buried."

Ibrahim leapt up. "So where is it?"

"Back at the old camp site. It'll be in the same place, husband. Still safely buried."

"But where at the old camp site?"

"Why, under the rug ... Oh." Hajar looked down at the rug with dawning comprehension. "You ... you'll be able to find it?"

Ibrahim sat down again and put his head in his hands. "I hope so, but I was thereabouts last night, and I couldn't have said where our tent used to be. If I cannot find even that, how will I know where to dig?"

Ibrahim returned to the old site the next day with a mattock and spent the next three days digging, but he did not find the black stone. After the three days, he went back to his tent and saw to the needs of his flock before trying again. He prayed to al-Ilah for help, reasoning with the silent god that if he did not find the stone he could not construct the altar. That did not work either, and Ibrahim started digging again.

So it was for the next twelve years. Ibrahim would guide his flock to find forage; never going more than a day or two's travel from the burial site, and hurrying back to dig over the spot as often as he could. He became known to his neighbours as Mad Ibrahim, but he refused to explain his obsession with digging over the desert. Two years after he lost the stone, the monsoon came early and stayed late, the rains building into flash floods that washed over the old site. The water scoured away the marker stones he had erected to show where he had already dug, forcing him to start again. The rains also engendered new vegetation however, and within a month, he was able to move his camp back to where it had been before, now spending every spare moment at his self-imposed task.

The years passed. Isma'il grew into a sturdy boy and took over the management of the growing flock, guiding them to the grazing lands every morning and back again in the evening. They moved camp several times, but Ibrahim refused to travel further than two days away, needing ready access to the old camp site. Brothers and sisters were born, and Hajar had her hands full cooking, cleaning and educating the children. Ibrahim became, if anything, more obsessive in his quest as the years rolled on. He dug trenches across the old camp site, shifting mountains of sand and soil that the children played on, but he did not find the black stone.

"It's there," he told Hajar every evening. "I can feel it. I'll find it tomorrow."

Sometimes a traveller would pass by, and Ibrahim would invite the man to share his tent and his food, offering the hospitality so important for dwellers in a hostile environment. If he felt he could trust the man and the man was in no hurry to move on, he would offer him employment digging up the desert. When this happened though, Ibrahim dug less, spending his time watching the stranger in case he found the holy object and made off with it.

After twelve years, the whole of the old camp site had been dug over, some parts more than once, and Ibrahim fell into despondency. "Al-Ilah has abandoned me," he lamented. He despaired of ever finding the holy stone and sat day after day on a mound of dug over sand and rock, refusing to do anything.

"Go build your altar to your god without the black stone," Hajar said. "Your god will surely forgive your carelessness."

Ibrahim forbore from mentioning his wife's culpability in the matter. It would not help and would more than likely divert attention onto his own shortcomings. "It wouldn't be the same," was all he would say.

"Go up to the mountain, father," Isma'il advised. "Find the old altar and pray to al-Ilah there where he once was. He may hear your words clearer than he does down here."

Ibrahim nodded. “You’re wise beyond your years, my son. Pick an unblemished kid from the flock. I’ll sacrifice it on the altar, and al-Ilah will hear me when the hot blood splashes the rock.”

The journey to the high ledge took Ibrahim the best part of two days. The old trails which he had not walked since bringing down the black stone had become obliterated and fresh rock had fallen on the steeper parts. He managed the climb without incident though and reached the ledge with its weathered altar in the afternoon of the second day. Leaving the kid tied to a shrub, Ibrahim brushed the altar clean before washing it carefully. He made a small fire and burned a fingernail-sized piece of frankincense, wafting the sweet smoke over the altar.

At dusk, he laid the bound kid on the altar rock and stood over it with his stone knife at the ready. “Hear me, al-Ilah. Your servant, Ibrahim, son of Azar, offers you a sacrifice of a young unblemished kid from his flock. Draw near, O Great One, Merciful and All-Knowing, as the life is spilled for you.” He grasped the kid’s head in one hand, bending it back and drawing the flint edge of his knife across the taut throat. The goat gave a single terrified bleat before its blood gushed out over the rock.

Ibrahim stood back and raised his bloody hands to the heavens and prayed again. “I am thy loyal servant, al-Ilah. Hear me and accept this sacrifice of blood. Show me where your holy black stone is buried so that I may fulfil your wishes and build an altar to you where all men may worship.”

The mountain, the ledge and the altar remained silent. No blue flame appeared, and no sign was given that the prayers had been heard.

Ibrahim sighed. "I didn't think it would work," he muttered. "Al-Ilah is gone from here, else why would he tell me to build an altar elsewhere?"

Night fell and Ibrahim felt the pangs of hunger. He built up the fire and skinned the sacrificial goat, roasting a leg over the flames. The fat from the thigh he added to a pinch more frankincense and burned it, letting the commingled scents ascend to the heavens. When he finished his meal, he carved off meat from the carcass for the following day and took the rest to one end of the ledge for whatever scavengers might be attracted by the smell of blood. He curled up by the embers of the fire with his back to the stone block and fell asleep.

He dreamed. Ibrahim saw himself stride down the mountain with his fourteen-year-old son under one arm and the great block of the black stone under the other. Despite the size of this boy and the swollen rock, he had no difficulty negotiating the rocky terrain, almost seeming to float rather than walk. He reached his tent and entered, but now he carried only the black stone. He pulled back the rug and dug a hole, burying the holy object.

Do not disturb this stone, he heard his dream self tell his dream wife.

He looked up and saw the goddess, Astarte, the bright evening star, falling in the west. For an instant, it touched the tip of the mountain before disappearing. Ibrahim turned within his dream, and the walls of the tent vanished. To the southeast, he saw the twin rounded hills called the Breasts of Uzza lying one directly behind the other. The next instant, he stood on the ledge again and saw his body curled up by the fire. A flash of fire leapt from Astarte behind him and traced a glowing line over the desert. Another came from the Breasts of Uzza intersecting the Astarte line exactly where ...

Ibrahim woke in the cold dawn with a smile on his face. *Thank you al-Ilah.* He hurried back to his campsite on the plain below. "I know where the stone is, Isma'il. Your advice was sound. Al-Ilah accepted my sacrifice and showed me in a dream where it's buried."

He and his son went to the site that evening and built a fire, waiting for Astarte to cross the heavens. While the goddess moved slowly toward the west, Ibrahim walked back and forth until the two hills of the Breasts of Uzza lined up one behind the other. He piled rocks in a small cairn and walked away, keeping the two hills in line, again marking the spot with rocks. As Astarte neared the peak, he saw it was setting slightly to one side of the mountain, so he ran until the bright star hung just above the darkness of the peak. He gave his son a rock and bade him watch as the star set.

"Watch that it goes down behind the highest part of the mountain. Move to the side if you need to, but when it dips out of sight, put the rock down."

He left his son and moved back a hundred paces or so and found another rock, waiting in the chill night air as the great star fell toward the peak. Ibrahim found himself slowly walking north, then south a bit, then north again, correcting his position as Astarte fell behind the peak and Ibrahim dropped his rock, placing another one on top of it.

"Isma'il, return to the fire," he shouted, and his son called back an acknowledgement.

When dawn arrived, Ibrahim went to the cairns lining up the Breasts and Isma'il to the rocks marking the setting of Astarte. Keeping the markers in line, each one slowly walked until their paths crossed.

Ibrahim looked down at the sand then across to where he had dug up the desert. "I was digging in the wrong place all these years. I put my reliance on my own memory rather than rely on al-Ilah."

Despite the guidance of his dream, it still took time and a lot of digging to find the black stone, but eventually the light of day shone once more on its glassy surface. Ibrahim sat holding it for a long time, carefully wiping its surface clean of every trace of sand and dirt. Isma'il admired it and sat close, gazing at it reverently.

"I was there when you found it; father, but I don't remember it. It's beautiful."

"Yes, it fell from the sky under the direction of al-Ilah. He has returned it to me at long last."

"And now?"

"Now I'll build an altar to al-Ilah and incorporate his holy black stone so that all men may come to know him."

"Where, father? Here, where it lay all this time?"

Ibrahim shook his head. "I've thought about this over the years. I think I must take it north along the trade road, until I find a place where all men come."

They packed up their tent a few days later and set off for the north, moving at the speed of the grazing goats. They passed through San'a and Najran, but Ibrahim shook his head and pointed north. Always the western mountains were on their left hand and the sandy desert to their right.

Though Ibrahim was of the tribe of Ya'fi and the tribes whose territory they passed through were sometimes less than friendly to foreigners, the tribes allowed travelers on the trade roads as everyone benefitted from their presence. Besides, shrines to various gods, both general and local, were situated along the road and protection was given to all who made offerings on the altars. Ibrahim sacrificed at every altar on the road, but he prayed in the privacy of his tent each night to al-Ilah, bowing down before the black stone. When they came to the town of Ta'if, he hesitated and looked around carefully before shaking his head. "Close, but not here," he muttered.

The road ran northwest from Ta'if, and a few days later, they found a small village nestled in a narrow valley and watered by the Well of Zamzam. The trade route continued north, but it was crossed here by another that ran down to al-Bahr al-Ahmar called the Long Sea by others and also east toward faraway Dilmun.

"This is the place," Ibrahim declared. "The place where I shall build the altar to al-Ilah."

"What is the place called?" Isma'il asked.

Ibrahim did not know, but a fellow traveller on the road told them. "This place is Makkah."

***

Men worship gods and women worship goddesses. Not always, but if the choice is there, men and women will follow the deity who most closely resembles them in form and temperament. Gods are often represented by the dynamic forces that affect us all, such as the storm, the killing sun, thunder, the desert sandstorms, war and strong drink; whereas we women choose goddesses who represent the calmer aspects of nature like beauty, love, the fates and children. Yes, I say 'we women,' because my name is Hajar. History has all but forgotten me, except as the wife of Ibrahim and the mother of Isma'il. That is often the fate of women in a man's world.

I suppose, now you will ask how it is I can write this account when few women are ever taught how to read and write? The truth of the matter is that I can do neither, for who squanders education on a girl? I learned the home skills I would need at my mother's knee and have never needed more ... until now. I would like to have written these words myself, but all I can do is recite my tale to a scribe, and he writes my words down. I suspect he embellishes the account – he smiles and shakes his head – but he is my beloved great-grandson, Mus'ad, and he is good to me. He will make me sound more like a chieftain's wife than the partner of a humble shepherd, putting words of which I scarce know the meaning into my mouth. He is a good boy, and I love him dearly – *yes, write that down Mus'ad, for it's the truth* – but I fear someone reading this account years from now will not see me in it at all.

Men have their little secrets that they learn when the priests of male gods perform the sacred rites. From them, they believe a male god made the world and everything in it when his seed spurted out, in much the same way a man believes he only needs a woman as a fallow field to receive his own life-giving seed. How little they know! A very long time ago, in the days when mankind was first formed from the primal clay, it was not a male god who knew how to fashion them but a female, the first goddess – the Great Mother Goddess. Back in those early days, women ruled the tribes and the tribes lived in peace with each other, for all humans, men and women, were related to one another.

Now it is different; men rule and women have been relegated to the home and hearth. It is sacrilege to suggest the Great Goddess made a mistake when she fashioned men, giving them strength and desire, for these are qualities a woman values in a man. But strength should be used in the service of family and tribe and desire in the courting of a mate. Men now misuse these attributes, employing strength in pursuit of wealth and power and desire has turned to lust and rape. I do not believe a goddess sanctioned this change; it can only have come from a god who valued men above women.

Which god is responsible? I have my

suspicions, and they are not pleasant. Do I dare voice my suspicions? This is not an idle question in view of the power men now wield over women. I could be tried for heresy under these male-god laws and condemned to death. Being the wife of Ibrahim and the mother of Isma'il would not save me, even in my dotage. *Don't deny it, Mus'ad, just write it down, there's a good boy ... yes, that too, for it's my account you're writing.*

The beginning was nearly forty years ago on a day that is lost in so many other days, for ours is a simple life without the need of naming the days or months, of writing or reading, of counting higher than the goats in one's flock or the beads in a necklace. It was a day like those that went before and those that came after, save in one aspect – my husband found a new god. Yes, it was the day he descended from the mountain, bursting with the news of a flame and a voice in his head.

I do not like to speak ill of the dead and less so of my late husband for, despite his many faults – he was a man after all – he was always a loving husband and a good father to his children. However, it must be said that he was a simple man. I asked him how he knew it was a god, and he gave me his reasons. One was the vision was of a blue flame that burned without fuel and gave no heat.

Gods and goddesses take many forms, and I suppose it is not impossible that one could appear as a still, blue flame. The Great Goddess is often represented as a tall, beautiful woman with wide hips and full breasts as befits the Eternal Mother, but I have seen the ancient figures that primitive tribes own, rudely carved stone images that hint at nothing more than the creative force within women – coarse images all breast and pudenda. But I have never heard of her, or any other of the great pantheon of lesser gods, being represented solely as a flame. How could one form any emotional or spiritual connection with something so inhuman? However, there is a class of spirit who come from the flame. The djinn were created from a smokeless fire, the priests tell us.

Ibrahim said the spirit on the mountain spoke to him in words as clear as two people speaking together in a tent. Yet the words were not formed in the air but rather within his head. They were words of command but also with an undercurrent of amusement as if two old friends whiled away an hour over a jar of wine. *That's Mus'ad talking, I don't drink wine.*

Now I have spoken to many gods and goddesses over the years and sometimes my prayers have been answered, but never by a voice sounding in my head. The gods speak by signs – a bolt of lightning, the flight of birds, the behaviour of the sacrificial animal or the fall of divining sticks – but I have never heard a god speak with words. Yes, I suppose it is possible, but I have heard voices in the desert where there were no people – voices that sought to deceive me. I know them for what they are, those creatures born of fire, the arch-deceivers, the djinn and the ifrit and worst of all, the shaytan.

My husband believed he had met a god, but I believe he met nothing but a demon. *Write it, Mus'ad, I'll take my chances.*

There are hierarchies of demons just as there are hierarchies of gods and men, but from what Ibrahim told me, I do not think he met even one of those powerful beings called Shaytan or Ifrit. I think he found a lowly djinn. It was not able to perform miracles or conjure up fearsome visions but beguiled my husband only with fair words. Djinn are deceivers and pranksters, rarely causing direct physical harm, whereas an Ifrit can kill and a Shaytan will rend body and soul. A god can be equally deadly. I gave thanks to the Mother that my fool of a husband only met a djinni on the mountain.

He brought home the black stone with the news he was going to build an altar to al-Ilah in Makkah, many miles to the north, a small town nestled in a narrow valley connected by trade routes to the world. Ibrahim and Isma'il started building the altar, a simple structure consisting of an arc of stone and an oblong room open to the sky. The black stone itself, more of a deep reddish-brown in fact, was set waist high into the wall where all could see it. Everyone who came to the altar wondered at the nature of this stone, where it came from, what it meant. Anything used in the worship of a god automatically becomes sacred, so it was that any hint of it coming from a demonic source soon became heresy. The other gods of the tribes came to recognise the sanctity of this new shrine and had their devotees move their own worship to the Shrine of the Black Stone. They call this building the Kaaba now and venerate my husband and Isma'il, even as his god rises in power.

By the time Ibrahim was an old man, more than

a dozen gods had moved their centre of worship to Makkah. Perhaps it was because they sought the sanctity of the new shrine, or maybe it was to share in the wealth that pilgrims brought to the town. Chief among the early gods to make the move was Hubal, god of shepherds, perhaps because Ibrahim had been a shepherd when he found his god. Already, the followers of Hubal say he is al-Ilah, though my husband's fellow worshippers deny this. They hold that al-Ilah is supreme, though they hesitate to cast the other gods down or denigrate them in any way. I fear this will happen in time, for surely this must be the aim of the djinn. A demon does not have the good of men at heart and certainly does not hold the gods in esteem. I have confidence, though, that the Great Mother will survive as she has survived the coming of the lesser gods. How can a mere demon destroy the worship of one so powerful?

I am old now. I have survived my husband by thirty years and Isma'il by five. I have grandchildren and great-grandchildren in my house, but I shall not live much longer. I am content with my life, for I have lived it as the Mother Goddess commands, but … I wish I could feel confident about the future my children must live in. The strength of al-Ilah grows with every passing year and one day I fear …

Yes, make your mark on this account too, Mus'ad, as I'll make mine. I can recognise the tale it tells but not the words, for you've made me sound like an educated woman. No, I don't mind, dear boy. Put the manuscript away. It's in the hands of the gods whether it survives.

Hajar, wife of Ibrahim al-Azar

Mus'ad ibn Qedar ibn Isma'il ibn Ibrahim al-Azar

Chapter Two

Men are such fools. I feel nothing but contempt for those gullible creatures of blood and clay, barely more intelligent than the goats they herd or the animals they hunt. Humans have crawled over the surface of the land for thousands of years – quarreling, fighting, hunting and creating more of their kind – and I have had little to do with them. Why should I? Our interests are so different. I seek out knowledge, whereas a man seeks only to fill his stomach, keep warm and dry and rut feverishly and repeatedly on the belly of his woman. Our paths crossed only when I was hungry, and then my nature was more like one of the great predatory cats as I pursued my terrified prey, toying with him to heighten his terror and finally sucking him dry of energy and life as I feasted.

Men kill buffalo and deer, goat and hare, fish and fowl, consuming their flesh to sustain their bodies, secure in the knowledge that these lesser forms of life are put there for their enjoyment. Similarly, I hunt men, consuming their spirit and life to sustain my own. Well, that is not strictly true. A man will die if he does not eat, but I will only get hungrier. I tried it once, going a whole turn of the seasons without imbibing life. At the end of it, I was no weaker, felt no lessening of my faculties, so I decided the experiment was pointless. I broke my fast, slaying whole tribes and communities until I felt sated. Since then, I have exercised moderation, except when I feel bored. The taking of life is a proper thing for my kind. I am secure in the knowledge that these lesser forms of life – men – are put there for my enjoyment. They are as savage as me, in their way, toward other creatures, so I take from them no more than they deserve.

I have said that I am a djinni, being created from the smokeless fire, but that is not really accurate. I took that name originally because that is what men called me as their life force was wrenched from their quivering bodies. However, I am more than a djinni. I am a long-lived, possibly immortal energy being, having none of the weaknesses of physical life and being imbued with great power. I can fashion myself an apparent body when I choose or invade a living one, bending its actions to my will. I can, with a little effort, read the thoughts of men's minds and influence their actions without them being aware of my presence. In short, I am a god.

It took me a while to realise this, but given my attributes, it is obvious. I remember when I first came to this conclusion. I was resting on one of the smaller peaks of the south-western Arabian Peninsula, well-fed after feasting on a solitary traveller and in a good mood. Night fell, and I turned my mind inward in contemplation. The truth came to me suddenly, and such was my shock, for I had not previously considered my divinity, that I screamed aloud my joy. I know I have no lungs, vocal cords or mouth to shape a scream, but I can still vibrate the air around me and the effect is very like a wailing cry. Ask of Ibrahim the shepherd; he heard me.

I considered what it was to be a god. *I must get myself followers*, I thought, *but how to do it?* Could I just go to the nearest town and say 'I am a god, worship me'? I could imagine that causing fear which would not serve my purpose; or laughter, which would just result in wholesale slaughter. I will not be held up to derision. My alternative was to find another traveller, but this time talk to him instead of killing him. As it happened, a man came to me.

Ibrahim, or Ab'rim as he was then, climbed the mountain while searching for one of his goats. As he approached, I sifted his mind and discerned his purpose. The goat he sought was nearby, having fallen and bruised its leg. I waited for the poor, weak human to climb to my ledge. He displayed obvious fear, so I calmed him, stroking his mind and fostering the belief in my goodness. I showed him the goat, and he brought it to me. I told him it had a broken leg and affected a cure, loosening its muscles, and I knew I had him. He gave me a praise name – Aali – and I was content to use it for the time being. I dismissed him, and just to create a lingering sense of wonder, possessed him and augmented his night sight, so he could clamber down to his waiting flock.

I was interested to see if my interaction was sufficient and waited for the man's return. He came, bearing honeycakes, and I instituted a sacrifice, bidding he lay the food on a flat rock that his mind told me was an altar. His wonderment and awe was so great I decided to test him. How far could I push this weak man? I told him to bring his son to me as a sacrifice, and amazing to say, he did not at once reject the idea. He was horrified and saddened, but deep down I saw his acceptance of my command. I was a god, after all, and gods expect to be obeyed. Perhaps because I was a new god, I still harboured some doubts that Ibrahim would return.

He came, the fire of his zeal almost bursting into a flame of his own. I had thought about my command over the seven days and realised a god must be merciful as well as stern and the heartfelt intention was as pure as the action. It was a simple matter to pluck an image of his wife from Ibrahim's mind and convince him it was real. He took the imaginary lamb from her phantom arms and spilled its nonexistent blood on my altar. As an aside, I was glad no actual lamb had been sacrificed, for although I have killed animals before, I prefer not to. Animals have little choice in their lives, being governed by instincts and dominated by men, to their detriment. In many ways, I prefer the simple thoughts of animals to the self-serving thoughts of men. Anyway, Ibrahim's gratitude was overwhelming, and I locked him into place as my first disciple. I became al-Ilah, the Supreme God, in his eyes at least, and I named him Ibrahim Khalil Ullah – Ibrahim, Friend of God.

By chance, a star fell from heaven the previous night and had impacted lower down the mountain with great noise and light. The rocks shook, and I knew Ibrahim had seen it from afar. I told him to find the glassy fragment of the meteorite – well, of course it was. Do you think I believe stars can really fall? Men would know it only as a fragment of the sky god's realm, a thing holy and rare. I instructed him to make of it an altar down in the flat lands where all men could come and worship me.

He did it too, after he lost it, searched for it and eventually rediscovered it. I had nothing to do with that by the way. I visited him from time to time as he dug the desert over, but I was disappointed in him and debated whether to just kill him and start again with a more attentive fellow. In the end, I left him to it and wandered through other lands, sampling experiences and tasting the life forces of many men.

I returned many years later and was delighted to see he had found the black rock and carried it north to Makkah. He and his son, Isma'il, built the rock into a stone structure and worshipped there the rest of their lives. Their descendants did also, and I remained their god. I performed sufficient 'miracles' that nobody could doubt my power, and I made sure those who followed me devotedly benefitted from the association. They grew in wealth and influence and soon became a force to be reckoned with in that holy city. They named themselves Qurayshi after one particularly ruthless man some two hundred years after Ibrahim died.

Other gods came to Makkah, attracted to the god building, the Kaaba, but none were stronger than me. Many of these so-called gods were nonexistent, their worshippers bowing down to lifeless stone idols or carved wooden images, but a few were djinn. These I dominated and made subservient, for was I not al-Ilah? And so the years turned. I became stronger and nurtured the Qurayshi tribe. They became my right hand and instrument of my will. It was seldom strangers got the better of me.

Chapter Three

The land known as al-Yaman was always rich. Most of the land is as dry as the greater Arabian Peninsula, but the southwestern portion receives monsoonal rains. The coastal region is hot and humid and the swamps breed hordes of mosquitos and other biting creatures, but as the land rises further from the sea, the climate becomes more bearable and rich soils support an abundance of crops and herds. Legend has it that Ibrahim came from this region several hundred years before, more particularly from a tiny tribe called the Ya'fi, though this claim is hard to substantiate. The descendants of Azar, Ibrahim's father have all but died out save for the branch of the family that descends through Ibrahim's eldest son, Isma'il. The few that are left in al-Yaman eke out a living on poorer soil now, herding a few sheep and goats, and boast of their familial relationship to the chosen Prophet of al-Ilah.

Near to the remnant of Ya'fi, but not too near, lived Nazih ibn Salah, an honest, virtuous man sometimes simply called the son of righteousness. He was no longer a young man but enjoyed a reputation for hard work and honest dealing all his life, and he was looked up to by everyone in the vicinity of the mountain village of Ta'izz. He was a farmer, but he did not plant his crop, being content to nurture it and harvest it at the proper time. This crop had made him moderately wealthy, for he was a grower of *al lubn*, the sacred frankincense much sought after by priests.

Nazih's trees were scattered across the dry hillsides, and he walked the paths between them every day. He had done so for the last forty years, ever since his father Salah had died, bequeathing him the property. For several years, he had followed the ways of his father, intent more on guarding his trees from robbers than in fostering their growth, but as he grew in experience, he tried new things and found his crop multiplied under his ministrations. The trees themselves were ancient, having been in the family since the time of Nazih's great-great-grandfather, Saddam. That worthy warrior had been granted a measure of land with incense trees already in existence for saving the life of the tribal chief. Saddam's son, grandson and great-grandson had not made any notable improvements, being content to harvest the precious resin and turn their attentions to other more interesting matters.

Nazih had been different right from the start. As a boy, he had followed his father as he supervised the collection of the resin, but had quickly discerned the three workers his father employed knew little about the process. He asked for and received permission to visit other incense farms, and he slowly learned the correct techniques for harvesting the aromatic sap. Salah listened patiently to his son's explanations on how they could improve the yield from their trees but had done nothing. When the father died, the son took over the farm. All but six of the *al lubn* trees were left to Nazih, those six being left to his younger brother, Yasir. The first year, Yasir – being unskilled in collection methods and unwilling to take advice – had killed two of his trees and Nazih persuaded him to lease the survivors to him. Yasir, who understood the more conventional crops of the region, thankfully left his older brother to work the *al lubn* trees and took a share of the profits. Nazih gave his brother the proceeds of six trees each year, reasoning this had been his father's intention. Within five years, this was no imposition as his methods steadily increased the yield from his own trees.

The rains had been moderately good this last season, producing an abundance of foliage and flowers, though less seed had set. When the fruits matured, Nazih visited the trees and collected what seed he could, noting as always which trees produced the most viable seed. On this particular day, he was accompanied by his nephew, Wasim, his sister's son, a ten-year-old boy. Nazih had never married, and his sister, Ruwa, born late in life to their parents, had always seemed like a daughter to him. Her son became the grandson he would never have, and the two of them grew close, spending much time together. On their seed collecting days, Nazih counted up the seed pods on each tree and told Wasim, who made a notation on a piece of slate.

"Five on tree thirty-seven, Wasim."

The boy dutifully scratched on the slate with a piece of flint.

"Show me." Wasim held up the slate, and Nazih examined the marks. "Very clearly written, but how many tens should there be?"

The boy's lips moved as he repeated the number thirty-seven and calculated how many tens were contained within it. "Three, uncle."

"And how many have you marked?"

Wasim's shoulders slumped. "Four," he whispered.

"Never mind. Cross one out so I don't count it later."

His nephew scratched out the offending symbol and scanned the many marks on his piece of slate. "Why do we count the fruits on each tree, uncle? Wouldn't it be more profitable to count the pieces of resin you collect?"

"I do that as well, my boy. Come sit down in the shade, and I'll tell you what we're doing." Nazih dusted off two rocks. He sat down on one and adjusted his robes comfortably, while he waited for his nephew to settle down. "Now, tell me, why does a tree produce seeds?"

Wasim, who already knew where babies came from, looked sideways at his uncle, wondering if he was playing a trick on him. "Seeds are... seeds are a tree's babies."

Nazih smiled. "Indeed they are, and if I'm to increase the number of *al lubn* trees I tend, I must plant more. Therefore, I collect seed and plant it, raising the seedlings until I can harvest resin from them."

Wasim nodded. "I can see that, uncle, but why not just collect seed? Why do you count how many come from each tree?"

"A good question. Consult your slate, and tell me how many fruit pods were on ... oh, let's say, tree eighteen."

Wasim ran his fingers down the scratches on the slate, frowning as he sought to recognise the symbols representing that tree and its tally of fruit. "Sixteen, uncle."

"So many? Now, why are there sixteen on one tree and only five on another?"

"I don't know."

"Have a guess. Look around you, Wasim."

Wasim looked around at the hillside, already dry as dust despite the rains being only two months in the past. "Water, uncle? Did tree eighteen get more water?"

Nazih clapped his hands softly. "Excellent, my boy, a very good guess ... but, no that's not the reason."

Wasim looked down, crestfallen.

"Don't take it to heart; it was a very good guess. Really, there's no way you could know. Even I didn't know, until I started keeping records for each tree." Nazih paused, waiting until his nephew looked up questioningly. "I took a lot of resin from tree thirty-seven last year but only a little from tree eighteen." He smiled at the puzzlement on the boy's face. "It depends on how much resin they produce the year before. The more resin, the fewer seeds the next year."

Wasim thought about this revelation for a few minutes. "Why? Why should resin have anything to do with seeds?"

"Think of the resin as the strength of the tree. The more strength we take, the weaker the tree gets. The weaker it gets, the fewer seeds it can make."

The boy nodded slowly. "But why do you want to know?"

"If I'm to make more trees, I must gather seed. I must therefore not weaken my trees too much by collecting too much resin."

"But you have many trees. If each one only produced one seed you would still have many seeds."

"That's true, but it's not only the number of seeds that becomes fewer. When I plant seeds from weak trees very few seedlings grow. If I want lots of healthy seed, I must take them from a strong tree."

"Where do you plant these seeds, uncle?" Wasim looked over the hillside. "I don't see any young plants."

"You won't. I sowed my seed out there for the first year or two but very few sprouted, and those that did were eaten by wild goats and conies. Now I grow them elsewhere and only plant them out when they're a year or two old. I'll show you some later."

Nazih arose and led his nephew to the next tree, and they continued their rounds of his *al lubn* orchard. He collected seed from a few trees, putting the ripe fruit into little cloth bags and tying them with a drawstring, marking the bags with a knotted string to tell them apart.

"Why don't you collect every seed, uncle, if only a few will sprout?"

"I collect a few from any tree that produces plenty of fine grade resin, but I've learned to select my trees." Nazih walked up to one gnarled specimen and brushed his hands lightly over the foliage. The perfume of the incense wafted over them. "Examine this tree, Wasim. What can you tell me about it?"

The boy squinted up at it. "It's a big one … lots of leaves … but no fruit."

"I took all the fruit off it a few days ago. It had over fifty, if you're interested."

"Is that a lot?"

Nahiz squatted down and made marks in the dirt. "That many." He gestured at the tree again. "What's different about this tree?"

"It is bigger and has more leaves."

"What about the resin?"

Wasim stared, then frowned. "You've made no cuts. There's no resin forming."

Nazih nodded and smiled. "For many years, this was my best tree. It gave much resin and of high quality. For the last two years, I've rested it and it's rewarded me by yielding many healthy seeds. Many of them have sprouted, and I have several now planted out." Nazih beckoned and led the boy down the hillside and up onto the next one. "I bought this land three years ago, and I've been planting young *al lubn* trees on it this year. See?"

The sapling in front of them was no taller than Wasim. It had a single main stem and three small branches with a ragged crown of dusty leaves. A framework of cut thorn branches surrounded it, so Nazih had to lean in carefully to rub the dust off a leaf. "The thorns keep the goats at bay," he explained. Wasim was kicking at a clod of earth, and the old man put out a hand to restrain him. "That's part of the water retaining wall. When it rains here the ground is often so dry the water rushes straight off the hillsides and into the wadis. I made these broad basins around each sapling to keep the water in. Instead of draining off, it soaks into the earth and nourishes the plant."

"When will you cut it to get the resin?"

"In about another five years. Too soon and you weaken the plant. In the meantime, I watch my saplings closely and carefully remove anything that could damage them. I even take the flower buds off so it won't waste its strength making seeds."

"And this tree is the child of the big one we saw?"

"Yes. I hope that when I cut it, it'll produce top quality resin like its parent."

Wasim did not say anything, just screwing up his face in doubt.

"You don't think it will?" Nazih asked. "Yet a child resembles its parents. Two brown goats produce brown kids, do they not?"

"My father has two brown goats, but they produced spotted ones."

Nazih nodded slowly. "It happens, but I don't know why. I believe, though, that offspring usually resemble their parents." He grinned suddenly and squeezed his nephew's shoulder. "If I'm wrong, I've wasted a lot of time on these seeds and saplings. Do you want to come and see me cut a first time tree?"

"Yes, uncle. You've never shown me how you do that."

"Well, watch and learn, and maybe in a couple of years, I can hire you on as my worker." Nazih led his nephew back across to the hillside where the mature trees were scattered across the slope. They passed the one that supplied the seed and several others where Wasim could see the tears of the plant forming on the trunks. He inhaled the sharp perfume of the raw resin and hurried to where his uncle was standing beside a medium-sized tree. It towered above the boy, but his uncle could have reached almost to the topmost branches if he had tried.

Nazih squatted and beckoned. "Observe the unblemished bark, my boy, there're no flaws. The trunk's relatively straight, and it has three strong branches. Most of the other trees have already been cut, but because this one's just reaching maturity, I decided to cut it late and only subject it to the widening once."

"Widening?"

"I'll show you later. For now, watch and learn as I make the first cut. First, I strip away the outer bark and rub the trunk down with a cloth to remove loose flakes … if these loose bits are left, they get caught in the hardening resin and contaminate it. Now, I take my knife …" The copper blade shone warmly in the sunlight. "... and make a single, deep incision about two hands in length through the outer skin. Some men will insist the cut should be vertical, but I say it should curve around the trunk gently. And ... see there? The first drops form on the edge of the cut."

Sap, like drops of milk, formed in tiny beads along the cut surface, slowly growing in size. Some of them coalesced and trickled down the length of the wound, becoming stickier and less fluid as they oozed to the bottom of the cut. Behind the first hesitant drop, another formed.

"It smells like it, but it doesn't look like incense, uncle. Isn't it supposed to be brown?"

"There are different grades. What we offer up to the gods at home is lower grade and brown, as you say. The finer resin that we send to the priests in the great markets is yellowish or even, if very pure, a pale green colour. It comes out white but changes colour as it hardens."

"And that's all you do, uncle? Just that one cut and then you collect the resin?"

Nazih smiled. "Well, there's a little more to it, but I'll leave that for another day. Are you hungry?"

They walked back down to Nazih's house, a stone cottage with a thatched roof, where he lived alone. The old man drew up a bucketful of cold water from the well and poured it while his nephew washed his hands. He then rinsed his own and dried them on the hem of his robe. On his uncle's instruction, Wasim took a small earthenware pot and approached the milk goat tied up in the shade of the house. She rose to her feet and stared at the boy, bleating softly. He stroked her and then squatted, feeling at her teats. The goat stood calmly and let the boy direct thin jets of creamy, white milk into the pot. After a few minutes, he got to his feet, cradling the pot in his arms and thanked the goat for her gift. She bleated solemnly and lay down again, her ears flicking the flies away.

Nazih had gathered a handful of dried dates, and they sat on the flagged stones near the door to the house, eating the sweet fruit and drinking the milk still warm from the udders. They sat in companionable silence for several minutes before Wasim wiped his mouth on his sleeve and pointed toward the valley road.

"You have a visitor, uncle."

The road that ran past Nazih's *al lubn* plantation was the main road north out of Ta'izz and people used it for a variety of purposes. However, no reasonable destination lay beyond Nazih's house for several days' travel, and as the man walking up the road was not leading a horse or a donkey, it was a reasonable assumption that his purpose lay closer at hand.

Nazih stared at the approaching figure until he turned off to come up the path toward the house. His eyebrows drew together as he recognised the man. "Wasim, go inside and fetch another cup. It's your uncle, Yasir." When the boy ducked inside, he allowed himself a small complaint. "May the gods give me patience," he muttered. "What does my little brother want of me now?"

He rose as Yasir drew near and advanced on him with his arms spread wide. "Brother, my house is yours. Enter and refresh yourself."

Yasir said nothing, and after a perfunctory embrace, stamped over to the well and waited for his brother to pour water for him. Nazih did so, and afterward dried his brother's hands and feet with a cloth Wasim brought over.

"Come to the house. Wasim should have … ah, yes, I see he has … thank you, Wasim … May I offer you a cup of fresh goat's milk, brother? A few dates perhaps?"

Yasir accepted a cup of milk and a few dates. He sat with his back to the house wall and consumed the food, offering no more than a few words of conversation. When he finished, he put his cup to one side and fixed Nazih with a calculating look.

"How's business, Nazih?"

"The gods have been kind, brother. And with you?"

"Father left you the easy part of the inheritance. I have to work much harder on my farm."

Nazih sighed. "I'm the elder son, Yasir. To me, by right, comes the larger portion. This was discussed and upheld by the elders ten years ago. Why do you raise it again?"

"Because it's not fair. You were left the *al lubn* trees which generate huge profits with no more trouble than having to collect the beads once a year. I, on the other hand, have many crops that need a lot of attention; and then when I do harvest them, I get little for them as everybody else's crops are on sale at the same time."

"There are other incense growers, you know. I, too, have to compete."

Yasir laughed bitterly. "There's never enough incense to satisfy the priests. You get high prices always."

Nazih inclined his head in agreement but said nothing, waiting for his brother to get to the point of his visit. Wasim stared from one uncle to the other, wide-eyed but keeping very quiet.

"If I had *al lubn* trees, I could be wealthy too," Yasir grumbled.

"You do have trees. Father left you six, which I care for."

"Then why don't I see more than a pittance from your profits, brother?"

"You have six trees out of ten times that number that I own. You get exactly one-tenth part of my profits, for no effort on your part."

"Yet you get richer every year and I poorer. How is that if you're not cheating me?"

"I can think of many reasons for that, brother," Nazih said calmly. "For instance, I work alone on my land while you hire laborers. And I spend little aside from my daily needs."

"You're telling me I'm a wastrel as well?"

"I didn't say that, but you have a young wife and she's often dressed in new clothes."

Yasir grimaced. "Shazi is another burden I bear."

"I wouldn't presume to advise you ..."

"Then don't."

"... but you should correct your wife if she oversteps her position."

"Beat her, you mean?"

"No, brother, I don't mean that. Sit down with her and explain your financial situation. Have you ever talked to her about trading and what your farm produces?"

"Of course not, that's my concern. Hers is the home."

“It’ll become her concern too if you can no longer pay for new clothes. Talk to her in kindness, Yasir. She’ll see the sense of it.”

Yasir shrugged and crossed his arms over his knees, resting his head on them. “It may be too late anyway. I’m going to have to sell the farm.”

“Sell it? Sell your inheritance? You cannot.”

“That's easy for a wealthy man to say, but I owe silver and my creditors won’t wait.”

“That's ridiculous. Anyone in Ta'izz would be willing to wait for what they’re owed. You tell them to come and see me. I’ll remind them of tribal charity.”

“They’re not from Ta'izz.”

Nazih stared at his younger brother, noting the trembling that Yasir tried to hide. “What have you done, son of Salah?”

“Send the boy away and I’ll tell you.”

Nazih stared a bit longer before turning to their nephew. “Wasim ...”

“I hear you, uncle. I’ll go and feed the goats.” Wasim jumped up and ran across the bare dirt to a stone barn and a holding pen in which a dozen goats were corralled. The animals saw him coming and ran to meet him, bleating for his attention at the fence.

“You have my undivided attention, Yasir.”

Despite the absence of the boy, Yasir was in no great hurry to reveal his troubles. He poured himself another cup of milk and sipped at it, staring out over his brother's *al lubn* plantation. “It started about three years ago,” he said at last. “I had a good crop of cucumbers, but so did everybody else in Ta'izz and the prices were so low I almost had to give them away."

"I remember."

Yasir nodded and continued. "I decided to try selling my cucumbers in San'a. I loaded up my three donkeys, borrowed another three and set off for the big city. I reasoned that there'd be more merchants in a big city and fewer gardens in which to grow food. If I got even slightly more for my cucumbers than I could get in Ta'izz, I'd make a small profit."

"Seems like a reasonable assumption," Nazih murmured.

"It was," Yasir snapped. "You're not the only one who can think." Nazih said nothing. "So, I arrive in San'a after seven days with three quarters of my cucumbers ..."

"What happened to the others?"

"It's hot on the plains and they rotted. Anyway, I sold my cucumbers for a very good price, and I could've sold my melons, pumpkins and oranges several times over, had I thought to bring them."

"So you sold everything and turned a tidy profit. Where lies the problem?"

"I'd never been to San'a before. I decided to stay a few days, see what there is to see." Yasir hesitated. "There's a ... a certain tavern there. They sell strong wine and ... entertainment."

Nazih groaned. "Tell me you didn't get drunk and were robbed."

"I wish that was all that happened. I drank a bit, I ... I spent silver on a girl, and I played dice with some pleasant fellows. Somewhere in the night, I fell asleep and woke the next morning in a room at the tavern with my silver gone, a headache replacing it and a man staring at me."

"So you were robbed."

"No ... yes ... maybe. I don't remember, but the man told me what else happened that night."

"Who was he?"

Yasir shuddered. "He said his name was Baqir of the Qurayshi and said his name as if he meant it."

"Baqir? To rip open? What is he, a butcher or something?"

"Possibly, but he wasn't talking about that sort of work. He said that I'd lost all my silver at dice with his chief and had gone on to lose more on credit – six silver pieces. It was his job to collect the silver from me, and he asked when I was going to pay."

"How much had you lost?"

"I forget. It doesn't matter. What matters is what came after. I explained that I had no more silver and could not get more until I sold more of my farm's produce. To do that I'd have to return home. He agreed, and I came back to Ta'izz. I loaded up everything I could, even the sacks of wheat I was saving for winter, and returned to the markets at San'a. I sold it all, and it came to a little more than I owed – eight silver pieces. I paid Baqir and took a room in a different tavern, meaning to return home the next day."

"What did you tell Shazi about all this?"

"She doesn't know. I told her I was robbed."

"Still, you had a small surplus at least, after you paid your debt."

"I had it when I went to bed, but with the dawn, Baqir was back. He demanded the same sum again, saying that although I'd paid the debt, I hadn't paid the interest owing on it."

"I hope you went to the town elders or the constable. A man cannot charge interest unless it's been drawn up in writing, signed and witnessed."

"I know that. I'm not ignorant of the law. He produced the document. Now, you know I cannot read well, but I could make out the interest rate, my signature and the signatures of two witnesses. I don't remember agreeing to it, but I must have as he had the paper."

Nazih shook his head and stroked his beard. "You think it was a forgery?"

"Who can say? It doesn't matter. I paid over what I had and left, telling Shazi I was robbed. We survived the winter on the sale of the incense from my six trees that you paid me, but next spring Baqir came to Ta'izz demanding a sum far in excess of the original sum. Interest on the unpaid interest, he said. This time he made threats."

"What sort of threats?"

"He gave me a month to find the silver and then he beat me badly. I couldn't stir out of my house for a week. He said if I didn't have at least half the silver at the end of that month, he would kill me and take my wife as a slave."

"By all the gods, brother, I hope you went to the village council about that, laid charges against him at the very least. A judge could hear the case and ..." Nazih's voice trailed away, and he looked at his brother with compassion. “You didn’t. I’d have heard.”

“I was ashamed. I sold some of my land and had enough to pay half what I owed by the end of the month.” Yasir grimaced. “Baqir looked disappointed. He took the silver and told me to have the rest by mid-summer or double if I wanted to pay the interest as well – and then he broke my nose, by way of a reminder.”

“So that was why you came to me year before last,” Nazih said softly. “You wanted your share of that year's incense in advance to pay your debt. Why didn’t you tell me why you wanted it, brother?”

Yasir would not look at his brother. “As I said, I was ashamed.”

“I gave you the incense. You paid off your debt. Why are you still in trouble?”

“I paid it all but a little bit – a few pieces of copper, nothing more. Baqir said it didn’t matter and went away. We struggled to survive that year, but we managed it. We even had a small surplus after the harvest. I thought everything was good, but just before last year's harvest, Baqir came back. He said the small unpaid amount of interest had grown, doubled and redoubled. He laughed when I reminded him he had said the little bit left unpaid did not matter. 'Of course it matters,' he said. 'Do you think I’m stupid?'”

“I don't suppose you ever got receipts for your payments or even a copy of the original agreement?” Nazih asked.

Yasir shook his head. "Baqir is not that sort of man, nor is, I suspect, his master. He's given me until next month to raise it all." He raised his head to look at his brother and his eyes brimmed with tears of despair. "What am I going to do, Nazih? I don't have the silver to pay him, even if I sell everything I have."

"And it sounds as if you will never find enough silver as he will come back asking for more each year." Nazih got to his feet and brushed down his robe. "I need to think on this, Yasir. Stay here, have more milk and dates." He turned and strode away over the courtyard to the barn and goat corral.

Wasim looked up from where he sat in the pen with his arm around one of the kids. "Is everything alright, uncle?"

"This morning was better than this afternoon," Nazih conceded. "But maybe tomorrow will be good again. We must trust in the gods, Wasim."

The boy got to his feet. "What's happened?"

Nazih stared down at his nephew for a few moments and then nodded his head. "I want you to help me." He turned and led the boy back into the *al lubn* plantation and up to his best-producing tree. He prised off a thumbnail-sized piece of resin and raised it to his face, breathing in the strong aroma. "Good. This'll be acceptable." Nazih led the way to the top of the hill and stopped outside a swept circle of ground where he took off his sandals, motioning to the boy to do likewise.

"This is holy ground. We must show respect for the god of high places."

Nazih walked to a small square-cut rock in the middle of the circle and knelt. He waited until Wasim joined him and then took his fire bow and a small block of wood with a charred hollow. In the warm, still air he sawed the bow vigorously and soon a spiral of smoke rose from the block. He added wisps of dry grass and blew on them gently, feeding the fire with tiny shavings of wood. When flames licked strongly at the shavings of wood, he placed the resin chip on the fire.

"Wasim," he said quietly. "Keep watch around us. Tell me if you see anything."

"What ... what sort of thing?" Wasim asked, round-eyed.

Nazih spared him a quick smile. "I doubt you'll see the god himself, but he may speak through a sign. Let me know if anything moves or if you see anything unusual." He bowed down as the blue smoke from the incense ascended into the heavens and murmured prayers to the god. After several minutes he sat up and looked at Wasim. "Anything?"

"No, uncle."

"Nothing? You are sure?"

"Only the hawk." The boy pointed into the sky.

A hawk, high up in the washed out blue of the firmament came soaring from the north on outspread wings. It circled the hilltop and stooped, descending rapidly to the north again, until it faded from sight in the distance.

"The god speaks," Nazih said with conviction.

"What did he say?"

“Nevermind. Come, we must go back to the house. Uncle Yasir is waiting.”

When they got back, Yasir was pacing the yard. Nazih took his brother by the arm, falling into step beside him.

“I’ve given your problem some thought, brother, and I’ll do what I can. When does Baqir return?”

“On the day of the new moon.”

“Ten days hence. It doesn’t give us much time, but it’ll have to do. Go home now, brother, and make a list of all your assets. Return here in two days with the list. Ten days hence we’ll meet Baqir together – here.”

“Everything? Am I to be beggared then? I thought you said you’d help me.”

“I will, brother, but first I must know where we both stand financially. Also I must find out from Baqir how much you owe.”

“I can tell you that.”

“Forgive me brother, but I’ll hear it from him. You’ve thought before that you’d paid him off and then discovered you hadn’t.”

Yasir returned to his farm, and Nazih thought for an hour before saddling up a donkey and riding into the town of Ta'izz. There he spoke with the elders of the tribe for some time. In the evening, two fast horses with trusted riders left the town – one headed north toward San'a and the other west toward Mocha. Nazih watched them both out of sight and then headed home to formulate the next stage of his plan.

Ten days later, Nazih stood outside a large tent he had erected in his courtyard. He had stripped his home of its finest furnishings and lined the tent with rugs and cushions and furniture. A jar of wine on the end of a long rope hung in the well cooling, and he had laid on a rich mutton stew with fresh baked bread, cheese and dates. It was important that he impress his visitors, so he had even spent silver to hire two servants for the day. One was on the road keeping watch now, while the other waved an ostrich-feathered fan to keep the ever-present flies at bay.

The first of his visitors arrived – his brother, Yasir. Shortly after him the chief of the Ta'izz tribe rode up on a fine stallion with two bodyguards on lesser mounts. Nazih greeted them all and sat them on his right hand, offering wine and dates. Chief Tahir accepted and extravagantly praised Nazih on the quality, but his two bodyguards refused, drinking only water and remained standing behind their chief. Yasir was restless, darting glances toward the entrance and sipping continually on his cup of wine.

"Where are the others, Nazih?" Tahir asked quietly.

"They'll be here." Nazih bowed and beckoned to the servant. "May I offer you goat's cheese, High One? I made it myself from my own flock."

While Tahir nibbled without much enthusiasm on the crumbly cheese, the next visitor arrived. The man, in long black swirling izar and black kufiyya with a gold wire headband, left his horse in the care of the servant outside and entered the tent, where

Nazih greeted him with great respect. “My lord, welcome to my humble tent. I thank you for coming.”

The robed man glanced across at the chief and nodded his head, his gaze slipping across the bodyguards dismissively, lingering for a few seconds on Yasir. “They’re not here yet?”

“No, my lord. You’ve met Chief Tahir ibn Tawfiq al-Ta'izz? Chief Tahir, may I present Judge Mahir Abd-al-Aziz al-San'a?”

The two men greeted each other with inclinations of the head and small gestures invoking the blessings of the gods. Nazih led the judge to his seat and personally served him with wine. Silence ensued for several minutes, and then the sound of horses' hooves came from the road.

“Ah, they’re here,” Nazih murmured. He arose and went to greet the men from San'a. Six men came to the tent, one imposing and confident, the others walking behind and to the side with hands on the curved daggers in their waist sashes.

“I am Baqir,” said the confident man. “Why are all these others here?” His gaze flicked over the seated men, a sneer forming as he saw Yasir, but his eyes widening when he caught sight of Judge Mahir. He covered it quickly and moved to the vacant cushions and settled himself. His men arranged themselves to either side. “Well, where is my silver?”

Nazih clapped his hands for his hired servants and told them to serve the meal. “Let us all partake of food and ask the blessings of the gods on our meeting.”

Baqir shrugged and started eating, drawing a disapproving look from the judge. Nazih gave thanks to the gods for the blessing of the food, then his other guests started their meal. He watched his guests eat, attentive to their needs, but only picked at the food himself, feeling his stomach clench within him at the task ahead. The servants cleared the meal away and brought round bowls of scented water and towels.

Judge Mahir belched politely and inclined his head toward his host. "Nazih ibn Salah, you have honored us with your hospitality, but you brought us all here for a purpose. Will you please state it?"

"Honored Judge, Chief of Ta'izz, Baqir, my brother, Yasir, I have asked you all here today that we might settle amicably a dispute that has arisen between my brother Yasir ibn Salah and this gentleman here, Baqir of San'a. My brother unwisely fell into debt while on a business trip to San'a three years ago and being unable to pay the debt immediately, incurred interest payments. Despite his every effort since, which included sale of some of his land, the entire crop from his farm and borrowing from me against future income from his share of my incense crop, he's still in debt. What is more, the amount he owes is now higher than when this affair first started. Have I fairly stated the circumstances, Yasir?"

"Yes, brother," Yasir mumbled.

"Baqir?"

"More or less," Baqir agreed. "But what need is there of talk? He owes me silver; let him pay. And while we're at it, why are all these others here? This is between me and Yasir."

"Chief Tahir is here because Yasir is from Ta'izz and Judge Mahir al-San'a because the initial debt was incurred in the town of San'a. As you may know, Baqir, the judge has legal jurisdiction over crimes committed in that area."

"Why are you saying crimes? There's been no crime committed."

"You don't dispute that my brother Yasir owes you silver? And that the present sum derives from interest owed on the original sum?"

"No, but that's not a crime. The law allows interest to be charged for an unpaid debt."

Judge Mahir leaned forward. "As the expert here, let me say that the law allows interest charges to be met providing certain conditions are met. The debtor must be aware that interest is being charged at a stated rate, and the document of debt must be signed by the debtor, the principal creditor and two witnesses without connection to either party. Also, that rate must not exceed fifty per cent per lunar month."

"All of which conditions were met," Baqir said with a cold smile.

"That isn't true," Yasir whined. "I didn't know what the interest rate was."

Nazih frowned but said nothing. *He said he did know*.

"Perhaps I could hear first from the contenders in this matter," Mahir said. "Yasir ibn Salah, will you go first? Describe to me, in your own words, what transpired."

"Transpired?"

"What happened?"

"Ah." Yasir started hesitantly but soon warmed to his task and managed to keep the whine out of his voice almost until the end.

The judge nodded and turned to Baqir, asking him for his version of the events. He spoke rapidly and succinctly and was soon finished. "So you see I'm now owed a hundred silver pieces."

"All of this should be easy enough to prove," Judge Mahir said. "Do you have the document of debt?" he asked Baqir.

"Of course." Baqir clicked his fingers and one of his men pulled a parchment out of a pouch and handed it across. He opened it, scanned it quickly and passed it to the judge.

Mahir examined the document carefully. He looked up at Baqir in surprise. "Khayri ibn Rashid al-Isma'il al-Qurayshi is your principal?"

Baqir nodded his head in assent. "I have that honor."

Mahir grimaced and continued his examination of the document. "Well," he said at last, "this all seems to be in order. Even the interest rate is high but acceptable – fifty per cent per month. I can find no fault with the contract."

"No," Yasir cried out. "I ... I don't even remember signing it. It must be a forgery."

"That's a very serious accusation," the judge said. "Can you prove it?"

"Let me see." Yasir held his hand out.

Mahir would not relinquish his hold on the contract but held it up for Yasir to see. Nazih also peered at the writing with interest. "Well, is it your signature?" the judge asked.

Yasir nodded and hung his head, his face pale and sweating.

"I agree," Nazih said. "However, there's one point I find curious. Perhaps you do too, Judge Mahir?"

"Perhaps," the judge said cautiously. "What is your curious point, Nazih ibn Salah?"

"Refresh my memory on another aspect of interest law, Judge Mahir. Isn't there a limit on how high a debt can mount?"

Mahir stroked his beard thoughtfully. "In absolute terms, no; but relatively, yes."

"What does that mean?" Chief Tahir asked. "For those of us who don't study law on a daily basis."

Mahir made a small moue of distaste. "If a man had a debt of a hundred horses at interest, he might owe a maximum of five hundred horses after a short time, which is a huge amount; but if a man owed a single copper piece at interest, his debt could not rise beyond five copper pieces. The law states that a man cannot owe more than five times the original debt in the original specie."

"Then I'm saved," Yasir cried. "My original debt was six silver pieces. My debt can only be thirty pieces, and I can borrow against my farm to raise that."

"Your monetary debt can only rise so far," Mahir said, "but unless you can prove that you made a reasonable effort to pay off the debt, then the courts will be forced to arbitrate between the parties for the outstanding amount. A judge could find against you and forcibly sell your farm to cover the debt. Why, a man could even be sold into slavery to pay his creditors."

Yasir paled and started to tremble.

Baqir stirred. "My principal would be content with this man's farm and his person as a slave."

"One moment, if you please," Nazih interrupted. "Judge Mahir, correct me if I'm wrong, but interest is charged on the full time period, isn't it? Not on a partial interval?"

"That's true. Interest is charged by a stipulated time period – a year, a month, a day, depending on the circumstances. Why, I once had a case before me where interest was reckoned by the hour and ..." Nazih coughed politely, and the judge smiled and stopped his anecdote. "Interest paid off before the stipulated time is calculated at a lower rate.

"The reason I ask is that in the original document the stipulated time period is one lunar month or twenty-nine days."

"What of it?" Baqir asked, frowning.

"I've talked to my brother and to many merchants making the journey between Ta'izz and San'a, and the average round trip is fourteen or fifteen days. If we allow another three for my brother to harvest his crops in Ta'izz, he's still back in San'a in eighteen days. Another day to sell them and he's paid off his debt well before the deadline of twenty-nine days."

"So?" Baqir asked truculently.

Mahir nodded. "Yes, I think I see where your argument is going. The original debt was six silver pieces. If the interest rate had applied for the full month, another three would be owed after that time. However, your brother returned and paid off the original debt in nineteen days. When informed the next day of interest due, he had only two silver pieces left over and paid that toward what he thought was his debt, whereas if it really was in nineteen … no, now twenty days, two silver pieces would have paid the interest debt off in full."

"Then … then I've paid it and owe no more!" Yasir cried.

"Except it wasn't eighteen, nineteen or even twenty days," Baqir growled. "It was twenty-five days at least. There's still silver owed."

"Hmm, I cannot see any way out of this," Chief Tahir mused. "It's Yasir's word against Baqir's. I believe Yasir, he's of the Ta'izz after all, but there's no proof either way."

Nazih sat in thought while the others argued. *The trouble is putting a date on events that happened nearly three years ago. If the inn keeper could remember when Yasir was there, but why should he keep records and my brother's not exactly memorable, so he won't remember him. His wife Shazi? No, her word would be worth little as she would, of course, lie for her husband. Wait, what did Tahir just say*?

"Chief Tahir," Nazih broke into the argument which was starting to get heated. "What was that you just said?"

"Eh? What? I don't know. When?"

"Just a few moments ago. You said something about taxes."

Tahir frowned and thought back. "Taxes? No, I didn't … oh, I recall. No, it wasn't about taxes." He laughed. "I said all this talk about dates and sums owed was taxing even my understanding."

"That's it," Nazih said with a grin. "Taxes."

"No, no, no. I said taxing, not taxes."

"I understand, Chief Tahir, but I'm talking about taxes – namely the property taxes we all have to pay every year around harvest time. Would you have those records, Chief Tahir?"

"Of course."

"They would show who paid their taxes, how much and on what day, wouldn't they?"

"Yes. Why?"

"An admirable thought, Nazih ibn Salah," Judge Mahir said, clapping his hands softly. "Chief Tahir, would you be please send one of your men to the village to collect the tax records?"

Tahir grumbled but sent his man off, and while they waited, they drank wine and listened to a fund of stories the judge had accumulated in his extensive travels. The man returned with the records within an hour and set them before his Chief. He in turn handed them to the judge.

Mahir pored over the entries but ignored them all until he came to that of Yasir ibn Salah. "Here we are. Yasir paid his tax on the sixteenth day of Imr'a. A sum of ... well, that doesn't concern us. Now, according to the document of debt, it was signed on the eighteenth day of Sam'r. That's a period of ..."

"Twenty-seven days," Nazih said smiling.

“As I said.” Baqir was triumphant. “It’s long enough for silver to be owed. That’s very nearly a full month.”

“Except,” Mahir said quietly, “if Yasir paid his tax in Ta'izz twenty-seven days after signing the document, it means that he paid over the silver he had in San'a no later than twenty days after the signing. It’s common knowledge that the journey between Ta'izz and San'a is at least seven days on foot.”

“Then the two silver pieces I paid would cover my debt!” Yasir shouted.

“Just a moment,” Mahir said. He bent over a tablet, making notations and calculations. “It seems that you were short by two copper pieces, Yasir.”

“It still adds up then,” Baqir said. “He owed interest on the interest when I came collecting six months later.”

Mahir calculated again. “Two silver pieces and one copper.”

“But I paid more than that!” Yasir cried. “Eleven pieces of silver, he said. I paid half then and almost all the rest by midsummer. And he broke my nose into the bargain.”

“Is that true, Baqir of San’a? You offered violence to this man?”

“It’s allowed,” Baqir snarled, “when a debtor refuses to pay.”

“I didn’t refuse, I just couldn’t pay.”

“Same thing.”

“No,” said the judge, “It’s not. When a man doesn’t have the required gold, silver or copper to pay a debt, you have various options, none of which include violence. You may forgive him the debt, you may wait for payment or you may put collection in the hands of the local Sharif who has jurisdiction over lands, men and property. Why didn't you do any of these?"

"I did. I waited for payment until midsummer."

"After breaking his nose."

Baqir shrugged. "I didn't think he was taking my demands seriously."

"Yet he'd just paid you five silver pieces and some copper. More than he really owed."

"I didn't know that for I don't calculate these things. I only carry out the commands of my chief."

"Khayri ibn Rashid al-Isma'il al-Qurayshi?"

"Yes."

"You cannot read and write, Baqir?"

The man shook his head. "A few words, enough to sign my name to something."

"Then it seems I must talk to Khayri ibn Rashid."

Baqir looked unsettled for the first time. "Why do you need to talk to him?"

"Yasir is now owed silver over this transaction, and he has a grievance concerning the broken nose. Khayri ibn Rashid has profited by the mistake and is accountable for the assault committed by one of his men."

"That's nonsense," Baqir blustered. "How can he be held accountable when he didn't even …?" The big man fell silent and looked away.

"He didn't know of your actions, Baqir al-San'a? Is that what you were about to say?"

"I … I'll make restitution," Baqir said. "There's no need to disturb the peace of al-Qurayshi."

"You, Baqir al-San'a? You would take on this debt personally? Now? Witnessed here in front of these people?"

"If I must. I don't want my master disturbed."

"Then let it be so," Judge Mahir said. He took out paper and quickly drew up an agreement whereby Baqir agreed to pay Yasir the sum of twelve silver pieces within a twelve-month period, one piece per month with no interest payment owing. He read it out slowly so everyone understood the terms and conditions.

"Why no interest?" Yasir complained.

"Charging interest caused this problem. You're the aggrieved party, but I thought you might like to charge none in return. Was I wrong?" Yasir hesitated a moment and then shook his head.

"Why twelve pieces?" Baqir grumbled. "He paid only eleven and according to you he really did owe two and a copper piece."

"The rest is compensation for the injury you did him."

Judge Mahir oversaw the signing of the document by the principals and witnesses, though in Baqir's case, his signature was almost illegible, so the judge appended a note attesting it as true. "Very well, then. This dispute is settled. Baqir will make payment of one silver piece on the next day of the new moon and on every new moon thereafter until twelve payments have been made." The judge glanced at Baqir's surly expression and added. "The payments are to be made to the Sharif of Ta'izz on behalf of Yasir ibn Salah."

Baqir and his men left first, saying little as they saddled up and rode out northward toward San'a. The Judge, Chief Tahir and Yasir left a little while later, thanking Nazih for his hospitality and for brokering the agreement.

"Baqir isn't completely bad," Judge Mahir said. "He's a violent man, but he has a reputation for caring for his horses. Does that sound strange?"

Tahir shrugged. "Should we care?"

"It ended well," Nazih agreed, "but I cannot understand why Baqir gave in so easily."

Mahir paused with his hand on the saddle of his horse. "You've obviously never met Khayri al-Qurayshi."

"No, Excellency, I haven't."

"I suspect Baqir was extorting silver from your brother without Khayri's knowledge. If he learns of this embezzlement, Baqir will die. Khayri isn't a forgiving man."

"But Khayri is a good man?"

"Only the gods can see into the heart of a man, but I think Baqir would die not for extorting the silver but rather for not giving Khayri his share. Khayri follows the god of the Qurayshi of Makkah, al-Ilah, and thinks that with the favour of a powerful god all things are lawful for him." Judge Mahir was silent for a few moments and then said quietly, "It is said that a man comes to resemble the god he serves. I think that might be true in this case."

When he was alone, Nazih climbed to the top of the hill once more and burned another fragment of incense, his prayers wafting up with the white smoke. Rising to his feet, he looked all about him, marvelling at the clear air and the feeling of contentment that filled him. Movement caught his eye, and he stared to the north. Below him on the road that led to distant San'a were gathered half a dozen horsemen. He could not make out who they were, but as he watched, they slowly started moving south in the direction of his plantation. Then he knew.

"Baqir," he muttered. "Why is he still here?" Nazih hurried back down to his house. One servant had put away the food and drink and left for the village, while the other was still engaged in cleaning up after the meal. He called the servant to him and bade him run to the village as fast as he could manage. "Find Judge Mahir and tell him that Baqir is returning. I fear he means mischief. If you cannot find him, bring the Sharif and his men. Hurry!"

Scarcely had the servant left when Baqir and his men arrived. The horses clattered up the stony path that led to the courtyard, and Baqir confronted Nazih, pushing him back with his horse. His men dismounted and fanned out, searching the house and barn.

"No one here," called one of the men.

"Good." Baqir dismounted and faced Nazih.

"Why are you here?" Nazih asked. "Our business is finished."

"Oh, yes, you'd like it to be, I'm sure." Baqir smiled unpleasantly. "If it weren't for your meddling, I'd have my silver by now and be well rid of this stinking village."

"You cheated my brother. Judge Mahir found against you according to tribal law."

"The gods know where you found a judge of the San'a, but it won't help you. Your brother may have escaped me, but you won't. I'll lose twelve silver pieces because of you, so I think it only just that you recompense me."

"But unlike my brother, I'll go straight to the judge."

"Yes, like I said, you're meddlesome. Well, you won't get the chance. You'll pay me now – twelve silver pieces."

"I don't have silver and even if I had, I wouldn't give it to you."

Baqir turned to his men. "Search his house and barn. Ransack them. A silver piece for the man who finds his hoard." He watched the old man as his men started, smiling at the look of pain that came over Nazih's face as his possessions were thrown crashing to the ground.

"Nothing, Baqir," said one of the men a little later.

"Where is it, old man?"

"I told you, I don't have silver."

Baqir slapped Nazih, and the old man reeled back from the blow. "This is an incense plantation isn't it? That's worth money. Show me then where your collected incense is."

"No."

"I advise you to think again, old man. Give me an incense brick worth twelve silver pieces, and we'll leave you alone. Refuse and … well, you really don't want to find out what'll happen to you."

Nazih considered. *If I delay them, the Judge or the Sharif will return and arrest them.* "Please try and see it from my point of view. An incense brick is worth far more than twelve silver pieces. If I got one out, you'd rob me of the whole brick rather than just cutting off a piece."

"So you do have incense. However, you wrong me by implying I'm not a man of my word. Give me incense worth twelve silver pieces, and I'll leave." Baqir watched the old man and saw the hesitation in his face. "Why do you delay? You owe me the twelve silver pieces I lost as a result of your meddling."

"Rather, it was your deceit that cost you the silver," Nazih said, playing for time. "If you hadn't deceived your master, you'd be free of this debt. What will your master think of this? Khayri al-Qurayshi, I think you said."

"He won't know. I'll take my silver from you and pay the fine the judge imposed on me. My master need never find out."

"But you're compounding your error by robbing me. A powerful man like Khayri will find out."

Baqir shook his head. "I'm not here to argue with you for I'm fast losing my patience. Produce the incense or die; it's all one to me."

"You'd kill me? Don't you fear the gods, Baqir of San'a?"

Baqir laughed. "The gods are like men, old man, vain and mercenary. As long as you praise them and offer them something, they're happy. Has your long life not taught you that gods can be bought and sold like any other commodity? I follow al-Ilah of the Isma'il Qurayshi, a most pliant and accommodating god. I can do as I wish and buy forgiveness with a sacrifice."

"You blaspheme, Baqir of San'a. Your so-called god, al-Ilah, is nothing but a djinni if he lets you behave like that. I call upon the older gods, the true ones, and goddesses too ..."

Baqir snarled and hit Nazih in the mouth, silencing him. He threw the old man to the ground and kicked him unconscious. "Find that incense," he roared to his men.

They eviscerated the house and barn but except for a few copper pieces in a box, an assortment of brass vessels and a small silver charm, they could find nothing of value.

"What about the incense trees?" asked one of the men. "We could scrape off the resin and sell that."

"If we had all day we could, but we cannot stay here. This must seem like a casual robbery." Baqir stared at the lower slopes of the hillside and the scattering of *al lubn* trees. "Cut them down. If the old fool thinks to cheat me, he'll do so at his cost."

His men grabbed axes or knives and those without metal implements used their hands to rip at the leaves and branches of the gnarled trees. They shouted with triumph as each tree fell and moved on to the next, slowly moving over the slopes. One man went across the wadi to the small trees in their thorn enclosures, but Baqir called him back.

"They are worthless; make sure of the bigger trees."

A cry of outrage and pain sounded behind them, and Baqir turned to see Nazih staggering up the slope toward them, blood streaming from his head.

"Stop!" the old man cried out. "You mustn't. These are trees dedicated to the production of incense for the gods."

Baqir pushed him to the ground again, but Nazih rose and clutched at the man's robes. Baqir cursed and stabbed out with his dagger. A look of agony twisted the old man's features. He coughed blood into his grey beard, crumpled and fell to the ground. As he fell, a high, thin scream split the air around the hill and every man stopped chopping at the trees and looked round fearfully.

"What was that? It … it sounded terrible."

Baqir shivered. His mind held an image of the blue flame of a demon. "It was nothing," he said brusquely. "A hawk riding upon the air, nothing more." He searched the heavens and pointed. "There's the hawk." The other men looked but could see nothing. They started edging down the hill away from the body of the old man and toward the security of their horses. Baqir knew his control was slipping so made the best of it. "Come, it's time we started for home."

A few minutes later, the horsemen rode out of Nazih's property and turned north toward San'a. When the Sharif arrived with his men, they found devastation around the house and barn. Shortly after, they found the body of the old man lying cold on the hillside.

***

I am Wasim ibn Juda ibn Junayd, and I am justly proud of my father and of my paternal family line, but I am also the son of Ruwa bint Salah, who was the sister of my uncles Nazih and Yasir. I was there on the day my uncle Nazih was killed, and I saw everything that transpired. Many years have passed since that evil day, but I remember it as yesterday for Nazih shaped me on that day as if he had foreseen his death.

I did not hear what passed between my uncles on the day I helped Nazih record his al lubn seeds as he sent me away to tend his goats while they talked. I can guess though as I heard most of it ten days later. After I helped my uncle sacrifice to the gods on the hill above his plantation, we returned to his house and I slipped apart so he would not notice me, yet not so far that I could not overhear what was said. I know if he had caught me eavesdropping, he would have been ashamed for me. If my father had caught me, he would have thrashed me and he has a strong right hand. I risked it, though, as I had my share of curiosity. What boy does not? I overheard a name – Baqir – and talk of Uncle Yasir becoming a beggar. I heard a time – ten days – and I resolved to be there too.

On the day of the meeting, I left home at dawn before my father could find me and set me to work. I ran over the hills to Uncle Nazih's plantation, climbing the far side of the hill that sheltered his trees and coming down past the small concealed cave in which he stored the scrapings of incense from his trees. I concealed myself in the goat pen for the animals knew me well enough not to be disturbed by my presence.

When the sun neared its zenith, I heard horses and risked a look over the low stone wall. It was Chief Tahir and two of his men. They did not see me and even the servant who tied up the horses close to the goat pen did not guess at my presence. A stranger arrived next, clad in black robes and an air of authority; then another group of horsemen arrived from the north. These men looked harder, cruel of feature like ... like the Badu or wandering tribes of the desert.

I have mentioned there is a small cave in this hill, no more really than a tunnel that burrows through the rock for the space of twenty paces. In it Nazih stored the bricks of incense he harvested each year, letting them dry and mature in the cool darkness that creates the best quality. My uncle had shown it to me once and told me the secret of its concealment. It lies amongst boulders and is guarded by an old, gnarled thorn tree, almost leafless, the only one left on the hillside. Peer over the boulders and all you will see is the trunk of the tree, but slip between the boulders and kneel so you peer between the roots and a cool blackness beckons. I was afraid of snakes and scorpions when I first saw the entrance, but my uncle laughed, telling me the pure odours of incense keep the cave free of all vermin. He was right, for I never saw even an insect or a spider in its darkness.

Then Baqir arrived with his men. I still remember that day so long ago when I witnessed my uncle's death. I do not think of him as often now as I once did, not because my love for him has faded, but because other things are ever battering at the gates of my mind. When I do think of him, his face is bright in my mind's eye and he smiles at me, forgiving me, which is more than I can do. I was only ten years old on that dreadful day, yet I always wonder if I could have done more to help him.

Baqir's men ransacked his house, throwing his possessions to the ground. Then they knocked him down and kicked him until he lay still. Tears filled my eyes, and I almost left, but it was too late to run when they started up the hill to destroy the trees. I made it back to the cave unseen and watched, my heart surging with sorrow and anger. I saw Baqir not twenty paces off, directing his men in their savage destruction, and I saw the blue fire about him once more. In those days, I knew nothing of the evil djinn and ifrit of the desert or of possession, yet what I saw made me shrink back as if the fire itself had eyes and might spy me cowering under the thorn tree roots.

I heard my uncle cry out, and I saw him running up the hill shouting at them to stop their desecration. I filled my lungs to cry the warning, but Baqir was faster and my uncle fell dead at his feet. Agony rose within me and was released as a formless shriek of despair. I thought then I would be discovered and share my uncle's fate, but the men looked up in the sky, thinking a bird had cried out. They ran to their horses and left.

If any of them had looked back, they would have seen a small boy appear out of the hillside and stumble to where the man they had killed lay. I knelt beside my uncle and lifted his head, cradling it while my tears spattered his face. His mouth and beard were bloody, but I wiped them ineffectually with my sleeve and sobbed his name.

"Bless you ... my boy," Nazih whispered.

"Uncle, you're alive!"

His eyes slipped past mine to the chopped and hacked trees. "Loo ... look aft ... my ... trees."

I promised him I would and babbled on about how his servant would return and we would bandage him up and heal him. Then we would catch the evil men and replant the *al lubn* trees. He never heard me and never spoke again, dying there on the hillside among the wreckage of his incense trees in the arms of a small boy who was powerless to turn back death.

The Sharif and his men found us there as the shadows lengthened. I was led away weeping to my parents, and the village gave my Uncle Nazih a fine funeral and buried him. A week later, I found that Nazih had left the plantation and house to me in his will that had been lodged with Chief Tahir. My other uncle, Yasir, contested the will but half-heartedly, as he owed his own farm to Nazih's efforts. The Sharif pursued Baqir and his men to San'a and beyond but never caught them. They disappeared into the desert where they no doubt fell in with the wandering tribes. Their natures were similar after all.

I have been to Makkah and worshipped at al-Kaaba with its three hundred and sixty gods and goddesses. I pay them all my respect for who knows when a man will have need of a particular deity, but there is one I will not worship. This refusal of mine has earned me the resentment of one of the dominant tribes of the area – the Qurayshi. They hold this god in high esteem, believing themselves descended from Ibrahim and Isma'il, who reputedly first found this god. Though what man of jazirat al-Arab does not claim descent from Isma'il? Yet they claim a closer relationship than other men, obstinately refusing to see what is plain to others.

This god of theirs they call al-Ilah as if naming him *The God* somehow elevates him above all others. Ibrahim, who first found this god, was a shepherd, and I think it possible that this al-Ilah is merely Hubal, the shepherd god, by another name. Hubal's symbol is the crescent moon and al-Ilah's is the bright star that falls to earth, yet I have seen banners where both crescent moon and star are found together. I have seen this fallen star too, the black stone Ibrahim and Isma'il built into the wall of al-Kaaba. I no longer tell people what I believe al-Ilah to truly be as I have to live and trade among them. Religion ever stirs up violence and hatreds in men. Al-Ilah is the god of the Qurayshi. Baqir was a man of the Qurayshi. Baqir was possessed by a djinni, a blue smokeless flame, the same flame Ibrahim saw on a mountain top hundreds of years ago, if the stories are right. I believe the being known as al-Ilah is a demon of the desert, a djinni, and for this reason, I will not sell my incense to his priests. This demon possessed Baqir, and my uncle Nazih died as a result. One can revenge oneself against a man, but how does one seek vengeance from a demon, particularly one who is worshipped as a god? I had a choice to make – to spend my life in futile bitterness or to put the past behind me and make the most of the life my uncle gifted me. I chose the latter.

I journeyed on from Makkah, traveling with my own camel caravans, across the sandy and stony wastes to far off Dilmun on the shores of the eastern sea. There I have spoken to men of other races, men who have beliefs very different from ours and who seek out knowledge for its own sake. I took a ship in Dilmun, perhaps the first man of Ta'izz to do so, and sailed north to the great city of Ur and south to Magan where men rip rock from the ground and turn it into shining copper. I learned much and brought this knowledge home to my own people. Most of the tribesmen do not want to know anything that will not help them grow more melons, raise more goats or harvest more incense, but my eldest son sits at my feet as I recount the tales of my wanderings and declares he will follow in my footsteps. I will take him with me after the next harvest and teach him three things: seek knowledge where it is offered, deal honestly with all men and honour the gods, but first make sure they really are gods.

Chapter Four

Makkah in the early days was a town surrounded by wilderness. Even after five hundred years or more, following the influx of so many gods and goddesses to the Kaaba built by Ibrahim, the town could justly be described as an ungodly place. How could it be otherwise? Those who called themselves gods were in fact djinn and their motives were largely selfish. I was different though. Conscious of my elevation in the eyes of men to the status of Supreme God, I acted the part, answering many prayers, manifesting miracles and attracting much support from the Qurayshi tribe. In case you think me too godly, my worshippers pay a price for my attention. I feed on them while they pray, but I refrain from killing them – usually anyway. I have learned to extract some of their life force in such a way that they feel exhilarated by the experience but drained. Thus both parties benefit.

The Qurayshi tribe proved to be a valuable investment. Their name means little shark, and if you have ever seen these fish in the great seas, you will appreciate why I like them so much. They are almost as bloodthirsty as djinn. The Qurayshi are descended from Isma'il through Nabit his eldest son and later through Adnan. It was at about the time of Adnan that the men of that family took to banditry to earn a living. They developed their martial skills and soon dominated the other tribes in the vicinity. Not much happens in Makkah and the surrounding territory without the Qurayshi having a hand in it. Every transaction involves a payment to the tribal coffers, every event attracts a fee and every person must pay a poll tax and a tax on their income, on a birth, a marriage or a death – all sanctioned by heaven, of course. I make sure my Qurayshi worshippers realise where their power and wealth come from, and they continue to offer sacrifices.

Sometimes I leave the incense-laden peace of the Kaaba and join a raiding party as they disappear into the desert. Usually I slip into the body of one of the men and savor his bloodthirsty thoughts and the exquisite thrill of one man killing another. In return, I offer him insights and give advice on the most interesting ways to torture a prisoner or to ransom him for profit. You can be sure that where a Qurayshi is involved in a particularly hideous killing or brutal rape, I am there. I need some relaxation from my godly duties, after all. The man, Baqir, was a favourite. He was a violent man with a pair of fine horses he tended to mistreat. I do not like that aspect of men, so I corrected it, earning him an enhanced repitation among the desert folk.

I was not there when Baqir of San'a committed his petty crime of robbing that poor farmer, Yasir, of his profits. I mean, can you imagine a god getting involved in anything so paltry? I heard of the affair several months afterward, when one of Baqir's men visited his relatives in Makkah. He boasted of the crime to a man who, unbeknownst to either, was harbouring a certain god and hinted that as the farmer was likely to default on his payments, violence would be necessary to convince him of his error. I listened with a little interest, being somewhat bored at the time.

I should say here that boredom seems to be an occupational hazard for divine beings. I have immense power, can bring about almost any desired result with little effort and quite frankly, see little challenge in everyday existence. I am always on the lookout for new experiences, or failing that, of particularly sordid or sanguinary ones.

Baqir's foray into al-Yamani promised a timely distraction. I tagged along in his body, enjoying the violence simmering beneath the man's outwardly calm exterior. He came south to collect a payment far in excess of the debtor's ability to pay and looked forward to inflicting pain. Instead, he was confounded by the farmer's brother and a judge of San'a. Unfortunately for him, this judge had not yet been bought by the Qurayshi tribe, and Baqir had to face an unbiased judgment. I was annoyed at having the prospect of bloodshed averted, and Baqir was on the verge of violence when the judge handed down his decision. I looked for other avenues of action, and my control of the Qurayshi man slipped for a moment. The blue light of my godhead glowed about him for a few seconds, but nobody saw it.

If Baqir had given in to his anger, he might have killed the judge and everyone else there. Then his master in San'a would have been forced to cut short his promising career as a killer. After all, even a Qurayshi chieftain cannot yet allow judges to be killed with impunity. I wanted to foster Baqir's abilities, so I calmed him and spread a few ideas about. I told him he could come back later and steal the incense grower's wealth. As it happens, Baqir was lost to me soon after. His enemies pursued him and drove him into the desert where he took up with the wandering Badu and died shortly afterward in a quarrel over a woman.

It seems petty, does it not? Here am I, the supreme god, acting to ensure that one man triumphs over another to the tune of twelve silver pieces and a little gratuitous violence. I should be wielding storms and earthquakes, making nations rise and fall or engineering destruction on a massive scale. Well, I suppose I would do that if I knew how, but do not lose sight of the facts that I am really just a djinni and it is only misguided men who call me a god. I do wonder sometimes if there really are gods. The fact that I have seen none does not necessarily mean they do not exist. This world came from somewhere, after all. And if there really is a god, what does he think of a djinni impersonating him? I may never know, so I will just go on playing my part. Maybe if I play it long enough, I really will become a god. Who is to say that is not how gods arise? I was a djinni thousands of years ago when I was born of the smokeless fire, but I am now worshipped, feared, obeyed, prayed and sacrificed to as if I was a god. My powers may grow with time; already I am the most powerful being in this part of jazirat al-Arab. Perhaps that is all divinity is – being stronger than anyone else.

Still, I wonder if that is all there is to being a god? Philosophers among men, and I have come across a few in the past thousand years or so, talk of the attributes of god not only in terms of strength and power but also in terms of justice and mercy. I cannot really comprehend this. Would the Qurayshi still respect me if I did not support them in their banditry? Would they still follow me if I displayed weakness? It is an interesting thought, and I am minded to try it. It would cost me little as even if the experiment failed and my standing among the gods suffered; it is easy enough to wait until my mistakes die and a new generation of faithful followers grow to maturity.

I met the boy, Wasim, many years later. He was a rich trader, and I was in the guise of a traveller. We met and we talked while we sat within a tent waiting out a desert sandstorm. He told me of his revered uncle and what the memory of this man meant to him. While inhabiting Baqir's body, I had heard the thin scream that frightened his men but was at a loss to explain it until Wasim revealed he had been responsible. He had hidden in the cave in the hillside that held the old man's stored incense and when he saw the death of his uncle had wailed in anguish. The reverberations of the cave lent his cry an unearthly quality. It occurred to me that I had had some part in Wasim's success as I had fostered the violence in Baqir that led to his uncle's death. Some people say that out of every evil intent comes a good result and see it as the workings of god. Well, perhaps they are right, for the old man's death certainly led to the boy's comfort. It was the workings of this god, al-Ilah, which produced such a favourable outcome. Alright, I admit I did not seek such a result, but why should I not take the credit? And having achieved this once, maybe I can do so again. Who is there to prevent me becoming a god, if I so choose? A real god? Show me one.

Wasim has shown me the way, rising from adversity and seizing the opportunity. Can I do less?

Perhaps I will try it. I could endeavour to be less bloodthirsty and look for the greater good. I will become a just and merciful god. Just do not expect me to go too far and become a loving god.

Chapter Five

Nobody can say when men first took the rocks of Magan with their blue and green tints and by fire extracted red metal from them. Legend has it the men of that day ran upon their hands because their feet were ill-suited for walking, having just climbed down from the trees of the thick forests that clothed the land. They were naked in those days and hunted with sticks and stones, but as they became more dextrous, they fashioned clothes out of skins, learned to seek out the flints that could be knapped into weapons and knives and tamed the fire that fell from heaven in the season of storms.

One day, as the story goes, a man sat down to cook the animal he had killed and gathered rocks for his fireplace. He chose rocks that pleased his eye with tints of green and blue and chalky limestone, and in the centre, he made his fire. The wind whistled down the valley and fanned the flames to a great heat, and to his amazement, a glowing substance trickled out of the fire and congealed into red copper. For a time, this metal was merely a thing of wonder, but men found it could be fashioned and sharpened into weapons of great power or into ornaments of surpassing beauty.

Thus, the age of copper was born, and men flocked to the hills of Magan, seeking the coloured rocks and striving to release the copper from them. Not all succeeded, but those that did, guarded their secret and grew rich. These men employed other people to dig the ore from the ground and crush it or to gather firewood. Their women would mould the wet clay from the river valleys into mud bricks with which to fashion kilns. Rapidly, the mountains lost their cover of trees, and the life-giving soil washed off the hillsides with the rain, exposing more ore. The copper miners grew in number and now had to barter the precious metal for fuel and food as their land could no longer be used for farming.

Many, many years later, Magan became a vital part of the empire that grew from the two great rivers to the north, the Dijlah and ul-Firat, and the cities of Babel, Ur and Dilmun. Another great civilisation, far to the east on a river called the Indus, also traded with Magan, and the copper miners of that land found their product in great demand. One of these miners and businessmen was a man called Ea-Sil.

Ea-Sil was a great believer in the division of labour. His business, inherited from his father and grandfather before him, had grown over the years to become one of the largest copper manufacturers on the Magan peninsula. His father had worn himself out trying to manage every aspect of the business, but Ea-Sil had no intention of following him into the family grave mound for many years. He delegated the different parts of the operation to family members, knowing this way he could cut costs and keep control. His youngest brother, Idin-Sil, concentrated on buying wood from wherever he could find it and turning it into high grade charcoal. The next oldest, Gimil-Sil, was in charge of the miners who extracted the raw ore from the ground. Rabi-Lug, a cousin two years younger than Ea-Sil, managed the actual smelting of the ore and casting the molten copper into ingots. Hafiz ibn Jabbar, husband of his sister, Barra, had responsibility for providing the large workforce with food and comforts and wet river clay to make the kilns. Hafiz's younger brother, Na'il, guarded the enterprise with his small army of bullies. Ea-Sil was also a great believer in ruling his little empire with a bronze fist and keeping the profits close. He paid his brothers and brothers-in-law well but made sure anything they owned remained within the family.

Ea-Sil conducted all his business in his upstairs room in the family house at Musqatti-Sil, the small port where the ships that traded in copper came to do business. This place of *letting fall the anchor* had been nothing but a fishing village in his father's day, but the deep water channel that came close inshore and jutting headlands allowed for a safe berth while loading and unloading. The House of Ea-Sil took it over and renamed it to distinguish it from other villages all along the coast with similar names. Over the years, Ea-Sil's family turned it into a flourishing trading port. Ea-Sil himself could have been the ruler of this port had he desired the responsibility, but he was content to let others govern the town and pay him for the privilege.

A soft knocking sounded on the door of the accounting room. Ea-Sil looked up from his consideration of the shipping charges levied on the load of timber brought in from Moehendus in the Indus Valley the day before. He frowned and set the tablet to one side. "Enter," he rapped out.

The door opened and a round, unbearded face peeked around the edge. "Sorry, master," said the youth in a soft but high-pitched voice. "You asked to be told when Rabi-Lug was ready to tap the kilns."

Ea-Sil beckoned the youth in and handed him the tablets with his correspondence. Although he did not fully trust any member of his family, Ea-Sil trusted this young man, the eunuch Nunna. He had bought Nunna's family at the slave markets of Dilmun ten years before and instantly saw the promise of beauty in the five-year-old boy. The father and mother entered his service elsewhere, and the boy was educated at Ea-Sil's expense in his household, learning how to read and write. He also became proficient in numbering and had his pure, young voice trained in song. When Nunna was ten, before the first signs of puberty sprouted to mar his youthful perfection, Ea-Sil left on a trading trip and arranged for the boy to be kidnapped and handed over to the gelders. When Ea-Sil returned a month or so later, Nunna's scars were well on the way to healing. The memory of pain and terror were longer healing, but Ea-Sil effected a rescue, blaming an enemy and promised him a life of ease and comfort by way of recompense for the loss of his incipient manhood. Nunna responded well to his master's lies, and he was often called to Ea-Sil's bed. The boy was grateful to Ea-Sil for rescuing him and happy to offer him whatever service he required. As Nunna was beautiful and accomplished, Ea-Sil enjoyed the eunuch's presence in his bed, but he valued his abilities as a scribe almost as much as his abilities as a catamite. Nunna was even trusted with the business accounts.

Ea-Sil nodded and gestured to the clay tablets sitting in their wooden frames under moistened cloths. “You will accompany me, Nunna. Bring a tablet and a stick.”

He led the way out of the door and down the stairs that clung to the outside of the mud brick house. His eldest child, a daughter of nearly eight summers, ran to him with an expression of joy. Ea-Sil stroked her head and gently pushed her back into the arms of his wife, Gurana. “Take a note, Nunna,” he said as they left the courtyard of the house and set off down the village street that ran inland toward the hills. “Surra is eight. It’s time she was betrothed. I have in mind the son of Az'il, the ship-owner. It’ll bind him to the family.” Nunna folded back the moist cloth and made a series of indentations in the soft clay with the triangular tip of his writing stick.

The road was dusty in the baking sun, and the heated air shimmered and created black pools that evaporated and reformed as they strode toward the hills. Close at hand, between this bay and the next, teams of men hauled wood from where bundles had been offloaded from the trading ships and stacked the logs into the brick kilns under the expert supervision of Idin-Sil and his helpers. Fires were lit under the logs and sealed off from the air, and days later, other men broke open the cooled kilns and started extracting the gleaming black chunks of charcoal. This was loaded into willow-stick panniers and hauled up the valley to the site where the copper ore was mined.

Clay from the riverbed was made into kilns here too, but these were very different kilns from the ones that made the charcoal. While air was excluded from the charcoal furnaces so the wood did not burn, the copper furnaces required a steady stream of air to fan the flames, generating sufficient heat to crack and melt the pulverised ore. Giant bellows made of leather pumped air into the pit furnaces, the interior fires flaring a white heat with every exhalation of these huge artificial lungs. The men working the bellows were naked, sweat pouring off them as they heaved and pushed. Overseers kept a close eye on them, ready to encourage them with a tickle of the whip or replace them as heat and exhaustion drained their limbs. Small boys ran around with hide buckets and wooden dippers, providing the workers with water or splashing the charring leather and wood bellows where the heat of the furnace threatened to set them alight. Over this whole vision of hell hung a choking pall of fumes that caught at the lungs; a stink made up of burning rock, smoke, sulphur and charred hair. Ea-Sil and Nunna watched this frenetic activity for a time, until Rabi-Lug saw them and ran over.

"Welcome, Ea. You're just in time to see us crack the new kiln."

"It does not look any different. What makes it so?"

Rabi-Lug saw where his cousin was looking and pointed off to the right. "Not this one, Ea. Over here."

Ea-Sil grunted and followed Rabi-Lug around the ordinary kilns and further up the valley. "What is different about this new furnace, Rabi?"

"You'll see. It's going to improve profits considerably."

"Possibly, but tell me anyway."

Rabi-Lug hesitated. "It's in the way the copper is produced … er, if it's all the same with you, Ea, I'd like my foreman to explain it."

"His idea was it?"

"No, no, of course not … well, partly … but he actually built it, so I thought …"

"Very well then. Let him explain. Who is your foreman?"

"Enki, a good man. He had his own operation in the west, until his tribal chief took over and threw him off his land."

Another few hundred paces brought them to tall wickerwork screens and behind these what looked like a rounded mud hut. Teams of men were again directing streams of air into the interior, and the domed wall shimmered with its internal heat. A burly man dressed in a leather apron hurried over and knuckled his brow to Rabi-Lug and Ea-Sil and then stared at Nunna with obvious curiosity.

"Enki, explain to the master what we're doing with this furnace."

The man frowned. "Er, we be making copper."

"I know that," Ea-Sil snapped. "That's what I pay you for. Tell me why this furnace is different from the other ones. What's this great dome structure?"

"Yes, master. Sorry, master. Well … the pit type furnace we always uses be easy to build and fire, but the copper it makes be not so good, hard to dig out and needs more …"

"Yes, yes, I know all this."

"Please, Ea," Rabi-Lug said hurriedly. "Let him explain in his own way. Then you'll be able to appreciate the differences more easily."

Ea-Sil nodded. "Very well." He stroked Nunna's cheek fondly and smiled. He pointed to the screens behind them. "Wait over there, your face is looking quite flushed. I'll call you when I need you."

Enki followed Nunna with his eyes and licked his lips before turning back to his masters. "As … as you knows, master, we digs a pit and lines it with stone. Then we adds charcoal in a layer and crushed ore on top of it, a bit more charcoal on top and then stone slabs over everything to keeps the heat in. Bellows blow air into it to keep it all hot as it burns. We keeps it going until all the charcoal has gone, several hours like, and then we waits for it to cool. Then we digs it out, knocks off the slag on the top of the copper lump, and we heats up pieces of the rough copper and pours it into moulds."

"And this thing?" Ea-Sil gestured at the domed furnace.

Enki grinned. "Same sort of thing, but we keeps it all above ground. We makes a big clay bowl with a wall all the ways round it and puts in a layer of charcoal, then a layer of ore, then a layer of charcoal, then a layer …"

"I get the idea," Ea-Sil said. "Alternate layers."

"Yes, master. Sorry, master. We builds the wall up as we go, nice and thick, and then covers the lot with rock slabs and plenty of wet clay. When we fires it up and blows air in, the ore melts and runs down into the bowl at the bottom."

"Which is exactly what you get with the old type, except this is obviously a lot more time-consuming to build. Why're you wasting my time, Rabi-Lug?"

"Please, Ea, listen."

"It be much more than that, master," Enki went on. "All the extra charcoal makes the fire hotter and the copper runs like water into the bowl and the … the slag sits on top of it, sort of floating like … like butter on milk ... or ... or scum on soup."

"Very poetic, Enki, but you still end up with a copper cake you have to free from the slag and refine."

"No, no, master, much better than that. Comes you round here and has a look." The foreman led them round to the rear of the dome where, low down, the dome blistered out into a swelling protuberance. "We calls it a nipple, master, 'cause it looks …"

"Yes, I can see that. What's it for?"

"Behind it is the bowl with the pond of molten copper," Enki explained. "When we knocks the end off the nipple, the copper comes pouring out in a stream down this 'ere groove and into these moulds, leaving the slag behind as it be sitting on the copper like. We won't have to melt it again to gets the pure copper."

Ea-Sil considered. "Show me one of these copper ingots from the new method."

Rabi-Lug swallowed. "Well, er … we haven't actually got any yet. This will be the first time."

Ea-Sil stared at his cousin and then at the foreman. “So you haven’t actually tested this furnace? You don’t know whether it’ll work?”

“It … it should, Ea.”

“It’ll work, master,” Enki said softly, barely heard above the wheezing of the bellows and the muted roar of the furnace.

“Very well then, show me.”

Rabi-Lug guided his cousin back, giving the foreman room to move. The man took up a long pole with a heavy blade on one end and positioned himself near the nipple. He called out to the other workers to stand clear and as they withdrew, flexed his muscles and swung the blade in an overarm stroke. The heavy metal smashed into the brittle clay of the nipple and shattered it. White hot metal sprayed out; Enki screamed and dropped his pole, stumbling back. Molten copper poured out as a thick column as blindingly bright as the sun, splashed into the groove, spattering globules in all directions, before running down and into the moulds. Dense clouds of smoke and fumes filled the air, the glowing copper showing fuzzily through it.

Ea-Sil applauded, clapping his hands and nodding. “Very good, Rabi. An impressive demonstration, but I'd like to see one of the new ingots before I make up my mind. Have Enki bring us one as soon as he can cool it off.”

Rabi-Lug grinned and then his smile faded as the fumes cleared. Enki lay on the ground on the far side of the furnace, rolling around in agony as several workers tried to help him. “He's hurt,” he cried, running forward.

One of the furnace workers threw a bucket of water over the hapless foreman, drawing forth a shuddering cry from the man. The workers drew back as Rabi-Lug dropped to his knees beside Enki, swiftly examining his torso and limbs. Several tiny scorch marks littered his broad chest, but a strip of flesh across the muscle of his left upper arm was blackened and raw. Only a little blood was oozing from the wound, and Rabi-Lug grimaced but nodded sagely, probing the wound with his fingertips.

"The metal has cauterised the wound. We must get him home quickly. You two ..." Rabi-Lug gestured to the workers. "... pick him up and take ..."

"I ... I be alright," Enki ground out through clenched teeth. "Aah ... leave me alone" He struggled to his feet and stood swaying for a few seconds before looking across at Ea-Sil. "Sorry, master," he muttered. "I knows what went wrong. I'll fix it for ... for next ... next ..." His eyes rolled up in his head, and he fell backward; the two workers designated to carry him just being able to break his fall.

"Take him down to his house and fetch a physician for him," Rabi-Lug ordered. He waited until the workers were out of hearing before turning to Ea-Sil with a worried expression. "I hope this unfortunate accident won't prejudice you against the new method."

Ea-Sil beckoned Nunna across. "Did you see that? Good." Looking back at Rabi-Lug he added,

"Let me see one of the new ingots, then I'll tell you what I think."

Rabi-Lug walked over to where the ingots were cooling in their small clay troughs. Waves of heat still emanated from the dull metal, so he took a bucket and poured water over the end ones. Steam billowed up as the water boiled and danced on the heated metal, but as he continued to pour, the sizzling died away. He poured another bucket over them and then squatted, gingerly touching the metal with his fingers. "Ow! Still hot." He took a mattock and dug into the ground near an ingot, prising up the bar until it snapped free from its neighbour. Bright copper showed in the wound. Rabi-Lug wrapped a piece of leather around the hot ingot and carried it over to Ea-Sil.

"Turn it over. Show me." Ea-Sil critically examined the small oblong piece of copper, paying particular attention to the gleaming strip where it had broken away from the ingot next to it. "What do you think?" he asked Nunna.

"Good quality, master," the eunuch replied softly. "It appears to be pure metal without any of the dross one usually finds. I think you could sell this without refining it further."

"That would be a great saving," Rabi-Lug said.

"How much more time-consuming is this method?"

"A bit," Rabi-Lug conceded. "But labour is cheap."

"Ea-Sil nodded. "What do you think, Nunna?"

"I think this method could increase your profits, master."

"And that's not all, Ea," Rabi-Lug said. "Enki and I have been talking about other methods, and we can take this process further. It would be easy enough to get tin from Persia. With that we could make bronze."

"That's what happens to my copper already. I sell the copper to Dilmun, and they make it into bronze."

Rabi-Lug nodded, eagerness showing in his sweaty bearded face. "But we could make it ourselves. Enki says that the cost of bronze is double that of copper or more and ... and if we could sell to Dilmun or ... or even bypass Dilmun altogether, selling direct to the inland tribes, we'd be looking at triple prices or more."

"How is it that Enki knows these things?"

"Well, he had his own copper smelting operation inland at Adis. One of the Dilmun bronze makers was a friend. He saw what was involved."

"Why didn't he make bronze himself if it's so profitable?"

"He says he was going to, but he lost his land before he could."

Ea-Sil thought for a few minutes. "Triple price, you think?"

"Or more."

"There's a lot to be calculated here. I want you and Enki to come and see me tomorrow. You will have all the figures and costings ready for Nunna. I'll consider this fully, before I reach a decision."

"You won't regret it, Ea."

Ea-Sil put his arm around his cousin's shoulder and smiled coolly. “If I do regret it, Rabi, be assured that you’ll regret it more.”

He received them in the main store house adjoining his house in the town of Musqatti-Sil. The large stone and mud brick structure was lined with bales of cloth, sacks of incense, dried fish and meat, spices, ivory, hides, dates, rare timbers and ingots of copper, as well as pearls from Dilmun, glass beads and rhinoceros horn. Ea-Sil traded in anything that could turn a profit, and his ships plied the routes between Ur and Dilmun to the north, the ports of Persia and Moehendus of the Indus Valley to the east and Yaman and Punt to the southwest. The contents of the store changed every time one of his ships docked, but as often as not, left traces behind to add to the rich aroma that pervaded the air. Rodents abounded amidst the bales and stacked bundles of trade goods, but a dozen sleek spotted cats from Kush plied their trade within the store and kept their numbers in check.

Ea-Sil's servants had cleared a space in the middle of the room and set up a table and four stools. A shaft of sunlight arrowed through a high skylight, illuminating the patch of floor where Ea-Sil sat on one long side of the table, and Nunna with wax tablets and writing implements at one end. Facing him were two stools, as yet empty. One of the cats lay in Ea-Sil's lap, and he stroked it absently as he waited for his cousin and the foreman to appear. Nunna poured water from a jar into a clay cup and carried it round the table to his master. He took it, thanked him with a nod and continued to contemplate his own thoughts.

"Master," Nunna murmured. "They're here."

Rabi-Lug and Enki entered the store. The injured foreman had his burned arm bandaged and salve smeared over the blistered burns across his chest. His face was pale beneath his weathered face and bags beneath his eyes spoke of a sleepless night. Rabi-Lug, by contrast, appeared well rested and moved confidently, his teeth showing in a broad grin.

"Sit." Ea-Sil gestured to the two stools. Rabi-Lug murmured a greeting and sat down, while Enki's descent was little short of a collapse. "How are you feeling?" Ea-Sil asked in a disinterested tone.

"I ... I be ... well, master," Enki whispered.

"Good. Then let's get on with this. Rabi-Lug, you have some figures on the costs involved in setting up this new copper refining method?"

"Yes, Ea, and on the bronze smelting."

"Tell me."

Rabi-Lug did so at great length, pulling figures and descriptions out of his memory, pausing while Nunna made entries in wedge-shaped script on his clay tablets and then continuing with his narrative. When he finished, Ea-Sil sat silent for several minutes before asking Nunna to read back some of the figures. He asked questions, and Rabi-Lug and Enki answered with Nunna making more notes.

"Nunna, please summarise these figures. Leave out all the details but give me the profit owing on each method."

"It will only be approximate, master. Rabi-Lug has made assumptions that may not hold up when ..."

"An approximation will suffice."

"Yes, master. In what units do you want the profits? Gold, silver, copper?"

"Relative will do. Use our present monthly total of copper ingots as your base line."

Nunna bent over the wet clay tablets again. His lips moved as he sounded out the figures to himself and made fresh marks on a new tablet. After several minutes, during which Ea-Sil's fingers drummed out an impatient rhythm on the table top and the cat on his lap leapt down, he looked up.

"I have it, master. If we take our present monthly copper production by the old method as one, then – and this is only if Rabi-Lug's figures are correct – using the new method will increase our monthly production to one and three-fourths …"

"That can't be right," Rabi-Lug interrupted. "I calculated at least twice as much, maybe more. You've added something wrongly."

"Respectfully, no," Nunna replied. "I've had to add in more factors than you gave me, such as the replacement of slaves and extra guards for the added copper."

Ea-Sil laughed harshly. "That's why you work for me, Rabi-Lug. Don't think you know more about this business than me. Go on, Nunna."

"Making our own bronze is harder to calculate as we have to buy tin ore or maybe even tin bars to add to the copper. I can only estimate the actual cost of this, as we don't buy it at present. Further, we'll have to find room for this ore in our ships, perhaps displacing other valuable cargo. Then there's the problem of Dilmun." Nunna stopped and looked meaningfully at his master.

Ea-Sil smiled and nodded. "Tell them. They should know the reason why we don't go ahead with this ... if I so decide."

"Dilmun buys our copper and trades some of it on to the cities of the Two Rivers and Moehendus. They also make bronze and trade it with the wandering tribes of the interior. They make considerable profits from their trade. It's possible that if we try to circumvent them, they'll stop all trade with us. That would be disastrous."

Rabi-Lug and Enki sat glumly, striving to digest this unwelcome information. "So we don't make bronze then?" Enki asked.

"I haven't made that decision," Ea-Sil replied. "Nunna, what's our profit if we turn all our copper from the new method into bronze?"

Nunna shrugged delicately. "If Dilmun does not act against us, almost certainly four, maybe as high as seven. There are too many imponderables at the moment."

"That's a lot of profit," Rabi-Lug said.

"If Dilmun acts against us, our income could disappear entirely," Nunna added.

"I think the risk is too great," Ea-Sil commented. "However, I'll give this matter more thought before I decide. In the meantime, Rabi-lug, Enki, you'll say nothing."

"Of course not," Rabi-Lug said quickly. He saw the meeting had ended and got to his feet, followed a moment later by Enki. "Thank you for listening to our proposal, Ea."

When the two men had left the storeroom, Ea-Sil told Nunna to take the clay tablets back to the office and join him on the roof of the house. He climbed the external stairs slowly, fending off inquiries from servants and his wife. The roof was flat and made of strong timber beams coated with asphalt and covered with reed mats, through which the preservative had soaked in places. A sturdy railing surrounded an area measuring about ten paces by twelve and a linen awning was rigged to provide respite from the fierce Arabian sun. The only furniture was a cushion-strewn couch and a low table. The roof was the private preserve of Ea-Sil and no one came there without his express permission.

Ea-Sil paced slowly, hands clasped behind his back. He avoided the patches of asphalt seeping through the mats without conscious effort and turned his mind back to the meeting and the great profits on offer if he took the risk of incurring Dilmun's displeasure. *I'm wealthy already, and my present operations will continue to garner me profit. What need have I of more*? He bared his teeth in a fierce grin. *You can never have too much wealth. Yet I risk all if I go down this path.*

Nunna slipped onto the roof and saw his master deep in thought, so he squatted in the shade and turned his mind to a contemplation of what mattered most to him. *Ea is worried. He tries to hide it, but I can see. I wish I could remove that worry from his mind.* He thought back with gratitude to the man who had bought his whole family from the slave market at Dilmun, educated him and then rescued him a second time from the gelders. He shivered despite the heat and felt a faint burst of anger toward the men who had robbed him of sons. *If Ea hadn't returned when he did, they might have sold me on and my life would be ... No matter, I have contentment. That will suffice*. Nunna looked critically at Ea-Sil as he paced the roof, his long robes flapping in the breeze off the sea and his beard and long hair gleaming. *A hard man, cruel but capable of acts of kindness. He despises his brothers and keeps them in his fist, but he provides for his wife and children. And I hold his heart. How may I serve him better*? He recalled the figures from the meeting without effort and considered the problem of Dilmun. *Dilmun is the thorn in the foot*.

Ea-Sil walked to the railing and looked out over the township toward the docks and further, over the charcoal furnaces of the foreshore to the valley where smoke and dust billowed as his workers clawed ore from the ground and drew the red copper metal from it. Nunna rose and crossed the roof in bare feet, putting a hand gently on his master's shoulder. Ea-Sil turned, anger flashing across his face for an instance before a look of naked lust replaced it. He turned to the young boy and kissed his upturned face.

"Come, Ea," Nunna said softly. "Your mind is in turmoil. Let me soothe your body and spirit." He took his master's hand and led him to the couch.

Ea-Sil responded vigorously, lying down with the youth and parting his robes. For several minutes they were lost in familiar motions and afterward lay together panting. Nunna rearranged his clothing and leaned over to pick up a small packet from beside the couch.

"Kath, master?" he asked. He offered a handful of leaves wrapped in clean cloth. Ea-Sil took one and popped it into his mouth, chewing on it slowly. Nunna did likewise and lay down in the arms of the older man, chewing on his leaf. As usual, his head started to spin from the effect of the drug, and he felt his heart beating rapidly. This effect passed quickly, and he was enveloped in a feeling of euphoria. The problem that had been taxing his mind suddenly seemed inconsequential.

"I think I know the answer, master."

Ea-Sil stirred and dragged his attention away from a contemplation of the clouds. "What is that you say, my darling? You know, you have the softest skin." His callused hand stroked Nunna's thigh.

"Dilmun, master. I believe I have a solution to your problem."

"Have you indeed? Well, tell me later. I have other things on my mind right now." Ea-Sil turned the youth onto his belly and covered his neck with kisses.

Nunna waited for his master to finish, impatient to offer his idea, but reluctant to interrupt Ea-Sil's pleasure. At last the older man lay back, red in the face and sweating. Nunna waited a few minutes until his breathing slowed and tried again. "Dilmun, master?"

Ea-Sil yawned and scratched, adjusting his robes. “Go on, then. What is it you have to say?”

“I think I know how you can test the waters of profitability without risk ... well, without much risk.”

“I'm listening.” Ea-Sil's hand stroked Nunna's hair, but his thoughts were already far from their physical passion.

“Tell Enki to build a new copper furnace and also one for smelting bronze. Buy enough tin to make ... say, one hundred bronze ingots. Don’t take them to Dilmun or the Two Rivers to sell, but to Moehendus or somewhere people won’t know you made the ingots. You can say you bought them in Dilmun and are trading them on. This way you get a good price without the viceroy of Dilmun finding out. Once you know your profit on one hundred ingots, you can calculate whether or not to continue.”

“An interesting idea. Let me think on it.”

“I would advise you not to think too long, master. There’s a Moehendus ship docked now. I believe she carries tin. If she sails north, there’s no telling when more will be available.”

Ea-Sil waited a day before he decided. His first act was to call Enki in and quiz him about bronze making.

“I’m sorry, master, but I don’t knows how much tin you’ll need.”

“The question is not a difficult one. I wish to make one hundred ingots of bronze. How many copper ingots will I need and how many tin ingots?”

“I don't knows, master. I’ve never made bronze before.”

“Then how were you going to make it back when you had your own land? Or is that just a fable to impress Rabi-Lug?”

Enki shook his head vehemently. “I haves seen it made,” he assured Ea-Sil. “But I haves never known the ... the ... how much copper and tin to put in. It was a secret.” He shrugged. “How hard can it be? We trys one lot and if it doesn't work, we trys another.”

“May the gods save us,” Ea-Sil muttered. “Alright, tell Rabi-Lug what you need. We have refined copper bars already, but we need a bronze smelter. How long will it take to make a hundred ingots.”

“A month? Two?” Enki ventured. “If we gets the ... the amounts right straight away.”

“Too long. I need them in no more than twenty days. Build as many bronze smelters as you need but deliver those bars to me.” Ea-Sil sighed. “I will instruct Idin-Sil to release more charcoal to you and Hafiz to find more food for your workers. Just get it done.”

When Enki had left to start his work, Ea-Sil sent a runner to find Nunna. The runner found the eunuch down at the docks and passed his message along.

“Please tell the master I’ll be with him in about an hour.”

The runner was appalled. “I cannot take that message to him. You must come now.”

"In an hour." Nunna started toward one of the ships and then turned back to the fearful messenger. "Tell him I'm on his business and my success is vital for the enterprise. I'll be with him in an hour."

"What enterprise?"

"You don't need to know." Nunna hesitated. "Tell him I speak with the Moehendus captain."

Nunna arrived back at Ea-Sil's office in just over an hour to find his master in a foul mood.

"Where have you been? I sent for you hours ago."

"Forgive me, master, but I was working on your behalf to secure the tin essential for our ... your project."

Ea-Sil grunted. "And did you get it?"

"The captain of Vishnu's Arrow is a petty nobleman of Moehendus by the name of Sakindar. He is ... er, partial to youths and I ..."

"I didn't give you permission to offer yourself to another."

"No master, nor did I do so. It was enough that I kept him company and shared a jug of wine. He enjoyed my conversation, and I sang to him." Nannu smiled gently, and Ea-Sil flushed and looked away. "We talked about many things – poetry, dance, hunting, the weather ... and tin ore."

"Continue."

"Captain Sakindar's cargo is partly tin ore bound for Dilmun. He stopped here to offload some spices, but he sails tomorrow. We got to talking about tin ore, and he told me a few interesting facts about it. The ore is not rich in the metal, but he estimates there is enough tin in his one load to make twenty thousand bronze arrowheads – that's about forty thousand shekel weights of bronze.”

Ea-Sil whistled. “That’s a lot of bronze. Do you have any idea how much tin that represents?”

“No master, though, he did show me his cargo of ore. I must admit it looked just like ordinary rock to me, but he boasted of its value. I asked him whether he would sell me some, just a little bit which would not be missed by his buyer. He laughed, but I pressed him and he agreed ... for a price.”

“Of course. What did he want for it?”

“Me.” Nunna smiled. “I told him he’d have to ask you, but I didn’t think you’d agree.”

“Quite right ... but we do need the ore.”

“We settled on ten shekels of gold for a sackful of ore.”

“What? That’ll beggar me. I won’t pay it. Why, I'd rather he took you.”

“Of course, master. Only you can decide whether I’m worth more to you than ten shekels of gold.”

Ea-Sil grumbled for a while, but eventually he gave in and took ten shekels of gold from his strongbox, handing them over to Nunna. “I want a receipt,” he said.

Nunna made to hand back the gold. “He won’t give a receipt for fear of Dilmun finding out. He made that quite plain.”

“Oh, very well, but make sure it’s good ore in the sack.”

“Inasmuch as I don’t know what tin looks like, I’ll do my best.”

Nunna tucked the gold into the sash of his robe and taking two slaves with him went down to the docks again. Leaving the slaves on deck, he entered the captain's cabin and handed over just five shekels of gold, keeping the other five safely hidden in his sash. “Our agreed price, Captain.”

Sakindar bit each of the bits of gold to test their purity and pronounced himself satisfied. “I suppose you want a receipt?”

“No need, Captain Sakindar. I’ll take my ore and depart.”

Sakindar smiled and put his arm around Nunna's shoulders as he walked him to the door. “You know, you could earn yourself a gold piece if you'd stay with me an hour or two.”

“Captain, I’d love to, but my master is very strict and would beat me if I dallied.”

“Then sail with me to Dilmun and afterward to Moehendus, and let us enjoy each other's company. I can offer you love, but a beautiful youth like you will have no problem finding rich benefactors in either city should you decide not to stay with me.”

Nunna took Sakindar's hand and kissed it. “Alas, I cannot. My master keeps me closely guarded. Besides, I owe him a debt of loyalty.”

Sakindar sighed and shrugged. “A pity. You’ve quite captivated my heart. If you change your mind, look for Vishnu's Arrow twice a year. You’ve only to say the word …”

Amid further protestations of love and regret, Nunna took his leave and supervised the transport of the sack of tin ore to Ea-Sil's storehouse.

Within ten days, Rabi-Lug and Enki had reduced the tin ore to five silvery bars and put aside a hundred bars of refined copper. Enki had also prepared the kilns necessary for smelting the bronze but at this stage requested a meeting with Ea-Sil and Nunna.

"I has the copper and the tin ready to go, but I don'ts know the proper mix to use," Enki said.

"Also, we've only five bars of tin," Rabi-Lug added.

"Those fornicating bars cost me two gold shekels each," Ea-Sil snarled. "I can't imagine how I'm going to get that back by trading mere bronze. It's all your fault, Nunna."

"Yes, master. However, the seller had all the advantages, as we needed to obtain the ore secretly. If this works, we'll be able to strike a better deal next time by buying it openly. The costs will fall."

"If there is a next time. Perhaps I should just stop this right now."

"Of course that's for you to say, master, but having expended so much to get this far, it would be a pity to lose it all when a little extra could open up a whole new market."

The others sat and waited for Ea-Sil to make up his mind. At last, he nodded. "We continue."

"And the mix?" Enki asked.

"We'll have to experiment," Nunna said.

"We don't have much tin to experiment with," Rabi-Lug observed. "Give us some idea of where to start."

Ea-Sil looked at the eunuch. "It's on your head. Tell them what you know."

Nunna frowned and chewed on his bottom lip. "It would be better to use too much tin to start with. We can always resmelt with extra copper if the bronze is no good."

"Can you have bronze that's no good?" Rabi-Lug asked.

"I would imagine so, if the formula is a secret. If it didn't matter what proportions you used, everyone would make it."

"So what do we do?"

"Try two different mixes. Then we can compare them and maybe get an idea whether we need to alter the proportions. Use a five to one and a ten to one mix. That way we have extra tin bars to use if we get the mix right."

"We're not going to get one hundred ingots of bronze with those ratios," Ea-Sil grumbled.

"Unless the right mix turns out to be twenty to one," Nunna said. "With respect, master, there was no way of predicting how much tin we'd get or need."

Enki got straight to work, firing up the kilns and melting the copper and tin bars, heating the crucibles until the metals melted and ran together. He stirred the mix with a granite spoon that had a long wooden handle and when the glowing liquid appeared uniform, carefully tipped it into the prepared moulds. When they had cooled, he took two bars and cleaned them up, chipping away the sand and grit that roughened the surface of the ingots. He also took them to a blacksmith and gave him instructions. Later that day in the storeroom, Enki laid two bars of bronze in front of Ea-Sil.

“They don’t look much different,” Ea-Sil said. “One is lighter in colour …” He picked them up. “… but not in weight.”

“They be different, and I don'ts know, it might be important. I tests them after I casts them,” Enki explained. “This lighter looking one be harder than the other, but it also snaps ... it break easy. I had a blacksmith beat out a bit as if he were making a sword. It was hard work, and he snaps it. It takes a lot of work to makes it into a cutting edge but the edge keeps sharp for a long time. The darker coloured one be softer…”

“Meaning?”

“It can be beatens out easily and it bends rather than snap. It gets sharp, but also blunts more easily than the lighter one.”

“Which is which?” Nunna asked.

“The light, brittles one be the five to one mix.”

“I assume that a warrior wants a sharp blade but not one that breaks in his hand,” Rabi-Lug mused.

“But also one that stays sharp,” Enki added.

“So which is it to be?” Ea-Sil asked.

“Neither,” Nunna said. “And both. We must make a mix that lies somewhere between the two. With luck, we will find a bronze that is hard but not brittle and keeps its sharpness.”

Enki took all the bronze bars and melted them all down in a single crucible, recasting them in fresh moulds. Then he took the bars and a sword fashioned from one of the bars back to a meeting in the storeroom. He laid the sword on the table and stood back with a smile. “I thinks we is very close.”

Ea-Sil picked up the sword and tried the edge. "It's sharp now, but will it last?"

Nunna took the blade and wielded it experimentally. "Does it flex or snap?"

Rabi-Lug left the bronze weapon on the table. "What is its mix?"

"The edge lasts well," Enki said. "I has not made it snap, but when it be hit by other bronze, the note be too high. One of the slaves was a soldier, and he says a high note means the mix be wrong. Too hards, he says. This mix be two parts tin to fifteen parts copper, being made up of both of the first batches."

"Who is this slave that used to be a soldier?" Ea-Sil asked. "Can he be trusted?"

Enki hesitated. "Ranu. He be a slave. Where be he going? Who can he tell?"

"You're right. There's no cause for concern." Ea-Sil looked at Nunna and one eyelid drooped. Nunna nodded discreetly.

"If two parts to fifteen isn't quite right, where do we go from here?" Rabi-Lug asked.

"We changes the mix again," Enki said. "If the bronze be still too hard, we must add more copper, a little at a time. I says we melts down all the bronze we haves, including the sword, and adds an extra copper ingot. That will makes one part tin to er .. .er ..."

"Eight of copper," Nunna finished for him.

Ea-Sil shrugged. "Do it, but remember the time. We've used fourteen of the twenty days already."

Two days later they reconvened, and Enki showed his new sword. "I am nots sure whether we have the right mix or whether we needs a bit more copper. It still has a high ring but the note be not as ... as flat as before. I thought to ask Ranu, but he hads an accident yesterday. He ... he fell into a fire."

"A pity," Ea-Sil said, "But unimportant for our purposes. Do you propose adding more copper, Enki? You've only four days left."

Enki scratched his head. "I thinks this mix be good but ... well, if you asks me ...one more bar."

"Two to seventeen," Rabi-Lug clarified.

Another two days passed, and Enki reported back with another sword. This time he wore a broad grin. "Wes got it. Two parts to seventeen gives us a nice hard bronze, easy to gives an edge to, bendy and …" He turned the sword sideways and brought the flat of the blade down on the edge of the table. It rang with a pure, mellow note. "… it even sounds nice."

"Good." Ea-Sil nodded. "How many bronze ingots have you made of this mix?"

"Counting the two that makes up the sword, there be nineteen."

"And how many more can you make from the remaining tin?"

Enki frowned and concentrated. "Er, twenty… um, seven, I thinks."

"Twenty-five and a half," Nunna corrected. "That makes a total of forty-four and a half."

"Half?" Ea-Sil queried. "Where does a half come from?"

"Two parts in seventeen is the same as one part in eight and a half. Perhaps if Enki was to resmelt the tin slag, he might be able to get a little more tin, even enough to make up that other half bar."

"Very well. Enki, you'll see if you can find any more tin. You'll also make as many bronze ingots as you can using this successful mix. I want these ingots cleaned and ready in two days time. Use as many men as you need."

When Rabi-Lug and Enki had left to put Ea-Sil's orders into effect, Nunna stretched and yawned. "Have you given any thought to whom you will entrust the sale of the bronze, master?"

"There's no one I trust except you, darling boy, and I'm not letting you out of my sight. I'll take the bronze to Dilmun myself and you'll accompany me."

"Moehendus might be safer, master."

"I've decided on Dilmun."

"Who will you leave in charge here in Musqatti-Sil?"

"Idin. He's moderately competent. I'll leave him full instructions."

Forty-seven bronze ingots were packed in a wooden chest and carried aboard one of Ea-Sil's own trading ships, a small coastal dhow, for the voyage up the gulf to Dilmun. The captain took them out of Musqatti-Sil harbour within the hour, gulls screaming a farewell. They tacked north up the Magan Peninsula and then ran before the southeasterlies into the gulf, dolphins riding the bow wave. The coastal mountains were barely visible on the horizon, hidden in wreaths of cloud despite being far out to sea and at the mercies of tide and wind. Ea-Sil stood in the prow of the little ship and rejoiced at the wind blowing in his hair.

"I'm quite invigorated by the salt air, Nunna," he declared. "Let's go down to the cabin." He proceeded to forcefully exercise his sexual rights over his slave. While his master slept in post-coital exhaustion, Nunna came on deck and stood looking out at the far off land, thinking thoughts that would have shocked and angered Ea-Sil.

The trip took several days, even with the wind chasing them over the waves. They sailed through the night as the captain was loath to put ashore. He explained that though the land was technically Magan at that point and soon would be Dilmun territory, the writ of the kings did not extend this far. They would be safer at sea, so he hung lights at the prow and masthead and maintained a watch in the darkness. As they drew closer to the island of Dilmun, the gulf narrowed and the nature of the waves and wind changed. Their progress slowed and other vessels converged on their course. The captain ordered his men to arm themselves, and he positioned himself near the steering oar at all times.

"Pirates?" Ea-Sil asked.

"Unlikely this close to Dilmun, but I believe in being prepared."

No other ship approached them however, and a day later, the captain slipped his dhow into a dock in Dilmun's outer harbour. "You can wait a day or two on board if you like. The harbour master will then find a place for us in the inner harbour. Or you can disembark now and go overland into the city."

"We'll go ashore," Ea-Sil said. He instructed Nunna to bring a single bronze ingot and their luggage and strolled down the gangplank. Nunna found transport to the city on donkeys, and after a dusty and dry two hours, they entered the bustling city of Dilmun.

The streets of the city made the foundries and furnaces of Magan seem quiet in comparison; people crowded the narrow roads, and everyone seemed to be shouting, arguing and attempting to sell all manner of goods and services. Gaily coloured sailcloth formed awnings over either side of the streets, and rows of stalls, tables and pens sold spices, cloth, jewellery, slaves, livestock, food, hides, ivory and timber. Prostitutes postured in doorways, leaving little to the imagination, and tumblers and jugglers entertained any who would look their way. To walk the length of a city street was to be assaulted by colours, by sounds, by movement and the pungent aromas of thousands of close-packed humans, their animals and their produce.

Nunna stared at the seething chaos with trepidation, though his heart beat faster and he could not tear his eyes away from the sights. "It shouldn't be hard to sell our bronze here, master," he shouted above the din. "Where should we start?"

"Be silent, you fool," Ea-Sil snapped. "You're not to mention our purpose here, unless I give you leave." He looked at the bustling crowds and frowned. "We must find the House of Enlil. Make inquiries. I'll wait here." He sat down in the forecourt of a small tavern and ordered wine.

Nunna returned within the hour and guided his master and their donkeys through the streets to an imposing walled courtyard halfway up the hill topped by the viceroy's palace. A guard at the door bid them wait in a shaded alcove while he conveyed their names to the master of the house. After a few minutes, he returned and ushered them into the presence of Rua-Enlil, trader of Dilmun.

A burly bearded man in brightly coloured robes arose from a couch as they entered the room and advanced toward them with arms outstretched in greeting. "My dear Ea-Sil, it has been a long time." Rua-Enlil embraced him and then stood back, examining him closely. "The years have been kind to you, old friend. Are you well? Do you prosper?"

"I'm well enough, Rua, but you – you must be doing very well." Ea-Sil looked around the richly appointed room and at the gold thread in their host's garments. Envy tightened his features, and he made an effort to relax.

Rua-Enlil nodded affably, his sharp eyes noticing his guest's reaction. "The viceroy has honoured me with his custom, and through him, I have access to the royal house of Ur." He ran his gaze over the youth standing near the door and smiled lasciviously. "And who's this delightful paragon of beauty?"

"That's Nunna, my body servant."

On hearing his name, Nunna advanced and went down on his knees gracefully. "My lord," he murmured.

"By all the gods, he's a feast for the eyes." Rua-Enlil grasped Nunna's face in one hand and turned it upward, gazing into the youth's dark eyes. "Is he cut?"

"Yes."

"Of course. How else will you preserve that beauty and keep him bonded to you? How old was he?"

"Ten."

"Ah, right on the cusp. A wise decision. Who did you use? Gazirra or ibn Walid?"

"Ibn Walid."

Rua-Enlil nodded. "More expensive, but he does excellent work. An absolute minimum of scarring and doesn't cut so deep as to deny them pleasure. I always say a boy who can still enjoy being used will give greater pleasure to you. What did you pay?"

Nunna did not hear his master's reply as his mind was shouting at him. *He knew? He knew! But he came and saved me from the gelders when I was taken ... How did he know where I was? Because he organised it. He paid for me to be ... to be ... cut? This was planned? He deliberately robbed me of my future. And just for his pleasure ...*

"Nunna. Nunna!" The youth focused and saw Ea-Sil staring at him, holding out a cup of watered wine. "Sit over there until I need you."

Nunna took the cup and moved away, his mind still in turmoil.

Ea-Sil and Rua-Enlil chatted of inconsequential matters for several minutes, both deliberately avoiding the matter of business. They sipped on their cups of chilled wine, waiting for the right moment. It came.

“There’s talk of war in the north,” Rua-Enlil said casually.

“There are always wars,” Ea-Sil agreed.

Rua-Enlil sighed. “What a terrible world we live in. Luckily, an astute man can turn a profit no matter what the circumstances.”

Ea-Sil nodded. “It’s often a matter of being able to supply the right item at the right time.”

Rua-Enlil drank deeply and put his cup down carefully on the table. He folded his fingers and regarded his guest intently. “You have such an item?”

Ea-Sil gestured to Nunna, and the young man brought over a small leather bag and handed it to his master. Ea-Sil took out the bronze ingot and laid it on the table.

The merchant of Dilmun studied the bar of metal but did not reach out to pick it up. “Where did you get this?” he asked.

“I made it,” Ea-Sil replied. “I have forty-six others.”

“I don’t see a viceregal imprint on the bar.”

“What’s a viceregal imprint?”

“The viceroy of Dilmun controls the trade in bronze throughout his territory. Every bar that is bought and sold must carry the stamp of legitimacy imprinted on it by his inspectors. It’s a sign that taxes have been paid on it. If your bars don’t have the imprint, they cannot be sold in Dilmun.”

“Hmm, I didn’t know this. How much is the tax?”

“Not much,” Rua-Enlil said softly, “But if you took these to the inspector, he’d confiscate your bronze, your other property and perhaps your head. You aren't a licensed supplier." He stared at Nunna with a predatory smile on his face. "What would become of your beautiful boy then?"

"So I cannot sell them in Dilmun? I paid a small fortune to make them."

Rua-Enlil picked up the metal bar, weighing it in his hand. He held it so the light reflected off it. "It looks to be good quality. May I ask the ratio you used?"

Ea-Sil hedged. "You know about bronze? You make it yourself perhaps?"

"I have a licence," Rua-Enlil admitted. "If you don't want to tell me the ratio, perhaps you might confirm if it was say ... one to eight and a quarter. That's what I use."

Ea-Sil nodded. "Very close. If you're licensed, you could buy my bronze and pass it off as your own."

Rua-Enlil sighed again. "I could, but as your mix is different from mine, the inspectors might notice. While the risk of detection is small, it's not altogether absent. Tax evasion carries a heavy fine, but fraud attracts the death penalty. I regret I must decline your offer."

"And no one else in Dilmun will buy it, I suppose?"

"If you approached anyone else, they'd denounce you immediately. It's only because I'm a friend ..."

"So there's nothing I can do?"

The merchant merely smiled. "Ea-Sil, we're friends aren't we? I could take a risk and buy your bronze, for the sake of friendship. I'd have to try remelting the bars and ..." Rua-Enlil glanced across at the Magan man, "... adding more tin? Ah, I thought so. You used eight and a half. I was right. I tell you, Ea-Sil, I know my bronze. Anyway, all this would be time-consuming, and my servants, while loyal, would wonder where the bars came from. I couldn't offer much – say five gold shekels for the lot?"

Ea-Sil groaned. "I paid twice that for the tin alone. The copper's worth more too."

"Seven pieces, if you'll lend me the boy for an evening. Fifteen, if you'll sell him outright."

Ea-Sil hesitated and Nunna tensed. "I … I think I must now decline."

Rua-Enlil shrugged. "A pity. Well, there's always the road west, if you can smuggle it past the border guards. You could try selling it to the wandering Badu tribes of the interior. They care nothing for where the metal comes from, and they'd pay a good price – if they don't just rob you and leave your bodies for the jackals." He laughed and stood, signalling an end to the meeting. "Come and see me on your way back, if you're still alive. If the boy has his beauty after the desert sun has taken its toll, I'll buy him off you so your trip isn't totally wasted."

Nunna spoke to Ea-Sil out on the street. His mind still raged with the revelation his master had arranged for his gelding five years before and the apparent rescue had all been for show to bind him with bonds of gratitude. Part of him wanted to strangle the man, though the greater part, obedient to years of loyalty, still proved a restraint. He thrust the feelings of violence away. "Thank you for not selling me or hiring me out, master."

"The man sought to cheat me," Ea-Sil growled. "I wasn't about to reward him for that."

"Nevertheless, I'm grateful."

"I've lost money hand over fist with this debacle, and it's all your fault. I should sell you. I'm sure I could get a better price from one of the brothels."

Nunna said nothing, but he considered what he would do if this happened.

"I suppose I'll have to throw more gold after that which I've lost," Ea-Sil grumbled. "When the ship docks in the inner harbour, we'll collect the bronze and have it transported by camel west into the desert."

The work fell to Nunna once more. He found them cheap accommodation and arranged the hire of three camels on a caravan heading west in five days time. While he waited for the ship to dock in the inner harbour, Nunna sat cross-legged on his thin straw mattress at the foot of his master's plush divan bed and sewed pockets in tough canvas to hold the bronze bars. They could not risk them being discovered, so Nunna used the pocket cloth to line a series of leather panniers which they filled with cheap trading goods. He explained to Ea-Sil when his master complained about the expense, "I've made inquiries. The viceroy's border guards examine the loads of all caravans leaving the city. If they find unmarked bronze, they'll arrest us. If they find empty panniers, they will get suspicious, so we must put something in them."

"But seashells? They'll think us mad."

"Better to be laughed at as ignorant foreigners than suspected of a crime. Besides, shells are drilled and strung together as beads in the interior. It's a cheap but not a ridiculous cargo – unless you'd rather pay five times as much for cloth or twenty times as much for spices."

Ea-Sil shook his head. "Do as you see fit but don't bankrupt me. If you do, I'll sell you to a poxed whoremaster."

Five days later, they passed through the border inspection without the slightest suspicion falling on them that the panniers contained anything more than loose seashells. The guards dug their hands into the shells, sifting them through their fingers and laughed.

"You haven't done this before, have you? These loose shells will all be chipped and broken by the time you reach your destination. You should've packed them tightly in small bags."

When the caravan moved away from the inspection point, Ea-Sil turned on Nunna angrily. "Why didn't you pack them in bags? You're losing me yet more money."

"If they were in bags, the guards could remove them easily and see that something was sewn into the lining. I've brought material and thread. When we stop tonight I'll make bags and transfer the shells into them."

They fell into a routine that consumed their days. The caravan moved at walking pace, heading roughly toward the setting sun at the slow amble dictated by the slowest camel. Nunna and Ea-Sil rode their own mounts, and their pack animal followed on a tether. Nunna quickly got used to the swaying motion and looked out over the dunes each day as if he sailed a dhow across a limitless ocean. The sun was fierce, burning their skin, and they adopted the dress of the desert people – a long flowing izar that trapped cooler air close to the body yet allowed it to circulate and a checked cloth kufiyya secured with a piece of rope.

They arose with the dawn and stopped to set up camp at sunset, sometimes at a well or water seep, more often just in the shelter of a pile of rocks. The camels were hobbled and left to forage amongst the spindly bushes and sparse grasses, while the caravan riders built a fire against the cold nights and prepared a hot meal. Ea-Sil's hire of the camels included their food and bedding and the protection that came from companionship in the wilderness, but they set their blankets apart from the other merchants. Ea-Sil demanded this because he disdained the company of men he regarded as being of lesser station and Nunna had no choice but to do as his master wanted. In truth, Nunna enjoyed sleeping farther from the fire. It was colder, but he liked lying on his back staring up through the cold, clear air at the stars scattered like the shards of the sun on a warm sea. Also, sleeping apart gave him time to think. Not that he was often alone as Ea-Sil demanded sex from his slave with increasing frequency and violence. Nunna submitted, not knowing how he could refuse, but the pleasure had gone from the act now that he knew the truth of his condition.

Nunna lay alone one night, half a month after leaving Dilmun. His whole life, or at least as far back as he could remember, had been spent as a slave of Ea-Sil and for the last five years as a catamite created solely for his master's sexual pleasure. *I loved him – I gave him my heart, yet he did that to me*. For the first time in his short life, Nunna thought about leaving Ea-Sil, running away. *I could do it easily out here. At home, I'm watched and I could never make it over the mountains, but out here on a fast came l…* He tracked a shooting star as it streaked across the heavens and imagined it was himself racing westward ahead of the caravan. *Where would I go? How would I live*? He contemplated his talents. *I can read and write. I can do business accounts. I can sing ... and I suppose I can always sell my body. No. I don't want to do that again. Still, if I had to, at least I would have a choice. I've none with him*. Nunna started to shake with anger toward Ea-Sil and was grateful he slept alone that night. *I could kill him so easily*.

The nights without Ea-Sil's company were Nunna's favourite time for other reasons too. He could bundle up in his blanket, look at the stars and dream. He had little to do during the day except stay on his swaying camel, but the harshness of the desert intruded on his thoughts. His daytime world was dominated by the reds, yellows, greys and browns of the land and the washed out bowl of pale blue above him, pierced by a disc of white heat as fierce as any of Enki's furnaces. Nunna would guide his camel out of the line so he did not have to stare at the animal and rider in front and try to empty his mind. Distracting him though were the sounds of the desert, not at all the silent place he had supposed. He could hear the creak, rasp and clink of leather and metal gear, the moans of complaint from the camels and the occasional rumble of flatulence, a shouted command once in a while or the high-pitched whistle of a kite invisible in the glare above him. The wind, as hot as from a furnace, would lift the sand grains, making them rustle and whisper and dry his lips and skin, bringing scents of death and burning rock to his nostrils. Nunna rubbed mutton fat on his exposed surfaces but did not mind that his youthful looks faded and coarsened. Ea-Sil left him alone now, partly from anger at the youth's lack of passion and then from a lack of interest as body odours increased. Nunna rejoiced but was careful not to show it. Ea-Sil's anger could easily tip over into a severe beating or a spiteful rape.

Several small groups of wandering Badu saw the caravan and intercepted it, wanting to trade. They had little to offer, save goat meat, milk, clarified butter and skins and showed no interest at all in Ea-Sil's bronze, though they traded a few bags of shells. The caravan leader raised his eyebrows in surprise when the bronze came out the first time, but his only comment was that Ea-Sil would find good offers for the metal in the markets of Makkah. This was not the first time Nunna had heard of the western town, but previously it had only been in terms of the caravan's destination. Nunna now cultivated the caravan leader's friendship and learned all he could.

"I'm Firuz bin Jawid. What's your name, pretty boy?"

"I'm Nunna. I've heard the name Makkah before, but I know nothing about it."

"Not many live within the town itself, but many come there to trade. It lies in a narrow valley between high hills and rocky crags. The blessings of the gods are upon it, despite the brackishness of its water."

"Why do you say that?"

"You haven't heard of the Kaaba?" Nunna shook his head. "It's a small square stone building that was fashioned by Ibrahim himself a thousand or so years ago. He fixed a black stone given to him by God into the wall and three hundred and sixty gods and goddesses are now worshipped within its precinct. Perhaps you've heard of Hubal? No? Then what of al-Ilah, Manet or Uzza? They're all worshipped hereabouts … but perhaps al-Ilah more than any other." Firuz smiled at the youth riding alongside him. "What god do you follow? The god of love, perhaps?"

Nunna shook his head. "I've as little time for gods as they've had time for me."

Firuz nodded somberly. "Maybe you'll find one in Makkah. They seem to have a god for everything. Back home in Persia, we have fewer gods but a great many demons."

Nunna laughed. "Perhaps you would recommend a god?"

"Any except al-Ilah." Firuz looked around as if worried he might be overheard. He guided his camel closer to Nunna's and lowered his voice. "Al-Ilah is a violent god only suitable for tribes like the Qurayshi. They're capable of anything, as is their god. One could almost suspect they followed a djinni." Shouts arose behind them, and they turned to see a belly strap on a camel had snapped, spilling the contents of someone's panniers over the sand. Firuz turned his camel and rode back to supervise the reloading of the merchandise. Nunna resumed his place in the column.

"Think you're too good for me now, do you?" Ea-Sil sneered. "Can't wait to run after the first man who speaks nicely to you? You know he just lusts after your tender buttocks, don't you? Well, remember that you're mine. I own you, and you're not opening your cheeks for any man, unless he pays me good gold first."

Nunna said nothing but eased his camel away until he rode alone. Tears formed, but he brushed them away angrily.

A month later, they reached the *Well of Beginnings*, which Firuz informed them was only a day's travel from Makkah.

"Why the *Well of Beginnings*?" Nunna asked. "Surely the *Well of Endings* would be a more appropriate name?"

"Indeed it would, beautiful boy," Firuz agreed, his teeth showing white amidst his dark beard. "That is if it hadn't been named by a traveller leaving Makkah."

Ea-Sil was furious at both Nunna and Firuz for this exchange and would speak to neither.

The caravan camped at the *Well of Beginnings*, though the sun was still a full hand span above the horizon. Firuz explained these were Qurayshi lands, and while the tribe would probably respect the sanctuary of the Well, they were less respectful of traders on other parts of the road.

"You mean they're bandits?" asked one man.

"Not exactly," Firuz replied. "That tribe controls Makkah and surrounding lands. They demand that travellers, traders, pilgrims even, pay a duty for using the road. However, they'll only exact payment if they find us on the road itself. We're exempt here at the Well and once we reach Makkah."

"So they'll be waiting for us when we leave the Well tomorrow?"

"Maybe, maybe not. There are other roads that they patrol. It's as the gods will."

One god evidently willed the Qurayshi should tax Firuz's caravan, for a dozen men on camels waited for them on the road an hour after dawn. The leader of the ambushing party sat relaxed on his mount and lifted a hand in greeting as Firuz neared.

"May the blessing of al-Ilah be upon thee, Firuz bin Jawid," he called.

Firuz signalled the caravan to halt. "I see you Abd-Ilah ibn Hadi al-Baqir al-Qurayshi. To what do I owe this honour?"

Abd-Ilah laughed, showing white teeth. "I ask you to make an offering to al-Ilah."

"Gladly," Firuz replied. "It was my intention to do so at the Kaaba this evening."

"Then I'm glad to save you the trouble." Abd-Ilah's smile vanished, and a subtle hand signal drew his men up alongside, their hands resting lightly on the hilts of their swords. "You know the routine. Please dismount and unload your trade goods that we might assess your road tax."

One of the traders behind Firuz snorted and said, "Why do we lie down for these dogs? We outnumber them."

"Truly," Firuz murmured, "And there'll be twice as many of us when they have separated our heads from our bodies. We must pay the road tax, so let them collect it."

Grumbling, the men of the caravan dismounted and unloaded their camels, and each trader stood beside his bales and open panniers as Abd-Ilah walked along the line with Firuz, examining the merchandise.

"Don't try and hide your valuables," Abd-Ilah said, "For if I find you out you'll pay extra."

The Qurayshi calculated a tax on some items, less on others, and ignored some altogether. One man had gold ornaments and was forced to hand over one part in ten, another had spices and paid likewise, but a third had cured leather and lost only one part in twenty. A trader of salt was waved away without tax.

"We can get all the salt we need from the western sea. You'll find it hard to sell that in Makkah."

Nunna watched the men coming closer to Ea-Sil's panniers. He saw the smug look on his master's face and felt a fresh wave of anger wash through him.

Abd-Ilah paid only cursory attention to Ea-Sil's panniers of seashells. He took a single bag and tossed it to one of his men. “Give it to your wife, Shihab.” He nodded and turned away. “We’ll let you get on your way Firuz, but next time, make sure you carry more valuable merchandise. This was almost not worth the trouble.”

“Abd-Ilah ibn Hadi,” called a clear young voice. “Have you checked the bottom of the panniers?”

“Silence, you fool,” Ea-Sil hissed as he whipped round, his face contorted in rage.

Abd-Ilah looked curiously at the angry man and the beautiful youth. He snapped his fingers, and his men ran forward, tipping the bags of shells out onto the sand. The cloth lining to the panniers tore loose and a single bar of bronze fell free.

“Well, what have we here?” Abd-Ilah picked up the bar and weighed it in his hand. “Search the panniers. There may be more.”

When all forty-seven bars lay gleaming in the sun, Abd-Ilah asked Firuz, “Did you know of this treasure?” The caravan master shook his head. “You swear? On whatever god you hold dear? On your life?”

“I didn’t know of it, I swear” Firuz said calmly. He stared at Ea-Sil and Nunna as if daring them to call him out on his lie.

"Then you're not held to be concealing taxable goods, Firuz bin Jawid. Instead, I shall confiscate all of this bronze."

"No, you cannot!" Ea-Sil screamed. He rushed toward Abd-Ilah, tugging at the dagger in his belt. One of Abd-Ilah's men knocked him to the ground, and Abd-Ilah stood over the fallen man. "The bronze bars have no markings. They're illegal anyway, so as I represent the Banu Qurayshi and we're the law hereabouts, I'll confiscate the metal. Be grateful I don't notify the authorities in Dilmun of your transgression." He turned away as his men started loading the metal onto their own camels.

Ea-Sil staggered to his feet and stared at Nunna. "You've ruined me, you ungrateful whelp." He put his hand on his dagger and strode forward.

Nunna fell back a few paces and then stopped. "No more, master, I'll take no more. Ea-Sil, I deny you," he cried and ran forward to meet his former master.

They met and Ea-Sil struck Nunna. They struggled; a blade emerged, flashed and turned. Both man and youth fell to the sand, but only the youth arose, the dagger in his hand, blood spattering his robes.

Abd-Ilah's men swiftly disarmed Nunna and held him fast. They brought him to their leader and forced him to his knees.

"You've murdered him, boy," Abd-Ilah said. "What was he to you?"

Before Nunna could answer, one of the traders called out, "They were father and son."

Abd-Ilah's eyes widened. "The penalty for parricide is death," he said softly.

"He wasn't my father," Nunna said into the shocked silence. He stared in fascination at the crumpled, bloodied corpse of Ea-Sil on the ground; head tilted back, his blood-streaked beard jutting at the sky. Already a fly crawled on his face, investigating the fluid in one half-open eye. "He wasn't my father."

"What was he then to you?" Abd-Ilah asked. "You traveled with him from Dilmun, and you are of an age to be his son." Nunna shook his head, and he asks again. "If not a son, what then? A nephew? Cousin?"

"I was his slave."

"His slave?" He shrugged. "The penalty for killing your master is the same as for killing your father. Firuz, you knew of this boy's status?"

"I suspected it, but it could as easily have been a father-son or uncle-nephew relationship. This knowledge answers questions I had."

"What questions?"

"He's of an age where a youth strives for a beard, yet his face is as smooth as if he shaved. His voice is high but mellow, and I often saw the man lead him off into the night. I believe he's a gelding, a body-slave to cater to that man's sexual appetites."

"We geld camels and horses," laughed a man, "but I've never seen a gelded man. Why do they do it? Is it to tame his wild spirit?"

“You’re a fool, Zaahir,” said another man. “They geld young boys so they can use them as they’d use a woman.”

“What? They cut off their ... they make them into women?”

The rest of the men laughed and continued to talk over Nunna as if he was a piece of baggage.

“Gentlemen,” Firuz chided. “This talk is unseemly, especially in front of the lad.”

“You’re right,” Abd-Ilah agreed. “We’re here to decide whether he dies for killing his master, not for being gelded, which is no crime.”

“Is there any doubt of his guilt?” asked the man who had called Zaahir a fool. “He admits he’s a slave, and we all saw him kill the old man.”

“The penalty for that is death,” a man said. “Is there any reason for that to be delayed?”

“How?” Zaahir asked, his eyes glittering. “Stoning?” He looked around. “There are few stones here, but many a few miles further on.”

“Let him die the same way he killed his master,” said another man.

“Yet in all this he remains calm,” Firuz said. “Look at him. This is a youth, a boy almost, who knows he faces imminent death but is unconcerned. I’d like to know why.”

“He’s a cold-hearted killer.”

“No, I don't think so,” Abd-Ilah said. “I think we should hear from the boy. Even a convicted killer has the right to a final statement.”

“This isn’t a court of law,” Zaahir protested.

“All the more reason. Well, boy, do you want to plead for your life? We’ll listen.”

Nunna stared at him blankly, as if he had already moved from life into death and the men were talking a foreign tongue. He shook his head and looked down at the sand.

"You see, he doesn't want to talk," Zaahir said. "Let's carry out the sentence."

"We should take him back to Dilmun," one of the traders said. "He came from there."

"He was going to Makkah, and he's within the jurisdiction of my tribe, the Qurayshi," Abd-Ilah replied. "Our god al-Ilah will judge him after we've executed him," he added piously.

Nunna looked up at the name, recalling what Firuz had told him. "I've heard of al-Ilah, but I would hesitate to call him a god. He sounds cruel."

The Qurayshi men growled in anger and two stepped forward as if they would send him to their god immediately, but their leader halted them with a gesture.

"You're not helping your case, boy, if you insult our god. Yet even now, if you speak, I'll listen." Nunna said nothing, and Abd-Ilah stared at him. "Tell us your name at least? Your family? Do you want to go into death as an unknown?"

Nunna sighed. "My name is Nunna. My father's name is unimportant as the family history stops with me. I was five years old when I was bought in the slave markets of Dilmun with my parents by Ea-Sil ... him ... a copper maker of Magan."

"You were a gelding before he bought you?"

Nunna laughed bitterly. "No. For five years he raised me in his own household, teaching me to read and write, to do his accounts and to sing for his pleasure."

"And you repaid him with death?" Zaahir asked.

"I can honestly say I loved him then. When I was ten, my master went away on business, and while he was away, I was kidnapped from his house and taken into the hills where they … they … cut me. A month or so later, my master returned, learned of my fate and rescued me. I continued in his service, partly as a scribe but mostly sharing his bed."

"Did he mistreat you?" Firuz asked.

Nunna hesitated but then shook his head. "Not really, not at first. Remember I was a slave. I didn't want my new role, but I felt gratitude to him for rescuing me from a horrifying experience and for keeping me in his household. When I healed, he took me to his bed. He was my owner, and I was his slave. If I didn't obey, I was beaten. I learned to put my mind elsewhere when he used my body. After a time, I came to take pleasure in it as much as one takes pleasure in anything done well. I had no future so sought solace day by day. I could use my skill to put him in a good mood so I wouldn't get beaten for other things."

The Qurayshi men looked at him again with a predatory gaze. Most of them had never even heard of a eunuch, but they all imagined what it would be like to lie with one.

Nunna shuddered under their gaze. "That's all. I decided I had had too much and killed him at my first opportunity."

"That's not all," Firuz said. "All this happened in Magan. How is it that you were journeying from Dilmun to Makkah?"

"Does it matter?"

"No," Abd-Ilah agreed, "but I too am curious. Indulge us."

Nunna sighed again. "That man is ... was a copper miner and smelter in Magan. He owned a trading empire that bought and sold all manner of goods but mostly copper in Moehendus and ..."

"Where?" Zaahir interrupted.

"Moehendus in the Valley of the Indus, far to the east," Firuz said. "Go on, Nunna."

"And in Dilmun," the boy continued. "Then he got the idea he could make more gold by making bronze and selling that instead. We came to Dilmun with these bars but found that the bronze market was closed to us. We weren't a recognised maker of bronze and couldn't sell it. We would've been arrested. A ... a friend of ... his recommended we bring it to Makkah, so here we ... I am."

"You've told us that while in Magan you slept with your master Ea-Sil, if not with enjoyment, at least with resignation, yet across the desert this had changed. I saw you, Nunna, so don't deny it. He took you roughly, and I saw not love but hate in your eyes. What changed you?"

"Something he did." Nunna looked Firuz in the eye. "In Dilmun, my master told me that he paid the gelder to have me cut so I would become his body slave, his bedmate. He lied to me, letting me believe he'd rescued me and loved me, when all along he was the one who robbed me of my manhood and my future, just so he could have an object for his lust. I hated him, yet I would have run from him if I could rather than kill him."

"Why didn't you?"

"Where would I run? How would I live? I could perhaps find service as an accountant, a scribe or a singer, but my voice and my beardless face would attract notice. A eunuch is good for one thing only it seems." A certain amount of bitterness crept into Nunna's voice. "If I ran, I would become a whore to many men; if I stayed, to only one. I decided to stay. Then, when I saw that Ea-Sil was to get away with his bronze smuggling, I decided to strike back at him where it hurt most – his profits."

"And you killed him," Abd-Ilah said.

"I didn't mean to. I meant only to hold him close and tell him how I despised him. I knew that would earn me a beating, but I no longer cared. Then he drew a dagger, and ... and he died. I don't know how it happened. I have no training with arms. I've never even held a dagger before."

"The result is the same," the Qurayshi leader said. "You killed your master. We may now understand why, but it doesn't excuse the deed. You murdered, and the penalty for murder is death." Abd-Ilah drew his sword, curved and bright in the sunlight. "In view of your suffering at the hands of this man ..." He nodded toward the swelling body of Ea-Sil, "... I'll offer you a swift death. Prepare yourself, lad."

Nunna shuddered but bent his head so he would not see the killing stroke delivered.

"Wait. A moment, please," Firuz said, stepping close to the kneeling boy. "Abd-Ilah ibn Hadi, what is the penalty for murder?"

"What in the name of all the gods are you talking about? Haven't you been listening? It's death, and if you'll stand aside, I'll carry out the sentence." Firuz did not move. Abd-Ilah spoke again in a lower voice. "You draw out the waiting for the lad, Firuz. Stand aside."

"Death is one penalty, but there's another among my people. I understand that the same rule applies here. I'm talking about blood money."

Abd-Ilah lowered his blade. "That only applies if the dead man's family call for recompense instead of the life of the transgressor. Ea-Sil's family is not here to ask for it."

"If they were here, you'd be bound to follow their wishes."

"That's true," Abd-Ilah agreed. "But even if they did that, the lad cannot pay anything. He's a slave and penniless. In such a case, his life is forfeit."

"Unless another pays the blood price for him."

Nunna looked up to see Abd-Ilah gazing quizzically at the caravan master. "You, Firuz?"

"Why not? I have no family. Who can object to how I spend my gold?"

"Why?"

"He's a handsome youth with a quick and ready mind," Firuz said. "He'd be useful in my business, and I enjoy his company."

"And his firm, rounded buttocks," Zaahir guffawed.

"This talk is all meaningless anyway," Abd-Ilah said. "The dead man's family isn't here to demand the blood price, so the penalty is death." He raised his curved sword again.

"Put it to the god," Firuz said. "A blood price can be held for the family to claim within a year. I claim the justice of the god on this lad's behalf."

Abd-Ilah lowered his sword again, frowning. "Which god's mercy do you invoke?"

"Al-Ilah."

The leader of the Qurayshi smiled and sheathed his sword. "You agree to be bound by the decision of the god? Whether the verdict is death or gold? And the price?"

"Yes."

"Then we'll invoke al-Ilah and we'll see."

The caravan was sent back to the *Well of Beginnings* to await the outcome of the invocation. Nunna was bound and thrown over the back of a camel, and together with Firuz and the Qurayshi men, they rode into the desert heading for a range of hills that thrust up through the sand.

"We're not going to the Kaaba?" Firuz asked.

"It's not necessary," Abd-Ilah said. "We can invoke the presence in any high place."

"And the god will come?" Firuz persisted. "Most gods stay near their main altars and answer only to their priests."

Abd-Ilah laughed. "Not al-Ilah. My name means servant of al-Ilah, and that's an apt name, for everyone knows the god stays close to my family. My ancestor, Baqir, was the first to feel his blessing, and he'll answer me before any of those grasping priests in Makkah."

"So you'll be able to interpret his wishes?"

The laughter was more general this time. "You'll see," Abd-Ilah said. He turned and reprimanded one of his men who was beating his camel to make it move faster. "Don't do that Zorah. You know al-Ilah hates cruelty. Do you want to bring his wrath down upon us?"

Evening fell as they entered the foothills and they dismounted and moved higher on foot, Nunna stumbling along at swordpoint. The first stars came out as the sun dipped below the horizon. The evening was beautiful, the air cool and even Nunna looked around with an expression of contentment.

They arrived at a great horizontal slab that had fallen away from the rocky crags above. The upper surface of the stone was stained dark with old blood and ashes that smelled faintly of incense. They made Nunna kneel in front of the altar and ranged themselves around him with Firuz on one side and Abd-Ilah on the other.

First Abd-Ilah and then the other men of the Qurayshi started chanting in a strange tongue. The syllables were fluid, running into one another, the rhythm rising and falling. The only recognisable word for Nunna was al-Ilah, constantly repeated. The cooling breeze had died away but instead of feeling warmer, Nunna started to shiver as if the heat of his body was being sucked from him.

"He comes," Abd-Ilah murmured.

There was a streak of light in the sky as if a star had fallen, and they all looked up, but there was nothing in the heavens. When they lowered their gaze, a blue flame tinged with green sat on the altar, unmoving, feeding on nothing.

"Al-Ilah," Zaahir shouted out. "God is Great!"

"O al-Ilah," Abd-Ilah said, "We have come to petition your justice. This man ... this youth is a slave who killed his master. This other man, Firuz bin Jawid offers the blood ..."

I know why you have come.

Nunna heard a voice but not one that is warmed by lungs, shaped by lips and tongue. It sounded in his head as if it was his own thought. *Is ... is this a god*? A feeling of amusement washed over him.

I know you Nunna. What is your life worth?

"Y ... you know m ... me?" Nunna stuttered. "My n ... name? How?"

Your minds are laid bare. Firuz bin Jawid, how much is this life worth?

"I don't know, my lord," Firuz whispered. "Tell me, and I'll pay it."

There was silence on the mountain for a space. Nunna stared at the still blue flame, scarcely believing it was a god he saw. The harder he stared, the more he found his eyes sliding off to one side as if it deflected his gaze. The inner voice came again.

Hear then the judgment of al-Ilah. Blood has been spilled, but in the absence of kin to demand the death penalty, the blood price may be paid. Firuz bin Jawid will pay the sum of one hundred gold pieces for the boy. There was a muffled gasp from the men, and Nunna's hopes fell. *Abd-Ilah ibn Hadi, you will hold the blood money in trust for a year from this day, paying it to the family of Ea-Sil of*

Magan when and if they request it. You will send a messenger to the village of Musqatti-Sil in Magan to tell them the gold awaits them. If they are unwilling to make the journey to Makkah to collect the gold, it reverts to the Qurayshi.

"I will pay it," Firuz murmured.

The voice continued but unintelligibly for all the men except Abd-Ilah. The men of Qurayshi prostrated themselves, and Firuz followed them. Nunna hesitated and then bowed his head in submission. The blue flame winked into nothingness. The visitation of the god was over.

They arose and descended the mountain. At the foot, Abd-Ilah and his men mounted their camels and prepared to leave Nunna and Firuz.

"I'll collect the blood price from you tomorrow, Firuz, when your caravan arrives in Makkah. Have it ready." Abd-Ilah turned his camel and clicked his tongue, urging it into motion. His men followed. The man and the boy watched their shadows disappear into the night.

"How can you afford one hundred gold pieces?" Nunna asked.

"I'm a rich man," Firuz replied, "though my riches are at home in Persia. But by some happy circumstance, I carry exactly one hundred gold pieces in my strongbox."

"How ...?"

"One might expect a god to know these things ... or a djinni. I saw and heard nothing tonight that convinced me of al-Ilah's goodness."

"I did," Nunna said. Then he looked sideways at his new master. "Or maybe not. You'll no doubt expect much of me for such a price. Have I exchanged one tyrant for another?"

Firuz turned and took him by the shoulders, gazing deep into his eyes. The moon was rising, and the man's face was plain in its bright light. "I want nothing not freely given," he said. "When I pay the blood price in Makkah tomorrow, we'll find a lawyer and I'll draw up a letter of manumission – of freedom," he added, seeing Nunna did not know the other word. "It'll be dated a year hence, when all claims by the family of Ea-Sil are void. At that time, you're free to go where you will."

"But you'll use me for a year first."

He smiled. "As I said, only what is freely given. Your companionship, your learning ... I haven't heard you sing yet." Firuz laughed. "Maybe love. That's your decision though." He waited, looking at the boy in the moonlight.

At length, Nunna nodded. "I'll be a good servant to you for a year. After that, we'll see."

"Then let's go back to the *Well of Beginnings*."

Chapter Six

Ah, mercy feels good. I really recommend it. It felt truly godlike to spare the gelded youth. I have always held the power of life and death over these human creatures, but usually it has been my pleasure to take life and give death. It was a new experience to abstain this time.

I have given some of my followers a word whereby they can claim my attention no matter where they are. Of course, I limit this great gift to those who are the most faithful in my service. Abd-Ilah is one of these. He knows the word that will invoke my presence, even though we may be many miles apart. When he called, I was busy receiving the praise of my priest in the Kaaba. He was offering up handfuls of incense and petitioning me on behalf of many. I encourage my priests to be profligate with incense, not that the sweet odour pleases me, but rather because I enjoy seeing them spend such a lot of their income on something that ends up as smoke. They extract huge fees from petitioners, and it is only fitting some of that money goes to their god who makes all things possible rather than just filling their coffers. They also pay with their life force, but that is another story. Priests never live long as a result, but there is always another eager to step up when his predecessor dies.

Anyway, I was saying I was being worshipped in the Kaaba, when I felt the word of power used by Abd-Ilah. The prayers of the priest were stale and uninteresting, so I answered the call; I doubt the priest even noticed my absence. I streaked across the intervening skies, homing in on the uprising prayers, and settled on the altar in the desert east of Makkah. Abd-Ilah and his men were there with two strangers. I never wait for men to voice their concerns as it takes too long, and their words seldom hold as much meaning as their private thoughts, so I sampled their minds and discerned the purpose for which I was summoned.

The youth's mind interested me. I have met brave men before and eaten my share of them. No man knows what happens when the weak flame of his being gutters and goes out, but some face extinction with equanimity, remaining calm and refusing to give in to the panic that tugs at the hems of their garments. Others howl their fear and plead for just one more breath, just one more sunrise before going down into darkness. This youth was one of the brave ones, and I wondered why. His life had barely started, yet he was prepared for death. I delved deeper and found he was gelded. I had not come across one of his kind before and wondered why any man would mutilate himself like this when procreation plays such a large part in men's aspirations. Then I saw the castration had not been voluntary and this act lay at the root of his present troubles.

What would a god do? I wondered. I dipped into the mind of the other stranger. I met the usual emotions of lust, pride and avarice, common to so many, but also intelligence, pity and a fledgling love. Curious. This Persian was prepared to pay to keep the youth alive. The only question in his mind was how much could he afford. His thoughts told me he had a hundred gold pieces in the strongbox in his caravan. That should suffice.

Abd-Ilah and his men were known quantities. They would obey their god without question, but it is a wise god who gives his followers what they want. The men wanted blood, but they could get this almost any day, so it did not dominate their thoughts. Their other desire was for gold, and this was harder to come by. I could deliver this to them.

Blood has been spilled, but in the absence of kin to demand the death penalty the blood price may be paid. Firuz bin Jawid will pay the sum of one hundred gold pieces for the boy.

The Persian should never have had that sum in his head. Well, we would see how strong his desire for the boy really was. There was one other necessary command. As it stood, the blood price was owed to the absent kin. I had to make sure the Qurayshi, in particular Abd-Ilah and his men, got their hands on it.

Abd-Ilah ibn Hadi, you will hold the blood money in trust for a year from this day, paying it to the family of Ea-Sil of Magan when and if they request it. You will send a messenger to the village of Musqatti-Sil in Magan to tell them the gold awaits them here. If they are unwilling to make the journey to Makkah to collect the gold, it reverts to the Qurayshi.

If I knew Abd-Ilah, he would be unlikely to make too great an effort seeking out the dead man's family. When his relatives failed to appear, he would willingly take the gold for himself. Abd-Ilah is a favourite of mine. I like to be able to give him what his heart desires.

I left them to it and returned to the droning prayers of the priest in the Kaaba. I paid little attention, being more concerned with my recent decision and the feeling this act of mercy engendered in me. It felt good, and I contemplated the idea that there was more to being a god than I first thought. Gods among the people of jazirat al-Arab are many, and most govern just a tiny bit of creation. A shepherd god looks after shepherds and goats, a war god is bloodthirsty and a goddess of love favours unmarried girls and courting couples. I was trying to be a greater god, so I must perforce be interested in a wider range of things. I loved death, but I also helped shepherds, traders, warriors and even women seeking revenge on occasion. Perhaps I needed to exercise a gentler side too. There is another god like this, and if I do not want to be eclipsed by him, I should make the effort.

I have never met this other god, and I daresay he is just another djinni making a living, but I have heard about him. He comes from the north from the land of Canaan and Sinai. Once he was a mere hilltop dweller, a solitary flame, called an *El*, but now it seems he has become the sole god of a people who also, like my Isma'ilites, spring from the loins of Ibrahim, though from a younger son called Isaac. These people, who are called Jews, are starting to move within jazirat al-Arab, and unless I want them to invite their god down to Makkah, I will have to do something.

I could strive to be as popular to the Jews as this *Yahweh* is in the Jew's homeland, but I think the easiest course is to get rid of the Jews themselves. If they perceive jazirat al-Arab as being inhospitable, they will leave, and without them, my worship will dominate.

Chapter Seven

Miriam, daughter of Eliezer, bobbed her head respectfully under the firm gaze of her father and then looked boldly at her betrothed. The blacksmith's son was the only single male Jew in Makkah, aside from his father Abbas, and the only possible choice for a young woman fast approaching her prime. The two fathers had arranged the betrothal six months before without consulting either son or daughter, the union of the families being the concern solely of the men. They would be married when Miriam turned sixteen, less than a year away, by which time Simeon would be nearly thirty. In the six months of their betrothal, they had never talked together without one of the parents being present, nor did they wish to do so. Talk would come later, after they were married.

Simeon, son of Abbas, smiled, his white teeth showing in his dark beard and placed a handful of iron hinges on the counter of Eliezer's shop.

"Shalom, Eliezer. Shalom Miriam," Simeon said. "My father sends his greetings and hopes that these hinges meet with your approval." He smiled again at Miriam. "You are well, Miriam?"

Miriam bobbed her head again. "Yes, thank you, Simeon." When she married, she would pass from the authority of her father to the authority of her husband, so she owed respect to both men. She did not mind, for there was no other possible action, but sometimes she wondered what it would be like to choose for herself. Her twelve-year-old sister, Ruth, had no eligible male picked out for her, and she often made up stories in which she caught the eye of some handsome, rich hero. *Father would still have to approve the marriage*, she thought, s*o where's the difference? Besides, Simeon is a decent man.*

Eliezer examined one of the hinges carefully and worked the action. "These are good work, Simeon. Miriam, don't stand there gawking, child. Find a chair for our guest; pour him a cup of well water."

Miriam ducked her head and hurried off, but Simeon called after her. "No need, I cannot stay." She did not hear, and Simeon smiled awkwardly at her father. "I must get back to the foundry, Eliezer. We have a large order of chain links to make up. We'll be busy for most of the week."

"The Lord provides by sending us work. You and your father will still come for the Sabbat meal this week?"

"Of course, Eliezer. You honour us."

"The honour is ours," the shopkeeper replied. "Besides, you're family ... well, almost. We must discuss your marriage."

"Thank you, Eliezer. However, it is my father with whom you should discuss marriage plans. I'm a dutiful son as Miriam is a dutiful daughter."

"We're both blessed," Eliezer said complacently. "Well, off you go then, lad. You mustn't keep your father waiting."

Miriam returned a few moments later, carrying a stool in one hand and a cup of water in the other. She looked around the small shop in dismay. "Simeon has gone?"

"He has work to do, child, as have you. Give me the water, for I thirst." Eliezer drained the cup and handed it back to Miriam. "Where is your mother and Ruth?"

"Mother's in the kitchen, supervising Josea's lessons, father. Ruth is ... is helping her."

Eliezer grunted. "Find Ruth and return. I have work for both of you."

Miriam hurried into the dwelling at the rear of the shop and into the kitchen where her mother was preparing the noon meal, while her six-year-old brother, Josea, pored over a page of parchment, laboriously copying the letters of the alphabet. For a moment, she felt a pang of envy that her brother would become so much better educated, while her lot in life was to become just a wife and mother. She knew how to read and write and work with numbers, and of course, she was trained in the womanly skills of managing a household, but she sometimes wished for more, for the freedom to. *May the Lord forgive me my ungrateful and unworthy thoughts. Josea is a boy – of course he must be well educated. I am just a woman.* "Mother, have you seen Ruth? Father wants us both in the shop."

Her mother, Anna, looked up from peeling vegetables and pushed back a stray lock of hair that had escaped from her scarf. "I told her to beat the blankets, but I don't hear much work going on outside."

"I'll find out," Miriam said hurriedly, stepping to the door. She looked around the small yard, but her twelve-year-old sister was nowhere to be seen.

A rope tied between the house and a pole supported a blanket and another lay on the ground nearby with a wicker paddle beside it. *Where is she*? Miriam opened her mouth to call and then thought better of it. “You’re seeing him again, aren't you?” she muttered and ran over to the gate that let out onto the lane at the back.

The lane was deserted, so Miriam set off quickly for the Street of the Tailors. As she turned the corner of the lane, she took out her headscarf and slipped it over her hair. Informality was fine at home and even in the shop if there were no customers present, but in public she knew she should be seen as a well brought up Jewish girl. She bent her head as she hurried down the streets, avoiding the sometimes hostile glances of the Arab men.

The hostility was not personal but had more to do with her father's attitude to the polytheism common in Makkah. When Eliezer had first arrived in the town two years before, he had made it quite plain he regarded his Jewish god, Yahweh, as infinitely superior to the stone and wooden idols of the Kaaba. This view had met with good-natured tolerance at first, but as Eliezer's disdain grew greater and his comments more pointed, tolerance turned to irritation and occasional bursts of anger. People still frequented his shop, but business had fallen off. Lately, Eliezer had moderated his tongue, but it was still too early to see if relations with the townspeople would improve.

Their family had been the first Jewish one in Makkah, though they were joined the next year by

Abbas and his son. It had been natural for Miriam and Simeon to be betrothed by the two fathers, but there was no younger brother for Ruth. Although only twelve, Ruth was far more interested in marriage and family than Miriam and lacking a suitable boy of her faith, had looked elsewhere. She had found a youth she thought she loved in Saleem, son of the tailor Salih. He was seventeen and apprenticed to his father. He was also a worshipper of the god Shams and unaware of the young Jewish girl's infatuation.

Miriam found Ruth hanging around a stall in the Street of the Tailors. She was pretending to examine the samples of cloth but keeping an eye fixed on the shop opposite. The open front of the shop held two men sitting on a rug on the ground, the older one carefully cutting cloth and the younger one dexterously sewing the cloth into garments.

"Father's looking for you," Miriam murmured as she joined her sister. "And you know he'd beat you if he knew what you were doing."

Ruth smiled at her elder sister before returning her attention to Saleem. "Isn't he beautiful?"

"Men aren't beautiful," Miriam chided. She looked critically at the young man. "He's handsome enough, sister, but he's not for you."

"Why not? I'm attractive," Ruth preened unconsciously, "... and I'd make him a good wife."

"He also worships a false god, and father would beat you if he knew you were looking at any man like that, let alone an unbeliever. Now come away. Father wants us both to work in the shop, and mother's already wondering why you didn't beat the blankets."

"I did one of them ... but Miriam, why should you get the only eligible man in Makkah and I have to become an aging spinster?"

Miriam laughed and took her young sister by the arm, dragging her away. "Because I'm the eldest and because that's what father arranged. You know that. Besides, other Jewish families will move here and one of them will have just the young man for you. You're very young yet."

"You think so? You've heard something. There are other families moving here?"

"Not exactly, but ..." Miriam stopped and took Ruth's face in her hands, looking into her eyes. "You cannot speak of this to anyone, sister, but I overheard father talking to Abbas about buying a site for a synagogue. Two families aren't enough for a synagogue."

Ruth's face lit up. "Then there must be others coming here." She broke free and twirled, dancing a few steps. "My husband is coming," she sang. Several passers-by gave her dark looks, and one muttered something under his breath.

"Enough," Miriam said sharply. She took her sister's hand and ran with her back to the lane and then into their back yard. While Ruth folded the first blanket, Miriam quickly gave the second a cursory beating and folded it too. She pushed her sister through the back door and into the kitchen, holding up the blankets for her mother to see. "All done, mother."

"It took you long enough," their mother grumbled. "Come and give me a hand with the bread now."

"Sorry, mother. Father wants us in the shop." Miriam put the blankets on the table and hurried Ruth out of the kitchen. Eliezer snapped at them when they entered the front shop, demanding to know where they had been. Ruth glanced at her sister and hung her head, saying nothing. Miriam bobbed respectfully and apologised. "I'm sorry, father. Ruth was in the middle of beating blankets in the yard, so I helped her finish. Was that wrong?"

Eliezer harumphed and muttered something indistinctly, tugging at his long beard. "Well, now you're both here, you can make yourself useful. I want the floor swept carefully and mopped, and I want it finished by mid-day."

"Yes, father," the sisters said in unison. They set to with a will, while their father sorted out his merchandise into pleasing arrangements on the shelves, counters and barrels within the shop. They were no more than halfway through their tasks, sweeping dust and debris out into the street and swabbing down the floorboards so they gleamed, when the door was thrown open and three Arabs entered.

Eliezer immediately stopped what he was doing and hurried to meet his customers. "Greetings Nasib ibn Qadir al-Qurayshi," he said unctuously to the young but tall, spare-framed leader of the trio. "How may I be of assistance?"

Nasib bent his neck graciously and indicated his companions with a flick of his wrist. "Baqi ibn

Khalil, Fuad ibn Najib." He settled his sleeves and looked slowly around the shop, pausing momentarily on the two sisters before dismissing their presence and moving on. Satisfied there were no surprises in wait, the tall man turned back to the Jewish shopkeeper. "Eliezer ben Daud, you know why we're here."

Eliezer licked his lips and glanced from Nasib to his companions and back again. "Er, I'm not sure that I do ..." His voice trailed off expectantly.

"We're a tolerant people, Eliezer ben Daud, as is evidenced by the three hundred or more gods that are worshipped in the Kaaba. We'd welcome one more, even your Yahweh, if you sought to come in peace, but you don't. You seem determined to cause trouble in Makkah."

Eliezer glowered, and he glared at the speaker. "I do no more than worship God ..."

"By denying all others," Nasib broke in. "All we ask of any man that comes to Makkah is that he pay his taxes, obey the laws and conduct himself with decorum."

"I do all those things," Eliezer retorted. "But I obey a higher authority. Our prophet Moshe said, when he brought our people out of the land of Egypt, 'Thou shalt obey the Lord thy God', by which he meant Yahweh."

Nasib shrugged. "No one is telling you not to worship your own god unless doing so disturbs the peace, but you seem set on insulting our own gods and setting yours up over them."

"Moshe also said 'Thou shalt have no other gods before Me.'"

“Precisely. You must stop saying this, Eliezer ben Daud.”

“I cannot stop worshipping the God of my fathers.”

“I told you he wouldn’t listen to reason,” Fuad complained. “He’s a foreigner and doesn’t appreciate that his god is just another one of the many gods that abound everywhere.”

“That’s true,” added Baqi. “Every man thinks that his own god is the lord of creation and cannot see that the man in the next village thinks the same thing of his own god.”

“That’s not true,” Eliezer protested. “I don’t equate Yahweh with the petty demons and false gods that inhabit every hilltop, thicket or spring. Yahweh is the God of Everything and demands exclusive worship.”

“From his own followers, certainly,” Nasib said. “But there’s no necessity for anyone else to worship him.”

“I’m not asking them to; only to acknowledge His pre-eminence.”

“Impossible,” Baqi said.

“Sacrilege,” Fuad added.

“That’s not going to happen, Eliezer ben Daud.” Nasib hesitated, flicking another glance at the sisters who were bent over mop and broom but listening avidly. “As representative of the Qurayshi clan and of the Elders of Makkah, I formally ask you to cease your proselytising immediately and to refrain from talking about your god with the native inhabitants of the town.”

“And if I don’t?”

Nasib sighed. “We’re a peaceful community, but you’ve thrown a hive of bees into our midst. If you don’t cease your disruptive works, we’ll eject you and your family from Makkah.”

“I won’t go, nor will my friend, Abbas the blacksmith, and furthermore, there are another seven families coming to Makkah. You cannot obstruct the Lord's people.”

“I knew it,” Ruth whispered excitedly.

“Please be under no illusion, Eliezer ben Daud. We mean what we say. You have a choice – cease talking to others about your god or leave Makkah. You have a month ...”

“Too long,” Faud said.

“You have a month,” Nasib repeated. “Choose wisely.”

“I’m not leaving, nor will I cease to talk about my God.”

Nasib ibn Qadir bowed to the shopkeeper, then turned and left, his companions following with no more than cursory nods of dismissal. They stood outside the shop and talked amongst themselves in low tones.

“He won’t obey,” Fuad said.

“That is also my thought,” Nasib agreed.

“What then are we to do about it?” Baqi asked.

“I’ll pray to al-Ilah for guidance,” Nasib said. “But I think we must be more persuasive.”

“I doubt he’ll listen to reason.”

“Maybe not to reason, but maybe to emotion.”

“You have an idea?”

Nasib nodded. “Let me pray on the matter first.”

Eliezer did not discuss the matter with his family, despite queries from his daughters. He told them to mind their own business and that afternoon went to see Abbas the blacksmith. He was gone a long time and stamped back into the home in a foul mood. Anna, his wife, knew of his moods and was careful not to provoke his anger. Without the release afforded by a loud argument, the fury still burned within him the next day and he snapped at everyone, finding fault even when he was obeyed instantly. When one of the farmers did not bring round his promised produce, Eliezer's anger broke out, and rather than waiting patiently or sending a message by a youth from the street, he ordered his daughters to go.

"Husband, you cannot mean to send our daughters out unaccompanied?"

"Hush, wife. When I want your opinion I'll ask for it."

"The streets aren't safe ..."

"Enough. They're going." Eliezer glowered at Miriam. "You know the way to Gamil's farm?"

"Yes, father."

"Then take this message to him and bring me back his answer." He handed over a scrap of paper with scribbled writing on it. "Go straight there and straight back. Don't start conversations with any men nor visit the markets either."

The girls ran out into the street, and Miriam led the way by a circuitous route across town. The streets were unusually full of people, and they sometimes had to slow or wait for crowds to pass. Few people spared the sisters more than a glance.

“Why so many people?” Ruth asked. “And where are they going?”

“It must be a market day, but I thought I knew all those.”

“Perhaps we should follow along and see. Come on, Miriam, it's more or less on our way.”

“Father said we should avoid the markets.”

“He'll never know and besides, we’re only going to see if there is one, not stop and buy things.” Ruth pulled free of her sister and joined the crowds walking toward the centre of town. Miriam called to her to stop but then shrugged and hurried after her.

Within a few minutes, it became obvious that there was no market ahead of them. Miriam recognised the tall cubic building in the square over the heads of the crowd and tugged at Ruth's arm. “It's the Kaaba,” she whispered. “These people are going to worship. We shouldn’t be here.” Miriam tried pushing back against the flow of people but to no avail. They were both carried forward into the large square now filled with worshipers. All around them, people began to pray, filling the air with their cries and supplications.

“Who is your god?” asked a woman beside Ruth. “Why aren’t you praying?”

Ruth stuttered and looked to Miriam for support. The older girl leaned over and said, “We worship Yahweh, and we are praying. We do it silently.”

“What a strange thing,” the woman said. “How will your god hear your prayers unless you shout them aloud? Who is this Yahweh anyway? I've never heard of him."

A man nearby overheard them and said, "Yahweh? Isn't he a northern god? One of those sky gods from Canaan or Egypt? Someplace like that."

"I heard he was the Jewish god," added another man. "You know, the one who's been causing all that trouble in the Kaaba." He looked suspiciously at the two girls. "Who are you? What tribe do you belong to?"

"We must be going," Miriam said. "We've said our prayers, and our father will expect us home immediately." She took her sister by the hand and tried to force their way through the crowd. Several members showed annoyance at being pushed and remonstrated loudly.

"Wait. Stop them. They're Jews and have been preaching against our gods."

The cries of annoyance turned to anger and hands grasped at the two girls, preventing them from going any further. They were ringed in by faces showing anger, curiosity and a leering expectancy.

"Wh ... what do we do?" Ruth whispered.

"I don't know," Miriam muttered back. "Try not to show you're afraid." She sought out the man who had first accosted them and addressed herself to him. "Why do you molest us? We're two well brought up girls of the town going about our lawful business. If you have a grievance against us, call the Sharif and let him adjudicate."

The crowd relaxed a bit and the grip on their arms and clothing eased. The man scowled. "I can call the Sharif if you wish, but all I want to know is your tribe. Tell us that."

"You know it already, else you wouldn't ask. We're Jews of Makkah."

"And followers of this Yahweh?"

"Yes," Miriam said boldly. Ruth nodded.

"You aren't welcome in this town, Jew girl. Your god causes too much trouble."

"It's not our god who causes the trouble but rather you unbelievers."

The crowd started murmuring again and pressing closer. "Call the Sharif, have them arrested." "Throw them out of town." "Beat them." The jostling got more violent, and Ruth cried out in panic, clutching at her sister's arm.

The crowd in the direction of the Kaaba stirred and parted reluctantly to let a tall spare-framed man through. The young man stood and stared at the two girls for a few moments, stroking his short dark beard. "What is this disturbance on our holy day?" he asked.

"These Jews are creating a nuisance," one man said.

"They called us unbelievers," cried a woman.

The young man nodded. "I'll deal with this now."

"Who are you to just walk over here and tell us what to do? We're going to teach these girls a lesson."

"I am Nasib ibn Qadir al-Qurayshi. Does any man dispute my right to deal with it?"

"Al-Qurayshi? No, no, of course not." The crowd moved away from the man and the two girls, leaving them in a small open space.

Nasib nodded. "Good. Follow me, daughters of Eliezer ben Daud."

"We ... we should go home," Miriam said.

"Your choice is to follow me or stay with these people." Nasib turned and walked off. Miriam and Ruth looked at each other, then at the watching crowd and hurried after him.

"Where are we going?" Ruth asked. "Are you taking us home?"

"You know our father, don't you?" Miriam said. "You were at the shop yesterday."

Nasib said nothing, just led the girls at a fast pace through the crowd, skirting the Kaaba and into one of the empty streets beyond. Miriam and Ruth started to turn aside from their course, but Nasib clicked his fingers and two men came running to catch them. "I'm sorry, daughters of Eliezer, I must insist you accompany me."

"Our names are Miriam and Ruth," Miriam said, "And our parents will be worried. We should go home as quickly as possible."

"Your parents won't miss you for an hour at least," Nasib said with a smile. "It'd take you that long to get to Gamil's farm and back."

"H ... how did you know we were going there?" Ruth asked.

Nasib did not answer but pointed at a doorway. "We've arrived. Miriam and Ruth, please enter and enjoy my hospitality. If al-Ilah smiles, you'll be home by sunset."

The doorway led into a small two room dwelling. The larger room in front was windowless but ventilated and lit by an opening high above them. The walls were bare stone and mortar, unadorned by either curtain or picture. Furnishings were simple: a large divan couch, a rug covering almost the entire floor, a low table, a jug and cups, a covered earthernware bowl and numerous cushions. The sisters caught no more than a glimpse of the other room as the two men with Nasib walked through into it and shut the door.

Nasib gestured to the furnishings. "Please make yourself as comfortable as you can. I'll bring food soon. I apologise for the lack of amenities, but if your father is reasonable, you'll both soon be home."

"Our father?" Miriam queried. "What has this to do with our father?"

Nasib smiled and bowed. "Until later." He closed the street door behind him, and the girls heard the clack of the lock engaging. Miriam tried it anyway, but the door was locked.

"What's he talking about?" Ruth asked. "Has he gone to tell father we were near the Kaaba? That's not our fault; we were caught up by the crowd."

"I don't know." Miriam paced along each wall, examining the surface and turning her face up to the skylight above them. She tried the door that led to the inner room, but it too was locked. Faint sounds came from within, but she paid them no heed, continuing her examination of their cell.

"I've got to ..." Ruth blushed and fell silent. She crossed to where her sister stood and whispered in her ear, "Miriam, I need to ..."

Miriam pointed to the covered earthernware bowl. "I think that's what that's for."

"No!" A look of horror crossed the younger girl's face. "I ... I couldn't ... not ... not being watched."

Miriam smiled gently and nodded. "I'll ask, but I know what the answer will be." She rapped on the inner door, paused and rapped again. It opened a crack, and one of the young men peered through. "My sis ... we ... need to ..." She blushed herself at having to talk to a man about it. "We seek relief."

"Relief?"

"To ... to pass water."

"Ah." Comprehension dawned on the young man's face. "Use the bowl." He shut and locked the door again.

After holding out for nearly an hour longer, Ruth took the bowl behind the divan couch and telling her sister to guard the door and not to look, squatted and managed to relieve herself. When she finished, Miriam did likewise but with considerably less fuss.

They sat on the divan and sipped water from the cups and watched the angled square of sunlight that streamed in from the skylight creep across the wall.

"The man's been gone for hours," Ruth whimpered. "We should be home by now. I mean, so he's complaining to father that we were there, but how long does that take? Father should have come for us by now. I'd rather have one of his beatings than just sit here waiting."

"I think his grievance is a little more serious," Miriam murmured. "He's the man who came to see father yesterday while we were cleaning the shop. Nasib, I think he said his name was. He doesn't like Jews and wants them out of Makkah."

"Why? What have we ever done to him?"

"Weren't you listening to him and father?"

Ruth shook her head. "It was boring."

"He objects to the fact that our god, Yahweh, is more powerful than any of their gods."

"Well that's just silly. Does he think it's our fault?"

"I really don't know what he thinks, sister. I just know that he doesn't like Jews and he's the only person who knows we're here. He may not even have gone to see father."

They sat in silence for a time. Miriam considered knocking on the inner door again and asking for food. From the position of the sunlight, it was past noon. However, she did not want to get another refusal so sat thinking instead, damping down her pangs of hunger and hoping Ruth would not ask. Finally, the latch on the outer door rattled, and a key turned in the lock.

Nasib entered and quickly closed and locked the door again. He nodded at the sisters sitting on the divan before crossing to the inner door and rapping on it, entering when a man opened the door. He reappeared a minute later and set down some food on the low table – bread, goat's cheese, dates, a handful of almonds and two apricots.

"I'm sorry I was delayed," Nasib said. "Please, you must be hungry." He gestured toward the food. Ruth immediately grabbed an apricot and bit into it, but Miriam shook her head.

"Why are we here, Nasib ibn Qadir? Did you see our father?"

Nasib broke off a piece of bread and pulled up a chair, sitting across the table from them. He chewed reflectively and swallowed. "I have seen your father. I mean no disrespect, but in some ways he's an unreasoning man."

"I haven't found him so," Miriam said carefully.

"In the matters that concern a young girl perhaps not. In matters that lie between men, I find him less than cooperative."

"That's something that you must discuss with him then. I couldn't comment on the concerns of my elders."

Nasib nodded and smiled. "You've evidently been well brought up. I wouldn't ask you to comment on the issue that lies between your father and the elders of Makkah, but as you're forced to accept my hospitality, I seek only to apprise you of the reason for your detention."

"You said we'd be home by evening," Ruth said. "You promised."

"I actually said soon, young woman, but alas, the decision isn't mine to make."

"Whose decision is it then?" Miriam asked. "The leader of your clan? The Qurayshi? Can we appeal to him?"

"In this affair, I can be regarded as the leader of my branch of the clan. But no, the man holding up your timely release is your father."

"Our own father? I cannot believe that."

"Believe it. He puts his god before his own flesh and blood."

Ruth burst into tears. Miriam put her arms around her sister and comforted her. After a few minutes, as Ruth's sobs subsided, Miriam turned back to face Nasib and regarded him coolly. "Our father holds the Lord our God in the highest regard, as is proper. We'll abide by his decision to put the Lord first."

"Commendable. It means you cannot leave here though."

"You mean to keep us captive forever?"

"Unless your father relents, I cannot release you. My bargaining position would be untenable."

Miriam picked up a few almonds and chewed them slowly while she considered Nasib's words. At length, she said, "As this dispute touches upon our freedom, may I ask the nature of it? It would make the waiting easier if I knew what was at stake."

Nasib smiled. "You wouldn't understand."

"Try me," Miriam challenged. "I am no woman of the Arab tribes nor a child."

"Nor, it seems, are you one to remember your place when a man speaks."

"Your women are kept uneducated and subservient in all things, Nasib ibn Qadir. Do not deny it, for I have talked with your womenfolk in the marketplace. Among my people, a woman is not prevented from learning, and my parents saw to my education. I can cook and clean as well as my mother ... *Lord forgive me the sin of pride* ... in all aspects of the home. I know needlework; I can shear a sheep, card, spin and weave the wool into garments. Turning to other matters, I can read and write Hebrew, Aramaic and Arabic, I can calculate numbers. I can sing and recite poetry, and I am ... well, very nearly word perfect in the recitation of our Holy Writings. Don't tell me I'm uneducated ..."

"Enough, Miriam, daughter of Eliezer," Nasib said with a laugh. "You don't have to convince me further of your abilities. I'll tell you what I can but don't be surprised if the subject of our discussion goes beyond your normal experience."

Ruth tugged on Miriam's arm. "I'm tired. When can we go home?"

"I don't know, sister. Why don't you have a rest while we wait?" Miriam gathered together some cushions and blankets and made Ruth comfortable on the divan couch. She and Nasib took some food and water and two chairs across the room and arranged themselves so their talking would not disturb the sleeping girl.

"Very well," Nasib said. "Let me start by probing the extent of your knowledge and also explore some facets of your belief of which I may be unaware."

"Then be aware, first, that I'm untrained in theological matters, for this is an aspect of life that's usually kept from women, save for the knowledge necessary for the home. I'll answer to the best of my ability, but my words may be unintentionally false."

"I'll bear that in mind," Nasib said. "Now, the Jews are known to have one god. Is this because you believe there's literally only one god or because others exist but you don't worship them?"

"There is one god."

"Really one or functionally one? By that I mean that some people like the Egyptians worship Ra and Atum and the Aten all as aspects of their sun god. So too do the Hindoo of the east. I forget the names, but their supreme god has aspects that reflect creation, preservation and destruction."

"Our Holy Writings say 'The Lord thy God is One God.' By this, I presume them to mean he's a solitary god." Miriam smiled. "He'd have to be as we believe him to be the only god."

"How then do you regard what others worship as gods?"

"False gods. We've had our share of those in the past, as our Holy Writings say, but for fifteen hundred years or more we've followed the One True God."

"Interesting. My tribe and my family have followed our god for much the same length of time. Does this god of yours have a name? I've heard him called Lord and God and Yahweh."

Miriam bent her head for a few moments, composing her thoughts. Then she looked up at Nasib and said hesitantly, "The Lord our God is Holy and is most often referred to as Lord or God or the Holy One of Israel. He has a name, for when our prophet Moshe saw Him in the burning bush; he identified Himself as the God of our forefathers and gave his name. I will forebear to utter the name by which he is known for fear that I might inadvertently link it with that which is unclean."

"This is the name Yahweh?" Nasib asked. "Your father uses it. Why not you?"

"I'm but a woman and in my ignorance I might bring dishonour on the Holy Name. My father is more experienced in worldly things and can guard his tongue. It's his choice to use it and mine to refrain." Miriam bent her head, and her lips moved in a silent prayer. "Even this name is likely not the real one. I've heard that the High Priest may utter the real name once a year in the Holy of Holies within the temple at ... at Jerusalem."

"This is the temple that the Romans destroyed a hundred years ago?" Nasib asked softly. Miriam did not trust herself to speak but nodded instead. "Pray take a moment to compose yourself," he said kindly. Nasib got up and poured a cup of water, bringing it back to Miriam. He waited while she drank and wiped away her tears. "Do you feel able to continue?"

"Yes. Thank you."

"Let's return to this matter of false gods. How do you define a false god?"

Miriam's lips twitched into a smile. "Any who is not the Lord our God."

Nasib chuckled. "Alright, so you regard Hubal the god of shepherds to be a false god. Also, presumably, our other local gods such as Manaf of the sun, Kain of the waning moon, Quzah who holds the rainbow, Uzza of beauty and Ilat the Mother?"

"Yes. I'd point out that the Lord holds the sun and moon in his hand and stretches out the rainbow. He's a shepherd to our people, of surpassing beauty, and He created the first mother, Eve, from Adam's rib. You have many gods, each in charge of one small aspect of life; we have One who controls all."

Nasib stroked his beard thoughtfully. "You say your god is of surpassing beauty. Have you seen an image of him?"

"No, for we're allowed no graven images of the Lord."

"Then how do you know he's beautiful?"

"I confess I don't, for no man may look upon the face of God and live. But it's said that when Moshe came down from the mountain with the Law, his face shone. He only saw God from behind, yet the sight filled him with glory. Also, how could a god who is just and merciful and has given us all the beauty in the world, fail to be beautiful too? Can the creation be more beautiful than the creator?"

"Ah, Miriam, daughter of Eliezer, maybe some parts of creation."

Miriam hung her head and blushed, wishing Simeon her betrothed had said those words.

"I think, too, you do yourself an injustice. Although just a woman, you've explained your god to me better than many men would be able to do so. Tell me, Miriam, what does your god tell you to do when living amongst unbelievers?"

Miriam thought for a few minutes. "I cannot think of specific injunctions, but we're enjoined to be modest, chaste and hardworking, to keep ourselves apart and to do all things to glorify God."

"Do you also preach to the unbeliever?"

Miriam allowed herself another smile. "If we're asked questions like you're doing now, we'll answer, but as for preaching, no. What would be the point? The Lord our God entered into a covenant with our forefathers, the sons of Israel. The Law of Moshe was given to the Jews only, and the Prophets came to the People of Israel not the Gentiles."

"So an unbeliever, a Gentile, would never be allowed to worship your god?"

"I ... I'm unsure on that point, but my father once spoke of an Aethiop who converted. He gave up his false gods, was circumcised and became a believer. It's very uncommon, I think. Most outsiders who become Jews do so by marriage."

"How does that work?"

"If a Jew and an unbeliever marry, the unbeliever must convert and the children are raised in the Faith." Miriam coloured slightly. "This, too, is uncommon, but I've heard of it."

"And if the unbeliever won't change? Must love go unrequited?"

"If he wouldn't change, it wouldn't be love. Besides, the love for God must always be stronger than mere earthly love."

"But far better to have both?" Nasib asked.

The corner of Miriam's mouth twitched. "Love between a man and woman is not strictly necessary, at least not at the start. A man and a woman can learn to love over a lifetime. My parents did. Isn't this the case among your people too?"

"It is," Nasib conceded. "Most marriages are arranged, and this is to protect both man and woman from making a mistake. Sometimes, if the woman is attracted to a suitable mate, the match is allowed to go ahead. Was this the case with you and Simeon ben Abbas?"

"You touch upon personal matters, Nasib ibn Qadir. Let's just say that our fathers arranged it and my heart's at peace."

Nasib smiled. "I wish you every happiness. If I might return to the subject of our respective gods, am I right in understanding you've never seen your god?"

"No man ... or woman ... may see God and live. His power and majesty would burn us away."

"Then how do you know he exists?"

Miriam stared. "What do you mean? Of course he exists. The Law of Moshe and the Words of the Prophets all tell us ..."

"And you believe what you're told without question?"

"When our priests tell us, yes. And my father. He wouldn't lie."

"It must be wonderful to have a father and priests who are incapable of lying."

Miriam frowned. "That isn't what I'm saying. All men are fallible and capable of untruth, but I believe they don't lie about God."

"I hope they don't, Miriam, but what if they've been lied to? What they, and you, sincerely believe may not be truth but mere tales passed down by men."

"No. No, I cannot believe that." Miriam shook her head, a look of unease on her face.

"Leaving aside belief in what you've been told, then, how else do you know your god exists?"

"I ... there's beauty in the world. A cool sunrise, the flaming glory of a sunset, a shower of rain, a rainbow, the stars, a flower ... the laughter of a child ... the look of love that passes between my mother and father. These are things that reflect the goodness of our God."

"And yet all these things would be explained by the people of Makkah as being the gifts of one or other of their gods. Who's to say they aren't right and you wrong?"

"The laws that are given to us by Moshe and the Prophets. These are good laws that protect everyone, even widows and orphans, and provide justice for the man sinned against. Aren't these provisions of a loving god? Our God."

"Tell me one of these laws."

"I ... I'm not skilled in ... Give me a moment." Miriam thought hard, remembering her lessons. "The prophet Zechariah, enjoins us to defraud no widow or fatherless boy ..."

"The code of the Qurayshi tells us that widows of fallen warriors should be married to kin of the fallen man and her former children raised as his own. I'd say this law of an unbeliever was as good as your Zechariah's. Our code goes further, too, offering protection to our beasts of burden. Tell me one of your laws concerning justice."

"I cannot remember it exactly, but if an injury is done to someone, the law calls for it to be returned upon the sinner, eye for eye, tooth for tooth, hand for hand and foot by foot. Isn't this perfect justice?"

"I suppose it is, but what if the injury is accidental? Then you have two men maimed. In my tribe, we allow recompense to be made to the injured party – so many camels for an arm, so many for an eye. If a man causes the death of another unlawfully, the next of kin may demand the death of the killer or they may choose to accept compensation that allows the family of the murdered man to support themselves. Doesn't that sound more reasonable?"

"I'm no scholar that I can argue my faith by quoting from the Holy Books, Nasib ibn Qadir."

"Nor do I wish such dry knowledge, Miriam daughter of Eliezer. I seek to know your god through your mind."

"You should ask my father. He knows much more than I."

Nasib smiled. "I'd rather ask you. Would it surprise you to know that, unlike you, I've seen my god?"

"Which god is this? You have many."

"The people of Makkah have many gods, but I have only one. His name is al-Ilah."

Miriam frowned. "That name just means The God in your tongue. It's a title not a name."

Nasib clapped his hands gently. "Our beliefs have a point of similarity. You have one god; I have one god. We both refer to them by title rather than name."

"Yes," Miriam agreed. "And we both believe that our god is the only true one. I cannot see that we'll find other points of similarity."

"Hmm, I wonder. A little while ago, in passing, you referred to the prophet Moshe as seeing god in a bush, I think you said. Can you explain that please?"

"A bush? Ah, yes, the burning bush. Let me think a moment." Miriam concentrated, remembering her lessons. "When Moshe lived in the land of Midian, he tended goats, and one day he saw a fire burning in the heart of a bush ... a thorn bush ... yet there was no smoke and the thorn bush wasn't consumed by the fire. He turned aside to look, and a voice called him by name. 'Here I am,' he said, and the voice from the middle of the burning bush said it was holy ground and instructed him to take his sandals off. He did so, and the voice went on to identify itself as the 'God of Abraham, Isaac and Jacob.'"

"We share a common ancestor," Nasib said gently. "For I'm descended from Abraham, whom we call Ibrahim, and from his eldest son, Ishma'il. It was they that found the black stone which forms the central holy place of the Kaaba. Do you think that the prophet Ibrahim – Abraham – could lead his descendants into error? It is written that the god of Ibrahim is al-Ilah, and here you say that the god of Abraham is Yahweh." Nasib looked into the young girl's eyes. "Miriam, do we worship the same god after all?"

“No. The Lord our God is One God.” Miriam started to cry. “I don’t know,” she whispered. “You’re confusing me.”

The room grew dark, and Nasib produced small oil lamps and lit them so that small pools of butter-yellow light illuminated the two of them but left the sleeping girl in shadow. Nasib also spread a blanket over Ruth and put another one beside Miriam.

“To confuse you is the last thing I want,” Nasib declared. “Come, dry your eyes.” He handed the young woman a clean cloth. “I had thought to show you my god so you’d know that al-Ilah truly exists, but I can see that you’re not ready for such a revelation.”

Miriam wiped away her tears and blew her nose gently while looking at the young man over the edge of the cloth. “Show me? How? Can you conjure your god at will?”

“I’ve been given a word of power wherein I can petition my god and know that he hears my prayer. It’s not given to everyone, but I’m directly descended from Isma'il and head of my clan.”

“You can command your god?”

“Of course not. That’s blasphemy. I can ask him and know that he hears me. Because of my favoured position, there’s a good chance that he’ll answer my prayer.”

Miriam thought about this for a few minutes. Ruth stirred on the divan and almost woke before muttering something and turning over. “What would your prayer be?”

"That al-Ilah would manifest himself so you might acknowledge his existence." Nasib shrugged. "It doesn't matter. You aren't ready."

"What sort of manifestation?"

"You aren't ready."

"If I was," Miriam persisted. "What sort of manifestation would it be?"

"Who am I to know the mind of god? As I believe al-Ilah and your Yahweh may be the same, perhaps something that you could accept – a burning bush maybe."

Miriam's mouth fell open. She shut it hurriedly and swallowed. "I ... I'd like to see that."

"I've told you you aren't ready. I made a mistake bringing you and your sister here and thinking that I could talk to you about the matters that concern the Elders of Makkah." Nasib stood up. "I'll have you and your sister escorted home."

"No ... yes ... thank you, Nasib ibn Qadir." Miriam arose and looked in confusion at Nasib. "Then you're giving up trying to evict us from Makkah?"

"No, but I'll no longer do it by threatening Eliezer's beautiful children. I hoped you might still be able to think for yourself, but it appears your mind is set about with fables and closed to truth. Well, no matter. I'll think of something else. Please wake your sister, we'll leave immediately."

While Miriam roused Ruth and explained the situation, Nasib brought the other two young men in from the back room and had them prepare torches to light the way. They set off through the darkened streets, the two young men leading the way and

Nasib bringing up the rear. There were few people out, and they quickly reached Eliezer's shop.

"I won't cause trouble by coming in to confront your father but will leave you here," Nasib said. "I'm sorry to have upset your pretty lives, daughters of Eliezer."

Miriam told Ruth to stay where she was and drew Nasib aside, speaking to him in a low voice. "What must I do to convince you that I'm ready to see your god?"

"What are you saying?" Ruth asked, staring at her sister talking so intimately with their captor.

Nasib smiled in the darkness. "Acknowledge that al-Ilah may be your Yahweh."

"How can I do that? I don't even know if al-Ilah exists, and if he does, whether he's truly a god and not a demon."

"You could tell the difference?"

Miriam hesitated. "Yes. Yes, I could tell the difference between good and evil."

"Then I'll take you to see al-Ilah. Tonight."

"Tonight?" Miriam said sharply. "I cannot go now."

"Miriam, what is it?" Ruth called out. "What's wrong?"

From inside the shop came a clamour of voices as they recognised Ruth's call.

"It must be now," Nasib said. "Hurry. You must choose."

The front door of the shop opened, and Eliezer looked out. Abbas and Simeon stood just behind him, peering into the night. He saw Ruth and the two young men with torches. “Ruth, daughter, is that you, child? Come inside. Where’s your sister?”

“I ... I’ll come with you tonight,” Miriam said quietly.

“Come then.” Nasib turned her and pushed her down the street into the shadows. “Gafar, Issa, leave the other girl and come quickly.” The three men and Miriam ran off into the darkness, leaving Ruth crying out her sister’s name and Simeon bellowing his anguish as his betrothed was snatched from him again.

“Where are we going?” Miriam panted as they ran through the streets. “The Kaaba?”

“Not there. The building’s tainted by the presence of three hundred false gods. I’ll take you out to a desert shrine. We should be there around daybreak.”

Nasib and Miriam rode through the night on camelback. Miriam had never ridden one of these beasts before so hung on tightly behind the young Arab as he guided the camel through the desert and parched scrubland. The swaying motion disturbed Miriam for some time, and at one point, it grew so bad she nearly asked to be returned to Makkah. She persevered though, and after a while found the required reaction to their mount’s motion that enabled her to relax and enjoy the journey.

Miriam had been well brought up and lived her whole life in towns. She had seldom seen the desert except in glimpses at the edges of the builtup areas and never at night. The waxing moon spread a silvery light over the sand and rock, turning every shadow into ink and the scrubby bushes and tufts of grass into unfamiliar darkened shapes. The air was cold, and she shivered in the blanket Nasib had provided, but the gentle wind carried with it scents of rock and dust and spices. It all suddenly seemed very romantic and dangerous, being carried off into the night by a handsome young man.

She shivered and wondered if she had done something really foolish. *Nasib is leader of his clan, he must be a responsible man. Also, he's never acted with impropriety toward me*. She relaxed a bit but still played over several romantic scenarios in her head. More than one involved Simeon coming after them to rescue her or realising he should be more forthright in his approach. Being betrothed at the instigation of their fathers meant she did not know how he felt about her. *Does he love me? Do I love him? Does it matter if we're to be married*? She found her thoughts turning to the silent man in front of her and her future. For a year, she had known that to marry in her faith, she must accept the man her father chose for her. There was only one eligible Jewish man in Makkah, and she was fortunate that one man was reasonably good looking, hard working and stood to inherit a decent blacksmithing business. Miriam knew she would be looked after all her life if she married him. *If? I mean when ... but ... do I want more than that? Imagine if there was more than one eligible man in Makkah – maybe father would've allowed me some say in my own marriage*. She shrugged. *If wishes were loaves, we'd all eat well.*

Nasib stirred in front of her as she shrugged. "Are you well, Miriam? Do you need to walk around or relieve your body's burdens in any way?"

"I ... I'm alright, thank you, Nasib." Miriam looked out over the scrub filled land toward a distant range of hills. "Do we have far to go?"

"Those hills ahead. We'll be there just before dawn. If you're tired, slip your feet into the saddle girth and rest against my back."

Miriam said nothing for she knew she could never do that. *I shouldn't be alone with any man, even my betrothed, yet here I am. And now he invites me to rest my head on his shoulder*? Despite her qualms, she soon found her head drooping and after almost slipping from her seat, dug her feet under the saddle girth and tentatively leaned her head against Nasib's shoulder. She fell asleep before she realised it, her arms encircling his waist and her nostrils breathing in the strong manly scent that emanated from his body.

The motion of the camel changed and Miriam awoke. Ahead of them, the hills were limned in the first light of dawn and the land rose up about them. The camel snorted and blew, complaining about the slope, and Nasib eased back on the pace.

"You're awake, Miriam? Good. We're nearly there."

Miriam released her hold on the young man and sat upright, thankful the darkness still hid her blush of shame. *How could I hold him close like that? The Lord be praised no one saw me*. Despite her thoughts, her heart still beat faster than it should and her hands remembered the touch of his muscled body.

A few minutes later, Nasib brought the camel to a halt and forced it to its knees so they could dismount. He hobbled the animal and left it to graze, striking off up the hillside with Miriam. The darkness was lightening by the minute, and by the time they reached a horizontal slab of rock that had evidently served as an altar recently, the first rays of the sun were stabbing over the edge of the hills.

"Have you thought about what would convince you al-Ilah and Yahweh are the same?" Nasib asked. "If you have, don't tell me. I'll petition god."

Miriam nodded. "I've thought over your words, and I think it's unlikely they're the same. If your god manifests, I believe I'll know him for a demon. That knowledge may mean my death, but I'm prepared. The name of the Lord my God is a strong tower. In it I'll find safety."

Nasib lifted his arms to the heavens and started praying, interspersing the mellifluous phrases with a single word of an unknown language loudly spoken. After several minutes, he lowered his arms. "Now, we wait for a sign."

It came – a streak of light across the heavens as if a fragment of the sun plummeted to earth – then nothing. The hillside and the altar were unchanged.

"That's it?" Miriam queried. "That's your sign from god?"

Miriam.

"Yes, what?"

"I didn't say anything," Nasib said.

Miriam.

The hair on the back of Miriam's neck lifted. "I ... I am here. Sp ... speak."

Remove your sandals for you are on holy ground.

Miriam bent and fumbled with her footwear, casting it aside. A flicker caught her eye, and she saw a thornbush nearby burst into flames. She gaped and soft mewling noises came from her throat. The fire blazed, yet through the roaring flames she could see the bare branches of the bush standing unsinged, every leaf in place and unmoving, despite the ferocity of the conflagration. With a moan, she sank to her knees.

"My ... my Lord and my God, h ... h ... how may I s ... serve thee?"

I am the god of Ibrahim and Isma'il.

"Such were the words given to Moshe the prophet, but I'm a lowly servant girl, Lord. Tell me how I may serve thee."

Be faithful. Be strong. Tell others what you have seen here today.

Miriam fell forward on the ground and screwed her eyes shut against the glare of the fire that burned yet did not consume. "I will obey, Lord."

Then go with my servant Nasib and tell of what you have seen.

Miriam half rose and opened one eye then looked around in amazement. The light and fire in the thornbush had disappeared, leaving the plant untouched. The rocks and scrub were once more an ordinary hillside in the strengthening morning light.

"You ... you saw, Nasib? You heard the Word of God?"

“I saw the burning bush, just like in your story, Miriam, but I heard nothing save the sighing of the wind and the cry of the kite high in the heavens. If God spoke to you, he spoke to you alone.”

“But you have seen God before. Is this how he appeared to you?”

“As a flame and a voice within my head. Never before as a burning bush. Perhaps he appeared this way so you’d recognise him.” Nasib paused. “Do you recognise him?”

Miriam nodded. “I ... I had no presentiment of evil, and the god appeared to me as he appeared to the prophet Moshe. I’m indeed blessed among women. You called al-Ilah and my God answered. They must be the same.”

“What will you do?”

“What God bade me do. Tell everyone what I’ve seen.” Miriam started back down the hillside to where they had left the camel. She smiled and her face almost glowed in the morning light as she thought of her God and the privilege she had been given to bring this news to the other Jews of Makkah.

***

I am the daughter of Eliezer ben Daud and his wife, Anna. I am the wife of Simeon ben Abbas and mother of three sons and two daughters, all of whom are married and have families of their own. My husband, Simeon, is an Elder of the Synagogue here in Makkah, and I have status within our community. I have lived a full life and have few regrets, having come to love my husband after a marriage arranged by my father and Simeon's. I am looked up to by almost every Jewish mother, woman and girl, and after prayers when the men stand around and talk about learned things, the women come to me for my advice. It may be something simple, like 'Ruth, what would you recommend for lifting bloodstains from linen?' or more important, like 'Ruth, my son Elias is of an age to be betrothed. Do you have in mind a suitable girl?'

Yes, I am Ruth, the only living daughter of Eliezer and Anna. Late at night, in the dark when the household is quiet and Simeon is snoring beside me, I sometimes think of Miriam, who was once my older sister and of her unforgivable sin. Nobody talks of her, not even my parents, for she was shunned shortly after she returned from the desert. The charge was blasphemy, but it could as easily have been fornication had Simeon sought to press his case. If our community had been larger than just the two families, the penalty may even have been death, but shunning was almost as severe. No man or woman, not even a family member, could greet her, offer her a cup of water or piece of bread or even acknowledge her presence. My heart broke, but she brought it on herself.

I cannot know what was in her mind that night, but I know with a certainty that her mind was pure and filled with the love of the Lord our God before we were kidnapped. Her mind was filled too with understanding; at least as much as a woman may grasp of spiritual matters, and thereby lies the problem. A man learned in the Law and the Prophets could have stood against the blandishments and cunning traps of Nasib ibn Qadir (cursed be his name). My sister stood no chance. A woman does not speak in synagogue, is not educated to the same degree and must always defer to a man, so any arguments she could muster were but a pale imitation of the Truth held in the Torah.

I was with Miriam in the room when Nasib talked to her and led her astray. Sometimes when I lie awake at night, I think about what I could have said, support I could have given, that might have saved her life. I can think of words now, but then I was only twelve years old and largely ignorant of scriptural matters. I ate Nasib's food, I lay on his couch, and I went to sleep after a short time, being bored with all the talk. Later, I awoke and lay still, listening.

I heard how Nasib introduced the blasphemous idea that the Lord God of Israel was somehow the same as his own god, this al-Ilah, just because that name means God and because their Ibrahim worshipped him. Miriam so readily accepted that Ibrahim was the prophet Abraham. I know, Abraham's eldest son was called Ishmael, but I think this is coincidence. I have listened to the women talk in the market and their legends talk of Ibrahim and Isma'il living their whole lives in Arabia, whereas we know from the Torah that Abraham came from Ur of the Chaldees and moved down into Canaan that later became the land of Isaac and Jacob. Abraham knew the Lord God and would not have been deceived by what can only be a shaytan, one of God's adversaries.

I thought Nasib had failed in his attempt to deceive Miriam when he agreed to return us to our parents. I rejoiced that Truth had won out over Falsehood. And then something happened right outside our house, even as our father came out into the street. I do not know what it was, but Miriam and Nasib stepped aside and talked. Between one breath and the next, my sister Miriam was lost to me. She ran off into the night with Nasib and his friends, leaving me alone to face my father.

Miriam came home the next morning, bubbling over with her experiences and eager to share them with everyone. She burst into the kitchen and cried out, "I have seen God! I have been to His holy mountain and heard His voice in the burning bush, just like Abraham."

Father rose so quickly from the table he knocked over his chair and sent plates crashing to the floor. He strode over to his eldest daughter, screaming "Blasphemer!" at the top of his voice and struck her, knocking her down.

Mother cried out in anguish but did not intervene, knowing the accusation was correct. Everyone knows that no man, or woman either, can see God and live. Josea started crying, and I picked him up and comforted him. Miriam picked herself up shakily, and through her own tears, said again, "I have seen God." She held out her hands to her parents, but Mother hung her head and Father glared.

"I won't have a blasphemer in this house," he roared. "You're no longer my daughter."

“Father, no. I saw God in a burning bush, and He spoke to me, telling me He was the God of Abraham. He commanded me to tell everyone that the al-Ilah they worship here is the same Lord God of Israel.”

“Enough! I won’t have such words uttered in my house. I disown you, blasphemer.” Father picked Miriam up and threw her bodily into the street, slamming the door in her face.

We all sat in the kitchen crying, while Miriam wept outside, calling upon us to listen. After a bit, she went away, and we heard she went to Simeon’s house. He would not listen either and repudiated his relationship with her, breaking off his betrothal. What is more, he publicly accused her of fornication, as she had been alone with Nasib overnight. This last accusation shattered her, as the charge of blasphemy had not. She left, weeping, and we saw her no more.

Miriam disappeared from Makkah many years ago, and I do not even know if she still lives. I think of her sometimes when I lie awake at night and wonder just what it was she saw that so convinced her. I have never heard of a demon that could possibly mimic the Lord God in His glory, yet what else could it be? A pale imitation of God could perhaps mislead a person weak in faith. Yet Miriam was strong in her faith, so what happened? Sometimes I wish that I, too, could see what she saw, but when I think that, the shadows press close and the room grows cold as I imagine coming face to face with Miriam’s demon. I pray fervently until the terror passes, which it always does, but then the next night, my thoughts return to her. I know what I must do. I must cast my sister from my mind entirely. Everybody else has expunged her from their lives, and I must do the same or else I will risk my very soul by seeking knowledge of al-Ilah.

I have no sister. Miriam died many years ago on the day that I was kidnapped and released. There is no god but Yahweh, the Lord God of Israel. His name is a strong tower which will protect me. Anything else is but a demon howling in the wilderness.

Chapter Eight

I miscalculated. It seems that even a god can be wrong. I thought I could get rid of the Jews and their strange god by subverting their faith. It seemed like a reasonable plan. I can assume pretty much any shape or form and to blaze up in the middle of a thornbush without consuming it is a simple thing for me. Add in a few carefully chosen words lifted from the girl's mind, and I was masquerading as this Yahweh of the Jews. Nasib ibn Qadir acted under my instructions. He is of the inner circle of Qurayshi, one of the few who has the word that will summon me. He was to kidnap the daughters of the troublesome Jew and sow the seeds of doubt into one or both minds. He would never have succeeded with a man trained in their faith, but I thought an untutored female mind would be vulnerable. And I was right in this.

Nasib brought the elder girl to my desert shrine and summoned me as previously arranged. It was a small matter to pluck the images from her mind and duplicate them. I am a fire that burns without consuming, so placing myself in a bush matched the girl's conception of her god. What is even better, I did not have to lie. Djinn lie, so a god should represent the truth as much as possible. If I mislead, it is because the human misleads himself not because I have uttered a falsehood. I am a flame; it is my nature. The girl's concept of her god was as a flame. She made the connection and misled herself. She thought she could tell the difference between good and evil, but those attributes depend on actions, and as I did nothing to alarm her, her fears came to nothing.

Similarly, the tale in her head told of ground made sacred by the god's presence, so I uttered the words she expected to hear. It could be true after all, if I am to be a god, then the ground where I am should be holy. Lastly, she knew her god as the god of Abraham and Isaac. I believe this Isaac was a younger brother to Isma'il in Jewish lore, but from what I can discern, I have my doubts as to whether their Abraham is the same man as the Ibrahim who became my first follower. It does not matter. Once more, I did not lie, for I never claimed to be the god of her Abraham and Isaac. I said, "I am the god of Ibrahim and Isma'il." The girl made the connection in her own mind. She was not a fool; I could see she was an intelligent girl, but she wanted to believe and convinced herself.

All this was according to plan. I knew the other Jews would not automatically accept her words, but I thought her presence among the others would slowly taint their minds. A Jewish community that was less than pure would poison the faith of others as they arrived, and soon they would be no more than another clan worshipping the gods of the Kaaba. Well, that did not work out. Family is obviously of less importance to Jews than their relationship with their god. The girl became an outcast and of little use to me. Her sister, Ruth, even married Miriam's betrothed, both families having decided the elder daughter was dead to them. Well, that was nothing to me, for the girl was not one of my believers.

It occurred to me that it did not matter having another powerful god in Makkah, as long as he did not interfere with me. Now I speak of this Yahweh as a powerful god only because of the things he is reputed to have done. The stories that were in that girl's mind amazed me. This god raised men from the dead, healed, inflicted injury, disease and death, parted the sea, brought plagues on whole nations and stopped the sun and moon in the sky. I hoped this was mostly fabrication; after all, I could not do a fraction of that, and I am the most powerful god in the Kaaba. So either this Yahweh is extremely powerful or he exists only in the minds of his believers. And if he exists, where is he? The Jews of Makkah erect no shrine or temple to him, nor, when they built their temple, or synagogue as they call it, was there an altar or an idol they identified as their god. I listened in on their prayers, watched them closely, ready to flee when Yahweh appeared, but he stayed away. Had these men forgotten the word of power that called their god to them?

I sought out other settlements of Jews in nearby towns and found the same thing; they prayed together and called on the name of their Lord, but he never answered. I even went as far as Jerusalem, the seat of Jewish worship, but found nothing. Either every Jew has forgotten the word of power or else they have no god, worshipping only an idea. Therefore, I have nothing to worry about. Yahweh remains a god of Israel, not of Makkah. The Jews of al-Arab are just another tribe, worshipping an impotent god like the other three hundred or so little gods of the Kaaba. I stand supreme, and I can afford to be magnanimous in victory. Let others worship who they will, the Qurayshi worship me and I will keep them in power in Makkah.

So, I am supreme in this one town. Is this sufficient? Gods of other nations rule over much larger territories, and I do not even hold sway over the jazirat al-Arab. If I do nothing, if I am content to rule my oasis and ignore the wider world, then sooner or later a bigger, more powerful god will come to Makkah and I will find myself in a struggle for supremacy. I cannot allow that to happen. I must extend my rule beyond Makkah and bind the other tribes of al-Arab to me. I will send out selected men as emissaries to the tribes, supporting them through miraculous events, and bind them to me. Nasib ibn Qadir shall be the first. I will send him to the warlike Badu of the deep desert for their bloodthirsty lifestyle appeals to me.

I must become more militant, a god of warriors. My people will take command of the whole of jazirat al-Arab and bring my worship to all peoples, all tribes and clans. Men will sacrifice to me and die in battle with my name on their lips. “Al-Ilah!” will become known and feared throughout the lands.

Chapter Nine

Shaiba ibn Hashim prided himself on his success in life. The name Shaiba meant old man, but he was now in the prime of life. The grey hairs that had been present at birth, hence his name, had spread until at fifty, he was almost completely grey-headed. His body did not look old though. Tall, spare of frame and with a hawk nose that spoke of Badu within his ancestry, he was a fierce polytheist who loudly decried the popularity of the two great monotheistic religions – Judaism and Christianity – that flourished along the borders of and even within jazirat al-Arab. He resisted what he regarded as new-fangled nonsense and put his faith in the beliefs of his forefathers. As head of the Banu Hashim clan of the Qurayshi, he was in a position to make life very uncomfortable for any man who sought to worship one god to the exclusion of all others.

He stood now on the edge of the great open place surrounding the Kaaba and stared toward the stone edifice, his face mirroring the emotions that warred within him. Twenty years before, as a young man ready to make his name, he had made a rash vow to the gods of the Kaaba.

"Gods of my forefathers," he had said. "Give me sons. Give me ... ten sons, and I'll offer up one to you as a sacrifice."

The gods of the Kaaba listened to the prayers of young Shaiba ibn Hashim, and in due course, he became father to six daughters and ten sons. On the birth of his youngest boy, the previous year, he remembered his oath and considered his options. First he waited a year. Children often died in infancy, and it would be pointless making the offering if his tenth child died. All his sons were strong though, and on the first anniversary of the youngest's birth, he faced up to the decision ahead of him. There was no question that he would honour his vow. Only a fool cheated the gods. The only question was which son would be sacrificed. The choice was difficult as Shaiba loved all his sons for different reasons – this one was clever, this one a fighter, this one handsome, this one gentle and so on. In the end, unable to make up his mind, he cast lots and settled on his second youngest son, Abd-Ullah, born three years before.

Still, Shaiba hesitated. He loved little Abd-Ullah and thought to cast the lots again but knew that was not fair on his other sons, whom he loved equally. *If only I could offer up a daughter*, he thought. He felt a twinge of guilt as he loved his beautiful daughters too. ... *but sons are sons.* He decided to broach the subject with the priests of the Kaaba and see if there was any way out of his dilemma. So now he stood on the edge of the open place wondering what he would say to the priests. He shrugged and strode forward to meet the priest standing in the doorway of the sacred building.

"I have come to fulfil an oath I made twenty years ago."

The priest of Hubal heard the words of Shaiba and rejoiced inwardly. The Banu Hashim was a powerful clan, and although he knew the chieftain favoured the gods of the Kaaba equally, it was good to have the mighty bend their knees to him. “What oath is this, Shaiba ibn Hashim?” he asked. “Could it be that the gods have blessed you with ten sons, as you prayed so many years ago?”

Shaiba grunted but hid his annoyance. The priests were fond of playing with one without regard for a man’s position or importance. “I made an oath to offer up one of my sons if the gods blessed me with ten of them. I’m here to fulfil my oath.”

“Very good, Shaiba ibn Hashim,” said the priest. He looked around. “But where is the boy?”

“I selected my son Abd-Ullah by lot, but I wish to petition the gods to spare his life.”

“The gods have a right to his life if that was promised,” observed the priest. “Do you seek to cheat the gods?”

“No,” Shaiba said stiffly. “But the gods may accept a price for my son’s life. I’m here to offer it.”

The priest of Hubal smiled and rubbed his hands together. “Enter into the Kaaba, and we shall put your petition before the gods.”

The inside of the windowless structure was dark, lit only by small guttering oil lamps that tossed the shadows around the chamber. Images of the gods seemed to bend and sway as if in some arcane dance. The air was still and heavy with the sweet smell of incense mixed with sweat from the twenty or so priests in attendance. The priest of Hubal took his place in front of the altar of his god and spread his arms wide, waiting for the buzz of interest around the room to die down. A scattering of other petitioners hurriedly finished their business and moved to the shadowed edges of the room where they stood silently and listened as the priest started to speak.

"Shaiba ibn Hashim, you have come before the assembled gods of the Kaaba to offer a sacrifice of wealth in place of the sacrifice of blood you promised twenty years ago. Know that the gods expect your sacrifice to be a worthy one."

"I offer ten camels, strong bulls and fertile cows in equal part."

"Let the god Manaf answer," cried the priest of Hubal.

The priest of Manaf took a bundle of arrows from a cedar chest and advanced to stand in front of Shaiba. He held the arrows aloft and prayed to his god before casting the arrows to the ground. The wooden shafts clattered and scattered. The priest bent over them, noting the directions the iron tips pointed and which ones were touching.

"Manaf rejects your offer."

"Then I offer twenty camels, bulls and cows as before."

This time the priest of Uzza came forward and gathered up the arrows before praying and throwing them down.

"Uzza rejects your offer."

"Thirty camels."

"Nebo rejects your offer."

"Forty."

"Shams says no."

"Fifty." Shaiba felt a trickle of sweat run down his back. He was a rich man, but there was still a limit to what he could afford. He took a modicum of comfort in the fact that the gods must surely know how wealthy he was and would not beggar him.

"Ya'uq rejects your offer."

"Sixty camels, bulls and cows, including five cows in calf."

The priest of Dhushara went through a great show of casting the arrows and consulting them. "Dhushara rejects your offer."

The bidding climbed to one hundred camels, and Shaiba was drenched with sweat. He was nearing the limits of his disposable wealth and knew he would have to allow his son Abd-Ullah to be sacrificed after all. He saw the priest of Hubal step forward and cast down the divining arrows with a supercilious sneer.

"Hubal rejects …"

"But al-Ilah accepts your offer," interrupted a voice from the shadows.

The priest of Hubal turned swiftly, an oath half-uttered on his lips, as a young man, scarcely bearded, stepped out of the darkness and smiled at Shaiba.

"Al-Ilah accepts your offer of one hundred camels, Shaiba ibn Hashim."

"What are you doing, Makram ibn Ruh?" the priest of Hubal snarled. "You're not a priest and cannot speak for your god. Leave us now. Shaiba, Hubal rejects your offer."

Makram walked around the priest, reaching out and touching his robes with a frown on his face. "Do you really want to pit Hubal against al-Ilah? Here and now? My god speaks to me and tells me he accepts this generous sacrifice." The young man searched the priest's face for an answer but found only fear.

"I … I … Hubal accepts the offer," the priest whispered.

"Excellent. Shaiba ibn Hasim, please deliver the camels to the stockyards tomorrow morning. Priests will be on hand to dispose of the animals." Makram walked with Shaiba into the bright, hot sunlight of the open space. "You must really love Abd-Ullah your son," he said. "Look after him, for the gods value him highly."

***

The city of San'a in al-Yaman had grown over the years and had become the capital city in the territory of jazirat al-Arab ruled by the Christian Emperor of the Kingdom of Aksum, the Negus Abraha. In an effort to convert the pagans of the jazirat, he built a great church or *ekklesia* in the city, which the locals called al-Qulais. To secure his rule over the tribes, Abraha played one off against the other, offering rewards to one until others united in jealousy and then shattering the rebellious confederation by offering bribes and titles to opposing factions. He made Muhammad ibn Khuza'i a king and ordered him to go northward into the lowlands of the jazirat, subjugating and spreading the word of the Christian god and of his Emperor.

For a time, the people welcomed Muhammad and his men, offering them the hospitality due to a guest, but Muhammad grew haughty and took as his due what was freely offered. He sneered at the faith of the people, calling their gods demons or mere lumps of clay or wood, and the people grew angry. By the time Muhammad reached the land of Kinana, his progression more closely resembled a conquest rather than a peaceful journey, and one Urwa ibn Hayyad, a man of the Hudhayl, took an arrow and pierced Muhammad so he fell down dead.

Muhammad's brother Qays fled back to San'a and told Abraha. The Emperor flew into a rage and swore to raid the tribes of the lowland, burning and pillaging, and raze to the ground all the temples dedicated to pagan gods.

This oath of vengeance soon came to the ears of the Qurayshi of Makkah, and their anger against Abraha grew great. Hotheads among the younger men of the tribe, determined to strike back at the tyrant and lacking military might, settled on a deliberate insult. A small group journeyed down to San'a and under the cover of darkness crept into the great church of al-Qulais and defecated on the altar.

Abraha lost his temper and marshalled his army, assembling forty-thousand men to stamp the Qurayshi and their temple of the Kaaba into the dust. His own elephant, Mahmoud, led the army, and several other elephants accompanied the slow-moving force. Various tribes in the path of the army – the Banu Kinana, Banu Khuza'a and Banu Hudhayl – rose up and attacked but were defeated with great loss. Inexorably, the army of Abraha drew close to Makkah.

Shaiba ibn Hashim was an old man of seventy-three in this Year of the Elephant, but he was not about to flee from the approaching army. His family and business was centred on Makkah, and those things concerned him more than the possible risk to his own life. In particular, his beloved son, Abd-Ullah, ransomed twenty-four years before from the gods of the Kaaba, had recently married a comely girl, Aminah bint Wahb, and she was expecting their first child. Shaiba made sure the woman was taken in care by other members of the family and sent into the hills surrounding the town until this unpleasantness with Abraha could be resolved. Abd-Ullah would normally have been home looking after his wife, but he was on a business trip in Yathrib in the north, so Shaiba was happy to perform that duty.

The sun was warm, and the town was quiet with so many people fleeing to the hills, so Shaiba sat in the courtyard of his house with a few close friends and chewed strong khat leaves as they waited to see what would happen.

"We cannot just sit around and wait, friend Shaiba. We must do something."

Shaiba smiled and set his box of leaves to one side. "What would you have us do, Asif? We cannot oppose Abraha militarily, and I won't flee to the hills." He stretched and cracked his knuckles before taking up another khat leaf. "The gods won't desert us."

The youngest man there, Basit, grunted. "I notice the priests have all fled though."

"I think the priests have less faith in the gods than most," Dawud observed. "I have to admit that most gods don't seem much concerned with us. I mean, I've never sacrificed to Manaf, the sun god, yet he still shines down and warms my old bones. Does he actually do more for someone who sacrifices to him?"

"I agree that's likely for most gods," Shaiba said, "but I've seen a few things in my time, and I wouldn't like to neglect that which I don't fully understand. Al-Ilah, for instance."

"Oh yes, al-Ilah," Essa laughed. "You're Qurayshi, and head of Clan Hashim, dear friend. You have to say that. How about the rest of us? I'm not sure I want to rely on a shepherd god's dubious fighting skills when it comes to Abraha's forty-thousand men."

"And elephants," Basit added. "Don't forget the elephants. I've never seen an elephant, let alone a white one like Abraha's personal beast."

"Have faith, dear friends," Shaiba said. "We're in the hands of the gods."

A knock came at the gate of the courtyard. A servant ran across and opened it, exchanging a few words with the man outside before pointing across at the group of old men.

The man hurried across and bowed. "Shaiba ibn Hashim," said the man, "I bring news from Yathrib." He pulled a letter out of his dust-stained pouch and handed it across.

Shaiba took the letter and turned it over in his hands for a few moments. "Forgive me, friends. I must read this." He broke the seal and opened up the folded paper, scanning the contents quickly. His eyes widened and he gasped. He read the message once more before his hand dropped to his side, and he slumped back in his seat.

"What is it, Shaiba?" Dawud asked. "News of Abraha?"

"It's from Yathrib," Essa chided, "not the south. What's happened? Has your son lost all your money?"

Shaiba looked at his friends, his eyes glistening. "My son is dead. Stricken down with a nameless disease. My darling Abd-Ullah whom I ransomed from the gods."

"They won't be denied," Essa murmured.

Shaiba's friends offered up their condolences and withdrew a few paces to allow their friend the opportunity to weep in some privacy. Instead, he took several deep breaths and folded up the letter, tucking it into his sash. "Let al-Ilah's will be done," he said firmly.

"Will you go to Yathrib?" Basit asked. "You'll need to make the arrangements."

Shaiba shook his head. "I cannot leave Makkah with Abraha on our threshold."

"But he's your son," Asif protested. "You must go. None will think the less of you."

"My son is dead and in the arms of al-Ilah. My duty is now to the living – his wife and unborn child, and also the people of this town."

"Come, Shaiba, you're in the throes of grief and refuse to give into it. What can one man do against forty-thousand? Go to your son. Leave Makkah in the hands of the gods."

The old chieftain stood silently for several minutes, looking toward the surrounding hills where his family had fled to safety. “I will go to Abraha,” he said quietly. “I will persuade him not to attack Makkah.”

His friends tried to dissuade him, but Shaiba was adamant. He settled his affairs and made provision for Aminah and her unborn child just in case the petition to the Christian King went badly. Essa volunteered to accompany him, and the next day, the two men set out on fast camels for the south. Another day found them amongst the forward scouts of the army, and they brought them into the company of the king.

“You are welcome, Shaiba ibn Hashim,” Abraha said. “You and your companion. Your wisdom is known and spoken of even as far away as Aksum, and I hope that we can settle this business before it’s too late.”

“Your majesty, that’s my hope too,” Shaiba replied. “For the tribes of Makkah are fierce, and many men would die if you attacked.”

“You’re vastly outnumbered,” the king pointed out. “Your tribesmen would be the ones to die.”

“That’s in the hands of al-Ilah.”

Abraha nodded piously. “Indeed. All things are in His hands.”

“If god was willing, your majesty, what would persuade you to spare Makkah and return to San’a?”

“I’ve no interest in Makkah, nor in its people, Shaiba ibn Hashim. Men of your tribe, with the blessing of the priests of your Kaaba, defiled the church of the One True God. For that blasphemous act, I and the Lord God will have justice.”

"And what would be just in your eyes, your majesty?"

"Gold. I'll have to build a new church as the defilement of the old one renders it displeasing to God. Such good works are expensive. Gold to my own weight … a hundred times over."

"There isn't that much gold in the whole of jazirat al-Arab," Shaiba said uneasily. "A new church could not possibly cost that much."

"There's more. As well as the gold, I require every man of the party who defiled the church to be handed over to me."

Shaiba shuddered at the thought of what Abraha would do them before they died. "I don't know the names of these hotheaded fools, but surely reparations could be made for their lives?"

"There's more. This whole affair was instigated by the wicked men posing as priests of your pagan gods. I'll return with my army to San'a if you'll pay a tribute of one hundred times my weight in gold, hand over the defilers and tear down the Kaaba."

"Blasphemy," Essa hissed.

"Peace, brother," Shaiba murmured. "Your majesty, we could perhaps find some gold, and I can put it to the clans that they deliver up the hotheads, but you ask too much when you demand we destroy our holy place."

"I don't want to seem a hard and uncaring man," Abraha said. "I'll forego the gold, if you deliver up a single man for punishment and tear down the altars to your pagan gods. In return, to show my magnanimity, I'll build a magnificent church to the True God in Makkah, so all may worship in the light of his Blessed Son's sacrifice."

"I cannot make that decision alone," Shaiba said. "I can carry your words to the Elders though."

"Do so, Shaiba ibn Hashim, but do so quickly. My army will be on the doorstep of Makkah in three days. Accede to my demands … no, my requests, and I'll spare the town, destroying only the Kaaba. Refuse, and I'll stamp the place flat and put every man, woman and child to the sword."

Shaiba and Essa bowed and backed out of the king's presence. As they mounted their camels under the watchful eyes of the guards, Shaiba said, "The gods of the Kaaba will defend it. They'll fight against this Christian adversary and overcome him. Their servants won't be dishonoured."

"As god wills, so let it be done," Essa agreed.

The Elders of Makkah were in an uproar when Shaiba reported on Abraha's words. "We're doomed," Ziad bemoaned. "We cannot stand against an army of forty-thousand."

"Nor can we agree to his terms," Shaiba said sharply. "What do you want to do? Flee the town and let it be destroyed?"

"What else can we do?"

"Trust in God."

"Really? Which one do you think is powerful enough to destroy Abraha?"

"There's only al-Ilah. Flee the town if you will. I'll stay here and await the god's actions. We're all in his hands anyway. What he wills, will come to be." Shaiba got up and left the meeting.

Many more people left Makkah that day, but Shaiba sent word to the hills that the heads of the clans should return to the town to show their support for their god. The men returned, but so did Aminah, the widow of Abd-Ullah. Shaiba was horrified and drew her aside to remonstrate with her.

"My husband is dead, father-in-law. I returned that I might stand in his place beside you," Aminah said.

"You're a brave woman, Aminah bint Wahb, and a worthy wife of my beloved son. If you bring forth a son, I prophesy that he'll be a mighty warrior, conquering all."

"If it's al-Ilah's will, let it be so."

The day had started hot and bright without a breath of wind, but slowly dark clouds formed in the east, creeping across the sky toward Makkah. Faint rumbles could be heard within the cloud, and streaks of light shot through it.

"There's a storm coming."

"It doesn't look like any storm I've seen."

"Well, we'll know soon enough. It's heading straight for us."

Abraha's army reached Makkah, the dust of his approach climbing high above the almost deserted town. The tramp of eighty-thousand feet could be heard long before the first men appeared, but when they did, they halted an arrowshot from the town's boundary markers and waited.

"Why do they wait?" Essa asked nervously. "They must know we cannot stop them."

"Abraha will want to enter first, I imagine," Shaiba said. "There, see …" he pointed. "He comes on his elephant."

A massive pale grey animal moved slowly, ponderously out from the army lines, a mahout on the animal's neck and an ornate chair strapped to its back. The figure of Abraha, clad in gleaming chainmail, sat in the chair and haughtily regarded the town and the waiting figures of its citizens as he drew nearer. The mahout tapped the elephant's head, and it curled back its trunk and let loose a screaming bellow. The people waiting at the edge of the town – fifty men and one pregnant woman – drew back in alarm.

"I've never seen an elephant before," Essa muttered. "What do we do?"

"We're in al-Ilah's hands."

The elephant moved forward, and behind it, the army surged into motion. The mahout urged the beast into a lumbering run, and it spread its great ears, the trunk questing forward, its great white tusks raised. Then it reached the town's boundary marker and stopped so suddenly the mahout almost lost his seat and King Abraha swayed forward. The animal shuffled and backed away while the mahout beat it about the head with a stick, yelling at it to advance again. The elephant refused. It stood there at the edge of the town, swaying its massive head back and forth and emitting a deep rumbling sound.

"What is it doing?" Essa whispered.

Shaiba smiled. "I see the hand of al-Ilah in this."

“What about that storm?” muttered one of the Elders. “It’s getting very close.”

“That too … maybe. Who knows?”

Abraha spoke sharply, and the mahout turned the elephant and it moved away, back to where the army had once more stopped. Moving in a circle, the elephant broke into a run again and charged the people in the town. Once more the beast stopped dead, refusing to advance beyond the town’s boundary markers. Again it was turned, moving in a wider circle before charging the town from a different angle, and again the elephant refused to cross into Makkah. This time, the beast settled awkwardly and sat, refusing to budge. Abraha cursed loudly and leapt down from the elephant. He called his men forward, and the army cheered and started running.

“God stopped the elephant. Can he stop an army?”

The first of the dark clouds swept across the town, and the forefront of the advancing army fell into shadow. The sound of whistling and sighing came from above, and things fell from the sky, streaking down at an angle and plunging into the running men. Screams erupted, and the army front disintegrated as men sought shelter from the falling things. All thought of advancing into the town disappeared, and the front lines turned and broke, forcing their way back into the ranks behind.

“What’s happening?” screamed an elder.

“Stones,” yelled another. “Stones are falling from the sky.”

The rain of missiles grew heavier and swept across the front ranks of Abraha's army. The King himself fell and then sought shelter beneath upturned shields. For a time, all was chaos, and then the strange storm continued on its way into the western mountains, leaving the plains outside Makkah looking like a battlefield. Many men lay dead, tossed about like straw in a windstorm; others sobbed and cried out, dragging themselves away. By far the larger part of the army was uninjured, having been outside the fall of rocks, but they saw in the swift destruction of their fellows a sign from God – from their Christian God – that the expedition was cursed. They turned and started on the long trek back to San'a. Abraha was mortally injured, but he lived long enough to reach his capital city.

The people of Makkah returned to their town and tended to the injured soldiers, letting them go back to their homes when they recovered. They buried the dead and set about resuming their normal lives. The miraculous deliverance of the town was a subject of discussion for a long time, the events and their causes growing more unlikely with every retelling.

"What do you think happened?" Asif asked. "Did al-Ilah really send a flock of birds to drop rocks on the enemy?"

"Does it matter?" Shaiba queried. "However it happened, Makkah and the Kaaba were saved."

"I'd still like to know. I was there, and I didn't see any birds, but what else can it have been? Rocks don't just fall from the sky?"

"I didn't see any birds either, but I saw the rocks fall. I picked some up, and they were hot. Some even looked as if they'd been cooked in an oven."

"Well, that's just ludicrous," Basit commented. "There're no ovens in the sky. I think there were birds, but they were in the clouds and we didn't see them."

"Or a whirlwind," Essa said. "It carried rocks aloft and then dropped them."

"All things are possible for al-Ilah," Shaiba agreed. "Whatever method he chose, he saved Makkah, so we can be grateful."

The other Elders nodded. "Praise be unto al-Ilah."

Aminah bint Wahb, the daughter-in-law of Shaiba, delivered her baby a short time later in the month of Rabi' al-awwal. Her child was a boy, small but healthy and with a good pair of lungs. Aminah wept for joy, but also in sorrow that her husband, Abd-Ullah, six months dead, was not there to rejoice with her. She named her son Ahmad.

***

As was the custom of those times, the women of the Badu, the wandering tribes of the desert, came to Makkah a few months later looking for boy children to raise. Women of the towns often gave their children into the care of Badu women as the harsh life of the desert people produced a healthier and hardier race of men. A Badu woman would approach a young mother and offer her services, bargaining with the family for a good fee for rearing the child. Every Badu woman found a baby in Makkah that year, save one, Halimah bint Abi Dhuayb. All the other women of her tribe found suitable babies for generous payment, but the only child left for her was Ahmad the son of Aminah. The widow had no money to offer as a fee, but Halimah relented when she saw the child, taking him without recompense.

Ahmad went back into the desert with Halimah a few days later. She acted as wet-nurse and foster-mother to the infant and renamed him El-Amin after his mother back in Makkah. Halimah and her husband had other children, including a baby not much older than El-Amin, and as soon as the child was weaned, his foster-father, Sa'di, would take him out with the older children and instruct him in the ways of the desert people. He learned the value of every item within a Badu camp: the proper behaviour of a child in front of adults, the resolution of disputes between children and every aspect of Badu life.

When he was two years old, Halimah took him back to Makkah to visit his mother but pleaded with Aminah to be allowed to keep him a while longer. His mother desired her son's presence in her home but could see how healthy he was and acceded to Halimah's wishes.

"You'll look after him?" Aminah whispered, clinging to her son in the doorway of her home.

"He's as my own child," Halimah assured her. "He'll be reared as an upright man of the Banu Sa'd."

When he was six, El-Amin was given added responsibility by his foster-father. He led a flock of his sheep out to graze and put the boy in charge of them, giving him a staff and warning him not to let the animals stray. But in the lonely spaces of the desert, the boy's thoughts turned inward, and he contemplated his own young life and what his future might hold. The harsh light of the desert played tricks with his eyes, and the heat stupefied him. Sometimes he spoke to the empty air and listened as if someone replied.

Sa'di found him one day with his flock scattered and strode to where the boy sat oblivious to his charges. "Why are you neglecting your flock, El-Amin?" he asked harshly.

The boy looked up, his eyes unfocused and dreamy. "They speak to me," he whispered.

"Eh? Who speaks to you, boy? The sheep?"

"Two men in white. They say they've come to cleanse me."

Sa'di looked nonplussed. There was nobody in sight and as he had approached, seen nothing but the sun's dazzle around the boy. "Cleanse you? Cleanse you for what?"

"They say that'll be revealed."

Sa'di wondered if a djinni had appeared to the boy, but a djinni would scarcely talk of cleansing him. He took El-Amin, and together they rounded up the sheep and returned to camp.

"I think he must be returned to his natural mother," Sa'di told his wife that night. "I fear that something in the desert has marked him and may do him harm if he stays."

Halimah sorrowed for she loved El-Amin. “It shall be as you say, husband.”

So El-Amin went back to his mother, Aminah, in Makkah, where he once again became Ahmad. He missed his foster parents and his brothers and sisters, but he was aware of his duty to his mother and his grandfather, Shaiba ibn Hashim. There was little for a boy to do in a small household, so he would often go to the centre of the town, to the great open place, and contemplate the worshippers attending the Kaaba. Other times he would wander to the outskirts of town and sit and stare at the hills or watch the travellers as they arrived in the great caravans.

Shaiba was a very old man now, but he took Ahmad in hand and introduced him to commerce. The boy would sit in a corner at the trading post and watch the transactions that took place or bring his grandfather coffee or cool well water when he called for it. The old man also told him about his father, Abd-Ullah, as he knew next to nothing about the man who had sired him but died in Yathrib before he was born.

“Mother, I’d like to see my father’s grave.”

Aminah looked up from her cleaning and regarded her tall, thin son carefully. “Time enough for that when you’re older.” She broke into a fit of coughing and had to sit down for a few moments. “In a few years, I’ll ask your grandfather to take us north.”

“My father’s name means servant of God,” Ahmad said. “I’d like to see his grave. The men dressed in white said I should ask you.”

"What men in white are these? Have you been speaking to strangers?"

Ahmad smiled. "They're no strangers, and they too are servants of the Most High."

Aminah was suddenly glad she was sitting down, for she had heard the stories that were told of her son. Her resolve wavered. "You're only seven. That's very young for such an arduous journey."

"Please, mother."

She nodded. "I'll ask Shaiba ibn Hashim if he can make room for us in one of his caravans."

Two weeks later, Aminah and Ahmad set out for Yathrib with a caravan carrying hides to the merchants of that town. The journey took nearly a month at the slow pace of the caravan, and a few miles from their destination, Aminah collapsed, spitting blood. She recovered enough to take her son to his father's grave, where he prayed, but the effort exhausted her. A physician in the town recommended the sea air as a restorative and with the help of Shaiba's agent, arranged for her to be taken to Al-Abwa on the sea coast. The sea air did not help, however, and she died a few days later.

Ahmad's grandfather's agents in Yathrib saw to the funeral and burial of his mother and had the boy brought back to Makkah, where Shaiba took him into his household. This arrangement was not to last either as the next year, Shaiba ibn Hashim at eighty-one years of age was gathered to his forefathers.

Ahmad's uncle Imran, full brother to Abd-Ullah by Shaiba's wife Fatimah bint Amr, took the orphaned boy into his home, knowing the growing lad was one of his father's favourites. Imran, also known as Abu Talib, was a successful trader in his own right and regularly sent caravans to the incense lands of southwest Arabia and the ports that plied the Indian trade, and also to the great cities of the north – Jerusalem, Damascus and Antioch. He worked Ahmad hard, training him in the ways of commerce. Abu Talib was not of the ruling clan of the Qurayshi, but he had position in the community, being the custodian of the Kaaba. He knew, though, Ahmad would not be in line for any high position within the tribe, so he trained him toward a calling that would provide him with a good living – that of trader and merchant.

When Ahmad was ten, Abu Talib took him on the expeditions to trade in incense and rare woods from India. He liked the lad and took a lot of trouble with him, making sure he understood the reasons for his trading decisions. Ahmad was quiet and studious, listening to advice and paying attention to detail. On his second visit to the southwest, Abu Talib allowed Ahmad to initiate a small trading transaction of his own. He bought a quantity of almonds and dried apricots in Ta'izz and resold them in Makkah, turning a small profit which he handed over to his uncle.

The next year, Abu Talib took his nephew north to Syria. The twelve-year-old was very excited at the prospect of journeying outside jazirat al-Arab and seeing other people with strange beliefs. His tribe believed in many gods, but his uncle believed only one of them, al-Ilah, was truly worthy of worship as the Supreme God. Ahmad was less sure. He was still visited by the men clad in white raiment, though less frequently, and he wondered how these beings fit into Arabic theology. In his mind, it stood to reason one god must be above all others, but nobody he knew, not even the priests of al-Ilah, knew about the white men of the desert.

"Men dressed in white, you say, boy? I think the sun must be affecting you."

"They say they're servants of God."

"You mean angels? Al-Ilah speaks directly to us, boy, he doesn't need messengers. And he wouldn't talk to a child."

"Yet they do talk to me. If they're not from al-Ilah, who are they from?"

"You're imagining them or else they're djinn of the desert. Pray hard to al-Ilah that you never see them again, boy."

The caravan wound its way slowly northward, passing into lands ruled by very different people – Jews and Christians. Ahmad learned that even among these people who said they worshipped a single supreme god, there was much disagreement. With his uncle's permission, Ahmad listened to preachers in Judea, Samaria and Syria, but though he learned a lot, none of the knowledge helped him in his search for truth.

Then they came to Bosra in southern Syria. Abu Talib had decided only a few days before that the city would be his first major trading stop and planned on spending several days there. On the approach to the city, while several miles out, a man walked into the road in front of the camels and signed for them to stop. Abu Talib quickly scanned the surrounding hills and woods for any hint of an ambush but found none. He gestured for the caravan to halt, and he slid down off the lead beast, his hand close to his sword.

"What's your business, friend?" Abu Talib asked cautiously. "We're bound for Bosra and mean to be there by nightfall."

"I am Bahira," said the man. "I'm a Nestorian monk, and I've been awaiting your coming."

"You were waiting for me? How can that be? Even I didn't decide to come to Bosra until a few days ago, and nobody knew of my decision save my companions."

"There's One who sees all, even into men's minds and hearts. He bids me welcome you and offer you shelter for the night, and sustenance."

"My thanks, but I think we'd better press on for Bosra."

"You won't get there by nightfall, and I've the best water in the neighbourhood. Besides, the Most High has bid me welcome you, and I must believe there's a reason. Would you resist God?"

"Since you put it like that, Bahira, I most willingly accept your hospitality."

Bahira led the way along a track that led into the hills, and the camel train followed. The monk's abode was a dry and spacious cave in the hillside beside a bubbling spring that collected in a fern-lined rock basin before spilling out into a tiny brook that disappeared among the trees. An open grassy area near the cave was large enough for a single tent and there was ample space for others beside the brook. Forage was plentiful, and the members of the caravan quickly set about erecting their camp and seeing to their animals.

The monk pointed to a small flock of sheep penned near the rock basin. "Take, slaughter them according to your custom and partake of the food God sends."

The men did so, and soon the sheep were roasting over fires. When they sat down to eat, Bahira refused the meat, saying, "I have taken a vow and must abstain. Eat plentifully though for God has given of his bounty." He gave thanks to his god and sipped water and ate raw vegetables, while his guests devoured the roasted meat and bread fresh-baked in the ashes.

Ahmad ate sparingly and stopped before he was full, not wanting to give in to gluttony. He caught Bahira's eye and asked, "Holy man, may I ask you a question?"

Bahira stared at the lad for a few moments before answering. "Ah, here's the reason the Lord called to me. Ask away, young sir."

"You're a Christian, aren't you? Why then do you hide yourself away in this cave? All other Christians I've seen have been in the towns and cities."

Bahira nodded slowly. "When our Lord God created the first man, Adam, it was in a garden. Later men, fallen from grace, built cities so they could hide from the Face of God. Later, prophets such as Abraham, Moses and Jesus were all men who lived in the wild places. It is here that God may see man clearly and where men may be granted a vision of God."

"We believe that Abraham, or Ibrahim, from whom I'm descended, lived as a shepherd, but was not Moses a prince of Egypt? Surely then he was a city man?"

"Not so, young sir, for though he was raised in pharaoh's court, he fled to the wilderness of Midian where he saw God in a burning bush. After he led the Children of Israel out of bondage, he lived the rest of his life in Sinai."

"And Jesus? Didn't he preach and die in Jerusalem?"

"You've been well educated, young sir, but Jesus only preached in the cities so he could reach the ears of the ungodly. After each time, he went back into the wilderness so that he could be once more fortified by God."

Ahmad nodded, thinking about the monk's words. "You say much that's wise and thought provoking, holy sir. May I sit at your feet and learn from you?"

"It was for this that the Lord guided you here. Yet you're still a boy. You must ask your guardian Abu Talib."

Ahmad turned to Abu Talib. "May I, uncle? Please."

Abu Talib considered the matter carefully, weighing up his trust for the holy man and the safety of his nephew. "How long would you want to remain?"

Ahmad smiled. "As long as he has things to teach me."

Abu Talib grunted. "That could be years." He looked across at Bahira. "Forgive my concern, holy man, but this boy is my favourite nephew. How can we guarantee his safety?"

"No man would disturb my solitude, but if you want, leave two men to guard him. As long as they remain silent, I am content."

"Very well. Ahmad, you have three days. At noon on the third day, my men will bring you into Bosra from where we leave for Damascus."

"Thank you, uncle."

The next morning, Abu Talib took the caravan into Bosra, leaving Ahmad in the care of two of his most trusted men. When the camel train was out of sight, Bahira instructed the two guards to retire out of earshot and sat the boy down under a tree near the brook. He examined Ahmad in silence for several minutes, raising a hand in caution once or twice when the lad opened his mouth to ask a question.

"You must learn to listen and observe, young sir."

"Indeed, holy sir, I'm more than willing to do so, but how will I learn unless I ask questions?"

Bahira smiled. "Put your faith in God and all necessary things will be revealed to you. Now, Ahmad son of Abdullah, tell me of your life in far off Makkah. Is it true that Arabs are polytheists? Do you worship many gods in this Kaaba of yours?"

Ahmad opened his mouth to reply hotly and then contained himself, considering his words. "Holy sir, may I speak plainly, for I don't wish to cause offence?"

"Please do, for it's necessary that we utter the truth."

“Then I must tell you that I find the worship of many gods to be abhorrent. I believe that there is One True God.”

“And does this single god of yours have a name?”

“His blessed name hasn’t been revealed to me, but some of my tribesmen call him al-Ilah.”

“That means The God in the Arabic tongue, doesn’t it?”

Ahmad inclined his head in agreement.

“The Jewish god is single also,” Bahira said. “His name is Yahweh, but he’s sometimes referred to as El or Elohim, the latter term being the plural form of God which implies the Jews were once polytheistic.”

“And the Christians? Some people say one God, others three.”

“Christians are divided on this. You’ll hear of Jehovah, which is the Latin form of Yahweh, but there’s also the Logos and Parakletos.”

“Three Gods then. The Christians are polytheists.”

Bahira smiled wryly. “Some men have strayed from the path of true knowledge, but by the grace of God will return to the fold. The Roman Church believes the Father to be one with the Son – the Logos – and the Holy Spirit or Parakletos. They say they are three and yet the three are one. The Bishop of Rome calls it a sacred mystery, but I call it confusion.”

“What do you say, holy sir?”

Bahira noticed one of the men guarding Ahmad had crept closer while they talked and was listening intently. He opened his mouth to rebuke the man and then closed it again. *What does it matter if another listens? The truth is there for all.* For a moment, he thought he saw a blue glow about the man's head but when he looked it was gone. He rubbed his eyes and turned his attention back to the youth.

"I say there's one God, the Father, His Son who is a created being and the Holy Spirit which is God's Will," Bahira said.

Ahmad considered these words, turning them over in his mind. "You've told me that the Christian God is Jehovah. Who then is this Son you talk of?"

"The Son is the Logos, the Word of God, the firstborn of all creation. It's possible that the Logos was the only thing that God created, for through the Logos everything else came to be."

Ahmad frowned. "If God only created one thing, and this Logos the rest, then does that not make the Logos more powerful than God? Surely that cannot be."

"Have you heard of Words of Power? Single words that if uttered will shatter rock, tumble mountains, part the seas or strike a man dead?"

Ahmad stirred uneasily. "These are myths, stories to frighten children."

"Not so. They exist."

"You …?"

"No. I seek knowledge in other areas. I've no wish to wield such power, but it illustrates my point. God created a Word of Power and imbued it with His Strength and Wisdom, so that that one Word, when uttered, could bring into being all of creation. This Word is the Logos, the Son of God. By this creation He became the Father."

"This … this means God had a wife? If you're saying Ilat, the mother goddess of the Arabs, is the wife of God, I'll listen no further." Ahmad started to rise, but Bahira motioned him to sit again.

"I mean no such thing. That would be blasphemy. God is all-powerful and does not need the female essence to bring new life into being. He created the Son using the power of his own Holy Spirit."

"I'm confused."

"It's a lot to grasp when first you hear it," Bahira conceded. "Think on it a while, young sir, and I'll fetch us some food with which to refresh ourselves."

While Bahira was away, Ahmad thought on the holy man's words, striving to fit this new-found knowledge into his understanding of his own god. He too, noticed the man sitting close by but also paid him no heed, his mind being on other things. Bahira brought food, and they dined simply on bread and cheese with tart apples to follow, sitting silently while they ate. After they tidied away the scraps and gave thanks for the food, Ahmad cleared his throat.

"Holy sir, I think I can comprehend the existence of the Logos, the Son of God, but when we travelled through Jerusalem, I met a Christian who talked of Jesus as being the Son of God. Was he mistaken?"

"Indeed he was not, though there are some disputes within the congregation of Christians as to the status of Jesus bar Joseph. Jesus claimed to be the Messiah, the prophesied Son of Man who sits upon the right hand of God. That he was the Son of God, the Logos himself, few Christians will dispute, but not all are in agreement as to his nature. Some, like the bishop of Rome, say that he was God himself, the second part of their blasphemous trinity, but others, more reasoning, say that he was truly man."

"If he was truly man, then how could he be the Logos?"

"That's the crux of the matter. I follow the teachings of Arius of Alexandria in this. The Logos existed from the first moments of creation but gave up his heavenly life to enter the body of a man born of woman, so that he might lead all men to God. He was executed by the Romans and died for all men, so that they might enter heaven."

Ahmad looked astonished. "The Logos is dead?"

Bahira smiled. "No, they only killed his fleshly body. The spirit within was resurrected and ascended to heaven, where he once more rules with God – under God."

"This is all very perplexing," Ahmad said. "I've heard tales from other travellers about the gods and heroes of other nations, and some of these have similar stories. I cannot recall the details, but they talk of a son of Zeus who was raised up, then hung upon a tree and finally raised to glory."

"I think you're referring to the tale of Dionysus, or perhaps the Egyptian Osiris, both pagan gods. There are definite similarities to the life of Jesus, and as the stories predate Christianity, we must assume they prefigure the Truth of Jesus. Perhaps they're even inventions of the Adversary, whom you call Shaitan."

Ahmad nodded. As the afternoon progressed, he listened to Bahira as he told the full story of Jesus' birth, ministry and death. The holy man went on from there to talk about the teachings of the Christ and the similarities and difference with the faith of the Jews.

As night fell, the two of them retired to the cave to sleep. One of Abu Talib's men slept outside in the tent they had thought to share with their master's nephew, but the other insisted on sleeping across the cave entrance. Ahmad welcomed the sole company of Bahira and plied him with questions until the fire burned down to sullen embers and the moon rose, sending them yawning to their beds.

On the second day, Bahira continued to teach young Ahmad, either sitting beneath the tree by the brook or else climbing to the top of a nearby hill where they could see Bosra in the distance. The two guards climbed the hill also, grumbling at the extra effort in the hot sun, but still remained attentive to the possible dangers. They saw no one on their rambles though, except for a solitary shepherd and his flock. Bahira used the sighting to talk again about Jesus' ministry, striving to turn this young Arab boy toward an acceptance of Christianity. Once more, the man who had sat close by was within earshot.

Toward nightfall, Ahmad spoke up about Jesus in a forthright manner. "I've learned that the two great religions of Judaism and Christianity have many similarities. They're both based on One God, their beliefs are similar, their values alike and they share many prophets like Abraham, Moses, Isaiah, Jeremiah and such, but differ mainly in that the Jews don't accept Jesus as coming from God. From your words, I've learned that Jesus is a true prophet of God, but that his message to man has been corrupted. Is this a true assessment, holy sir?"

"It's close, young sir, but you mistake my teachings if you regard Jesus as merely a prophet. He's the Son of God and ranks above any of the prophets that have gone before. Put your faith in him and heaven will be your reward."

"How can I put my trust in a prophet whose message has been corrupted? God will surely not allow his Word to be altered or destroyed."

"What? You look for another prophet? One who'd supplant the message of the Christ?"

"It may be that the gospels of the Christians are not God's final word."

Bahira laughed. "No man comes to God except through the Christ say the gospels. Beware of setting yourself up as a false prophet, young Ahmad. You lack understanding, despite my efforts, for I've spent a lifetime in the study of God and you but days."

"I wouldn't presume to set myself up, holy sir, but if God sees fit to raise me up, I'll do his bidding."

They parted then, each feeling his pride impugned by the other, and Ahmad slept that night in the tent with his uncle's servants. In the morning, the men packed up the tent, ready to start for Bosra, but Ahmad took a silver cup and went to Bahira's cave.

"Holy sir, I thank you for your hospitality and your thought provoking words. I beg you to accept this small gift as a token of my appreciation. It was given to me by a prince who came seeking knowledge, but I've no use for baubles such as this."

Bahira turned the cup over, marvelling at its ornamentation. "It's a costly gift, Ahmad ibn Abdullah. I've nothing to offer in return."

"There is no need."

Bahira grimaced and made to hand back the cup. "You've seen my home. I've renounced the world and have no use for wealth."

"Then sell it and give the money to the poor." Ahmad bowed. "Goodbye, holy sir."

Abu Talib spoke to his servants immediately upon their arrival in Bosra. Then he asked his nephew how the visit with the holy man had gone. "Did you learn much from Bahira the monk?"

Ahmad considered the question carefully, picking the words of his answer. "He taught me more than he thought, uncle. I learned that Jews think themselves a chosen people but reject Jesus the Prophet. Christians accept Jesus but corrupt his teachings. I don't think either religion is suitable for the people of Arabia."

"I'm sure you are right, nephew. Maybe one day you'll find the best one – or maybe you know him already. I've always thought al-Ilah should be our one god."

Ahmad said nothing but thought about the men in white back in the desert outside Makkah – angels, as he thought of them now. He wondered what they would say, both concerning Bahira's teachings and about Abu Talib's belief.

Chapter Ten

I will not go down without a fight. I have been a god for nearly three thousand years, been worshipped as al-Ilah by hundreds of men and have affected the lives of countless others. Who does he imagine he is, this Ahmad who now calls himself Prophet of God? He is just a man like any other … No, perhaps not quite like any other. If I am honest, I must admit he was a strange boy and has grown up into a single-minded man. I have watched him grow and change, yet I cannot fully grasp what happened.

As always, I have supported my Qurayshi, dominated the lesser gods of the Kaaba and fostered the growth of Makkah, keeping it the holy city of God. I was present when the Christian king of Aksum, Abraha, led an army against Makkah, and I played a part in its defence. I stopped the king's white elephant in its tracks by creating the image of a ravine in its animal mind. Of course it stopped; an elephant is no fool. I like elephants and would never hurt one. Then the army of the king was destroyed but not by me. I have wondered whether another power was at work that day; for while I engineered the violent thunderstorm that swept down upon them, I did not bring the hail of stones from the sky. They came from beyond, but from where exactly I cannot say.

I should explain that although I am very powerful, I have my limitations. For one thing, I seem to be tied to the land. I can rise up through the air, accelerating upward through cloud and dust storm into regions that burn bitterly cold, where the air is thin and even birds struggle to breathe, but I can rise no further. Where the pale blue sky becomes a deeper shade, cobalt, Persian or even indigo, my strength fails me, and I find myself falling back to earth. Well, the rocks fell from the heavens above me, streaking earthward in myriad tiny trails of fire. Only one in a hundred of these missiles reached the ground, most burning up like coals, yet even then they wrought havoc among the Christians of Aksum and San'a. Was there a god above me sending them, or are they something natural? It is like the black stone – that meteorite that fell so long ago and is now part of men's religion. Did that too come from a god above, or was it a natural event?

I suppose it matters only that it might be construed as evidence of a higher being, some entity more powerful than me – a true god, if you will, this one that Ahmad calls Allah perhaps. Well, if it comes to a contest between al-Ilah and Allah, I have some advantages. I have been around far longer, and my followers number in the thousands. Allah's worshippers are few – Ahmad (who now calls himself Muhammad), his wife Khadija, Ali, Abu Bekr, Abu Talib and a handful of young men. My only mistake has been to allow this new religion to develop so far. No further though. I will raise the tribes of Makkah against this self-styled Messenger of God and stamp out his fledgling religion.

When Ahmad was a boy, I paid him no attention. I cannot be expected to follow the lives of everyone, let alone an ordinary boy. I wish now I had, for if I had visited him in the desert as he tended his foster father's sheep, I could have put the lie to his tales of angels. Things dwell in the lonely places, I grant, but they are usually djinn that seek to harm people. I cannot know for certain, but I believe his men in white were creatures of the smokeless flame and breathed mischief into his ears. Certainly he was strange from then on. I find it hard to believe a true god would use such a half-hearted method.

One of my most ardent followers in those days was Abu Talib, and when he took his caravans south or north on trading expeditions, I sometimes accompanied him. On occasion, I took the form of a man, but more often I was a flame dancing unseen in the desert glare. On the expedition to Syria, I had come along as a man, interested in the insights a human form gives me on the habits of men. The boy, Ahmad, intrigued me too, and I was one of the men Abu Talib selected to watch over his nephew when he left the boy with Bahira the monk. That monk's mind was an experience, let me tell you. I dipped into it, and the things that man believed was almost beyond belief! His was an uncritical mind that tended to embrace the wonderful, colouring ordinary events with the miraculous and inventing details freely. I think the solitude of years had damaged his faculties.

I encouraged Abu Talib to leave the boy there, and though the man whose form I took was a stranger to him, I engendered complete trust in Abu Talib's mind. I wanted to be there when Bahira spoke to Ahmad. The boy's mind was already filled with a mish-mash of belief in angels and a god he called Allah, and I thought it would do him good to mix all this up with a warped view of Judaism and Christianity. Either the boy would throw everything over and come back to the pure worship of al-Ilah, or the contradictions and ambiguities would drive him mad. On the contrary, neither happened. The boy absorbed parts of both religious doctrines but fed them into his own framework and set his ideas fermenting for another thirty years.

Ahmad came back from Syria and settled into an ordinary life, and I lost interest in him. I busied myself elsewhere, cementing my position as the god of the Qurayshi, and I even allowed a degree of resurgence in idolatry. After all, none of those little gods could threaten me and having a choice of worship kept the population calmer. Makkah was divided peacefully between the idolators and my worshippers. Why should I care about a handful of Allah worshippers?

The followers of Ahmad/Muhammad grew in strength however, and his preaching started to disturb the peace. The Elders of Makkah decided on a compromise. They would allow Muhammad to preach his one god Allah as long as he would allow the existence of the other gods as intermediates between men and his rather distant Supreme One. I did not think it would work, but it seemed reasonable to try. I decided to help matters along. I donned the disguise of a man's body and went to listen to him preach in the streets. He talked for a long time, but eventually he came to a passage where his Allah is supposed to have told him,

He saw of the greatest signs of his Lord. Have you then considered al-Lat and al-Uzza and Manat, the third, the other?

I think he meant only to show how much greater his god was than the goddesses worshipped in Makkah. Muhammad hesitated for a moment, perhaps at having mentioned the names of the three goddesses.

I immediately asked in a persuasive voice, "These are exalted females aren't they? Will they intercede for us?"

Muhammad stuttered, seeking guidance from his memory and finding none. "Yes, they … they are exalted females, whose intercession is to be hoped for." He looked decidedly uncomfortable and prostrated himself to Allah. His listeners, mostly idolators, imagined him bowing down to the goddesses and were delighted, joining him in the prostration. A few minutes later, Muhammad got up and hurried away. My laughter followed him, for I had shattered his faith in front of everyone.

However, the next day he was back, claiming a vision from Allah through angel Jibreel while he slept. "There is no god but Allah," he declared. "The words spoken by me yesterday were not from God but were put into my mouth by Shaitan. I repudiate them." Interestingly, he looked straight at me as he said it, though he can surely have had no knowledge of my true nature.

In retrospect, I should have stamped out the young Muhammad and his worship of Allah in the formative stages. By dismissing him as unimportant, I allowed his ideas to gain a toehold in Makkah. Forty years later, I was faced with a battle for men's minds and hearts. I made another mistake by ridiculing him and trying to get him to compromise. Even then I could have won, but he was a slippery man. Well, it is not too late to remove him by force.

Chapter Eleven

Juda ibn Anwar was up before dawn. The day promised to be a hot one, and he wanted to practice his archery and sword skills, before the heat of the day grew too exhausting. He rode out into the desert and tied his stallion in the sparse shade of a solitary thorn tree before pacing out his archery range. A straw target lay on the ground from when he had last practiced here, so he set it upright and wedged it with a rock. He counted off fifty paces and strung his bow, flexing the springy wood and then sighted along his arrows, discarding one that had warped. Juda fitted an arrow and drew it back smoothly before releasing it immediately. The arrow flew in a flat trajectory and pierced the edge of the straw target, clattering to the ground on the far side.

"Fool," he muttered. "Better one arrow sighted properly than three released in haste."

Juda took more time over the second one, drawing back and holding the tension until even his iron muscles started to tremble. He eased up on the string and lowered the bow, nodding to himself. *A deep breath, hold and release slowly, then another*. The bow rose again smoothly, and the string came back. As the point of the arrow passed the target, he released and the arrow sped across the fifty paces and buried itself to the feathers in the packed straw of the target's centre.

"Better." He shot again, almost as slowly, and one after another, four arrows joined the first one. The arrow that had gone through the target had snapped off a flight feather, but the others were still in good condition, so Juda retrieved his shafts and paced off a hundred steps. Slowly, he prepared and again loosened his arrows at the target, sending all five into the middle of the straw bundle.

The range increased. At one hundred and thirty paces, Juda started to miss the target and stayed at that range, firing off his five arrows again and again, until he was hitting the straw centre four times out of five. He recovered the arrows for the last time and walked back to his horse, wiping the sweat from his eyes. His mouth felt dry and dusty, so he swilled water and spat it out twice before drinking. A movement caught his eye, and he squinted at the thin column of dust far out over the Makkan plain. *A horseman – riding fast and in this direction.* Juda unstrung his bow and packed it away before taking out his curved scimitar.

He moved away a dozen paces and examined the blade carefully for imperfections. The edge, ground sharp and gleaming brightly, displayed a flawless curve. Juda smiled and took a spread-legged stance, raising the sword above his head. Holding the pose for a dozen breaths, he leapt forward, the blade slashing through the air. Abruptly, he stopped, pivoted on his left foot and swung the sword sideways. Iron control terminated the slash and started it back in the opposite direction before stopping again and thrusting forward.

Again and again, he thrust and cut, blade high and blade low, his feet dancing as he went through the forms of death. He was aware of the approach of the horseman, saw him slow and stop his mount nearby and sit watching him in silence. The newcomer did not interrupt as Juda completed his exercise, ending spread-legged again with sword upraised. He waited until his breath slowed, before he lowered it and kissed the gleaming steel.

"Well, Basim, what brings you out here?" Juda did not look at the man but walked back to his horse and replaced the scimitar in its scabbard.

"News, Juda. From the north."

"Say then." Juda started checking his horse's saddle girth.

"The Qurayshi are defeated."

Juda stopped what he was doing and turned to face Basim. "What? That's not possible."

Basim shrugged. "I'm only telling you what I heard."

"Didn't Abu Jahl meet up with the caravan then? Did the Muslims attack them one by one like cowards?"

"They could tell you more in town. We're just getting the story of what happened, but there was disagreement between Abu Sufyan and Abu Jahl at Juhfah. The caravan was south of there already, and the Banu Adi and Banu Zuhrah came home at once."

"The fools. They went there to do a job, and they left with it half done."

"Be fair, Juda. Most went to safeguard the caravan …"

"Then they're fools, as I said. The caravan was part of it, but this was a good opportunity to draw the Muslims out of Yathrib and destroy them once and for all. What did the others do?"

"They continued on to the wells at Badr where Muhammad met them with three hundred men."

"Al-Ilah preserve us. Three hundred only? And how many were left of the Qurayshi?"

"A lot had left, but … well, six hundred at least."

"So with odds of two to one, we still lost."

"Not just lost, Juda. Many of our leaders were killed, including Abu Jahl."

"May the gods forgive them." Juda regarded Basim with a stony look. "What are the elders planning on doing next?"

"They didn't say, Juda, but they asked for you as one of the war leaders. Will you return with me now?"

Juda went in to the Council of the Elders, when they arrived back in Makkah. He listened in silence to the full description of the battle and the round of excuses following. The talk fell away into a general silence, and the representatives of the clans and tribes looked at one another.

At length, Abu Sufyan ibn Harb, the nominal head of the Qurayshi since the death of Abu Jahl, stood and addressed Juda. "Come then, Juda ibn Anwar, you're renowned as a fighter by the Banu Makhzum. How would you have won this battle?"

Juda stood and regarded the assembled heads of the clans and the surviving war leaders. "Who am I to say? I wasn't there. Perhaps it couldn't be won."

"What? We outnumbered them. Why didn't we win?"

Juda looked slowly from man to man, seeing anger in some faces, perplexity in others and even some fear. “I can think of good reasons,” he said quietly, “but they’re not ones you wish to hear.”

“Don’t treat us like children,” Abu Sufyan said angrily. “We’re all men. Tell us what you think.”

“Very well.” Juda scratched absently at his beard, while he considered his words. “First, it’s possible that their god, Allah, fought on their side.” Several of the men muttered, and Abu Sufyan glowered. “I mention this solely because the Muslims will claim it. Three hundred of their men routed six hundred of ours. Why did our gods not prevail? Perhaps because this Allah of theirs was stronger.”

“You tread a dangerous path,” Abu Sufyan growled. “Are you secretly a convert to this pernicious doctrine?”

“No. I’m Banu Makhzum and loyal to al-Ilah and the old gods. I speak of Allah only that you might see the danger into which this ill-considered battle has tipped us.”

“Ill-considered? Are you saying we should have let the Muslims capture my caravan unopposed?”

“Not at all, but the actions of the Makkan warriors were not well thought out and poorly executed.” A murmur of rage rose from his listeners, and Juda raised a hand. “You asked my opinion, so hear me out. The first fault is that you had no overall commander. Abu Sufyan was guarding the caravan, Abu Lahl led a contingent of men from Makkah, and several other nobles took groups from their own clans. Everybody wanted the glory, but nobody would let another man tell him what to do. When it came to the fighting, you had no plan. Every man fought as he wanted to, as if he alone fought against one enemy. And how did the Muslims fight? By your own admission, they had a plan. They fought under one commander – this Muhammad."

"You said first," Abu Sufyan said sourly. "What other faults were there?"

"The Makkans didn't want victory badly enough."

"That's nonsense," Abu Sufyan retorted. "Every noble who answered my call did so in the hopes of much booty."

"Exactly. Our men hoped for mere monetary gain, but the Muslims wanted victory for their god, Allah. They had more to lose and fought harder."

"I suppose you're saying you should have led us."

Juda shrugged. "I'm a trained war leader. Why not use my skills instead of leaving me at home?"

The Elders of Makkah thanked Juda with ill grace and dismissed him. Juda went back home, and later that day his father came to see him. Anwar ibn Mukhtar was a sub-chief of the Banu Makhzum clan of the Qurayshi and was a rich and influential man, one of the Elders. He grimaced at his son but refrained from saying anything until he had washed, given thanks for the meal his son's wife served him and eaten his fill. Juda waited patiently and served his father hot milk with honey after the meal with his own hand.

"You didn't make yourself any friends today," Anwar said, holding his cup out to be refilled.

"Couldn't you have sweetened your message a little? Like this milk?"

"Would you have me lie, father? We lost at Badr, because we fought like we always do – for personal honour and gain. That's good enough for warfare between tribes, but it's suicide against a disciplined army, no matter how small."

Anwar sipped and belched politely. "The Muslims don't have an army. They were lucky. Next time we'll beat them. You'll see."

"Forgive me father, but I must contradict you. The Muslims are disciplined. They share a common faith that offers them everything, even if they should be killed in battle."

Anwar looked away. "So do we. Our gods look after us."

Juda smiled grimly. "Yes, we pray for rain, or for a good harvest, or victory in war and sometimes it rains, we get a good crop once in a while and we win battles, but that is more likely because we train well. Our gods may or may not help us. But let me ask you this, father, what does the warrior who falls in battle gain from dying for our cause?"

"You're talking nonsense, my son. A man fights for his honour and that of his family, his clan, his tribe. If he dies, he knows he's done his duty."

"Yes, and he knows that he leaves his wife a widow and his sons fatherless. If he's really lucky, his wife will remarry and his sons will be raised as another man's. Do you know what a Muslim gains?"

"You're going to tell me, I'm sure."

"Paradise, father. A man who dies for Allah and the man they call his Messenger will live again in Paradise with food and drink and companionship for all eternity." Juda shook his head. "I don't believe it, but his followers do. And what about the man who refuses to embrace the Word of Allah? I'll tell you – he inherits eternal torment in a fiery hell. That's incredible incentive for the faithful and worrying for any man who even suspects Muhammad is what he says he is."

"Are you, too, a follower of this Muhammad?"

"Much of what he says is good and reasonable, but …" Juda shrugged. "I'm still a loyal follower of al-Ilah."

"I'm glad to hear it, my son. Don't stray from the paths of your ancestors."

"I can still see why the followers of Allah are so determined."

"You give them too much credit," Anwar said. "The Muslims are poor and most of them have kin here in Makkah. They won't risk the safety of their families."

"Yes, they're poor, but they're united. Muhammad tells them that family and tribe means nothing now and that the only loyalty they have is to their brothers in Allah. The worshippers of other gods won't harm their families, because they fear blood feuds among the tribes; but if you go against the Muslims, they'll think nothing of killing their own fathers or brothers or sons."

Anwar stirred uneasily. "Are they madmen? Remember your own brother, Tahir, was captured at Badr. Will they kill him too?"

"They've asked for a ransom, and I believe they need the money more than they need blood. Besides, they won't want a blood feud with the Banu Makhzum. Perhaps they are madmen, but holy madmen. You won't succeed against them using the normal rules of warfare. Give me command of a thousand horsemen, and I'll wipe them from Madinah."

"Madinah? Where's that? I thought they were in Yathrib."

"They've taken to calling Yathrib, Madinat al Nebi – The City of the Prophet."

"What? The Muslims are a small minority there. Do they have that much influence?"

"Father, with respect, you taught me that in warfare, good intelligence is like a sharpened blade. Even though I've been denied a place in the Makkan army, I've endeavoured to know what goes on amongst our enemy. Shortly after Muhammad arrived in Madinah, the chief of the Banu al-Najjar, Asad ibn Zurara, died, leaving no natural heir. Muhammad's great-grandmother was from that clan, and they accepted the Apostle as Asad's successor. The Muslims are now in a strong position in Madinah."

Anwar shook his head. "I had no idea."

"Will you speak for me to the Council of Elders, father? Persuade them to give me an army and I'll wipe out the Muslims."

"I know for a fact the Council won't sanction a slaughter. It's not the Arab way. We must seek a compromise."

Juda's fists clenched in rage, but he was careful not to show his father disrespect. "The Elders seek to compromise, but Muhammad won't. He seeks only our subjugation or destruction." He turned away and busied himself with the milk pot, pouring a small amount of the now tepid liquid into a cup and adding an ample amount of honey as sweetener. Juda sipped and when he felt himself calm, turned back to his father.

"We were defeated at Badr, where we lost many of our leaders. It's reasonable to suppose that their families will, sooner or later, want vengeance. Let me, I pray, accompany the next force to be sent against the Muslims."

Anwar considered his son's request. "I'll put forward your suggestions to the Council."

Anwar ibn Mukhtar kept his promise, but only the letter of it rather than the spirit. He put his son's suggestion forward but would not back it up with his own support or even mention his reasons. Consequently, Juda was not called on for any of the small, unsuccessful raids sent against the Muslims. Juda kept silent and continued his training, while the population of Makkah became increasingly frustrated with their inability to exact vengeance.

One of the other tribes raided Makkah, killing one man and driving off a large flock of goats. Juda was asked to take part in a retaliatory raid. Fifty men were recruited, but as each man had to supply his own camel, weapons and food, it was two weeks before they set out. During this time, the raid had been discussed and terms set with the local Badu to guide the raiding party across the desert.

Consequently, the element of surprise was lost and the tribe was in hiding. The Makkan warriors killed two men, burned a tent and captured a lame camel; small recompense for the initial raid. Juda complained loudly about the lack of security involved.

"How can we possibly succeed when we talk about the raid for weeks beforehand and ask the Badu to guide us, when the Badu are also paid by our enemies?"

"This is how it's always done," he was told.

Juda went on another two raids of neighbouring tribes but with as little success. The enemy invariably knew they were coming, and even when they did stand and fight, there was much posturing and name-calling but very little actual fighting. He thought about the logistics of a raid and discussed it with his friend Basim.

"I agree, Juda, but this is the way Arabs live. How can we change things? They hear about our plans just as we hear about theirs."

"What if they didn't hear we were coming? If we surprised them, we could kill many men and take all their camels and goats."

"That's what we try and do anyway. You can't stop people talking."

"No, but you can limit the spread of information," Juda said. "Look, one of the first things we do is talk to the local nomadic Badu and arrange for guides ..."

"We need guides."

"I'll get to that. Now the Badu are probably the same ones that the enemy tribes use as guides, and inevitably, somebody talks. So, we don't approach the Badu. We don't hire guides. We don't shout it out to everyone that we're going on a raid."

"But we need guides."

"No, we don't. Not for short distances. I could guide a raiding party to any oasis within a week's ride of here. Another point – we ask for volunteers and then wait for days or weeks while everyone discusses it and gathers their weapons and food. Meantime, anyone passing through Makkah knows exactly what we plan to do. What if we told a few men – say twenty – to get ready but didn't tell them where we were going until after we left?"

"They'd never agree to go. Would you? You'd want to know."

"Well, we've got to do something. We spend time and money on a raid and for what? A handful of goats or a camel or two."

"It's how we Arabs have always done it."

"Then it's time for a change."

A week later, Juda quietly gathered together a dozen of his father's camels and arranged for them to be grazed near a hill an hour's ride west of Makkah. In the panniers, he secreted food and water together with extra bows and arrows, swords and lances. When he was certain that there was no talk in the town about his preparations, he personally asked his closest friends to join him for archery practice and wrestling. A dozen accepted, and they openly rode westward, singing and laughing.

At the arranged grazing site, Juda told his friends what his true intentions were and offered them the opportunity of great sport and profit against the Thaqif.

"When do we go?" Arfan asked.

"Right now."

"But we have no weapons, only our bows," Nefu said.

"I've brought weapons for everyone."

"And food?" Da'ud asked.

"Yes."

"Water?" Da'ud persisted.

"Yes."

"What about our fathers?" Ikrimah asked. "We should tell them."

"If you want to tell them, go ahead, but we won't be here when you return."

"We'll need guides," Arfan said.

"I'm your guide."

Basim laughed. "So this is what you meant. I'll go with you willingly, Juda ibn Anwar."

Some of the other young men were still a bit diffident, but they agreed to go along with Juda's plan as long as they had the option of pulling out if things went badly. Juda smiled and agreed.

The journey to the territory of the Thaqif took two days, and they achieved total surprise. The tribesmen were tending their herds without a thought of attack as Juda led his companions in a charge. They left six Thaqif men dead and drove off a herd of thirty camels, together with harness and blankets. A joyful party entered Makkah a few days later, the young men singing the praises of their warleader.

The successful raid did not change the views of the leaders of Makkah. They stared enviously at the captured camels and harness but refused to let Juda lead another raid against the tribes.

"You go against custom," Abu Sufyan said. "Do as your ancestors did and the gods will smile on us."

"As they did at Badr?" Juda muttered, but he bowed his head in submission to his elders.

A year after the defeat at Badr, Abu Sufyan raised an army to attack Madinah. The command of the cavalry, some two hundred strong, was offered to Ikrimah ibn Abi Jahl. Juda was furious he had been passed over for command and voiced his anger to his father.

"This is a mortal insult. I'll challenge Abu Sufyan."

"Don't be a fool, my son. This is only a means of chastising you for your ill-considered raid on the Thaqif. You're not banned from the army, only from command."

"So you'd have me fight as a common foot-soldier? I'd rather stay home."

Anwar shrugged. "You're a man and must make up your own mind. But think on this – your friend Ikrimah is named a cavalry commander. Go with him as one of his riders and be seen as a willing instrument of our victory over the Muslims."

Juda accepted his father's advice, and Ikrimah welcomed him as his unofficial deputy. The army marched north and in an attempt to achieve a measure of surprise, avoided the main caravan route, skirting the hills and bypassing the town to arrive at the Hill of Uhud just to the north.

The Quryashi formed up in front of the Muslims, their banners flying, and their women, who had accompanied the army, as was the custom of the time, started calling out, taunting the enemy, singing and reciting poetry to fan the flames of courage in their own men.

"Hear then the Daughters of Quraysh and know that we offer kisses to our brave men. Our beds are scented with rose and musk and to them shall come the victors. Make sure you are among them, else our love shall be for braver men."

Talha ibn Abdul Uzza stepped out between the two armies and challenged the Muslims. Ali ibn Abu Talib immediately ran out and swiftly slew him.

"Allahu akbar," shouted the Muslims. "God is most Great."

Talha's brother Othman stepped out and repeated the challenge, whereupon Hamza ibn Shaiba, the Prophet's uncle, strode out and killed him. Again the Muslims called out praise to Allah. Then with a shout of triumph, the small Muslim force rushed forward and fell upon their enemies, dealing them savage blows. The Makkan cavalry, under the command of Ikrimah and Juda on the right flank and Basim on the left, maintained their position, having received no orders to attack.

"We should attack anyway," Juda urged. "Our leaders just want to deny us the glory."

"Maybe," Ikrimah agreed. "But do you see their archers on the hill? If we attack, we'll be cut to pieces. Wait in patience, my friend. Our time will come."

It came. Such was the zeal and fury of the attacking Muslim army that it burst through the Qurayshi line and descended on the Makkan camp. Many men immediately ceased fighting and started to search the baggage. The archers saw their fellow Muslims break through the lines and start plundering the enemy camp. Fearful they would miss out on booty following another swift God-given victory, they broke ranks and ran to join in the looting.

"Now we have them," Juda exulted. Ikrimah nodded and swung the horsemen around the lines, joining up with Basim's men, and together the cavalry drove into the rear of the disorganised Muslims, hacking and slashing as the horses stumbled over the rocky lower slopes of the hill.

Juda used his lance at first, but it broke as he impaled his second victim. He drew his curved scimitar and leaned low in the saddle, slashing at the running men, spraying blood over his horse and covering his arm and face. He grinned through the mask of blood and spurred his mount onward, heading for the banner of the Prophet.

The Prophet's standard bearer was slain, and the banner of Islam fell. A cry went up that Muhammad was dead. Many Muslims panicked and ran for cover on rocky Uhud. Muhammad himself was struck by a stone and wounded, but his followers rallied around him, fending off the determined attacks of Juda and Basim. They carried the Prophet unconscious from the field, leaving it in the hands of the men from Makkah.

The Qurayshi stripped the dead of their armour and began to saddle their camels and horses, preparing to return to Makkah. They shouted and laughed, rejoicing in their victory. Juda and Ikrimah rode up with their men and found Abu Sufyan about to depart.

"Complete victory is within our grasp," Juda declared. "Take up the sword once more."

Abu Sufyan shook his head. "It's too dangerous."

Juda snorted derisively. "We've shattered the Muslim army. We should follow up our efforts and remove the threat once and for all."

"If they're defeated, they'll trouble us no more," Abu Sufyan replied. "Besides, we're not equipped for a siege should they retreat inside the town."

Juda and Ikrimah watched the Qurayshi men depart, and followed reluctantly, knowing they were not strong enough to capture Madinah by themselves.

"At least Muhammad's influence will fade after this defeat," Ikrimah said. "His reputation cannot survive being let down by his god."

"I wouldn't be too sure," Juda replied. "His men love him."

Juda was right. The reputation of the Prophet did not suffer by his defeat, as it was perceived he had, as a mere man, listened to the young hotheads rather than as a Prophet to the Word of Allah. "If

God had spoken to him," people said, "he would have won, no matter the odds."

The next year, Muslims and Makkans once more met at Badr, but this time there was no fighting. The two armies confronted one another, but each occupied a strong position and would not be enticed into battle. The coastal tribes watched both sides and came away from the inconclusive meeting more impressed with Muhammad than with Abu Sufyan.

The Muslims of Madinah were farmers for the most part and traders only when an opportunity arose. Consequently, the wars left them little affected. The Qurayshi, however, lived by trading with Yemen and Syria, and the stranglehold the followers of the Prophet held over the trade routes crippled the economy of Makkah. They still desired the overthrow of Islam but increasingly could not see how this was to be accomplished. Juda knew that his words would never be accepted by Abu Sufyan, so he refused to be concerned with the Madinan problem and spent his time leading raids on the inland tribes, well away from the followers of Islam. Basim joined him in this pastime, though Ikrimah grew closer to Abu Sufyan, striving for a position of authority within the Makkan forces.

A year or two later, Muhammad led his followers on the Umrah, the small pilgrimage to Makkah. As was the custom for religious festivals and pilgrimages, they came armed with only short swords or daggers and laden with animals for the sacrifice, hoping that the Qurayshi would allow unarmed pilgrims into the town. Instead, the

Qurayshi mobilised an army and met the Muslim group some distance from Makkah and drew up across the route to the holy city. Despite outnumbering the almost unarmed pilgrims, they were painfully aware of the fighting prowess of the Muslims, so they did not attack.

Muhammad also did not want to shed blood while engaged in his holy purpose, so he sent envoys to the Qurayshi asking for talks.

"We haven't come to wage war but to perform the Umrah," Muhammad said. "I know the war has weakened the Qurayshi, so, if you wish, I'll conclude a truce with you. You'll vow not to interfere when I preach to the unbelievers. If I have a victory over the unbelievers, the Qurayshi may choose to embrace Islam. If you don't accept the truce, then we fight and Allah will definitely make us victorious."

"You cannot think of complying with this man's demands," Juda said to Abu Sufyan as the commanders discussed Muhammad's words. "We outnumber them, and they are poorly armed, besides being weighed down with sacrificial animals. Fall on them and destroy them."

Basim added his support. "It's our best opportunity. If you won't do it, only say the word and Juda and I will lead our cavalry to victory."

Ikrimah stood up and denounced his former friends. "Their words are folly. Is this how peaceable men should act? I say, let the Muslims worship in Makkah. They gain strength when we oppose them, so let's weaken them with kindness."

The Qurayshi grumbled at the proposed terms of the treaty and argued both for and against Juda and Basim on the one hand and Abu Sufyan and Ikrimah on the other. In the end, they agreed that Muhammad could enter Makkah but not that year, because of the ill feeling between the two groups. Interpreting this as a sign of weakness by their leaders, many ordinary men within Makkah started to think Islam must indeed be the True Faith.

"How else can it grow in strength whether the followers of the Prophet win or lose? Surely the power of their Allah is stronger than the power of al-Ilah."

Muhammad and his followers turned back from Makkah, having secured the right to return the following year to complete the Umrah. Muhammad declared it a victory and said he had a revelation from God where Allah told him, "Truly we have granted you a manifest victory."

The pilgrimage took place the next year, and Muslims had access to Makkah once more. They made use of it to preach to their unbelieving kinfolk. His friend, Walid, who had embraced Islam after being captured at Badr, approached Juda.

"Juda, my friend, examine your heart. Don't you see that the Apostle of God is Allah's chosen Messenger and has come to unite the tribes in true worship? Join us and your reward will be great."

Juda's response was noncommittal, but he spent time thinking about this new religion and the way in which it was inexorably growing. He discussed it with his friend Basim, revealing his own brother

Tahir was also a Muslim, having converted after Badr.

"Speak with him," Basim said.

So Juda wrote to his brother and invited him to Makkah.

The brothers embraced and retired to an inner room. "You're looking well, brother," Juda said. "Your new lifestyle agrees with you." He offered Tahir some khat leaves but was refused on the grounds that the leaf was a drug.

"Allah has blessed me manyfold," Tahir went on. "You, however, look burdened with cares, if I may say so."

Juda chewed his khat, a feeling of euphoria creeping over him. "I'm well but strangely discontent. It's almost as if history is passing me by."

"The future lies with Islam, brother. Surely you can see that."

Juda nodded slowly, welcoming his drug-induced clarity of mind. "I've thought about this a lot in the last two years, and I've discussed it with my good friend, Basim. Traditionally, we've worshipped many gods, but the Qurayshi have tended toward al-Ilah. Is this god not just another name for your Allah?"

"Categorically no! Al-Ilah of the Qurayshi is a demon, a djinni and will burn in hell for all eternity along with his followers. Embrace the True God, Allah, and hearken to the words of his Prophet Muhammad."

"Your faith is condemnatory. Surely a good man of another faith can still attain Paradise?"

"No. Only by making the Shahadah, the Declaration of Faith, may he be saved."

"Remind me, brother. What is this declaration?"

"There is no god but Allah, and Muhammad is the Messenger of Allah."

Juda considered the words. "It's no great thing, it seems. If Muhammad's god is Allah, then it's reasonable to suppose he must be the Messenger of his god. As for Allah being the One God, I am starting to think that may be the case. Muhammad is certainly blessed by his God."

"Then make the Declaration, my brother, and enter into the peace of Islam."

"You make it sound easy, yet I'm known as an enemy of Islam. I've taken up arms against Muhammad and have slain his followers."

"The Prophet doesn't hold that against you."

"You sound very sure."

Tahir smiled. "I've talked with the Prophet personally on this very subject. He said a man like you wouldn't be able to keep away from Islam very long."

"He said that?"

"His very words. Accompany me back to Madinah and make your Declaration before the Prophet. Your friends Basim and Ikrimah too, if they are of like mind, for Muhammad values them highly."

"I must think about this, brother. Our father is resigned to losing you, but I don't wish to cause him pain by abandoning him also. Then there is

Abu Sufyan. He hates Muslims and will not willingly let us go."

"As you will, but don't delay too long. No man knows when he'll be called before God, and I would sorrow to see you burn in hell for eternity when a few words spoken from the heart would admit you to Paradise." Tahir rose and took leave of his brother, returning to Madinah that same day.

Juda thought on his brother's words for the rest of that day and examined his heart and innermost thoughts. He went in to his father and broached the subject to him.

"A man must make his own way in the world," said the chief of Banu Makhzum. "Do as you see fit."

"Do I have your blessing, father?"

Anwar ibn Mukhtar put his gnarled hands on his eldest son's shoulders and peered into his eyes. "You have it, my son."

Juda took his leave and went out into the early evening cool of the city. He walked the streets with Basim for a time, and they prayed quietly outside the Kaaba, addressing both Allah and al-Ilah but were answered by neither. Then they went round to the house of their former friend, Ikrimah ibn Abi-Jahl, who had shared the cavalry command with them at the battle of Uhud.

"We're considering going to Madinah and becoming Muslims," Juda told Ikrimah. "Will you come with us or at least give us your advice?"

"By all the gods, have you both taken leave of your senses? You fought against them and without a doubt incurred blood debt. Do you think the next of kin of those you slew will just forget it? You're dead men."

"My brother says we would be welcomed there …"

"He's biased."

"And the Prophet has added his welcome."

"I wish you wouldn't call him the Prophet," Ikrimah grumbled. "He's just a troublemaker who has forsaken the ways of his people."

"I think he's a lot more than that. Come, my friend, think on it. Whether he wins or loses a battle, his strength grows. His people are united across family, clan and tribe and willing to die for him. That speaks of a lot more than just being a troublemaker."

"He divides families. Even your family is split."

"There's no enmity. My father and brother still love each other."

"Perhaps, but not all families are so fortunate. Some Muslims have killed their own kin, and Makkans have killed Muslims. You cannot tell me this division is a good thing."

Juda interrupted. "You believe in the old gods, don't you? Have they ever commanded you to do something?"

Ikrimah raised his eyebrows in surprise. "Of course."

"In speech? What did they say?"

"Well, of course not in words, but they've made their wishes known in the flight of birds, the fall of the arrow sticks …"

"I know, my friend, I've experienced that too, and more, but that's all open to interpretation. What would you do if a god – any god – spoke to you in clear words that you didn't have to interpret? Would you obey him?"

"Of course. What are you saying?"

"Allah talks to Muhammad in clear words, we're told. The Muslims are left in no doubt as to the will of God."

Ikrimah laughed. "That's just Muhammad saying what he wants. If you don't believe me, look at the affair of Zaid ibn Haritha and his wife Zainab bint Jahash."

"Zainab? One of the Prophet's wives?"

"His seventh. While we're on the subject, why are Muslims allowed only four wives, but Muhammad has at least nine or ten?"

Juda grimaced. "Presumably, Allah has allowed him a dispensation ..."

"Exactly. And who tells us Allah's decision? The man who benefits by it. Do you remember what his young wife, Aisha, said? She said, 'Your Lord certainly seems anxious to gratify your desires.'"

"I'm not sure ten wives is exactly a benefit," Juda murmured.

"You know what I mean. Back to Zaid. Remember he was a slave adopted by Muhammad? Well, he marries Muhammad's cousin, Zainab, and a little later, Muhammad sees how attractive she is and lusts after her. What does Zaid do? He divorces his wife, so his stepfather can marry her. But Zainab is pious and refuses to marry Muhammad, so ... what happens? Yes, Muhammad has a revelation from God. Suddenly, it's God's will that they marry, so what else can she do? She has to obey her god."

"But if it really was a command from Allah …"

"Then of course, they'd have to obey. I can see that, my friend, but you must admit it's very convenient. Whatever Muhammad wants, his god is only too happy to grant. And who is it who reveals God's wishes? Muhammad. It's just too convenient and self-serving."

"Yet if he is truly a Messenger of God …"

Ikrimah shook his head. "Your heads have been turned by foolish tales of wonders, my friends. Give up this mad scheme of yours."

Juda and Basim rose to take their leave. "We cannot. We must follow the dictates of our hearts and our heads. We shall go to Madinah and see if Muhammad will accept our swords."

"Know that if hereafter I meet you in battle, one of us will die," Ikrimah said solemnly.

"As God wants," Juda replied.

Juda saddled his horse, took his weapons in hand and left Makkah that night. Basim accompanied him. The guards on patrol saw them leave and notified Abu Sufyan, who in turn summoned first Anwar ibn Mukhtar and then Ikrimah ibn Abi Jahl to give account for the men riding toward Madinah. Juda's father hedged, avoiding a straight answer, and asked what business it was of Abu Sufyan.

Ikrimah spoke plainly. "Juda and Basim ride to Madinah with the express purpose of converting to the faith of Muhammad."

"They are traitors," Abu Sufyan cried. "I'll have them captured and returned to Makkah where they'll stand trial for their lives. They blaspheme against the gods of their forefathers."

Ikrimah, though a young man, stood in defiance of the Qurayshi leader. "Oh Abu Sufyan, guard your tongue, I beseech you. Juda ibn Anwar and Basim ibn al-Walid are misguided, I admit, but they are free to follow whatever religion they choose. If you oppose them, you oppose me also, and I'll ride with them to Madinah."

Abu Sufyan grumbled about the disrespect young men showed for their elders, but he took no action.

The night was cloudy with an almost full moon intermittently showing the road to Madinah as it wound through the lava fields and low hills. Juda rode with only one eye on the road and one ear on the night sounds as he discussed with Basim the changes that had come over their lives. The faint clink of a metal harness went almost unnoticed, and it was only the movement in the shadows that brought him fully alert.

You fool. What will you tell your ancestors when you appear before them, killed while daydreaming? Juda drew his sword and spurred his horse toward the waiting men, Basim only a heartbeat behind him. Just as they reached the riders, the moon lit up the scene and revealed two older men with their swords sheathed. Juda pulled his horse to a halt and challenged them.

"Who are you to ambush peaceable travellers? Speak now before we cut you down."

"Peace be with you, Juda ibn Anwar," said a gravelly voice. "And you, Basim ibn al-Walid. It is I, Amr ibn al-Aasi of the Banu Sahm. Don't you recognise me from the cavalry charge at Uhud? My companion is Othman ibn Talha, Custodian of the Keys of the Kaaba."

Juda controlled his nervous horse as it stamped and circled. He peered closely at the two men in the moonlight and nodded his acceptance, sheathing his sword. "What are you doing out here unaccompanied by your followers?"

"We could ask you the same thing," Amr said. "But we heard that you journey to Muhammad to declare for him. We would join you."

"You wish to make the Declaration of Faith?" Juda asked. "Then we welcome you as future brothers in Allah."

The four men made their way to Madinah together and both parties, Muslims and unbelievers, were impressed that such notable persons had made the Declaration.

***

Muhammad, having achieved a treaty of peace with Makkah and attracted four such famous men, started to look further afield for converts. He sent an envoy to the Banu Ghassan of Syria, asking the chieftain to embrace Islam. The chief accepted him favourably, but the envoy was accosted and killed by a minor Ghassanid chieftain on his return. Envoys were widely regarded as sacred persons by the Arabs, so this breach of custom was viewed with horror. Muhammad immediately organised an expedition to punish the Banu Ghassan. Three thousand men were raised, and the Prophet's adopted son, Zaid ibn Haritha, placed in command. Under him were Jaafar ibn Abi Talib, the brother of Ali, and Abdulla ibn Rawaha. Juda and Basim accompanied the force but held no positions of authority.

The army moved north out of Madinah, and for the first day, the prophet accompanied them. After emotional farewells, Muhammad turned back and the army set off through the sandy wastes to Syria. As in almost every raid that took place, security was lax and the enemy knew of their approach long before they reached Banu Ghassan lands. The enemy chieftain mobilised the local tribes and gathered an army to oppose the Muslims at the town of Maab.

Muslims boasted they faced a hundred thousand or more unbelievers, but the truth was barely a twentieth of that number could be supported by that inhospitable land. Even this smaller force outnumbered the Muslims, and they halted for two days wondering what to do. Many were in favour of sending a message back to Muhammad and asking him for a course of action, but that would have entailed a delay of over a month. Instead, Abdulla ibn Rawaha fired up the spirits of the Muslims.

"Oh my brothers, you came out to seek martyrdom by fighting against the enemies of Allah and His Prophet, but now you seem afraid. We don't face the enemy armed only with our own strength but with that of God Himself. There are only two possible outcomes – total victory or martyrdom – and both are equally glorious." The Muslims cheered and voted for an immediate attack.

They met the enemy on a mountain ridge to the east, but as there was not enough room to fully engage the enemy, the Muslims withdrew to the village of Mota that sits upon a small plain. As was usual, the two forces drew up in ranks opposite one another, and as nobody seemed inclined to challenge the enemy in single combat, the Muslim leader, Zaid ibn Haritha, decided to set an example of heroism.

"Why do we delay? The sooner we die for Allah and the Prophet, the sooner we'll be in Paradise." He took up the white war banner, which the Prophet had given him and charged into the enemy. Their spears swiftly killed him.

Jaafar, as second in command, snatched up the fallen banner and raised it aloft crying out, "Paradise, Muslims. Remember Paradise." The enemy closed around him, and after a bitter struggle in which he received many wounds, he fell dead.

Abdulla, the third leader, hesitated and then, ashamed of his indecision, raised the banner again and ran into the midst of the fighting. Within minutes, he too was dead. The Muslims, now leaderless, were driven back in disorder.

Juda and Basim fought in the ranks, taking direction from the junior officers. Juda was wounded with a cut to his chest. He lost a lot of blood and retired to have his wound bound up. Basim fought on and when he saw the Muslim lines disintegrate, knew he had to do something. He called in a loud voice for the white war banner, now speckled and streaked with martyr's blood and lofted it, summoning the men to rally round it. As the men formed up, he led them away slowly, fighting continuously until they left the field of battle. So intense was the fighting that Basim broke sword after sword, snatching up a new one from the fallen as blades shattered in his hand.

The Muslims camped for the night, but their position was precarious as the Ghassanid forces were only a short distance away and more footsoldiers were arriving every hour. Basim knew the next day would prove decisive, and unless help came from somewhere, the Muslim force was doomed. He had many campfires built and under cover of darkness, ordered his cavalry to withdraw behind a hill. Then as day broke, they galloped out under fresh banners, making as much noise and raising as much dust as possible to join the encampment. The Ghassanids believed reinforcements had arrived and withdrew, allowing the Muslims to safely retreat.

The Muslim forces returned to Madinah, but news of their defeat preceded them. People lined the road and threw dirt at them, yelling, "Cowards! Runaways! You are the army of God, yet you fled." Juda felt his face burning with shame despite his bloodied bandages, but he bore the insults bravely, looking with envious eyes at his friend Basim who rode a fresh horse at the head of the army. The people called for the army to be punished for running away, but Muhammad spoke up in their defence.

"These men are not runaways, but have judiciously withdrawn so that, Allah willing, they might fight again another day." The people still grumbled though, so he had a vision that night. "I saw the martyrs of Mota in Paradise, reclining on couches of gold and eating of wholesome fruit and drinking pure water from the fountains of Heaven. Zaid ibn Haritha was there, as was Abdulla ibn Rawaha, and Jaafar the son of Abu Talib was an angel with red wings stained by his martyr's blood." All muttering ceased at this obvious sign of Allah's pleasure at the noble sacrifice of the Muslim fallen, and Muhammad went on to honour one more warrior.

"Our beloved Basim ibn al-Walid broke several blades in the service of Allah at Mota. Henceforth, he shall be called *Saifullah*, Sword of Allah."

Juda ground his teeth when he heard this. "It should've been me. If I hadn't been wounded in Muhammad's service, I would've rallied the army and mine would now be the honour." He started to avoid Basim, being eaten up with envy.

The next year, Muhammad decided it was time to return to Makkah, the Holy City, and take possession of it. He led an army of ten thousand south to Dhu Towa just outside the city, where he divided his men into four columns, each to enter the city by a different route. Abu Sufyan had come to meet Muhammad and was now sent ahead to reassure the people.

"Stay in your houses," said the old Qurayshi chief. "Or remain in the courtyard of the Kaaba and no harm will come to you. The Muslims are an unstoppable force, and we must bow to the will of God."

The four columns now advanced on Makkah, and three of them entered the city unopposed. The fourth was under the command of the Sword of Allah, and his old friend, Ikrimah, faced him, leading a group of loyalists against the invading Muslims. Basim threw his cavalry forward in a charge and routed Ikrimah and his followers, killing twelve of them.

Basim spoke to the bodies on the ground. "He who opposes Allah and His Messenger invites death." Juda was present and shook his head at his former friend's coldness toward men they both knew.

Muhammad's men occupied Makkah and arrested men whose names were on a list the Prophet had made of the enemies of Islam. Ikrimah was on that list, and he fled for his life.

The apostle of God now rode into the city on his camel and made the seven ritual circuits of the Kaaba, touching the black stone with his stick every time he passed it. He then performed the midday prayers in the courtyard and called upon Othman ibn Talha, the Custodian of the Keys of the Kaaba to unlock the small cubical building. The Prophet entered and found paintings and idols of gods and people inside. He ordered all the idols destroyed and all the paintings erased, except those depicting the Prophet Jesus and his mother Mary.

Now that Makkah was cleansed of idolatry and had become a Muslim city, Muhammad set about urging surrounding tribes to do the same. He sent Basim to the Banu Jadheema clan of Banu Kinana, unaware that many years before, Basim's uncle had been killed by the Banu Jadheema and there was blood-feud between them. The Sword of Allah was under orders to avoid bloodshed, yet when he had disarmed the clan, he had a number of them bound and ordered them to be beheaded.

"You cannot do this, Basim," Juda said in a low voice. "These men surrendered peaceably and have entered into the protection of Islam."

"Don't tell me what to do, Juda ibn Anwar. I command here, and these men have dishonoured my family. For that they must die."

The Apostle was horrified when he heard the news and made a public statement in the courtyard of the Kaaba, "Before God, I am innocent of these deeds of Basim." He dispatched Ali with a large sum of money to pay blood money for any who had been killed.

The incident did not discourage the Prophet from sending Basim on other missions, for he recognised the iron will and steadfastness of the Sword of Allah. Basim rode northeast to Nakhla, to the Banu Sulaim, with the intention of destroying the shrine of the goddess Al-Uzza. The custodian of the shrine heard about the approach of the Muslims and feared for his life. He hung a sword about the neck of the idol and urged her to defend herself while he fled to a nearby hill. Basim entered the shrine and hacked the idol to pieces in a fury.

Juda accompanied Basim but was conscious fate had passed him by. Basim advanced in Islam, whereas Juda merely watched. He had no hope now of supplanting his former friend but still hoped to temper his excesses.

Muhammad continued to use Basim, appointing him one of his commanders on the campaign against the Hawazin. For the first time, the Muslims outnumbered the enemy; yet for a time, it looked as if the followers of the Prophet would be swept away by the fierce fighters of the Hawazin. Superior numbers won the day, however, and Muhammad made it plain that angelic forces had once more aided the faithful.

Juda continued to watch over Basim, but increasingly became just another fighter in his command. He ceased to have any effect on Basim, and found it very hard to save any lives, even those of women and children, or ameliorate his former friend's savage violence. Basim could never carry out an assignment without killing someone. His faith burned fiercely and he would accept no excuses or pleadings from those he was sent against.

The Prophet used him for difficult and dangerous tasks where an iron will and a granite heart were needed. He recognised in the years ahead, when the message of Islam spread out to bring all peoples to a worship of the True Faith of Allah, strong commanders would be needed, ones who would not shirk this duty and who would not flinch from the task. The Apostle of God saw in Basim ibn al-Walid a commander who would instill fear in the hearts of the enemies of Islam, but recognised Juda ibn Anwar was not such a man.

Chapter Twelve

So close. I came so very close to stamping out the fledgling religion of Muhammad, but I miscalculated. My first mistake was that I misjudged the fanaticism of the man who calls himself the Messenger of God and the strange effect he had on people; and the second was that I relied on humans to do my work. Never rely on humans; they are weak and self-centered. Use them and discard them by all means, but if you rely on them, they will let you down every time.

When Muhammad fled Makkah, I thought I would be able to tighten my grip on the polytheists and other-theists that stayed behind. After all, I have been managing quite nicely so far. I do not begrudge people a belief in the minor gods of the Kaaba as long as they recognise that I, al-Ilah, reign supreme. What I could not stand was that someone should introduce a new god like this Allah and then have the temerity to say he was the only god. What do they think I have been doing these last few thousand years? Al-Ilah, the god of the smokeless green-tinged blue flame, has made a name for himself and is known, loved and worshipped by thousands. Well, maybe not loved but certainly respected.

Muhammad claims Allah speaks to him through angel Jibreel – another being I have not encountered in desert or city – but I speak to my chosen ones direct without intermediaries. In every generation, I pick one or two men I favour with my special attention, speaking to them, advising them and answering their prayers. Ikrimah ibn Abi Jahl was one of them. This young man was easily moulded as his early life was governed by two character flaws. The first was his desperate need to gain the approval of his father and the second was his jealousy of his kinsman Juda ibn Anwar. Both stemmed from his insecurity. Sometimes I can use flaws like this, and I often visited Ikrimah, though he was never aware of it. He prayed to me, and I spoke to him, but he never knew I was inside him controlling him.

The father, Abi Jahl, was a cracked vessel. Tyrannical to his family, he crushed the spirit of the young Ikrimah. Abi Jahl was a ruthless man and ever mindful of his position within Makkan society. He ridiculed the young Muhammad and later threatened his safety so much the man fled. If he had been less antagonistic, the Allah worshipper may have remained in Makkah and his god may never have amounted to much. I blame myself for that. You are surprised? I can recognise my faults as well as the next god. I was so sure that Muhammad's delusions were those of a half-witted shepherd boy from the desert who sees mirages and believes them to be real. I had never come across Allah or one of his angels, so naturally I did not believe they existed. Is that so hard to understand? I am a being of the flame, and I am aware of many others like me, though weaker. These other flames are djinn, though they pretend to be gods. I was a djinni, but now I am a god. This Allah, if he exists, must surely be a djinni too, pretending to be a god, but I have never found him.

So Muhammad fled from Makkah and gathered supporters in nearby Yathrib. I spoke to Ikrimah. He whispered to his fatherm and they set out to destroy Muhammad at Badr. The result was unexpected, but there were so many leaders there, no one of them was going to allow himself to be ordered by another and so lose standing in front of everyone. A divided leadership led to a shattered army. Still, some good came of it, as the Makkan leadership became consolidated under Abu Sufyan. Some success followed but still the power of the Muslims grew. I put the idea of assassination in Ikrimah's mind, but the leaders of Makkah prevaricated and the opportunity was lost. Interestingly, Muhammad used assassination to rid himself of troublesome enemies, so I wonder if Allah whispered in his ear as I did in Ikrimah's.

I left Ikrimah and followed Juda and Basim from Makkah to Madinah, and at the battle of Mota, I took over Basim's will, entering him and controlling him, lending him a djinni's love of blood. He became a violent man without honour, and I thought by this to make people loathe and shun Muslims. It did not work as Muhammad threw Basim against his worst enemies, utilising his djinni-given violence.

You may ask why I do not just possess Muhammad and subvert his religion from within. It pains me to admit it, but I cannot. For some reason, his mind is impenetrable, and I am forced to work through those around him. I even tried to kill him once, possessing a man in his entourage and attacking him with a dagger. Needless to say, my attempt was unsuccessful, and I found my dagger turned against me.

For a time, I thought it might be possible to destroy Islam, but that passed by the time Muhammad conquered Makkah. Then I thought I could just wait until the man died. I reasoned that any set of beliefs that relied so heavily on personal divine revelation must surely founder with the death of the Messenger. After all, Allah spoke to no other Muslim, only Muhammad. Well, that idea crumbled too. Abu Bakr succeeded Muhammad, and Umar succeeded him in turn. Certainly there was a falling away of the weaker elements and of those that resented Muhammad's power, but the new faith proved remarkably resilient. By the time Umar took the reins of power, I knew I could no longer hope to conquer Allah.

I still had not seen him, you understand, and I did not know whether he really existed as a god or djinni or was just something Muhammad's mind had dreamed up. I had the same problem with that other solitary god of the Jews and Christians. Was Yahweh a real god or just a djinni? Was he the same as Allah? Or are all gods imaginary? Except me, of course, and that rag-tag collection of godlings that Muhammad drove wailing out of the Kaaba into the desert. There are others too, I think, far to the east and to the northwest, for I sometimes feel a vibration, a quiver, which touches my flame as nothing physical can do. I feel it faintly when one of the djinn is close by, so for me to feel it across the gulf that separates Arabia from India or Europe must mean some powerful beings reside there. One day I shall have to go and see, test their strength, but not yet. There are more important things to do.

It pains me to admit it, but I have taken one of Muhammad's ideas as my own. Before this Messenger came along, Arabs believed in many gods but thought little about what happened after death. If they considered the matter at all, they imagined themselves somehow reunited with their ancestors. Muhammad introduced the idea of a Paradise, green and wet with bubbling fountains, plentiful food and soft breezes – everything their harsh desert life is not. Virgins await them there, especially if they die at the hands of unbelievers, and I have seen the effect these promises can make on men. The Muslims do not fear to die with such a reward awaiting them. They will perform any unpleasant task; kill even close kin with alacrity, if they think Paradise awaits them as a result.

I now promise my followers the same thing and embroider it when necessary. They obey willingly and will do almost anything for me. Is there really a Paradise? I do not know. I have never seen one, unless you mean the time long ago when men were so sparse on the earth that they lived in relative harmony with the animals. Does a man go to Paradise when he dies? I doubt it. The life force of a man flickers weakly at best, not like the strong motionless flame of djinn. I have caused men to die, many times, but I have never seen his weak flame continue past the death of his body. I believe the flame dies along with the physical part, and I see no reason to support the idea that Muslim, Jew or Christian is any different. Djinn are the only ones that can live without a body, and we have no need of women, virgins or otherwise, or of verdant fields and cool springs.

I can see now the Muslims are going to win – at least for now. The heirs of Muhammad will insist on faith in their Allah and eventually take over the known world. So where does that leave me? Do I attempt a rearguard action against Islam, or do I seek another destiny? Islam only has room for one god, so if I stay, it must be as a djinni rather than as god. Will the Muslims allow a djinni to exist in their domains or will I be hounded out? Not that any man can hurt me, but what if there really is an Allah? I shall have to think on this some more, but I can see my life is about to change. It is time I left Makkah and perhaps even Arabia. I can wander the world and see what it has to offer, but I shall keep close to the people I know. It has been a long time since I fed on men's lives, but I can remember the sweet taste. It beckons me again.

Chapter Thirteen

A brisk northerly wind whipped up white caps on the choppy sea within the harbour of Ceuta on the North African coast. Over a hundred ships rode at anchor, straining against the ropes that held them in serried ranks. The wind hissed through rigging and buffeted the horde of tiny craft that sought to service the ships, carrying stores and weapons and soldiers on board. The wharves were likewise bustling with activity; men shouting orders, ropes creaking as bales of provisions were lowered into the waiting boats before being rowed laboriously out to the ships. The scene was a blaze of colour with the banners of each tribe, clan and family involved in the loading, flying wherever its members were active.

Sharif ibn Malik stood in the lee of a stone warehouse and watched. His heart pounded and his hand gripped the pommel of his sword, imagining he was already in the land of the infidel, helping to bring the Word of Allah to the benighted unbelievers. Then he glanced once more at the choppy water, and his stomach clenched at the thought of actually entrusting himself to its fluid movement. *We should go by land*, he thought. *Never mind that it's thousands of miles further and populated by Christian nations. We're people of the land, the desert. Water is for drinking, not sailing on.*

Thoughts of the land route around the Mediterranean led Sharif to think of Damascus. He had been born there thirty years before, and it was there that he had entered the service of Tariq ibn Ziyad a scant five years ago. Born of an Amajegh father and Syrian mother, Sharif had gravitated toward the Berber warrior already making a name as a war leader. Tariq had been named the deputy of Musa ibn Nasair, the governor of North Africa, and last year al-Walid, the Umayyad Khalifah, had summoned the two powerful men to his capital city to plan the invasion of Christian Spain.

Musa had sent Tariq back to the Berber lands to raise men for the Muslim army. Sharif had gone with him, renewing his acquaintance with the Amajegh tribes, getting in touch once again with the old half-forgotten customs, long since submerged in the language and customs of Muslim Arabia. In truth, Sharif regarded himself as an Arab now, viewing the men from his father's tribe as backward savages, often still clinging to their old gods and their old ways. He made a point of preaching to them, bringing his relatives to the pure light of Allah and ruthlessly slaughtering any who apostasised as soon as he turned his back. The younger men had flocked to the green banner of Islam, eager for adventure and plunder from the rich Christian lands across the sea. They were aboard one of the ships now, waiting for the arrival of their captain.

A man cleared his throat just behind him, and Sharif swung round, his hand pulling out his sword, cursing his own inattention. He blew out his breath noisily and visibly relaxed as he saw the man step out of the shadows.

“Rais. I could have taken your head off, startling me like that.” Angrily, Sharif shoved his sword back into its iron-studded leather scabbard.

The swarthy man in front of him grinned, revealing broken teeth. “You were the one daydreaming, Sharif. If I wanted you dead, I could have slipped a dagger into your kidney before you even knew I was here.”

Sharif smiled and nodded. “And why are you here, if not to kill me and assume my position within Tariq’s staff?”

“Our men are aboard, everything’s loaded. When does the great man arrive, and when do we leave?”

“He arrives when he arrives, and we leave when Allah the Merciful wants.” Sharif relented and put his arm around his friend. “I expect him today, my friend. As for our departure …” He shrugged. “That depends on the wind changing … that’s to say, on the will of Allah.”

“Then if we cannot hurry either along,” Rais declared, “let us away to a tavern I know and raise a flask of wine or two.”

Sharif looked around quickly for eavesdroppers or spies. “Have a care, Rais ibn Rasheed. Such an idea will see you lashed outside the mosque as a warning to all drunkards.”

His friend laughed and started away from the waterfront, tugging the other man along. “Who said anything about getting drunk? I just enjoy the taste of grape, and we’ve nothing else we need attend to this afternoon.”

Sharif allowed himself to be persuaded. They wandered through the narrow streets of Ceuta away from the bustle of the port and into a more secluded and deserted quarter of the town. Rais knocked gently on a door set into a high mudbrick wall. A panel slid back and an old man peered out, looking suspiciously from one man to the other.

"Come, let us in, old man" Rais said. "The sun is hot, we've been working hard and we thirst."

"We only have water and milk," grumbled the greybeard.

"Then that'll have to do," Rais declared. He winked at the old man, who muttered and closed the panel before opening the door. They passed through a narrow passage into a spacious courtyard shaded by lemon and orange trees; the scent of the blossoms hung thickly in the air, and the sound of splashing fountains and the song of small birds drove back the heat of the day.

The old man led them to a bench and a low table under a high lemon tree. Rais murmured to him and slipped him a silver coin. A few minutes later, a young boy appeared with a tray balancing a jug of wine, two cups and a platter of bread, goat cheese and olives. The boy put the tray down on the table and walked off.

Rais poured the wine and lifted his own cup. "Let us drink to a successful war. Plenty of dead infidels and much gold."

Sharif grimaced and looked about the courtyard, seeing other groups of men eating and drinking. They were talking too, but he could hear nothing above the sound of the water and songbirds.

He sipped at his own cup guiltily. “We shouldn’t be drinking,” he muttered.

“So says the Quran and the ahadith,” Rais said with a grin. “Yet we do it all the same. Why is that?” He popped an olive into his mouth, chewed carefully and spat the stone onto the ground.

“The Prophet warns us to beware of intoxicating drink, which is wine and distilled liquors, yet many men – good faithful Muslims in all other respects – still drink. Certainly the Khalifah al-Walid and the rest of the court in Damascus drink, often to the point of intoxication and debauchery.”

Rais swirled the dark purple liquid in his cup. “You’re a good Muslim, my friend, yet you’re drinking the fermented juice of the grape as am I. I know my reason, but what’s yours?”

“Probably the same. I can reason that the Prophet warned against intoxication rather than wine as such. If I’m aware of the effects of wine, I can drink it as part of a meal and stop before I become intoxicated. Thus I can obey Muhammad and not shame the Khalifah who succeeds him by abstaining when he doesn’t.”

“Excellently put.” Rais refilled his cup and splashed a bit more into Sharif’s. “Drink up. We’re a long way from being drunk.”

The boy brought a chicken and lemon dish served with rice, and the two men ate from the single dish, picking up their food with the right hand and shaping it before slipping it neatly into their beard-fringed mouths. When they finished, they washed in rose-scented water and dried their hands on clean linen before settling back with a fresh jug of wine.

"Tariq's given you the command of a troop, my friend," Rais said quietly. "This war will bring many opportunities for honour and wealth."

Sharif nodded. "He's honoured me already, though maybe because I share Amajegh blood with him."

"I think there's more to it than being a Berber. Many men are Berbers, yet you've been chosen above them."

"That's true. It must be because I've great talent for leadership."

Rais grinned. "Now you go too far. However, you have great opportunity, my friend. Make the most of it."

"Oh, I will." Sharif sipped in silence for a few minutes. "Have you ever sailed before?"

"On a river. My parents were originally from Egypt, and I've sailed the current a few times. Never on the sea though. And you?"

Sharif shook his head. "I've crossed the Nile a few times on a ferry. I've always trusted in a camel or a horse under me, never a boat. I am … apprehensive."

"How bad can it be? When the wind comes about, we sail for Spain and we'll be no more than a day, maybe a day and a night in the crossing. We're men. We can bear anything."

"I've heard that men vomit so much they pray for death."

"I think that must be exaggeration. Some men make it their livelihood, sailing the oceans and seas for trade or fish. Certainly it's never bad on the river. Why should the sea be different?"

"Well, it's in God's hands," Sharif said.

"Yes, as Allah wants." Rais looked thoughtfully at his friend. "You must have the ear of Tariq, being one of his commanders. What's the plan once we land in Spain?"

Sharif looked into his wine cup, not meeting the other man's gaze. "I'm not in Tariq's confidence."

Rais belched loudly and poured himself another cup. "I'm not asking for confidences, my friend, but all I know is that we're to sail against Christian Spain. I would just like to know what to expect. Are we landing on secluded beaches for instance, or must we sail into well-defended harbours? If the latter, perhaps I should stop drinking right now and beg forgiveness of Allah for my sins."

Sharif laughed. "There's no need to give up your wine just yet. I meant it when I say Tariq doesn't confide in me, but I do know that we're heading for the Rock, near a place called Algeciras. The enemy expect us to force a landing at the port, but we'll land near the Rock and march around the bay."

"And what do you know of the enemy?"

"Only what most men know. Spain is held by the Visigoth king, Roderic, and his Christian nobles. They're good fighters by all accounts."

"But we're better."

Sharif grunted. "Maybe, maybe not, but we do have one thing in our favour. We're fighting to bring the Word of Allah to the infidel. God must certainly be on our side in this endeavour."

Rais nodded sagely. “It stands to reason, but don’t the Christians claim their god is on their side too?”

“What of it? Allah is the True God and Muhammad is his Prophet. Can any man stand against them?”

“A man in our troop said the Christian God was the same as Allah. If this is so …”

“It’s not.”

“You’re certain?”

“Yes. I’ve talked with Christians before, in Damascus. They believe in three gods whom they call the Father, the Son and the Spirit. The Jews are closer to the True Faith, believing in only one god whom they call their father, Yahweh. Christians have added the Son, who is no more than the Prophet Jesus, but they’ve raised him to be the equal of his Father.”

“Shocking,” Rais murmured. “And the Spirit?”

Sharif shrugged. “Trying to discuss this with a Christian is like catching a fish with your bare hands. Their logic is slippery. Some say the Spirit is a dove, others that it is Jesus’ mother, Mary, and others that it’s the power of their god and not a person at all.”

“How can any religion be so unsure of itself? When the Prophet was in doubt, Allah revealed the Truth to him immediately.”

“Well said, Rais ibn Rasheed, for the Holy Quran says, ‘Truth has come and falsehood has vanished; verily falsehood is doomed to vanish.’”

“Prophetic words indeed. The truth of Allah has come, and the falsehood of Christianity is doomed to vanish. Sharif, my friend, I'm greatly heartened by your words. I was feeling apprehensive about our enterprise, but now I'm assured of our victory. Nothing can stand against us." Rais poured them both another drink and clinked cups with his friend.

A distant cheering carried to them as they sat in their secluded courtyard and both men looked up questioningly. Several men at other tables stopped their own drinking and conversation, and one of them hurried out into the street to find the cause of the disturbance. He returned within minutes, excitement making him stumble over his words.

"The wind has changed. It blows now from the east."

"You hear that?" Rais asked. "We could claw our way to Spain with an east wind, and if it changes more …"

Sharif drained his mug and stood up, swaying slightly. "I must report to Tariq's headquarters. We could get the order to sail at any moment."

"I'll come with you," Rais said, "for I think you have drunk too much, my friend. If any question us, I'll lie, saying you've been working on the ships and that's the reason you're unsteady on your feet."

"You'd do that for me?" Sharif put his arm around Rais' shoulders and started toward the door to the street.

"Of course. If you're judged intoxicated, you'll suffer for it, but I know that wasn't your intent. Does not the Holy Quran say of God, 'He invites you to forgiveness of your sins and a respite till an appointed term'?"

"I'm not sure that's precisely what's meant, my friend, but I'll accept your help with thanks."

They hurried through the streets and bypassed the harbour, meeting no one that challenged their sobriety. They turned up the hill that led to Tariq's headquarters to the house that had once been that of Ceuta's mayor. The guards passed Sharif through but turned back Rais.

"I'll get down to our ship," Rais said. "Join me when you can."

Tariq ibn Ziyad stood in the small courtyard of the house surrounded by a dozen men in flowing robes. He nodded at Sharif as he entered without breaking his flow of speech and pointed to a diagram drawn in the dust.

"We're here in Ceuta with our fifteen thousand men, and here …" Tariq tapped with his stick, "… is the Christian king, Roderic, with his army in Toledo. It's a long way away, but you can be certain he'll march to meet us when our army lands on his shores. Up till now, we've just been raiding their shores, sending small forces across the sea to burn farms, destroy crops and vineyards, loot a town or two. But this has all changed. The Commander of the True Believers, Al-Walid ibn Abdul Melik, Khalifah in Damascus, has commanded that we invade Spain and bring its inhabitants to the sword or the True Faith. This I've vowed to do, and you, my brave commanders, will lead the men into battle, knowing you do your duty for Allah, the Prophet and the Khalifah."

The commanders applauded, and Tariq went on to assign specific duties to each of them. "Now,

Sharif ibn Malik, why were you so late to this meeting?"

Sharif bowed low. "A thousand apologies, my lord. I was dining when I heard the wind had changed. I came as quickly as I could."

Tariq stared unsmiling at a faint stain of purple on his commander's lips. "I'm sure I don't have to remind you that we're doing God's work here. You wouldn't sin in any way and jeopardise this enterprise, would you?"

"N … no, Sir, of course not."

"Good. Then I'll give you an honourable duty. You'll be the first to leave harbour and the first to land on the coast of Spain, securing the landing site for the rest of the fleet. I'll be following with a tenth of the army a day behind you, the rest landing later."

Sharif trembled slightly but hid it with a deep bow. "You do me great honour, Sir."

"Secure me the beach, Sharif, and we'll see about the honour."

At Tariq's signal, servants brought bowls of water and clean linen towels, and they all performed the ritual ablutions, cleansing the body of impurities before they approached God. Sharif trembled again, knowing that fermented juice had passed his lips, but he offered up fervent silent prayers to Allah for forgiveness, vowing never to repeat his sin. Tariq then led his commanders in prayer, standing in rows on prayer mats and facing east toward Makkah.

They stood in the Niyyat posture, focusing their minds and shutting out the world. "Allahu akbar, God is great!" they declared, before bringing their hands down below their navels and reciting the opening supplication. "Glory to You, O Allah, and Yours is the praise. And blessed is Your Name and exalted is Your Majesty. And there is no deity to be worshipped but You. I seek refuge in Allah from Satan, the accursed."

Tariq and his commanders continued through the formal words, standing or bowing from the waist as the formula required. They dropped into the Sudjood, the prostration and through the other actions, careful to hold their bodies exactly as prescribed. They reveled in the words, reciting them clearly, offering up their prayer and declaration of faith. Some of the commanders were not Arabic, coming from tribes that had accepted God and His Apostle during the Muslim surge across North Africa. Rather than use their native tongues, they had to recite the ritual prayers in Arabic, the mellifluous syllables rolling off their tongues fluently from repeated use.

Prayers complete, they rose and took their leave. Tariq called Sharif aside and spoke to him softly. "Your ship will leave before nightfall. The wind is coming round to the south, so the fleet will lift anchor tomorrow morning. We'll not be far behind you, so make sure all is in readiness for our arrival."

"It will be done, my lord."

Sharif bowed and let his commander and the other officers precede him, then he walked slowly down to the harbour, his mind on the coming crossing to Spain. He found Rais on the docks, sitting on sacks of wheat to be loaded onto the ships and talking with an old man. As soon as Rais saw Sharif, he stood and greeted him. "What news?" he asked softly. "Do we sail?"

Sharif nodded. "Before dusk. We must be well clear of land before nightfall."

"That soon? Then I must hurry home and say goodbye to my wife."

"I didn't know you were married, Rais. When did this happen?"

"Three months ago." Rais grinned. "You have your duties to occupy you, but common soldiers like me need a bit of warm companionship of an evening."

"There are women of the town," Sharif said, gesturing vaguely.

"You've picked up bad habits in Damascus, my friend," Rais said primly. "I'm a good Muslim; I cannot just fornicate with a whore."

"But … but marriage – who is she? How was it arranged?"

Rais laughed. "It's only a temporary marriage. She's a Berber girl of good standing in the community. Comely too and as agile as a young she-goat. Don't worry, my friend, I'll pay her well and divorce her before we leave."

"Pay her? Divorce? Wouldn't it have been easier just to hire her by the hour?"

"And commit the sin of fornication? I'm a good Muslim; I cannot bed any woman out of wedlock, and only a whore would lie with a man unless she was married to him."

"But how can a marriage be one of convenience?"

"I'd forgotten you're Sunni, my friend, and no longer believe in Mut'ah. I'm Shi'a though, and for us, a temporary marriage is a very useful thing."

"But to divorce her so easily? I mean, what will she think?"

"Do you imagine she didn't enter into this willingly? She knew what it meant to marry a man of Tariq's army. She's Muslim too and fears fornication and the loss of her honour. She's married now, divorced tonight and will walk away with a useful dowry. Oh, she's a woman – she'll scream and weep and abuse me soundly – but I'll fill her belly once more and give her gold, and she'll see me off with a smile. I'll be here when you sail, my friend, never fear."

"I never doubted it," Sharif muttered, shaking his head. "Go and do what you must, but be here again in an hour or I'll sail without you."

"I'll be here. I wouldn't want to miss those pretty little Spanish girls."

"More Mut'ah marriages?"

"Of course not." Rais managed to look shocked. "They're Christian infidels. I can rape them without sin." He bowed and hurried off, leaving Sharif staring after him.

The old man smiled toothlessly. "You want me to find you a girl, master? You said yourself you have an hour."

"No. Go away."

"For a little extra, I can find a girl to marry you for an hour."

"Get out of my sight, old man."

"A boy then?"

Sharif growled and started to draw his sword. The old man turned and hobbled away as fast as he could. Sharif forgot about him and went in search of a boat to carry him out to his three ships anchored in Ceuta harbour. He found one of his own boats still loading stores and had the sailors row him out to the nearest of his ships, the Barak – meaning blessing. From its pitching deck, he could see his other two ships, the Bahadur, meaning bold, and the Basil, meaning valiant. *What possessed me to name them thus*? he asked himself. *Now they'll have to live up to those names*.

He found the captain of the Barak in the hold, attending to the stowage of cargo and called for his attention. "Ho, Theodoulos, are you ready to set sail?"

The captain finished what he was doing before turning round. He wiped his hands on his stained robe and grunted non-committally."

"You're ready?" Sharif persisted.

"Close enough," Theodoulos admitted. He looked up at the scudding cloud and spat on the deck. "If the wind comes round another point or two, we can clear the harbour tomorrow morning maybe."

"Make it two hours. We have orders to sail before sunset."

Theodoulos scowled. "We'd be safer in harbour overnight than standing out to sea." He turned and let loose a full-throated roar of rage at his workers. "Drop that barrel, you son of a poxed goat, and I'll slit your fornicating balls off and send them back to your diseased wife!" He turned back to Sharif and continued as if nothing had happened. "The seas off Ceuta are shallow and treacherous. We should wait until morning, so we can see where we are."

"You wish to tell that to our commander, Tariq ibn Ziyad? I thought not. We have our orders captain, so whether we're ready or not, we sail in two hours time."

The captain shrugged. "If we must sail, then earlier is better. We need to anchor offshore, and we need light to choose our anchorage."

"Can't we sail through the night? Tariq expects us to be in Spain tomorrow."

"Saints preserve us," Theodoulos muttered. "You won't be happy until we're all dead and in heaven."

Sharif stared. *I forgot my captains are Coptic Christians*. "You can do it?"

"You won't find another captain who can. Yes, I can do it."

Sharif sent orders across to his other two ships to prepare for sailing in as little as an hour's time and then went aft to the tiny canvas cabin set up for the commander's use. He opened a carved chest beside the cot and took out a roll of parchment. He studied it, weighing up his resources and preparations against the task set him by Tariq. Sharif would have preferred to discuss the plans with Rais as he had difficulty in thinking complex matters through, but in his absence resorted to a low vocalisation as if the other man was there.

"Three ships, a hundred men, no horses, arms and provisions for a week. Is it going to be enough?"

Rais was not there to answer, so Sharif muttered an objection for him. "Depends what we're supposed to do. If it's only to guard a deserted beach, then yes, it's enough. If we're expected to overcome Roderic's army, then we're dead men."

"There may be some troops, but there shouldn't be any army. We're under orders – land and secure the landing site for the rest of the ships."

"And we land here? By the Rock? Why not in Algeciras?"

"You think a hundred men are enough to take the town? I don't, and obviously Tariq does not either. We are to land here …" Sharif tapped the drawing on the parchment, "… just inside the bay and landward of the Rock. When the army arrives, we march around the bay and take the town."

"Unless they're waiting for us."

"That's as God wants." Sharif rolled the parchment up again and put it back in the chest. He went out on deck again and scanned the fleet, judging its state of preparedness. Boats were still ferrying supplies out to the others, but his ships sat alone, though their decks were feverish with activity. The captain ambled up to him, the crush of armed men on the deck parting reluctantly to let him through.

"We're ready, Sharif ibn Malik. Give the word, and we'll haul the anchors up."

"Is Rais ibn Rasheed on board yet?"

"No."

"Then we wait."

Sharif knew little about the sea, but he knew ships needed the wind more or less behind them to sail across it. He looked at the direction the banners on the mastheads were pointing as they snapped and cracked in the wind and then at the breakwaters guarding the harbour entrance. *I don't see how we can do it. We'll hit the rocks. Perhaps that's what the oars are for.* He frowned and thought about calling the captain back but hesitated. Men stood all around him, men that would be looking to him for leadership in the days to come. *If I appear fearful, they'll despise me. Better to die than to lose their trust.* He swallowed and looked at the heaving grey sea and the white caps of the waves and wondered whether drowning was a painful death. *Trust in the captain*, he decided. *He doesn't want to die either.*

A sailor called that a boat was approaching, and Sharif saw Rais in it. Minutes later, his friend was aboard, wet but grinning, and he worked his way through the throng to Sharif.

"You see, I made it."

Sharif shook his head. "Your … wife is happy?"

"Wife no longer, and happy? Well, let us say content, and I'm pleasantly tired."

"Not too tired to sail, I hope?" Sharif saw the captain looking at him and nodded, raising his arm in assent.

A shout went up from the sailors, and the triangular sail unfurled, the pressure of the wind throwing the ship to the right as it swung on its anchor rope. Water sprayed aboard and soldiers grabbed for supports, cursing the laughing sailors.

The prow came round to face the harbour entrance, and the anchor rope tautened under the strain. Theodoulos yelled for the anchor to be lifted, and as it came free from the sand and mud of the harbour bottom, the ship shot forward, the prow dipping almost under the water.

The wind gusted fiercely from the east, carrying the Barak swiftly toward the rocks of the breakwater. Men started crying out in alarm, but Theodoulos merely looked from the sail to the prow to the sea, sparing only a glance for the oncoming rocks. He shouted out a command, and the sailors pulled on the ropes. The wet sail flapped, knocking an unwary soldier to the deck. The sail cracked again as the ship came about, floundering in the water for a moment before the ropes were released once more and the wind filled the canvas. The ship leapt forward again on a course that carried it toward the tip of the breakwater.

"Now!" yelled the captain. "To your oars and row for your lives." The sailors leapt to their stations and dug the oars into the foaming water. The blades dug deep, and they strained to push the boat forward.

Sharif forced himself to walk slowly over to the captain and stand silently by him, desperately wanting reassurance that they were not all about to die but reluctant to disturb the concentration of the only man who could save them.

"You have a question?" Theodoulos asked quietly, his eyes never leaving his ship.

"Why didn't we use the oars to leave the harbour?"

"This wind would have blown us onto the rocks even without the sail."

"So why use the sail?"

"For speed. If we wallow in these seas it's all over."

"Are we … will we hit the rocks?"

"Maybe. That's in the hands of the Lord. What are the other ships doing?"

"Eh … what?"

"The Bahadur and Basil. I dare not look. Have they come about?"

Sharif looked astern and saw the other two ships in his little fleet crashing through the waves behind them. "Yes, they are rowing also, but they're further from the rocks than us."

"They were anchored further to the south. They'll reach the open sea without any problems."

"And … and us?"

"The wind has backed to the east when I hoped it would swing to the south. It'll be a close run thing. If you're a religious man, start praying."

"I have confidence in you, captain." Sharif spoke loudly, so the men closest to him could hear and be heartened. In his heart, he offered a quick prayer to God.

The breakwater rushed closer, and the men fell silent, staring at death. The captain did not flinch, calling out his commands and his men instantly obeying him. At the last moment, when it seemed they must splinter themselves on the rocks, the rudder oars bit deep and the ropes were slackened, spilling air from the sail. The ship shuddered and turned, losing speed but easing away from the tip of the mole. Before the vessel could flounder and lose steerage way, the captain ordered the ropes pulled taut again, and the ship lurched back toward the rocky finger of the breakwater but slipped past so close the seagulls perched on the rocks took to the air in fright. Moments later, the Barak ran before the wind and along the coast before easing out into the open sea. The sailors shipped their oars and let the wind do the work. Off to the east, the Bahadur and the Basil plunged through the waves on a parallel course.

Around him, Sharif could hear men offering up thanks to Allah, and he quickly offered up his own before catching the captain's attention again.

"We are on course for Spain?' he asked.

"Yes, but not for our destination," Theodoulos replied. "To get to the Rock, we must go north, and the wind is still set from the east."

"You cannot do it?"

"Yes, I can do it, but it won't be a comfortable trip."

"Just do it."

Theodoulos laughed. "As you will, Sharif ibn Malik, but I think you haven't travelled much by sea to be so nonchalant."

The captain brought the ships about on a new course, angling across the east wind. The vessels heeled over, men cursing as they slid over the sloping wet decks. Adding to their discomfort was the motion of the waves now taking them from the sides, the ships rolling and pitching in a complex motion that soon had many of them, Sharif included, vomiting on the slippery boards. The cold sea spray and biting wind added to their discomfort. Theodoulos had his sailors dip buckets into the green seas and sluice the decks clean until nightfall, when it became too dangerous to move about in the darkness. Lamps were lit, but only a few of them, helping more as a guide for the other ships than as illumination.

Sharif emptied his stomach and dry retched for a while before drifting into an exhausted sleep. Rais was unaffected by the motion, though the stink of vomit made him nauseous. He sipped a little wine from a flask to settle his stomach and ate a little bread. He remained by his friend's side and occasionally wiped the salt spray from the sleeping man's face or restrained him when the ship plunged into a deeper trough. In the middle of the night, the wind eased round to the south, and a little later, the motion of the ship became less chaotic.

Dawn broke gray and uninviting, and Sharif rose and washed his face in a bucket of cold seawater before waving aside the offer of food and staggering across the deck to talk to the captain.

"You do this for a living?" Sharif croaked.

Theodoulos smiled. "You've had the worst of it. In conditions like these, I'd normally be at anchor in some sheltered bay or running before the wind. However, we're under orders to reach Spain, so we must make the best of it."

"And have we? Reached Spain, I mean?"

"There." The captain pointed forward to a bank of low cloud. "Behind that cloud is dry land."

Sharif grunted and closed his eyes for a moment. "If you say so, captain. And the Rock?"

"The wind turned south in the night, and we're heading straight for Algeciras Bay. We'll be there in an hour or two. Perhaps you'll join me for some breakfast?"

Sharif shook his head. "What of the other two ships?"

"They kept station in the night. See?" Theodoulos pointed.

The sun rose, burning off the cloud and revealing the sheer seaward side of the Rock. The three ships steered for the open bay but hugged the shoreline so as not to betray their arrival to any watchers in the town of Algeciras, but their precaution was in vain. A thin column of smoke arose into the clear sky, and as they neared the beach, they could see men watching them.

"They're expecting us," Rais said with a smirk of satisfaction. "Good. I feel like slitting a few Christian throats."

Appreciative laughter arose from the men nearby, and Sharif clapped his friend on the shoulder. "Just make sure none of them escape. We don't want Roderic's army down on us before the main fleet arrives."

The Barak turned toward the beach, and with the sail furled and the oars driving the ship forward, it surged into the shallows and scrunched into the sand. Rais and half a dozen men were over the side before the ship stopped moving and ran up the gently shelving sand toward a group of men forming themselves into a loose line.

Rais threw himself forward with the cry "Allahu akbar" and sword raised high, his men a breath behind him. Sharif jumped down onto the sand bellowing for the soldiers and the sailors to follow him, but by the time he arrived panting at the scene of the skirmish, it was all over. Ten men lay dead, only one of whom was a Berber, and a pale wounded man bit back his pain and watched his captors.

"One prisoner for you to question, Sir," Rais said.

Sharif squatted down beside the man and looked into his eyes. "What is your name?" he asked in Arabic.

The man said nothing but flicked a glance toward Rais and back again.

Sharif repeated his question in Arabic, enunciating clearly, then switched to the Berber tongue. Rais added Coptic and Hebrew but with no greater success. "What's the point of a captive if you can't question him?" Sharif stood up and looked around. "We need to set up a perimeter with scouts to warn us of enemy approach."

"I'll see it's done," Rais said. "What do you want to do about him?"

"He's no use to us. Kill him and put all the bodies out of sight in the bushes."

"Shouldn't we give him the opportunity of converting to Islam, Sir?"

"How are you going to induce him to make the Declaration if you can't speak his language? He can't tell us anything, but if he escaped, he could certainly tell others about our strength. He's a liability, so kill him."

Rais nodded and drew his sword, whereupon the wounded man started gabbling, his rising voice ending in a bubbling shriek.

Sharif brought all the men ashore, including the sailors, and had the ships secured. Rais had the dead men hidden and sent scouts out to the rutted dirt road that skirted the bay. He also sent a pair of men scrambling up the rock to watch for the main fleet. Many men were feeling the effects of seasickness, so Sharif ordered a hot meal to be prepared and led the men in prayer to Allah. Theodoulos, his fellow captains and a handful of sailors stood apart and offered up quiet prayers to their own Christian god.

When the men were fed, rested and made their peace with God, Sharif led them out along the bay road for a mile but encountered no signs of human life. He left twenty men under the command of a junior officer with orders to guard the road and kill anyone who came upon them from the direction of Algeciras.

"If you're badly outnumbered, fall back to the ships, but send a runner back with a warning."

Sharif marched his men back to the ships and sent a group up the Rock to relieve the watchers at the top. He sat in the shade of a tree and watched as the men set about unloading the ships of everything useful. Rais came across and sat down beside him, offering him a skin flask.

"Wine?" Sharif asked. "Not for me."

"I wouldn't think of it," Rais replied. "Not when we're engaged in holy work." He looked up at the position of the sun. "When can we reasonably expect the fleet?"

"Theodoulos says with a south wind they can make the crossing in five or six hours. They were to leave at daybreak, but that could easily be delayed."

"Before dark, though?"

"As God wants."

Evening came and there was no sign of Tariq or the fleet. Sharif ordered more food prepared, the lookouts on the Rock relieved and the outpost on the bay road supplied with food and bedding. Setting a number of extra guards along the beach in both directions, they settled down for the night. The night hours passed uneventfully, and after dawn prayers, the lookout on the Rock signalled ships were in sight.

Sharif ordered Rais up to have a look and report back as quickly as he could. He arrived back on the beach, scratched, bruised and sweat-stained. His clothing was ripped, and he was nursing his hand.

"A bloody monkey bit me. The cursed thing tried to snatch …"

"The ships?" Sharif interrupted.

"Oh, yes. There's about fifty sail south of us, the closest perhaps an hour or two away." Rais held his hand up, scowling. "The son of a she-goat tried to rob me of my food and bit me when I tried to stop it."

Sharif hid a smile and said, "Get your wound washed, and let the physician put a poultice on it. I cannot have my lieutenant incapacitated at the start of the campaign."

The first ships put into Algeciras Bay around mid-morning, and by a little after noon, Tariq and his commanders had set up a command post on a clear space at the foot of the Rock a hundred paces or so inland from the landing beach.

Tariq listened to Sharif's report and nodded when he described the dispositions he had made with his small advance force. "Well done, Sharif ibn Malik. You've acquitted yourself with honour. It won't be forgotten." He turned away and called over his aides. "Assemble the men, and I'll address them. Adil, you have men prepared for your duty? Good, then get ready. You know the signal."

The men crowded around. The sailors had been brought up to hear the words of their war leader; the scouts and lookouts were withdrawn so they could be heartened by his words. When all were assembled, a banner was raised, and a few minutes later as the first thin plumes of smoke arose from the beach, Tariq ibn Ziyad mounted a low dais and addressed his troops.

"Warriors of Allah, rejoice, for you've been chosen for a special duty, that of conquering Spain, the Iberian lands and the kingdom of the Christian Visigothic king, Roderic. Behind you, by my orders, our ships burn, so there's no going back." A muttering of disbelief changed to anxiety and rose to roars of dismay as the men caught sight of the columns of smoke. Horns sounded loudly, and the commanders called for quiet. Over a period of many minutes, order was restored and the men turned once more to their leader, eager for words of reassurance.

"Oh, my noble warriors, where will you now flee? The sea lies behind you, the enemy in front. Your only hope now is your courage and loyalty.

Remember that in this land you're like an orphan sitting at the table of a greedy man. Your enemy lies before you with a huge army, men in abundance, but all you have are your swords and your courage if you're to snatch your lives from the grasping hands of the enemy. Don't delay, don't hesitate and don't fear to grasp success; for if you do, your enemies will take courage from your inaction. Not for us the horrors of having to besiege the enemy behind strong city walls, for our little force landing here has provoked the king of this land to venture forth and meet us in battle. Warriors of Islam, don't believe that you face danger alone for I'll be leading you. I'll be in the forefront of battle where the chance of life is least, exposing myself freely to death."

Tariq fell silent and looked around the sea of upturned faces, seeing fear and resignation in many but also a fierce determination in others. He smiled. "My glorious warriors, you'll suffer but a short time and afterward enjoy supreme delights. Our fates are bound together. If you fall in battle, so shall I – or survive to avenge you. If you fall in battle with the infidel, remember the delights of Paradise that await you. But if you fight bravely and survive, conquering our enemies – ah, then think of what will be your reward. In this land are many ravishingly beautiful Greek maidens, their delectable bodies draped in sumptuous gowns decked with gold and pearls and precious coral, and they live in the palaces of kings. The Commander of the True Believers, Khalifah Al-Walid ibn Abdul Melik has chosen you from all his Arab warriors to lead this attack that will defeat the enemy and bring the Word of Allah to the infidel. Such is his confidence in your bravery. For himself, the Khalifah desires only that the Word of God shall be exalted here – the spoils belong to you.

"Remember that I'll lead you in battle, and as the two armies meet hand to hand, you'll see me seeking out Roderic the Visigothic king, tyrant of his people and God willing, bringing him to combat. If I should perish, don't lose heart but choose from amongst you an experienced hero to lead you. Defeat Roderic, kill him, and his soldiers will lose the will to fight, but you, whether under my command or under the command of another, are assured of victory for you fight for Allah, for his Prophet and for the Khalifah Al-Walid."

Tariq's speech came to an impassioned end, and his soldiers cheered him mightily over and over – "Tariq!" they cried, "Tariq! Tariq! Tariq!" – the noise sending flocks of birds beating into the skies and the apes on the Rock chattering in fright.

"Listen," Sharif cried, "Even the monkeys on Gibr al-Tariq flee from the mention of his name."

The commanders formed the men up into squads and set them off onto the bay road, each man carrying his weapons and a pack of rations. The sailors marched too, grumbling but resigned to their new life in Tariq's tiny army. Less than two thousand men faced the might of the Visigothic Kingdom, but their hearts were strong and their hopes high.

Algeciras fell without a fight. Most of the townsfolk fled into the country, and the small garrison of soldiers surrendered immediately. They were given the option of converting to Islam or dying in their faith. Many were Jews who had already been given a similar choice by the Christian authorities, and these ones readily made the shahadah, reasoning life as a Muslim could scarcely be harder than life as a forced Christian. The bulk of the captive soldiers were Christian and most chose to die in their faith. Tariq had brought interpreters with him for just this purpose.

Neither Sharif nor Rais were called on for the executions, but they watched with great interest, curious as to the mettle of their enemies. One by one, the Christians were led forward, their hands tied behind them. They were made to kneel, and an Arab soldier struck off their heads with a blow or two of their sword. Blood collected in pools on the paving stones of the town square, and the few townspeople who had been captured were employed to drag the bodies and severed heads aside. The civilian population was also invited to convert, but if they declined, their lives were spared though their names were registered.

"Only those who bear arms against us will be killed, unless they become our brothers," Tariq declared.

Most of the soldiers executed met their death bravely, calling on their god, the saints or on Mary to receive their souls, or else cursing their killers.

"They have a goddess called Mary?" Rais asked. "I thought you said they worshipped three male gods, Father, Son and Spirit."

Sharif shook his head distastefully. “They call her the mother of god.”

“Mother? That’s blasphemy. How can God have a mother?”

Sharif shrugged. “Don’t ask me. I only repeat what I’ve heard. Christians have a god they call the Father, another they call the Son and this woman called, Mary, who apparently lay with one and gave birth to the other.”

“What revolting beliefs. Allah be praised we’ve come here to bring them the pure truth of His word.”

The last of the enemy soldiers died, and Tariq immediately set about moving his army out of Algeciras and onto the road leading north and east past the bay and the Rock now called Gibr al-Tariq. Word had come in from scouts that an army was gathering somewhere on the coast, and Tariq was eager to meet it.

There were horses in Algeciras, a few well-bred mounts owned by the officers and gentlemen of the town and a dozen lesser beasts. These were commandeered, and the senior officers now rode at the head of their squads. Sharif was given a swaybacked mare and told to take his men and an interpreter out into the countryside to forage for provisions and to give warning should the enemy seek to surprise the main force. The mare could barely make it into the first range of hills, so Sharif dismounted and led it instead.

The hillsides were dry but pleasant in the sunshine, and insects buzzed and chirred in the vegetation. The hillsides smelled of honey and thyme with just a faint tang of salt from the distant sea. The soldiers moved quickly and almost silently, keeping their senses alert for the presence of the enemy or for an opportunity of plunder. They happened on a poor farmhouse and captured an old man and woman with two youths. The soldiers liberated the livestock and helped themselves to grain and root vegetables before turning to their human captives.

"Do you accept Islam?" Sharif asked through an interpreter.

"What's Islam?" asked the old man after a few moments.

"Submission to the One True God, Allah, and to his Prophet Muhammad."

"We're Christian."

"I know. I'm giving you the opportunity to embrace the Truth."

"We have the Truth," said the old woman. "We go to church every Sunday."

Sharif shook his head. "We're wasting time. Either embrace the truth of Allah and his Prophet or die and burn in hell forever."

The woman started weeping, as did one of the youths, but the old man defied them. "If we die in the Lord, we shall go to heaven. It's only heathens like you who will go to hell."

Sharif shrugged. "Kill them all."

They moved on from the farm, and Rais walked alongside his friend.

"Are we going to kill everyone we meet?"

"Only those that fight us or defy us."

“It seems that with every Christian dead there will be none left to farm the land.”

“We’ll bring in good honest Muslims from Africa. Besides, we won’t kill everyone. Many will see the sense of converting.”

“Another thing – where are these sensuous young women Tariq promised us? That old woman did not ignite my lust in the slightest.”

Sharif laughed. “Have you yet seen one of the palaces he said they live in? Don’t worry, my friend, we’ll find many young girls who will embrace you and God’s Word.”

“One or the other, please. If they convert, they are much harder to persuade. Give me a nubile young Christian girl with whom having relations is no sin.” Rais thought for a moment. “She can convert afterwards, if she likes.”

The route of Sharif's group of soldiers paralleled the coast road for several days. At the prescribed times, Sharif stopped his men and they set out prayer mats, faced east and performed the ritual prayers. After each approach to Allah, they felt refreshed and strengthened in their resolve. They ate well, supplementing their rations with produce from the farms and anything else they could glean from the land. On the third day, they found a small village and surprised it, throwing a cordon of steel around it before the inhabitants could flee.

A mixed group of men, women and children were herded into the middle of the village and made to kneel, the men apart and children below puberty with the women. Rais and several of the men eyed the girls and women and grinned, anticipating delights to come. Sharif mounted the old mare once more so every person could see him and addressed the villagers through the interpreter.

"I am Sharif ibn Malik, representative of Lord Tariq ibn Ziyad and servant of Khalifah Al-Walid. I come to conquer and to bring the Word of Allah which was given to his Prophet Muhammad for the benefit of all who hear it and take it into their hearts. I recognise that as Christians you are a people akin to us. We're descendants of Abraham and believe that the man you call Jesus was a Prophet of God. Where you have gone astray is to think this Jesus was more than a man. Your religious leaders have subverted the teachings of the Prophet Jesus, and so Allah sent the Prophet Muhammad to correct these mistakes and bring all men back to the True Faith of Islam, which is Submission to God.

"I call on you now to admit your heresies and to embrace the True Faith. Declare that Allah, the Merciful, the Compassionate, is God and that Muhammad, peace be upon him, is his Prophet, and we'll welcome you as brothers. Cling to your heresies and you'll die. It's your choice."

Nobody said anything for several minutes, and then one of the captives slowly rose to his feet. Immediately, two of the Berber soldiers forced their way through to him with swords drawn and curses on their lips. Sharif called to them to wait and addressed the man.

"What say you? Do you speak for these people?"

The man licked his lips and looked around him. "I have no authority in Almisa save over myself, but I have a question."

"Speak then. If you're civil you need have no fear."

"If we convert to … to … what did you call it? Islam? What's to prevent us turning back to the faith of our fathers once you have gone?"

Murmurs of anger came from the Muslims and fear arose from the captives. Sharif signalled for silence. "Once a man has embraced the True Faith, turning away from it is apostasy and the penalty can only be death."

The man grimaced. "Then forgive me, noble sir, but you put us in a difficult position. We live in a Christian country, and if we turn from the Church and you leave our village, our lives are forfeit; yet if we don't, you'll kill us. How can we decide?"

"If you don't convert, you die now, for a certainty, and unshriven by your priests. If later, your Christian neighbours put you to death for being Muslim, you have the reward of Paradise to look forward to. Certain death and the risk of hell now, or possible death and Paradise later. I think your choice is straightforward."

The man thought for a moment and then nodded. "My name is Pietro. I will become your first convert. Tell me what to say, and I will say it."

"Come out then, Pietro, and join your brothers-to-be. I'll rename you Basir, which in the Arab tongue means wise, for you're displaying wisdom. Anyone else? Man or woman? Child even?"

The captives hesitated, weighing the odds, and then a few stood and when beckoned, came out to stand beside Pietro. The others knelt and looked at their captors sullenly.

"No more?" Sharif asked. "Come, it's no hard thing to take the Truth into your hearts."

One more man got up and joined the converts, but the rest stayed where they were, their lips moving in prayer.

"Very well, you've made your choice." He turned to Rais and the men of his squad. "Choose from among them the women and girls that please you and take them aside. I'll spare them for your pleasure. As for the rest, send them to the hell prepared for them by Allah." Sharif turned away as his men moved in with drawn swords.

Rais moved swiftly, striding into the little group of women and grabbing a dark-haired girl by the wrist. "This one is mine." A woman next to the girl wept and clutched at Rais, and he kicked her aside. The girl started screaming, but Rais ignored her cries and dragged her away.

"No!" yelled a male voice. "Maria!" A man among the ones marked for death, hurled himself forward, snatching a dagger from his clothing. He dodged one of the Muslim soldiers and ran to where Rais still struggled with the girl, his dagger raised.

Rais saw him coming and threw the girl to the ground, stumbling back to avoid the dagger sweeping down at his chest. A soldier raised a bow but could not clearly sight the man and lowered it again. Rais fumbled for his sword but tripped and fell as he dodged another sweep of the man's blade.

Sharif muttered an oath and stepped forward, his sword raised. He thrust it at the man and scored a wound across his chest. The man dropped the dagger and fell to his knees near the girl, his hand outstretched to grasp her. Sharif turned toward Rais and reached down to help him to his feet, a grin on his face. He did not see the man grasp his dagger again and rise to his feet, but he heard a cry of alarm from a soldier and felt a blow to his back. He turned quickly, agony already spreading through his body, and swept his sword blade across the man's guts, disembowelling him. Sharif stood swaying, hot blood soaking his tunic and spreading down his legs. The world tilted, and the ground leapt up to greet him.

Rais called out hoarsely and sprang to his friend's side, dropping to his knees in the dirt. "Sharif, my friend, are you …?" He saw the pooling blood and knew the wound would be swiftly mortal. "I will avenge you, Sharif ibn Malik."

Sharif opened his eyes and stared past his friend to the cloudless blue sky. "I … I thought … I had …" He coughed and stifled a cry of pain. "You … are in … command, Rais ibn …" His eyes wandered and became still.

***

Rais got to his feet slowly, his hands clenched and his face reddening in passion. "He has slain Sharif ibn Malik. They have slain our commander." He glared at the kneeling men and then at the women and children. "Kill them all. Every one of them. Let them all burn in hell as cowardly traitors."

The soldiers hesitated. "All? What of the ones who seek to convert?"

"They are not yet Muslim, but traitorous Christians. Kill them too."

"My lord," Pietro screamed out. "Have mercy. Even your commander, the noble Sharif, called me Muslim. He named me Basir – wisdom – for my actions. Be merciful, I beg you."

Rais stared at the grovelling man and nodded. "I'll spare you, Basir." He threw his sword at the man's feet. "Your first duty as a Muslim is to kill the infidel. Kill this woman he called Maria."

Basir picked up the sword and advanced slowly on the cringing girl. "Forgive me, Maria," he whispered.

"You … you're damned, Pietro," Maria replied. "I spit on you."

"I … I cannot do it." Pietro turned to Rais and dropped the sword. "Please, noble sir. Don't ask me to kill the people I've known all my life. Anything else."

"Then die with your friends." Rais called out to the soldiers. "Do your duty and kill the infidels. All of them." He picked up his sword and thrust it into Pietro.

The killing done, Rais ordered all the bodies to be heaped together and the town set alight. When the flames had taken hold, he led his soldiers away, Sharif's body wrapped and slung over his swaybacked mare. Forsaking the hills, Rais led his men down onto the coast road to meet up with Tariq ibn Ziyad and deliver his friend's body for burial. Where the road dipped down to the coastal plain, Rais stopped and looked back at the funeral pyre that was once a thriving town. Despite the loss of his friend, he grinned, and blue fire sparked in his eyes. He hoped his next assignment would involve the killing of many Christians.

***

I am Rais ibn Rasheed and my duty in life is to kill Christians. I followed my friend Sharif ibn Malik over to Spain when our commander, Tariq ibn Ziyad, invaded. I was with Sharif when he died, and I have risen in Tariq's army in his stead. I would give up my position, wealth and fame though, if I could just undo what happened that day in the small Andalucian village of Almisa.

I did not know him long, which may surprise you given the depth of feeling I have for him. I was born and raised in a small goat and olive village in Sinai in the hills not far from the Egyptian border. It was so small and my hatred for it so great that I do not even remember its name. My father was Rasheed ibn Rasheed, the younger Rasheed being a worthless son of the hard working older one. My grandfather loved me and told me tales of faraway places he had once seen. When he died, my father beat me and put me to work, working the press that squeezed the green oil from the olives. My father was a mean-spirited man who envied my grandfather and lost no opportunity belittling him to any who would listen. I could not escape his voice, and day by day, he destroyed the image I had of the old man. I was told the older Rasheed had never stepped outside the village and every story he told was nothing but lies. There was only one place safe from my father's poisonous tongue – my heart; there I kept the memory of my grandfather alive.

One day when I was eighteen and almost resigned to a dull life pressing olives and tending goats, a squad of soldiers of the Khalifah marched into our village, a young, handsome hero at their head. All my grandfather's stories came rushing back, and I knew if I let this 'story' leave my life, there would never be another one. I volunteered for the Khalifah's army. My father refused to give his permission, and being a good Muslim son, I could only obey when he ordered me to my room. He forgot to order me to stay, however, and that night I broke through the mud daub wall of the house and ran to catch up with the Khalifah's men and the shining hero, Sharif ibn Malik.

Alright, I am no god-cursed sodomite that I should lust after him, nor so weak in my mind that I feel an attraction for this man, Sharif, but I was young and impressionable. He literally saved me from the boredom of village life and the tyranny of my father. I still call myself Rais ibn Rasheed, but in my own mind, Rasheed is my grandfather not my father.

Naturally, Sharif had no idea I revered him, and I was careful not to let my actions or words become unseemly. I am not tall, but I am strong. I learned the skill of a warrior quickly. By the time Sharif's band of men reached the Berber lands of Al-Jazair and Al-Maghrib, I was a trusted aide and a feared soldier of the Khalifah. I was also a drinking companion. This is another aspect of my life I suppose I should not voice abroad too much. The Prophet warns against intoxicating liquids like wine and beer, but I think he was warning against their adverse effects on weak men rather than telling us to avoid the grape which was, after all, created by God. There are always men who obey the letter of the law rather than its intent, so I am circumspect when I drink and thus harm no one.

Women are another weakness of mine. I was raised to respect women. Though I had the normal urges of a young man, it was relatively easy to keep my mind focussed on Allah and put the sight of a slim ankle or wisp of hair away from thoughts. Of course, in a village, you know every woman and they all know you. If I had stayed, my father would have arranged a marriage with a girl from a neighbouring village, as the women in my village are all related to me, though some quite distantly.

As a soldier, I came across women I did not know wherever I went and not all of them were as chaste-minded as a Muslim woman. The first time the soldiers took me to the bazaars of Alexandria, I was shocked. There were many Arab women to be sure, but also Jews, Copts, Christians and a stew of races from farther afield. Their mode of dress was varied too, from almost completely covered to almost naked. Strangely, even the near-naked women went about their business unbothered by men – except for callow youths like me who stared openly.

Worse was to come when the soldiers took me to a tavern. Women danced there and shed what remained of their clothing. They were non-Muslim women, and I suppose whatever god they worshipped allowed such behaviour. I spoke of it to my companions, and my concerns amused them.

"Be thankful for infidel women, young Rais," said Sakhr, pushing the gold disc of his authority to one side as he leaned close to me. His breath smelled pleasantly of herbs mixed with wine, and his hand rested companionably on my shoulder. "Muslim women are chaste and modest, as is only proper, and a man can only slake his thirst for such a one in marriage. An infidel woman, though, knows no better, as you can see." Sakhr's discourse broke off as he inspected the obvious charms of a dusky beauty dancing close to us. "Take her, for instance – literally if you care to. She offers her charms for all to see, and more besides if you have ready coin."

"More?" I said. "What more do you mean?"

"Have you never lain with a woman, Rais? Spent your seed in her tilled field? We must change that, eh fellows?" Sakhr appealed to the other men watching the dancers. They agreed, laughing. "Take this copper coin and go to her when she stops dancing but before another man buys her services. Offer it to her and say, 'Lie with me, daughter of sin,' for Sin is the land she comes from. For copper, a woman will admit you to the heaven that lies between her legs."

I looked at him askance, doubting his sincerity, but not wishing to be thought timid did as I was instructed. She slapped my face and flounced away, calling me all manner of terrible names. Worse even than this was the laughter of my fellow soldiers and the triumphant grin on Sakhr's face. I slunk off into a corner and hid my face in the shadows.

So it came about that despite the ribaldry of my fellow soldiers, I achieved my aim. The girl, whose name was Ahloua – I have never forgotten it – had seen more than I and discerned the reason for my rudeness. She found me in the shadows, shared a drink with me and then, for a gift of silver not copper, took me to her cot in an upstairs room. I learned that night why Allah created man and woman and why he made one part to fit in another and give pleasure to both.

I said goodbye to Ahloua the next morning, though I thought my heart would split in two with sorrow. The girl was businesslike from, I suppose, long practice. She bade me return when I had more silver, and then, seeing my downcast face relented, telling me with silver and a pleasant manner, I would find as many women as I wanted. She was right, and often I did not need to pay silver before we got down to business. However, women must make a living too, so I always gifted them some little trinket they could sell. I made a point of never leaving with a harsh word uttered by either of us.

I have had my share of Muslim women too, but you must not think that they would offer themselves for money or gifts like an infidel. They are considerably more trouble to bed, so unless they are very beautiful, I generally will look elsewhere. A Muslim girl will hold out for marriage but luckily there is a way round this. The Qur'an in Surah An-Nisa, ayat twenty-four states 'All married women are forbidden you except those whom your right hands possess. Other women are lawful for you, provided you seek them with dowries from your own property, taking them honourably, not in debauchery. Those whom you marry for a fixed time, in Mut'ah; give them their dowries, and there is no blame on you concerning whatever you mutually agree after what is appointed.'

What this means is that if I, as a Shi'a, find a willing Muslim girl, I can marry her for a fixed time – a week, a month, a year – and then divorce her, giving her a dowry which she will then use to find another husband. She benefits and I do too, so everyone is happy. The Sunnis say the Prophet abolished Mut'ah, but then the Sunnis are mistaken in many things.

So we wound our way slowly westward across North Africa, visiting remote villages, spreading the word of the upcoming invasion of infidel lands by our Lord Tariq and promising great booty for any man brave enough to join our venture. We found one or two in each village men, and as soon as we put together a score of volunteers, we sent them ahead by the main road under the guidance of an officer. In all, we probably added a hundred men to Tariq's army.

When we reached Ceuta, where the fleet was assembling, it was our task to whip the farm labourer's and layabouts into something that might pass muster for a trained army. I know, I had only a year's start on most of them, but already I could hold my own with any man in Sharif's squad, including Sakhr. Well, alright, maybe not Sakhr, not every time, but I was good. We drilled them to hold a spear and not to flinch when men come yelling at them with weapons raised to take their lives; we showed them how to wield a sword and counter an enemy's thrusts and cuts; we instructed them in the use of bow and arrow until they could hit a target forty paces away seven times out of ten. They were not skilled warriors, but they would swell the numbers, and maybe they would learn how to kill before they were killed.

Sakhr, as ranking officer in Sharif's squad, should have had his ear, been his trusted lieutenant and confidant even though Sharif did not like him. He was a good fighter and had earned his commander's trust. It was just a pity that the son of a whore was surly and pig-headed. It got him killed just a month before we sailed.

I had married again, a raven-haired Berber beauty with gold rings in her ears and nose. We made an arrangement for a temporary marriage to last until we sailed, and I settled a suitable price with her father. Naturally, her charms called to me, and I tried to avoid my duties toiling in the hot sun with half-trained soldiers. Sakhr had never forgiven me for turning the tables on his jest back in Alexandria and lost no opportunity to mock my efforts with women. Now, he pulled me out of my wife's tent to go into the hills with him.

"You've become soft," Sakhr sneered. "The only weapon you can raise is the one between your legs."

I said nothing, for as well as being surly and pig-headed, Sakhr has an evil temper. I knew I was in good shape, better than he, so I let the snide comment pass.

"Draw your sword and let us plumb the depths of your failing," Sakhr told me when we were alone.

This I did not like, for Sakhr was a better swordsman than I and we were not on the practice field using blunted blades. If he killed me out here, he could claim it as an accident. I did not even have a relative to avenge me. However, I could not avoid it, so I pulled my sword out and faced him.

For a time, I was able to parry his blows, though I was forced to give ground. I looked for a way to pierce his defence, for I saw he was angry and I feared for my life if I just let him attack. My only hope was to outlast his fury. Already he was tiring, trying to beat me down with the sheer ferocity of his attack, and then he over-extended himself and I slipped inside his guard. We grappled, each holding the other's sword arm and grunting with the effort.

"Let's call it an even match, Sakhr," I said. "In truth, Sharif would have our balls if he found us fighting with naked blades."

Sakhr nodded and I felt his muscles relax. "Your sword skills are laughable," he said. "I should put you on report."

"I have other abilities," I replied, starting to feel annoyed.

"Ah, yes, your much-boasted about spear. Let us hope the Spanish army is made up of women so you can prove your prowess."

"I can shoot the bow better than you. Also, I'm faster ..."

Sakhr laughed. "I've no doubt if we ever have to retreat, you'll beat us all back to the boats."

That got me angry. If he had been any other than the squad leader, I would have called him out for it. You do not call a man a coward, unless you are prepared to back your words up with actions. He saw it in my face and smiled.

"Think you can run faster than me, Rais? A hundred gold dinars say I can beat you back to camp."

I was tempted. A hundred dinars was a fortune that neither of us had but that he, as an officer, would find easier to borrow. I was fairly certain I could win that race, but that would not expunge the slur he had cast on my name. "That's an easy course, all downhill, and proves nothing." I turned and pointed in the opposite direction. "Race me to the top of the hill, if you're not afraid." Crudely put, but he was angry. He ran well, I'll say that for him, but he was a big man and I beat him to the summit. I could have beaten him easily, but I paced myself, knowing this race was not the end of his efforts to belittle me. It would not end until one of us was dead.

He was deeply flushed, and his breath came in great whooping gusts when we topped the hill; so before he could catch his breath, I challenged him again.

"I've seen girls run faster when striving to protect their modesty," I sneered. "Is that the best you can do?"

He drew his sword and came at me, staggering and slashing wildly. I dodged but did not draw my weapon. Instead I picked up a rock and threw it at him. He yelled and came at me again. I ran, enticing him on with taunts, staying just out of reach. His breath came faster, his face turned scarlet and he roared with rage as he stumbled after me. I led him on until we reached a steep part of the track, where the rock was shattered and loose. I turned and picked up a rock, taking my time, and bounced it off his skull. He went down like a tall tree when it feels the axeman's blows, sliding and tumbling until he fetched up against a large rock.

I climbed down to him and pelted him with pebbles, until I was sure he was not shamming. Sakhr was dead, his eyes staring blindly from a blood-covered face. I said a prayer for him – he was my brother in Allah, after all – and then I went back to camp to report his death in a fall while we were exercising.

I paid blood money to Sakhr's relatives back in Syria. It was not required strictly as no one knew I had killed him, but I was mindful of the Holy Qur'an at Surah An-Nisa, ayat ninety-two where it says a believer is not to kill a believer except by mistake. Ayat ninety-three says because I killed Sakhr intentionally, my lot is Hell, but I will trust in Allah the All-Knowing and Compassionate. He knows that I killed in self-defence. I wanted to go a little bit further than I had to, so I sent Sakhr's relatives ten dinars in gold, telling them it was his share of the booty.

Sharif reprimanded me for carelessness, but

only mildly as Sakhr outranked me and if he challenged me to a race up the hill, well of course I was not to blame. He waited a week for decency and then promoted me to his position.

Three weeks after, we sailed for Spain, and a week after that, Sharif was dead, killed by an infidel while protecting my back. What can I say? We are all in God's hands, and we live or die by God's will. All I can do now is make sure my friend, Sharif, is adequately avenged. I have vowed a thousand infidel deaths for his, and I am nearly halfway there. For the last three years, I have not even lain with a woman, not a Jew or a Christian, for everyone I find I kill. When the thousand are dead, then I will drink wine in remembrance of my friend and put the memory of his death behind me, but until then – forgive me if I do not talk further – there is a village only ten miles from here and my sword hungers again.

Chapter Fourteen

I have decided, and my decision is good. I am tired of being a god – well, of masquerading as one anyway. I will be true to my nature and be a djinni once more. In truth, it is easier, for no one expects anything of you. Most people do not even know I am there. I drift into a life, feed on the energies of the man or woman, kill if I am so inclined, and move on. What could be easier or more natural?

I left Arabia and its peoples for a time when it became apparent Islam was a force to be reckoned with. I journeyed east for a while, seeking nothing in particular, just sampling the lives of the different peoples who inhabit those lands. I killed often, sometimes to feed, other times just to feel the horror and dread within a man's mind as he faces extinction. Every man professes to believe he will continue to exist in some form after the fleshly body has been rendered unfit for use, but when faced with the last breath, the last beat of the heart or the last fading thought, they all doubt – even holy men and priests. Sometimes I play on that doubt, revealing myself at the last moment, telling them that as they are possessed by a demon as they die, their fate will be to burn in hell forever. It is all nonsense of course. Men's flames flicker and go out; they do not exist elsewhere. I do though. I absorb their energy and go on to my next victim.

I can, as I have already said, exist without killing. I can lap gently at the sea of energy within a person, feeding without depleting their resources. I could go through a city, filling myself to bursting point, and not a single human would be aware I was there. I have done so. When I was a god, men and women prayed to me, and this directed energy fed me too. But feeding in this manner is like eating a bowl of plain unsalted rice or a loaf of unleavened wheat bread. It fills, but it does not satisfy. I seek the succulent meat off the bone, spiced sauces and sweetened desserts, you see? I know enough about humans to borrow their metaphors. How could I not when so often their thoughts sustain me?

I journeyed east as far as the land of Chin and then came back through the jungles of the south, travelling as far and as fast as I liked, or stopping off at some interesting place to absorb the customs of a people. I saw neither gods nor many demons, though I try to be circumspect in my actions, moving on before my depredations start to be widely noticed. I found a few places where some demon or another wrought havoc among a local population and heard stories of others, but always the stories ended with relief coming from some supernatural source. Men do so love a tale of wonders, and what can be more wondrous for a short-lived creature than to hear of immortal beings?

There was one demon though. They call them rakshas in India, and there was this one in the north where the land hurls itself skyward, clothed in forest below and ice above, who was different. I did not seek him out, and he did not seek me. Our paths crossed, and I doubt he was even aware of me. He came raging down a river called the Alaknanda, killing as he came, but then I saw him spare a girl, a child, and wondered why. When he left, I asked the child, but her grief at the death of her parents obscured all other thoughts. I granted her the peace of a gentle death and moved on.

I was back in the region of Arabia about forty years after I left, but what a change had come over the place. I was right to think Islam was an unstoppable force, but it was not the Islam I fled from. I think Muhammad's greatest mistake – or possibly Allah's – was to bring the message to men. Men are vile creatures, ever ready to tread another man into the ground or stab him in the back, so as to gain some advantage. It was no different in this new religion, this new way of life. Men clambered and fought to the top of the pile, all for the sake of power. I do not know if Muhammad intended his own descendants to succeed him, or whether he thought the most able man should follow him, but within those forty years, his own relatives ruled and died, and Muawiya, the son of Abu Sufyan, rose to the Khalifate and founded the Umaiyid dynasty.

Two sects now make up Islam, Shi'a and Sunni, splitting the movements between those that think Muhammad's successors should be descended from Ali, the cousin of their Prophet, and those that think their leader should be chosen by the Muslim community as a whole – in other words, the man with the strongest army. None of this really matters to me, of course, but there is one great advantage to this internecine conflict – the more men are divided, the more they kill each other and often in inventive ways.

The Muslims swept across North Africa and across into Christian Europe. I followed, finding men I could manipulate or encourage into excess. One such was Rais, a common soldier. I was with him on the crossing to Spain, inuring him against seasickness, giving him strength and fueling his lust. With me in control, Rais was the first into battle, the fiercest fighter and the most virile of men.

I was with Rais for nearly ten years. When his friend, Sharif, died, he vowed vengeance, and I fostered these notions. He decided a thousand Christian deaths would be the blood price and set about achieving it. For five years, he built himself a fearsome reputation as a warrior, but as Spain became settled, there were fewer opportunities for bloodshed. By seven years, his tally stood at eight hundred. Tariq had long since been recalled to the court of the Khalifah, and Musa was now governor. His ideas of rule were less sanguine, and he viewed Rais with some disdain, keeping him attached to the court where he could do no harm.

Islam has always allowed for Jews and Christians to live amongst them, following their own beliefs. They are called dhimmi and count as second-class citizens, but as long as they pay their taxes, they are afforded a measure of the law. Rais could not stand this law and looked for ways to circumvent it. Under these laws, a believer may kill a dhimmi, but under no circumstances may a dhimmi kill a believer. Rais used this, picking fights or accusing innocent men and then killing them. The deaths of a few would have gone unremarked, but each death meant a loss of revenue for the governor, and in the end, he decided it could go on no longer.

Governor Musa sent Rais on a punitive expedition into an area still controlled by Christian knights. He then sent news of the expedition to the enemy. Rais and his men were captured and tortured.

I must say the Christians are quite inventive when it comes to pain. I helped matters along by inducing Rais to utter some particularly revolting blasphemies and then reveled in his agony as they slowly took him apart. When he died, after a deliciously long time, I possessed a few Christians for a number of years, but for some reason, it was not the same. Perhaps it is because I was born of the Arabian wastelands, and I found myself wanting to be back there. I went the long way round, overland through Europe and through the Bosphorus, until I came to familiar territory.

There are demons in Europe – I even interacted with a few, including an interesting female one, a succubus – but not as many as Christians believe. Curiously, the flame of these European demons is red-tinged as mine contains a hint of green. I have no idea if this is significant.

I have to admit, the world is a wonderful place for one such as I. There is so much pain and suffering I can make a living wherever I go. Arabia, the East, North Africa, Spain, Europe and Syria – they all give me pleasure, but I am after other sensations. Where shall I go next?

Chapter Fifteen

Aaliyah bint Fuad was born in Fustat on the banks of the Nile and lived there all her life. She married, was widowed under unusual circumstances and married again; yet never saw the need to travel further than an occasional trip to Alexandria to sell her leather goods. Later, when the Sultan of Egypt, Salah ad-Din Yusuf ibn Ayyub, commonly called Saladin, raised a wall around both Qahira and Fustat, she seldom left its confines, doing business within the city and letting buyers come to her.

Her father, Fuad ibn Nazih, had been a smalltime tanner and had plied his smelly business well outside the town limits. Fuad married and had a dozen good years with a woman he grew to love, before the bloody flux carried her off. He was blessed with two sons and a daughter and died when Aaliyah, the youngest, was only thirteen. Her brothers died before her father – one of disease (the same flux that took his mother) and the other from a knife in the back when he was hurrying home one dark night. Aaliyah inherited her father's business at a tender age, but she never considered the option of selling it or letting a cousin or uncle take it over. When challenged by her male relatives, she pointed to the example of Sauda bint Zama, wife of the Prophet.

"Respectfully, Oh brothers of my father, was not Sauda bint Zama, second wife of the Prophet, also a worker in leather. We are told she had a thriving business when she married."

"Presumptuous child," scolded one uncle. "The Qur'an at Sura al-Ahzab, ayat thirty-three tells wives to stay in their homes not to indulge in business, which is the affair of men."

"Then forgive my presumption, uncle, for doesn't that ayat refer to the wives of the prophet? I'm not a wife yet, and when I am, I'll listen to the counsel of my husband. For now, I'll manage my father's leather business, which he left to me as my inheritance."

Her uncles left without addressing another word to her. Aaliyah hitched her dress up and started trampling the hides as she had seen her father do, and after a few years of hardship, the business started to grow. She bought slaves, black men from Nubia, and had them educated in the Qur'an, for she believed all men should come to knowledge of God. She was an imposing woman, slim and taller than most women, and she developed strength of body to augment her strength of spirit.

Aaliyah was eighteen when her uncles arranged a marriage for her. It was in her mind to refuse, but her Aunt Hadya pointed out she had no father or brother to perform this vital duty for her.

"How else are you going to find a husband? Will you go out on the streets like a common whore and meet a man that way? It is the duty of the men in our family to find you a husband."

Aaliyah reluctantly agreed to the marriage, and Shadi ibn Masood from distant Al-Jazair, a small man with a small business – he was a dealer in mud bricks – moved in with her, paying her, fittingly enough, a small dowry. Within a year, Shadi had

spent all her money and bankrupted his own business. Then he started to run up debts. They had a son which she insisted on naming Fuad in honour of her father, but even he was little recompense against the steady destruction of her life. She remonstrated with her husband but was first ignored and then beaten. She called on her family to intervene, but they were aghast that she would try and involve them in a matter that concerned husband and wife. She decided to try and divorce her husband, and the decision caused an uproar.

"You'll bring shame on our family, foolish woman," said her uncles. "Go home and learn to be a submissive wife."

"God gave me a mind, and my father gave me the opportunity to use it. I'm more than just the wife of a wastrel," she retorted, but her uncles refused to listen. She told Shadi what she intended to do.

"You cannot do this," Shadi howled. "I'll not allow it."

"It's not for you to allow or disallow, husband," Aaliyah replied, meeting his outraged gaze instead of replying with downcast eyes.

"The Qur'an doesn't allow it," Shadi said smugly. "You may take it to a judge, if you want to make a fool of yourself." He then took a stick thicker than his thumb as prescribed by law and beat her.

Aaliyah hired a lawyer for gold in hand. He shook his head at her intention but took her money and then her suit before a judge. The judge listened to both sides and then passed down his judgment without even retiring to consider his decision.

"There's provision under Shari'ah law for a woman to divorce her husband. This is called Khula. However, there are certain circumstances pertaining to the granting of this Khula. When a woman decides to marry a man, she has made a conscious decision to accept the man as head of the household in all things. This entails obedience to his will on her part and a duty of care on his part. Should there be a desire for divorce on the part of the woman, she must first have made every effort to address the problems inherent in the marriage. A woman cannot demand a divorce; she can only ask her husband for one. A husband who cares for his wife will grant her request, if it's plain that the marriage has broken down without possibility of reconciliation. This hasn't happened here.

"The woman, Aaliyah bint Fuad, has demanded a divorce, contrary to law, and the husband, Shadi ibn Masood, has made it plain that he doesn't desire a divorce, because he believes he can be reconciled with his wife. Therefore, there can be no divorce. Although the woman's property is her own, inherited from her father, and the husband should be supporting her from his income rather than living on the profits of her business, yet this is no reason for a woman to divorce a husband where the man doesn't agree to it. Let the husband work and support his family, as he should. Woman, learn to live with your husband in the submissive manner proper to a Muslim wife."

When they got home, Shadi beat Aaliyah again for putting him through the shame of a court appearance and knocked out one of her teeth. He then took what money there was in the house and went into the city, spending it all on drink and prostitutes.

Aaliyah thought about her situation for several days and then went to her husband and bowed before him. "Legally the business is mine, husband, but I'll do as the judge orders. You shall work by managing the tannery, and I'll stay home like a dutiful wife and look after our son."

"That stinking place? There must be something else I can do."

Aaliyah shrugged delicately. "That stinking place makes us money. Do you know how to keep accounts, go to the buyers and bargain for the best prices or how to go about finding skins?"

"No."

"Then managing the tannery, though smelly, is something you can do to earn money. You should know how leather is made if you're to manage the whole business one day."

Shadi reluctantly agreed and every day went off to work outside the city limits, returning each evening reeking of urine, excrement and rotting meat. He complained bitterly, but Aaliyah praised him for his diligence and at the end of the month gave him gold for his efforts.

"You've done well, husband, and you're worthy of your reward. Take it and do as you see fit."

Shadi immediately left for the taverns and brothels, as Aaliyah knew he would. That night, she locked and bolted the doors and the main gate, leaving only the side gate unlatched. The side gate was only used by the night soil merchants when they took the household waste to the tanning works along with the waste from the city. She had devised a plan, but it relied on Shadi coming home drunk and using the side gate.

Do I dare essay this? What if I fail or I'm found out? What else can I do? I must do something.

Midnight passed and the sky started to lighten in the east. Aaliyah began to worry that her husband was sleeping off his excesses somewhere in Fustat, but then she heard the catch on the side gate click and the gate swing open. She drew a shawl about her and hurried out with a hooded lantern, careful to let no ray of light illumine the courtyard. *It's not too late …*

"Woman? Ish … ish that you? Where's the … where's the fornic … fornicating lantern?" Shadi stumbled and almost fell, uttering a crude curse. "I'll thrash you, you … you bitch, if you don' …"

"I'm here, husband."

"Wha … where?" Shadi peered into the blackness.

"Right in front of you. Give me your arm, and I'll guide you to bed."

Shadi shuffled forward and tripped over a wooden bench carefully placed across the path. He fell forward onto his face with a yell, and as he did so, Aaliyah lifted the hood from the lantern. Shadi looked up, squinting, and Aaliyah cracked him on the head with a stone. He collapsed back with a groan.

"May God forgive me," she muttered, "but there should be a provision for a woman to rid herself of a worthless man." She stared down at her husband's unconscious body and breathed a faint laugh. "It seems I must find it myself if the Law won't help."

Aaliyah set the lantern down and dragged Shadi over to where the tall pot of nightsoil stood. She removed the top from it and peered in, her eyes watering from the ammoniacal stench of its contents. With a great effort, she hauled her husband upright, blessing the fortune that made her strong and he small, and stood him beside the jar.

"Such a waste of good urine," she murmured, grasping Shadi's ankles and tipping him headfirst into the jar of nightsoil.

Shadi revived as he went into the noxious liquid and started struggling. Aaliyah looked in horror at his thrashing feet and backed away. Her conscience screamed at her to pull him out, but she hesitated, and when she did finally take hold of his ankles, he had ceased all movement. She pulled him out anyway, splashing herself liberally in the process and stared at her husband's contorted face in the light of the lantern. She shuddered and closed her eyes, aghast at what she had done.

Turning away at last, she stripped her stinking dress and shawl from her and went into the house to wash and check on little Fuad, and then she ate some food, knowing she would need her strength. She also peeled a small onion. Dawn arrived, and dressing in her wet and noisome clothes again, she unbolted the main gate and went out into the road.

"Send for the Shurta," she told the first man she saw. "Someone has murdered my husband." She also sent a man to take a message to her Aunt Hadya.

Her Aunt Hadya, the Shurta deputy chief, Abd-al-Aziz, and his assistant, Shukri, arrived by the time the sun had risen a span into the eastern sky, along with a crowd of interested sightseers. The assistant closed the gates to keep them out while the Shurta deputy walked over to the body of Shadi. He looked down at the corpse with a cloth held over his nose.

"What happened?" Abd-al-Aziz asked Aaliyah.

"I don't know. My husband went into the city last night. I came out this morning, and he was ... he was there." Just before the Shurta had arrived, she had rubbed onion juice into her eyes and they now appeared red and inflamed, tears streaming down her face. The stench of the nightsoil covered any odour the onion might have. Aunt Hadya put her arm comfortingly around her niece.

"Lying just there?"

"N ... no. He was in the jar. I hauled him out."

Abd-al-Aziz ventured a quick look into the pot before withdrawing. "You said he was murdered. What makes you say that?"

"Would any man choose to kill himself like that?' asked Hadya scathingly. "And how could you accidentally fall into the jar? Somebody put him there."

Abd-al-Aziz grimaced at the old woman's tone. "Who?"

"How should I know?" Hadya asked.

Aaliyah shook her head. "I cannot imagine. My husband was well-liked in the town of Fustat."

"Oh? Who told you that?" Shukri asked, coming up behind her.

"He did. Isn't it true?"

Shukri snorted, but Abd-al-Aziz said gently, "All men have enemies. Shadi obviously did."

"But you'll find these enemies?"

"I'll make enquiries. Is there anything else you can tell me?"

Aaliyah frowned and seemed to hesitate before replying. "We had gold in the house, honoured sir. Twenty dinar from a large sale of leather this week. I thought my husband only took some of it when he went out last night, but this morning it's all gone."

Hadya tut-tutted. "That man loved his drink."

"Drinking is against the Law of God," Shukri said.

"So is murder," Abd-al-Aziz observed.

"He sinned, and he paid the penalty. Perhaps it was God's will," Hadya said.

"Or another's."

"What do you mean?"

"Robbery can be a motive for murder," Abd-al-Aziz said.

"You didn't hear these robbers?" Shukri asked.

Aaliyah shook her head. "I didn't know it was gone until this morning. And my … my husband could've taken it all last night."

"There is, of course, another possible motive," Shukri pointed out. "I understand you sought to divorce your husband."

"That is true," Aaliyah confirmed. "However, the judge found against me and bid me reconcile with my husband. I did that, and we … we … and now this happens." She put her face in her hands and rubbed a finger into her eyes, reanointing them with traces of onion juice. Fresh tears trickled down her face. Hadya put her arm around Aaliyah again, but the young woman was so tall it looked as if she was comforting the older woman.

"If the court wouldn't separate you, did you seek to separate yourself by other, fouler means?" Shukri persisted.

"How can you say such a thing?!" Hadya exclaimed. "Aaliyah is a model of hardworking chaste womanhood, obedient to family and husband. She comes from an excellent family, far better than yours, assistant Shukri."

"Of course," Abd-al-Aziz said. "But we must, however, explore all possibilities."

The assistant went and looked in the jar. "Why is there so much? Don't you have your waste taken away daily like everyone else?"

"We own a tannery and for this we purchase urine from the collectors. Naturally we use our own as well, but it's more economical to save it and transport it with the other collections."

"So it was bad luck you had a full jar sitting here." Shukri bent over Shadi's body and poked a large bruise on his forehead. "Violence has been done. He was struck with something."

"Probably to subdue him before putting him in there," Abd-al-Aziz observed. "But why bother killing him? If the gold in your house was the object of a robbery, why kill him as well?"

"Unless he knew them," Shukri said. "We must question his known associates."

"That'll not be easy. You'll have to send men into the brothels and taverns. Get started on that," Abd-al-Aziz ordered. He waited until his assistant had left and then spoke quietly. "I'll send men to collect and prepare the body for burial in the absence of his family. Aaliyah bint Fuad, we have only your word on the events that happened here last night. There were no witnesses. When we track down Shadi's associates, are we going to find contradictions to your story?" He stood and stared at Aaliyah for several minutes, but she returned his gaze, striving to be neither too bold nor too meek. "I think there's more to this tale, but I'll leave you for now. Maybe we'll talk again. You realise that if we recover your gold, most of it will go toward Shurta expenses?"

"The gold's not important. Just find the killers of my husband."

"And if there is no gold?"

"Then I'm sure you'll do your duty."

Aaliyah buried her husband, and as the days became weeks and dragged out into months, she waited for the Shurta deputy to find some discrepancy in her story. She put the guilt she felt behind her, knowing she had done it to survive, but half expecting God's vengeance to find her out. The thunderbolt did not fall, however, and Aaliyah strove to take her mind off the possibility of catastrophe by losing herself in her work. She found a woman to look after Fuad during the day and spent from dawn to dusk at the tannery outside the walls of Fustat, thinking only of animal skins, urine and leather. However, the guilt of the murder nagged at her.

Despite her late husband's efforts, the business still ran smoothly, and Aaliyah now had several slaves to help with the drudgery. Raw skins were bought from herdsmen and shipped up or down river to the primitive docks at Fustat. They were collected and brought by donkey to the tannery. Aaliyah had an arrangement with the nightsoil collectors of Fustat and Qahira to buy quantities of human urine, and with the butchers to buy sheep, goat and calf brains. Small children were given the job of collecting dog dung and paid small copper coins for basket loads.

Typically, the skins arrived stiff with dirt and dried blood and often crawling with maggots. The first task was to make them supple again, so they were soaked in vats of water. Slaves pounded the skins with wooden mallets to soften them, and then trained men and women stretched the stinking skins over wooden frames and carefully scraped the insides free of rotting flesh and fat. Aaliyah always oversaw this task and often sat down with her slaves to take part because a slip of the knife could ruin a hide. When the inside of the skin had been scraped clean, it was time to remove the hair.

The nightsoil was filtered to remove the solid waste that inevitably ended up in containers meant only for urine. The human excrement was sold on to farmers to use as fertilizer for their crops. The urine was left to stand in large vats, and when sufficiently rotted, the scraped skins were immersed in the noxious brew. Swarms of flies were always attendant on the vats and clustered around the people working there, but they could be ignored. Poles could be used to manipulate the skins, mixing and swirling the urine, but vigorous action could damage the skins, so the soaking hides were trampled under bare feet. Aaliyah always made a point of joining her slaves in this unpleasant task and had often explained her reasoning when questioned about the foul smell clinging to her feet even after she washed.

"Nobody likes to do that job, not even the slaves. I could compel them to do it, but they work much more willingly if they see me share their labours."

A day of trampling in the urine and the hair would start to pull loose from the hide. While still wet, the slaves would rip and pull at the short hair, thoroughly denuding the skin. Aaliyah dealt with the almost finished product, scraping it gently with a sharp knife to completely depilate it. If she was not yet ready to further treat the hides, she oiled them and set them aside.

The remaining processes of turning depilated hides into leather were equally odoriferous, involving the use of the dog excrement and animal brains. First Aaliyah prepared vats of water in which oak bark and leaves had been soaking for several weeks. These hair-free skins were spread out and the dung of dogs smeared all over them and rubbed in well. A new slave asked her about this process.

"See how the untreated skin is springy and when you bend it, resumes its old position," she replied. “After we rub it with dog dung and wash it out, the hide is soft and flexible.”

“Why do we use dog dung, mistress? Cattle dung is far more plentiful and cheaper.”

“It does not work. For some reason the dung must come from a meat-eater. Cat dung would do, as would that of pigeons or foxes …” Aaliyah grinned. “… but where would we find enough?”

She instructed the slave to take the dung-covered skins down to the river and wash them thoroughly. “Make sure there is no trace of dung left, for we want no more maggots in the skins.”

When the washed skins came back, they were soaked in the tannin-stained water in the bark vats for a few days and then taken out and left to dry in the shade. The resultant leather was pale tan in colour, soft and flexible. The last task was to carefully cut away the edges that had nicks and scratches, holes and strips of hair that had escaped the flensing process. The finished product was stacked away in the storehouse.

Aaliyah knew from long experience that different treatments produced different types of leather. Some types were more suitable for saddles and horse or camel gear, other types for shoes. A method she used increasingly was preparation with brains. It was more work but produced softer leather if done properly and fetched a higher price. The old tanners used to say each animal had just enough brains to cure its own hide, implying that different types of brains were needed depending on the animal skin being treated. Aaliyah had experimented and could discern no difference in the finished product whether she used the brain of the animal itself or the brain from another species. Sheep and calf brains were the easiest and cheapest to obtain, so she used those.

She took some of the hides that had been stripped of their flesh, fat and hair but did not go into a urine bath. Instead, brains were cooked and mashed into slurry and then rubbed into the hide, skin side first and then hide side. It called for a lot of effort, and the brain mix had to be kept warm, so large rounded rocks were heated in the fire and used to smooth the skin. After a day of rubbing brains into the hide, it was soaked overnight in water.

The next morning, each hide was staked out taut and wooden wedges used to push the water out of the hide. Over and over, the wedge was pressed into the skin, forcing water out of the pores and sweeping it away. When no more could be squeezed out, a different instrument was used – a stick carved and polished into a round, smooth, blunt point. For the rest of the day, the strongest slaves pushed this stick over the taut hide, working over every part of it, and when every point had been stretched, shifted the orientation of the skin and did it again. Aaliyah would examine it at intervals and point out bits that had been missed.

“It is still moist,” she’d say. “Unless you squeeze and work every drop of water out of it, it will become stiff again. See the fibres in the skin? Those must all be loosened and stretched.”

When the skin was dry to the touch, a slave took the hide by each end and passed it around a well-smoothed stake set in the ground. He pulled it this way and that, back and forth, squeezing out a little more water, and heating it by friction as the fibres were stretched further. Finally it was draped over a smoky fire, so the smoke could penetrate the leather, preserving it and preventing water from getting back into the fibres. These brain-cured hides were also stored but separately from the urine-cured ones.

Once a month on average, Aaliyah loaded her leather sheets onto donkeys and took them into the markets of Fustat. Her father had sold them singly at a stall in the bazaar, but Aaliyah had tracked down the main users of leather and persuaded them to buy from her in quantity for a discounted price. Now she had no more than half a dozen customers and took the leather to their shops directly. She made a little less money per hide but was assured of a market and wasted less time trying to find buyers.

On one such delivery day, about a year after the death of her husband, she was waiting in the shop of the noted shoe merchant, Kamil, while he conducted business with another customer in a back room. Aaliyah left her bundle of leather on the counter and walked around the shop, examining the finished wares and observing the work of Kamil's many assistants. Some men cut the leather using a pattern, others punched holes in the leather and others stitched, drawing a thread made of twisted intestine through the tiny holes.

She watched the stitchers for a time and then asked, "Wouldn't it be easier to pull the thread through if the holes were bigger?"

One man ignored her, but a young lad agreed. "The problem is though, that if the holes are larger, the shoes are not waterproof. Keep them very small and the thread draws the leather tight."

"Ah, I see. You know your business."

The older man grunted. "He will know it in time, if he controls his tongue and pays attention to his job."

The lad laughed. "Take no notice of Ali. You're the tanner aren't you? This is fine leather you make."

Aaliyah thanked him and would have asked his name but the curtain to the back room was swept aside and two men entered. One was short and stout with a full beard and glittering eyes that flicked an intense gaze around the room, missing nothing. The other was tall and spare of frame with a carefully trimmed beard. He looked to be a young man as his beard and hair showed no trace of gray.

"Ah, the very person I was talking about," the short man said. "Latif ibn Yaqub, this is my tanner, Aaliyah. If there's anyone in Fustat or Qahira who can help you, it's her."

The tall man bowed politely and fixed the tall woman with an interested look. "I am delighted to meet you, Aaliyah. Kamil has told me of your expertise in making leather."

Aaliyah nodded back politely and then stared at the short shop keeper. "Let me make something abundantly clear – I'm nobody's tanner. I'm my own woman, and I answer to no man. I'll sell my leather to any man prepared to meet my price, but I can also choose not to sell to him."

Kamil flushed and looked away. "Yes, er … well, I didn't mean to give offence." His eyes lit on the pile of leather on the counter. "I see you've brought more leather. At the, er … usual price?"

"Yes. You wish to examine it?"

"No, no, no, that won't be necessary. Highest quality, you know," he muttered to Latif. "Well, I'm a busy man." He bowed briefly to both and hurried off to examine the leather.

"A woman of fire," Latif murmured.

"I, too, am busy," Aaliyah said. "If you'll excuse me?" She adjusted her shawl to cover her hair completely before stepping out into the street.

Latif moved slightly to block her exit. "May I speak with you for a few minutes?"

"You're in my way, ibn Yaqub."

"My pardon." Latif moved aside and followed her out of the shop. "I would still like to speak with you."

"Where are you from, ibn Yaqub?"

"Latif, please. I'm from Damascus."

"In Damascus perhaps a man may speak to an unattended woman in the street, but in Fustat such a thing is frowned upon. There are standards."

"Of course. I don't wish to give offence. Perhaps I could speak with your husband?"

Aaliyah caught her breath. "I … I'm not married."

"Your brother then? A male relative?"

"No." A slight smile tweaked Aaliyah's lips. "There's my son … but he's not yet two years old." She controlled herself and added. "I don't live with a male relative, and I manage my business alone. If you have something to say to me about leather or tanning, you may call on me at the tannery. Take the south gate and follow your nose and the flies." She walked away and did not look back.

"After noon prayers tomorrow, then," Latif called after her.

An hour after the Dhuhr prayers the next day, Latif presented himself at Aaliyah's tannery outside the southern walls of Fustat. A slave let him in and conducted him to the shaded central tent where she kept records of every consignment of skins and every delivery made to her buyers. She was writing on a sheet of paper when he walked up, so he waited in silence until she finished, sanded the ink, blew off the excess and slipped the sheet into a box containing similar records.

"You have a fine hand, Aaliyah bint Fuad. That's uncommon in a woman."

"I'm an uncommon woman," Aaliyah agreed. "My father believed that both male and female should be educated, for did not God create both men and women to praise him?"

"Indeed." Latif paused for a moment, uncertain whether he should pursue this line of conversation. After a few moments, he decided against it. "May I speak with you about another matter?"

Aaliyah arose from the carpet where she had been sitting and bowed. She indicated a place on the carpet. "Please accept my hospitality, Latif ibn Yaqub, though I'm afraid that I can offer you only plain water and dates."

Latif bowed in turn and sat cross-legged. "Water and dates were offered to the Prophet and accepted with praise for Allah and the giver. I can do no less, Aaliyah bint Fuad. May the blessing of Allah the Merciful, the Beneficent, be upon you."

Aaliyah sent a slave scurrying for the provisions and sat down opposite the man. "My tent is a less than salubrious place to talk," she said. "The smell of the vats is particularly noticeable today."

"It's an honourable odour, being that of hard work and the production of a valuable commodity."

While they waited for food and drink, Latif and Aaliyah sat and casually examined each other, sending fleeting glances and following the contours of chin and cheekbone, arm and hand, the pleasing folds of robes and head-shawl, the glint of gold and silver from rings and anklet and the gleam of dark, deepset eyes. When the provisions arrived, Aaliyah served her guest with her own hand and waited until he had eaten and drunk his fill before speaking.

"What did you want to say?" she asked.

"So direct," he murmured. "I've seen the quality of the shoe leather you produce, and I can see from the size of your works and the number of slaves you employ that you run a successful and efficient business. May I ask what leathers you commonly make?"

"Mostly brain-cured for shoes and dung-cured for harder leather. I also experiment with other methods from time to time."

"Parchment?"

Aaliyah shook her head. "There's little demand for it here in Egypt. I have all the work I need with my leathers."

"There's going to be a demand for it," Latif said, leaning forward slightly, though whether in excitement or from a desire to be more private, Aaliyah could not determine.

"In Alexandria or Damascus or Jerusalem, no doubt, but not here in Fustat," she said. "Papyrus is far cheaper and easier to make here in the land where it grows."

"But it isn't as useful as well-made parchment. Have you forgotten that Salah ad-Din has become Sultan of Egypt? He intends to move his entire seat of government to the court in Qahira. For a government to operate efficiently, it needs mountains of records – records written on parchment."

"If that's so, then I'm sorry that I cannot help you,"Aaliyah said.

"Perhaps you might, if you're willing."

Aaliyah looked away and fanned at the ubiquitous flies. *He's attractive, but do I need him*? *No. Ah, but do I want him? Fool. Remember what happened with the last one. Could you live with doing that again*? "What did you have in mind?"

"You have a successful business and a reliable work force right here in Fustat. I have the knowledge of how to make good quality parchment. I propose a partnership. You provide the site and the labour, I provide the expertise."

"And the profits?"

"Split equally between us."

Aaliyah considered the proposal for several minutes, staring out over the urine vats, while her mind weighed the advantages. "Why don't you set up in business for yourself? That way all the profit is yours."

"That's true," Latif said. "And I had considered it, but I'd have to find land and build the vats and pits necessary, hire men or buy slaves, buy skins, obtain supplies of lime … all this is expensive and time consuming." He shrugged. "I have little money."

Ah, there we have it. Greedy, like all men. "So you want me to set you up in business and then only take half the profits? I think not. If I do it, I'll take three parts out of four."

Latif showed his fine white teeth in amusement. "Making parchment's a delicate affair. Not at all like your coarse leathers. Equal shares."

"I'm sorry you've had a wasted trip, ibn Yaqub. Perhaps you should wait until you have some money backing you before you try entering the parchment business."

"I doubt I'm the first to contemplate supplying the government with parchment, and many will try for a share in the market."

"This is supposed to convince me? You tell me now that should I invest in this, not only will I have only a half share in the business, but my own share must decrease with time."

"Only if you hesitate, Aaliyah bint Fuad. The first person to supply fine quality parchment to the government will win the contract. We're looking at hundreds of dinars every year."

Aaliyah raised her eyebrows. "That much? How many sheets of parchment?"

Latif shrugged. "A thousand at a time? Probably more. Every decision made by the judges must be recorded, every promulgation laid down by the Sultan, and then the imams will want their sermons taken down for posterity."

"Even if we were the first, others will come along and supplant us."

"No, for our parchment will be superior, and we'll have a government contract. Trust me in this, for I've learned at the feet of masters."

"Where?" Aaliyah asked curiously.

"In Damascus, Anatolia …" Latif shrugged. "Are we partners? Equal shares?"

"Three shares out of five. I have all the initial expense."

"Your expenses reimbursed twofold in the first year. After that equal shares."

Aaliyah watched the man's eyes for signs of guile but saw none. "Very well. We try it."

"Excellent. Now, what I'll need first …"

"Shouldn't we draw up an agreement first and have it witnessed? I omitted this once before and regretted it." *Ah, and that's not all I regret.*

Latif nodded. "As you wish. Draw up a contract, and I'll sign it. Now, I'll need five vats measuring at least three paces in length, and plenty of water. Fifty skins to start with, adult goat or similar, but as equal in size as possible. Also, a sack of pumice rocks, a dozen bags of lime and …" Latif went on to list a dozen items, ticking them off on his fingers before bringing out a neat list. "I hoped you might agree," he said with a smile.

That afternoon, Aaliyah had three of her slaves start to scrub out two of the urine vats, and another two constructing new ones. Latif borrowed a small amount of money and hurried into town to start looking for other supplies. Aaliyah handed over the silver with few qualms. *If I'm wrong, it's a small loss*, she told herself. *I think he's honest – at least as honest as any man can be.*

While Latif was away, another visitor came to call at the tannery. Aaliyah's breath caught in her throat when Shurta Deputy Abd-al-Aziz strode in, pushing her slaves aside. He looked around the yard, caught sight of Aaliyah and stalked across to her.

"Deputy Abd-al-Aziz, what a surprise to see you. Have you caught the killers of my husband?"

"I've found out a few things, Aaliyah bint Fuad, that puzzle me. Perhaps you can shed some light on them."

"If I can," Aaliyah said cautiously, feeling a tremor start in her throat.

"We found out your husband's drinking companions on the night he was murdered. I've only just come to see you because two of them were so inebriated they could remember nothing useful, and the third had left Fustat. At first that looked highly suspicious so we searched for him and a month ago found him in Alexandria."

"Oh … er, so you found the gold on him?"

"After a year? We questioned him at length and though he is of necessity vague about what happened so long ago, he did remember one interesting thing." Abd-al-Aziz glared at Aaliyah, waiting for her to look away. After a minute, he scowled and continued. "He remembers that your husband Shadi had only a little gold with him."

"Well, he would say that, wouldn't he?"

"He distinctly remembers your husband complaining that you'd given him only a little gold despite him having earned more. What do you say to that?"

Aaliyah shrugged. "I'd say he's telling the truth, he's deliberately lying or he doesn't remember."

Abd-al-Aziz stared. "Explain yourself."

"The easiest explanation is that he no longer remembers something that happened a year ago. He was drunk, and if he knew Shadi, the chances are that they'd often drunk together. He may be confusing that occasion with another, when he had less to spend. If he had something to do with the robbery and killing, then obviously he'd lie. On the other hand, he may be telling the truth. Maybe Shadi only took a little gold but told his drinking companions there was more at home. Someone, who may just have overheard him, decided to follow him home and see if there was more."

"If this man is guilty, we can charge him with robbery or even murder, but if it was just someone in the tavern who heard Shadi's words, we may never know."

"As God wants," Aaliyah murmured. "Even if the man you question is guilty, how will you know unless he confesses? Where are the witnesses necessary to convict him?"

"You sound as if you don't want him punished."

"If he's guilty and you can prove it in a court of law, then of course he must be punished. Anything less would be unjust and an affront to God. It is better for a guilty man to go unpunished than for an innocent one to suffer. Allah will judge all on the final day."

Abd-al-Aziz stroked his beard and regarded the tall young woman thoughtfully. "You're not afraid of Allah's judgment?"

Aaliyah hesitated. "I? Why should I be afraid?"

"Aaliyah bint Fuad, I know you're guilty of your husband's death."

"B … but I'm not. How can you say such a thing?" Aaliyah paled and looked away. "You have no proof."

The Deputy Shurta showed his teeth in a savage grin. "So you admit it?"

"No. No, of course not. You're guessing and trying to trap me into an admission of guilt."

"You're innocent of his murder?"

"I have said so."

"Do you swear by Allah and the Prophet that you didn't kill your husband? On Allah and the Prophet?"

Aaliyah recoiled and hid her face. "I… I cannot."

Abd-al-Aziz moved closer so that not even the old slave by the gate could possibly overhear them. "There are no witnesses to hear us, Aaliyah bint Fuad. Admit your guilt and ask forgiveness of God."

"You'd arrest me," Aaliyash whispered.

"I could witness against you, but you'd deny the charge. That wouldn't stand up in a court of law."

"I know that as a woman, my testimony is half that of a man's."

"Is murder less than fornication? Allah bids us bring four witnesses against a woman on a charge of adultery. Shall I bring fewer against you on a charge of murder?"

"Then why are you seeking to have me admit guilt? You're but one witness."

"I won't bring you before a judge, Aaliyah. Nobody saw you kill your husband, so there are no witnesses. No witnesses, no case."

"Then why?"

"For the sake of eternity. You've murdered your husband, and when God judges you, you'll burn in hell forever. Admit your guilt before me and God, seek His forgiveness and you may avoid this fate."

Aaliyah shuddered and sighed. "I had reason."

The Deputy shrugged. "So I've heard, but it doesn't excuse you. Shadi will also be standing before God to be judged. Perhaps it's worse for him. You sent him off before he could repent of his wrongdoing. You at least have that opportunity."

"Even so, I cannot. I don't regret my action." *Ah, but I do, every night.*

"Then I'll pray for you." Abd-al-Aziz turned on his heel and strode away.

Latif arrived back from the city a short time later with his purchases, and Aaliyah made an effort to hide her agitation. She followed her partner round as he examined the cleaned-out vats, the goat skins soaking in water and the quality of the tannin in the oak leaves and bark imported from Syria. He pronounced himself satisfied.

"As soon as your slaves finish cleaning the skins, we can start."

"Then let's join them. The more hands at work, the sooner they'll be ready."

Latif looked surprised. "I'd heard that you get your hands dirty in your business but wasn't sure whether to believe it."

"Believe it." Aaliyah pushed up her sleeves and pulled a skin from the vat, taking a knife and starting to strip the fat and shreds of flesh from its inner side. Latif watched her for a few minutes before shrugging and pulling out a skin of his own. Together, and aided by the slaves, they stripped a dozen skins before 'Asr prayers and another dozen before Maghrib prayers at sunset.

Each time they washed themselves thoroughly, unrolled prayer mats and faced Makkah. The slaves joined them for they were Muslim too, and when the sun had set, they left the slaves in the care of the foreman to feed them and bed them down for the night and walked back toward the city.

Latif lingered at Aaliyah's gate, and she could see he wanted to say something but did not quite know how. She decided to ease matters for him.

"I cannot invite you to eat with me, Latif. Except for my housekeeper, there's only my infant son at home."

"Of course not." He looked around in the gathering dusk, but the streets were deserted. Lights showed in the windows and doorways of houses and smoke curled skyward, carrying with it the aromas of the evening meals cooking. "I wouldn't want to invite scandal."

"Thank you," Aaliyah said. "It's one thing to be associated in business, another to be seen together socially."

Latif nodded. "I saw the Shurta Deputy as I came back this afternoon. He stopped me and asked me my business. He seemed … I don't know … agitated? Concerned that I was in business with you. Why should that be?"

"I don't know."

"I know it isn't because of your business reputation. I checked that most thoroughly before I approached you. It's something else. Everyone I talk to says you're a fine, upstanding woman, but …"

"But what?"

"I don't know. They never say." Latif cocked his head to one side and looked quizzically at Aaliyah's shadowed face. "Is there anything I ought to know?"

Aaliyah hesitated for so long Latif thought she was not going to answer. "There's nothing that concerns our business association."

"And on a more personal level?"

"There is no personal level, Latif ibn Yaqub. Now, I bid you goodnight." Aaliyah turned and entered her compound, closing and latching the gate behind her.

The next day, while the slaves finished off the raw skins in the water vats, Latif mixed up a solution of lime very carefully.

"It can burn your skin if you're not careful. Mix it slowly and always stir the vat with a long pole." He studied the cloudy liquid and nodded his satisfaction. "It's ready for the first skins." He took a clean skin and laid it on the surface of the lime solution, pressing it into the cloudy liquid with a pole and folding it with the hairy side outermost. He repeated the procedure with the next one, pushing it to the bottom of the vat and laying alongside the first one. One by one the other skins joined the first two, until all fifty skins were in the solution.

"Now what?" Aaliyah asked as Latif stepped back and laid down his pole.

"The skins stay in there for eight days – a bit longer if the weather turns cold. Early morning, noon and evening, each skin is to be lifted with the pole, agitated gently, and laid back down."

"Easily accomplished." Aaliyah issued instructions to the foreman, and he detailed a man to carry out the duty.

"That's really it for now," Latif said. "Why don't you show me how you make ordinary leather while we're waiting?"

Aaliyah raised her eyebrows. "I thought you were just interested in making parchment. Making leather is a filthy, back-breaking job. Why would you want to do that?"

"Well, I don't really, but we're partners."

“Partners in parchment making,” Aaliyah said sharply. “There’s nothing in our contract about sharing the profits from my leather making.”

“Of course not,” Latif said with a smile, “but you helped me prepare the parchment skins. The least I can do is help you with your leather.”

For the rest of that day and the next eight days, Latif worked willingly, following Aaliyah’s instructions and as his skill increased, matching her hide for hide. Rather than lose output to the parchment manufacturing process, Aaliyah calculated she had actually gained through Latif's presence.

On the ninth day, Latif prepared another vat of limed water and with the help of the slaves, transferred the skins from the old vat into the new one. “As before,” he said. “Move them three times a day for eight days. Now, back to the dog dung … or is it brains today?”

Aaliyah decided she was getting the best of the agreement she had entered into with Latif. He was a hard worker and did not mind getting filthy in the process. He had a good eye for a bargain, but he was not a miser. As they worked and prayed side by side over the next eight days, her feelings for him thawed, and she found herself wondering what it would be like to know him on a personal basis. *Would he be different? He seems different*. She thought about how she might manage this and decided to ask her Aunt Hadya for advice.

Aunt Hadya was horrified. “You’re in business with a man and now you want to … to know him better? What's the matter with you, girl? Don't you care what people think?"

"I've done nothing wrong. I haven't even put myself in a position where people might talk."

"Have you been alone with him?"

Aaliyah shook her head. "I've only seen him at the tannery or on the public roads."

"Who else was present at the tannery?"

"The slaves were always present, even when …"

"The slaves don't count," Hadya snapped. "Girl, you're putting yourself in a dangerous position."

Aaliyah looked uneasy. "Nothing has happened. I wouldn't let it."

"I believe you for you're not that stupid. However, it's not what I believe that's important. What of other people? Many in the city must know you're seeing this man alone at your tannery day after day."

"The slaves …"

"Forget them," Hadya cried. "They mean nothing. Just be thankful they cannot testify against you either."

"So what am I to do, Aunt Hadya?"

"Be quiet. Let me think." She sat and stared at the blank wall opposite for several minutes. Then she nodded in satisfaction. "Go home. From now on, when you go to the tannery, make sure someone else is with you at all times – find a girl of near marriageable age, two if possible, and give them work. It need be nothing difficult, but they must have instructions not to let you out of their sight." A thought struck her, and she paled visibly. "You … you haven't been intimate with him already, have you?"

"Of course not. If I had, would I have come to ask your advice?"

Hadya grunted. "Thanks be to Allah for that mercy. So, hire the girls, and leave the rest to me."

Aaliyah hired two girls who were cousins of Kamil the shoemaker. Kamil's wife swore they knew how to work soft leather, so Aaliyah had them cut and stitch scraps of leather into bags and then embroider them with fine stitchwork.

"There's more money to be made in the finished article than in the basic material," she told Latif when he asked about their presence. "I haven't made a decision as yet, but I've employed these girls to cut and sew some of my leather, so I can judge the worth of my idea."

Latif nodded, dismissing the girls as unimportant. "A man called Firdos ibn Nazih has invited me to dinner. Do you know of him?"

"He's my uncle, brother to my father."

"So he's not just a merchant of Fustat extending hospitality to a fellow merchant?"

Aaliyah grimaced. "It could be. I'm not in my uncle's confidence." *Is this Hadya's doing*?

The skins reached the end of their second eight-day soak in lime water, and Latif showed the slaves how to take them out and wash them thoroughly in fresh water. "Ideally, running water, but we must make certain we remove all traces of the lime. It has done its work." The skins were washed and then soaked another two days in fresh water before being taken out and the hair carefully scraped off them while they were still wet. The scraped hides were immersed again.

Two days later, Latif mentioned that he had had dinner with Firdos, Aaliyah's uncle. He said nothing further, but she thought she could detect a slight smile around the corners of his mouth. She was curious but did not want to admit to it. Finally, Aaliyah could stand no more. She straightened from the urine vat, brushed a strand of hair that had escaped her shawl back from her face and looked at Latif who was still bent over the skins.

"Well, what was it about? What did Uncle Firdos invite you for?"

"Nothing much." Latif kept plying his paddle, the stale noxious fluid swirling with every stroke.

"Was it about business or … or something else?"

Latif sat back and looked at Aaliyah calmly. "Business of course. What else would two merchants talk about?"

Aaliyah frowned, not quite sure in her mind what she expected to hear. "That's all? Did you reach agreement?"

"It's too early to say. We had a free and frank discussion though, and we expect to meet again."

"But what…"

"Now, I think it's time we prepared the parchment, don't you?" Latif rose to his feet and walked over to where the skins were being stretched taut. "Pumice comes next. Shall I show you how?" He ran his hands over the scraped and hairless hides, feeling for any irregularities. "See this one,"

Latif commented. "See how the grain is rough here and … here too. Also this area is too transparent. That tells me the skin was stretched improperly." He cut the cords holding it to the circular frame and bundled the skin up, throwing it to one side.

"We just throw it out?"

"We could prepare it and still sell it to a minor official, but we're trying for a government contract here. Until we get it, I don't want substandard parchment produced under our name. Word gets around and the slightest thing could jeopardise our bid. These others are good, though." Latif pointed to half a dozen stretched hides. "We'll work on those today."

Latif took the sack of pumice and sorted out several handfuls of the pumice dust and two hand-sized pieces of the light volcanic rock. Turning the dried skins flesh side uppermost, he sprinkled them with water and pumice dust, then started rubbing with the rocks, making sure every scrap of the taut hide was covered, that the fine abrasive powder cut into the drum-hard surface. As each one was finished, he put the moist hides aside on their stretching frames to dry in the shade.

"Another two days and we do it again."

After evening prayers, Aaliyah allowed Latif to escort her home again on the public roads but this time at the gate, she invited him in.

"My housekeeper is here with my son and her half-grown son. It'll be quite proper."

"Perhaps, but I think I must decline. Besides, your Uncle Firdos has invited me to dine again."

"You didn't tell me."

"I didn't think it necessary."

"You'd better go then. You don't want to keep him waiting." Aaliyah watched Latif turn away and could stand it no longer. "Wait!" When he turned and stood looking at her in the dusk, she had difficulty finding words.

"Why does … what are you talking about … with my uncle?"

Latif looked at her for long enough to make her squirm with embarrassment. "I rather think that's between your uncle and me, don't you?"

"If it's about business – parchment making – then it concerns me. We're partners."

"Yes, we're partners, Aaliyah, but not everything I do concerns our business together. Your Uncle Firdos doesn't speak to me about parchment or leather."

"Yes. Yes, of course. I'm sorry I asked; it was rude of me."

"There's nothing to forgive." Latif bowed. "Until tomorrow then." He turned and strode off into the night, leaving Aaliyah feeling embarrassed but also highly curious.

The next morning, she sent a message to the tannery to say she would be late and hurried into the city instead, calling on her Aunt Hadya. In her aunt's home in the women's quarters screened off from the rest of the house, she sat on embroidered cushions and drank sweetened tea with her aunt. After talking about the health of her son, Fuad, and enquiring about the numerous other family members, Aaliyah got straight to the point.

“The man I’m in business with, Latif ibn Yaqub, has dined on two occasions with Uncle Firdos. What were those meetings about?”

Hadya raised her eyebrows. “You ask me? How should I know?”

“I … I thought, with him eating here …”

“Naturally, I don’t eat with the men, so how could I know what they speak of?”

“He hasn’t said?”

“Why would he? What my husband talks about to his guest is his own business.”

“But he’s your husband …”

“I would never presume to intrude on my husband’s affairs,” Hadya said primly. “If he wants me to know, he’ll tell me.”

“How is it that Uncle Firdos even asked Latif to dinner? Was that your doing?”

“I was concerned about you being in the company of this man whom we know nothing about. I merely suggested to your uncle that maybe we should find out if he is honourable.”

“And is he?”

“That’s for your uncle to say.”

Aaliyah left shortly afterward with her curiosity unassuaged. She hurried to the tannery, where she found Latif busy pumicing the last of the batch of skins for the parchment production. He had found another three that had been improperly stretched, but he was content with the others.

“May the blessings of Allah be upon you this beautiful morning, Aaliyah,” he said goodhumouredly. “You are well?”

"Well enough, I suppose. Did your dinner go well last night?"

Latif smiled. "Yes, thank you. Your Uncle Firdos has a good cook."

"That would be my Aunt Hadya's cooking. What did you talk about?" she asked bluntly.

"Aaliyah, you have a real problem with your curiosity, don't you? It concerns me that a person can have no secrets around you."

"So there are secrets? What are you hiding from me?"

Latif walked away, heading for the shaded central tent. Aaliyah followed, her face flushed and her limbs trembling with the knowledge she was displaying rudeness but unable to help herself. Latif pointed to a cushion and sat on another one close by. He waited until she seated herself.

"Now, suppose you tell me why you're curious about my affairs to the point of impoliteness."

"I'm sorry," Aaliyah muttered. "I'm just concerned that our business deal's in jeopardy."

"I can accept that you don't fully trust me yet, but do you think your own uncle would plot to defraud you?"

"Why not? My husband …" Aaliyah closed her mouth quickly.

"Ah, yes, your husband, Shadi ibn Masood. I've heard about him."

"What have you heard?"

"That he defrauded you and nearly bankrupted your business. That he betrayed your marriage bed. That he drank and whored and gambled. That he died in a disgusting fashion. That you killed him."

Aaliyah paled and her eyes opened wide. "All true," she whispered, "Except … except the last."

"Please don't lie to me, Aaliyah."

"I'm not lying."

"You know you are."

"Why are you trying to make me admit it? Are you in league with the Shurta Deputy? Are you seeking a public confession, so you can have me executed for murder?"

"No, Aaliyah. Let the Deputy find his own witnesses if he can. I want nothing from you but the truth."

"But why? Why do you want to know?"

"So there are no secrets between us."

"You're a fine one to talk. You keep secrets from me."

Latif smiled. "I'll tell you what I talked to your uncle about, if you tell me the truth about your husband's death."

Aaliyah thought for several minutes and then shrugged. "If you seek to use the information it'll do you no good. I'll deny having said it."

"I promise I'll speak of it to no one without your permission."

"Then you're correct," she murmured, after a glance to make sure the slaves and the cousins of Kamil were nowhere close. "I killed my husband Shadi." She breathed out, hard and long. "It feels good to have said it."

"How did you kill him?"

"I hit him with a rock and tipped him headfirst into a tall jar of urine."

"Was there no other course of action you could have taken?"

"I would rather not have killed him, if that's what you mean; he was the father of my son, Fuad, after all. I tried to divorce him, but the Law doesn't allow for a woman divorcing her husband unless the husband agrees."

Latif nodded. "Khula. If I were a less pious man, I would suspect the law was unfair. However, that ruling came from Allah via the Prophet, so we must assume it's for the best."

"It didn't help me, though. With divorce ruled out, I must wait for him to die to be free of him. I chose to hurry things along."

"Why that method? It's rather gruesome."

"I didn't have much choice. I could hire assassins, but word would have got back to the authorities. I'm not proficient with arms, so I couldn't waylay him one night. I could've smothered him while drunk one night or poisoned him, I suppose, but it would be quickly known I'd done it. This way I could put the blame on robbers seeking to silence him. I have my little son to think of. I cannot deprive him of father and mother together."

Latif was silent for a long time. At length he stirred and said, "I know he was a wicked man, but even a wicked man can demand justice from God. And the guilt must burn you. Have you asked forgiveness of Allah?"

Tears formed in Aaliyah's eyes. "How can I?" she asked miserably. "I would give much to be free of the burden of my guilt, but I had to do it. How can I truly regret my action when it has freed me from tyranny?"

"Then you must atone."

"How? If I admit my guilt, I'll be executed and then Fuad will be an orphan."

"Blood money," Latif said softly. "You must offer Shadi's family gold to avert their wrath. You could make a payment without revealing why. You would know, as would Allah and I, but no one else. It might help you come to terms with your guilt."

"I … I'll think about it." Aaliyah's mind whirled as she contemplated the possibility of being at ease with her conscience. She almost forgot why she had unburdened herself in the first place. "So what then is your secret?"

"My secret?"

"What you were talking to Firdos about."

"Ah, that. Well, your uncle wanted to know what sort of a man was getting involved with you, offering business partnerships and who knew what else. He asked many questions, and by the end of the first evening, he suggested I marry you to avert gossip."

Aaliyah's mouth fell open and one of the many flies around them flew in. She coughed and spluttered and eventually spat it out, while Latif sat and watched her, smiling. "I hope you told him 'No'."

"No?" Latif's smile vanished. "You don't want to get married?"

"Ah, I get a say in it, do I? I thought here were two men arranging a woman's life again. My uncle's arranged a marriage for me once before and look what happened then. I'm quite content to remain single, so you can go and tell my uncle his deal is off. Whatever he offered you to take me off his hands …"

"He didn't offer me anything," Latif interrupted. "I told him at the dinner last night that I wouldn't marry a woman who didn't want me. The only way I could know if she really wanted me was to ask her myself. Alas, it seems she doesn't want to marry."

"I don't trust men."

"I'm not surprised, but you went into business with me anyway. That must mean you trust me."

"That's different, we have a legal contract."

"If we married, we'd also have a legal contract – one that you would write yourself and that I would sign, binding myself before God and the Law to follow its provisions."

Aaliyah considered his words for many minutes. "You would do that for me?" she whispered. "Knowing what I did?"

"Yes." Latif leaned forward and took Aaliyah's hands in his own. "Will you marry me, Aaliyah bint Fuad, tanner of Fustat?"

***

I never trusted her, but then I suppose, in my profession, a man should not easily trust another. I lived my life in the Shurta and for the Shurta, I and my father and my grandfather before me. I rose to the position of Wali al-Jara'im of the Sultan's Enforcers, but at the time of the murder of Shadi ibn

Masood, husband to the tanner, Aaliyah bint Fuad of Fustat, I was only Deputy Chief of Shurta, Abd-al-Aziz ibn 'Abbas ibn Baha al-Wahal. Even then, as a middle-ranking police officer, the position paid moderately well and allowed me many opportunities to become wealthy through bribes and gratuities. What? You cannot be surprised – everyone does it.

It was obvious from the start that the tanner was lying. She presented me with some improbable story of robbers stealing gold from her house while she slept and then murdering her husband by drowning him in his own urine. Now you tell me – is that a reasonable story? Shadi ibn Masood was scum, I admit, and had his enemies, as do we all, but none that would be that vindictive or innovative. I know, I asked around. There were some who would casually kill for a copper coin, but they would stab their victim or bludgeon him to death in an honest manner. Dead is dead, after all, and you cannot talk when your breath is stilled. Why would a robber go to the trouble of taking Shadi to the jar of urine in the courtyard and drowning him in it to silence him? Far simpler to cut his throat. No, either the method of his death meant something to the killer, or it was the only method readily available.

Aaliyah bint Fuad had a motive to kill her husband. She had tried to invoke the law of Khula to rid herself of a useless man, but the judge found against her. I can imagine her state of mind, faced with a lifetime married to that man, waiting and hoping he would die while she was still young enough to get remarried. One can hardly blame her for hurrying the matter along. Except, of course, that it is against the laws of God and man, which I am here to enforce. Still, there are ways out of any situation. Aaliyah found a way out of her marriage; there was a way out of my investigation too, had she the wit to find it. I tried to hint at it by telling her that the stolen gold would have to pay Shurta expenses. She knew there was no stolen gold, so how did she imagine I was going to use it to pay expenses? She should have offered me more gold as an extra fee, an incentive, then I could have made a great show of looking for the murderer, found some itinerant ne'er-do-well, and had him quickly executed for the crime. Case closed. Instead, I had to keep the investigation open officially and that looked bad on my record. Stupid woman.

I knew early on that I would not be able to lay the blame at the woman's door. You need witnesses to convict someone, and the only person with Shadi that night was Aaliyah. She was hardly likely to testify against herself. The law against fornication requires me to find four witnesses of the act, and it seems reasonable to suppose you need at least that many to convict someone of murder. Aaliyah bint Fuad was not a professional criminal, she had a conscience and it troubled her. If I could find no witnesses, the only other way to find justice for Shadi ibn Masood was to persuade her to confess. I had to move softly here, for pressing her too hard would have the opposite effect. She would become defensive. I needed her to think about her crime and with the knowledge I also knew of her guilt, hope she would eventually give herself up.

It might have worked, but one Latif ibn Yaqub, a Jewish convert from Damascus turned up. He was a parchment maker and was looking for a business partner when he arrived in Fustat. As the woman was one of the foremost leather manufacturers in the district, it was not surprising he found her or formed an association with her. It is possible she led him on, seeking the respectability of marriage, though I found no evidence of impropriety. She was always properly dressed with full robes and headscarf, showing only her face, her hands and her sandaled feet. She never met him alone; though they worked with only the company of slaves until the cousins of Kamil the shoemaker went to work for her. She was strict in her observance of prayers, and if she was a little lax in her behaviour in public – walking the streets and conducting business without the company of a male relative – it fell short of scandal.

What I did not see coming was her marriage to Latif ibn Yaqub. Firdos ibn Nazih, the woman's uncle, evidently arranged it, and by all accounts, they are content. They have children. They are persons of note in the community and regularly give alms to the needy.

She has even found a way to still her conscience, and I would wager half my hidden wealth that Latif was the one to think of it. A year ago, after a particularly successful year in which their parchment business won several contracts to supply royal and gubernatorial courts throughout North Africa and Syria, Aaliyah announced that in honour of her first husband so cruelly murdered, she was making a one-time payment of five hundred gold dirham to his family in Al-Jazair. She was widely praised for her generosity and her new husband was lauded for his open mindedness.

They elected to travel to Al-Jazair themselves, to the home of Masood, carrying a banker's draft for the sum. I offered to perform that task for them for a small fee, say one hundred dirham, to spare them the arduous journey. I pointed out that Shadi's family were not to know the full amount being offered and if they got most of it they would be grateful. Payment of the blood money would give a good conscience, no matter the amount, I told them. Aaliyah and Latif thanked me but declined my assistance. So the murder of Shadi proved to be a profitless investigation for me. Whether or not the woman will get away with it entirely depends on the arrangement she made with God. Blood money should suffice, but I suppose she will not know for certain until she stands before the throne of Allah on the Day of Judgment.

She will not be alone before God. I have killed my share of men and more, but only in obedience to my duty to the Sultan. Being Wali al-Jara'im, of course, my duty is whatever I want it to be, and I have grown rich in his service. I am an old man now with sons and grandsons, and one day soon I will be called to Allah. I have no doubt I will be judged favourably for I have always said my prayers, given alms to the poor and followed the dictates of the messenger He sent to guide me so long ago.

Just after the death of Shadi ibn Masood, a blue flame appeared to guide me through the intricacies of that and other investigations – a still flame such as the angels in heaven wear. Yet the flame was personal, rather than just a messenger of God's Will, and often pointed me toward a wrong-doer, revealing which men and women had been forsaken by Allah and whose deaths would not be laid at my feet. Of course, I followed the dictates of the angel, for not to do so would be to insult God. If my actions sometimes seemed crimina, or at least to skirt the law, I told myself God must have a reason. Allah would not lead me into wrong-doing.

I have not seen the blue flame since I retired to my country estates, except … perhaps once, though I cannot be sure. My eldest grandson, Abdul-Rahman, who is himself rising through the ranks of the Shurta, came to see me. He seemed disappointed to see me in such good health and did not stay long. I bade him farewell in the shadowed portico, and for an instant, I thought I saw a familiar blue light bathing his head. He stepped out into the bright sunshine a moment later and the flame vanished. One of my servants died a day later, and my grandson sent me one of his to take the dead man's place. It is kind of him, but I know him and his mind. I think I do not have long to live.

Chapter Sixteen

Why did I ever bother with that god thing? Yes, it felt good to be worshipped and obeyed, but really the energy sustenance I got from prayer was a mild and insipid fare compared to the rich taste of a man in agony. I think it is far better that I stay true to my nature as djinn and feast on death. A man once asked me – I was sitting opposite him in his hovel, extracting his life painfully – why, as all men died, I did not just prey on old men and take my food as they slipped naturally away into death. That man extended his life by an hour while I explained the difference to him, though in the end I do not think he appreciated it.

Old men so often have a sour outlook on life, wanting to die, and this attitude flavours the energy within them. Their life force has only a tenuous hold on their bodies, and when I feed, the unwholesome mess just oozes away. With a younger man or a woman with children, the hold on life is fierce and they struggle to resist me. When I feast on their life, I rip it bloodily from their shrieking bodies, gorging myself on their vital energies.

Why do I tell you all this? Is it that I seek to somehow justify my existence? By now you will know that by human standards, I am a savage, cruel monster who thinks only of himself and cares nothing for the innocent men, women and children slaughtered to feed my ravening flame. Why then should you care one iota for me or my story? You are probably hoping some god will come along and kill me. Well, they have had thousands of years to do so, and the fact that I am still alive speaks volumes about these beings – if they truly exist. A god is nothing but a demon that has become successful enough to fool his worshippers and cares nothing for their well-being. I was like that once, but I am too honest to be a god. I prefer to be true to my nature and openly so. Perhaps that is why I have taken steps to ensure my story is not forgotten. I want you to realise that the gods you worship are shams, unworthy of your high regard. They are dishonest, pretending to be what they are not. I, on the other hand, openly acknowledge what I am.

Lest you still think me totally undeserving of your sympathy, let me remind you that I have feeling for the weak. What weak, you ask? I who kill women and children when the mood takes me? Well, women can be cruel too, and children grow up to be adults and I see inside them. I see their inner thoughts and know each one of them is descended through generations untold from bloodthirsty ancestors who achieved the supremacy of their race, their species, over countless corpses. Let us say I represent those corpses, and I avenge them by wreaking retribution on their killers and seeking to ease the burden, when I see others like them suffering at the bloodstained hands of humanity. Who are these innocents? Look around you, they are everywhere – from the corpses that grace your dinner tables, to the beasts that plough your fields or carry your goods or are kicked out of the way in your streets – killed because they inconvenience you. Do they deserve their fates? I think not.

I wandered down over that strip of land connecting Africa to Europe and Asia – a tiny area that three great religions fought over – Judaism, Christianity and Islam. When I came through, I followed the crusaders out of Christendom, seeking to wrest the Holy Land from the grip of Islam. Fortunes swayed back and forth, cities falling, armies being destroyed, populations becoming decimated, first one side and then the other. I was the only winner, for Christian and Muslim taste very much the same to me. I found, too, I was not alone.

I suppose that should not have surprised me. After all, back in the days before men walked upon the earth, I had seen blue flames like me formed in the explosive conflagrations of gas and oil in the desert. It is in the nature of djinn to seek solitude, and competition for food can keep us apart. Wars, particularly large and bloody ones, provide a surfeit of death and demons congregate to follow the armies. I have seen djinn are created equal, but they do not all develop as I have done. My flame is larger, stronger and fiercer than most others, and other djinn flee from me or are devoured. The European demons that followed the nominally Christian armies are mostly small and weak, though I glimpsed a few as strong as I. Their flames burn with a reddish tinge. I do not know why this is, but it may have something to do with the means of their creation. In all other respects they seem the same as djinn, and I treat them the same – feeding on the weaker, avoiding the stronger.

And so I came down to the land of Egypt to the capital city of Fustat and its administrative hub,

Qahira. In later days, they amalgamated to form the bustling city of Cairo, but in the days of the great Islamic conqueror, Salah ad-Din Yusuf ibn Ayyub, or Saladin as he was known to the crusaders, the cities were separate, though enclosed by one wall. I left my fellow demons to feast on dying men in the armies and went south, seeking new experiences, novel ways of inflicting pain and misery. Any strong emotion is worth tasting and hard times produce them. I sampled what a community had to offer, killing sometimes, and moved on until I came to Fustat.

I dwelt within the poorer quarter of Fustat, moving from man to woman to man again, persuading them to crime or mischief as I pleased, sampling their greed, their cruelty or their pain and moving on. Sometimes I stayed outside of people, merely observing them, learning about the human condition before slipping inside another unwilling body and possessing them. So I came to Shadi ibn Masood, a man no better and no worse than those around him and with little to commend him. To tell the truth, I was a little bored with the petty crime of Fustat and was sitting inside his nervous system, enjoying the sensations that came to me via his outward senses. I could detect a growth in his bowels and necrotic tissue in his liver but neither concerned me. I am seldom interested in a man dying of disease; I prefer the red and raw taste of violent death. So I went with Shadi ibn Masood as he staggered home, fell with him to the ground when he tripped over a bench and lay looking up at his wife, while she struggled with a strong emotion.

I entered her and found her thoughts of murder slipping away as she came to a realisation of the enormity of the crime she contemplated. She/I hit him with the stone and dragged him over to the jar of urine. I had never seen anyone drowned in urine before, so I left her to stagger back indecisively and invaded him as the cold liquid shocked him into consciousness.

Shadi held his breath as a reflex action without conscious thought, and his immediate thought was to extricate himself. As the realisation that he was upside down in a container seeped into his brain, he started to panic, and the air in his lungs became rapidly depleted. He struggled and kicked but could get no purchase in the tall jar. I think if he had rocked from side to side he might have been able to tip the jar over, but it never occurred to him. As his need for oxygen became acute, he inhaled. As the noxious liquid rushed into his lungs and stomach, he suddenly realised where he was and he vomited. After that, death intervened rather quickly, cutting short my experience, so I reentered the woman.

She dragged her dead husband out, and I watched with interest as she prepared her story for the authorities. The onion was a nice touch. Tears always move people. The Shurta arrived, and I lost interest in the woman. I could see from her memories that her life was dull, and she would hardly be likely to murder again, so I left her. There was another person present who got to meet many murderers, and I could pick and choose another host. I crossed unseen into the Shurta Deputy Abd-al-Aziz.

My thought was to stay with this upright symbol of authority only long enough to find someone truly depraved and use them as my vehicle of delight. Instead, I found my Shurta host had a wealth of opportunity, and I could use him to indulge my every whim. He had ambition, that quality that will so easily lead a man to excess. Strangely, he was aware of my presence almost immediately and feared me, until I revealed I was an angel sent to guide him to great things.

Under my tutelage, Abd-al-Aziz rose to become the commander of the Sultan's feared secret police. I could have taken him further perhaps, even made a bid for the throne, but I saw in him reluctance. I did not push him. I had no need – I had all the death I wanted. When he retired, I transferred to his able grandson, Abdul-Rahman, and I raised him to his grandfather's position, where he spread death and destruction far and wide, until even the Sultan started to fear him and had him poisoned.

It was not an easy death. The Sultan had Abdul-Rahman brought before him in chains and the poison administered in front of him. He watched him die in agony, every muscle in his body going into spasm, until he died of suffocation. All the while, the Sultan watched him and ate and drank his own tasted fare. I swear he derived almost as much enjoyment from the death as I did. I stayed within the Sultan, driving him to excess, until he met with an untimely fate, and moved on.

Many years later, I found myself in Baghdad when the Mongol conqueror, Timur the Lame, invaded the city and put twenty thousand of the inhabitants to the sword. Timur shipped the artisans of that city east to distant Samarkand, and I went with them, eager for something new.

Chapter Seventeen

The city of Bukhara is a very clean city, at least in the more well-to-do areas. The Sultan and his ministers have, over the years, passed many edits banning spitting, urinating and littering in any public place, resulting in pristine building walls and spotless city streets, particularly around the mosques, minarets and madrasahs. The worst that will happen is the summer winds will blow dust through the streets, and in this eventuality, men are employed to carry great skins of water through the streets and sprinkle the contents to lay the dust. As a result, the population is well behaved, though they do grumble when the taxes are collected, for all this splendour must be paid for.

Bukhara is a Muslim city, and there are few public entertainments to be enjoyed by the populace beyond the occasional execution of wrongdoers by throwing them from the lofty Kalyan minaret. That is not to say Bukhara is a city without a culture though, as many artisans and craftsmen live there, many uprooted from Baghdad when Timur the Lame destroyed the city and its inhabitants a few years before. These artisans decorated the mosques and madrasahs with beautiful ornate designs, employing subtle colours that reflected God's creation without copying it. Blues and greens were favourite colours and lent a cool look to an otherwise hot city. The craftsmen from Baghdad were famous for the quality of their furniture and for their jewellery, and their adopted city now became renowned for these same qualities.

The citizens of Bukhara are, for the most part, good Muslims and readily follow the precepts of Islam that are referred to as the Five Pillars – the Recitation of the Creed, Prayers five times a day, Giving of alms to the needy, Fasting during the month of Ramadan and Making the Hajj pilgrimage to Makkah at least once in their lives. This last pillar is difficult for the poorer members of society, but often the more well-to-do will subsidise their less well off brethren.

Bukhara has one other claim to fame. Within its walls is a shrine dedicated to its most revered son, the Sufi Master Shaykh Baha ud-Din Naqshband, founder of the order that is now known as the Naqshbandi Order. Disciples who studied under the Master carry on his teachings, having attained wisdom after many years of study and meditation. One such Sufi teacher, not yet called a Master but who had already started to attract students, is Fadi al-Asim. Fadi set up his small madrasah in an alcove formed when some substandard mud brick crumbled in a hot summer years before. The authorities would have repaired the damage, but Fadi moved in and not even the Vizier wanted to move a holy man. So Fadi stayed, making the alcove his home and later school. Several years later, two students decided they wished to study at the feet of one who had studied at the feet of Naqshband himself.

Ala al-Din approached the thin man sitting in the crumbled mud brick alcove and prostrated himself. "Master," he said, "I wish to learn of your wisdom."

"Get up," Fadi replied quietly. "I am neither one set in authority over you, nor am I holy that you should revere me."

Ala did as he was told and sat crosslegged in front of the turbaned Sufi master. "Will you take me as a student, Master?"

"Are you a good Muslim?'

"Yes, Master."

"And you're fluent in Arabic?"

"I am, Master."

"Then recite the Qur'an to me."

Ala hesitated. "All of it?"

"Start with al-Ma'ida, The Table Spread. I'll tell you when to stop."

Ala swallowed and composed his thoughts, searching his memory for the right words. Then he took a deep breath. "In the Name of God, the Beneficent, the Merciful. Oh you who believe! Fulfill your contracts. The grass-eating quadrupeds are made lawful for your food…"

Ala's voice settled into a drone as he recalled the verses so lovingly learned over the years, mentally blessing his schoolteacher who had taught him the Holy Words, though little else. He worked his way methodically through the messages given to the Prophet by Allah all those years ago, finally reaching the one hundred and twentieth ayah of al-Ma'ida. "God is in the kingdom of the heavens and the earth and whatever therein, and He alone has power over all things." Ala stopped and looked at Fadi expectantly.

"Did I say to stop? Continue with al-Anim, The Cattle."

Ala stifled a groan and recommenced his recitation. Less than halfway through the sura, Fadi held up a hand. Ala completed the ayah he was reciting and sat silently.

"You did well to complete the ayah," Fadi said. "Why did you do it, when I told you to stop?"

Ala licked his lips. "The Holy Word shouldn't be cut off half-uttered."

"That's true, but you should then have spoken the next two ayat, for they complete the sense of the first one."

"I'm sorry, Master."

"Don't apologise to me but rather to God, for they are His words."

Ala said nothing but waited for Fadi to say something more. When he did not, he tried to think of a suitable comment or question but could not think of anything appropriate. As the minutes slid by, the opportunity to speak also slipped away, and now he was too embarrassed to open his mouth.

As the shadows crept toward evening, Fadi smiled. "Good, you know how to keep silent. Your memory is faulty though. You made three mistakes in al-Ma'ida. Do you know what they were?"

Ala shook his head. "No, Master," he whispered.

"Then go and find out. Search your memory and read your Qur'an. Come and tell me tomorrow morning what your mistakes were."

Ala rose to his feet, bowed and left the alcove without saying anything, his mind already turning over his words, looking for the errors.

He returned the next day immediately after dawn prayers and sat down in front of Fadi again. "Greetings, Master. I've returned as you bid."

"And did you find the three mistakes you made in al-Ma'ida?"

"I searched my own memory most diligently, comparing it to the written Word, but could only find two mistakes, both of them small."

"It isn't the size of the mistake that's important," Fadi said, "but rather the presence. Tell me of the two mistakes you found."

"The first was in ayah seventeen, where I said 'kingdom of the heavens and the earth.' I should have said 'dominion of the heavens and the earth.'"

"And the second?"

"In ayah forty-five, where I said 'a life for a life, an eye for an eye, an ear for an ear' missing out 'a nose for a nose' between eye and ear."

"Good. The third mistake you made was in ayah eighty-six, 'As for those who disbelieve and belie Our signs, these shall be the inmates of the flaming Fire.' You said 'inhabitants', whereas the Word of Allah says 'inmates.'"

Ala frowned. "I don't remember saying that. The correct version is fixed firmly in my mind."

"Then you must ask yourself whether you should trust your memory or mine."

"If you say it, it must be so," Ala admitted grudgingly.

Fadi did not comment but instead sat watching the young man for several minutes, watching his ill temper dissipate and agitation wash over him.

"The Qur'an," Fadi said at last, "Is it the Law of Allah or just guidance for the Faithful?"

Ala frowned. "It's the Law of God as given to the Prophet, peace be upon him."

"Tell me then of the ayah from al-Ma'ida that you recited yesterday. The one where it says, 'The grass-eating quadrupeds are made lawful for your food.' What does this mean?"

A look of unease crossed the young man's face. He licked his lips. "It … it means that four-footed animals that eat grass are lawful to eat."

"Are there any restrictions?"

"Yes, they must be slaughtered in a lawful manner, their throats slit so that the blood spills out upon the ground. This is halal."

"And if they're not killed in such a way?"

"Then they're haram, forbidden."

"So both the animal and the means of its slaughter must be halal?"

"Yes, Master. So it is written."

"Name me the beasts that are halal."

"Cattle, sheep, goats, camel … er, rabbit … deer …"

"Always deer?"

"Except when one is on pilgrimage."

"What about the pig?"

"The pig is haram."

"The donkey?"

"The donkey is haram."

"And the wild ass?"

"... er, also haram."

"Not so, for the prohibition is against domesticated donkeys only. What of those creatures that fly?"

"The duck, the goose, the chicken, the quail. That's all I can remember."

"The locust?"

"And the locust."

"There are others. What of animals that live in water?"

"Fish only, Master."

"So these lists of halal and haram animals are in the Qur'an?"

"Er, no, master. The Word guides us, but the ahadith inform us of …"

"But you said the Qur'an was the Law of God not just guidance."

Ala looked unhappy. "Yes, Master, but the guideline that one should only eat grass-eating quadrupeds is the Law of God, whereas the lists of halal and haram animals come from the ahadith. Thus, the Word has the force of Law, and the ahadith provide the details by which we live."

"Distinguish between the Qur'an, the Sunnah and the Hadith."

"The Qur'an is the very Word of God as spoken to the Prophet, peace be upon him, and written down by him. To read it, is to hear the Word of God anew. The Sunnah is the collected sayings and deeds of the Prophet, peace be upon him …"

"I think we can dispense with the added blessing when we talk," Fadi interposed quietly. "I'm sure the Prophet knows you hold him in the highest regard."

"Yes, Master. So, er … the Sunnah are the words and deeds of the Prophet, peace be … and the Hadith are traditions relating to the Prophet, peace … gathered by men wise in the ways of Allah."

"A man decides not to eat meat. Does he sin?"

Ala bit his lip and frowned. "No, for the Qur'an tells us what is lawful, but puts no compulsion upon us except to avoid what is haram."

"Very good. I am that man, Ala al-Din. As a Sufi, I eat no meat."

"M … may I ask your reasoning in this regard, Master?"

"You may, but not today."

Ala looked around and saw the sun was still ascending the sky. "It's not yet noon, Master. May I not hear from your own lips what led you to this decision?"

"No. East of the city is a low, conical hill. As the road passes the hill, a narrow track leads to a cave. Go there and meditate on the Word of God. Don't return until you can recite the whole Qur'an without a single mistake and discourse on any part of it. Knowledge of the Word of God is the first duty of a Muslim. Think too on what we've discussed today."

"But, but …" A look of dismay swept over Ala. "How long must I be gone?"

"As long as it takes, young man. A year at least, I imagine. Do you think the way of the Sufi comes easily? This is but the first step. If you cannot manage it, don't return. Go now."

Ala arose and sorrowing, did as Fadi al-Asim had told him.

***

A year later, almost to the day, Fadi al-Asim sat in his little alcove meditating. Knowledge of his wisdom had grown over the months attracting other seekers, and a youth sat crosslegged to one side of the Sufi master, remaining silent and still. Ala al-Din approached the alcove slowly, bowed and sat down. He was thinner than he had been a year earlier and his clothing more ragged. His eyes gleamed as though fixed on something of supernal interest.

Fadi saw the young man arrive but shut the knowledge out of his consciousness, while he wrestled with the idea in his mind. An hour later, he reached a tentative conclusion and tucked the finding away for future consideration.

"You have returned, Ala al-Din," Fadi observed quietly. "How have you spent the intervening time?"

Ala flicked a glance at the youth sitting silently beside him, but did not ask the question that tickled his curiosity. "I have followed your instructions, Master."

"You're now conversant with the Holy Word of God? In its entirety?"

"I am."

"What says Baraah, ayah twenty-seven?"

Ala answered without hesitation. "Then God will turn Merciful after this to whomsoever He pleases, and God is the oft-forgiving, most Merciful."

"And an-Nur, ayah four?"

"You shall scourge those who accuse the women who protect their modesty, while failing to bring four eye-witnesses, fourscore lashes, and you shall never accept their testimony, and they are the wicked ones."

"Good. Now you can tell me why I, as a Sufi, don't eat meat despite it being a halal food."

Ala smiled. "This was harder than learning the Word of God. The Qur'an is an unalterable set of instructions so that man may submit himself to the will of Allah. Your desire to not eat meat is not something handed down but is something that originates within your mind. As such it's harder to grasp, but I believe I've done it."

"Go on."

"The central concept is desire, Master. As a good Muslim and as a Sufi, your prime concern is gaining knowledge of Allah. Anything that distracts you from this task is bad. Food is a distraction but a necessary one or the body dies. But we desire succulent foods such as meat, and it leads us away from God. The distraction of food can be lessened by making it less interesting, for instance, by removing meat from the diet. The Sunnah states that the Prophet existed mainly on dates, water and barley bread. It's likely he ate meat, but not regularly, nor much. It's obvious his gaze was fixed on God, and as we try to emulate his example, we should likewise seek to give up eating meat, adopting a simpler diet."

"Interesting," Fadi commented. "You correctly identify desire as an enemy of proper living, yet you miss the reason for abstaining from meat." He glanced at the youth who had been following the discussion. "Safna Bukhara, what do you say?"

"I, Master? Had I the choice, I would say little, for when Allah speaks, ineluctable truth floods our minds, but when man speaks, lies enfold us."

Fadi smiled fondly. "Nevertheless, Safna, what say you on the subject of why I don't eat meat?"

"You love Allah with your whole body and mind. Thus you must also love His creation. Loving His creation, how can you bring yourself to kill? Isn't all life sacred?"

"Safna has it," Fadi said simply.

Ala scowled. "What of vegetables, then? Aren't they part of Allah's creation? You still kill them for food."

"A good question, Ala," Fadi said. "How would you answer him, Safna?"

"I'd point out that a wheat plant produces an ear containing a dozen or more seeds, each of which has within it the fulfilment of the plant's purpose. Eating some of the seed doesn't deprive the wheat plant of life. Similarly, the flesh of a date may be eaten, and the stone planted to produce another plant. Yet again, we may remove a leaf from a lettuce plant without injury to the plant."

Ala grunted. "But by the same argument you eat eggs, I suppose?"

"Not so," Fadi said. "Animals are a more elevated form of life. By eating an egg, you kill the infant bird inside it."

"Then milk, or cheese, or butter?"

"The milk of a goat more properly belongs to its kid. Likewise the butter and cheese formed from the milk. If we eat or drink these foods, we deprive the young animal of its necessary sustenance."

"You're telling me I must give up meat and milk if I'm to become a Sufi?" Ala asked.

"Not so," Fadi answered. "No man may tell you what you must or must not do; only Allah and his Messenger speak to your inner self. A Sufi may eat meat or he may not; that's his own choice."

"And what of you, Safna of Bukhara?" Ala asked roughly. "You are Turkic and one of the pagan inhabitants of this region. Have you given up meat to follow this Sufi?"

Safna stared at the ragged young man for several minutes and then answered softly. "My people were pagans, but I follow the true faith of Islam. I seek knowledge of Allah wherever I may find it."

"But you've given up meat?"

"That's between me and Allah, but as it is a stumbling block for your faith, I'll tell you. I, too, hold all life to be sacred."

Ala turned back to Fadi, his face set in a grimace. "And has Safna also spent a year learning the Word of God? Has he given up all to sit at your feet?"

"No man's journey is the same as another's, Ala al-Din. No two men come to Allah in exactly the same way. Be concerned with your own path, not that of a fellow seeker."

"So I, an Arab of good family, am to be subjected to hardship, while this son of pagan peasants sups at the table of learning? Is that the way of Sufi?"

Fadi's eyes glistened as the young man spoke, and he sighed when he finished. "You must ask yourself, Ala al-Din, whether this life is for you. I offer my hand to welcome you, and I bid you learn the ways of Allah. Stay, my brother in Islam, don't give in to the vanities of ordinary existence. You have much to learn."

"Yes, I see that despite my knowledge you regard me as an ignorant lout. Is this … this boy here to be a Sufi, or does he stay for other things?" Ala sneered at them both. "What does he do for you, old man?"

"I think, Ala al-Din, you'd better leave us. Plainly this life isn't for you. I'll pray that Allah will open your heart and humble your pride. Then you …"

"Oh, I'm leaving, old man." Ala rose swiftly and stalked to the alcove entrance. "I'll leave you to enjoy your boy, you teacher of falsehoods. But don't think I'll forget you … or you, Turk." He turned and strode swiftly away.

"Master, why didn't you tell him that I, too, have studied the Qur'an?"

"Why didn't you?"

Safna thought on this question for a short while. "It's as you said, Master, each man's path is his own. My knowledge of God's Word shouldn't be a stumbling block to his advancement. Yet … yet I feel that perhaps I could have done something, said something, which would change his mind."

"You're that persuasive, Safna?"

“I … I don’t know, but shouldn’t I have tried? He’s one of the faithful, after all.”

“Then hurry after him, Safna Bukhara. Persuade him to stay.”

Safna jumped to his feet and hurried off in the direction the other man had taken. Fadi remained sitting in a meditative position but closed his eyes, shutting out the gentle susurration of the city’s bustle. Time passed and footsteps approached the alcove.

Fadi opened his eyes and looked up at Safna. “Did you find him?”

“Yes, Master.” The youth sighed and sat down in his accustomed place. “I called on him to stop, and when he did, I pleaded with him to return, but he abused me for my efforts and pushed me to the ground.”

“What did you do?”

“Nothing, Master. I lay there until he left and then returned.”

“Safna, think. Where did you err?”

The youth frowned. “I should have tried harder?”

“Are you really that persuasive that you can turn a man from his chosen course?”

“Obviously not, Master,” Safna said with a rueful grin. “What, then, should I have done?”

“You believed yourself to be that persuasive though.”

Safna thought for a few minutes. “I erred in believing I could change his course.”

“Define your error.”

Safna thought again. “My error was one of pride, Master. I believed that I could persuade him where you, a Sufi Master, had failed.”

“I didn’t fail, Safna.”

The youth frowned again. “If you didn’t fail, then why did he leave?”

“He left because he loved himself more than God. I didn’t fail because I didn’t try to change his course once he’d decided upon it. Each man comes to God by himself, Safna. I’ve been trying to tell you this. You know God’s Word; your faith is bolstered by the Five Pillars of Islam ...” Fadi permitted himself a small smile. “Or it will be once you complete the Hajj, but you don’t govern men’s desires, nor do I, nor does the Sultan – only Allah writes in a man’s heart, and what he writes there will only be revealed when he stands before God on the Day of Judgment.”

Safna bowed his head. “I’m sorry, Master.”

“Don’t be,” Fadi responded sharply. “You’re doing it again. You’re telling me that you’ve failed me. You haven’t. You’ve only failed yourself. If you must apologise, apologise to yourself.”

Safna cocked his head to one side and caught Fadi’s gaze. “Sorry, Safna,” he murmured, his lips creasing into a smile.

Fadi shook his head but smiled also. “Come, Safna, we cannot waste the day in idle frivolity. You’ve seen me sit day after day, not moving, not speaking, my eyes closed. What is it I do?”

“You think about God?”

“More than just think, Safna. What I do is called Muraqaba.”

"Will you teach me this skill, Master?"

"Yes, but don't think to learn it in a day. It took me many years to perfect it, and even now I sometimes fail. Never think that because I sit here and you there that I am further along the path to enlightenment than you. We all make our own paths."

"I'll be patient, Master. I have but set my first foot upon the path."

Fadi nodded approval. "Muraqaba is about the heart, young Safna. The senses bring information of the outside world into the mind, and the mind influences the heart. Every sensation tells the body that pleasure or pain can be taken from the world, and every experience binds body and mind to the world. For the vast majority of men and women, that's all they know. The world spreads before them, around them, through them; and with every waking moment spent in contemplation of the world, in the enjoyment of its pleasures and in the avoidance of its unpleasantness, so too, is God pushed from our hearts. That's the tragedy of the world – that we can only know God through our hearts, and yet man seeks to cut himself off from knowledge of God."

Safna sat and thought about this in silence, and Fadi did not seek to hurry him. *Haste is the enemy*, he reminded himself. The youth stirred at last. "My heart listens to your words, Master, but the mind counsels otherwise."

"What does your mind say?"

“My mind says that God created the world. How then can it be evil, turning us away from God?”

“I didn’t say the world was evil, yet great evil can come from the world.”

Safna frowned. “You seek to confuse me, Master?”

“Not so. The confusion lies in the minds of men. I seek to pierce the veil and let God’s light shine on your heart.”

“Don’t just pierce, Master, but rend and tear the veil that keeps me in darkness.”

“All things come from God and are good. Yet there are those who would obscure the Words of God that lie plain upon the face of creation – men and shayatin take the goodness of God and make of it a thing to deceive others.”

“There really are shayatin?”

“There’s one that walks the streets of Bukhara. I’ve seen it myself.”

Safna shivered and looked about him as if he might spy the evil spirit stalking along the sunlit streets and through the shaded groves. “How may we guard ourselves, Master?”

“By keeping our hearts pure and focussed on God Most High. You must learn to control your bodily senses so that only goodness can enter, cutting yourself off from false ideas and wickedness. Turn your full consciousness toward God and say three times, ‘My God, you are my goal and your good pleasure is what I seek.’ Then bring to the forefront of your heart the Name of the

Essence – Allah – and focus on its meaning." Fadi smiled. "What is its meaning, Safna?"

"The God, the One, of Whom there is no likeness."

"Yes, Allah – Essence without likeness, for there are none like Him. He's present here with us now as we speak; He watches everything, sees everything and hears everything. Worship God as if He stood before you, for though you don't see Him, He sees you."

Once more, Safna thought long and hard about the Sufi's words. "And … and that's all there is to it? Keeping God in our hearts?"

Fadi permitted himself a dry chuckle. "If that were all, young Safna, every man would be a Sufi Master and the world would be Paradise. The world constantly intrudes upon us. In every waking moment, sight and sound and taste and smell and touch distract us from our contemplation of the Almighty. Can you shut out the world so that your thoughts are pure, undistracted?"

"I think so, Master."

"Show me."

Safna scratched his armpit and settled himself in a comfortable position, sitting crosslegged with his hands lightly resting on his knees. His eyes unfocussed and stared at the wall of the alcove beside Fadi's head. His breathing slowed, and the muscles of his face relaxed.

Fadi watched him closely, and after a few minutes quietly suggested he close his eyes. The youth did so, and the two of them sat in silence and unmoving for many minutes.

"Alright, open your eyes, Safna." The youth opened them, blinked and yawned; then he grinned. "Were you successful?" Fadi asked.

"I believe so."

"Truthfully?"

"Yes."

"You blinked repeatedly as if your eyeballs were dry, and you should moisten them. You swallowed. Your eye moved slightly when someone shouted in the street. You heard me when I suggested you shut your eyes and when I told you to open them again. Your toes moved once, and a muscle in your thigh jumped twice. Your nostrils twitched when the aroma of cooking …"

"Enough, Master. I take your point. All these things intruded upon me. I cannot shut out the world."

"Yes, you can, Safna Bukhara. Be in no doubt in that regard. You just need training."

"You can do it, Master?"

"Sometimes, and when I do, my heart is filled with the most ineffable joy, because it's as if God sat with me and His love enveloped me. For now though, that's Muraqaba, the goal toward which we all strive."

"How do I train to achieve this goal?"

"Imagine you stand outside a walled courtyard. It has no doors, and the walls are smooth and unclimbable. Inside you can hear men praying fervently, and you want to join them. How do you do it?"

"I could call to the men to throw a rope over the wall."

"You'd disturb their prayers."

"Then I'd have to climb the wall myself."

"How? The walls are as smooth as glass."

Safna considered the problem. "What is outside this courtyard?" he asked.

Fadi smiled. "It's your problem and your imagination. What would you like to have outside it?"

Now Safna grinned. "I would stack boxes, furniture, bales of wool against the wall and climb up those until I reached the top and then jump down the other side."

"Very good. The walled courtyard is your heart and the men praying inside it the love of God. To reach it, you must use anything lawful you have available to you. There are ways to scale the wall of the heart, and they are Shari'a, Tariqa, Haqiqa and Marifa."

"The words mean law, path, something and knowledge, but I don't see how they help."

"Come," Fadi said. "It's nearly time for prayers. Let's go and wash ourselves to prepare to approach God." The two men crossed to the public ablution fountains and carefully washed themselves according to the prescribed rituals. They joined the crowds of worshippers at the mosque of the shrine of Shaykh Naqshband and for a time, lost themselves in the bliss of praising God. Afterward, they ate a small meal of vegetables and bread, washed it down with pure water and sat in silence, contemplating their creator.

At length, Fadi spoke. "As you say, Safna, Shari'a means Law. It encompasses the Way of

Submission given in the Qur'an and Sunnah. Every Muslim is aware of Shari'a and attempts to follow it. For those of us that seek to be Sufi, Shari'a must be carried out completely. We seek to prove our love for God by complete submission to the Will of God, by rigorous self-discipline and a constant attention to our conduct. If any man has a lawful grievance against us, then we've failed."

"There are many who follow the Law, yet aren't Sufi."

"I rejoice that there are many, Safna, and I wish that all men would Submit to the Will of Allah, but even if all men prostrated themselves, only a few would be Sufi, for the Shari'a is but the first step. Until a man or a woman can conquer his or her body, purifying the spirit, there can be no advancement."

"A woman? Can a woman become Sufi?"

"Of course, for God made the mind and heart of woman as well as of man. A woman who can focus her mind and her heart is as capable of knowing God as any holy man. In some ways, a woman is supremely suited to know God as God has given her a creative function and emotions suited for love. However, there are not as many Sufi women as Sufi men, for the world puts obstacles in the way of women. Their bodies intrude more, snatching them back from a contemplation of God into the everyday tedium every month. They must conquer the desire for a husband and for children, and they must ever guard against the impure thoughts of men."

"Guard themselves how, Master?"

“Anything that binds them to the world will keep them from a pure knowledge of God. A husband will put demands of the flesh on her, and children will occupy every waking moment. Even unmarried though, her body is a source of lust for men who are unable or unwilling to control themselves. This is why the Qur’an bids a woman cover the parts of her body that might excite lust, and some authorities go even further, bidding her cover every part so no man is stumbled by her presence.”

“That’s good, surely?”

“Perhaps, yet if a man lusts after a woman because he sees her hair or leg or even her private parts, isn’t this a failing on his part, rather than on hers? Who is it that shows the lack of control – the man or the woman? Who is it that sins – the man or the woman? If we all lived according to Shari’a, truly Shari’a in our hearts, then we’d all wander naked and be filled only with love for God. That day may come, or even a day when women are as welcome in Sufi as men, but that day is not yet.” Fadi smiled. “We’ve digressed somewhat. Let’s return to the stages of perfection.”

“You said Tariqa, the path, comes after Shari’a, the law.”

“Don’t think of them as consecutive steps upon a road leading to God, Safna, for you’re already on the path that is Tariqa.”

The youth raised his eyebrows at this. “I am? When did this happen?”

“The day you came to me, for I’m Naqshbandi Sufi, and by coming to me, you chose the path of Naqshband.”

“So I’m already upon the path.”

“Yes, but don’t get complacent, for you have far to go. Remember in those early days I tested your resolve by making you fetch and carry for me, do all those degrading tasks? I’d normally have done them all myself with a glad heart, but they were a ready means of testing you.”

Safna smiled and bowed from the waist. “It gladdened me to do that for you.”

“Not everyone reacts as you did.”

“Ala al-Din?”

“Yes.”

“And that’s the path, Tariqa? Serving you?”

“Never me, only God. And that’s but the first thing. Next are the prayers. If you were to go to one of the other schools of Sufi, you would learn other prayers. Because you came here, you learn the Naqshband prayers. These prayers are the awrad and must be perfected. I’ve never let you recite them aloud, and I won’t until I’m certain you have them right. They are prayers that enable you to experience visions from God. If you were to make a mistake in the recitation, it would be a most grievous sin and would block you from the love of God.”

“Visions from God?”

“Yes, sublime visions, and the experience of these visions is Haqiqa.”

Safna thought about these things for a time. Fadi let him think, turning his own mind inward, contemplating without fear the growth within his own bowels that was only just starting to cause him pain.

"Master, I'm confused. You said there were four steps of which Tariqa was the second and Haqiqa the third, but now you say mastery of Tariqa gives you the visions. Does that not mean that the visions of Haqiqa are really part of Tariqa?"

"No, for the visions are but the manifestation of Tariqa and lead to full Hariqa. There's no definition that comes readily to mind as there is for the other steps, but I could say that Hariqa is the knowledge that comes from this close communion with God as evidenced by the visions. God enables me to see things that aren't apparent to other men."

"What sort of thing, Master?"

Fadi shrugged delicately. "I can see that you've drunk bad water recently. You have a looseness of the bowels."

Safna grinned and shook his head. "Not me. I feel as healthy as ever."

Fadi made no comment. "Marifa is also knowledge and knowledge that comes only from God. Haqiqa is knowledge from God about the world and what's in it, whereas Marifa is knowledge that comes from God and concerns God and the unseen world."

Lessons only occupied a fraction of the time Fadi al-Asim and Safna Bukhara spent together, for a Sufi's life is a full one. The Five Pillars of Islam ruled them – the recitation was constantly in the forefront of their minds; they offered up the ritual prayers with other Muslims; they fasted when

Ramadan came around each year; they dreamed of making the Hajj pilgrimage to Makkah. These things were easy for men who loved God, but the fifth pillar, giving alms to the poor, was harder for men already poor.

"Don't think in terms of money or material wealth," Fadi counselled, "But rather in terms of what you can do with the little you have." He led Safna round the city at regular intervals, finding the poor and diseased and washing their sores, binding their wounds and ministering to them as best he could. Neither did he overlook the plight of animals. "Allah created all things, even the lowliest animal. If an animal suffers, don't you think God feels its pain? How can I pass by the kicked dog, the beaten donkey or the sparrow with a wing broken by a stone from the hand of a thoughtless boy?"

Safna looked incredulous at first but watched as his teacher ministered to every person or animal in need. "Even a murderer?" he asked.

"Who am I to judge what's in a man's heart? Only God can do that."

"And a pig? Surely you wouldn't minister to such an unclean animal."

Fadi sighed and suppressed a shudder. "Even though it makes me unclean. Didn't God also make the pig?"

Safna was not always with his Sufi Master. He had been born in Bukhara of a Turkic family and owed his family much, spending what time he could helping his relatives.

Fadi also had other duties. Safna was not his only pupil, any more than Ala had been. Many youths and young men, often from good families, attended his lessons, and if none of them matched the piety of Safna, it was not for want of effort. *All men come to God by a different path or not at all,* he reminded himself.

Fadi had one other duty which he shared with other Sufi Masters of the Naqshbandi Order – that of guiding the spiritual progress of the ruler of the empire, Timur the Lame.

Timur was the ruler of an empire that stretched from Anatolia to India, from the Aral Sea to the Indian Ocean. His father was Taraghay, chief of the Barlas tribe from the steppes, and he had married into the family of Temujin the Khan of the Mongols and Khagan of the Mongol Empire. Timur could justifiably have called himself Khan after he wrested the western half of the Khanate from the Chagatai successors of Temujin, but he was content with the lesser title of Amir. A brilliant military leader, he was more at home in the saddle or at the head of an army than within the palace of Samarkand, frustrated by the interminable processes of government. Now an old man of nearly seventy, he had fixed his unwavering gaze on the Ming Dynasty of China and looked forward to being in the field again. He was a Muslim, but his faith was less one of conviction and more one of necessity. Islam provided a basis for bloody warfare against unbelievers and kept the native populations in check. Timur had religious advisers, as well as political and economic ones, and although he had already decided on war with China, he still gathered his advisers around him to tell him what he wanted to hear.

Timur's principal religious adviser was the Hanafite scholar, Abdul-Jabbar Khwarazmi, but the Amir listened to anyone he felt might have the ear of God. He sent an officer up from Samarkand to Bukhara to collect the Naqshbandi Sufi Masters, including Fadi al-Asim.

Fadi entered the throne room with his fellow Sufis and bent his knee to the Amir. The sun-browned, wrinkled old man with the walking stick that was the ruler of the Khanate nodded and smiled pleasantly before inviting them to sit on cushions.

"I go to conquer China," Timur said. "What advice do you have for me?"

The senior Sufi, Gafar al-Fathi, got to his feet and bowed. "Excellency, keep the love of God in your heart." He sat down and another Sufi Master arose.

"Great One, keep the Law of Allah always in your mind's eye."

"Excellency, remember to approach God in prayer regularly."

"May the shahadah be ever upon your lips."

"Great Amir, deal justly with the peoples you conquer and bring them all to the True Faith."

One after another, the Sufi Masters offered their advice, mindful the Amir held the power of life and death in his fist. No one wanted to contradict Timur's decision to invade China, so they only sought to ameliorate the harshness of war. Finally, Fadi al-Asim rose to his feet and bowed.

"Amir, to kill is wrong."

"What?" Timur's eyes flew open, and he stared at the thin old man standing before him. "What did you say?"

"I said that all life is sacred. Do not kill."

Timur scowled and looked around the circle of Sufi Masters. Nobody met his gaze, averting their eyes as his smoldering stare swept across them. "Is this the advice of a Sufi or just that of a senile old man?"

The senior Sufis hummed and hahed but eventually admitted that as each Sufi found his own path to God, every statement made by a Sufi was equally valid.

Timur turned his attention on Fadi once more. "Do you dispute that God has given me overlordship of the Khanate?"

"No, Amir."

"And over the empire of the Ming Chinese?"

"That I cannot say, Amir, for God hasn't spoken to me concerning this."

Timur grunted. "Much blood was spilled in conquering these lands that you admit God gave to me. Was I wrong to kill all these people?"

"My lord Amir, that's between you and God. All I have to guide me is God's word that all life is sacred."

"The Prophet Muhammad killed men – or at least caused them to be killed. Was he a sinner?"

"The Prophet, peace be upon him, cannot be guilty of sin. When men died at the hands of the faithful, it was because they fought against God and his Messenger."

Timur nodded appreciatively. "So as long as I kill God's enemies, I'm blameless?"

Fadi hesitated, seeking the right words. He heard a murmur of caution from the other Sufis but put them out of his mind. *My path is not their's.* "My lord Amir, if an infidel seeks to kill you because you're one of the faithful, then you may defend yourself, even to the man's death. Whether you choose to exercise this warrant is another matter. God tells us all life is sacred, yet allows us to kill in self-defence. Wouldn't it be better if we could defend ourselves without killing?"

Timur's face looked as if he had swallowed a draught of bitter willowbark. "It's men like you who make me glad I'm a warrior. Still, even you Sufis will agree that the Chinese are infidels and they attack us, who are faithful. We're justified therefore in defending ourselves."

The senior Sufi agreed solemnly, but Fadi did not take his seat. He looked around the throne room and shook his head. "Where are these Chinese infidels that attack us? My lord Amir, are you not gathering an army to attack them? How then, can their deaths be justified?"

Timur scowled and his hands gripped the arms of his throne tightly. "Do you seek death, Sufi?"

"No, lord Amir, yet death will find us all when God wills it. You sent for me and asked my advice. I've given it as I understand it from my study of God's Word. If I'm to die, let it be because I've obeyed my Amir and my God."

The old Amir stared at Fadi and then abruptly chuckled. "You're a brave man, Fadi al-Asim, yet I reject your advice. I'll conquer the Chinese in God's name, and you'll accompany me so that you may see God's Will unfolding."

Fadi bowed. "Let it be then, as God wants."

And so, on the sixth day of Rajab in the year eight hundred and seven from the time of the Hijra, the armies of Timur the Lame, Amir of Samarkand and effective Khan of the Chagatai Khanate marched north from his capital city to bring the Word of God to the infidel Chinese at the point of the sword. Not a man in that host doubted he could accomplish this task, for Timur was a consummate warrior and an experienced general. The soldiers of the Amir wondered at the season of campaigning, however, for it was still in the dead of winter and it was well-known Timur preferred the spring for his conquests.

"It's because the land of the Chinese is so far away," one aide explained. "By the time we approach the borders of China, it'll be spring."

For now, though, it was winter and a colder one than many had experienced. The army quartermasters, used to more clement campaigning weather, had omitted crucial cold weather supplies, and a week out from Samarkand, the first deaths occurred from frostbite.

They came to the Sayhoun River, the Great Pearly – named for its pearl-coloured waters – but found it frozen solid and marched along its western bank. The army followed its meandering loops northward. Instead of living off the land, the men found themselves reliant on the stores in the great ox-drawn wagons. Water was unexpectedly harder to come by, and every evening when the army made its camp, the men were forced to dig through ice a man's height thick to get at the milky water beneath. The next morning before they set off, they had to break through the refrozen water to fill the water skins. Fuel became scarce in the frozen landscape, and while men and horses could remain warm during the day, many died of the extreme cold during the winter nights.

Fadi had little to occupy him during the march. He was only there to witness the unfolding of God's Will over the infidel Chinese at the hands of Allah's Instrument, Timur the Lame. On most days, he rode in one of the wagons or trudged through the snow with the soldiers. He made friends with some and found some enjoyment telling the rough and ready warriors of the finer points of worship.

"This thinking youse do is all very well," one man said, "but it's the soldiers of the Khan what gives youse the ease to do it. Where would youse be without the fighting men?"

"Not trudging through the snow," Fadi admitted. "I do see your point, though constant warfare doesn't enable a man to grow close to God."

"Don't think we don't love God, 'cause we do, but we has our duty to the Khan." The soldier looked askance at the thin Sufi wrapped in wool garments. "I hear yer stood up to the Khan hisself. It's more than I'd care to do."

"Don't make too much of it," Fadi said with a smile. "It's easier to be brave if you have no fear of death."

The soldier thought about this for twenty or so paces. "I don't fear death in battle against the infidel, for thens I go straight to Paradise, but if one's Lord kills yer, what happens then? Does yer still go to Paradise?"

"I believe so. I have faith in God that He'll allow no injustice to take place."

The soldier laughed out loud, and then apologised. "Sorry, but I sees injustice wherever I looks. Yer sees a lot of it when yers a soldier. It's always the common people whats suffers after an army goes through, and where's the justice in that? They didn'ts ask us to come, we probably kills their family or robs them of food or fuel, and theys not better off whens we leave, so what's fair about that?"

"Indeed, but that injustice is caused by men. God has the power to change things, and he will; though you may have to wait until you stand before him to be judged."

"May that day be far off," the soldier muttered.

"As God wants," Fadi agreed. "Where are you from, soldier, and what's your name?"

"A little village in the mountains – Mula. Poor soil and poorer people. I couldn'ts wait to get outs. I am called Changa, son of Ulan."

"But you're a Muslim?"

"I knows me Qur'an, more or less, and I cans read it even, but not much else. I says me prayers whens I ain't fighting. I don'ts have no alms to give, and I can'ts afford to go on Hajj excepts the Amir he takes us to Arabia."

"You can still better yourself in the eyes of God," Fadi said. "You don't have to be a scholar to do so. There's always the path of Naqshbandi."

"I heards of that," Changa said in surprise. "He was a saint or something froms Bukhara."

"Indeed. Shaykh Baha ud-Din Naqshband was my teacher, and he set out eleven steps that a man can follow that will lead him to God. Would you like me to teach them to you?"

The soldier scratched at his beard and looked away. "I can'ts pay yer. I spents all my money on … in Samarkand."

"I don't want pay or even a promise from you that you'll listen. I believe that every man takes his own path to God, and I wouldn't presume to dictate your path."

Changa shrugged and adjusted the heavy pack on his back. "Off yer goes then, but I makes no promises."

"Shaykh Naqshband set out eleven steps by which a man might grow close to God. They're simple steps but require effort. Taken to heart, they mean that you're only eleven steps from God. We'll start with the first today – that of hush dar dam, awareness of breathing."

"Well, I have that one already," laughed Changa. "I know I breathe."

"Ah, but do you pay attention to it? Without breath we're dead, but who ever listens to what goes in and out of our lungs? It's perhaps hard to do now as we trudge through the snow, but when you're at rest, close your eyes and draw in a breath. Listen to the sounds the air makes as it rushes into your nostrils; smell the odours it contains; let the breath fill your mouth so that you can taste it. Where has that air been? Think on where it's going and what will happen to it. Draw the breath in and feel it rush down your throat and into your lungs. Feel your chest swell – hold it – and release it. Be aware of the difference between inhaled air and exhaled – dry and moist, cold and warm. Repeat this exercise until you're familiar with every aspect of breathing."

Fadi walked in silence for a while, hearing the soldier snort and rasp as he breathed the frigid air. "When you know how to breathe, you must forget it."

"Forget it? How can I forget how to breath?"

"Your body won't forget, but you must thrust the conscious thought of breathing from your mind. Breathe deeply and evenly and the action will calm you. Now insert thoughts of the Creator. Consider how he's given you the gift of breath. Think of every good thing God provides, and do this with every breath you take until you think of Him continually. Praise God with every inhalation, give thanks with every exhalation."

The army camped for the night, and the soldier and the Sufi parted, each to his own tent. The air was bitterly cold, and Timur called his generals to him. Fadi was summoned too, for the Amir desired him to see every aspect of the campaign.

"The weather is extreme," Timur said. "My scouts tell me the snowdrifts are deeper the further north they go, so we'll cross the river and move to the east." He coughed and spat into a linen cloth.

“My lord Amir,” said the senior aide, “Let me fetch a physician.”

Timur shook his head. “It’s only the cold air.”

The aide swallowed but persevered. “My lord, a winter chill can be serious …”

“Enough!” Timur snapped. “Would you have me coddled while my army braved the cold? We cross the river tomorrow at … what’s the name of that place? The ruins?”

“Otrar, my lord,” one of the generals said. “It’s a place of ill-omen. We’d be better off advancing north another day before we crossed.”

“Am I surrounded by superstitious peasants? We go east now.” Timur stared around at his military men and aides, his gaze alighting on the old Sufi Master. “You, Fadi al-Asim, what say you? Does a faith in Allah allow for superstition?”

Fadi bowed. “Superstition is worship of the pagan gods of old. The True Faith has no part in it.”

“Hah, you see? The Sufi has his uses after all.” Timur swept out of the tent and the generals also departed, some of them casting sour looks at the old man.

“Couldn’t you have lied?” murmured one of the junior aides. “The Amir will now lead the river crossing, and he’s not well.”

“How long has he been sick?”

“A week, ten days. He coughs blood in the mornings or when he exerts himself.”

“What do the physicians say?”

“He won’t see them. He says it’s nothing. Al-Asim, I’m worried about him. He listens to you, won’t you say something?”

Fadi looked around to see whether they were overheard. They were not, but he lowered his voice anyway. "God alots a span to all men."

The aide looked shocked. "Surely not."

"He's an old man and in ill-health. If he were in his palace at Samarkand and being attended by his physicians, I'd say he had time to be sure of his heir. Out here in the bitter cold and without rest or medicine …" Fadi shrugged. "It's as God wants."

"As are all things," the aide said piously. Then a moment later, "Is there nothing we can do?"

"His strength is his pride. Timur the Lame won't capitulate."

And so it was. The next day, the army of Timur crossed the frozen Sayhoun River and camped among the ruins of Otrar. While his army crossed, the Amir went hunting and in the course of chasing a wolf on the ice, was thrown from his horse. Though he broke no bones, his lungs refused the burden put upon them, and he collapsed. Timur lingered another week and then, wasted and weak, slipped into death.

The generals called off the expedition to China and returned with their Amir's body to Samarkand. It was embalmed in musk and rose essence, wrapped in pure linen and encased in the finest carved ebony before being entombed in the Gur-e Amir that had been designed for his son.

Fadi al-Asim also did not long survive. When the Amir had been laid to rest, Fadi spent several weeks recuperating his strength before setting off for his home city of Bukhara. On the way, his caravan was attacked by bandits, and he was killed.

It was remarked afterward that one of the bandits, a sour fellow by the name of Ala al-Din, marked the holy man for death and took pleasure in the sin. What became of the killer is not known, but the Sufi Master's body was buried reverently in Bukhara.

Ten years passed. Changa the soldier took heed of the words of the Sufi and left the army. He educated himself in language, writing and mathematics and even took lessons that he might speak well. Only in times of stress did he lapse back into the patois common to his people, but those times were increasingly infrequent. He could now converse fluently in Turkic, his native Farsi, Arabic and even in the various dialects of the Indus Valley. Spurred by that one day's conversation with the Sufi, he studied under a Naqshbandi Sufi in Bukhara for a time, and though he dedicated himself to the eleven steps introduced to him by the man he called his teacher, Fadi al-Asim, he knew he would never be a true Sufi. His other teacher, Sufi Master Safna Bukhara, knew it too, and he took him aside and released him from his vows.

"Changa son of Ulan, I release you from the Way of Sufi. Some men are called to take the Staff of God, but others are called to other things."

"Each man makes his own way to God," Changa replied. "I must find my own path."

"Do so then, with my blessing and that of our Master Fadi al-Asim."

Changa bade him farewell and left Bukhara, journeying first to his home village of Mula in the high mountains. Whatever fond memories he had of it evaporated as he beheld the tiny gathering of mud huts and the tired, bowed men and women who worked the dusty fields. This was his home no longer. He knew it but had to return, if only to say farewell to the few people who remembered him. His parents were long dead, and even his brothers and sisters were buried in the untidy graveyard outside the village boundaries. He had lived as a soldier, risking his life in every skirmish or battle, yet he ate well, enjoyed the attentions of physicians and had opportunities to relax. His relatives, on the other hand, were tied to a relentless cycle of scratching a living from the parched and stony land. They took what joy they could from their existence and gratefully fled it when death presented itself. Changa found a nephew, a sister's son, a wizened man who looked older than him. He made the nephew a present of his money, and then he blessed him in Allah's name and turned his face eastward.

Changa had had his fill of the western lands when he marched to the shores of the Bosphorus under the banner of Timur. He killed many men, sacked, burned and pillaged towns and cities and raped his share of women. He desired to turn his back on this part of his life, not just figuratively, but because he did not wish to revisit the scene of his many sins. Changa thought for a time of trying to atone for those sins by tracking down the relatives of his victims and paying them blood money. It was an impossible task, for who takes down the names of the men he kills or asks after the family of the woman on whom he takes his pleasure? He decided if he could not correct his wrongdoing, he could perhaps make up for it by spreading the Word of

God in new lands. The writ of Timur and his successors reached into India, and as he knew something of their languages, Changa decided to go there.

It was a long way from the mountains of his childhood to the plains of India and beyond. It was a journey akin to the one every man makes as he ventures forth in the world, but unlike a youth, he was in no great hurry. He was already a man of fifty years, so if he wished to see the white ramparts that he had been told lay beyond the dusty expanse of India, he could not dawdle. Changa walked the whole way, stopping at any city, town or village he chose to work for a few coins or to earn a meal and a bed by telling stories or giving instruction in the ways of Allah.

As he approached India, the familiar ways of Islam disappeared and Changa found himself introduced to strange gods and demons. He found gods with dusky skin and four arms dancing upon snakes, fierce goddesses wearing kirtles of human skulls, gods that were half ape and half man, elephant-headed gods before which the people offered rice and spices and flowers. It was very strange and very wrong, but he knew enough about human nature to realise he would make no friends by rejecting their gods out of hand. Instead, he sat down in the street outside their dark temples and preached the Holy Word of Allah to any who would listen.

People stopped to hear what he said and argued their own beliefs. Changa listened and answered calmly and with logic, and when he moved on, he sometimes left people who had made the shahadah and embraced the Word of Allah. He passed through into lands where even his knowledge of languages failed, so he stayed longer, picking up a smattering of different tongues. Changa found he was welcomed as a holy man and given alms by the people. He spoke of the Qur'an and of Allah and His Messenger, and they rewarded him with rice and vegetables.

As in most places, however, not everyone was friendly. He was attacked several times, probably because he was a stranger. As he usually had nothing to steal, they learned to leave him alone. Changa could have defended himself as he had training in combat, but his Sufi teachers had instilled in him a reverence for life, so he took their blows without protest. He met other men with a similar reverence, men clad in saffron robes who shaved their heads and spoke of the Way. Their way was not his way though, as they worshipped no god but only a holy man rather like Muhammad titled the Buddha. This man spoke of a Way, but it was a way not to God but to nothingness. They were gentle people though, and he was content to sit in their silent company, while they each meditated according to their custom.

There were Muslims in this land, but not many and fewer as he moved toward the White Mountains. When he felt the need, Changa would seek out a mosque, share Jumu'ah or sit in the doorway of a madrasah, listening to the imam instruct the children on the Holy Word. Afterward, one of the elders would invite him to break bread with him and question him about the world that lay beyond their town. He answered civilly and offered a blessing for their charity before moving on.

One day as he rested on one of the narrow paths above a rushing, tumbling river in the foothills of these white-peaked mountains, the clouds shredded and in the distance he saw a great ice-covered rock thrusting up into the azure sky. A fellow traveller called it Nanda Devi and said the mountain was a goddess. Changa knew better, but kept his silence so as not to offend him. The sight was certainly beautiful, and he offered up praise to Allah for His creation.

Changa met a demon here. It was not a djinni, for djinn are creatures of the desert, but was, he believed, a demon of India they call a raksha. A generation or so before Changa arrived, a Sultan of Delhi, Muhammad bin Tughluq, had carried bloody war into the mountains in an effort to crush native resistance to his rule. It is said he was thrown back by heroes who could not be killed. Stories grow in the telling; so when these tales were recounted to Changa by farmers and traders, he smiled politely and assumed they resulted from national pride. When one man told him a hero of those times still lived, he went to see for himself.

The hero lived in a lonely place near a memorial that had been erected to the Hindu fallen of that war. That should have, perhaps, alerted Changa; for djinn dwell in such places and it was likely a raksha had similar habits. He camped near the memorial, meaning to seek out this hero the next day. Instead, the demon found him that night.

Stealthy footsteps on the path brought him awake and alert, and he grasped his staff. Although Changa would not strike back against a human foe, he might have to ward off a predatory animal. It was no animal but rather a man, tall and lean with broad shoulders and deep-set eyes that threw back the firelight at Changa in winking points of blue.

"You're welcome," Changa said. "May I offer you what little I have?"

The stranger's voice rumbled deeply like thunder in a far off chasm. "I'll share your fire." He sat down across the fire from Changa and stared at him. "Most men fear to tread these paths even in the light," he observed. "How is it that you aren't afraid?"

"I fear only God. My name is Changa, and I come seeking a hero who once fought here."

"You may call me Pandalis." The stranger smiled, his teeth sharp and white in the firelight. "I am that hero you seek. Now tell me, what god do you fear?"

"There is only One," Changa said calmly. "Allah, the Merciful and Beneficent."

Pandalis hissed and drew back. "You're Muslim. I killed many Muslims once; perhaps it's time for one more."

Changa's heart beat faster, but he was also filled with joy. This man called Pandalis hated Muslims, and if he was killed by an infidel because of his faith, he would go straight to Paradise. "I won't fight against you, Pandalis, for I'm a man of peace and long ago renounced violence."

"You don't fear me?"

Changa smiled and shook his head. Then he blinked for it seemed as if the heated air above the fire made the man's face shimmer and move. A moment later he recognised him for what he was as he dropped onto all fours and his shape flowed and morphed into a great grey wolf of the hills.

"Duh yer fer me nuh?" the wolf asked. Changa heard a word that sounded like a curse, and the creatures jaws shortened and became more human. "Do you fear me now?" it repeated.

He could not help himself. He laughed and shook his head again.

Anger flowed from the strange shape in front of him. "I'll rip you limb from limb and gnaw on your entrails. You'll die screaming and calling upon me to end your miserable life."

"If you must," Changa said, though he did not feel brave. "But the one I'll be calling on will be Allah. You may rend my body, but my spirit goes to God."

The wolf sat back on its haunches, and its limbs became arms and legs. "Why do you believe your spirit lives on when the body dies? I've seen many men die and none survived."

"I know, because I've communed with Allah for many years. He doesn't lie, and He tells us the faithful will be in Paradise."

"You really have no fear, do you?" The wolf turned back fully into a man.

"You're not going to eat me?"

"Not tonight, but unless you wish to die, you'll be far from here by sunset tomorrow. A man's life has little taste unless he's in terror, but I'll feed anyway tomorrow night if I find you." Pandalis' body disappeared and a still, blue flame hung in the darkness at about chest height. Then it drifted off down the trail until it was lost among the trees.

Changa left after the dawn prayers, at which time he also gave thanks to Allah for his deliverance. On the way down the mountain, he thought about what the raksha had said and he reached a decision about his future. He would settle down in one of the towns that had a small Muslim community and offer his skills and knowledge. He was not Sufi, but he knew enough about their ways to arm others against demons. *Fear will kill you, but knowledge of Allah will drive fear from your heart.* Changa could not think of a better way to live.

Chapter Eighteen

I was going to say that I loved Timur the Lame, but that would not be right. Djinn cannot love, so I will amend my statement to say I appreciated him. Great conquerors are good for those in my business, and the Mongol Khans excelled in their trade. Thousands died and I was there for many deaths, feeding on the sweet rich taste of men's pain and terror.

When I left Egypt, I wandered north, following the extended wars between Christian and Muslim. When the Christians withdrew to their own cold lands, I remained in the Muslim cities of Syria and Palestine. I still fed well, for Muslims kill other Muslims with almost as much enthusiasm as they kill infidels. Their religion is a hard one, born in a hard land and fostered at the teats of greed and rivalry. I could never understand why my kind did not flock to the Muslim nations, for there was more death than even I could handle. It may be that djinn are not common, or it may be that they stayed away in fear. After all, I have seldom met stronger djinn than me.

I was in Isfahan in Persia when the city surrendered to Timur. He displayed the leniency he often did when a city surrendered, but like so many others, they took it for a sign of weakness and rebelled. When Timur returned at the head of his army, he ordered the population to be massacred. Over seventy thousand men, women and children were slaughtered, their heads cut off and fashioned into tall towers. I walked the blood-drenched streets of the city both in the form of a man and within the body of men as I chose, watching the inventive cruelty of men unleashed on helpless victims. I feasted, as you may imagine, but there were too many deaths to enjoy properly. I would rather drink deep at the agonised thoughts of a single man as life is slowly and painfully extracted from him than sip at a thousand butchered in blinding blood lust. Still, I had my fill of both.

When Timur's army left Isfahan, I joined it. Death followed wherever they went, and when they ran out of victims, they died themselves of disease and hunger. I was on the campaign that led to India and the capture of the city of Delhi. Thousands were killed and many more captured. Timur complained that the Sword of Islam needed further washing in the blood of infidels and ordered the captives to be killed. Any man in his army who did not bring him the heads of his captives would himself be executed. Ten thousand more died in an orgy of beheading.

The army moved back across Asia to Baghdad and another swathe of killings, this time of fellow Muslims who defied the Khan. Twenty thousand died, and the city's artisans and craftsmen were taken away and lodged in Bukhara and Samarkand. After the feasting of the last twenty years, I was content to relax in a peaceful city, though the term is relative. The inhabitants of Isfahan, Delhi and Baghdad would have thought Bukhara a model of peace and equanimity, but beneath the surface lay the usual undercurrent of violence. It is hard to keep a peacetime army as the trained killers need an outlet for their talents. That is why the next war is always just a stone's throw away.

China was Timur's next target and such was his eagerness to conquer that nation that he left the comfort of Samarkand and headed north in one of the bitterest winters known. Success can blind a man to his own failings, and Timur's fault was always that he rushed from one task onto the next without due consideration to the practicalities. He disliked setting up the apparatus of stable government in the lands he conquered and would rather punish rebellion than maintain peaceful relations. On his Chinese expedition, he set off in the dead of winter rather than waiting for spring and paid the penalty for his rashness. He died and was taken back to Samarkand for burial.

I never met the Sufi holy man, Fadi al-Asim, but I knew of him through the mind of a nasty small-minded man called Ala al-Din. He hated the Sufi, and I could feel that hatred from afar and was attracted to it. I was there when he killed his former teacher, and I wondered at the calmness of the holy man's mind as he died. It was enough to make me follow the Sufi's body back to Bukhara, where I saw a former soldier in the Amir's army start to learn the ways of Sufi at the feet of one Safna Bukhara, himself a pupil of the holy man. Being well fed and always having access to violent men in the poorer quarters, I stayed to see what would happen and saw a truly perplexing thing. This soldier, this killer called Changa, forsook violence and embraced the spirit of Islam. I dipped into his mind, thinking this was all some clever ruse for some nefarious purpose, but it was not. The change was deep-seated and genuine.

This man Changa fascinated me, and even when he ceased to follow the Path of Sufi, I followed him on the lesser paths he took. He journeyed across Asia to the dusty plains of India and then up into the forest-clothed foothills of the mountains they call Himalaya. There he met a demon.

No, it was not me. I could have revealed myself to him at any time, ripped his life from him and savoured his fear, but I chose not to. I was more interested in seeing what he did, so I left him alone. I watched as another being of flame, a raksha of India, attempted what this djinni refrained from doing.

The raksha clothed himself in a handsome human body, but I could see his inner flame and knew him for what he was. He changed into a wolf, the better to rend his victim, but I scarcely saw him for I was engrossed in the vision of a human unafraid of ghastly death in the jaws of a demon. I could have intervened, but I was entranced; I was amazed at his lack of fear. Apparently the raksha was too, for he merely warned him off, became a blue flame and disappeared without harming him.

I considered following the raksha, for he was one of the strongest of the brethren of the flame I had ever encountered. He was strong, maybe even as strong as I – I could tell by the vibration in his flame – but the only way to test it was to fight him. I decided to leave him to his mountains and go back to the deserts I knew so well. I was not afraid, you understand, but if he was stronger, he would kill me as I would kill him if I overcame. I was not ready to take that chance.

I left them both to it and became flame again, soaring through the middle air like a bolt of lightning until I came again to the plains. There I resumed by normal life, wandering, following my interests and preying on humans. But the mind of Changa still bothered me, and I knew I had to learn more about this god that was taking over the world, this Allah who, as far as I knew, still lived back in his little black box in Makkah. Perhaps one day soon I would pay him a visit and test his strength.

Chapter Nineteen

The man woke in the pre-dawn darkness and lay for a moment in the warmth of his blanket before easing himself onto the hard-beaten earth floor of his home. He shook his wife's shoulder until she broke out of sleep with a muttered greeting and then padded outside in his long shift. The sky outside was still star-strewn, but the first greying of approaching dawn was visible in the east. He hurried along the path that led to the midden, where he relieved himself with a sigh of pleasure.

He drew water up from the well and washed himself thoroughly before drawing more for his family. The woman had dressed and now came out of the tiny house with the children and led them, yawning and protesting, toward the midden. The man took water inside and poured some into a pan, putting it onto the small fire his wife had prepared in the hearth. He went back to the door and looked anxiously down the path.

"Dilak, hurry up, it's nearly dawn," he called.

"I'm coming, Atam," his wife called back from the darkness. "Have you dressed yet?"

Atam grumbled but went into the bedroom and stripped off his night shift before drawing on his clothes. He yawned and then went to the chest in the corner and drew out four prayer mats, carrying them through into the kitchen. Outside, he could hear the sleepy chatter of the children and the sharp tones of his wife as she hurried them along.

"Quickly Berna … no, dry yourself Emin. Come along. Atam, where are you? The sun is almost up."

Atam checked the water was heating and walked calmly outside with the mats, unrolling them and positioning them, his own in front and the other three a few paces behind. "Take your places and we will start."

The eastern sky was pink now with the light growing by the minute. Atam stood and raised his hands to the heavens, his wife and children following his lead. "Allahu akbar." Atam then folded his arms across his chest and recited the first chapter of the Qur'an from memory. He was in the habit of adding in verses that taught a lesson to one or other of his children, but today he reverted to a favourite of his.

"He it is who sends down water from heaven, then we bring forth with it buds of all plants; from it green foliage from which we produce grain piled up in ears; and of the palm trees, of the sheaths of it come forth clusters of dates within reach and gardens of grapes and olives and pomegranates, alike and not alike; see the fruit of it when it yields the fruit and the ripening of it; verily, in this are signs for people who believe."

Atam continued on through the forms, making the utterances in Arabic as prescribed, and finished just as the sun eased over the horizon. They each rolled up their prayer mat and carried it inside before breaking their silence.

The children chattered as they broke their fast with bread, eggs and milk, while the adults ate similar fare but added freshly brewed and sweetened coffee. Atam ate quickly, knowing he must be in the fields soon.

"Busy day, husband?" Dilak asked, her mind already thinking about her own day.

"When isn't it? It'll be harvest soon and there won't be enough hours in the day, but for now I can do the work I've put off. The children can work with me."

"Berna is growing up. It isn't seemly that she works in the fields. She should be learning the skills of a wife and mother."

Atam shrugged. "You know best, but send Emin out at least."

"When he's fed the chickens and milked the goats."

Atam nodded and stood up. He walked to the door then turned and stood hesitating for a moment. "I didn't want to say anything too early, but I think we can afford to do Hajj this year."

Dilak put down the dregs of her coffee and stared at her husband. The children paused in their chatter and looked at their parents. "Hajj?" Dilak asked. "Do you mean it?"

"I … I think so … no, I mean yes, we're going on Hajj."

"Are you sure? It would be the most wonderful thing."

"The weather has been good and the wheat, oats, barley and beets are growing well – the olives too. If Allah favours us with a good harvest, we'll be able to afford it." Atam smiled quickly and left before his wife could say anything else. He picked up his hoe from the side of the house and set off for his fields, his shadow long as it swept over stands of rippling grain. *Allah, let it be a good harvest. This may be my last chance to do your bidding.*

There was a small field planted in root vegetables – sugar beet, turnips and parsnips. It was in the lowest section of their land, where water collected when it rained, and even now at the far end of summer, the soil was moist and friable. Atam started at one edge of the field and shuffled along the first row, chopping out the weeds and heaping the earth up around the lush growth of the crops where the rains and animals had collapsed the mounded ridges. He shook his head at the rich growth of weeds that had sprung up in the last week, weeds that sucked the goodness out of the earth. At the end of the first row, he turned and worked his way back down the next one, the morning sun already raising a sweat through his freshly laundered green thobe. He brushed the sweat from his brow with the back of his hand, adjusted the taqiyah on his head and bent to his work again.

Mid-morning his son Emin appeared and Atam set the eight-year-old to collecting firewood from under the tall poplar trees on the northern edge of the field. As the sun neared noon, his eleven year old daughter, Berna, ran up the path to the field with two prayer mats and a basket containing food and water. She put them down and ran off home, racing to get home before noon prayers.

Atam glanced down at the shadow puddling around his feet and then quickly up at the blazing sun in a gray-blue sky. "Emin," he called. "It's time for Dhuhr. Hurry."

Emin came running, leaping over the plants and down the uneven furrows. Atam held the water flask for him so he could wash his hands. "Now hold it for me," he instructed.

The prayer mats were already set out, so they lost no time getting into position and for many minutes lost themselves in the joy of worshipping their God. After prayer, they ate their meal, sitting in the small shade of the poplars.

An hour after eating, Atam finished weeding the field. They gathered up the basket, prayer mats, hoe and the bundle of dry sticks Emin had collected and returned to the house. The chickens, which had been let out of their pen to scratch and forage, ran up as they approached, their bright eyes eager for any scrap. They investigated the sticks but finding nothing to eat wandered off to search elsewhere.

Atam and Emin washed themselves and drank deeply from the cold well water before setting off for another part of their farm. The small fields of wheat, oats and barley were lush with the swollen ears starting to turn yellow. Sprinkled through the fields were cornflowers as blue as rain-washed sky and poppies like drops of fresh blood. Atam looked at his fields for a long time, praising Allah for the beauty of the world. When Emin started fidgeting, Atam squatted beside his son and pointed out the wonders of the coloured petals, the sturdy stalks and the burgeoning grains in the ears.

"Give thanks to God every day for the things He provides – food for our bellies and beauty for our minds."

Emin listened and then picked a poppy flower apart; dropping the petals one by one and watching them flutter to the ground. "What's Hajj, father?" he asked.

"You know what Hajj is. It's one of the five pillars."

"Yes, but what is it?"

"One of the commands we're given is to travel to Makkah and worship at the Kaaba. A person is to do this at least once in his life if he can afford it."

"Have you ever been, father?"

Atam shook his head. "No, never. Once, just before I met your mother, I thought I might be able to get to Makkah. It wasn't in the month of Dhu al-Hajji though, so it would only have been Umrah not Hajj."

"What's Umrah?"

"It's the lesser pilgrimage to Makkah performed outside of Dhu al-Hajji. It's still worthy, but it isn't Hajj."

"But we'll go this year?"

"I think so, Emin. The harvest looks like it'll be a good one, and I've been saving some money."

"Is it a long way? Do we have to walk?"

"Yes, and no." Atam grinned and hugged his young son. "It is a long way. It'll take us a month to get there, and though I'll walk all the way, you'll probably ride our donkey or a camel."

"A camel? But we don't have a camel."

“We’ll go to ash-Sham and there pay for passage with a caravan going to Makkah.”

“When do we leave?”

“After the harvest. It’s three days to Ramadan, and then after that we’ll gather as much of the harvest as we can and sell it in Darson. Then we’ll leave.”

The month of Ramadan arrived, and the family rose even earlier in the morning. Now they had to eat a meal and say the morning Fajr before sunrise. Atam and Dilak would both fast during daylight hours, and for the first time, Berna would join them as her moon blood had started a month or two earlier. Emin was exempt, but would be making an especial effort this year by drinking only water and having a small amount of plain bread after the midday prayers. Everything else would stay the same, though Atam planned only light duties around the farm. This year, one thousand and sixty after Hajri, was a fortunate one. Ramadan fell just before the harvest when little remained to be done, and Dhu al-Hajji fell after the main harvest. It would be many years before these fortunate circumstances came round again.

It’s my last chance, Atam thought. *Please Allah, let it be.* He put a hand to his belly and pressed surreptitiously, but the pain was not much greater than it had been for the last month.

The sun rose on the first day of Ramadan, and the family went about their appointed rounds. Because they could neither eat nor drink between dawn and sunset, they guarded their strength, attempting lighter duties where they could. The day went slowly, but at last the sun slipped beneath the horizon, and they offered up Maghrib prayers together. Then they ate, hungrily this first day when their bodies were still unused to doing without food. The evenings were short as they were husbanding their lamp oil, but Atam read the Qur'an to his family for an hour before 'Isha, last prayers, and they retired for the night.

As the month progressed, the adults thought less of food and more of the reason for their fast. Atam, as head of the household, made sure his family appreciated why God had laid this obligation on them.

"Being God-given, it focuses our minds and hearts on God," Dilak said when Atam questioned his family during the heat of one day.

"Good. What else? Berna?"

"All Muslims do it, father." She cast her eyes down now in the presence of men, even her father, for now that she was a woman she must learn her place.

"Yes, that's true. Ramadan is one of the Five Pillars. But what is the benefit of all Muslims doing it?"

Berna shook her head and her mother answered for her. "If we know that Muslims everywhere are fasting at the same time, it gives us a wonderful sense of unity."

"Yes, excellent. Now, Emin, a question for you. How does it make you feel when you're hungry?"

Emin thought for a moment. "It makes me look forward to the evening meal."

“That isn’t a worthy thought, Emin,” his father reproved. “You should be thinking about God. What I asked though, was how it made you feel?”

“Grateful for food?” Emin asked hesitantly.

“Yes. Fasting makes us aware of others in the community who fast because they’re too poor to buy food. We live on a farm where we always have enough to eat …” Atam raised an eyebrow as Emin opened his mouth. The boy shut it immediately. “… But beggars and slaves often go hungry. Ramadan is a time when we remember those less fortunate than ourselves and even provide food for them.”

“Will we do that, father?” Berna asked.

“Yes. We only eat two meals a day this month, so the third we’ll donate to the poor. Four people will eat better this month because of our alms.”

Ramadan came to an end, and before it did so, the cereals turned golden brown, the green blades and stems becoming sere and dead. The fields now looked like waving cloth of gold strewn with rubies and sapphires. The harvest started, and from dawn to dusk the whole family worked to bring in the grain, to thresh it and bag the seed. Then they moved on to the root crops, though here they left some in the ground to sweeten in the first frosts. The olives were picked, and Atam loaded up the donkey and took the fruits in to the olive press in the village. He waited most of the day, but finally the olives tumbled into the press and the great stone turned to squeeze the translucent green oil from them. The first pressings were sealed in small jars for sale, but later pressings yielded an inferior grade of oil that the family used for cooking.

Fruits were picked as they ripened and some sold in the village, others stored in barrels and bins buried deep in the earth where the soil temperatures were always cool. Figs were split and dried in the sun and hung up in bags from the rafters of the house, alongside woven chains of onions and garlic. Hazelnuts and walnuts were swept up and left in the shell, also going into barrels to protect them from rodents.

Dilak made a tally of everything that was sold and all the stores put carefully away. Their harvest represented not only their survival, but also, this year, their holy pilgrimage to far off Makkah. As she added the columns of figures, she knew their margin was as thin as the paper she wrote on.

Increasingly, Berna helped her mother in the house, learning all the womanly skills she would need to set up house with the man her parents picked as her husband. She was twelve now and well into her monthly courses. When they returned from Hajj, Atam would open negotiations in the village for suitable suitors and start arguing the dowry. Atam and Dilak had agreed that twelve was a good age for a betrothal, followed by the marriage when she turned fourteen.

Emin was schooled. Three days a week, Emin went into the small madrasah in the village where an imam taught the children the Qur'an and also instructed them on reading and writing. On al-jum'a, the whole family accompanied the youngest member and stayed on to partake of communal prayers.

As the time drew closer to the date they must leave, Dilak grew more anxious. One evening, after the children were asleep, she took her husband outside where the first cold breezes from the mountains were chilling the plains. She drew her shawl about her shoulders and shivered.

"I'm worried, husband," she said simply.

Atam yawned, his mind on the work that remained before they could leave. "What about?"

"Are we going to be safe? It's a long way to Makkah and well, you only have a knife to defend us. What if we're attacked by bandits?"

"There's no cause for alarm. Come in now, it's cold and I desire you." He took his wife in his arms after an automatic look round to make sure they were unobserved.

Dilak slipped free. "Husband, please. Reassure me or I'll continue to worry."

Atam sighed and sat down on a wooden bench by the door, motioning his wife to join him. "We're safe because the authorities – the Dawlet-il Aliyyat-il Osmāniyye – control all the lands between here and Makkah. The presence of army patrols will prevent any attacks by the Persians."

"And bandits?"

Atam considered dismissing the threat but decided to be honest. "Bandits are a fact of life, but they won't trouble dirt-poor farmers taking their produce to market. Once we're at ash-Sham, we'll join a caravan which will take us to Makkah in complete safety."

"I'm not worried about losing our food, but we'll need silver also."

“Fifty dirhams at least, so we must hide it well.”

“We have that much?”

“Yes. Don’t worry, Dilak. I’ll take care of you and our children.”

“You’re sure, husband? Berna is of an age she’d be most attractive to evil men.”

“You think we should leave her behind? Your sister, Leniya, may look after her for a price.”

Dilak shook her head. “No, she stays with me. Just make sure nothing bad happens.” She smiled and allowed her husband to take her inside.

They left their little farm in the care of Boghos, the husband of Dilak’s sister, Leniya, on the thirteenth day of Shawwal and struck north on the little country roads, seeking to meet the main road that ran east from Darson to ash-Sham. The caravan that went from Istanbul to Makkah, passing through ash-Sham, was already ahead of them and Atam drove them on to catch it.

“Why couldn’t we have taken it from Darson?” Dilak asked. “It’d be much safer to travel with it than on our own.”

“We cannot afford it,” Atam said. “The fee from ash-Sham will take most of our silver anyway.”

Atam led the way down the dusty road, leading their heavily laden donkey, and Emin ran alongside him, darting off onto the grass on either side after a butterfly or tossing stones at the crows that offered their raucous opinions from the shelter of trees. Whenever they met a traveller, the boy would dart back to the security of his parents and stare wide-eyed at the strangers. Berna and Dilak followed behind, ready to twist the tail of the donkey if it showed signs of faltering. They talked in low tones and hid their faces when strangers passed them, though Berna looked boldly at one or two young men until reprimanded sharply by her mother.

They caught up with the caravan on the fifth day and thereafter followed it at its slower pace. They were not allowed to travel within the caravan as they had not paid the dues, but by staying close, they hoped to benefit from the protection offered by the troops accompanying it. Either their ploy worked or else bandits were looking the other way, for they reached the outskirts of ash-Sham on the twelfth day after reaching the main road.

The caravan turned aside to camp outside the city where grazing and water was offered to the pilgrims for a modest fee. Atam left his family camped nearby and set off to find the Amir al-Hajj, the official in charge of the caravan. Along with a staff consisting of a judge, two notaries, a secretary, a treasurer, quartermasters and chefs, the Amir al-Hajj governed every aspect of a pilgrim's life from the moment he joined the caravan until they arrived at Makkah. Like all officials, he was guarded from the common people by layers of lesser officials, but eventually Atam got in to see the Amir.

"I am Abdullah ibn Shihab, the Amir al-Hajj of this caravan. What is the nature of your business?"

"My name's Atam Petrosian, your Excellency. I, and my family, wish to join your caravan."

"Speak so my secretary can hear you. What is your town?"

"A village, Excellency. Catafeli, near Darson. I have a small farm there."

The Amir turned to his secretary. "Do we have families from Darson?"

"Yes, Excellency."

"Good. He can travel with them. So, Petrosian, who is travelling with you?"

"My wife, Dilak, Excellency. Also my son, Emin, and daughter, Berna."

"Do you have a pack animal?"

"A donkey."

"Excellency," the secretary hissed.

"A donkey, Excellency," Atam repeated.

"Do you need others? What of food? Tents?"

"We have some of our food and a tent, Excellency, but … er, what would a donkey cost?"

"Five silver dirham, one way. Adults, ten each, children under the age of puberty, five dirham. Can you pay?"

Atam looked stricken. "That's ten dirham each, one way … er, Excellency?"

"No, to Makkah and back. Only the donkey is one way."

"Then yes, Excellency. I'll pay for three adults and a child. Also one donkey to Makkah."

Amir Abdullah nodded and dismissed Atam with the flick of a hand. "Pay my secretary. He'll give you a receipt. Guard it well."

Atam took the receipt and showed it to the soldiers as he led his family to their place in the encampment. He explained they would be travelling at a specific place in the caravan train and they would have access to some of the caravan stores and the protection of the soldiers guarding it. Dilak and the children looked around at the bustle of people and animals as if it was market day in a reasonably large town.

"Can we go exploring?" Emin asked, wide-eyed.

"No," his mother said. "It's nearly time for prayers, and I need you both to help me set up our camp. Later, we'll all go for a walk and see which others of our brother Muslims are with us."

"We're also getting an extra donkey," Atam said. "It'll be delivered soon, so look out for it and hobble it with ours."

"Where will you be, husband?"

"I have things to do."

Atam set off purposefully until he was out of sight and then found a place out of the bustle. He groaned and tenderly touched his belly, catching his breath as the pain bit deeper. He fumbled a small leather pouch out from under his thobe and broke off a tiny piece of the dried brown poppy resin in it. The taste was bitter and he grimaced but swallowed and within minutes the pain started to ease. Atam set off again, but this time with purpose, scouting the length of the caravan and examining the disposition of the soldiers. He saw an officer and waited around, trying to catch his eye.

After a while, the officer beckoned him over. "You want to say something?"

"I'm Atam Petrosian. I've just joined the caravan."

"I thought I hadn't seen you before. Armenian, eh? Well, we've a few of those. I'm Bölükbaşı Vazrig."

"Good-day, Sir," Atam said, bowing. "Forgive me, I didn't realise you were of such exalted rank else I wouldn't have bothered you."

Vazrig waved the apology aside graciously. "I'm Armenian too, Petrosian. We must look after one another, no?" He waited, watching Atam's face expectantly.

He expects a bribe. If I don't give him one, I've made an enemy. If I do and it's not enough, he'll still make me suffer. Atam took out his depleted purse and passed three silver dirham across to the officer. "A token of appreciation, Bölükbaşı Vazrig, from one Armenian to another."

Vazrig looked at the coins in his hand impassively for several moments and then nodded, tucking the silver away in his belt. "Is there anything you need, Atam Petrosian?"

"I've never been in a caravan before. Is it safe? It seems to me that so many people gathered together must surely attract bandits."

Vazrig laughed, exposing coffee-stained teeth. "Let them try. We're under the command of Amir Abdullah ibn Shihab, and he hasn't lost a man or a camel to bandits in five years."

"He's a good soldier?"

"The best."

"He's a good man too? The two attributes don't always go together."

Vazrig hesitated. "He's a hard man, savage almost, with wrongdoers, but fair. His justice is based on Qur'an and Sunnah."

"If he's of the Faithful, what more can one ask?" Atam agreed.

The caravan left ash-Sham on the twenty-eighth day of Shawwal, its numbers greatly swelled by pilgrims flocking to it. The camels and donkeys lumbered into motion with a great deal of noise, but the Armenian contingent far down the line did not start to move for nearly an hour. Each group had a soldier to watch over it and make sure it kept to its correct station, while Bölükbaşı Vazrig galloped up and down the line with a force of fifty troopers. Mounted on fiery Arabian steeds, they could answer any call or cover any threat within minutes of the alarm being sounded.

Atam and Dilak had made friends with an older couple from Darson, who had waited until they were gray-haired before making the Hajj. The man, Jannig Akhoyan, had made the trip before, when he performed Umrah as a young man with his new wife. He was full of useful information.

"We travel by day for now, but when we get down to about Jerusalem, we'll start to travel at night."

"Why is that? To avoid bandits?"

"No. The days are cooling with Dhu al-Hijjah at this season, but it'll still be hot during the day. So we sleep then and travel when it's cooler."

Jannig's wife, Marta, also had advice for Dilak. "I see you have brought food with you, but you'll need more before we get to Makkah. Don't buy from the traders who bring their wares out to meet the caravan. Their prices are too high. Come with me when we stop near the larger towns, and we'll buy at the local markets."

The journey down to Jerusalem was uneventful. The progress was slow, and after a few days, the Amir ordered that the caravan must travel longer each day in order to reach its appointed resting place. The whole route was mapped out, and it was essential they camp at the places set aside for them. Dust and flies occupied their days, and after the novelty of the long procession wore off, Emin stayed close to his parents or rode one of their two donkeys. Berna was more adventurous, eyeing with interest any young man who came near them. Whenever her mother caught her at her shameless behaviour, she slapped her, and once after she had actually spoken to a stranger, Atam had to beat her. Thereafter, Berna fashioned herself a headscarf similar to the ones Arab women wore. Beneath its overhanging folds she could watch men without the direction of her gaze being discerned by her mother.

They arrived at Jerusalem and camped well outside its walls. The Amir al-Hajj announced they would be stopping for one day to restock supplies, and then they would be travelling by night. Marta took Dilak and Berna into the city with one of the donkeys to buy food. Atam and Jannig stayed behind to work on worn shoes and mend torn clothing, talking together as they did so. Emin had found a stray kitten and sat quietly, playing with it.

An hour before sunset, as people were straggling back to the caravan and getting ready for that night's departure, there was a sudden commotion and Bölükbaşı Vazrig rode past with several of his men. The officer reappeared minutes later with a distraught looking Dilak and Marta.

"Atam Petrosian," Vazrig said solemnly, "Prepare for a shock. Your daughter, Berna, has been abducted."

Atam stared at the officer and then at his crying wife. "What happened?"

"A man … a young man … Berna, she was being disobedient again … he took her … I told her to stay close, but oh no, she had to … then suddenly she was gone."

Atam turned to Marta. "What happened?" he asked again.

"We were at the markets and your wife had to speak to Berna several times for looking at and then talking to a young man. When we were on the way home, this same young man suddenly appeared and beckoned. Your daughter ran off with him."

"Who was he?" Atam yelled. "I'll kill him if he's raped my daughter."

"Calm yourself," Vazrig said. "Everything that can be done will be done. My men are questioning people in the market, and I've sent a message to the Amir."

"Meanwhile my daughter's in the hands of those men."

"She went of her own accord by these women's accounts, and there was only one man. Her chastity may be compromised, but she should be in no great danger."

Dilak cried out piercingly at this thought. "What could be worse? The shame she's brought on us." A crowd started to gather, and Vazrig instructed people to stand back and go about their business. "The caravan will be leaving soon," he reminded them.

"We cannot leave while my daughter is missing."

"You'll leave with the caravan tonight. No doubt Amir Abdullah will ask me to stay behind with some of my men to search. Don't worry, Petrosian, we'll find your daughter and catch up quickly."

The Amir al-Hajj rode up and questioned his Bölükbaşı at length. While this happened, a soldier rode in from the city with news as to the identity of the young man. Amir Abdullah thought for a moment and then dismissed everyone except the Petrosian family and Vazrig. "The man is known to me …"

"This rapist is your friend?" Atam interrupted.

"I understand your concern, Petrosian, but don't interrupt me again. As I was saying, the man who ran off with your daughter is known to me. He's Yaakov ben Galon, a petty criminal in these parts. The unfortunate aspect of this news is that he's associated with a rather nasty fellow called Dov. It's possible that Yaakov will just have his way with your daughter and let her go, but if Dov is involved, he may sell her as a slave or even kill her."

"Death would be better than the shame her fornication would bring on us," Atam muttered.

"No," Dilak cried. "You mustn't say that, husband." She held out her hands to Abdullah. "Amir, please send your men to find my daughter. We'll pay everything we have, even if we can go no further toward the Holy City."

Amir Abdullah nodded. "You and your husband will continue on with the caravan. I'll take a squad of men and find your daughter."

"Excellency, shouldn't I conduct the search?" Vazrig asked.

"Not this time. I've long sought a confrontation with Dov. You'll get the caravan under way, Bölükbaşı, I have every confidence in you."

Vazrig saluted and turned away, calling to his junior officers.

Atam moved to confront the Amir. "I'm coming too."

"No, you're not."

"How will you prevent me, Amir? Will you bind me like a criminal?"

"If I have to."

"Amir, this is my daughter we're talking about. I beg you to let me accompany you. I'll put myself under your orders and do whatever you say, only let me come."

"And if she's dead?" Abdullah asked quietly.

"Then she'll need a relative to preserve her modesty."

The Amir thought for a moment and then nodded. "Very well. Can you ride a horse?"

"I've only ridden a donkey, Excellency."

Abdullah permitted himself a small smile. “Not quite the same thing. A soldier will take you up behind him.”

The Amir led a troop of ten men into Jerusalem with Atam riding behind one of the soldiers, terrified at being so high off the ground and moving at such a pace. They rode through the narrow streets to the home of the city chief of Shurta. Abdullah left his men outside while he went in to talk. He came out several minutes later and led his men back out of the city and eastward toward the hills. Atam wanted to ask what was happening, but the soldier he rode with did not know and steadfastly refused to bring his mount alongside the Amir’s so Atam could ask.

“Don’ upset th’ gen’ral,” was all he would say.

They reached the foothills as darkness fell, but nobody stopped for prayers. Atam was horrified but shut his eyes and went through the words in his head, hoping that Allah would accept them. The country changed to broken rock and loose shale, but there was still enough light in the sky to keep to the faint trail leading into the wilderness. They dismounted when the light became too poor for riding, and Abdullah left two soldiers to guard the horses, leading the other eight and Atam onward.

Atam stumbled blindly through the dark, barely able to see the man in front of him, and wondered how the Amir was able to tread the path so confidently. Presently a whispered command brought them to a welcome halt and Atam fumbled for his poppy resin. He grimaced at how small the piece felt, but broke off a fragment and swallowed it. Slowly the ragged pain in his belly eased.

The Amir came down the line of soldiers, whispering to each what he expected of them. As each one received his instructions, he slipped away into the night. "Petrosian, you'll come with me. The bandits are about a hundred or so paces away around a camp fire. The soldiers will work along the rim of the basin and surround them."

Atam wondered how Abdullah knew there was a camp fire when to his eyes the countryside was an impenetrable darkness, and then he caught a faint whiff of smoke in the still air. "You're going to confront them?"

"No, Petrosian, *we* are going to confront them." The tone in the Amir's voice hinted at amusement. "After all, the girl's your daughter."

Abdullah led the way again with Atam shuffling along behind the Amir who looked as if he was out for a stroll. They stopped just below a low ridge, the edge showing up dark against a sky faintly washed with star light. Off to the left and right of them, an owl hooted softly. "The men are in place," Abdullah said softly. "Are you ready, Petrosian?"

Without waiting for a reply, the Amir crossed over the ridge into a basin in which burned a low fire. The flickering flames seem to cast as much shadow as light, but Atam thought he could see half a dozen men sitting around the fire. Laughter and raucous conversation drifted up, and Atam stiffened at the sound of a female sob.

Abdullah strode down the slope and as the men around the fire became aware of him, they fell silent. Two of them rose to their feet and one drew a sword. Atam edged down behind Abdullah, but after the first glance, the men by the fire contemptuously ignored him.

"Who are you?" demanded a great bear-like man who stood with his hands on his hips. "Don't I know you from somewhere?"

"You should, Dov," Abdullah replied. "I've been hunting you these past few years."

Dov laughed coldly. "Be very sure you're prepared to catch what you hunt, son of Shihab. It may be the last thing you do."

"Let me kill him," growled the man with Dov who had drawn the sword. "Him and the little pig behind him."

"Go on then."

The swordsman moved past his leader and advanced on Abdullah, who sighed and drew his own sword. As the man swept his blade at him, Abdullah casually flicked it aside, moved past him quickly and slit the man open. The bandit fell to the ground with a surprised groan and expired.

"I've come for the girl, Dov. Hand her over unharmed and I'll walk away this time."

"You can have her when we've finished with her. Yaakov says she's as lively as a young goat."

"Now, Dov, and I'll let you live."

Dov laughed, his voice sounding mirthless and like the growling of a bear. "Best me, Amir al-Hajj and you can have anything you want."

Abdullah grunted. "Draw your sword then."

"No. I'll fight you without weapons."

The Amir curled his lip in disgust. "You expect me to wrestle you? You stink. Draw your sword or order your men to attack me if you're afraid to."

"For that you'll die slowly," Dov said. He did not move, but as Abdullah leapt forward, the Amir stumbled and dropped his sword. He fought to maintain his balance and managed it, swaying, a few paces from the bandit leader.

"You're stronger than I thought, Amir Abdullah," Dov said conversationally.

Abdullah said nothing. His muscles stood out and his eyes bulged as he strained forward, but it was as if he was bound with strong chains. "You … won't … win," he ground out between clenched teeth.

Dov chuckled. "I already have. Don't look to your soldiers out there in the dark. They won't move until I release them. Already one has forgotten to breath and has died."

"You … are … djinn."

"Not the first you've come across, I think. However, I'll be the last. If you have a god, offer up your prayers, for now you die." Dov gestured and Abdullah fell to his knees, his face swollen and red as he fought to breathe.

Behind him and partly obscured by the Amir's bulk, Atam listened with increasing horror. *Djinn? O Allah, protect me*. He saw Abdullah collapse and knew that in a very few seconds, the djinni's attention would turn to him. *Run* ... *or* … He snatched up a rock and threw it at Dov's head, screaming out a silent prayer as he did so. *You fool, that won't work against djinn.*

But it did. Dov's attention snapped from the fallen Abdullah to the scrawny farmer just as the rock cracked into the man's skull. He staggered back and collapsed. Abdullah drew in an agonised breath, then another and forced himself to his feet. Snatching up his fallen sword, he leapt forward with a savage snarl and hacked the bandit leader's head from his shoulders.

The other bandits surged forward as their leader died, but the soldiers, now released from the djinni's coercion, poured over the lip of the basin and cut them down. Renewed screams came from the shadows on the far side of the fire, and Atam ran over, shouldering soldiers aside. He found two half-naked women cowering on the ground, trying to shield their bodies with scraps of torn clothing.

"Berna?" Atam stared disbelievingly as one of the women turned a tear-streaked face toward him. She rose to her knees and stretched out her arms to her father, her garments falling aside as she moved. Atam recoiled, turning his head away. "Cover yourself, you whore," he rasped.

"Father, no. It's me, Berna, your daughter. Don't turn from me." She broke out into fresh tears, but gathered her clothes around her.

"You ran off with a man. You're nothing but a painted whore." Atam gasped as a stab of pain lanced through his belly, and he took out his dwindling supply of poppy resin with shaking hands. He broke off another piece and swallowed it.

"You … you're good for nothing. No man will marry you now."

Berna and the other woman started wailing again. Abdullah ordered two of his men to give their cloaks to the women, and he drew Atam to one side while they used the shadows to make themselves decent again.

"She's your daughter and needs you," Abdullah observed quietly.

"She has whored," Atam replied listlessly. "Better if she'd died."

"She was taken unwillingly, Petrosian. She had no choice but to perform an indecency. You should welcome her back, or if you think some blame attaches to her, then forgive her."

Atam shook his head. "I cannot. She's brought shame upon me and her whole family."

"Nobody need know. I'll swear my men to silence."

"I would know. God would know. Shame can only be expunged with blood." Atam paused, considering. "She must die for the honour of the family."

"You're a narrow-minded bigot, Petrosian," Abdullah said. "No, say nothing." He put a hand on the farmer's shoulder as Atam opened his mouth.

Atam felt his senses lurch, and he wondered fleetingly if he had eaten too large a piece of poppy resin. "I … I …" The thought died unspoken, and he stared incredulously at the scene around him. The fire flared brilliantly in the middle of the basin, throwing bright light in all directions, but also inky shadows that danced and flickered; yet the darkness was not really darkness, for he could see individual sand grains and the tiny creatures that dwelled among them. The men burned too, and he thought it must be the ruddy reflection of the flames until he saw the bodies did not. They lay still and cold, while the living moved among them with flames enveloping them. Atam tried to look at Abdullah, but his eyes slid away from the man. Every little sound was magnified, and Atam thought he could hear sand grains rasping against one another, the rhythmic breathing of every man and somehow, from far off in the direction of the city, a low babble of voices. The scent of the wood smoke and body odour of the dead bandits was sharp in his nostrils, and he could even taste the blood that soaked into the sand. He lifted his eyes to the heavens and saw a blaze of stars like nothing he had ever seen before. Instead of white pinpoints of light, he saw every colour pulsing and flaring. "How …?" he whispered. "What …?" Abruptly the vision faded, and he stood gasping, striving vainly to recapture the glory.

"You're eating poppy resin," Abdullah said. "You shouldn't be doing that on Hajj."

"I pray that God will understand, Excellency. I have good reason."

"Try and do without it, Petrosian. For the good of your soul."

"I … I'll try, but …"

"We should be getting back. We must catch up with the caravan tonight."

"Yes." Atam nodded. "Come daughter, your mother will be glad to see you're safe." He put out a hand to help her up.

"Father?" Berna cringed as if Atam might strike her.

"Come, Berna. I didn't know what I was saying. Of course you're blameless in this affair." He lifted her gently to her feet and embraced her.

A soldier, on the orders of Abdullah, carried her to one of the horses, and another soldier took the other woman. They left the bodies of the bandits where they lay and lit their passage back to the horses and beyond using brands from the fire. Atam found an opportunity to walk next to the Amir.

"Excellency, you called the bandit leader djinn. Was he really?"

Abdullah was silent so long Atam thought he was not going to answer. "The bandit leader was a man called Dov the Bear, a man with a long history of evil. Somewhere along the way he was taken over by a djinni."

"But you killed the djinni, didn't you?"

"You don't kill demons that easily," Abdullah said. "The man Dov died and stands before Allah now perhaps, but the djinni still lives and will do its evil elsewhere."

Atam looked around nervously. "Then it could invade one of us?"

"Not easily if you resist it. I imagine Dov asked the djinni to come into him. Anyhow, don't worry about these things. They are my concern as Amir al-Hajj. Your concern is your family and getting yourself prepared for Hajj."

It was nearly the middle of the night by the time they overtook the slowly moving caravan. Dilak and Marta folded Berna in their arms and rushed off into the darkness armed with water, towels and fresh clothes. Under the circumstances, the Amir could not send one of his soldiers along as protection while Berna washed and changed, so he performed this guard duty himself, standing out of sight but within call.

The caravan continued its slow way southward, turning more easterly and following the main pilgrim route into the Arabian Desert before swinging back toward the Red Sea coast. Atam paid more attention to his family and the new friends they had made on the journey, considering their feelings and striving to help them as much as he could. He also tried to recall the intense feeling he had experienced when colours, sounds, scents and tastes had all but overwhelmed him. Every time he thought about it, the memories slipped away. *It's as if it happened to somebody else who described it to me*. He wondered if the poppy resin had been responsible and was tempted to try taking some more to see if it happened again. *I'll need to for the pain soon enough, but for now I can resist. It's almost as if taking the poppy brings on the pain*. He pressed his belly softly but there was no answering surge of pain.

Excitement grew among the pilgrims and many started wearing *Ihram*. Atam explained to his family that it was not really necessary before they reached the *miqat*, which for this caravan was at Juhfah, some distance northwest of their destination. "We cannot afford to wear it too early; it'll be in a less than pristine state before we reach the Holy City. I'll buy what we need at Juhfah."

Jannig, his travelling neighbour, pointed out to Atam that if he waited to the last minute to buy the *Ihram* garments, the cost would be much higher. "Go and see Vazrig," he said. "He found our garments cheaply, maybe he still has some."

Vazrig was happy to relieve Atam of a little more silver, but the garments he found were of high quality and a spotless white. Atam took the clothes back to his family and showed them how they were to be worn.

"See, we men – that includes you Emin – wear these white, seamless lengths of cloth. The first is worn around the lower body and must cover us from waist to knee." He demonstrated by fitting it to his son. "The top one has to cover the upper part of the body. It doesn't have to be draped over the right shoulder, but it's easier to keep in place if it does." Again, he demonstrated with Emin. "See, you're the proper little pilgrim. Now, you must wear sandals or no footwear. Your choice, but you mustn't wear shoes, because the footwear must not come higher than your ankles."

"What about us?" Berna asked. "I'd feel embarrassed showing off my legs like that, and …" she blushed, "The top garment is … is indecent."

"Silly girl," Dilak chided. "Women don't wear the two pieces of cloth. We wear long white robes that cover us decently from head to toe." She slipped one of the robes over her daughter's head and adjusted the folds, tucking an unruly wisp of hair back under the headband. "There, completely modest. Wearing that you look like a true *muhrima*."

"And you like a true *muhrim*, Emin," Atam added.

"Now, put the *Ihram* clothes away until we get to the *miqat*," Dilak said. "We don't want to soil them."

Time passed. They slept as best they could through the heat of the day, waking for prayers at the appropriate times and walking slowly and steadily through the starlit nights. Sometimes they glimpsed the huge black expanse of the sea stretching away on their right hand, the moon tempting them away from the Holy City with a shimmering path of silver across the waters. Other times, the shadows of the desert seemed to harbour djinn and fierce animals, and it was only the presence of the caravan and Bölükbaşı Vazrig's men patrolling the edges of the road that kept them at bay. They were seldom troubled by the wandering tribes of Badu, or Bedouin as they were sometimes called, for Amir Abdullah had a fearsome reputation along the caravan route and his caravans were avoided by bandits.

They reached the road that led inland to Madinah, and looked longingly toward the other Holy City of Islam before turning south again. *Miqat* was near and people felt a surge of excitement.

Atam was excited at the thought of seeing the prophet's birthplace but also puzzled. In the last week or two, he had scarcely taken out his small lump of poppy resin. Once or twice he had guiltily eaten fragments, not because he was in pain, but because he felt if he did not the pain would return fiercer than ever. It had not returned, and this puzzled him. He knew he had a growth in his belly. When the pain first came a year ago, he had visited an itinerant apothecary who had diagnosed the crab claw growth. He could cut it out for a fee, but there was no guarantee he would not die under the knife. Left untreated, the crab's claws would dig deeper with passing time and he would die in great pain in a year or two. Atam had chosen to wait it out for his family's sake and had become reliant on poppy to reduce the gripe of the crab in his belly. For some reason, the crab was sleeping now, but Atam was not going to complain. He just had the horrible feeling that when it woke his death would come swiftly. *Just let it sleep until I see the Kaaba and celebrate Eid*, he prayed.

The caravan arrived at Juhfah just before dawn on the thirtieth day of Dhu al-Qi'dah. The Amir al-Hajj gathered everyone together and led them in the Fajr prayers before addressing them.

"Tomorrow is the first day of Dhu al-Hijjah, and today is the last day on which you can prepare for this great occasion in your lives. Every Muslim is obliged to perform Hajj once in their lives if circumstances permit and here you are about to fulfil the Fifth Pillar of Islam. We're at Juhfah, the *miqat* for anyone arriving in Makkah from the north, and it's here that we all adopt *Ihram*. I see that some of you are already wearing the required garments, but all of you must now prepare. You know what must be done, but I'll go over the main points again, for any person who fails to follow *Ihram* fails his God.

"First, you must be in a state of cleanliness. There's plenty of water here at Juhfah, and you are expected to use it, cleansing your whole bodies. A man may then trim his hair and cut his nails, for these things are forbidden during *Ihram*. You're also forbidden sexual relations, shaving, using perfumes and washing your hair with anything but water. You won't fight or quarrel with your fellow pilgrims, and in order that you refrain from this, you'll guard your tongue, saying only what is pleasing for the duration of *Ihram*. This injunction applies to animals – you'll kill no animal or insect during *Ihram* unless it seeks to harm you. Neither will you uproot any plant. All of you will have the seamless garments and robes by now, together with sandals. When you've finished washing and preparing yourself, you'll dress in these pure garments for your approach to the Holy City." Amir Abdullah looked over the sea of faces and smiled. "Go then and prepare yourself for *Ihram*. We leave tonight, and we'll get to the *Haram*, the holy land on which the City of Makkah stands, at dawn on the seventh day."

When the caravan halted just outside the Haram, where it would stay during the days of devotion, Abdullah announced that he would not enter Makkah himself, but that they would need no further protection from his guards. The pilgrims now moved on foot, bare or sandaled, and clad in their Ihram garments to the centre of Makkah, where the Kaaba lay in its great courtyard. They performed the initial circuit of the black-draped cube with its inlaid black stone, the tawaf al-qudum, shuffling around counter-clockwise in their thousands, calling on Allah to hear them – that they had arrived to be of service to their God. After this single circuit, they moved out to the village of Mina where tents had been erected for the thousands that poured into Makkah for the Hajj. They spent this first day of the days of devotion in prayer and reading from the Qur'an, preparing themselves spiritually.

"I feared that I'd never see this day," Atam told his family. "But Allah has blessed us. Tomorrow we go to the Plain of Arafat where we stay by the Hill of Mercy, approaching God in prayer and supplication, asking forgiveness for our sins."

"Then what, father?" Emin asked. "Do we go to the Kaaba again?"

"All in good time, my son. We must cast stones at the pillars in remembrance of our father Ibrahim's faith in Allah and rejection of Shaitan, and sacrifice the lamb for Eid al-Adha, the Festival of Sacrifice." He outlined the events of the next few days and what they meant in terms of their faith. "We offer these things up to God and then we feast on the sacrifice, a third for family, a third for friends and a third for the poor."

"Tell them about the sermon given on the Hill of Mercy, husband."

Atam smiled at his children. "You children know it already. It's the sermon the Prophet

Muhammad gave when he did Hajj. Can you remember what he said?"

Emin grimaced, but Berna said hesitantly, "It was about what it means to follow the Way of Submission to Allah, wasn't it?"

"Yes, daughter. Can you recall what points he made?"

"The shahadah," Emin cried. "There's only one God."

Dilak nodded, smiling. "And He's not to be represented by anything in His creation."

"All Muslims are equal," Berna said, "Except if they're very pious."

"Good. What else?"

"Men have to treat their womenfolk well."

"Of course. What else?"

"The Qur'an is the Word of God?" Emin asked, and his father nodded proudly.

"You must give alms," Berna added. "So that nobody is excessively rich or very poor … oh, wait, wait … Every person has a right to his life, his property and … and …"

"Honour," Emin finished.

"Excellent, my children. The only ones you left out were that you cannot charge interest on any loan you make, nor can you take the law into your own hands but must bring your grievance before the proper authorities."

"Like the Amir al-Hajj in the caravan," Emin said. "Why didn't he come into Makkah for the Hajj after coming all this way?"

"I don't know," Atam said slowly. "The rest of his men did, but he didn't." He rubbed his beard thoughtfully, remembering a time in the desert when he saw things so much more clearly. *There was something ... I learned something about Abdullah ... he ... he ... no, it's gone again.* "I don't know why exactly, Emin, but I don't think he can do Hajj."

***

I am in hell. I do not feel the burning flames of Jahannum, nor have I been judged before the throne of God, yet I must have done something terrible to suffer like this.

My name was Abd-al-Latif ibn Sharif, and I was born to a family steeped in the service of the Sultans. My grandfather and father before me were soldiers, and I learned to handle weapons almost before I could recite the Qur'an. Yes, I think of myself as a good Muslim, yet I find myself rejected by God for reasons I cannot explain.

I was born in the city of ash-Sham, also called Damascus, nearly forty years ago and served as a soldier in defence of the city from the age of fifteen. I saw hard service but acquitted myself well and rose in rank to that of Bölükbaşı, or captain under Mehmed Pasha. I had the opportunity of going on Hajj that same year, and I became troubled when I saw the depredations bandits made in their attacks on the small caravans that travelled to the Holy City. By law, the Hajj pilgrims are protected, but only if the bandits are good Muslims. Of course, strictly, you cannot be a bandit and a good Muslim, so bandits are usually infidels or apostates. The little caravans are virtually undefended as the men are armed only with holy thoughts, and I have yet to see the Holy Qur'an turn back a sword blade. I reasoned that a large caravan protected by a force of dedicated warriors could make the journey unscathed, and I approached my superiors with the idea.

They referred it to Sultan Ibrahim in distant Stamboul, and he thought the idea worth trying. That first year, a hundred pilgrims left the capital city with an escort of twenty soldiers and made the trip to and from Makkah without incident. The following year, double the number made the trip, again without trouble. I was rewarded for my idea with command of the yearly caravan. My position as Amir al-Hajj was prestigious, and I had a troop of fifty fine horsemen at my disposal. I set about organising the caravan for maximum efficiency and worked at identifying and neutralising the bandit gangs along our route.

It was on one such foray into the desert between Hajj caravans that I fell into unforgiveable sin and the certainty of hellfire. I still do not know for a certainty what I did to deserve my fate, but such things do not happen to men loved by God, so I can only assume I erred grievously. Pray for me, I beg.

I became separated from my men in the Syrian Desert. The group of outlaws we had been chasing were wily and desperate, but we hunted them down one by one and meted out the Sultan's justice on the spot. Night was falling when we set out after the last remnant of the gang, and in the darkness, I took a turn in the foothills that my men failed to follow. Yes, of course it was their failure. I was their leader; it was their duty to follow my lead, and they failed.

At length I found myself alone and faced a difficult decision. Somewhere ahead of me were three murderers. I could press on in the hopes of finding them and God willing, dispatch them. Or I could retrace my steps and hope to find my men. The trouble with that latter course of action was I would look at best a fool, and at worst a coward, so I pressed on alone. Eventually, I lost the trail and decided I could do no more that night. I unsaddled my horse and hobbled him, letting him forage among the sparse vegetation. For myself, I dared not light a fire, so I dug into my saddlebags and discovered a few dried figs.

I sat with my back to a large rock that held the last of the sun's warmth and munched on my fruit while my horse, a black shadow off to one side, nipped and tore at the stringy grass. The sky was littered with stars, and had not been for three murderers out there somewhere; I might have lost myself in the wonder of it. As it was, I stared out at God's infinity and wondered how many stars there were, until the moon rose and I grew tired. I said my prayers before retiring, facing toward the Holy City, and prepared to lie down.

A bright star leapt out of the east, passed soundlessly overhead in a brilliant streak of blue-white fire and disappeared behind me. I blinked, the image of the star showing pink against my closed eyelids before fading. Then a sound came from the direction of the star fall, a faint sound as of a stone dislodged and fallen against another. It came again, and I heard the sound of soft steps crunching in the gravel. *The bandits*, I thought. I stepped away from the rock into the open and drew my sword.

"Your sword is useless, Abd-al-Latif." The words slid over the cooling rock, and my horse whinnied and backed away, stamping his feet.

"If you believe that, come and try it out," I called back. "And how is it you know my name?"

A soft chuckle. "You told me yourself."

"When? Do I know you?"

"Not yet, Abd-al-Latif, but I have a feeling we'll get to know one another very well."

"Show yourself."

The footsteps sounded again, and a shadow detached itself from a greater one and walked out into a patch of moonlight. The man was tall, like me, and with a similar build. His face was in shadow still, framed by dark beard and hair. I saw a smile as a gleam of white in the darkness.

"I carry no weapon, Amir al-Hajj of the western caravan."

His words did not reassure me, and I hefted my sword, watching him closely. "First my name and now my title, but I don't know yours."

"I've gone by many names over the years, but you may call me Aali, or Ilah."

"A lofty name for such an ordinary man," I sneered. "Why are you here?"

That soft chuckle again. "Didn't you see the shooting star? I came for you, Abd-al-Latif ibn Sharif, but I think I'll have to rename you. Servant of the gentle, son of virtue really doesn't suit. I'm neither gentle nor virtuous."

"What is this nonsense?" I cried. "If you think to destroy my name, you'll have to kill me first."

"I think Abdullah ibn Shihab is better – Servant of God, son of the shooting star, for you shall be my servant, and I'm the son of the shooting star. Indeed, I've been called a god by one who knew me after a shooting star fell. Ibrahim, who built the Kaaba in Makkah with my black stone – you may have heard of him."

"You're mad and blasphemous. Ibrahim lived nearly four thousand years ago. You talk of times and abilities beyond the strength of men. And I'm not your servant – not now, not ever."

"You cannot stand against me. Kneel to the inevitable."

The man had been edging toward me, and finally I knew I would have to kill him. I raised my sword and leapt forward, screaming. In an instant, the man was enveloped in blue fire and the tendrils of flame rushed toward me and entered me. I threw my head back and howled like a lost soul, my jaws gaping as if I would swallow the moon, but all I swallowed was fire that burned in my belly, ran like a lightning bolt through my limbs and burst my head open like a ripe melon. I felt myself falling and tried to think of Allah in this instant of my death – but failed.

I stirred and opened my eyes. The moon had moved across the sky, and the stars had wheeled toward dawn. I sat up and looked around. My horse stood dozing a little way off, a motionless equine shadow, but … there was no trace of the stranger –

the man of blue fire. Did I dream him? Was he a phantasm sent by a desert shaytan to deceive me?

What is your name? The thought trickled into my mind, and without thinking, I replied, "Abdullah ibn Shihab." I knew that was not my name; it was that of the man of blue fire, but I could say no other. "Wh … where are you?"

Here. A pause filled with cold mirth. *Here, inside you.*

A feeling of horror swept through me. "What are you?" I cried and then, as I realised I was speaking to myself, "What am I?"

We are djinn. I thought that I would journey to Makkah once again. It amuses me to see it through the eyes of one of Allah's faithful.

"I … I won't do it."

My dear Abdullah, Servant of God, you have no choice. You'll do exactly as I say, willingly; or do exactly as I say, after.

"After what?"

The pain came flooding through my body, coursing along my veins, ripping out my sinews and burning them in acid flames. I gritted my teeth and held on, refusing to give in. My muscles went into spasm and I fell to the ground, arching my back, my bitten tongue gushing blood between my teeth. "No," I moaned. "I 'ill no …" Abruptly the pain ceased, and I lay panting and spitting blood, filled with a sudden elation that I had beaten the djinni.

The pain returned, tenfold greater, and my shrieks shattered the night air and sent the great star-covered bowl of the sky cascading in shards of black and silver as I passed out.

I recovered in the dawn light and stirred. *The pain will continue*, a voice in my head said. *I can keep this up for as long as there's life in you.*

"Why?" I croaked through my blood-filled mouth.

Because it amuses me. Will you obey?

"Yes," I whispered.

Good. Look over there by the tall rock. I've a present for you.

I looked and saw, in the morning light, the neatly severed heads of the three bandits I had been pursuing. I picked them up, trembling with fear and exhaustion, packaged them in a linen cloth and secured them to my horse after saddling him. He was well-trained and did not flinch from the bloody bundle.

As I rode back along the trail, I probed my mind as one does a missing tooth with the tongue, but found nothing but a cringing memory of incredible pain. I wondered whether the djinni had left me and if it would return, but tried to put that behind me. I had a duty to my men and my position as Amir al-Hajj. I would go to the Holy City, not as the djinni wanted, but because it was my duty.

My men had backtracked too when they found me gone and were amazed both at my injuries and at the three heads I had, praising me for my skill as a warrior. I let it be, knowing the truth would bring horror and condemnation. I felt a hiss of pleasure deep inside me as if I had stirred dead leaves with a stick and disturbed a deadly serpent. I knew the djinni was still with me.

I guided the caravan from Stamboul to ash-

Sham and then on to Makkah that year, as I had the year before, but this time, when I came to the edge of the Haram, the Holy Land, I found I could not enter. It was as if a wall of crystal stood before me. I could see no barrier, yet I could not advance. I made my excuses and retired to my tent.

"Allah won't let me pass," I murmured. "Your presence isn't welcome."

Fire burst through me but even as I took breath to scream, it vanished. *How can that be*? asked the djinni. *Try again*.

I did as I was told but with no greater success. We walked along a curved boundary for a thousand paces or so, long enough to see that the crystal wall extended around Makkah. Then we returned to my tent to await the end of the Hajj celebrations.

"There's always next year," I murmured, but a tiny part of me rejoiced that the djinni had been foiled. Alas, he heard my thought and I paid for it. Over the past few years, the djinni has heard all of my thoughts and I have suffered the flames of hellfire as punishment. Only one thing I ask myself now, one thought that the djinni allows me to think – why is it that Allah has sent me to hell?

Chapter Twenty

How can I be excluded from any place I want to go? What power has this Allah to keep me out? I have been in Makkah before, walked its streets and even visited the Kaaba, though admittedly before there was such a thing as Islam. Could that make such a difference? I even left my host for a while as he slept and tried to approach as a pure flame, but with no greater success. It puzzles me and disturbs me, for if Allah has such power, he may seek my destruction. I waited, expecting a thunderbolt, but nothing happened, so I took my servant, Abdullah, and went back to the service of the Sultan in Stamboul. Every year I guided the Hajj caravan to Makkah, and every year I found myself thrown back by the crystal wall.

Abdullah has just shrugged his shoulders, but does not know why. It is very simple really. I have been prevented from entering Makkah, but nowhere else, so what does it really matter? I will go and do other things, more important things, and leave Makkah to its jealous god.

I stayed in Abdullah ibn Shihab, for one does not waste a good servant. I even allowed him to remain as Amir al-Hajj, for it allowed me access to violent men in the cities we passed. I was prepared to stay like that for many years, harvesting human life when I needed it but otherwise just letting the years flow. I had no real purpose in my existence. Then something changed.

In the year 1060 A.H., Abdullah again guided the caravan south, but this time there was a man called Atam Petrosian who had brought his family on Hajj. He was a pitiful little Armenian farmer with a nondescript family, but unexpectedly he brought purpose into my life. When the caravan stopped at Jerusalem, Atam's wife and daughter went into the city after supplies. The wife claimed her daughter was kidnapped, but I do not think her abductor had any great difficulty in taking her out of the city and having his way with her. But instead of just releasing her so she could run weeping to her mother's arms, the fool decided to keep her and hand her over to his fellow bandits.

When Abdullah questioned the women, I plucked the image of the kidnapper from their minds and knew at once I was dealing with the Dov gang. Abdullah found out their current whereabouts from agents in Jerusalem and set out with his men and Atam to apprehend them, and if luck was with them, rescue the girl relatively undamaged.

In the five or six years I have used Abdullah, I have tracked down and killed every gang member who preyed on the Stamboul caravan, with one exception. The gang of Dov the Bear had always eluded me. Sometimes I thought it was because he could read my mind. Then, of course, I found out that he could. If I had had my wits about me, I might have guessed earlier; after all, if I can take over and control a man, what was to stop other djinn from doing the same? In fact, he made a good choice of victim as Dov's natural proclivities tended towards torture and death. There was a ripe field for him to reap.

He took me by surprise and gripped my mind and Abdullah's body in a vice of iron. It was staggering how strong he was, and I knew that for the first time in thousands of years I faced death. The obliteration of a human body while I am in it is nothing. Ordinarily, I would just flit like a gust of warm breath from the dying man to another in better health. However, this djinni also had my flame in his vice, and I could feel the life being squeezed out of me.

Atam Petrosian saved my life. The rock he threw stunned Dov's body and distracted the djinni. As his hold eased, I shook free and scooped up my blade, severing the bandit's head. The djinni, of course, was untouched and unharmed, but being forewarned, I knew he could not strike at me or those I protected again. The djinni fled. My men killed the rest of the gang, and we freed Petrosian's daughter and a drab they kept around for entertainment.

I have known men for many, many years, and nothing they do should surprise me, yet Atam the farmer did so again. He came out on a dangerous mission to rescue his daughter, and then, with her safe from harm, he turns on her, calling her all manner of names and wishing she was dead to save his honour. Honour – what a contradictory human concept. There was nothing honourable in his mind, and even I, the ravening wolf that feeds on human sheep, could see the injustice of it.

In disgust, I slipped into his mind and quickly altered his thoughts, rerouting the sparks of energy that coursed through the fibres of his brain. I was about to come out again when I noticed something sitting in his belly. If you have ever seen the gall formed on an oak tree by a little flying insect, you will know what I mean. The growth was like that, though larger, foreign and formless, and it was killing him slowly. I investigated it, passing my flame through it and testing its vigour. I gave thought to Atam Petrosian, the man and his recent actions, and felt a momentary flash of kinship for this weak creature. He had saved my life, so I saved his.

Now before you start thinking that I was acting contrary to my nature as a djinni, know that I was motivated by curiosity. Men die of many things but how a little thing like this formed of his own flesh could kill him, I did not know. So I experimented, cutting off the blood supply to the growth and starving it. It started to die, and I encouraged his natural bodily processes to take over the task of destroying it. This did not all happen at once, but I was able to start the process and add to it over the next week or so. By the time we arrived outside Makkah, I knew he would live. I was better than a surgeon, for I caused no pain, left no scar and charged no fee.

This got me thinking. I had a feeling that no matter how many times I approached Makkah, I would not be able to enter it. Therefore, what was the point of continuing? I had also, with the death of Dov the Bear, removed all the significant bandits and violent men along the route of the Stamboul caravan, so any further Hajj journeys were likely to be fairly boring. It was time I released my servant

Abdullah from his prison and went looking for something new.

Yes, I know, what has come over me? A century or so ago, I would not have thought twice about devouring the life of my servant once I had finished with him. I can only explain it as a realisation of my dependency on humans. If I am to feed on people, I should tend my food supply. Perhaps a bit of the farmer Atam Petrosian rubbed off on me as I cured his growth. Whatever the reason, I feel a desire to know more of the human body and how it works. I must look for a surgeon and learn how to look after my fragile meat animals. I already protect animals from the excesses of humans, perhaps I should extend that protection to the weakest humans.

Chapter Twenty-One

The plague swept through northern Iraq in 1799, leaving countless thousands dead in its wake. The city of Sulaimaniyah felt the force of the sickness too, and Ibrahim Pasha ordered the gates closed against refugees from the countryside. He was too late though, and the pestilence swept through the city, respecting neither rich or poor, nor faithful or unbeliever. It invaded the household of Sajjad ibn Zaki, minor wool merchant, and before it left, claimed the lives of Sajjad, his two sons and three daughters and his aged parents. It left alive, after a mild sickness, Nadira bint Khayyam, wife of Sajjad, mother of their children and despised daughter-in-law.

Her family, as plague victims, was buried in a communal grave, and after the burial, she returned to her house to find that one of her late husband's surviving brothers had claimed the house as his own and left her destitute. She complained to the imam, but her brother-in-law's testimony was held to be worth twice hers as set out in the Qur'an, and her eviction upheld. The secular city administration and the courts were in shambles, and Nadira, when she applied for a legal ruling, was told to wait six months and then apply for her case to be heard. Meanwhile, she was afforded a pallet in a women's refuge as charity and left to her own resources.

Nadira had helped her husband with his trading accounts and knew how to read and write in Arabic, Kurdish and Hebrew. She also had some mathematical ability and an enquiring mind, so she thought it would not be hard to find work. However, few merchants wanted to hire a widow without dependents as they felt her proper place was in the home rather than at work. After a few jobs that lasted at most a few days, she found a caravan owner, Murtada, who needed a reliable person who could read and write to manage his city business when he was out of town. He took Nadira on, but because she was a woman, she could not work in the same room as him and could only work when he was away. Nevertheless, it provided enough money that she could pay for her food and board in a small house that Murtada provided for rent.

The work was interesting, but there was never enough of it to occupy her mind. She thought of her husband and children whenever figures and words left a space in her mind, and she often made up the accounts with tears in her eyes.

One day as she sat in the caravan merchant's office, drafting a letter to a customer, she heard cries from outside. She put her pen down and listened for a few moments and then went to the door. Outside, a woman lay in the road, holding her belly and screaming with pain. Nobody paid any attention; one man even stepped over the woman without stopping.

Nadira hurried over and knelt beside her. "What's wrong? Tell me."

The woman turned a sweaty face toward her and gasped, "Baby."

"Who's your midwife? I'll send for her."

The woman cried out again. "Dead, in the plague."

"Your husband then. Family? A sister?"

The woman shook her head. "There's no one … Oh!" She doubled over as another contraction shook her.

Nadira appealed to the passers-by. "Help me. This woman needs a midwife. Send for one quickly."

"That's not my concern," said one man. "Let her husband look after her."

"Where's her husband?" asked another. "Why is she outside unattended?"

A woman started forward to help but was called back sharply by her male companion.

Nadira cursed beneath her breath and struggled to lift the woman to her feet. "Come with me then. I'll look after you." She helped the woman into the room the caravan owner used as an office and laid her down on the rug. "I must examine you," she said. "Don't be concerned, for I've had children of my own and there are no others to see you."

The woman struggled with her modesty, blushing deeply, but at last nodded and looked away. Nadira lifted the woman's dress and stripped away her sodden underclothing. Her belly was swollen and taut as a drum. Gently, she eased the woman's legs apart and peered between them.

"Your … er, parts are er … parted." Nadira did not know what to call them; no one had ever told her and it was not a question one asked. "I don't think your baby will be long delayed. I'll fetch water and cloth."

In fact, it was another six hours before it was all over. The cry of the muezzin penetrated their room for the noon and late afternoon prayers, but both women had their attentions elsewhere. Nadira hoped God would understand and continued to clean away the blood and faeces and grip the woman's hand as she strained to deliver her child. The woman's screams lessened in intensity as exhaustion set in, and it was with a groan of relief that the baby finally slithered out onto the rug. Nadira cleaned the boy off as best she could, wiping away the blood and fragments of membrane.

"You have a baby boy," Nadira said. "What will you call him?" Then she laughed. "I don't even know your name. I'm Nadira."

"Fathiyya," the woman whispered and then a look of panic swept over her face. "It hurts. Is there another one?"

Nadira looked. "It's the afterbirth." She tied a cord around the umbilicus in two places as she had seen the midwife do with her own youngest child, and then, lacking a knife, bit through the tube, spitting out the blood. She wrapped the afterbirth in a cloth and set it aside before wiping the woman clean and rearranging her dress. Then she sat back and watched as Fathiyya gave her firstborn son his first meal.

A little before sunset, Murtada returned and stared in first amazement and then in growing anger at his office and the two bedraggled women in it.

"What's happening here? What have you done, Nadira? It stinks in here."

Nadira hastily adjusted her headscarf and dress. "This woman collapsed in the street and none would help her, so I brought her in here."

"What's that to me? Where's her husband?" He peered suspiciously at the woman and baby propped up against the wall. "Does she even have one? Is she a whore perhaps?"

"Her husband died of the plague," Nadira retorted, "As did mine, and …"

"My rug!" Murtada screeched. "It's ruined. That cost me a hundred dirham. She must pay for it."

"Where's your charity?" Nadira chided. "Would you have her give birth on the bare ground? Doesn't our faith speak of protecting widows and children?"

"Enough!" Murtada cried. "Take this whore and her whelp and get out. If you don't, I'll call the authorities and have you arrested for … for gross indecency."

Nadira helped Fathiyya to her feet and with the baby wailing in protest, stepped out into the street as the muezzin called Maghrib prayers. Nadira sighed and offered up another silent prayer to God for his understanding. There was no way she could get clean in time for worship. "Fathiyya, you've somewhere to go? I'd offer you my house, but it belongs to that man in there and I don't think he's feeling generous."

Fathiyya nodded. "I can go to my cousin's house. She sometimes gives me shelter." She shifted her baby to her other arm and looked down at the ground. "I cannot offer you any," she whispered.

"It doesn't matter. I'll find somewhere."

Fathiyya turned and walked away without another word, and Nadira sadly watched her go. "May the blessing of God be with you."

Nadira was evicted from her house, but not until the next day. She again went searching for work and accommodation and found it with an elderly physician, Faruq ibn Haroon, who funded a small hospital at the rear of his house. The women who performed the menial duties like cleaning, feeding and washing the patients had all run away or died of the plague, so he was willing to hire a replacement.

Her days became filled with work, always backbreaking and often dirty, but ultimately satisfying. She worked, ate, prayed and slept, and as the months passed, her pain of loss lessened. She found she could think of her family and smile, remembering the little things that had brought them joy. She kept herself apart from the other hired women, preferring solitude to aimless chatter.

One day, about a year after her arrival at the private hospital, she was washing down the bedboards where a man had just died, when Doctor Faruq came into the room.

"Can you read Hebrew?" he asked.

"Who, me, doctor? Yes."

"Good. Come with me." Faruq led the way into his office and motioned Nadira to a chair. "This letter arrived from Darband. Can you read it?" He handed her a piece of folded paper.

Nadira perused the letter quickly and nodded. "It's from a man called Elisha ben Josea. He asks if you can operate on his three-year-old son who has a harelip."

"Hmmm. Yes, I can do that – perhaps. I'll write and tell him I need to see the child first, but … if I write the letter in Arabic, can you write what I say in Hebrew?"

While Doctor Faruq scribbled away on a tablet, Nadira looked around the room with interest. Bones lay on a table near the window, and she wondered whether they were human or animal. There was a bookshelf on the far wall with a long row of leather-bound tomes. She got up and crossed the room to the books and looked at them, hesitantly reaching out a hand to touch them.

Faruq coughed gently, and Nadira turned quickly, dropping her hand to her side. The doctor smiled. "You like books?"

"Yes, doctor, but I've never seen inside one unless you include account books."

Faruq got up and came around his desk to stand beside her. "These books are my most proud possessions after my Qur'an and ahadith. They're full of the accumulated knowledge of all the great surgeons from Greek times onward – al-Zahrawi, Ibn al-Quffi, al-Baladi, Ibn Khatima and the wonderful Ibn Sina." He smiled and touched one volume lovingly. "I even have one of my own."

"May … may I see it?"

Faruq took the book carefully from its place on the shelf and opened it at random, handing it to Nadira. She took it gingerly and looked at the neat text, her lips moving slightly as she formed the unfamiliar words.

"You can read it?"

"Yes, doctor."

"And understand it?"

"A little, but some of the terms are obscure … to an ignorant person like myself, I mean, Doctor Faruq. I'm sure your words have an evident clarity for the learned."

"You're kind to say so, Nadira, though I think I detect false modesty. You're intelligent for a woman. What terms don't you understand?"

"Well, this passage here, where you talk about removing a stone from the bladder using a catheter through the urethra of the member. A member is a person, and a bladder is a container made of a sheep's stomach, I believe, but I don't know the terms catheter or urethra." Nadira frowned. "Nor, I admit, why you'd have a stone in a bladder in the first place, or need to take it out."

Faruq smiled but stifled a chuckle. "That passage comes originally from al-Majusi, nearly nine hundred years ago. The bladder in question, Nadira, is the one we have within our bodies that fills with urine. Sometimes the tissues around the bladder swell or else a small stone forms within it, and the tube leading to the outside, the urethra, is blocked. To remedy this, I insert a thin tube up the urethra and into the body, draining the backed up urine and sometimes flushing the stone out too. Left untreated a patient suffers excruciating pain. Oh, and the member mentioned is the penis of a man."

Nadira looked horrified and blushed, dropping her gaze.

"I don't say that either to titillate or to shock, Nadira. In surgery, there's no male and female, only the relief of suffering." Faruq took the book back and put it carefully in its place.

"Yes, yes, I can see that," Nadira said after a few moments. "So you'd cut open women as well as men?"

"I've done so. Of course, one has a female member of the family present to guard against any accusation of impropriety. One must always be careful not to upset religious or moral sensibilities."

"Wouldn't it be more seemly then to have female surgeons to operate on women?"

Now Faruq did laugh, but not unkindly. "I fear the learning required would be far beyond a woman's capabilities. Stick to caring for the sick and midwifery. They're proper pursuits for females."

Nadira nodded. She indicated the books on the shelf. "These books are full of wonders. Would you permit me to look at them?"

"To what purpose?"

"Because they're full of wonders, Doctor Faruq. As you've said, I'm intelligent for a woman, but I lack understanding of medical things. If I read these books, I could learn only so much as my female brain could take in, but I'd learn to appreciate the knowledge of surgeons such as you."

"It'd be no bad thing to have such an appreciation," Faruq mused. "When would you want to read?"

"When my duties permitted, doctor, and under your supervision, of course."

"I'll think about it. You may get back to your work now. I'll let you know when I've finished the letter for you to translate."

Nadira returned to her duties, and later that day, Faruq called for her to translate the letter into Hebrew for his Jewish patient in Darband. He watched while she carefully formed the symbols and examined it when she finished.

"You have a good hand, Nadira. I've decided that for an hour every afternoon after Dhuhr prayers you may use my office to read what you will. You'll be excused your other duties during that time."

And so Nadira started to read from the medical textbooks of Doctor Faruq. To start with, he was always in the office, often watching her to see that she treated the books with proper respect; but as he came to observe her enthusiasm for learning, he left her alone more and more. Sometimes she was so engrossed in what she was reading that she could scarcely close the book when her hour was up. Faruq increased her reading time to an hour and a half and then to two hours every day. There were many words that puzzled her at the beginning, but as the months passed, Faruq's explanations made sense, and she began to grasp some of the complexities of the subject.

Sometimes Faruq would turn the tables and interrogate Nadira, asking probing questions that tested her understanding of a subject. She displayed an excellent memory and was quick to make connections between seemingly unrelated topics.

One morning, about a year after she started her reading, Doctor Faruq called her into his office as soon as she walked into the hospital. "I'm operating on a patient this morning. I'd like you to assist me."

"An operation, Doctor? You want me to operate?"

"Certainly not. That wouldn't be appropriate. You may watch though, and hand me instruments as I need them."

The operating room was a small one on the opposite side of the hospital from the beds where recuperating patients lay. A single raised bed stood in the middle of the room with a skylight positioned directly above it. Small tables stood on either side of the bed with metal instruments, dishes and bottles neatly arranged on them. At a nod from Doctor Faruq, two orderlies entered, bearing a man on a stretcher whom they laid gently on the central bed. The orderlies looked at Nadira with some curiosity, but said nothing and closed the door behind them when they left. The man on the bed groaned softly, and Faruq drew back his covering sheet to expose a chest and stomach in which a hole gaped wetly, oozing blood. The doctor leaned over the man and probed the wound area gently with his fingers.

"This man, who was brought in last night, is an officer in the Pasha's guard. He tripped and fell on a spear which has pierced his abdomen. As you can see …" Faruq turned the man gently to one side, "… the point didn't come out the other side, so we're limited to damage that's been caused within the body cavity. Tell me Nadira, what organs lie below this part of the belly?"

Nadira leaned closer, ignoring the metallic odour of the blood, the man's sweat and the fumes of poppy that still clung to him, and cast her mind back to the books with their drawings of the human body. "Left side, too high for the kidney but possibly the spleen. Almost certainly the intestines."

"Good. Well, let's have a look. First, we administer a small amount of opium to render the man unconscious … thus. Surgery would be impossible if he was thrashing around and screaming in pain. Then we prepare." He indicated a large dish and poured some red-tinged liquid into it. Wash your hands in this liquid, Nadira. It's spirits of wine and will keep your hands clean."

"Wine, Doctor? The Qur'an prohibits alcohol."

"I'm not asking you to drink it, just wash your hands in it, yes, that's the way… no, don't wipe your hands on your dress … hold your hands up and let the air dry them."

"Why spirits of wine? Why not good clean water?"

"Didn't you read Ibn Sina and al-Razi on the prevention of infection?"

"Yes, Doctor, but I didn't fully understand it."

"I'm not sure if any man does – fully. It seems that every object, including our hands, though they may appear to be clean, is really carrying tiny unseen bits of dirt that can infect a wound and cause it to suppurate. Spirits of wine either wash the unseen dirt away or render it harmless somehow. For now, it's enough to know that it works." Faruq indicated the motionless patient. "Shall we start?"

Nadira gulped but nodded, standing, at the doctor's suggestion on his left so he had freedom of movement but she could also reach all the instruments.

"When I ask for an instrument, pick it up halfway down its length, dip it in the alcohol and pass it to me handle first. I'll also need sea-sponges from time to time, and I'll pass these back to you when they're full of blood. Squeeze them out in the bucket, rinse them in alcohol and squeeze them out again before handing them back to me. Any questions?"

Nadira shook her head and then asked, "Won't it hurt him dreadfully when you cut into him?"

"It would if he was awake, but somehow unconsciousness blocks pain. Now, pass me the first knife. I cut the abdomen … thus. In every operation there's a choice. A large cut enables us to see more but heals slower and with greater blood loss. A small cut is kinder on the patient, but it then becomes harder to examine the internal injuries. I prefer a smaller cut if I can." Blood welled up as Faruq sliced through the body wall, and Nadira, under direction from the doctor, soaked it up with sponges. Faruq pointed out the layers and structures as he cut deeper – skin, fat and muscle, blood vessels and membranes.

The sides of the incision fell apart, revealing a mass of dull pink and purplish coils and glistening organs, together with a stink of faeces. Faruq sniffed and grimaced. "Not a good sign. It indicates the intestines have been punctured." He applied an astringent to the cut surfaces and the blood flow abated somewhat. "Does the sight disturb you, Nadira?"

"I … I'm alright, Doctor, but it's very different from the line drawings in the books."

Faruq drew aside the coils of intestine attached by sheets of mesenteric membrane to the body wall. "It makes you appreciate God's handiwork," he observed. "The guts don't just sit in the bowel but are each supported in their place by membranes … ah, here, see? The spear point has pushed the coils aside and sliced through one side of this one and … yes, here, it's punctured another coil. See how the faeces slip out into the body cavity? That alone could kill him, so I was right to operate."

"Yet if it remained within his intestine it wouldn't harm him," Nadira said. "Does it make that much difference? Faeces are revolting but the same no matter where they are."

"Again, one might think so, but the intestine is the proper place for faeces until they're expelled and cause no disease, but the body cavity is not their natural abode and if present will cause inflammation and rot."

Doctor Faruq threaded silk onto a fine needle and had Nadira wash it carefully in alcohol. "Are you a seamstress, Nadira? Then you'll appreciate this." He took the first coil of the intestine and carefully washed it in alcohol before gently pressing the ripped sides together. He pierced first one side with the needle and then the other, drawing the thread after it. Looping the thread over the wound, he repeated the action close to the first, then again, gradually closing the wound. Then he tied it off and trimmed the ends of the silk thread with a sharp knife. Faruq looked at Nadira, noting her alert concentration and came to a decision. “Would you like to sew the other one up?”

“Me?” Nadira’s eyes opened wide. “I thought women weren’t allowed to do surgery.”

“That’s true, however, I can think of no statement in the Qur’an or ahadith that specifically prohibits it. By custom, women are excluded from such activity, but I think to save a life we might make an exception.”

“How would I be saving a life?”

“The punctured coil lies deeper, tucked between others. Your fingers are slimmer and more supple. You’ll be able to do a neater job than I, and in a case like this, a neater job may mean life instead of death. Are you willing?”

Nadira nodded nervously.

“You won’t be able to tell anyone of it. If this became public, we’d both be censured.”

“I’m willing.” Under Faruq’s guidance, Nadira threaded more silk and washed it in alcohol and delicately reached down through the living intestines to suture the puncture wound.

“Very neatly done,” Faruq murmured as she tied off the thread. “Now we can clean up and get out of this man’s body.”

He showed Nadira how to use thin strips of stretched sheep intestine instead of silk for the sutures in the body wall. The man was still unconscious, so Faruq called the porters in to remove him to the recovery ward, a room with two beds in it.

“I’m pleased with the way the operation went,” he said. “I have every hope of his speedy recovery, but we must keep him on liquid food only for a few days. Solid food will strain his intestines. You may also give him poppy if he complains of pain and have his sutures bathed in dilute alcohol twice daily."

Nadira took charge, but made sure there was always another woman in the room whenever she changed the dressings or ministered to the man. He recovered consciousness and complained of being sore, but otherwise was amazed to be alive.

"You've saved my life."

"Doctor Faruq operated on you. He's a skilled surgeon."

"And he has beautiful angels to assist him," the man said with a smile. "I am Karim, of the Pasha's guard."

The woman with Nadira clucked her tongue disapprovingly, and Nadira hid her answering smile. "No talking. Rest and gather your strength."

Karim gathered his strength but still tried to talk to Nadira. From asking around, he knew she was a widow, and he was interested. Every time she came into the room, he would try to elicit conversation from her. Sometimes he would tell her of his brother, Nabil, also a guard in the Pasha's pay but stationed in Sayyid. Other times he would smile and compare her to Hur'In, 'a companion pure, most beautiful of eye.'

"Hush," she would say, trying to look severe but melting under the compliment. "You'll get us both in trouble."

"It would be worth it," he would murmur in reply.

Then on the fifth day, he said he felt hotA despite the cooling breeze that blew through the room. He was thirsty and his mind wandered.

Nadira put the back of her hand against his forehead and frowned. "Are you in pain?"

"A little, but mostly just hot. I feel as if a fire has been lit inside me."

She brought him an infusion of willow bark to bring down his fever, but it had no effect. Sponge baths of cool water gave Karim some relief, but within an hour he was thrashing on his bed and moaning. Nadira went to see Doctor Faruq, who came to examine his patient himself.

"The fever's a worrying sign. Keep up the cool baths and the willow bark. I have to go out of town for three days. If he's no better by the time I return, I may have to open him up again. Maybe we missed some dirt or else a stitch has pulled out."

By the evening of the next day, Karim was weak and his speech rambled. He tossed off all his bedding and only lay still when sponged with cool water. Nadira examined his incision carefully and worried about the livid streaks in the otherwise pale skin. Karim's condition worsened, and the next morning he lost consciousness, though he still moved weakly and moaned. The wound in his abdomen was inflamed, and Nadira wrinkled her nose when she caught the first stink of putrefaction.

"He has an infection," she told the woman with her. "He must be cleaned up – inside."

"Doctor Faruq doesn't return until tomorrow night."

"He could be dead by then."

The woman shrugged. "Insha'Allah."

"We must do something."

"We can do nothing. It's in God's hands."

Nadira sat with Karim and watched as life slipped away from him. "Is all Doctor Faruq's work to come to nothing?" she muttered to herself. "And what of mine?" She had a sudden dreadful thought. *What if it's my stitching that's given way and spilled faecal matter into the body cavity? I've never done stitching like that before, so I could easily have made a mistake*. The more she thought on it, the more certain she became. *If he dies, it'll be my fault. I'll have killed a man*. She reached a decision and called the porters to her.

"Take this man to the operating room."

The men eyed her askance and one of them said, "We don't take orders from a woman."

"No, but you take them from Doctor Faruq. He left specific instructions for the care of this man, and I can only carry out those instructions in the operating room."

"Why didn't he tell us then?"

"I don't know. You can ask him when he returns – maybe when you tell him you refused to let me do my work."

The men grumbled but took Karim on a stretcher to the operating room. "What are you going to do to him here?" the same man asked.

"That's my business and none of yours." Nadira closed the door after the porters left and started assembling the things she would need – spirits of wine, needles, silk, sheep gut thread, swabs and a sharpened knife. She prayed to God not to let the man die because of her mistake.

The man lay motionless on the raised bed, naked save for a cloth draped across his private parts, and Nadira fleetingly considered that if anyone entered the room now she would face a charge of gross indecency. No matter that the man was unconscious, a woman and a man could not be alone in a room together unless they were married or closely related. *But I cannot have anyone in here with me. What I mean to do is just as bad.* She took a deep breath and started palpating Karim's abdomen as she had seen Doctor Faruq do. The flesh felt hot and the belly was hard and distended. The line of the incision was livid and weeping thin yellow pus.

Nadira washed thoroughly with the alcohol and swabbed down Karim's abdomen, carefully paying attention to the incision. When she realised she was just putting off the moment of cutting into the man's flesh, she threw the cotton swab aside and grasped the knife. *Allah help me.* Holding the sharp edge uppermost, she sawed through the sheep gut thread and gently pulled it free. The edges of the wound parted slightly and then held, stuck together by congealed blood and pus.

She grimaced and turned the knife over, slicing firmly along the line of the incision. Blood spurted out, spattering Nadira's face, arms and dress. With a cry of disgust, she dropped the knife and stepped back, watching in horror as a flood of blood and runny pus poured out and started dripping onto the floor. She wiped her face with the back of her hand but only smeared herself more, so she washed in the alcohol, mopping her face and stinging her eyes.

"Help me, angel."

Nadira whipped around and stared aghast. Karim was awake and looking at her with beseeching eyes. At once, her disgust left her and she saw only a man in distress. She prepared a little narcotic on a cloth and held it over Karim's face until his eyelids fluttered and closed. Then she picked the knife up off the floor and washed it in the bloodstained alcohol before opening the incision further, dabbing on astringent as she went to control the bleeding.

The coils of intestine lay in puddles of blood, glistening wetly. She mopped at the fluids with bundle after bundle of cotton, absorbing the blood. Eventually, all the excess was gone, and she started looking for signs of damage. To her surprise, she found her own stitches intact, but one end of Doctor Faruq's stitching had pulled free and faecal matter was again oozing out into the body cavity. Blood was also collecting, so she searched for the source and found it, below the gut and mesenteries, a nick in the body wall and a vessel that weakly pumped blood out of the body.

What do I do? Nadira stood and stared down at the blood slowly welling up from the cut artery. *Think, Nadira. You've read all those books. You must stop the bleeding ... but how*? She picked up the bottle of astringent and after cleaning away the blood again, dabbed it on liberally. The stream slowed and almost stopped but then it broke free and pulsed again. *Can I sew it perhaps*? She threaded silk onto the needle and washed it in alcohol and used more swabs to clean the site. *I cannot even see the vessel, so how can I sew it*? She dropped the needle back onto the table and hit the bed with her open hand in frustration. *What would Faruq do*? *What would the surgeons of old do*? She tried to recall passages from the books and at one point considered leaving her patient to search for the required knowledge in one of them.

If I cannot see the vessel, it's because it's buried in the flesh. I must cut away the flesh so I can see the vessel.

"And then what?" she muttered. "The vessel is so small even I with my slim, supple fingers couldn't stitch the ends closed."

Then think of something else ... Could I plug it? With what? Could I tie it off? Nadira took some of the washed silk thread and fashioned a loop which she dropped over her little finger and pulled on. The loop tightened around her flesh. She loosed it and fashioned half a dozen more. *Just in case*.

Nadira fetched more cotton cloth from a cupboard and eyed with distaste the heap of bloodied cloth piling up on the floor. The light was failing too. Somewhere in the course of her concentration, the muezzin had called 'Asr prayers, but she had failed to notice. *Another sin*. She took out some oil lamps and lit them, arranging them to cast their light on the opened abdomen. At last, she was ready and set to work, mopping up blood and then applying astringent. As the flow lessened and she could see where the blood was coming from, she made a delicate cut across the puncture. Mop and cut, then mop again. It was slow work, but Nadira did not dare move any faster, fearful that in her ignorance she would do real damage.

After several minutes, the ragged ends of the artery were freed from their surrounding tissue and the blood, also freed from the constriction of the flesh, pulsed more strongly from one of them, merely oozing from the other. The flow weakened even as she watched, and she knew her patient could not last much longer. She took a looped thread and slipped it over the pulsing end, drawing it tight. The flow abruptly ceased and Nadira smiled. She tied off the other end of the artery and doused the area liberally with alcohol before starting to draw the cut flesh of his belly together.

With a start, she realised she had not fixed the stitch in the intestine, so she rapidly threaded another piece of silk and did so, adding a few more for good measure. She dabbed alcohol again, and this time, satisfied that she had done everything she could, set about stitching Karim's body wall back together again. Nadira worried if she had done the right thing; the man lay very still, pale and hardly breathing.

Nadira had finished and was wiping the blood off his body when the door burst open and the porters rushed in, together with a woman from the hospital and an imam and his assistant. They looked around in mounting horror at the blood-spattered floor and bed and the pile of blood-soaked cloths. The imam's eyes grew wide at the sight of Nadira, her dress smeared and streaked and blood on her hands and face.

"What in the Name of God have you been doing, woman?" the imam croaked. "If you really are a woman and not some foul demon from hell."

"That is Nadira bint Khayyam," said the woman called Raja. "She works with Doctor Faruq, altogether too closely if you ask me. I wouldn't be surprised if they're fornicating."

"You have a foul tongue," Nadira said sharply. She addressed the imam. "I'm Nadira bint Khayyam, and I am indeed Doctor Faruq's assistant. This man on the bed is one of his – one of our – patients. I was attending to him when you entered."

The imam edged closer, careful not to let blood touch his garments. He peered at Karim closely. "You've cut into him and stitched him up like a … a leather bag."

"Yes. He was bleeding inside and I had to stop it. As I said, he's a patient and I was trying to save his life."

"Only God saves lives," the imam snapped. "Would you add blasphemy to the charges against you?"

"No. No, of course not."

"Why did Doctor Faruq not perform this operation?"

"He's out of town," said Raja.

"And he left this man in my care," Nadira added.

The imam stroked his beard thoughtfully. "So Doctor Faruq told you to cut into this man?"

Nadira shook her head. "No. The man got sick after he left, and I judged it necessary to operate before he bled to death."

"You judged? You take that upon yourself too?"

"I only meant that in my opinion ..."

"Enough. Your guilt is clear, Nadira bint Khayyam. You'll face charges of blasphemy, attempted murder and indecency in that you're alone in a room with a man. However, we'll wait until Doctor Faruq returns before deciding whether he shares your guilt or we should add disobedience to your crimes. Porters, take this woman away and lock her up."

The porters grasped Nadira's arms and then hesitated. "Where should we lock her up?"

"Don't you have a secure room here? One with a lock?"

"Only Doctor Faruq's office."

"Then put her in there."

As the porters started marching Nadira out, she called out to the imam, "Somebody must look after my patient."

"It will be done, woman, and while you wait for justice, pray that the charge doesn't become one of murder."

"May I have water to wash in? Clean clothes?"

The imam watched Nadira hauled away and told Raja. "See to the injured man and when you've attended to him, take water and clean clothing to the prisoner."

"Let her rot is what I say," Raja muttered.

"You'll do as I say, promptly and cheerfully," the imam rejoined. "If not, you may yet join her. I'm unconvinced the woman could do this without others knowing. Have you been protecting her?"

"No, no. Of course not. I'll do what you want immediately." The woman bobbed her head submissively and hurried away.

"Stay here and see that it's done," the imam told his assistant.

An hour later, Nadira was clean and in fresh clothing and had been brought a little food, water, and a blanket. It was dark now, so she said her prayers and rolled herself in her blanket. In the morning, she was allowed out of the room long enough to attend to her bodily needs before being locked up again. She spent the day sitting comfortably in Doctor Faruq's chair and reading his medical books. In one of them, she found a description of tying off cut arteries and was pleased to know she had done it correctly. The day passed slowly, and as the time for Faruq's return approached, she found herself worrying he would be blamed for her misdeeds. *He warned me against doing surgery ... but I could not let Karim die. Or would he have lived anyway? Maybe I mistook the situation.* The door opened and Doctor Faruq walked in, the woman who had informed on her fussing behind him.

"Be quiet, Raja," Faruq said testily. "Of course, I can go into my own office. Now go away." He glared at the woman until she turned and stalked away. When she was out of sight, Faruq gestured to Nadira. "Come on, quickly. You have to get out of here."

Nadira jumped up and ran to Faruq. "What's happening, Doctor? Have they told you what I did?

I'm sorry, I didn't mean for you to get into trouble. Is Karim alright?"

"Karim? Oh, you mean the patient you operated on – he's dead. No, don't start crying, we haven't got time." Faruq ushered Nadira out of the door and along the corridor to the door that let out on the alleyway. "Don't talk now, just come with me. I've no doubt Raja is fetching the imam and police."

Faruq checked the alley was deserted before slipping outside with Nadira. He hurried her along the alley and into one of the main streets, keeping to the shadows. After several twists and turns, they arrived at a stable near the city wall. Faruq rapped on the door. It opened a crack and a turbaned head peered out.

"You got here quickly, doctor. Did anyone see you?"

"I don't think so. Bilal, this is the woman I told you about. Nadira, this is an old friend. You can trust him with your life." Faruq essayed a quick smile. "In fact, we'll both have to."

"Doctor, by saving my son, you've already done more for me than I can repay," Bilal said. "My service is yours, before God."

"Thank you, Bilal. Now, Nadira, the charges against you are serious, and you must flee the city immediately. Bilal will escort you out of the city and up into the hills, where I regret he must leave you. Go to a little village called Sira, to the house of Fazdi, a Kurdish Jew. He owes me a favour, and I've told him to expect you. Wait there until I can clear up this mess."

“Have I made a lot of trouble for you, Doctor? I’m sorry, but I acted with the best of intentions.”

“I’m sure you did, Nadira, but why did you operate again? You must have known that was dangerous, both for you and the patient.”

Nadira told him, quickly describing the symptoms and how she had acted.

“And had the stitches pulled out?”

Nadira hesitated and then decided which stitch had failed was unimportant. “Yes, one. I repaired it and found an artery which was also cut. I tied it off and sewed him back up.”

“Yes, I saw that. Fine work but too late.” Faruq shrugged. “You never really get used to losing a patient but the important thing is to learn from it. What did you learn from this one?”

“To … to check thoroughly before finishing. If I … if I’d checked the stitches and found the cut artery the first time …”

Faruq nodded. “And I share the blame, more in fact, because he was my patient and you were just assisting me.”

“But I shouldn’t have operated again.”

“Medically, you had no choice, Nadira. I would’ve done the same had I been here. Where you erred was to be the wrong gender. If a man had performed that surgery, nobody would be angered, but because you’re a woman …”

“Because I’m a woman, I’m little better than a demon from the desert,” Nadira said bitterly. “It seems I must find another interest to occupy me.”

“Maybe for a little while, but I’d hate to lose you as my assistant. I’ll try and convince them that you acted with my full knowledge and authority. I think the civil authorities will agree, but the imam and religious leaders cannot see beyond accepted custom. Now, go with Bilal and wait until I send for you, no matter how long."

While they were talking, Bilal had saddled two donkeys and loaded them with saddlebags. They led them out of the stables and along the street toward the north gate of the city.

"If anyone asks, you're my sister, Batul. Cover your face and don't speak. As your brother, they'll expect me to answer for you."

As it happened, the guards let them through without question, though one of them commented that it was late to be travelling. Bilal said their father was sick, so he and his sister were going home to tend to him.

"May the blessing of God be upon you," the guard called after them.

The night was dark, but the road stood out pale across the countryside in the starlight. The road wound its way over a low range of hills and along a broad valley before veering to the east. They came to a crossroad where a few huts huddled close. Bilal pointed to the road that ran toward the mountains.

"I can go no further if I'm to reenter the city before daybreak. Go up this road until you get to the town of Sira and the house of Fazdi. There are no side roads and no other towns or villages, so you cannot get lost."

"Thank you, Bilal. I am indebted to you."

"Doctor Faruq saved my son's life. It's the least I can do to repay him. Go now, with God's blessing."

Nadira was exhausted by the time the eastern sky lightened, and after she prayed, she found shelter among the rocks near a stream and was asleep almost as soon as her head touched the ground. She woke in the early afternoon, prayed again and set about making something to eat from the provisions in the saddlebags. There was a bundle in the bottom of the bag that contained jars of ointments, packets of powders and a flask of Spirit of Wine, all neatly labelled. There was also the copy of Doctor Faruq's medical book in the bag, and she blessed his thoughtfulness in packing it. She read it while she ate dried fruit and bread. From the description Bilal had given her, Nadira estimated it would take her another twelve hours of travel to reach Sira, maybe more if the way was rough and she travelled at night, so she determined to press on for at least another three hours that day, sleep overnight, and reach her destination the next day.

Nadira never reached her destination, for when she woke with the dawn the next day, she found half a dozen men sitting around watching her as she slept. She scrambled to her feet and straightened her dress, her heart starting to hammer in her chest.

"Who are you?" she stammered. "What do you want?"

A lean, middle-aged man with a badly healed scar marring an otherwise unremarkable face got up from the rock he sat on and sauntered toward her. "What is a woman doing travelling unattended?"

"It's a matter of necessity," Nadira said, thinking fast. "My … my uncle is sick, and I journey to tend him. There was no one to accompany me."

"What, no husband, no brothers, no sons?" Nadira shook her head. "So who is your uncle? Perhaps I know him?"

"Fazdi, of Sira."

The lean man peered closer at her. "You do not look like either a Kurd or a Jew."

"You know him? Then let me go to him. If you tell me your name, I'll commend you to him."

The man laughed. "I'm Elepas, and I doubt Fazdi would welcome news of me. I fired his grain harvest two years back. You want to know why? He failed to pay me to protect his property against bandits."

"Bandits?" Nadira could not think of anything useful to say, but she felt some comment was called for.

"Yes, like my son, Toomath, here." He gestured and a youth with a sullen look limped over to them.

"Why all the talk, father? Just have her and let's be done here. I need to see a doctor."

"Patience, Toomath. We talk because it pleases me to talk. Besides, women appreciate a little talk before pleasure." He hitched at his robes suggestively.

"I am … am a doctor," Nadira said.

"You? You're a woman. When was a woman ever a doctor? Do you perhaps mean a midwife?"

Elepas roared with laughter and the other men joined in. "You may need a midwife yourself in nine months, if I decide to let you live."

"Your son said he needs a doctor. What for? Maybe I can help. I've had training."

"Hmm. Have you indeed? Well, maybe you can. It'd certainly save a risky trip into the city." Elepas nodded, deciding. "Alright, Toomath, you can make use of her first."

"What's wrong?" Nadira asked the youth, "You're limping. Do you have an unhealed wound? A snakebite? A bone that's set crooked?"

The youth grinned. "I've something much more useful that you can do. I raped a poxed whore a month ago, and the filthy bitch gave me her disease. Can you cure it?"

Nadira paled and closed her eyes. "I … I don't know." She tried to remember something in the books she had read.

"Well, here's the deal," Elepas said. "Cure my son, and I'll keep you for myself only. Fail to cure him, and he'll pass on your failure to your own parts. Agreed?"

Nadira felt sick but could see she had no choice. "As Allah wills."

"Pray to your god if you want, but you cure him."

Nadira nodded. "Show me," she said to Toomath. He grinned again and lifted his robe, dropping his pants. Nadira thanked God she had been married and knew what a male member looked like. This one looked like nothing she had seen though. The member was red and just behind the head was an angry, weeping sore that leaked thin pus. She swallowed, forcing back her nausea.

"I need cinnabar. I must check my saddlebag."

Elepas gestured to one of his men. "Lemlas, check the bags for a weapon."

The man emptied the contents of the saddlebag out onto the ground and roughly opened the bundle, breaking one of the jars. Elepas snarled at him to be careful and picked up the medical text. He held it upside down and stared at the pictures.

"These are pictures of bones and guts. Maybe you really are a doctor."

"I told you I was, now may I prepare a cinnabar paste for your son?"

Nadira knelt and ground some cinnabar ore in a small stone pestle and added water to produce a thick paste. She saw Toomath grinning at her and making suggestive motions with his member, so she added some ground red pepper to the mix before spooning it out onto a piece of flat stone. "Here, smear this on the sore, liberally. It may produce a burning sensation, but if it's too much for you ..."

"You put it on," Toomath said, holding his member out.

"No. I'm not sure you can stand the pain and if I'm within reach, you'll hit me. Also, I don't want to touch that."

"I can stand any pain, you Muslim bitch." Toomath grabbed the stone and sniffed the paste before scooping some up with his finger. He hesitated, then dabbed some on the sore. One of the men laughed so he smeared the rest on. "There. There was no pain." Doubt suddenly flickered in his eyes and his eyebrows drew together. “There’s no pain,” he repeated, though less forcefully. Sweat broke out on his upper lip and his hands moved to cover himself.

“Are you alright?” Elepas asked, interest winning out over concern. “Is there pain after all?”

“A little,” Toomath admitted. “Nothing I can’t handle.” He drew his pants up and turned away, moving awkwardly.

“Don’t remove the paste,” Nadira called after him. “The pain shows it’s working.”

Elepas stared thoughtfully at Nadira and rubbed his chin. “What was in that paste?” he asked. “I’ve seen that cure applied before, and it caused no pain then.”

“Ground cinnabar and a little something of my own.” Nadira decided she would not be cowed by this oaf of a bandit. “Some people think when nothing seems to happen that nothing is happening. I added some red pepper to the mix.” She looked at Elepas boldly. “Perhaps I added too much.”

Elepas stared and then he roared with laughter. “A woman who thinks. How delightful. I shall enjoy you in my bed.” He wiped his eyes with a rag. “A doctor’s always useful to have around, but will you be too dangerous to keep alive? Will you try to kill me, woman?”

“I’ve caused one death. I don’t want to cause more.”

“Who …? No, never mind. I’ll keep you alive and well for now, Doctor Nadira, if only for my son’s sake, but I’ll keep my eyes on you.”

The little band moved off the next morning, downhill and away from Sira and Faruq's friend Fazdi. They kept to country paths and avoided the main roads and stole produce where they could without being seen. Nadira fixed a fresh batch of cinnabar and red pepper daily, but the sight of Toomath's attempts to hide his agony lost its appeal after a few days. The chancre did seem to be healing, so she dropped the pepper from the mix and put the difference down to his increasing health. A month later, Toomath was almost cured, and he declared his member ready to use again.

"Not on Doctor Nadira," Elepas reminded him. "She was only your meat, if she failed to cure you. She's to be my delight." Nadira heard him and concealed a shudder.

"Can we watch?" Toomath asked. "We've no other women."

"What do you take me for?" Elepas roared. "A savage? Of course, you can't watch." He shrugged and grinned. "You can listen to her cries of joy though."

"How about we raid a village first," Toomath suggested. "Who knows, perhaps we could all find women to enjoy."

Elepas considered and then nodded. "Very well. Send Lemlas to scout one out for tomorrow or the next day."

Lemlas returned late the next day with information on the town of Dowarta. "It's a little large maybe, some thirty men all told but some fine women, good flocks of sheep and silver."

“Thirty men are too many,” Elepas grumbled. “There are only seven of us. And what are we, shepherds? We don’t want sheep.”

Toomath laughed. “Unless we can’t get women. There’s silver though. That’s worth a try.”

Elepas shook his head. “Thirty men? We’d be slaughtered.”

“There’s a way,” Lemlas said. “Look.” He took a stick and sketched a plan on the bare soil. The other men crowded round to look.

“That’d work,” said one of the men.

“Might work,” Elepas corrected. “Then again it might not. If it doesn’t, we’re seven against thirty.”

“It’ll work,” Lemlas said confidently. “If it’s done right. I’ll take Jonas and drive the flocks, you and Toomath wait where …”

“Who’s chief here?” Elepas snarled. “Nothing happens without my say so.” He glowered at the ring of men.

“It’s a good plan though,” Toomath agreed.

Elepas grunted. “Jonas is wasted driving the flock. He’s too good a fighter. Let it be Berko who helps Lemlas.”

“So we do it?” Toomath asked.

“Yes, at dawn tomorrow. But we make a quick strike, kill as many of the men as we can in the confusion, grab some women and the silver and get back into the hills before they can regroup.” Elepas leered at Nadira. “When we get back, we can all have some fun.”

The gang set out for Dowarta shortly after midnight, carrying firepots and their freshly sharpened weapons. They left Nadira tied beneath a tree. Elepas squatted beside her before he left and told her to get some sleep.

"I want you well rested for tomorrow." He grinned and shoved his hand up her dress to leave her in no doubt as to why. Then he laughed and led his men off at a trot.

The moon was three-quarter waxing and set not long after they left, plunging the campsite into dark shadows. Nadira eased herself as best she could and tried to sleep. She dreaded what the next day might bring but knew if she was not rested, she could not help herself. Sleep eluded her though, and after a bit, she gave up and set herself to remembering what she could of Doctor Faruq's medical texts. Unfortunately, this led her into thoughts about her operation on Karim and what she should have done. *I killed him*. She went over every step of the procedure, weighing against what she read in the books and against Faruq's actions. *I did everything I could – except spot the cut artery the first time we went into him. But even Faruq didn't see that.*

Nadira dozed as dawn approached and woke up cramped and thirsty when the sun shone full in her face. The donkey grazed peacefully near the stream, and birds sang in the sunshine and among the trees. She looked around the deserted campsite, needing to relieve herself but seeing no way to achieve this. *I face horror enough today without adding to my shame by soiling myself.* She pulled against her bonds again but felt no give there. The tree was a slim one and there was enough slack in the rope to allow her to lean against the trunk and by pushing with her feet, ease herself into a standing position.

Nadira edged sideways, sidling around the tree. Her bladder felt like bursting, so she knew she could wait no longer. She eased herself into a squatting position. *Please let my robes not be in the way.* She urinated, feeling the hot liquid splash against her feet and calves. Afterward, she edged back to her previous position and sat down again, grimacing as the splashed robes clung wetly to her. She tried not to think about it, and the growing heat of the day soon dried the fabric.

Thirst became her overriding concern. As the heat increased, she felt her mouth dry out and she could not avoid the bright sunlight that bathed her prison. She looked longingly at the cool water in the little stream and thinking how beauty depended on one's frame of mind. *It looked lovely an hour ago.* Even the bright dragonflies skimming over the water or the little blue butterflies dancing above the turf no longer had the power to distract her. She closed her eyes, determined not to look at the cool water. *It only makes the thirst greater. Where are they? How long does it take to return from a dawn raid? That was hours ago.*

A horrible thought crept into her mind, more horrible even than the return of Elepas. *What if they never return? They were only seven against thirty. If they're all killed, nobody will know I'm here and …* Nadira shuddered. She started to pray and then remembered she was praying for shame and ignominy. *Death would be better.*

An hour later, the men returned. However, these were not men flushed with a victory over their enemy and laden with booty. Only five filed into the campsite, bloodied and filthy, and Toomath supported his father who cried out horribly with every jarring step. He laid Elepas in the shade and hurried over to Nadira and cut her free.

"Go to my father. He needs you."

Nadira stopped by the stream and washed herself, gulping down water until she could hold no more. She paid no attention to Toomath's increasingly angry urgings. "I cannot help him if I'm fainting from thirst. Now tell me, what happened?"

"They organised quicker than we thought they would. And they had guns – a handful of muskets, but Lemlas and Jonas were killed. A musket ball hit my father in the jaw. I think it's broken."

Elepas groaned mightily and tried to talk, but his speech was slurred and the effort caused him great pain. Nadira examined him and found the musket ball had hit the man's lower jaw on the left side, shattered the jawbone and ripped along the flesh in a bloody furrow to his chin. She probed gently and could feel the edges of the bone grating together.

"Can you fix it?" Toomath asked.

Nadira sat back on her heels and thought. *It'd be simpler if I just let him die. I've nothing but shame and degradation to look forward to if I he lives.* She saw Elepas looking at her beseechingly, and she swore silently. *I cannot just let him die. I must try to save him.*

"I've never set a broken jaw, but the surgeon al-Majusi has. He describes it …"

“Where can we find this al-Majusi?” Toomath interrupted.

“He died hundreds of years ago, but he described his operation fully in a book I read. I remember enough to do it.” *I think.*

“Then do it.”

“I’ll need some things first. Find me gold or silver wire, or if you don’t have that, then strong linen thread. I’ll also need a leather strap, cotton I can use as bandages, and a small spoon. Also bring me my saddlebag.”

Toomath sent men off to get what they could, and while she waited, she cleaned the furrow in Elepas’ jaw. The blood had dried, so she tried not to dislodge the hardened blood, but worked to clean the wound of fragments of dirt. When her saddlebag was brought to her, she took the small flask of Spirits of Wine and dampened a cloth.

“This’ll sting, but it’s important that you don’t jerk back. Can you do that? Don’t try to talk, raise your hand if you understand.” Elepas lifted a hand.

“What is this stuff you put on my father?”

“It’s called Spirit. It has the power to clean away dirt you cannot see.” She dabbed the wound, and Elepas’ hand gripped the turf. He stifled a groan.

“Good. Here are the other things, so we can get started. No wire?”

“Some jewellery. Should I unravel some wire from this brooch?”

“Yes.” Nadira cast her mind back to al-Majusi’s description of the procedure, while she prepared the other things. She had a small packet of dried poppy resin, but did not know how much to use. *A good dose, I think. Better if he loses consciousness.* She mixed a little alcohol and resin in a cup and added a little yoghurt one of the men had to disguise the taste of the alcohol.

She handed the cup to Toomath. "Spoon this mix into your father's mouth gently. It should deaden the pain or even make him sleep. I'm going to have to hurt him."

A little while passed, and Elepas' eyes fluttered and closed. He still mumbled, and his hand pulled at the turf, but his jaw now sagged rather than straining against the pain.

"Very well, let's proceed. I want one man to sit on his legs and two more to hold his arms. Toomath, sit behind him and hold your father's head very still." When everyone was in position, she slipped the leather strap into her patient's mouth and eased it back gently. In answer to Toomath's silent question, she explained. "I have to put my fingers in his mouth and hurt him. I don't want him biting me."

Nadira knelt astride Elepas' legs, conscious of the indelicacy of the position, but needing to be directly in front of him and close. She slipped the fore and middle fingers of her left hand into his mouth and gently felt the inside of his jaw, wincing at the unevenness her fingertips registered. Her right hand probed the outside of his jaw, the contours of the broken bone complicated by the open wound in his flesh. She closed her eyes, concentrating on the broken ends of the bone.

"He's lucky. I think the break is relatively simple … no, wait, there's another …"

With a sinking heart, Nadira felt the bone grate and shift in another direction. Elepas groaned as her fingers probed, and he strained against the men holding him.

"You can mend it though, can't you?" Toomath pleaded.

"I'll do everything I can." Nadira removed her fingers from the man's mouth and looked in at his chipped and broken teeth. "Let me see the silver wire you have." The wire was thin, but kinked and short. *Maybe it'll do for one break.* "And linen thread?" The men had unpicked lengths of thread from a shirt. It was stained and fraying but would have to do. She rinsed both wire and thread in the alcohol.

Nadira put her fingers back into Elepas' mouth, feeling the misalignment of teeth. "Alright, hold him steady. This is going to hurt him a lot." She pushed out with her left hand and it with her right, then as the broken bones shifted, added a vertical factor.

Elepas snapped out of his drug-induced stupor and bellowed, straining against the men holding him. He jerked his head back, fighting his son's hold and bit down simultaneously. Despite the presence of the leather strap, his teeth dug into Nadira's fingers, and she gasped in pain.

"Get his mouth open again."

Elepas screamed as his son dug his fingers into the angle of his jaw. As his jaws parted, Toomath slipped a small piece of wood into his mouth. Elepas gagged.

"Hold him." Nadira pressed hard and felt the bone crunch back into position. Elepas bucked and screamed before collapsing unconscious again. "Quickly, before he recovers." Nadira pushed the other fragment of bone into place and ran her finger over the line of his teeth. She nodded. "Give me the wire and …" She pointed to her bundle. "… and that blade."

She looped the wire around one of his back teeth, pressing the wire between the teeth with the short-bladed blunt knife. The metal dug into his gums, making them bleed, but when she tugged on the wire it did not budge. Next, she threaded it between two teeth on the other side of the broken jaw and wound it tight, anchoring the two fragments together. There was still a short length left, so she ran it back to the first tooth and wedged it into place. "Now the thread," she muttered.

Nadira performed a similar action with the linen thread, tying the small broken fragment to each of the larger pieces, binding the teeth in Elepas' jaw together. When she had tied the last knot and wedged the loose ends between the man's teeth, she peered in, examining her work. *It looks untidy, but it should work. If there's no sideways pressure on the jaw, and he doesn't eat for a month …*

"Your father mustn't chew any food for a month. Can you make sure he doesn't?"

"What does he eat then?"

“Soft food. Milk, raw eggs, mashed vegetables, broth. Whatever you can reduce to slurry. It’s vital that his jaw remains as motionless as possible until the bone can heal.”

Nadira bound Elepas’ jaw with a cloth strip tied over his head, and then they made him comfortable in the shade. She then attended to the other injuries sustained in the raid, though none were severe. She did not ask what had happened at the village, but she pieced the events together from remarks the men made as they sat around and watched her work.

They had meant to fire the wool of the village sheep and drive the animals through the town, creating confusion. As the villagers poured out of their huts, they would be cut down. A simple plan, devised by simple men, and it had foundered on the reaction of the sheep. Instead of stampeding through the village, the terrified animals had broken down the barriers and scattered in all directions, bleating in fear. The men of the village ran out, but not in great confusion, and rapidly saw what was happening. The villagers also had guns, old muzzleloaders and had used them. The first one injured had been Elepas, and when he was shot, the fight went out of the others and they fled.

An hour later, when everyone sat nursing their wounds, Toomath looked around the glade and frowned. “Who’s keeping guard?” he demanded.

The men looked at each other questioningly. “I thought Lemlas, when I didn’t see him,” said one.

“He was killed,” Berko muttered. “But if not Lemlas, then who?” He got to his feet, grasped his spear and died. He tumbled backward to the ground, his throat spurting blood. An instant later, the roar of a musket reached them as other balls whined off the rocks. The others sat stunned for an instant before leaping to their feet or diving for cover. Toomath fell, clutching his leg, and another man screamed as a shot shattered his hand. Nadira lay where she had thrown herself, not daring to move.

"Cease fire," called a voice from the trees. The blue smoke dissipated on the breeze, and in the silence, the bandits could hear the sound of men moving on all sides.

Toomath raised his hands in supplication. "Don't shoot. We surrender." The other bandits raised their hands too, as several men ran out with muskets at the ready.

Nadira sat up and looked at the men in surprise. "They are the Pasha's men," she called. "Do not resist them." The soldiers hauled her to her feet and brought her before their officer.

He dismissed his soldiers and looked her over carefully, stroking his moustache as he did so. "You don't look as if you belong here. What's your name, and why are you here?"

"I … I'm … Amia, guest of the house of Fazdi in Sira. I, and my donkey, was captured a month or more ago. With your permission, kind sir, I'll return to my village."

"Not so fast, woman, for you've the look of a certain Nadira bint Khayyam who fled from Sulaimaniyah. Are you she?"

Nadira did not answer.

"Whoever you are, your integrity has been compromised by living with these men and you share their guilt. I could hang you along with them, or go out of my way to take you to Sira. If Fazdi knows you as Amia, well and good, I'll release you into his care. If he doesn't know you, you'll hang in the town square. What do you say?"

"I am Nadira."

"I thought so." The officer grimaced. "Know then that I'm Nabil, brother to Karim of the Pasha's guard in Sulaimaniyah. The authorities tell me you were responsible for my brother's death."

***

My commanding officer sent for me as soon as the news of my brother's death reached Sayyid. Being a compassionate man, he granted me leave to ride for Sulaimaniyah at once. Even so, I did not arrive until four days after his death and three after his burial. I paid my respects at his grave, and then silently vowing vengeance, I went to the hospital of Doctor Faruq ibn Haroom. The killer had worked here, and I meant to confront the murderer. I found instead, a mild-mannered elderly man and a revelation that shocked me to my core.

"I fully understand your desire for vengeance, Officer Nabil," the doctor said. "However, there are some things you should know."

"Don't think to fob me off with tales of disease and accident, Doctor Faruq," I replied. "I've talked to the religious and secular authorities and know the woman, Nadira, killed my brother. Don't deny it."

"I won't deny it, but know also that she saved his life."

"You're talking in riddles. How could she both save his life and take it?"

"Nadira bint Khayyam was … is … an exceptional woman. But for her gender, she'd be an exceptional surgeon. She came to work for me, and I saw her qualities and fostered them. When your brother, Karim, was brought to me, I let Nadira assist with the operation."

I frowned, not quite believing him. "A woman? Assisting in surgery?"

"It's uncommon but not unheard of. Besides, women make excellent midwives and nurses. This one, I judged, was something more. I showed her the workings of the human body and demonstrated how to sew up a torn intestine. Then I let her try."

"You had the temerity to let an untried woman loose in my brother's body?"

"Under close supervision – but I needn't have been there. She performed like a person born to the craft."

"And then she killed him."

Faruq shook his head. "It was my operation; I cut and stitched everything apart from that one rip caused by the penetrating spear point. My fingers were too large to get that deep, so I let her stitch – under supervision. I then sewed your brother back up and went away believing him safe."

"And then she killed him."

"Do you want to know what happened or are you intent only on what you want to hear?"

I ground my teeth in frustration at the drawn out story but nodded. "Go on."

"While I was away on business, your brother

developed a fever, his wound wept pus and blood and his belly became hard like a boulder. If I'd been here, I'd have operated on him at once, but I wasn't. Instead, Nadira was here and after some hesitation – understandable given the low esteem in which we hold women – she operated, alone. It's a measure of her courage that she took this course knowing she'd be castigated for it."

"So it was down to her actions," I said. "If she hadn't operated, you would have when you returned the next day. Then Karim would still be alive."

"If she'd waited, your brother would have died before I got back."

"So she operated and still my brother died before you got back. Tell me, doctor, isn't it written in medicine that inaction is better than faulty action?"

"Yes, but it's also written that not to act, when the course ahead is plain, is culpable. Let me tell you what she found when she operated the second time. Blood had filled your brother's belly and fragments of faeces floated in it. She drained him, cleaned him and repaired the torn intestine that had pulled free of the stitches …"

"That if she'd sewn correctly in the first place, wouldn't have pulled free," I interrupted.

"No, it was my stitching that was inferior. Nadira then found the source of the bleeding and tied it off. She cleaned up and sewed your brother back up before they broke in on her with their wild charges."

"If she did all this, how is it Karim died? And why do you say she saved him and killed him?

Doctor Faruq sighed. “She saved his life by operating, for unless she’d sewn the intestine back up and tied off the artery, your brother would definitely have died. By operating, she sought to save him, but the very operation that could save him, killed him. He’d lost too much blood already.” The doctor leaned across his desk and looked me directly in my eyes. “Your brother was dying, no matter what anyone did. Nadira at least tried to save him. You owe her thanks for that.”

This was more than I could accept, so I left the doctor and reported to the general of the Pasha’s guards. He gave me the assignment of tracking down Nadira bint Khayyam. I accepted willingly and with a squad of soldiers set off on horseback. We had no idea in which direction she had gone, so we tried every road out of Sulaimaniyah in turn, moving into the hill country to the north when all else failed. We were camped near the town of Dowarta one night, when we heard musket fire and investigated. The eradication of bandits is everyone’s business, so we tracked them to their lair and captured them.

Finding Nadira in the camp was unexpected and welcome. I decided I would take her back to Sulaimaniyah to face the courts and hang the bandits right then and there. Then I discovered the bandit chief Elepas, lying in the shade, unconscious. The woman had operated on him, and when I examined her work, I was staggered by her skill. I have a lot of experience with wounds, both on the battlefield and from brawling, and I have witnessed the butchery that passes for surgery among the army doctors. This woman was obviously inexperienced but was still far ahead of them.

It almost seemed a pity to hang the bandit chief who displayed such a fine example of her dental work, but a bandit is a bandit and does not even deserve the formality of a trial. I had my men string the four survivors from the shade tree. The three conscious ones gave my men much amusement as they writhed and finally died, but the bandit chief just hung from the rope's end and slowly strangled. I cut him down when he was dead and hacked off his head, meaning to take it back with me as evidence of Nadira's activities. If the court needed further proof of her work as a surgeon, this head would provide it.

We were no more than two day's ride from the city, but I had no suitable means of transport for a woman and could not countenance her sitting astride one of the horses; so she must perforce ride the donkey and we must match our pace to that of the sorry beast. We camped that first night beside a small river, and I worried about keeping her secure while we slept.

"I don't want to tie you up overnight, but I will if I must. Will you promise not to try and escape if I leave you unbound?"

"I'll stay," she said. "I could scarcely elude a squad of soldiers anyway."

We ate our rations around a campfire, augmented with a brace of rabbits one of the men shot. After the meal, I took Nadira aside and spoke with her over a cup of coffee, for I still hungered to know the truth about my brother.

"Women normally become midwives or nurses if they enter the medical field," I said. "Why are you different?"

"I don't know." Nadira sipped her coffee, ruminating. "I think it was when I saw the books in Doctor Faruq's office. I saw there was so much more that had been discovered, and it awoke in me a desire to learn, and having learned, use my knowledge to help people."

"It's not something the Qur'an looks kindly on – women working outside the home."

"I'm a widow, and I have no family to look after me. I must work or else beg in the streets. I like medicine, and I'm told I have some proficiency at it. Why then, shouldn't I be a surgeon?"

"Still, I've seen you at prayers this last day. You're devout – surely the Word of God must give you pause?"

"The Qur'an doesn't prohibit a woman from working. Even one of the Prophet's wives was a worker in leather with the Apostle's approval. Should I fail to follow where she would lead?"

I nodded, not really interested in following this particular line of discussion. "Did you really feel that after what … a year or two of study … you had enough experience to take a man's life in your hands?"

"If Doctor Faruq hadn't been away, I wouldn't have attempted anything. I judged that greater harm would come to your brother if I did nothing, so I reopened his belly. I repaired his intestine and found and tied off a broken artery that caused his internal bleeding." She sighed deeply. "He died anyway and his death will always weigh heavily on my soul." She looked up at me. "I'm sorry, intensely sorry, that I caused Karim's death. I admit my guilt, and I'll face the court at Sulaimaniyah without protest."

"Even without the charge of causing death, you face serious charges."

"Do you know what they are?"

"You'll be charged with blasphemy, of course, for daring to contravene accepted custom by working in a man's profession – and fornication."

"What? I've never …"

"Only the suspicion has to be there. When you were taken with my brother's body, four men saw that you'd been alone in the room with Karim. No matter that he was at death's door and his blood was spattered everywhere. Their minds are so sordid that they can imagine little else." I sipped the cooling coffee, wondering whether to remind her she had been alone with the bandits too. Whether or not they had raped her, she would be guilty of fornication in the eyes of the devout, for women are ever the temptress and men too weak to resist their wiles. I decided not to remind her; she had enough to worry about.

"I'm as good as dead," she said – I thought remarkably calmly.

"The sentence for either crime is death, and while you may be able to escape one charge, you won't escape them both." I stood and tossed the dregs of the coffee in the fire, making it crackle and hiss. "I have to check on my men. Will you wait here for me?" She nodded, and I strode off, impressed with her reasoning and her courage.

I returned an hour later. I had joked with my men for a space and then reset the guards, posting them to north, south and west. I beckoned to Nadira and led her east, and though she walked alone into the dark with the brother of the man she had killed, she did not hesitate. A hundred paces or so later, I stopped and turned to her.

"You're Shi'a, aren't you, Nadira?"

"Yes, what of it?"

"It doesn't matters to me, for I'm Sunni, but a week's travel to the east is Persia, where Shi'a dominates and where women are more accepted as man's equal. Your donkey is another fifty paces away, saddled and burdened with your saddlebags. Go with my blessing, Nadira bint Khayyam, and follow your calling."

"You're releasing me? Won't you get into trouble?"

I shrugged. "Maybe. It's time I was moving on anyway."

"But why?"

"Must you have a reason? Let me just say that I have a fondness for soldiers and healers. I'm one and you're the other. Now get out of here before I change my mind."

Nadira pressed my hand and murmured a blessing before vanishing into the night. I turned and trudged back to the camp, sending another man east as guard and repositioning the one in the west further to the north. In the morning, I raised the alarm and led the pursuit west onto the main road into the city of Sulaimaniyah where the supposed tracks of Nadira's donkey were lost in the multitude of prints that filled that great thoroughfare.

Chapter Twenty-Two

Humans are so weak and vulnerable. In the years since I cured the Armenian, I frequented many universities and inhabited many surgeons, driving them to perform acts in the pursuit of knowledge that horrified them even as I controlled their actions. If you were to examine the history books of this time, you would find many Arabic surgeons executed for their crimes against God and man. Or maybe you would not, because Islam does not like to record its mistakes.

After a while, I tired of this mischief and sought out the horrors of the battlefield. Men died for my enjoyment, but when I had fed, I felt unsatisfied. I am not sure why this should be, unless it is boredom. There is no real purpose to my existence – I kill to feed, then I kill again. Surely there must be something more, though why after thousands of years it is really only affecting me now, I cannot say. I will have to think about it. Maybe I need a challenge, but who could stand against me – save, perhaps, a true god – if any such beings exist?

I slowly drifted eastward over the next hundred or so years, amusing myself by finding inventive ways to make men suffer and then stimulating surgeons to find ever more inventive ways of repairing the damage. Women interested me anew, but not, of course, as objects of sexual desire. The attitude of Muslim men to women has changed over the last thousand years. Muhammad blew hot and cold with women, rescuing them from the drudgery that was their lot in pagan times, but then wrapping them in loose garments for fear that their god-given bodies would inflame weak-willed men. I could never understand how men were thought to be intelligent and reasoning, yet were such fools for women that a glimpse of ankle or the shine of washed hair escaping from a head scarf drove all sense from their minds. And then these same men had the effrontery to blame women for their own masculine failings. I have asked imams and mullahs and scholars of Qur'an and hadith and Sunnah, and ordinary men, but all I get is 'It is written,' or they look at me as if I am mad for even asking the question. Does nobody think for themselves anymore?

I came to Iraq as a soldier and passed into another. This man had a brother working for the Pasha in Sulaimaniyah, so I made him join the guard too and he was assigned to Sayyid. This Nabil, for that was his name, rose through the ranks under my tutelage, and he soon became an officer. Then his brother Karim died, killed by a woman who cut him open, they said.

I was intrigued by the feelings Nabil had for his brother. Love - that peculiarly human failing, a grief that reached far deeper than mere sorrow; and a desire for revenge that pleased me, for it promised new deaths. I put it into the mind of the Commander of the Pasha's Guard in Sayyid that he should allow Nabil to attend his brother's funeral. That is what happened, and though he was late for the funeral, he asked after the facts concerning the woman.

I sampled the doctor's mind as he talked with Nabil, and I saw he held the woman in such high regard he had risked his own life to help her escape the city. I also saw in his mind her destination. I encouraged Nabil to report to his general in the city, and he gave him the assignment of tracking down his brother's killer. As I said, humans are so weak and vulnerable and so easily led. They all thought it their own decision, because most men cannot feel my presence unless I desire it.

The bandits were an unexpected bonus. We were heading toward Sira when a deputation of men met us to tell of a raid on their village. Nabil told them they would look for them and rode on. We knew where the woman was, we thought, so there was no great hurry. We could easily take a few days to bring some bandits to summary justice. Nabil's scouts picked up the trail without any difficulty, and the oafs had not even set guards. We shot one and captured the rest and then found there was a woman living with them. Well, there is nothing to say a woman cannot be as murderous as a man, so I was looking forward to feeding on her death throes along with the others.

Except the woman proved to be Nadira. She had tended the wounds of the bandits and especially that of the bandit chief. I examined him, and my medical knowledge was available to Nabil also. He was amazed, and I was surprised at the skill she showed. We spared her life at the camp, though there was very little doubt she would be executed for fornication and blasphemy when we took her back to Sulaimaniyah. Naturally, I slipped into her to experience the mind of this skilled surgeon. I saw she remembered almost everything she had seen and easily recalled any diagram or paragraph in the books she had read. All she needed was practical experience to become a very great surgeon indeed. I came out of her to consider my findings.

For some reason, I found myself disposed to spare her and that shocked me. I have no feelings for humans beyond the savage joy of harvesting them for my pleasure or manipulating them on a whim, yet here I actually wanted to release her. What was the reason? Had this human somehow tainted my demon mind? Do I now seek meaning in my life rather than just pleasure? And what meaning would that be?

I have often given protection to animals when they are mistreated by men, for they are totally at their mercy. Here was another weak vessel totally at the mercy of savage men. But she was a woman, and I kill women as well as men ... so why do I feel inclined to spare her? Well, what would happen if I did spare her? She might feel gratitude, but only to the man who let her go, not to me for she has no knowledge of my existence. Even if she did, what could she possibly do for me except feed me? Despite this, I feel inclined ... Yes, I will give her that chance.

I was willing to just release her, but Nabil actually resisted me. Rather than force him, I persuaded him to question her at length and listen to her replies. Nadira convinced him with her honesty and selflessness.

The next night, Nabil placed the guards in such a way as to leave key trails unguarded. He gave her a donkey and bade her take the road east to Persia as she is Shi'ite and that country favours that sect. I hope Nadira made it to Persia for I am of a mind to find her later and see what she made of her life. But for now, I will go west again. European powers have increasing influence over Arabia and the fractured Muslim world. I can see war coming – a great war, a war such as the world has never seen – and I mean to be part of it. I will not lose my interest in medicine or my search for some meaning in my life, but war and death still call to me.

I come to reap the rich harvest of death in the west, and who knows, one day I may come for you. Keep an eye out for the still blue-green flame of my being and be afraid.

Chapter Twenty-Three

The moon slipped toward the Aegean Sea, casting its obligatory silver path across the still water but showing no sign of enemy activity offshore. Second Lieutenant Mustapha Celik scoured the sea with his binoculars for any sign of the British and French fleet but saw nothing. He thought he could hear gunfire far to the south, but there was certainly nothing offshore from the headland of Ari Burnu. He sighed as the moon dipped out of sight and the full blackness of the predawn sky fell upon him. He put his now useless binoculars away and pulled out a packet of cigarettes, tapping one loose and fumbling it into his mouth. The match flared as he struck it on his boot, and he inhaled the raw smoke into his throat, feeling the welcome rush of nicotine into his system.

"Nothing to see now," he muttered, as if talking to the night.

"No, Sir," said a voice from the darkness. "Shall I stand the men down?" The unseen speaker paused for a moment. "They're tired, Sir, and if we have to face the enemy tomorrow …"

"Small chance of that, Sergeant Kaya. The British would be fools to land on that little beach below us, and whatever else they are, they're not fools. No, we'll see no action yet. But yes, stand the men down and tell them to get some sleep." Mustapha dropped the butt of his cigarette to the ground and stepped on it, extinguishing its tiny glow.

"Yes, Sir."

Mustapha could almost hear Sergeant Kaya's crisp salute, and he turned back to the seascape as his night vision slowly returned. *Nothing out there*. He followed his sergeant back along the narrow track that wound through thick scrub up to a small plateau poised above the thin strip of beach below. Mustapha could not see the beach, but he could hear the slow slap and suck of the waves on its pebbled slope. *Nothing tonight*.

The track climbed, switching up and down along the narrow ridge that led to their camp on the plateau. A muted challenge was answered with a quiet reply from Sergeant Kaya, and they entered the darkened clearing. A dozen men stood staring out into the silent blackness with rifles at the ready. Despite intense curiosity, nobody said anything, instead waiting to be told whether their lives were about to be put on the line again.

"Alright, men, stand down," Kaya said softly. "Keep your rifles with you, but get some sleep if you can. Bey and Yilmaz, take sentry duty up and down the ridge, fifty metres distant."

"Which Yilmaz is that, Sergeant?" The voice sounded amused.

Kaya sighed, the joke wearing increasingly thin. "Berk Yilmaz, now hop to it." Berk's brother, Coskun, sniggered and muttered something to one of the other men.

"Settle down," Sergeant Kaya snapped. "Get some sleep. We'll be moving at dawn."

Mustapha yawned. "What time is dawn, Sergeant?"

"A few minutes before six, Sir."

Mustapha nodded. "Get some sleep." This time he saw, rather than just sensed, Kaya's salute, outlined against the starry sky. He withdrew a few paces and found himself a sturdy shrub and sat with his back to it, staring out down the scrub covered hillside to the beach about a hundred metres below. *I should get some sleep. God knows I'm tired enough, but I just fee l…* He sat and thought about what he felt but found it hard to pin down. *Just uneasy, I suppose.* The hiss and suck of the surf far below mingled with the subdued clatter of pebbles on the beach soothed him, and he dozed fitfully.

A little later, he awoke with a start and sat still, wondering what it was that had awakened him. The night was as it had been, dark and silent except for the sounds of waves and the breeze through the vegetation. Somewhere close to him a man coughed – *that wasn't it.* Mustapha took his pocket watch out and flipped the catch, releasing first the metal lid and then the cracked glass cover. He touched the face gently with his fingertips, feeling the positions of the hands. *Ten past four.* He listened, straining his ears in the dark and heard it again, the soft slap of water against something flat and solid. *But what? A rock? A piece of driftwood ... a boat*? Mustapha put his watch away and scanned the darkened shore with his binoculars. *Nothing.* He looked further out, slowly sweeping through the darkness out to sea and something pale came and went … then again. *There's a boat out there ... with men in it.* His heart started hammering with excitement.

Lieutenant Celik called softly to his sergeant. "Wake up the men – quietly. I think there's a boat down there."

Within minutes, he had his men assembled and he issued his instructions. Corporal Demir asked whether a runner should be sent to Company Headquarters, but Mustapha shook his head. "We've nothing to report as yet." He led his men quickly but quietly down the narrow track that descended to a little hillock not more than sixty metres above and slightly to the north of the unnamed beach below. Swiftly, Sergeant Kaya set up the machine gun so it covered the beach and Corporal Demir positioned the riflemen behind the cover of rocks and bushes.

Mustapha checked his watch again. *Twenty past four*. The sky had paled somewhat in the last few minutes, though sunrise was still an hour and a half away. Through his binoculars, he could see faint patches of white where the waves broke and further out … He hissed through his teeth.

"There's a boat …. no, two more. It's the British invasion."

"I cannot see anything," Kaya murmured. He took the binoculars when Mustapha passed them over and focused on the waters of the bay. "I see them, Sir," he muttered excitedly. "At least three below us and …" He shifted the direction of his scrutiny. "… more to the south."

"Wait until they disembark and then send them to hell."

"Yes, Sir." Sergeant Kaya scrambled away to issue his lieutenant's orders, pointing out where the boats now lay.

The light increased a little and now many dark shapes could be seen creeping shoreward, their progress delineated by the disturbance of individual bow waves. Mustapha saw the barrel of the machine gun slowly track one of the boats as it edged closer. He felt for his watch again. *Half past.*

There was a loud splash and a muffled cheer as a man leapt overboard from the leading boat. He struggled through the waist deep water, his rifle above his head. Behind him, the boats forged ahead, and Mustapha readied himself to give the command, when the machine gun broke into its metallic chatter. Fire stabbed out in the darkness and tiny white fountains stitched their way over the dark sea and intersected the wading man. He disappeared in a flurry of water, and as the rifles joined in with their crack and zip, dozens of other men leapt into the water and splashed toward the beach.

A few more of the attackers fell, but with hundreds of targets in the water, the defenders' fire seemed less accurate. As soon as they reached the beach, the men threw themselves behind boulders or bushes, anything that would offer a modicum of protection, and opened up with random return fire. In the darkness, all the attackers had to fire towards the flashes from the guns, but the bullets from the beach started to rip through the foliage on the hillside, edging ever closer.

Mustapha called to cease fire and without targets to aim at, the bullets came no closer.

Gradually, the gunfire from the beach fell away, and in the silence, Mustapha became aware of firing from north of the Ari Burnu headland and also from the south of their position.

"This is more than just a probing expedition," Sergeant Kaya whispered. "It must be the invasion."

"Detail a runner to go back to headquarters. Tell them we're under attack just south of Ari Burnu."

When the runner had sped off through the undergrowth, no doubt glad to be heading away from the danger, Mustapha withdrew his own squad to a position about fifty metres away and further up the slope. In the growing light, he could make out more activity in the small cove and movement on the pebbly beach. He listened, and heard distant voices, shouted commands, but could not make out what was being said.

"I think they're talking English, but I cannot understand it. The accent's different."

"Conscripts from the British Empire colonies perhaps," Kaya volunteered. He pointed. "See, they're coming up the hill."

"Then we must dissuade them."

The machine gun opened up again, followed by rifle fire, and after a few minutes, the surviving climbers ran for the partial cover of the beach. Mustapha had his men fire the occasional shot to warn the attackers they were still there and instructed them to pick targets as the light grew.

"Nearly dawn, Sir," Kaya said softly. "Some of the men will want to say prayers."

"We're in the middle of a battle, Sergeant."

"Yes, Sir. Of course, Sir."

Mustapha bore the silence for a couple of minutes. "They can take it in turns," he growled. "No more than one man in three away from his post."

"Thank you, Sir … on behalf of the men."

"They're allowed to wait until after the battle, you know. Other commanders would insist on it."

"The men know, Sir, and are grateful for your mercy in this regard."

"Ah, get out of here," Mustapha grumbled. He watched his sergeant withdraw and start plucking the men away from their posts, wondering just why men placed such reliance on something they could not see or hear. *I believed in God once, but one day that belief just sort of ... evaporated. Why? What made me see it as a sham*? He knew many men in the army of the Ottoman Empire were nonbelievers, or at least secularists, and there was no discrimination against apostates, in the army at least, though the mullahs ranted and raved.

Dawn arrived and with it their isolated position on the low ridge became apparent. Rifle fire from the beach increased, pinning his men down, and they were unable to deter the enemy pushing up through the scrub. Mustapha was of half a mind to withdraw his men to the next hill while he waited for reinforcements, and then his mind was made up for him. A flash of light from out at sea caught his attention, and he watched, puzzled for a moment as a smudge of smoke drifted across the naval ships far out to sea. Another flash, then another, and a shell screamed overhead, exploding with a muffled crump in the hillside several hundred metres away. The next shell was closer, and then closer still.

"Fall back to the next hill," Mustapha called, and Sergeant Kaya immediately saw to the men's retreat. After a hurried scramble to the next summit, they set up positions again and watched the shells now falling on and around the little plateau they had defended minutes before. The bombardment ceased, and the tiny figures of the attackers swarmed over the plateau below them.

"Where are our reinforcements?" Kaya grumbled. "A strong push now, and we could throw them back off the beach."

"Patience, Sergeant. The enemy has probably been landing up and down the coast. Trust headquarters to know what's happening. If they think we need support, they'll send it."

"Yes, Sir, but what do we do in the meantime? There are only a dozen of us."

"Harass the enemy, slow him down. If we can't hold them, we fall back to the next hill."

The enemy started off the plateau, pushing along the ridge toward them, and Mustapha directed machine gun and rifle fire at them for half an hour before pulling back along a thin, sheer-sided ridge to the next hill. Behind them, the Kocacimentepe Range stretched inland, the land rising in a series of steps. On either side were other ridges, some scrub-covered, others bare, and as the sun slowly rose, rifle and machine gun fire erupted from them as other units of the Turkish Army focused on the invaders. The progress of the enemy was slow, but more men poured off the beach, and the single company of the Second Battalion, Twenty-Seventh Regiment of the Turkish Ninth Division, could not hope to hold them. They fell back to prepared positions on Canak Bayiri.

The gunfire became constant with Mustapha and other officers organising a concerted effort to pin the invaders down. One of the other lieutenants had recognised the attackers as being Australian and New Zealand troops, perhaps with some British mixed in. Somehow this knowledge made it easier to fight back; they were no longer nameless men trying to kill them.

Word reached the company on Canak Bayiri that Colonel Mustafa Kemal had brought the Fifty-Seventh Regiment to an unnamed knoll along a ridge to the south of them. The knoll was immediately dubbed Kemal Tepe and morale soared to have this redoubtable warrior leading them. The Turks started to counterattack, driving the Australians back from the high ridges, containing them on the lower hills where they proceeded to dig in. Colonel Kemal brought up artillery and pounded the Australian positions and with his men attacking in force, drove the invaders off the hill. Some of the enemy were captured in this counterattack, and this confirmed the identity of the attacking force.

The Australians now pushed inland from the south, occupying a broad knoll on which a solitary pine tree flourished, but again, as the Turks counterattacked, were pushed back, the former fluidity of the armies settling into static defence. Both sides took losses, but as darkness fell on that first day, the Turks were poised to drive the Australians back into the sea.

Colonel Mustafa Kemal called his surviving officers together that evening to harangue them. “I mean to drive these invaders from Turkish soil. We attack at dawn tomorrow in full force.”

A major of the Fifty-Seventh cleared his throat nervously and saluted. “Colonel, we … we desire victory most strongly, but we haven’t the strength to do it. We’d be slaughtered.”

“Don’t you remember my words earlier, Major? I don’t care if we all die. Other troops and other officers will replace us and get the job done. Do you think you know better than I how to fight this battle?”

“N … no, Sir, but …”

“You’re relieved of command, Major. Get out of my sight.”

The major, pale-faced and sweating, swallowed nervously. He saluted and marched out of the tent.

Kemal looked around the other officers, none of whom would meet his eye. “Is anyone else a coward?” He waited a full minute, but there was no response. “Very well then, this is what we’ll do tomorrow at dawn. Third Battalion will …”

“Sir.”

The colonel looked up, surprised and angered at the interruption.

Mustapha Celik saluted crisply. “Sir, may I speak?”

“What’s your name, Lieutenant?”

“Second Lieutenant Mustapha Celik, Colonel of the Second Battalion.”

"And you want to advise me on the course of this battle, Second Lieutenant? From your vast experience?"

"No, Sir … well, yes, Sir. I mean, I was there when they first landed, and I've watched their progress from dawn today."

"And you believe this gives you insights into how the enemy thinks?"

"No, Sir, but I can see he's determined and fights bravely, as have our own men."

"Go on."

"The enemy has dug in along their front and they can be pushed back, Sir, but not by us, not without reinforcements."

"So you favour giving them time to dig in more deeply."

"No, Sir, but the alternative is to attack them with too few troops and exhausted men. If we're thrown back, our men will lose heart, see the invaders as too strong for them. I believe it would be better to contain them and bring reinforcements up. Then we can push them into the sea."

Colonel Kemal stared at this young Second Lieutenant that dared cross swords with his commander and noted the subtle way in which the other officers held their bodies, drawing back so as not to be associated with this self-destructive fool. "Are you afraid, Lieutenant Celik?"

Mustapha drew himself to attention. "Sir, order me to attack and I'll do so willingly and to the death."

"I may hold you to that. Very well … dismissed … all of you. I'll let you know your orders before dawn."

The other officers avoided Mustapha when they stepped outside the tent, certain his career was over and perhaps his life too. Mustapha also worried, for Colonel Kemal had a reputation as a hard man who got things done. *He'll get this done too, and if I stand in his way, I'll be destroyed.*

As it happened, though, he was not. Colonel Kemal issued orders that the Australian and New Zealand forces were to be contained. They were to be allowed to capture no further foot of Turkish soil, though, and if they advanced, they were to be thrown back or destroyed. He had a special task for Mustapha. He was to take his squad down the hill to cover the knoll with the solitary pine tree and prevent the crooked lines of the invaders from being straightened out.

The colonel's aide watched as Celik saluted and strode off to find his men. "That's an impossible task, Colonel. How can a single squad exert enough pressure on the Australians to prevent them shifting their lines?"

"Sometimes you have to give a man an impossible task to test his courage and resolve. Reinforcements are on their way and we'll attack tomorrow, but for now I put this man in a dangerous position so I may judge him. If he fails, it's no great matter."

Mustapha moved his squad under cover of darkness. The moon provided some light and the occasional flash of fire from a sniper in the

Australian lines gave them an idea of their target, so he strung his men across the hillside and had them dig foxholes in the stony soil to give them cover the next day. "We've been given the task of pinning the enemy down today," he whispered to his men. "Don't take unnecessary risks, but any movement in their lines is to be fired upon."

The dawn flooded the hills with light but because of the sun behind them, the valleys remained in shadow until the sun had risen higher in the sky. When the sunlight did sweep across the hillsides, it was already hot. The slopes where Mustapha positioned his men were steep and afforded little cover apart from the low scrub. Every inch of depth in the foxholes gave that little bit of extra security, but because they could not leave their refuges without being exposed to enemy fire, every necessity had to be performed within its confines. By noon, each man's retreat stank, but the odours were preferable to the dangers.

The knoll beneath them was criss-crossed with rudimentary ditches and hastily erected parapets. As the Australians moved along them, Mustapha's men caught glimpses as they hurried from cover to cover and snapped off quick shots. Occasionally, they were rewarded with a cry or an arm flung high, and once or twice a head thrown back in final agony. Their fire was returned, but because they did not move, there was less to attract the eye and far fewer casualties.

Toward noon, their diligence was rewarded. Unaccountably, a battalion of Australian soldiers made an appearance on the far side of the knoll and proceeded to march across the open ground between the lines. The lone pine on the Turkish side of the knoll witnessed their deaths as Mustapha's men opened up a hail of bullets and slaughtered them. A few survivors reached the safety of the dugouts, leaving their comrades littering the open ground. The Australians kept their heads down the rest of the day, and after nightfall, Colonel Kemal sent a runner to recall Mustapha's squad. He had lost three men to enemy fire but had accounted for many more of the enemy.

"You did well, First Lieutenant Celik," Colonel Kemal said. "Are you ready to do it again?"

Mustapha drew himself up, proud of his promotion on the battlefield. "Yes, Sir. We'll drive them into the sea."

The next day, Kemal launched his counterattack with the avowed intention of driving the allied invaders back into the sea. He had six regiments and attacked with five, keeping one in reserve. The Fifty-Seventh advanced down the ridge at the northern end against the New Zealanders and made good progress at first. As they advanced, however, they came into plain sight and one of the warships out in the bay opened fire, scattering the Turks and breaking up the attack. Elsewhere, the Turks attacked vigorously, but enfilading fire from the dug in Australians prevented the Turks closing with their enemy. Late in the day, a Turkish force stormed one of the ridges that fell away to the southwest of the knoll with the lone pine and got so close to the Australian lines they could hear the enemy talking to each other and calling out their commands. Artillery opened up at point blank range and drove the attackers away. Late at night, Colonel Kemal could see he had failed to dislodge the Australians from their positions and called off the attack.

Mustapha had fought alongside the men in his squad and other members of the Twenty-Seventh Regiment as they rushed into the gully from their position on the heights and then laboriously fought their way up the scrub-covered slopes. They advanced into a hail of bullets and soon resorted to crawling through the dust, taking advantage of a clump of roots, a boulder or just a slight irregularity in the ground in a desperate effort to survive. Mustapha saw his men fall, some fatally, others crying out from their wounds, men he had known the past year or more, and he felt a rising anger against these men who had come halfway across the world to invade his homeland.

He charged up the slope, pistol in hand, and came face to face with two Australians trying to pull a fallen comrade back to the shelter of the trenches. Without hesitating, he shot one man in the face and cannoned into the other one, clubbing at the man with his pistol while fending off the man's frantic attempts to claw his face. Mustapha heard himself scream and wondered if he had been hit, and then realised the man under him was not moving any more. He staggered to his feet and looked down at the dead man, oblivious to the bullets now whipping waspishly around him.

He's just a man ... a man like me. He might have a wife, a family at home. Why did he come here? What harm had I done him? Something slammed into Mustapha's left arm, spinning him around, and as he dropped to his knees, another bullet slammed into the ground in front of him, throwing up dirt into his eyes. He cried out and launched himself blindly down the slope until caught and held by his own men. Sergeant Kaya told two men to take Mustapha back to the lines, but he refused to go.

"I'm not about to desert you," he said. He rubbed at his eyes, and one of the men poured water from his canteen, washing some of the debris from his lieutenant's face. "I'll be alright; I can see now." He clapped the soldier on the shoulder with his good arm. "Thank you, Private Bey."

"You've been hit in the arm," Kaya protested. "At least have it seen to by a doctor or medical orderly."

"It's fine. It went through the flesh and missed the bone." Mustapha gingerly felt his arm and winced at the stab of pain. After a few moments, he found he could still move his hand, even if it did hurt abominably. "We've got a job to do."

Kaya grunted, knowing it was pointless to argue. He ordered the men back to cover and had them keep up a steady fire at anything that moved. "If you'd have given us some warning, Sir, we could've joined you in your suicidal attack."

"I didn't even give myself warning. I suppose it's too late to try again?" Mustapha raised his head above the scrub, and a flurry of bullets made him duck for cover. Somewhere to the right of him a man cried out briefly. “What are our losses, Sergeant?”

“Two killed – Osman Sahin and Volkan Sener, six or seven wounded.”

Mustapha swore. “Both good men. Why, Kaya? Where’s the sense in it?”

Kaya shrugged. “It’s God’s Will, Sir. At least they died fighting the infidel. They’re in Paradise.”

“I know what you mean, but even by your belief that’s not true. Those men up there, the British and Australians, don’t war against the Faith. They’ve no interest in proselytising, only in adding Turkey to their Empire. My men weren’t killed because they were Muslim but because they were the enemy.”

Kaya shrugged again. “It may be as you say, Sir, but either way it’s God’s Will. I think I’ll choose to believe they died for a good cause.”

“Oh, I’m sure they did, Sergeant. They died for Turkey. That’s enough for any of us.”

The fighting continued all that day and into the night. Mustapha and his men joined in the final assault on the lone pine knoll and were driven back at last. Under cover of darkness, they returned to their own lines. After sentries had been set, they fell upon food and drink, sleep or prayer, depending on their personal desires. Mustapha had his wound cleaned at last, but the doctor scratched his head when he saw the wound.

“You were very lucky, Lieutenant. From the entry wound, I would’ve bet on it breaking your bone, but it missed, exiting here. How were you holding your arm when you were shot? Really?

Then you're even luckier. It should've gone on to hit you in the chest, but it missed. You'd better give thanks to God, my friend." He probed the wound, searching for any fragments of cloth that might have been carried into his flesh, before thoroughly cleaning it and binding it tightly. "Come and see me – or another doctor – if the wound becomes inflamed. We lose more men from wounds than are killed outright in any battle."

Mustapha rejoined his men, ready for whatever was asked of them.

Colonel Kemal ordered another attack for the following day, across the series of ridges and steep-sided gullies. The allies had landed another four battalions the previous night, so the Turkish attack faltered in the face of withering fire. He pulled his troops back to consider his options, angry he could not dislodge the invaders.

"Give me reinforcements," Kemal demanded of his superiors.

"There are none," he was told. "Are you aware we're being attacked up and down the peninsula?"

"Give me reinforcements, and I'll drive these Anzacs from their beachhead. Then you'll have one less attack to worry about."

Kemal was sent five extra battalions, and on the sixth day after the initial landings, he threw his men into an all-out assault on the Anzac lines. By now, though, the enemy had dug a series of trenches and within these redoubts, resisted any attempts to overwhelm them. Reluctantly, Colonel Mustafa Kemal withdrew to his own trenches, aware now that he could not win with his present strength.

Two days later, the Anzacs counterattacked, but with no greater success as the Turkish army had also constructed a series of unassailable defensive trenches. The war among the ridges and gullies of the Kocacimentepe Range settled into a stalemate.

Mustapha had lost another three men and seven were wounded in the previous days of attack and counterattack, but the idea of sitting around in dusty trenches, baking in the sun or shivering as rain swept across the hills, scratching at fleas and racked with dysentery, filled him with loathing.

"I'd rather we charged the enemy again," he confided to Sergeant Kaya a few days later. "This sitting around will kill me."

"Sir, may I speak freely? As … as a friend rather than as a subordinate?"

"Of course, Direnc. We've known each other for years, and I count you as a friend as well as an excellent sergeant. Say what you will."

Kaya nodded and collected his thoughts. "First, let me say that the men welcome this inactivity. For them, life's more certain without those savage Australians shooting at them constantly. Now, they only have to contend with bad food, filthy accommodation and the occasional sniper."

Mustapha laughed. "You surprise me, Direnc. I thought I commanded men who were lions – who broke their morning fast by eating Australians. Nobody wants to die, but I thought they'd have a bit more enthusiasm for the task at hand."

"They'll do their duty, Sir, but …"

"Not Sir, Direnc. Call me Mustapha. We're friends, remember?"

"I remember … Mustapha. As I was saying, the men will do their duty, as will we all, and they know that sometimes a soldier is asked to die for his country, but it's unfair to ask him to seek out death."

Mustapha frowned. "You think I'm asking them to do that?"

"You do volunteer the squad for patrol duty rather more often than do other officers."

"And have we lost any men on these patrols?"

"A broken ankle, scratches and scrapes … no, Mustapha, no losses."

"There you go then."

"But why, Mustapha? As you say, we've known each other for years, and you've always been a thinking man, never one to rush into a dangerous situation without scrutinising it first. What's changed?"

"I'm not sure. I don't want to die, or even …" he flexed his wounded arm, "… get wounded, but my feelings have changed." Direnc said nothing, and Mustapha considered further. "I've always prided myself on being a calm, reasoning man," he said slowly, "But in the last few weeks, I've been gripped by anger. Anger at those sons of whores out there." He gestured towards the Australian trenches. "How dare they invade us?"

"I dare say the men in their trenches have as little to say about national policy as the men in ours," Direnc observed.

"I know that," Mustapha snapped. He let his breath out in a rush and took several deep breaths, forcing back his anger. "I'm sorry, Direnc. I'm not sure who I'm really angry with. It isn't the poor fools on either side who get themselves killed, or even the generals who order the men to their deaths. I suppose I blame the politicians and rulers, but they're only following an outdated notion of honour and glory."

"You sound a bit like a Marxist."

"In a way, but they want war just as much as anyone else – class war will kill you just as dead as military war."

"And you don't want war? You certainly seem committed to this conflict."

"What would happen if I threw away my uniform and gun? I'd be shot for cowardice and desertion. No, thank you."

Direnc thought about his friend's words for several minutes. While he thought, he rolled himself a cigarette and lit it up, inhaling the harsh smoke. "So what are you trying to say?"

"I've seen a lot of death, Direnc, more than just the few here at Ari Burnu. One nation invades another and men die, women are raped and children orphaned – and for what? Any gains one nation makes are squandered within a generation or two, a couple of hundred years at the most. Then enemies become friends and friends, enemies, and it starts all over again with someone else."

"I never took you for a student of history, Mustapha. Didn't you grow up on a farm?"

"You could say that."

"Then where did you see all this death before you arrived here? You're too young to have been in the war with Russia."

Mustapha shrugged. "It's not important; I'm just ranting because life is meaningless."

"There I must disagree with you," Direnc said. "Allah created this world with a purpose and man is here to be in subjection to Him."

"Ah, yes, I'd forgotten you were religious."

"You make it sound like something to be ashamed of."

"If you'd seen …" Mustapha muttered. "I don't want to offend you, old friend, but religions are as bad as nations for killing their followers."

"Oh, come now. Religions are a force for peace – well, Islam is anyway. The Christian nations have always waged war against us."

"Yes, they have, but the conflict hasn't been one-sided. Muslims have invaded Christian lands before. I remember in Spain …"

"You remember?" Direnc laughed. "You'll be telling me next you were there."

Mustapha snorted derisively. "I'd have to be over a thousand years old to have been there, but there are such things as history books, my friend."

"Well, of course, but Spain just proves my point. Muslims invaded Spain, but only to bring the Word of God to the heathen. It was a holy work."

"I've no doubt the Christians and Jews felt grateful as they died under the sword."

"Only those who refused to convert were put to death."

"Ah, yes, the People of the Book who are our brothers before God. Admit it, Direnc, foul deeds have been committed in the name of Allah and his

Apostle. Small wonder the Christians fear and hate us."

Direnc Kaya drew his brows together in puzzlement. "I know you aren't a religious man, Mustapha, but this goes too far. You're on the verge of slandering God. Beware the Day of Judgment."

"Fiery hell for eternity for merely questioning our Faith?"

"The Word of God is eternal and correct in every particular. It's there for all to read. There can be no questions."

"Oh, there are questions, believe me."

Direnc looked troubled. "You've fallen into error, friend Mustapha. I implore you to repent."

Mustapha only smiled and got to his feet. "I think there's a little matter of a patrol toward the enemy lines, Sergeant Kaya. Fall the men in; we leave in ten minutes."

The summer months were hot and dry. Rain did fall, as it falls every month in the Peninsula, but it provided little relief from the heat, dust and flies. The only thing that made conditions bearable was the knowledge the Anzac forces were suffering more. Every bit of food, every drop of water, every bullet, bandage and boot had to be brought in to the salient by ship, and often these supplies were put in peril by enthusiastic gunnery. The trench lines were essentially static from May to August, and the Turkish troops had little to do except pin the Anzacs down.

Patrols were sent out every night, not with any great hope of advancing the Turkish cause but to provide essential information on what the enemy was doing. Were the trenches being extended? Were units being moved around or concentrated at some point? What was morale like? Could the patrols overhear complaints or grumblings? Every bit of information that could be gathered was distilled into a report by the patrol leader and submitted to Mustafa Kemal. The Anzacs were doing exactly the same thing, of course, and sometimes the patrols would pass close by, each aware of the other's presence but unwilling to precipitate a confrontation.

Men died every day. The attrition due to constant sniping and shelling by artillery wore away as the companies and reinforcements were brought in. As summer neared its end, the commanders of the respective armies were contemplating fresh hostilities – a breakout by the Anzacs or an annihilation by the Turks. As these events were contemplated, the commanders called on their information gatherers to provide fresh intelligence.

Mustapha Celik was one of these intelligence gatherers. His enthusiasm for the task had been noted and whenever there was a particularly difficult task, his superiors called on him. They did so again on a hot night at the beginning of August.

"I've a very special assignment for you, Lieutenant Celik," Colonel Kemal said. "We know that the Anzacs are getting ready to breakout, but we don't know when or where. That's where you come in. You probably have the most experience with close patrolling, so I want you to get close enough to the Australian trenches to listen to their conversations. I doubt you'll hear anything definite, but even scraps of information can be pieced together."

Mustapha smiled and saluted and went off to collect his men.

"You're determined to get us all killed, aren't you?" Sergeant Kaya said bitterly.

"If you're afraid, I'll take Corporal Demir instead."

"I'm not afraid, curse you."

"Good man. Choose one other – someone quiet and who can understand English."

Kaya chose Private Selim Bey, and when the moon set, they slipped over the parapet of the Turkish trenches and crept into the scrub-choked ravines and gullies below the Australian lines. It was a little after one in the morning when they left, and it took them an hour to work their way close enough to the enemy trenches to hear what was being said. They lay just below the parapet of the Anzac trench in the deep shadow of the night and listened. Conversation was desultory among the soldiers and most centred on their families back home in Australia.

"This is useless," Mustapha whispered. "I'm going in. Wait here."

"What?" Kaya subsided as the shadow of his lieutenant drew back and disappeared into the night.

Mustapha unwrapped one of his leggings and wound it carefully around his head, covering his hair. He knew his complexion was entirely wrong for him to masquerade as an Australian, but he also knew there was a Gurkha brigade somewhere in the salient. *Maybe I can pass as one of them.* He lifted his head and peered over the lip of the trench, hoping he would not be staring down a rifle barrel. *No one*. He listened hard but could not even hear breathing, so he slithered over the parapet and landed softly in the enemy trench. Nobody was in sight, so he breathed a sigh of relief. His jacket was Turkish, so he took it off and put it back over the parapet before lighting a cigarette and sauntering slowly toward the sound of voices.

A turn or two brought Mustapha to a broadening of the trench where a shelter had been cut into the earth at the back of the trench. A hooded lamp sat on the ground barely illuminating half a dozen men sitting around in their shirtsleeves. A single soldier stood looking out toward the Turkish lines with his rifle in hand. One of the seated men looked up as Mustapha trod on a creaking duckboard.

"What have we here, then?" He got to his feet and half levelled his rifle, peering suspiciously at the darkened figure. "Who are you, mate?"

"Ah, good evening, Australian friends," Mustapha said. "I am Sub-Daffadar Harish Dai of the Twenty-Ninth Indian Brigade. It's a fine night for a walk isn't it?"

"Where's your flamin' uniform?"

"I'm not on duty, and it's a warm night, so I left my coat behind in my billet. My turban surely identifies me as a Gurkha."

"Your bloody Indian Brigade must do things differently then. Our Leftie would skin us alive if we wandered around looking like that. Who did you say you were?"

"Sub-Daffadar Harish Dai."

"I never seen a Gurkha before."

"Who the bleedin' hell do you think he is, wandering around the trench, then? A flamin' Turk?"

"Yeah, alright, of course, he isn't."

"Okay then, Subdaffy, pull up a pew and tell us abaht India."

"I'm sorry; Sub-Daffadar is my rank. It's Corporal, I think, but my name is Harish, and what is this pew you wish me to pull?"

There was a roar of laughter, and the men made room for Mustapha. "Have a seat, Harish" the man said. "My name's Jonno, this is Jimmy, Curly, Petey and Sebastian. He's a bloody toff from Sydney-side, but he's a decent enough bloke. You can call him Sebby – we all do. Fourth Infantry." He indicated the man standing sentry duty by the parapet. "That's Harry." The man glanced his way and nodded before returning his attention to the night.

"I'm very pleased to meet you," Mustapha said, bowing slightly to them all in turn. He sat down and pulled out his cigarettes. "May I offer you a smoke?"

"Those are bloody Turkish fags," Bluey said. "Where did you get them?"

"Our officers issued us with these. I believe they were captured."

The Australians took one each and lit up, inhaling tentatively. "Bloody Turkish rubbish," Petey said. He made as if to flick it away and then changed his mind. "No offence meant, mate, but your officers are pulling a fast one. Here, try a proper smoke." He passed Mustapha one of his own battered ones.

Mustapha lit up and hid his reaction to the harsh taste. "Different," he said. "Different, but better."

"So where you from, Harish?" Jonno asked.

"A small village in the mountains called Khela near the Nepalese border. They are mostly goat herders and farmers, but my father was a soldier, and his father before him." He looked around at the open pale faces of his new comrades. "And where are you all from? All from this Sydneyside like Sebby?"

"Hell no," Jonno laughed. "Me and Jimmy are from Brizzie, Curly's from Melbourne and Petey's from somewhere beyond the Black Stump."

"That's Nyngan to you, you bugger," Petey corrected. "Don't believe a word he says, Haris; he's an ignorant Queenslander who doesn't know enough about geography to scratch his own bum."

"And how is this war treating you?" Mustapha asked. "Is that a correct question to ask? For me, I'm enjoying it."

"How the hell do you enjoy it, Harish?" Jimmy asked. "Do you like squatting on your backside in the dust and mud, shitting your guts out and fighting flies and raggety-arsed monkeys?"

"You aren't professional soldiers?" The Australians shook their heads. "Ah, then that is it. I've known nothing else, so these things don't concern me."

"Good luck to you then, mate," Jimmy muttered. "You'll be all in favour of the push then?"

"Push?"

"I don't think we should say anything," Jonno cautioned.

"Ah, he's one of us. He probably knows more than us, being a bleedin' Corporal an' all. What abaht it, Harish? Are you ready for the attack?"

Mustapha hesitated, wondering how to draw them out. "The one on Canak Bayiri?"

"Canak what? Do you mean Chunuk Bair? Nah, that's not for us. We're heading for Hill 971."

"I don't think I know this hill. It hasn't been called that by our officers."

"The big one, 971, up there." Jimmy waved toward the rising ground of the Kocacimentepe Range.

"I don't envy you that task," Mustapha said. "There are many ravines in the way. Er, when are you going?"

"Now that's definitely something we shouldn't talk about," Jonno said. "Who knows who may be listening?"

"Balls," Jimmy muttered. "We're all friends here. Anyway, we don't know, Harish, me old mate. We've been issued with our rations for the next week, but it could be tonight or in a week's time."

"Won't be tonight," Petey said.

"Thank gawd for that," Curly added. "My gut's all in knots and I'd be farting and shitting all the way."

Sebby laughed. “Maybe that’d be a good thing. The Turks would think it was an artillery barrage and keep their heads down.”

The roar of laughter was warm and friendly, and Mustapha found himself liking these Australians. He reminded himself they were the enemy and invaders. Voices came from further down the trench, and the laughter died away.

“That’s the Leftie,” Jonno murmured.

“Leftie?”

“Lieutenant Sedgewick.”

“Ah, I’d better be going then.” Mustapha got to his feet quickly. “I don’t think he’d look kindly on me leaving my unit.”

“Yeah, officers are funny that way,” Jimmy said. “You’d better scarper then.”

“Goodbye, Australians. Maybe we’ll meet again.”

“Who knows?” Jonno said. “Maybe on Hill 971 in a few days time. God be with you, mate.”

Mustapha smiled awkwardly. “And with you … mate.”

“Go on, bugger off, Harish, or you’ll get caught.”

Mustapha turned and hurried away into the shadows and then along the trench to the spot where he had dropped into it. It was still deserted, so he climbed over the parapet and slithered his way back to where Kaya and Bey were still waiting.

“Lieutenant! Praise God you’re alright. I thought surely they’d captured you.”

“I hope it wasn’t too boring for you, Sergeant.”

"Not in the least," Kaya replied in a whisper. "We listened to men grumbling about the heat and missing their wives. Except that it was all in English, I could have been in our own trenches. Were you more successful?"

"Yes. Now come on, we're going home." Mustapha led the way back through the scrub to their own lines, giving the bird call that let the sentries know a friend approached. He directed his men to rejoin the squad and hurried off to find the Colonel.

"You did what?" Colonel Kemal exclaimed. "Actually into their lines and talked to them?"

"Yes, Sir. I told them I was a Gurkha from the Twenty-Ninth Indian Brigade, which I knew from our briefings were present, and …"

"You gave them classified information?" asked the Colonel's aide sharply.

Mustapha raised his eyebrows. "With respect, Sir, don't you think they know that already?"

"Yes, a stupid observation," Kemal confirmed. "Go on, Lieutenant."

"Well, Sir, they believed me, and I engaged them in conversation. I found out that a breakout is due in the next few days."

"You cannot be more precise?"

"The soldiers didn't know, Sir, only that they'd been issued with their rations that cover a seven day period. The breakout's in two parts, I think. I suggested Canak Bayiri, and they intimated that was a target but not by themselves. They are men of the Fourth Infantry Brigade and their target is Hill 971, which I took to be Kocacimentepe."

Colonel Kemal strode over to a large map spread out on a table and pored over it, pointing out things to his aide and a major who happened to be there. "He said the Fourth and the Indian Brigade, here and here. Surely the New Zealanders too. But how? We're dug in all along the ridges. It'd be a hard fight for every yard."

"Perhaps they'll try and bypass the ridges, working along the valleys," the aide suggested.

"I don't envy them then," the major commented. "There's no possibility of maintaining formation in those gullies, and we can pour fire down onto them from every position."

"Canak Bayiri was the other target. I would say New Zealanders again, and British. What units have we definitely identified?"

"Irish, Hampshire and Lancashire definitely, Sir," the aide said. "Wiltshire possibly. Warwick Ninth also."

Kemal tapped the map firmly. "We've no trenches on this spur until they reach Canak Bayiri. That's the way they'll come, I think." He turned and gestured to Mustapha. "Lieutenant, where do you want to be when they attack?"

"Wherever you put me, Sir."

"I'm serious. You did a good job tonight. You've earned the right to pick your battle."

"Then put me on Canak Bayiri, Sir. The Fourth are heading up Kocacimentepe, and I'd rather not kill men whose hospitality I've shared."

Kemal nodded seriously and then went to report to his own superiors. He was a skilled field commander with an eye for tactics and strategy, but he was still a relatively junior officer. The decisions to launch an attack or to move large numbers of men around the battlefield would come from the generals, not him, and the realisation rankled. He believed his superiors were too cautious and that desperate times called for daring actions. He knew how the allies would attack and what was needed for a successful defence, and the opening skirmish would be with his own generals.

The attack came five nights later. Just before dawn, the group attacking Hill 971 set off, travelling over unfamiliar terrain. The units attacking Canak Bayiri left at the same time, but initially had a better time of it, advancing along the Sahin Sirt spur that the Anzacs knew as Rhododendron Spur. They met with stiff Turkish resistance, though, and the advance was soon bogged down. As the New Zealanders advanced along the ridge, they found themselves exposed and vulnerable to Turkish fire and retired to a small plateau near the spur to regroup and try again under cover of darkness.

Mustapha and his squad were only a tiny part of the force defending Canak Bayiri, but losses among the men he knew were high. There was little cover on the summit as the soil was thin and stony and the trenches were shallow. They poured fire into the advancing men not only from Canak Bayiri itself but also from the hills to the north and south.

A naval barrage plastered the summit of Canak Bayiri that night, driving the Turks, including Mustapha and his men, from the peak. The New Zealanders, together with British units, stormed the top when the artillery bombardment ceased and took the hill. It proved impossible to hold, however, as the hills to the north and south were in Turkish hands and gunfire swept the exposed top.

The Turks counterattacked, charging up the eastern flanks of Canak Bayiri. Mustapha was in the forefront, encouraging his men onward, oblivious to the sleet of bullets directed at them. They reached the shallow trenches hastily dug by the allies and leapt down into them. Mustapha shot a man who came running toward him with bayonet fixed, and then his pistol clicked on an empty chamber. He reloaded calmly, while men fought and died around him, and then continued. A bullet plucked at his sleeve and another struck his boot, making him stumble, but he strode along the trench, firing at every enemy within sight. The gun failed him again, and he stuck it in its holster and took a rifle and bayonet from a fallen New Zealander, using that instead.

Resistance stiffened and the Turkish advance slowed to a halt. Men sought cover where they could, Turkish and allied soldiers often sharing different parts of the same trench, and kept up a constant sniping fire. Mustapha reloaded his pistol but hung onto the bayoneted rifle as well. He leaned back against the dirt wall of the trench and lit up a cigarette, blowing smoke upward as he calmed his racing heart. It was only a brief respite; as more New Zealanders poured along the trenches, Mustapha and his men continued the fight for control of Canak Bayiri.

Quiet Selim Bey was gunned down alongside him, so close he was spattered with the man's blood. The Yilmaz brothers, Berk and Coskun, died within minutes of each other, one by a shot to the head, the other shredded by shrapnel. Corporal Demir cried out and collapsed as a bullet shattered his knee. Sergeant Kaya fought on untouched, and Mustapha suffered no more than minor flesh wounds from flying fragments of stone. The enemy came too close for gunfire, and the armies fought hand to hand with bayonets, knives or teeth.

A New Zealand youth, seemingly only a child, thrust his bayonet at Mustapha. He knocked it aside and thrust back, the sharp point ripping easily through fabric and flesh to the life beneath. The lad screamed, high-pitched and in despairing disbelief, and dropped his weapon, clutching at the bayonet. He stared at Mustapha, the colour fleeing from his face, and then sank to his knees and onto his back, still clutching at the blade buried deep in his belly. "Mama," he whispered. Mustapha felt something grip his heart, and he choked back a sob, pulling the bayonet free. The boy sank onto his back, the whites of his eyes showing and scarlet blossoming on his tunic.

"Go with God," Mustapha muttered and stepped over the body, raising his bayonet to face the next foe.

A moustachioed man was next, older and more experienced, and Mustapha found himself battling to stay alive. He parried and stabbed, leaping aside and feeling blood trickle from a graze. He stumbled over the body of the lad, and it seemed as if the boy grabbed his feet, shouting at his comrade to finish him off, but it was only fear that gripped him. Sergeant Kaya shot the man as he raised his weapon.

The individual fights became a blur, merging into a melange of blood and dirt, terror and pain. Fighting became more difficult as the trenches became clogged with bodies. It eventually ceased at nightfall with the Turks in control of most of Canak Bayiri again. Mustapha organised his men, and a number of men from other units, because of the attrition of officers, into work details shifting the bodies of fallen Anzacs out of the trenches and piling them along the western sides. The bodies did not lie quietly but jumped and shook as bullets hit them. The allies kept up a barrage throughout the early part of the night but could not see their enemies were now partly shielded by the fallen bodies of their comrades.

Food and water arrived later, and Mustapha made his men get some rest, man about in two hour shifts. Exhausted men collapsed where they stood, and passage up and down the trench involved negotiating a careful route among unconscious bodies. Mustapha sat and smoked his cigarettes, his mind too active to rest as the stars slowly wheeled to their deaths far out over the summer sea. The anger that had buoyed him earlier drained away, and as the light slowly grew, he stared at the upside down dead face of a young New Zealander draped over the lip of the trench and found himself wondering who he was.

Somewhere a mother will grieve, a wife, a girl. Sons will mourn the death of a father and fathers the death of sons. And for what? Duty? Duty to whom or what, to a ruler's lust for power, economics, a faith, a temporary ideal? In a hundred years or less, Turks and New Zealanders, Germans and Australians will break bread together in friendship, and then what will the sacrifice of these thousands mean? Far better if we all sat down and broke bread together now and this dead lad could have returned to his family.

Dawn neared and soldiers awoke, offering up prayers as best they could. More men poured into the trenches, and Colonel Mustafa Kemal was there, striding along the trench, praising some, encouraging others, exhorting all.

"One last push and we'll drive the enemy back. We have the men, we have the equipment and we have right on our side. God is with us, men of Turkey, and by your efforts, we'll overcome. Arise now and throw back the invader in God's name!"

Kemal's words had the desired effect, and a great cheer went up as he led his men out of the trench and into the battle for Canak Bayiri. The Turks charged across the open ground screaming "Allah! Allah! Allah!" They swept over the Lancashire Battalion, killing them all, and drove the Wiltshires into the scrub-choked gullies. They poured down the spur, often moving so fast they intermingled with the retreating New Zealanders; the allied gunners further down the ridge killed friend and foe alike in their indiscriminate hail of fire. All the heights captured by the allies with such high cost of blood were lost in hours and the weary Anzacs thrown down into the gullies and behind their lines.

Mustapha was there at the last, firing his pistol and leading his men, but his heart was no longer in the battle. The curling crest of the Turkish advance faltered at last and drew back, but Mustapha remained where he was on the narrow ridge between Canak Bayiri and the ridge called Sahin Sirt. He stood and stared at the New Zealand lines, and his pistol dropped to his side. Bullets zipped past him and ricocheted from the rocks with waspish whines, but he paid them no attention. His only thought was, *What am I doing here*? "What in Allah's name has happened to me?!" he cried out.

"Lieutenant, get down!" Sergeant Kaya yelled from behind him. "Mustapha, for the love of God …"

A bullet slammed into Mustapha's chest, and he staggered back to fall at Kaya's feet. He was dead before his friend could bend to help him.

***

I cling to the thought that Mustapha Celik, my friend and commander, died with the name of God on his lips. When it is my time to go, I pray that I too may die with one of God's names still on my tongue so I will go straight to Paradise, there to enjoy every good thing, meat, wine and fruit served to me on a golden couch by handsome youths. I, too, shall have houris, ever young, ever virgin, amidst rich pavilions set among shady trees and cool fountains, and there I will remain forever.

Mustapha was my friend, and once upon a time, he had been a man of Faith, keeping to the Five Pillars, obeying the letter of the Law, a man to whom Allah and the Prophet meant everything. He grew up on a farm, was raised uneducated save for the teachings of the Qur'an and enlisted as a private in the Pasha's army. I knew him as a youth when we attended the same madrasah. My father wanted me to work for him as a merchant, but I wanted to see the world so I enlisted too. I arrived in the training barracks a year behind Mustapha and found him much changed. Somehow in that short year, he had gained an education and a calm outlook on life so unlike the brash farm lad back in our village. If I had not known him from before, I would have denied this was Mustapha Celik. Another thing that had changed was his attitude to the Faith. Our beloved country has always been on the borders of the Islamic world, and we have to fight to maintain our Faith, unlike the Arabs who live and work where the Prophet first received the Word of God. It seemed to me Mustapha had given up the fight and embraced the secular doctrines bandied about by Marxists and socialists.

We both trained, and after another year or two, we applied to become officers. Despite starting a year after my friend, I anticipated excelling in my examinations, for despite his new education he was still an ignorant farm lad, whereas I had completed my schooling. Furthermore, I prayed in the prescribed manner and did everything according to the Qur'an, whereas Mustapha spent more time contemplating the profane and carousing with whores. I should have passed the examinations and he failed, but it was the other way round. All I could salvage from my studies was a non-commissioned rating. Mustapha became a Second Lieutenant, and I became his sergeant. We remained friends, as much as an officer and a sergeant could, but the divide was greater than just rank. Somewhere in that missing year when he gained an impossible education, he also gained something else, something that led him down a path that would surely end in apostasy and death.

I grieved for him but knew it must be the Will of God. Our saying *Insha'Allah* is a very wise saying. All things happen through the Will of God, and nothing can possibly happen unless God allows it. So when we talk about something in the past, present or future, one should always say *Insha'Allah* or *As God wants.* By saying this, we do not run the risk of setting ourselves up as knowing more than God or desiring an outcome contrary to God's design. I grieved for my friend, Mustapha, for he appeared to be turning away from the Faith, but just thinking *Insha'Allah* enabled me to realise he could not appear to turn away unless God wanted him to. That realisation brought me peace.

War started in Europe, and as the Ottoman Empire was allied with Germany, we naturally joined on their side. Things had been going ill for us for some years, and we saw this as an opportunity to defeat Russia and regain our standing in the world. At least, this is how it was explained to me by others in our company. I have little understanding of politics, preferring to leave such matters to my betters. Mustapha explained it differently, and though his words seemed to make some sense at the time, on thinking about them later, I feared that he had lost his mind.

Mustapha told me stories – stories of warfare, stories of murder, violence and hate, and tied them all back to religion. Not all to Islam, I admit, for he seemed bitter about Christians as well as Jews and Muslims, but the common thread was all the ills of the world stemmed from the beliefs men had about themselves and their neighbours.

"Man desires what he doesn't have, and if his neighbour has it, he'll take it," he said. "Be it woman or camel or incense or land."

"Sometimes," I admitted, "But by no means always. The Word of God …"

"The Word of God is used by unscrupulous men to justify any action. Muhammad used it to destroy the pagan tribes and take their wealth. The caliphs used it to invade country after country, desiring wealth and power but using religion as an excuse. The Christians did the same when they tried to free Jerusalem and Tamerlane when he conquered and slew thousands. It happens right down through history, Direnc, and it's happening now."

"You cannot tell me that this present war is one of religion. We're Muslim but our ally Germany is Christian, as are our enemies the British, French and Russians."

"That's true, my friend, but each of these countries, each of these Empires, has been shaped by religion and the beliefs of the men fighting in their armies reflect the control religion has over them. Why else do Christian priests bless the troops before battle and our mullahs and imams do likewise? God is always on our side, they say, but isn't the god of the Christians the same as the one of Muslims? Why should he care who wins?"

His statements troubled me. "I cannot believe you're saying this, Mustapha. We know why God wants Muslims to win. It's so the True Word can be spread across every nation on earth."

"And then what?"

"What do you mean?"

"When the entire world is Muslim, when all men bend their knee in submission to Allah?"

"Then there'll be no more war, or poverty, or sin. All men will live in accordance with God's Word, in peace."

"Like Shi'a and Sunni, you mean? Or Syrians and Egyptians? Or Iraqis and Kurds? Why can't even two Muslims get along?"

I stared at my friend unhappily. "Why do you say these things, Mustapha? What has happened to you? You used to be devout."

"My eyes were opened, Direnc."

I suppose I should have asked him how his eyes were opened, but the look on his face scared me a little. It was the look a man might have when he teeters on the lip of a high cliff, knowing he must certainly fall, but also knowing there is a slim chance of survival if only he could fall into the water and avoid the sharp rocks. I feared what he might say, so after a moment's hesitation I upbraided him for casting the faith of his fathers aside so casually and I took my leave. I looked back and saw a wistful expression on his face as if he wanted to impart some great revelation, but I hurried on before he could call me back.

I avoided my friend for a time, as much as any sergeant can avoid his officer. I tried to make sure there was always someone else present or else be too busy with military matters to spend time alone with him. I am ashamed I forsook my friend at a time when he surely needed my help, but I was afraid.

News came of a British and French threat to the Canakkale Bogazi, the waterway that lies at the heart of our country's aspirations in the Mediterranean and Black Seas. Our company of the Second Battalion, Twenty-Seventh Regiment, Ninth Division, was sent to the Gelibolu Peninsula on the chance that they might land troops there. Intelligence indicated they might land them at the tip, so the men were glad we were placed in reserve in the dry hills near the headland of Ari Burnu.

Well, the world knows what happened next, so I will not repeat it. Suffice it to say, it was a long and bloody campaign with many men dying on either side. The Australians and New Zealanders were brave fighters, but they could not prevail against the righteous fury and bravery of the warriors of Islam.

Mustapha changed further. He was not so much brave as foolhardy, taking risks with his own life and those of his men. He became apostate, refusing to pray for himself; though he let his men do so. For that I am grateful to him as so many of our comrades needed the solace of prayer as the days went by. Then came that day at the end of summer when our colonel, Mustafa Kemal, led that wild charge across Canak Bayiri and drove the Anzacs from the summit. That charge was effectively the end of the enemy's campaign on Gelibolu. The war there dragged on another few months and many still died, but never again was our land in danger from that particular foe.

I wish Mustapha could have been there to taste victory, but as our charge drove the enemy off the summit, he stopped and just stared as the New Zealanders fired back. He cried out, asking Allah what had happened to him, and I believe in that instant he realised he had strayed from the path of righteousness. His question to God was a plea for forgiveness, and he died with the name of God on his lips.

"Blessed is the man who dies uttering the name of Allah, for he shall see Paradise."

Chapter Twenty-Four

I was right that war was coming to the West. I normally reside in lands where the Arabs hold sway, but there is no law concerning that. After Spain, if you remember, I spent a couple of hundred years drifting back through Christian Europe, sampling the horrors of medieval society. So too, this time, I came to Europe in the throes of the Napoleonic wars and followed the armies. Death was plentiful and I fed well, but I was also curious about modern surgery. It was as if I had stepped back in time. Muslim surgeons were far in advance of the West, though to be fair, the infidel doctors were catching up. Interestingly, the hey-day of Islamic inquiry had been hundreds of years ago; but as religion got its grips on men's minds, they ceased to look outward, being more concerned with god's Paradise. Christian nations were otherwise. Initially they were fixated on the Kingdom of Heaven, which, as I understand it, is like the Muslim Paradise but without trees and fountains, wine and delectable virgins. No wonder western minds turned from heaven in an attempt to better life on earth.

Muslim surgeons have had antisepsis and anaesthesia, brain surgery, dentistry and dietary remedies for a thousand years, but they have advanced little in that time. The Faithful are not allowed access to cadavers and cannot learn afresh what the insides of a man looks like. Christians have no such religious laws, and the battlefields provide a rich source of research material. They were slow to catch up, but catch up they have, and now I see them performing surgeries that would be the envy of al-Zahrawi, Ibn al-Quffi, al-Baladi, Ibn Khatima and even the wonderful Ibn Sina.

After Napoleon was finally defeated at Quatre Bras, I drifted, sampling rebellions and revolts, even sinking so low as to frequent civil executions. Greece and Serbia broke away from the Ottoman Empire – I was there. Poland, France and Germany suffered revolutions – I urged them on. The potato famine struck Ireland, and I even tried to foment strife between the peasants and the landlords, but I suppose they did not have the strength for violence. I cared a little for women and children dying of hunger but there was little I could do to ameliorate their plight, so I moved on.

The Crimean War involved me for a time when Great Britain, France and the Ottoman Empire fought against Russia. I have said it before, I am sure, but it is a constant source of amazement that countries can be at each other's throats one minute and the best of friends the next or vice versa. Perhaps I can see it more clearly because my point of view encompasses millennia. Prussians fight Austrians, and the French fight the Prussians; Russians fight the Ottomans, and the United Kingdom invades Egypt. All produced death in abundance and provided me with entertainment, but again I was assailed by thoughts that there must be some purpose in life, even for one such as me.

I went eastward once more, seeking out the uncomplicated, single-minded Muslim mind, and I came to the Ottoman Empire as it spiraled down into decadence and dissolution. The government had one last chance at greatness, and they took it, joining the European War on the side of newly founded Germany. That was a mistake, but who could have predicted it in 1914?

I found Mustapha Celik at the training barracks and invaded him, insinuating my cold flame along his nerves and sinews, his brain and bowels. I have grown adept at this over the ages, and if I do not wish a man to know I am present, you may be sure he remains ignorant of the fact. If he had been other than a simple farm lad, others might have noticed the change that came over him. However, he was far from his family, and his friend, Direnc Kaya, had not yet joined him, so none remarked on his sudden intelligence, his quick wit or rapidly developing secularism. I helped him become an officer, and when his division was sent against the Anzac forces, I made sure he survived. He was shot in the arm early on, and the path of the bullet would have shattered his upper arm and perhaps have carried on to do damage in his chest. I do resent it when someone tries to kill my host before I have finished with him, so I deflected the bullet from the bone and turned it aside so it missed his chest. The doctor spotted the marvel of the bullet's course, but his mind was wedded to science rather than miracles, so he did not make the connection.

I find I get bored more easily these days. I suppose it might be because I have done it all before. Hardly had I healed Mustapha when I was thinking of moving on. I contemplated taking over his friend, Kaya, but he is, if anything, more boring. I have had my fill of religious bigots who cannot see beyond the Qur'an. I thought about the commanding colonel, Mustafa Kemal. His mind was interesting, and I could see in him a real love of his country, not as the Ottoman Empire but as plain Turkiye. He wanted to turn Turkiye into a modern, democratic, secular, civilised country, far removed from the superstitious theocracies so beloved of Muslims. I wished him well, but I did not have the patience to see him through to his goal.

In the end, I stayed with my lieutenant a little longer, goading him into taking risks, playing with him and enjoying the heady taste of fear coursing along his nerves. Then, in mid-charge I abandoned him, leaving him none the wiser as to my presence. He stood, exposed and vulnerable on that ridge with bullets flying past him, and I picked up his last thought, heard his last words.

"What in Allah's name has happened to me?"

A poignant cry, for he really had no idea what had brought him to that place. The next moment, he was dead at his sergeant's feet and something extraordinary happened to me. I felt genuine regret.

I know what you are thinking – I am a djinni, a demon, I am incapable of kindness, of love, of good deeds. All that is true, yet I felt real regret that I had brought this man to his death. If I could have re-entered his body, re-energised his brain and mended his shattered heart, I would have. I could have created a travesty of life, a walking corpse, but Mustapha would not have been there. His fragile flame had already disappeared, and there was no bringing it back. I wept in silence, an invisible blue flame hovering over a bloodstained ridge in Gelibolu.

I could not bring him back, and he was unaware of my grief, so what could I do? Nothing. I left the land that would become Turkiye under Kemal and drifted east again, losing myself in the solitude of the desert for many years. I thought about whom I was and whether I should continue to be who I am. I do not know if djinn can kill themselves or even whether that was what I wanted, but for sixty years the world did not suffer from my presence.

I came back to the world of men at last, as I always do, but I thought this time I would try to do some good. If I could not save betrayed Mustapha, maybe I could save another. I thought it worth trying, if for no other reason than to see if it could be done.

Chapter Twenty-Five

The Rashidian household was a devout one but also a prosperous one. Muhammad Rashidian was a manager at a small bank in Tehran and as such enjoyed some status within society and a salary that enabled him to own a comfortable apartment in the city. His wife, Mobina, was university trained, though since the arrival of the children she had stayed at home to care for them. When the youngest daughter, Masouda, turned eighteen and enrolled at the university, Mobina had returned to the workforce, taking a job in a histology laboratory. It was not that they needed the money, but rather she wished to be a productive member of Iranian society. On her second day of work, hurrying to catch a bus, she was knocked down and killed by a car, which afterward sped away into the traffic.

After the funeral, Fatima Rashidian, the eldest daughter, took charge of the family, though she was neither male nor the eldest member. Her father did not object, and though her younger brother, Ibrahim, might have, Fatima quelled him with a look. Her eyes were reddened from weeping but her voice was firm.

"There's no reason things cannot continue as before. Mama would have wanted it so. Papa, you have your job that's paid the bills and will continue to do so. Masouda, you have your university studies, and Ibrahim, you must finish your schooling." Fatima looked around at her family members with what she imagined to be a stern but loving look. "I'll take over Mama's role. I'll adjust my own university hours, so I can be home a little after Ibrahim returns. I'll cook the evening meal, and when Masouda comes home, we'll do the cleaning together."

"Why don't we just hire a servant to do these things?" Masouda asked. "I'll be too tired to clean after a day's study, and besides, I'm going to be a dentist and dentists shouldn't have to clean houses."

"That means I shouldn't have to either," Fatima said. "Obviously, Papa cannot do it, or Ibrahim, and we cannot afford to pay anyone else, so we'll just have to."

"What do you say, Papa?" Ibrahim asked. "You're the man. Your word is law here." He looked sulkily at his sisters. "When I'm a man, I won't allow any woman to make decisions for me."

Muhammad sighed, his eyes vacant as if fixed on something not seen by anyone else. "What Fatima says makes sense. Let it be so." He got up and walked to the door. "I'm going to bed. I don't want to be disturbed."

The arrangement worked, and as the months went by, life returned to a semblance of normality in the Rashidian household. Muhammad's bank did well, and he earned a raise. He used part of this added income to hire a young girl from the poorer quarter to come in every afternoon to cook the evening meal and clean the apartment before they got home. As far as father and son were concerned, the girl was just hired help, no more deserving of thanks than a piece of furniture; but to Fatima and Masouda, she was a person with a fascinating background.

"What's your name?" Fatima asked. "And where do you live?"

The girl bobbed her head. "Maryam Bayat, Lady, from Shahr-e-Sang."

"That's miles away," Masouda exclaimed. "How do you get here?"

"On the bus, Lady."

By degrees, they found out that Maryam left home not long after daybreak, caught buses into the city centre where she worked in a laundry for half the day before coming on to the Rashidian household. She got home after dark each day. Fatima and Masouda were shocked that somebody worked so hard for so little return and implored their father to increase Maryam's wage.

"No," Muhammad said with finality. "The working class are bred to such labours. If I paid her more, she'd despise us."

Fatima and Masouda bowed to their father's will but made sure she left each week with a small gift of flour or butter or sugar. "We wish we could do more, but we've no money beyond what father gives us for the housekeeping," Fatima explained.

"You're very generous," Maryam said, kissing Fatima's hand. "I thank you, and my sister thanks you."

"You have a sister?"

"Zahra. She's twelve."

"And parents?"

"A father. Our mother died twelve years ago."

Fatima and Masouda caught the bus themselves every weekday, but theirs was a more pleasant trip to the Pardis campus of the University on Enqelab

Avenue in central Tehran. There, they attended lectures and practical classes on dentistry and others on various sciences, ethics, languages and Islamic studies. Their days were full, and though they took separate classes, Fatima being a year ahead of her sister, they met up for midday prayers and lunch in the company of other students in the shade of leafy trees where they discussed the world and how they were going to change it.

"America's the place to be," Hussain, a physics major affirmed. "They have the best universities, the best research laboratories and the best funding."

"You don't want to remain in Iran?" Narges asked. Her speciality was chemistry. "There are some good laboratories here, better every year …"

"You don't want to leave because Behrouz is staying," Masouda taunted. "His father will take him into the oil business."

Narges blushed. "So? I like him. What's wrong with that?"

"Nothing really," Amir said slowly, "But his father's very pally with the government and …" He looked around to make sure no one was listening to their talk. He saw a man lounging against a tree fifty yards away and speculated that he was SAVAK, the State Secret Police. Playing it safe, he leaned toward the others and lowered his voice. "The government isn't going to last much longer. I hear Khomeini will return."

Hussain laughed derisively. "Little chance of that. He's in exile in France."

"And he's coming back to set up an Islamic republic."

"The Shah won't let him do that, will he?" Masouda asked. "I don't think the Shah's very religious."

"Keep your voice down," Amir hissed. "You don't know who's listening." He glanced toward the tree, but the man had disappeared. He relaxed slightly and turned back to the others. "The people want Khomeini back and the Shah out. We … they've had enough of these crimes against the people. It's time for a return to solid Qur'anic values."

"Of course, we need the Qur'an," Fatima said, "But we're a modern country. The Shah has given us – especially women – a lot. I'd hate to see those advantages disappear."

"No need to worry," Amir assured her. "Khomeini knows everyone, women included, want him back. He won't take away women's rights."

"But an Islamic Republic will mean a return to full Shari'a Law, won't it?"

"You worry too much. The Imam will do what he must for the good of all, not just a minority as the Shah did."

"Imam?" Narges queried. "You call Khomeini an Imam?"

"Why not? He's Ayatollah already and our foremost Islamic scholar. As leader of the religious revolution, he deserves the title of Imam. Others are already referring to him that way."

The students were called back to lectures, but they met with friends every day, sometimes to discuss politics, sometimes the courses they were taking and other times just chatted idly about books, movies and music. Masouda tried talking to Maryam about these things as she cleaned the apartment.

“What books do you read, Maryam?”

The girl bent over her polishing and did not look up. “I can’t read, Lady.”

“What? Not at all? Well … er, what about movies?”

“Don’t have the money for things like that, Lady.”

“If I gave you the money for a movie, would you go?”

“Oh, I couldn’t, Lady. My father would beat me if I spent money on such things.”

On another occasion, she asked, “What do you think of the Ayatollah Khomeini, Maryam?”

“Oh, he’s very holy, Lady. My father says he’ll lead Iran back to Islam.”

“We’re already Islamic,” Masouda said sharply.

“Yes, Lady, of course, Lady. I’m sorry.”

The weather worsened as 1978 drew to a close with temperatures plummeting and snow and ice making the roads impassable. On several days, Maryam could not make it in to work, but the buses to the university were also not running, so Fatima and Masouda remained at home, studying and doing the household chores. Then the weather improved slightly, and the sisters headed back to lectures. At lunchtimem, the rumours flew.

“The Shah and Empress have fled the country.”

“They’ve gone into exile.”

“They’re dead, shot by order of Khomeini.”

The university authorities made a careful statement the next day, being careful to appear neutral, but confirming that the Shah had indeed gone into exile and the Ayatollah Khomeini would be returning soon. They advised students to go home and await further developments.

The city streets were already in turmoil when Fatima and Masouda boarded their bus. Crowds surged and the sisters saw with alarm that many men were armed. Shots rang out, followed by a stunned silence and then huge outcries. People ran back and forth, and whenever a westerner was spotted, the people would start shouting, "Death to America." Fatima pointed out the young men with rifles that dogged the footsteps of bearded mullahs. They wore green armbands and excitement seemed their most dominant emotion.

"I expect the Communists will be out in force too," Fatima commented quietly, so as not to be overheard by the other passengers.

"How can you know that, sister?"

"Amir told me. I think he belongs to Tudeh, the Communist Society of Iran. That means there's bound to be fighting. We'd best get home quickly."

That was not easy. When they got to the city centre to change buses, they found that services had been suspended indefinitely. No taxis were running, so Fatima and Masouda set off on foot. The streets were crowded, and there was an air of tension and subdued violence. A brawl started as they passed a group of men, with wild shouts and blows being exchanged, the violence leaping outward from its centre. Fatima hurried her sister away, taking to the back streets which were less busy. They passed a mosque, and as they did so, a young man carrying an assault rifle and wearing a green armband blocked their way. He looked them up and down and sneered, calling to his friends.

"Look what I've found. Two western whores."

"How dare you say such things?" Fatima snapped. "Apologise at once or …"

"Or what, whore? What sort of sluts are you, wearing such clothing?"

Fatima and Masouda looked at each other. Both were dressed in a similar manner with a knee-length woollen dress over slacks and a short winter coat. Scarves protected their necks from the cold, and a beret perched atop their lustrous black hair. Neither wore more than a touch of makeup – lipstick and eyeliner – and Masouda wore plain paste earings.

"What do you mean?" Fatima asked. "We aren't wearing anything …"

"You may as well not be. It's disgusting, showing off your legs in those trousers and flaunting your hair."

The other youths were pressing closer, lust in their eyes, and several guns pointed at them. She recognised the danger and decided now was not the time to argue. "P … perhaps you're right, Agha, but we wear only what the university permits …"

"You're students? What are you studying there at your rich man's university?"

"Dentistry."

"You want to be rich western dentists and rob the faithful."

“No, no, that isn’t so. We’re not rich, and we want to help people.”

“You would help Iran more by getting married and staying at home to raise children. Are you married? How old are you?”

“We’re not married, Agha. I’m only nineteen, and my sister’s eighteen.”

“Disgusting. You should be long married by now.”

“What are we going to do with them, Reza?” asked one of the other youths. He stared at Masouda and licked his lips.

“I think we must teach them that if they dress like whores, they must expect to be treated like them.” They shouldered their rifles and moved closer.

“Hold right there, Reza. You too, Abbas ... Hafiz.”

The youths stopped instantly and turned as a man in full black robes and turban walked out of the mosque. He stroked his beard as he crossed the street toward the sisters.

“What are your names?”

“Fatima and Masouda Rashidian.”

“Rashidian? You’re related to Muhammad Rashidian, the banker?”

Fatima nodded. “Our father.”

“I’m mullah Hussaini Nuri. I know of your father, and knowing his fondness for western ideas, it doesn’t surprise me he lets his daughters go out half-naked. Hasn’t he instructed you in the Word of God?”

"Yes, he has, mullah Nuri, and in the laws of Iran. We're quite properly dressed."

"Silence, woman! The laws of the cursed Shah no longer rule us. Soon, Imam Khomeini will return and bring back Islamic law."

"Under Islamic law …"

"You dare to tell me about Islamic law?" Nuri screamed. "Have you no shame? Must I give you a lesson in how a modest woman behaves?"

The sense of violence and hatred abruptly increased, and Fatima bit back her words. "N … no, mullah. Of course, you're correct. It's only the momentous events of today that made me forget myself. I … I apologise. Of course, the Shah is gone, and of course, Khomeini will …"

"Imam Khomeini."

"Yes, yes, of course, Imam Khomeini. He'll return and bring Iran back to the proper ways." She gripped Masouda's arm warningly.

"That's better," Nuri said, slightly mollified. "Very well, you'll return home immediately, and you won't venture out unless you're properly clad, covering your hair, and in the company of a male relative. If you don't, I'll have my men administer a proper lesson." He stood aside and waved them on. "Go, and think about what the Word of God means to you."

The young men stood aside reluctantly, jostling them as they edged past, but they did not follow or call out suggestively. The sisters hurried away and quickly turned a corner to be out of sight. Masouda shuddered.

"What horrible men. Should we go to the police?"

Fatima shook her head. "It wouldn't do any good."

"The old ways aren't really going to come back, are they? Women have fought to get the vote, to dress as we want, to go out alone, to … to marry who we want, not arranged marriage, or …"

"No, of course not, but while things are disturbed, violent ignorant men will cause trouble. We must just be circumspect."

University lectures started again after a few days, but two weeks after the departure of the Shah, Ayatollah Khomeini flew in on an Air France jet to Tehran airport. Millions turned out to greet him, waving, cheering and praising God. Women came in great numbers from all walks of life, for women had always supported Khomeini and knew that despite what the radical mullahs said, women would retain their god-given freedoms.

Muhammad Rashidian was increasingly nervous but blustered to bolster his spirit. "I've always supported Khomeini," he declared to his family. "Everyone knows this, and bankers will be just as important under the new government of Bakhtiar or even Bazargan as they were under the Shah. You'll see." His children smiled encouragingly, but did not see that there might be any problem. They knew very little about their father's work.

The weather improved slightly but was still cold. The students at the university gathered in the lee of the university buildings in small groups to discuss the political situation. Fatima and Masouda dressed much as they had before, but carried wide scarves now. If they were forced onto the streets again, they would take the precaution of covering their hair.

"It's not so very different," Narges said. "The Shah may have gone, but Prime Minister Bakhtiar continues in his absence."

"Nonsense," Amir declared. "Bakhtiar's days are numbered. Khomeini's Prime Minister Bazargan will take over, and we'll have stable, just rule under the Ayatollah. Better days are coming."

"Be careful what you say," Hussain warned. "Bakhtiar's still in control and that means the SAVAK could be listening."

Amir snorted. "Their days are numbered too. I'm not afraid." Nevertheless, he lowered his voice and glanced around. "I tell you, Khomeini and Bazargan will take power soon, ushering in a glorious period of Iran's history. Together with our friend and ally, the Soviet Union, Iran will cast of the shackles of the privileged and become a paradise for all workers."

"But Communism is godless," Masouda protested. "How can Soviet Russia be an ally of Khomeini?"

"Marxism isn't incompatible with Islam. You'll see. Very soon now, Khomeini will topple Bakhtiar's government, and then we Marxist's will rule with Khomeini as the religious figurehead for the masses."

"What about the mullahs and the Green Bands?" Fatima asked. "You must have seen them.

They're armed and dangerous. Are they just going to meekly step aside?"

"We control the Green Bands," Amir said. "The mullahs just think they do. When the time comes, they'll be the temporary police."

"In the meantime, they harass innocent women," Fatima said. She had told them what had happened to her and Masouda.

"More than just harass," Narges said. "I heard of women beaten because of the way they dressed, and even one raped. Also, they rob and kill any they suspect of being supporters of the Shah."

"Well, I'm sorry if women were attacked, but they possibly brought it on themselves if they dressed immodestly. You know the Qur'an says they should cover up. As for the Shah supporters …" Amir shrugged. "They're just getting a taste of what the rest of us have had to endure all these years."

"Yes, I've noticed you suffering," Hussain murmured. Amir glowered but said nothing.

"And that's nonsense about women bringing those attacks on themselves," Fatima added. "Do Masouda and I dress immodestly or provocatively? Does any woman at the university, for that matter? The Qur'an tells women to dress modestly, not cover themselves from head to toe. Yet you'd have us all in chadors or worse. At least the shah's regime freed women from that slavery."

"I'm not saying I condone attacks," Amir replied. "But think about where this behaviour leads. In the West, women flaunt their bodies, wearing bikinis and such. No wonder rape's so common there. Do you want Iran to become like the West?"

"No, of course not, but shouldn't men take some responsibility for crimes against women? Are men so weak-willed that the sight of a woman's leg or even just her hair or a bit of lipstick will cause them to lose all control?"

"Bravo!" Narges exclaimed, clapping her hands. "Answer that, Amir."

"I don't have to answer it. You're being ridiculous. You pretend to be Muslim, but in reality you're nothing but pawns of America. The revolution is here, and Iran will become an Islamic Republic allied to Soviet Russia, and then you'll find that all your antisocial ideas and behaviours are stamped out." Amir spat at their feet and stalked away.

"I had no idea he was so … so hate-filled," Masouda murmured.

"Marxist," Hussain said.

"Forget him," Fatima cautioned. "He's a minority. Khomeini will see that reason prevails. He won't alienate half the population because of an outdated interpretation of the Qur'an."

Three days later, the Rashidians woke to the sounds of shooting in the streets. They stayed home, glued to the radio, seeking explanations for the events taking place within their city and country. Khomeini had declared that Prime Minister Bazargan was doing God's Will and anyone who opposed him, opposed God and was a blasphemer. Within hours, the military might that backed the Bakhtiar government started to crumble, and fighting broke out in the streets. Within two days it was all over. The military withdrew from the conflict to prevent further bloodshed and disturbances, and the armed revolutionaries took over the government. The level of violence in the streets of the capital dropped, but Maryam took to coming to work in a chador.

"It's worse where we live, Lady. Green Bands stop every bus and threaten any woman who isn't properly covered up."

"It's monstrous," Fatima told her, "But go along with it for now. Khomeini will realise that extremists are doing this, and he'll stop them. We must just give him time. After all, he must be terribly busy."

The Family Protection Law was declared un-Islamic, and all the hard-fought rights of women were under threat. Female government workers were required to observe Islamic dress codes; women were barred from becoming judges. Beaches and sports were segregated on the basis of gender. The marriage age for girls, which had stood at eighteen, was dropped to thirteen. Divorce, once the right of any man or woman, was made the sole preserve of men again. None of these changes directly affected Fatima and Masouda, but they were uneasy at the thought that other more sweeping changes might follow. Then something happened that shook the foundation of their faith.

Maryam turned up to work one day with another girl, also chadored. "This is my sister, Zahra," she explained. "Lady, I didn't know where to turn. My sister, she … she needs to see a doctor, and I thought … well, I thought as you're training to be doctors …"

"We're training to be dentists, not doctors …"

Ibrahim had been in his bedroom but came out at the sound of voices and looked curiously at the two girls. "What are they doing here?"

"That's none of your business, Ibrahim. Please leave us."

"You can't order me around," he said sulkily. "I'm a man."

"You're a boy," Fatima snapped. "Now leave us, this is women's business."

He slouched off and went back into his bedroom.

Fatima turned back to Maryam. "As I said, we're training to be dentists, not doctors. What's the matter with you Zahra?"

The girl wept beneath her chador and veil. "Please, Lady, I'm bleeding … down there."

Masouda looked puzzled, but Fatima frowned. "Show me," she commanded.

Amid a lot of weeping and cajoling, they removed Zahra's chador and sat her down in Fatima's bedroom so she could lift her skirts.

"You've been raped," Fatima said flatly. "Have you been to the police?"

Zahra shook her head. "It wasn't rape."

"Don't try and tell me you consented to this. You're far too young to be having … having sexual relations. And the man who did this wasn't gentle. Who did this to you?"

"Her … her husband," Maryam whispered.

"Husband? You're married? How can you be married? You're only … what? Twelve? Thirteen?"

"Thirteen last month, Lady. Zahra isn't married now but she was yesterday."

"You're talking in riddles. How can she be married yesterday and divorced today? She's too young for either."

"Not divorced, Lady. When they changed the law, allowing young girls to marry at thirteen, our father advertised us. I'm not pretty and have been avoided, but Zahra is a flower and attracted immediate attention. A man came to my father and offered a hundred rials for mut'ah with Zahra."

"What's mut'ah?" Masouda asked.

Fatima paled. "I cannot believe it. Did Zahra give her consent?"

"She's underage," Maryam said bitterly. "Father makes the decision, but she's the one who must go through with it, and it hurts her."

"But what's mut'ah?" Masouda asked again.

"The full term is Nikah al-Mut'ah in Arabic, sister. It means marriage for pleasure; though in most cases, it's only for the man's pleasure. In Zahra's case, it means that a man can enter into a mut'ah marriage with her for a time as short as an hour and walk away when he's taken his pleasure. He pays a small dowry to the woman or in this case to her father."

Masouda gasped and blushed, looking from her sister to Zahra and back again. "That's … that's disgusting. You mean that sort of thing is allowed?"

"Depends who you listen to. Sunnis say not, but we're in Shi'ite Iran, so maybe. The Shah outlawed it, but I think Khomeini has just reintroduced it."

Masouda burst into tears. Fatima told her curtly to dry her eyes and get some bandages and antiseptic ointment. She cleaned away the blood and instructed Zahra to rub in some ointment. "She should really see a proper doctor, but this'll help in the meantime."

Masouda sniffed. "Can't she go to the hospital? She could say she was raped."

"She was. And no, she couldn't. If Iran is back under Sharia Law, a complaint of rape is tantamount to admitting to fornication." Fatima shook her head. "Is there anywhere you can take her where she'll be safe?"

Maryam thought for a few minutes. "Nowhere in Tehran that my father doesn't know. There is perhaps … yes, our mother's sister has married again and lives in Qum. If I could get her there, I think she'd hide us. But it's many miles, too far to walk, and I've no money."

"You must take the bus," Fatima said. "We've a little money saved."

Maryam protested she could not take the money, while Fatima insisted she did. After a short time, Maryam allowed herself to be persuaded.

"You should go immediately," said Fatima. "I'd walk you down to the bus station, but I have to prepare father's dinner. If he doesn't find it ready, he'll ask questions."

"I can take them," Masouda said. "I know the way."

"Then take Ibrahim with you. Nobody will look at you twice if a male accompanies you." However, Ibrahim was not in his room or in the apartment. "How like a brother. A nuisance when you don't want him and absent when you do. Masouda, you'll have to make dinner, and I'll take them."

Masouda laughed. "Papa will be even more suspicious if I make it. We'll be alright, there's no need to worry."

Fatima nodded. "I'm sure you will. Just keep to the main streets and keep covered." She hugged Maryam and then Zahra. "God be with you," she murmured.

"May the blessings of God be upon you," Maryam replied.

The three young women left the apartment, suitably covered, and Fatima busied herself preparing the evening meal. She found if she kept herself busy she did not think so much about what could go wrong or what might happen if Zahra's father discovered her. *Under Khomeini's new laws, he has the right to force her home and into renewed mut'ah, but that cannot be God's will. I cannot believe that.*

Time passed, and Masouda slipped quietly into the apartment, her fingers to her lips as Ibrahim entered on her heels and their father a few minutes later.

"Where were you?" Ibrahim asked. "And where are those girls?" Masouda shrugged and ignored her brother.

"What girls are those?" Muhammad asked.

"Maryam and her sister," Fatima replied. "She had a family crisis and couldn't come into work today, but she thoughtfully came to tell us so." *God forgive me my lies, though they aren't really lies; there was a crisis and she did come to tell us.*

Their father grunted and sniffed the aromas issuing from the kitchen. "Who did the cooking?"

"I did, father. Chicken horisht with polo, your favourite."

"You're a good girl." He gave Fatima an absent-minded hug. "You too, Masouda. And my pride and joy." He embraced his son, who smirked at his older sisters.

Over dinner, Muhammad Rashidian discussed the events of the last few days with his children, giving them instruction. "Ibrahim, you're nearly sixteen, you have charge of the house when I'm absent. Remember your sisters are unmarried and vulnerable. As things stand, they can probably still continue to go to their studies as long as they travel together, but if one needs to go out alone, you must accompany her. So, Fatima and Masouda, your brother is a man and not to be ordered around. Give him warning when you need to go out and ask him politely." He smiled reminiscently. "He's no longer your troublesome little brother."

"No," Masouda murmured to her sister. "Now he's our troublesome big brother." Ibrahim scowled but said nothing.

"Now," their father went on, "The Revolution has changed things. Fatima, on the weekend, take your sister – Ibrahim will accompany you – and buy some chadors. They'd better be plain black, at least until …"

"I'm sorry, father, but I'm not wearing a chador," Fatima said firmly. "They're a symbol of the oppression of women and unIslamic."

Muhammad stared, and then he frowned. "You'll wear one if I say so, by God. Do you think I tell you this lightly?"

"No, father, and I'm sorry if I oppose you on this, but Khomeini has called for modest dress and the hijab in the workplace. That means essentially what we wear already, but with a headscarf to cover our hair. I'm a good Muslim woman, Father, and I'll obey the Word of God and the legitimate pronouncements of the Islamic government, but not chador. The Qur'an calls for modesty only."

"I see. And you, Masouda? Will you obey me?"

Masouda hung her head. "No, Papa. I'm sorry, but not a chador."

"Order them, Papa," Ibrahim said eagerly. "They cannot disobey you then."

"Be quiet, Ibrahim, or go to your room. I won't order you to obey, girls, but I'm very disappointed in you both. Don't come crying to me if you're accosted in the streets." Muhammad pushed his plate away, his polo and horisht barely tasted. "I think I'll go out for a walk. I need some fresh air."

The sisters cleared away the dinner, while Ibrahim listened to the radio, tuning in to a succession of mullahs exhorting the populace to embrace the new Islamic state and to report any infringements of the law code.

“You hear that? You’ll soon be wearing chadors whether you like it or not.”

They returned to university and their studies, but travel became more difficult. The buses still ran but seldom on time as roving gangs of Green bands, with or without an accompanying mullah, threw up roadblocks and officiously examined everyone’s identification papers and harassed any woman who did not meet their rigid standards. Several women were hauled off and thrown into vans to be taken for questioning because their hijab was less than perfect. Others wore makeup and one mullah lost his temper with a pretty young woman. He screamed at her, spittle flying, then took a scrap of sandpaper from his pocket and proceeded to scrub the offending pigments from her face, throwing her crying and bleeding into the street.

The first time the Green Bands had picked on a woman, Fatima had stood up to protest, but they turned on her savagely and punched her until she collapsed sobbing into her seat. Not a single man intervened or even looked at the bullying, though several women fought back tears of sympathy. Any overt expression invited retaliation, so women quickly learned to look inward and ignore what was going on around them.

“It’s hopeless,” Masouda said to their friends at the university. “Iran is sliding back into the Middle Ages, and there’s nothing we can do about it.”

“I disagree,” Narges said. “I don’t think Khomeini knows what’s going on. He knows we women supported him all along, and he wouldn’t allow this oppression if he knew of it. We must tell him."

"How?" Fatima asked. "We can't just go and see him."

"We march. Tomorrow is International Women's Day, and women throughout Tehran and other towns are going to march and petition Prime Minister Bazargan to hear our pleas. He's Khomeini's minister, and when he sees how unpopular these things are – the hijab and the changes to Family Protection – he'll surely ask Khomeini to undo them."

"It could work," Fatima said cautiously, "But only if enough women march together. Bazargan won't listen if there are only a few hundred of us."

"There'll be thousands, millions maybe," Narges said. "Will you join us?"

Fatima smiled. "Just try and keep us away."

Fatima and Masouda left early the next day for the university, sneaking out even before their father left for work. Early as they were, meetings were already in progress is several of the rooms and lecture halls. They drifted from one to another for an hour, listening to snatches of speeches, to women complaining of oppression, and to men – Marxists mostly – pledging support. There seemed no central guiding body, with each meeting deciding for itself what to do, so Fatima had to make a decision.

"This one. They're going to march to Bazargan's office."

The women poured out into the university concourse and thence into the streets, completely blocking it and rendering impotent passing motorists. All they could do was rage and honk their car horns, yelling abuse. The women stated to chant, "Liberty, Equality, Freedom. Join with us to demand the rights that every woman has."

Fatima and Masouda linked arms with other well-dressed women and walked abreast, calling out to gathering bystanders to support their cause. Many people carried placards they must have made up before coming to the meetings. Fatima could see one just in front of them that read, 'Liberty and equality are our rights.' A little way back was another that read, 'Freedom does not need rules and regulations,' and further away were others, but their messages were indecipherable at that distance. Fatima was sure they were equally uplifting and logical.

"How can we fail?" she asked Masouda. "Bazargan must see we're sincere."

Not everyone was smiling now. Crowds were gathering, and the things they shouted were not supportive. A man ran out, his face suffused with rage, and spat at a marcher and punched at another. A man in the march grappled with him, and they fell to the ground, the press of bodies carrying them away. The calls became louder, more vindictive.

"Whores! Apostates! You'll burn in hell forever."

"Death to those that oppose the Imam."

A woman nearby tried to reason with the bystanders. "We don't oppose Ayatollah Khomeini, only the bad advice given him …" She was shouted down, and she rejoined the march, no longer smiling.

"Whores! Iran will be governed by the Qur'an and the Sharia. A woman's place is in the home. It's your God-ordained duty to bear children and serve your husbands."

The numbers of marchers was still swelling as women came out of office buildings. Many wore the hijab and several wore chadors, some of them stripping them off to reveal modest pant-suits and jackets. All around them, women were well-dressed and modestly garbed by any reasonable standard, but growls of rage rose from the ranks of watchers.

"Look at the whores flaunting their bodies." A man lifted his thobe and waved his penis at the marchers. "If this is what you're after, come and get it, whores." A roar of rage and lust arose from the men near him, and suddenly many men were doing the same, advancing into the stream of marchers, one or two of the younger men even masturbating in front of the women.

Masouda covered her face and hurried past, while other women just stared straight ahead, continuing to chant their slogans. "The chador is a symbol of oppression. Hijab is another. Women unite to keep your freedom."

A mullah started yelling, and the Green Bands fired their rifles in the air before shouting at the marching women. "The proper dress for a woman is the hijab, chador is better. God requires them to cover their hair and arms and legs and cleft – the parts that entice a man to sin. Cover up, you shameless whores!"

Thousands of women crowded the streets despite the efforts of the mullahs and their zealot agitators to disrupt the march. Now less well-off women flocked to swell the ranks, clad in skirts or jeans, boots, ragged dresses.

"Women, unite, don't be forced into chador …"

"Cover up, whores!"

"The mullahs say we must wear chador, that we can't be judges, that we shouldn't be educated. But for three generations we've been educated, unveiled and now we can even vote. Why must we give these freedoms up? Some of us are better educated than men, know Qur'anic law better than men – why can't they be judges?"

"Sacrilege!

The marchers neared Bazargan's office, and the women slowed, pushing bystanders aside. Their leaders continued to harangue them, leading other women in chants, laughing and talking. Fatima hugged the woman next to her, a stranger before today. "How can we fail?" she asked.

Men's shouting overwhelmed the chanting, and Green Bands swarmed out of the side streets, firing their rifles into the air and charging the women. Many were knocked to the ground and assaulted by the angry men. The comments from the bystanders increased in volume and hate.

"Look at that one there. I swear you can see her buttocks in those pants. Curse her for tempting me."

"They're harlots. No decent woman reveals her body thus.'

"Then if they're whores, let's deal with them properly."

"No woman reveals herself except to inflame a man. They're whores, deserving of death."

The marchers chanted outside the Prime Minister's office for an hour, but nobody came out to talk to them. In the face of increasing pressure from militants, they started to disperse. The smaller groups were harassed, and an organised paramilitary group calling itself Hezbollah, or the Party of God, actively started to attack the demonstrators.

Fatima and Masouda found themselves in a group of about a hundred mostly working class women herded south by Green Bands, away from the main body of demonstrators who were drifting back toward the university.

Fatima started to worry. "We should try and escape. I don't like this situation."

"How?" asked Masouda. She cringed as a young man charged in, scattering the women and knocking one to the ground. At once, other Green Bands started kicking her as she lay there screaming. After a few minutes, the screams died away and a volley of rifle fire drove the other women onward.

"The next time," Fatima muttered. It came, and as another woman was shoved to the ground, she grabbed Masouda's arm and dragged her into an alley. "Quickly. Run." They had gone no more than thirty paces when they heard a shout and saw half a dozen Green Bands charge in pursuit, followed by a mullah. They were caught very quickly.

The mullah stared at them and at their clothing, lingering over the parts of their anatomy that were visible beneath their clothing. "So you seek to escape the righteous condemnation of the people? You'll be questioned to determine the depths of your depravity. Take them to the Badrah Prison and lock them up."

The Green Bands hauled them away and together with about twenty other women from the small group, were loaded into a truck and driven to the Badrah Prison. There, they were hustled down steps to the underground cells and thrown into them, three to a cell. Fatima clung tightly to her sister and managed to share the same cell with her.

"Wh … what's going to happen to us?" Masouda quavered. She gripped Fatima's arm and looked around the dimly lit stone cell. A stench arose from a bucket in one corner, but apart from that, the tiny room was unfurnished. Light came from a single bulb high above them. There were no windows. Cold gripped them as if the room was a refrigerator.

"What's your name?" Fatima asked the other woman in the cell.

The woman looked at the sisters with a panicked expression. She was dressed in jacket and jeans with her hair unencumbered by any covering. "I … I'm Mazieh. I've got to get home or … or my husband will …" She put her face in her hands and sobbed. "I didn't mean for it to come to this. I'm pregnant, and I'm … I'm afraid."

Fatima introduced her sister and herself.

"What will they do to us?"

"That is with God," Fatima said. "There's nothing we can do, so I suggest we sit down and try to get some rest." She sat down and leaned back against the cold stone wall, putting her arm about

Masouda. Mazieh sat opposite but did not look at them, instead hugging her knees, her head bent.

An hour later, the cell door was flung open and an armed Green Band strode in. "Which one of you is Mazieh Rajavi? On your feet, whore, the judge wants to see you." He hauled the woman to her feet and pushed her out into the corridor, ignoring her tears. The door slammed shut again.

"She'll be alright," Fatima reassured her sister. "They aren't such monsters as would hurt a pregnant woman."

Mazieh was returned to the cell not long after, unconscious. She had been beaten and her clothes ripped. When the door closed, Fatima and Masouda tidied her up as best they could and made her as comfortable as possible.

Fatima raised one of the woman's eyelids and looked at the pupil. "She needs a doctor," she muttered. She went to the door and hammered on it for several minutes before a belligerent voice told her to shut up.

"The woman in here needs medical attention," she called.

"So? What's that to me?"

"She may die."

"As God wants."

Mazieh did not die, but neither did she recover, being still unconscious when the Green Bands came for the sisters. Fatima tried again to have a doctor called for the injured woman, but she was ignored and hustled down the corridor to an interrogation room.

A table occupied the middle of the room with two chairs on the near side, facing it. A table lamp with a bright bulb shone towards them, throwing the far side of the table and room into shadow. Dimly seen, the mullah who had arrested them sat facing them, flanked by two of the Green Bands. Other armed men stood in the room, cradling their weapons.

"Sit," the mullah said. He waited until both women had seated themselves and adjusted the light so it shone brightly into their faces. "What are your names?" Fatima told him and one of the men at the table scribbled down her answers.

"Why are we here?" Fatima asked.

"Silence! You'll answer all questions put to you, completely and truthfully. If you lie, you'll be punished. Do you understand?"

Fatima nodded, and Masouda whispered an affirmative.

"You're accused of apostasy. How do you plead?"

"Apostasy? No! How can you say that? How ..."

"Silence!" the mullah snapped again. "Answer the question. How do you plead?

"We're innocent."

"You lie." The mullah looked past them and nodded. A Green Band stepped forward and slammed the butt of his rifle into Fatima's shoulder. She cried out and fell sideways off the chair. A man helped her back up, roughly, and the mullah stared at her.

"The Holy Qur'an states that a woman should be modest and cover every part of herself except her face and her hands. Yet you sit here wearing trousers that show off your nakedness and flaunt your hair with the intention of inflaming the desires of any man who sees you. A person who deliberately disobeys and rejects the Word of God is apostate. The sentence for apostasy is death. How do you plead?"

"N … not guilty." Fatima screamed as the rifle butt descended again, and this time Masouda was also beaten until both women writhed on the floor.

"We'll try again," the mullah said calmly. "How do you plead?"

"Before God, we aren't guilty of apostasy, but …" She cringed as the Green Band moved forward again.

The mullah raised his hand, stopping the man. "Go on."

"It … it may be that we have … have erred in our understanding of the Qur'an, Excellency. We aren't trained in its study."

"No, you aren't. Do you accept my authority in religious matters?"

Fatima nodded, and Masouda followed suit.

"Then you're guilty. Do you repent of your behaviour and ask forgiveness of God?"

"Yes," Fatima whispered.

"How will you show your repentance?"

"How…?"

"Yes. Is your avowed repentance just another lie, or do you plan to show people you now support

Islam fully?" the mullah asked patiently. "If so, how do you plan to show it?"

"We … we'll wear hijab …"

"Good." The mullah nodded. "But chador would be better. What else?"

"I don't understand, Excellency. If we're covered, what else is there?"

"Your behaviour. You're women, and God has laid out for you your duty. It's to marry and have children, staying in the home to serve your husbands. Secular learning is unnecessary for a true Muslim, and universities are instruments of Satan. You should stay away from them."

Fatima felt hollow inside as her future threatened to drain away. "God gave me a mind …"

"Yes, but He gave you a woman's mind, and you should fill it with things that pertain to women like children and serving your Master. Leave intellectual pursuits to men who are equipped for it. What's your answer?"

"If … if the Ayatollah commands it …"

"The Imam has already done so," thundered the mullah. He slammed one hand down on the table. "I'm tiring of your excuses, woman. Either agree to give up your studies and stay at home, meekly submissive like you should be, or I'll send you to God's Judgment right now. A bullet is worth less than my time."

Panic bubbled close to the surface as Fatima forced her lips to move. "I … I … I ag … agree, Excellency."

"And your sister?" The mullah turned his ophidian attention to the younger girl.

"Y … yes. Her too. She'll do as … as I say."

"God will hold you to your vow. Take them back to their cell."

As the Green Bands hauled them upright, Fatima found the courage to ask, "How long will we be here?"

"Until I decide you can leave." He waved them away.

The cell was empty when they returned to it. The Green Band jailer shrugged when Masouda timidly asked about Mazieh. "She died. God's will, eh?"

"She might have lived if you'd got her a doctor."

The man shrugged again. "As God wills." He closed the door behind him.

Fatima went straight to the noisome bucket in the corner and squatted, leaning back against the wall to control her shaking. Masouda did likewise after her and joined her sister, sitting against the wall and hugging her for warmth.

"I thought we were going to die," Masouda whispered. "You should have just agreed with him immediately."

"They sometimes stone people for apostasy," Fatima replied dully. Now that the danger had receded, she felt exhausted and dispirited. "I had to try and extricate us from that charge."

"Well, I'm just glad it's all over. Do you know what the time is? Do you think we'll be home in time to make dinner?"

"I don't know. If he's going to let us go, why are we back here?"

No daylight penetrated the underground cells and no sound came from the corridor outside, so there was no way to mark the passage of time. Fatima counted to a thousand, and then again before she dozed. Hunger and thirst assailed them, and the cold stone sapped their warmth even through their winter clothing. Abruptly, the electric light snapped off, plunging them into stygian blackness. Masouda screamed, her cries quickly dying into whimpers as she clung to her sister.

"It's alright. It must be night time."

Masouda nodded and snuggled against her sister, her breathing slowing gradually and becoming regular. Presently she slept, and her sister cradled her head, stroking her hair.

Fatima knew that the mullah was taunting them and probably had no intention of letting them go. *We're going to die, and for nothing, because none of our actions are against God or Islam.* She murmured the shahada, finding strength from her declaration of faith. Sometime in the endless night she slept.

The sisters awoke when the light came on again. They yawned and stretched, looking expectantly toward the door, wanting someone to come in and give them food and water. After a bit, when nothing happened, they got up and stretched, loosening their muscles and used the stinking bucket again. Fatima's shoulder ached from the blows she had received, but she doubted there was any lasting damage.

The door rattled and opened, and a Green Band beckoned them out. “Come. Mullah Ebrahimi will see you again.”

“We’re hungry. May we have food?”

The Green Band shrugged. “I have none. Come now.”

“Water, then,” Fatima pressed.

The man scowled and pointed to a bucket. “Hurry then. It’ll go ill with you if you keep the mullah waiting.”

They hurried to the bucket and scooped up handfuls of water, drinking thirstily and splashing it over their faces. The Green Band pushed them away, cursing, and ushered them along the corridor to the interrogation room again.

The room was as it had been the day before, but this time an overhead light revealed its starkness. The table had been pushed back and two girls stood toward the back, where shadows still ruled.

“You have sought forgiveness of God for your actions, Rashidian?”

“Yes, Excellency,” Fatima said meekly, her eyes properly downcast.

“You know these women?” The mullah gestured toward the girls. A man pushed them out into the light.”

Fatima shook her head and then stared. The women had been beaten quite badly, their faces swollen and cut. “No, Excellency, I …”

“Don’t lie. I know you know them.”

Fatima peered more closely. “Maryam? And … and Zahra? What has happened?”

"Good. Then for the record, Fatima Rashidian, do you identify these young women as Maryam Bayat and Zehra Bayat of Shahr-e-Sang?"

Fatima saw no point in denying it. "Yes."

"The day before yesterday you helped them evade the law and gave them money for the bus to Qum. Don't deny it for a loyal patriot revealed your crime."

"I … I gave them money for the bus, I admit, but not to evade the law. They've committed no crime."

"You're lying again. Must I administer another lesson?"

"No, Excellency, … but ... may I ask what crime they're accused of?"

"Not just accused. They've admitted it. The charge against the younger one is theft against her husband and apostasy; against the elder, incitement to rebellion and apostasy. You're now charged with aiding a fugitive in the commission of her crime. How do you plead?"

"I … I … before I plead, Excellency, may I know the reason for these charges? I'm unaware of any theft or … or apostasy they might have committed."

"At thirteen, the younger one is the property of the father, and he very rightly gave her in mut'ah to a friend. The mut'ah was paid for and contracted for a period of a day and a night but after a single day, she fled, thus robbing her husband of his conjugal rights and her father of his property. Her sister aided her in this theft, and you aided them both. By law you're equally guilty. Don't think to deny it, for your plotting was overheard, and your sister was followed as she aided the fugitives."

"Overheard? By whom … Ibrahim? No, I cannot believe it."

"Praise be to God that one of the Rashidian family remembers their duty. Do you deny your involvement?"

Fatima sighed, feeling beaten down by her brother's treachery. "No, Excellency, but surely mut'ah without the girl's consent is illegal? It's rape, surely?"

"Her father gave permission. It's permissible."

"She was hurt by the act and needed the attention of a doctor."

"As God wills, but it doesn't alter her crime – or yours."

"God's Law is not for women, it seems."

"You blaspheme, Fatima Rashidian," the mullah snarled. "God's Law applies to both men and women. Women's place, as laid out by His Word, is as mothers and servants to their husbands. A proper Muslim woman knows this, and any of you women who seek to act independently, to interpret the Qur'an for your own ungodly ends, are guilty of apostasy and blasphemy. The penalty for that is death!" His voice rose to a scream by the time he finished, his face suffused with indignation and fury.

Masouda burst into tears, and Fatima froze, fear gripping her heart. "Excellency, please, we've … we've all acted in ignorance. We're all good Muslims, seeking to do what's right. It … it appears we've been misled. Isn't God all-Merciful? Can't we ask forgiveness of God and turn our lives around?"

"I'm not sorry," Maryam broke in. "If the Word of God says my sister must suffer forced prostitution, then it's wrong. The Qur'an has been written and interpreted by men for the benefit of men, not women …"

"Silence!" Mullah Ebrahimi roared. "You're a blasphemer and an apostate. Death is your lot, and you'll burn in hell forever. Take her out and lock her up. I'll sentence her later." He waited until two Green Bands had dragged her out before facing Zahra. "And what of you, Zahra Bayat? Do you choose death too?"

The young girl shuddered. "Please, Excellency, spare my sister."

"It's too late for her, she's dead. You may yet live, but choose swiftly for I'm losing patience with you rebellious women."

"I … I'll obey, Excellency," Zahra whispered.

"Good." The mullah beckoned a Green Band. "Take her to the forecourt and administer eighty lashes, then hand her over to her husband." He smiled grimly. "He may want to administer further punishment himself, as is his right."

The door closed behind Zahra, and the mullah turned back to Fatima. "Those two are young and not well educated," he said dismissively. "For you, there's no excuse. At your age, you should be married with a household and husband of your own. The fact that you're still unmarried is a wilful act of disobedience to the will of God. You must be punished, as must your sister, for she's also culpable."

"Have mercy, Excellency, please," Fatima said. "I … I misled by sister. The blame is mine."

"My heart is glad that you accept the blame, woman, for it shows that you may yet be forgiven by God. I was minded to have you executed along with the older Bayat woman, but God is merciful. Your sentence is one hundred lashes; your sister's is eighty lashes. To be carried out immediately. Contemplate your errors as you're punished and pray for forgiveness. Go and lead sinless lives from now on."

The sisters were taken out to their punishment, and the sole remaining Green Band looked at the smiling mullah. "Shall I bring back the Bayat girl for sentencing?"

"No need. Have her shot at daybreak with the other traitors of the Revolution."

The Green Band nodded. "She's fortunate then, for as a virgin she'll go straight to Paradise."

"I hadn't thought of that. Have her … rendered ineligible for Paradise before she's executed."

"Raped?" the Green Band asked cautiously.

"I cannot imagine God wants an apostate like that in Paradise. See that God's will is done. She won't have an opportunity to complain in the morning."

"And Rashidian? The father?"

"Bring him in for questioning. If he's this lax with his daughters' moral upbringing, who knows what else he's guilty of. Usury, perhaps. He's a banker after all, and when did those God-cursed parasites refrain from profiting off the misery of the Faithful?"

***

I thank God that He has seen fit to make me a Green Band, a trusted Fedayan of Mullah Ebrahimi and an instrument of the Revolutionary Komiteh. I was not always so, but God read my heart and found it pure, raising me up in His service.

I am uneducated, barely able to read or write, but I have an excellent memory and was the first in my class at the madrasah to learn the whole of the Qur'an. As the mullah in my childhood village said, 'What need has a man of worldly knowledge if he knows and lives by the Word of God?' I have found those words to be true, and the zealous display of my faith has stood me in better stead than the learning of useless facts about a thousand other things. Other boys in my madrasah went on to become merchants and traders, doctors and bankers, but I learned the use of arms. At the age of ten, I killed my first man.

There was a cadre of Iranian Freedom Fighters in a nearby town, and the mullah reported my abilities and devotion to their commander. I was summoned, and as a ten-year-old, I sat opposite him and his lieutenants, answering questions about the Qur'an and my commitment to Shari'a Law. He was pleased with my answers and my strict interpretation of Islamic Law, for under the rule of the Shah and the Western Satans – America and Britain – our beloved country had slid into decadence.

"You've answered well, Ali," said the commander. "But tell me, what is Shari'a Law?"

"It's the law in the Qur'an and the things the Imams said since."

"Does Shari'a Law take precedence over the law of Iran as set out by the Shah and the law courts?"

I had to think for a moment what precedence meant. "Yes."

"What's the penalty for theft, in the law courts?"

I frowned, for this was not something I knew about. I thought about what I had heard and hazarded a guess. "Prison?"

"And under Shari'a Law?"

"The hand is cut off."

"Which law is more just?"

I grinned as the question struck me as funny. "Shari'a Law, for the man won't do it again."

The commander joined me in a wintry smile. "And what is apostasy, Ali?"

"That's if you is a Muslim and you denies God."

"And the penalty?"

"Death."

"Do you want to join us, Ali?"

"Yes."

"Would you obey my orders, no matter what they were?"

"Yes."

"What if I told you to kill a man?"

I barely hesitated. "I'd do it."

The commander took me at my word. An instructor showed me how to fire a low calibre weapon and trained me in its use until I could hit a target at twenty paces nine times out of ten.

"To be sure of killing a man, you must be close, Ali, so close you can feel his heat, smell his fear and taste his blood when it splashes you. Bare hands are best, or a knife, but until you become proficient with those methods, a gun will do. You could easily kill him from cover, young Ali, you have the skill, but this first time, I want you to walk up to him, press the gun in his belly and pull the trigger. Can you do it?"

"Yes," I said very confidently.

"If you don't kill him, he'll kill you. What do you think of that?"

I considered this possibility. "If I die doing God's work, I'll go to Paradise."

"You're ready."

I was taken to a nearby town, and the man marked for execution pointed out to me. "What is his crime," I asked.

"Does it matter?"

"No."

I walked up to the man as he stood outside the mosque and pressed the gun in his belly. He looked down at me, more surprised than afraid, until I pulled the trigger. His robes and his fat muffled the report, and the gun bucked in my hand, but I was used to that. I tucked it back into my tawb and walked away, leaving him screaming in agony in the street. No one tried to stop me, and soon I was just another urchin lost among the crowd that gathered. The man died a day later – Insha'Allah.

I have added another ten years to my age, and I have killed many more men and women, all enemies of God. I became a Fedayan, vowing to serve God, the Prophet, and my Commander. My days became filled with a holy purpose. I did not let it worry me that most of my companions were older and more experienced than me, but set out to show that my faith was greater, my zeal more ardent and my ability with weapons more skilful. Of course, there is an injunction in the Qur'an not to shed innocent blood, but equally obviously, the men and women I killed were not innocent. All were guilty of crimes against God, and their deaths were pleasing to God.

Then the glorious day came when the Satan-backed Shah fled the country, fearful of the righteous anger of the people. The militant mullahs arose and called for soldiers in the fight to bring Iran back to the True Faith, and the local Komiteh, through my Commander, assigned me to Mullah Ebrahimi's Guard. We wore green armbands inscribed with the Holy Truth *Allahu akbar – God is great*. I felt as if God's name was written on my heart also, and I knew I had been summoned to this great purpose for a reason. God Himself had called me, and I was to be instrumental in bringing about the Islamic Republic of Iran.

Imam Khomeini returned to Iran to take up the reins of the country, bringing it back to God. Supporters of the Shah, backed by America, plotted against the holy revolution, and the mullahs called the Green Bands into the streets to fight for God and

Khomeini.

It is a symptom of how lax the country had become under the Shah and his minions that so many supported Satan's Lie even in the face of of the Islamic Revolution. We were kept busy chastising the ungodly and punishing those who sought to circumvent God's Laws. With the mullahs to guide us, we could do no wrong and we swept through the streets of Tehran, leaving order and godliness in our wake. It was at this time that a minor miracle occurred. I have already said I am uneducated, knowing only God's Word, but He has blessed me nonetheless, for as I took up the sword in defence of Khomeini and the Islamic Revolution, I was filled with ecstacy. I saw how an Islamic Iran fits into history, and suddenly my mind filled with words of which I scarcely knew the meaning; let alone how to use them in a sentence. Daring new thoughts occurred to me, and I saw visions inside my head of the march of God's purpose. I can only think these things happened to me because God has called me for a special purpose.

God guided my footsteps and kept me close to Mullah Ebrahimi on the day of the Women's March. The march is an example of what happens when men, or in this case women, become filled with pride. They believe their own thoughts and actions are worthy of consideration, instead of relying fully on God's Word. Any woman reading the Qur'an, or hearing a Friday sermon in the mosque or taking instruction from her father or husband, must know God's plan for her. It is to be quiet, chaste, modest, dutiful and industrious in the home, being at her husband's command in all things and producing and rearing children.

The women on the march, for all their talk of being good Muslims, had obviously lost sight of God and put more reliance on Western influences, as if Satan could promise them anything but hellfire for eternity. These misguided and in some cases evil women, instead of showing a wholesome modesty, flaunted their bodies, even their most private parts, knowing it would inflame the lusts of the watching men. I was happy to do the mullah's bidding and arrest some of these women.

Two of the women arrested were the sisters Fatima and Masouda Rashidian. I had never seen them before or even heard of them, yet something within me stirred when I saw them. It was not lust, for I was disgusted at their legs encased in tight trousers and the sight of their lustrous hair. Nor was it the presence of makeup, that paint that taunts men and drives them to impure thoughts. If it had been makeup, I might have followed the example of other Green Bands and removed the offending pigments with sandpaper or a razor. However, except for their trousered legs and hair, nothing made them stand out in my eyes, so I could not explain my interest in them. I locked them in a cell with another woman and went off duty.

I slept, and I dreamed of a woman. Not a lustful dream, you understand, but as if I was watching her from afar. I saw her come from Iraq and live in a series of small villages and towns. She was an extraordinary woman for she was a healer, a surgeon no less, yet also a dutiful and modest

Muslim woman. She married and had children, and they in turn had others through several generations. The meaning of the dream mystified me. Who was this woman, and why were her children important? Then God spoke to me in my dream, and I saw a pure blue flame. 'This is Nadira,' God said to me. 'Her descendants are Fatima and Masouda. Don't let harm come to them.'

I woke in a sweat, my mind whirling, and I wondered what to do. Should I go to the mullah and tell him of God's message to me, or act without telling him? Mullah Ebrahimi is a holy man, without a doubt, but we all have our failings. His is that he believes only his own motivation, being suspicious of anyone else's actions. Unless he is minded to release the Rashidian daughters, he will not follow my suggestion. Also, if I tell him it comes from God, he will think I am trying to weaken his position. I will have to look for a way to spare them without the mullah knowing.

I brought the sisters from their cell to the interrogation room and listened as the mullah put the fear of hellfire into them. He sentenced them to be lashed for their indiscretions, and I took them out to be punished. What to do? I could not imagine that letting them be lashed was not letting harm come to them, as God wished, but neither could I see a way to free them without the mullah hauling me before the local Komiteh and suffering their summary justice.

I took the sisters to the room where official beatings are carried out. The Instrument of God's Justice got up from his chair where he was idly picking his teeth and swaggered over, his eyes running up and down his new victims.

"How many?" he asked.

"This one twenty, the other ten."

"Twenty? Ten? That's hardly worth lifting my cane for."

I shrugged. "I don't sentence them; I only make sure the sentences are carried out. Get on with it."

"As God wants," the Instrument said. He forced Fatima to lie face down on a wooden bench and handcuffed her wrists to rings in the floor, then raised her coat above her trouser-covered buttocks. "Only twenty, you say?" He picked up a cane, no thicker than his finger, and flexed it. "Think on your sins, woman." He brought the cane down sharply with a loud thwack. Fatima jumped and gritted her teeth, holding back a cry of pain. The cane fell again and again, but Fatima had control now and shut her eyes, refusing to cry out.

The punishment finished, and Masouda took her place, shaking with fear. The ten blows fell swiftly, and though she was sobbing by the end of them, I knew there would be no lasting damage to their bodies. Whether their minds were damaged was another matter, but as God wants. I escorted them to the prison gates and past the guards. On the street, I gravely warned them to be more circumspect in their behaviour, and I might not be there to protect them another time.

"Why did you do it?" the elder daughter asked.

I shrugged, not wanting to tell them of my dream. That was God speaking to me, and I did not want to share the experience. Instead, I smiled and said, “As God wants.”

Chapter Twenty-Six

From Gelibolu to Tehran is fifteen hundred miles and sixty years, but I chose to travel slowly having no fixed destination in mind. I drifted down to Egypt and Arabia, Jerusalem and Damascus, visiting places I had been before and examining the changes that had taken place over the intervening centuries. Each place had changed enormously, but the people had not. They were just as venal and self-centred as before, but some, particularly the intellectuals, had a far wider knowledge even than the Arabic men of science. Another Great War swept over me, and in its aftermath, I saw conflict dig deep claws into Palestine. I remember when Jews once lived in a land they called Israel, and here they were again after wandering the world, claiming the right to live there as God-given. I also remember other gods and other peoples, and after so many conquests and slaughters, migrations and evictions, who can say they truly have an exclusive right to the land? Unfortunately, Jew and Palestinian both claim the same land, and I can see no peaceful solution.

The conflict in Israel promised to be long drawn out and bloody, but it did not hold my interest. After a war in which Israel demolished its neighbours in six days, I drifted north and east until I struck the two rivers and that crescent of fertile ground between them. From Baghdad, I travelled to the mountains and thence to the city of Sulaimanaya again and I remembered Nadira.

Nadira, if you remember, was that unusual woman with a remarkable surgical skill. I saved her life and pointed her toward Persia. I had always meant to find out what happened to her, but it was, of course, too late to find her a hundred and eighty years later. However, her descendants might be here if she remarried, and I might be able to find them.

I believe I have broken the bad news to you that the human spirit does not survive the death of the body. Well, let me be a little less categorical – I have seen no evidence of human survival. As far as I am concerned, the flame of a god and of a demon burns brightly and strong, though the flame of a demon can be snuffed out. I have seen it. Perhaps gods are mortal too, but I have no firsthand evidence. I have, however, been present at the deaths of countless humans, and though some flames burn brighter and stronger than others, they all gutter and fade away when the physical body dies.

I mention this not to upset you, but so you might understand my next revelation. The human flame dies and disappears, but there is a pattern of it in the human's fleshly descendants. The flame of a man and woman are … just so … how can I possibly describe what I see? Well, their son has an individual flame, but there are hints of the … pattern of his parents. His son has a unique flame also, but with a pattern that reflects both his parents. Even siblings may share characteristics of their parents' patterns, yet be unique.

What I am trying to say is if I was to happen upon a person who claimed to be a descendant of

Nadira, I could confirm it in an instant by looking for the trace of her unique pattern.

I followed her cold trail east into Persia, or Iran as they call it now, talking to people or delving into their minds, searching for some half-forgotten memory. I found it in a town called Marivan, just over the border, a tale of a female surgeon and her daughter, Estah, who moved on after a few years. Another trace at Sanandaj, then Hamadan and Borujerd, leading on to a woman called Mobina who married a man called Muhammad Rashidian and moved to Tehran.

Interestingly, every link in the chain was female, and they all had some connection to medicine, as if the calling was also passed down in the blood. Even Mobina was a medical technician. She and Rashidian had two daughters, Fatima and Masouda, who studied dentistry, and I was minded of that fine piece of dental surgery Nadira carried out on her bandit captor.

I followed the sisters, interested in their lives, and when they became involved in the protest marches, took over one of the Green Band fanatics, a killer by the name of Ali. The mullah Ebrahimi controlled the area of town where the Rashidian women lived, and I knew that sooner or later the sisters would be arrested. I wanted to be certain of being there. Having failed to follow up on Nadira, I now felt an urge to protect her descendants.

Ali the Green Band was no better or worse than many I have inhabited over the ages. Men will always find a reason to kill and justify that reason in the name of their God. Ali had been doing it since he was a child, and I doubted I could turn him from that course. Not that I wanted to, you understand. My only reason for being there within him was to protect Nadira's descendants.

The charges brought against the girls were the usual mish-mash of half-truth and self- interest. I suppose I could have gone into the mullah's mind and changed the charges or altered the sentences, but I am reluctant to enter the mind of a man well-versed in the Qur'an. Dealing with all those blind circuits and lack of reason makes me feel dirty somehow. I much prefer an obedient fanatic. Murder and cruelty are my stock-in-trade as a demon, and Ali was a fanatic. He knew the Qur'an moderately well for an uneducated man, but if there was ever a conflict between his conscience and the Word, he always took it to the mullah and followed his instruction. Ali was a simple man, and one with whom it was a pleasure to do business.

I escorted the girls to the punishment chamber and told the beater how many strokes to give them – twenty for the elder, ten for the younger. It was the best I could do for them. The punishment was impossibly light, but at least a beating was registered in the books. If I had let them go unscathed, questions would have been asked, and possibly they would have been punished again.

My purpose for being in Tehran was finished, so I left Ali considerably more educated than I found him – invading a mind is a two-way affair. I have access to all his thoughts, and he can access some of mine. If he has served me well, I am happy to leave him a little wiser. Also … there was something else … a pattern in his flame that puzzled me. It was faint, so very faint, but my memory eventually recalled its originator – one Firuz bin Jawid, a caravan master of ancient Persia. For the sake of a good man's memory, I left Ali intact.

I moved east again, seeking new sensations and interesting political situations. Afghanistan held me for a few years, when the Taliban fought against the Soviet invasion with the aid of American arms. I had some good times but moved on to Pakistan and thence to western India, where Muslims make up a large minority. I was in India once before, perhaps six hundred years ago, and I saw a demon, one of the raksha of India in the northern mountains. I was tempted to face him then to test his strength, but caution got the better of me. I am stronger now, far stronger and wiser, and it is in my mind to find this raksha and challenge him. I am in no doubt about the outcome of this challenge – it will mean death. One of us will die, and I cannot be sure it will be him.

So here I am at the possible endpoint of my aimless journey through life. I have been a demon, then a god and a demon once more. I have lived thousands of years, fed on multitudes of humans, entered many, observed hordes and taken the form of others, learning about men and women down the ages, particularly those followers of Allah. I have even posed as this god before he became strong, misleading many to their death. What does my long existence mean? Why am I here when so many of my flame brethren are not? Where do I go now, and what do I do? I have thought about this for a long time, and I think I know the answer.

I must draw this strong raksha to me, this one who calls himself Pandalis, and defeat him, cast him down into nothingness. If I can do this, then I will find my mission in life – to rid the world of demons and become the only one, rivalling the gods in their power. If I cannot overcome him, I will die and that too will be an agreeable outcome, for I am very tired of my mundane demon existence.

The only question is how to attract this strong raksha, but I think I know this answer also. He used to battle the Muslim invader of his country back then; I will provide him with another Muslim foe and draw him out to his death.

Chapter Twenty-Seven

Aali walked neither slowly nor quickly as he threaded the derelict streets of the Shastri Nagar district of Meerut. He was conscious of many eyes watching, not specifically for him, but for anything unusual, and he had no desire to attract attention. He was dressed in plain clothes, loose grubby trousers and kurta with a white taqiyah and sandals. Although a devout Muslim, his beard was short and untidy, displaying none of the discipline of the mind that peered out through dark, deep-set eyes. He moved through the narrow streets, unconsciously avoiding the filth that lay on the ground, his mind turning to his plan and what he would need to bring it to fruition. Time was of no great importance, but the act was. He refused to be hurried and accomplish nothing more than the handful of deaths in Delhi late last year.

The September bombings had spread a ripple of fear through Delhi, but they had quickly faded from the forefront of peoples' minds as the death toll had been light. The perpetrators had been amateurs, dressing in black, riding motor scooters and delivering small packages of low grade explosive. They had rapidly been caught and confessed. Aali vowed he would not make those mistakes – any mistakes. His bombers would not be caught, as he was preparing his men to blow themselves up along with their targets. Their acts of terror would stop the hearts of Hindus throughout northern India. What is more, Aali meant to survive and train another five bombers and repeat the carnage as many times as it took to achieve his end.

Aali stopped and leaned against a mudbrick wall, massaging the sudden stab of headache. He found he often got one when he his thoughts strayed toward his ultimate goal. *Forget it ... think of something else ... you have the men, what else do you need*? The headache faded, and Aali set out again. *Somewhere along here* ... He found the address he looked for, and after casting a quick look down the street in either direction, he knocked on the battered door. It creaked open after a few moments, and a Hindu woman in gaily coloured sari, gold nose ring and scarlet tilak on her forehead looked at him enquiringly.

"The advertisement in the paper … for the car?" Aali asked in Hindi.

The woman called back into the dim recesses of the hallway, and when a man came yawning from the shadows, she slipped out of sight. Aali repeated his request.

The man looked Aali up and down and then nodded. "Follow me." He closed the door and led Aali along the street a little further and down a side alley to a locked garage. He unlocked the padlock and lifted the creaking door. A rat scurried into the shadows but was ignored by both men. The car, a Maruti Suzuki Alto that had seen better days, glowered at the two men, sulkily sitting in its rust and dust.

"A fine vehicle," said the man. "Most reliable, most economical and very reasonably priced."

"Let me see the engine."

The man lifted the bonnet, and Aali could see that whatever the exterior looked like, the engine had been reasonably cared for. The man slipped into the front seat and after two false starts, turned the motor on. Aali listened and could hear a few noises that alerted him to potential problems. They were nothing a competent mechanic could not fix however, so he nodded, and the man turned the engine off.

Aali circled the car slowly, checking its rusted bodywork and the tread on the tyres. The spare was flat and bald, but the tyres on the car were no worse than marginal. "You have the papers?"

The man nodded. "Yes, all of them – registration, RTO tax receipt, insurance, no road tax though. I haven't used it this year. They're back at the house."

"And the asking price?"

"One hundred thousand rupees."

Aali sighed, hating the bargaining process but knowing he could not afford to stand out in the man's memory by not doing so. "It needs a lot of work. Forty thousand."

The man grinned and started extolling the virtues of his vehicle. "Ninety thousand."

"Fifty."

"Eighty."

"Seventy, but you throw in a tank of petrol."

"Cash?"

"Of course." Aali patted his pocket.

"It's a deal." The man took a can of petrol from the back of the garage and carefully filled the tank. "Shall we drive back to my house?"

The short drive back was relatively uneventful, though the man talked loudly and non-stop in an effort to drown out some of the strange noises issuing from the engine and exhaust. Aali paid the man and pocketed the papers before driving off.

His journey took him across the city to a slum area where the numbers of Muslims on the streets was a lot greater. He honked the horn at a wide wooden gate and waited. After a minute or two, a man peered out from a nearby window and nodded when he saw Aali. The gate opened, and he drove the car into a large courtyard where the dismembered remains of another four cars lay scattered over the baked and oil-soaked earth. Two men were bent over, looking into the engine of one of the cars, and he looked up as Aali drove in. He wiped his hands on a rag and walked over.

"Salaam, Aali." He looked past him at the Alto and grimaced. "Another wreck for me to fix up?"

"I have every confidence in you, Omar." Aali walked over to the man who had opened the gate and examined his face carefully. "May the peace of Allah be upon thee, Bahadur," he murmured.

"And on thee, Aali," Bahadur replied quietly. "That's the last of them? We strike soon?"

"As God wants, Bahadur. Are the others all here? I'll speak to you all at once, after midday prayers."

Bahadur led the way into the house adjoining the courtyard and down a long corridor, then up two flights of stairs to a well-appointed apartment at odds with the dilapidated house and the slum district it sat in. Another four men were in the room, sitting around and quietly talking. They all got to their feet and bowed deferentially as Aali entered.

Aali smiled and greeted each man in turn, exerting his charm so each man felt special. "Fadi, Ghalib, Hatim, Saif." He glanced at the wall clock. "Prepare to approach God in prayer," he instructed, and walked into the bathroom to cleanse himself, knowing the others would already have done so.

He walked back out into the living room of the apartment as the distant cry of the muezzin called the faithful to prayers. Six prayer mats had been set out diagonally, facing the position of Makkah, and Aali took his position, emptying his mind of everything but the contemplation of God. He led them into the ritual prayers, careful to perform it perfectly.

Afterward, they rolled up the prayer mats and stored them away in a cupboard before trooping into the kitchen where takeaway Chinese food was cooling. As they ate, Aali had each man go over his duties, paying especial attention to the tone of his voice, listening for any slight tremor or hesitation that might herald the onset of doubts.

"Bahadur, have you found all the fertilizer?"

"Yes, Aali. I have about a tonne of ammonium sulphate and sodium nitrate, stored separately."

"Fadi, you have the equipment needed?"

"Yes Aali. I've converted two of the basement rooms into laboratories. There are fans that vent the fumes via long pipes into the air high above the house."

Aali frowned. "Won't these pipes be seen and possibly be investigated?"

"They're disguised as television aerials. Further, I have glassware and plastic ware on hand, and I can get more at a moment's notice, if needed. A cylinder of gas and burners, also cooling coils, a deep freeze and a refrigerator."

"Ghalib, the detonators?"

"A little more difficult, Aali. I don't wish to attract attention, so I make discreet inquiries and buy singly at many different places. Many wealthy farmers have them to blow up tree stumps or large rocks. I have six blasting caps at present, but should have all ten in another week or two."

"Hatim, what are you gathering?"

"Hydrazine and aluminium powder, Aali. Hydrazine is difficult to obtain, but I have small amounts. Aluminium powder is easier, and I have several kilos."

"And Saif?"

Saif smiled. "Shrapnel. You asked me to get quarter inch ball bearings, but they are very expensive in the quantities we require, so I've come up with something a lot cheaper, easy to gather and is environmentally friendly."

Aali frowned again. Saif was the last member of his cell to join, and the only one with no criminal record. Furthermore, he had a sense of humour, which in his mind did not sit well with their purpose. "What do you mean – environmentally friendly?"

"Well, we seek to destroy the polytheists and infidels, but the earth is God's creation, so I could see nothing wrong in doing a little bit to clean up the city while fulfilling my duties."

"Explain yourself." The other men stared at Saif, sensing their leader's displeasure.

"We wanted about three hundred kilos of ball bearings, but the money you gave me was enough for only about fifty kilos, so I thought about what to do."

"You should have asked me for more," Aali commented.

"I considered it, but then I thought, maybe I can figure this out for myself. The ball bearings are to act as missiles, packed around the explosives to make them more deadly, but other things can do the same job, for instance, nails and glass."

"You should still have come to me."

Saif smiled. "Perhaps, but instead I employed a hundred boys to scour the rubbish dumps, the railway tracks, building sites, waste ground where buildings have been torn down, anywhere where there might be metal and glass. For a fraction of the cost, I have four hundred kilos of rusty nails, screws, bolts, nuts, shards of glass, metal turnings, old hypodermic needles, you name it. We have what we need, and the city is a little bit cleaner and a little bit safer for children – including Muslim children."

Hatim looked troubled. "Master, I thought we were attacking ungodly temples, those symbols of unbelief. Now Saif talks about killing masses of people with shrapnel. Doesn't the Qur'an say that killing an innocent person is an offence against God?"

Aali looked directly at Hatim until the man dropped his eyes. "The Qur'an says, 'The only proper recompense for those who fight against God and His Messenger and try to spread evil in the land is to be killed.' I ask you, who is it who fights against God and His Messenger?"

"The polytheists," Hatim said.

"Infidels," Ghalib added.

"The Word of God permits armed resistance when believers are under attack, or in freeing oppressed people," Aali went on. "Our people here in Meerut are oppressed, and how many times in the last twenty years have Hindu mobs killed our people, our women and children? Some people will ask whether a polytheist can be a decent man, and perhaps he can act decently to others of his faith, but the Qur'an tells us not to develop a waliy relationship with an unbeliever. Sooner or later, the unbeliever will turn on you and bring great harm to your loved ones. Better we strike first and safeguard them."

"We'd better hope there are no Christians among our intended victims," Saif commented. When he got blank looks from his listeners, he added, "You know, Christians, People of the Book."

"It's unlikely," Aali said stiffly. "That's why we're targeting Hindu temples. The polytheists are People of the Left Hand and are destined for hellfire. We're doing God's Work by helping them along to their fate." He looked around the faces, searching for doubt or wavering commitment. "If any man here isn't fully committed to military jihad, let him speak now. Anyone who wishes to depart may do so." Unobtrusively, Aali slipped his hand into his pocket and grasped his gun, slipping off the safety catch. *Nobody leaves alive unless they're committed.*

The men all looked at one another, but for a minute, nobody spoke. Then Saif cleared his throat. "We're all committed to God's Work, Aali. You're our leader, and we'll obey you without question, even to death." One by one, the others agreed, and Aali relaxed, slipping the safety back on his gun.

"Good. We've collected everything we need to make the explosives, and our mechanics are making sure the cars work reliably. I estimate that in another two weeks we'll be able to load up the cars and drive them to our targets."

"What are the targets?" Saif asked.

"You'll all be told when the time comes."

Aali separated the men into teams for the preparation of the explosives. First, he took Ghalib and Fadi into one basement room and instructed them in the use of the equipment and safety procedures. "You're preparing a chemical that's an essential component of an explosive, so handle it with care at all times. It won't explode by itself for it needs other chemicals, and even then it requires a detonator, but take precautions nonetheless. Methanol is poisonous and highly flammable, so keep the vent fans on and the windows open."

He demonstrated the technique, pouring water into a pan and adding ammonium sulphate and sodium nitrate, stirring them together. "The chemicals react to form sodium sulphate and ammonium nitrate, both of which are soluble. We must precipitate out the sodium sulphate, and we do this by packing dry ice around the pan. As the temperature of the mix drops, the sodium sulphate will crystallise out." He demonstrated, using ordinary ice. "Dry ice will be delivered this afternoon. Now, filter the liquid and discard the crystals. Lower the temperature further, and ammonium nitrate crystallises out. Save these crystals, and set them out to dry. I'll show you how to purify the crystals later." Aali left the two men to it.

Bahadur and Hatim were given another task. "When the ammonium nitrate has been prepared and purified, you'll stir it into the hydrazine until no more can be dissolved. I stress that this is a risky procedure; so much care must be taken. Anhydrous hydrazine is corrosive, flammable and poisonous. The reaction creates a foam of bubbles, so make sure the container is large enough." Aali demonstrated with a small amount of ammonium nitrate and hydrazine. "Thus. Ammonia is produced, so be careful to vent the room well. When no more ammonium nitrate will dissolve, pour the liquid carefully into bottles and refrigerate it."

"And what do you want me to do?" Saif asked.

"I want you to supervise and help both groups. First in the preparation and purification of the ammonium nitrate and then in the preparation of the explosive."

"And what will you do?" Saif asked with a grin.

Aali just looked at Saif for a few moments and then turned and left the room without saying anything. Saif shrugged and started examining the equipment in both rooms before hauling chemicals to the first preparation room. Aali returned when the dry ice arrived and showed them how to precipitate first the sodium sulphate and then the target chemical. The first batch of ammonium nitrate crystals was formed that afternoon.

After a few days, they settled into the rhythm of their work. The supplies of raw fertilisers decreased steadily, and plastic bottles of purified ammonium nitrate started to accumulate. As soon as these built up, they were taken to the hydrazine room and made up into the liquid explosive. Fine aluminium powder was added to the hydrazine to give it that extra bit of explosive power. Saif aided both groups, and Aali kept an eye on all aspects of production, making sure everything ran smoothly.

By the end of the first week, when the men had the production worked out well, Aali took Saif to inspect the five cars that had now been repaired and tuned. One by one, under the eyes of the mechanics, they tested each car and made sure it was running smoothly. They took them out for test drives, checking the suspension and brakes.

"Excellent work," Aali said at last. "I'll pay you the sum agreed upon and a ten percent bonus." He pulled a wad of cash from his pocket and counted a large sum of rupees.

The mechanic took the money and pocketed it, but his assistant looked thoughtful. "Why do you need these cars?" he asked. "It seems like a waste of money to do up old cars when for the same price you could've bought better ones."

Aali kept a pleasant expression on his face, but his hand slipped into the pocket that held a gun.

"That's my own business, but if you were concerned for my wealth, why didn't you raise this point earlier?"

The assistant looked down, embarrassed. "Then you wouldn't have given us the job."

The mechanic glared at his assistant. "Enough of this rudeness, Salah. Apologise to the gentleman at once."

Salah muttered an apology. Aali relaxed and said, "I will, however, satisfy your curiosity. I'm training up salesmen to travel around the countryside and sell clothing. I need reliable cars, so they can meet deadlines. If I bought newer cars, I still couldn't be certain they wouldn't break down. But this way, I have them checked over and repaired by a reputable mechanic. I think it's worth it."

When the mechanics had left, Saif asked a question. "Why did you tell that young man a story like that? No explanation was needed."

"True, but he may have gone away and thought about it some more. Maybe he would talk to others. This way his curiosity is satisfied."

"And afterward, when the bombs have gone off?"

"We move somewhere else and do it again with another house, another mechanic. This house will be destroyed, leaving no evidence."

However, the young man's curiosity was not satisfied, and the next day, he returned asking to talk to Aali. He was shown into a back room where Aali and Saif said they would talk to him. Salah entered and noted the presence of the two men and their unsmiling demeanour.

"Why have you returned?" Aali asked.

Salah licked his lips nervously. "I … I've thought about the reason you gave for the cars, and … and I don't believe you."

"So? Why should I care? It's my own business."

"I know one of the men who work for you – Hatim, though that's not his real name. He got out of prison last year. He assaulted a Hindu shopkeeper."

"The man tried to cheat him. I know all this, Salah, but I believe a man deserves another opportunity."

"And there's the ammonia stink, and … and I saw fertiliser being carried in by Bahadur."

"Which means what exactly?"

"You're making explosives." Salah saw Aali look meaningfully at Saif and suddenly realised his peril. "I want to help," he hurried on. "I think you're going to use the cars to blow up Hindus, and I want to help you."

Aali took his gun out and laid it on the table, pointing the barrel at the young man. "I think you're a police agent sent to investigate us."

Salah blanched. "No, Excellency, I'm not. Ask anyone, they'll tell you I took part in the riots last year. I'm faithful to Islam; I uphold every Pillar – well, except Hajj so far, because I cannot afford it. I want to kill Hindus, Excellency, but everyone's too scared – except you. You're planning something, and I want to be part of it."

Aali looked at Saif. "What do you think?"

"I don't think he has the wit to be a police agent, but we cannot allow him to walk out of here, thinking those things. He'll talk and ruin everything. Kill him."

Salah moaned with terror and dropped to his knees, his arms out in supplication. "Please, Excellencies, have mercy on one of the faithful. I won't breathe a word to anyone. I'll do whatever you ask."

Aali picked up the gun, slipped the safety off and cocked it.

"Of course," Saif murmured, "There's another option."

"What?"

"Let Salah prove himself. He can stay here tonight under guard, and tomorrow he can test one of the explosive systems."

"Test one of …? Yes, that needs to be done."

"Er, how are they tested, Excellencies?" Salah asked hopefully. "By fuse or timer? You … you aren't … suicide bombers?"

"No, Salah," Aali said with a wry smile. "We'll be using timers. You'll test one of those for us … unless you would prefer …?" He held up his gun and raised his eyebrows enquiringly.

"Oh, no, no, Excellency. I'm very happy to test the explosive for you to the greater glory of God."

The next morning, Aali and Saif carefully loaded a single one litre bottle of the finished hydrazine explosive into a padded wooden box in the boot of one of the cars and with Salah, drove for an hour until they reached a lonely stretch of open countryside.

"This will do," Aali said. He took the padded box and carried it a few hundred metres to an open patch of ground. Saif carried the detonator and timer, and Salah struggled under the weight of a car battery. Aali set the wooden box on the ground and unscrewed the lid, lowered the detonator into the liquid and securing the wires that led from it with a rubber bung firmly set in the bottle's neck. He attached these wires to the timer, a short metal cylinder wrapped in black tape.

"It looks amateurish," Aali said, "But I'm assured it'll work. It contains acid and a spring. A current of electricity will break a vial of acid which will slowly eat through a wire, releasing a spring which will make the connection with the detonator wires and … boom."

Salah licked his lips nervously. "How long?"

"The wires can be different thicknesses, depending on how long a delay you want. I've done a lot of testing before deciding on one to test with explosive. This timer should take five minutes, with an error of perhaps thirty seconds either way – plenty of time for you to get clear."

Salah swallowed. "Me?"

"Well, you did agree to test the explosive system," Saif reminded him. "Or have you changed your mind?"

"No, no, I'll do it. What must I do?"

"These wires here must be attached to the terminals of the car battery."

"Er, won't that, er, stand out when we do it for real. I mean, attaching wires to a battery …"

"In the real thing, the explosives will be in a car, the battery will be the car's battery and the wires will be merely a phone charger that's plugged in to the cigarette lighter. Nobody will even see it being done, let alone take any notice of it. Now, both of you walk back with me."

"Should I attach the wires?" Salah asked.

"Not yet."

Aali and his companions walked back to the car in silence. "Now, let's imagine that the bottle over there is the car, earlier parked near a Hindu temple. We're waiting for people to arrive … and now they have. The bomber will now walk calmly to the car, attach the wires, lock the car again and walk calmly away, not hurrying but not dawdling either. The bomber has five minutes to get clear. Do you understand, Salah?"

"Five minutes, you say?"

"Plus or minus thirty seconds. It took us only four minutes to walk back just now, so I want you to do exactly the same. Pretend these are city streets and you're the bomber."

Salah nodded, wiped his hands on his kurta, took a deep breath and set off for the target. Aali and Saif lounged against the car, watching him.

"I'm not sure he's going to be suitable," Saif murmured. "He seems very nervous and police will pick that up."

"Let's see how he does with this test. Sometimes a man settles down once he sees the reality of the situation."

Salah reached the explosives and waved at them. Then he squatted beside the battery and picked up the wires.

Saif glanced at his watch. "Shall I time how long ..."

The plain lit up as if a gigantic lightning flash had struck Salah. An instant later, the sound cracked across the intervening space, and the two men were buffeted by a shock wave. Tiny pebbles pinged against the metal of the car, and Saif clapped a hand to his cheek, too surprised to cry out. Dust enveloped the site where Salah had squatted a moment before.

"All in all, a very successful test," Aali murmured.

Saif stared at him and lowered the hand from his cheek. "You knew, didn't you? There was no timer." He glanced at his hand and saw there was blood on it.

"Of course, there wasn't. Salah was unreliable, a danger to our operation, however keen he said he was to kill Hindus. So I used him to test the explosives, which had to be done. I think it went well, don't you?"

The blast site was completely free of dust and gravel and any trace of vegetation. There was also no sign of Salah or the battery. Saif walked away from the site and after a hundred paces or so, found a fragment of the battery and a little further away, a smouldering piece of a sandal. He brought that small memento of Salah back to the car.

"What do you want with that?" Aali asked. "Do you regret his death?"

“No. He gave his life for a good cause. Perhaps God will allow him into Paradise.”

Aali laughed. “Believe that if you like. He was just another foot-soldier in the fight against the ungodly.”

“And I’m another?” Saif asked.

“You’re more than a foot-soldier.”

“But still expendable?” Saif persisted. “When we plug the cigarette lighters in, should we also expect an instantaneous reaction?”

“No. Salah’s death was necessary. I haven’t trained up my men to squander them in this first strike against the enemy.”

Saif grinned. “I think I’ll still utter God’s name as I plug the lighter in, so if anything … goes wrong … I’ll find myself in Paradise.”

“That’s a good rule for life, Saif. Keep God’s name forever on your lips, and He’ll remember you at the Judgment.”

They returned to Meerut and discussed their findings with the other men. Nobody was much concerned that the timer had not worked.

“As God wants,” Bahadur said. “I didn’t trust the man anyway.”

“Tomorrow we load the cars and you find out your targets.”

The inner door panels of the cars were easily removed, and the collected shrapnel from the city streets and wasteland was packed into the spaces encased in cloth bags. A five litre bottle of the hydrazine explosive was nestled among them and a detonator fitted, the wires running through a rubber bung, to one of Aali’s taped timers and thence to the plug that would be inserted into the car's cigarette lighter. The door panels were refitted, and the attaching screws glued in place. Each car held ten litres of the explosive and about eighty kilos of shrapnel. The six men stood and looked at the cars in silence, each man imagining the devastation and loss of life that would be caused when the cars blew up for God's greater glory.

"And now I'll tell you your targets," Aali said. He took them all back upstairs to the kitchen and spread out a map of Uttarakhand. Here are the target towns – Nainital, Rudraprayag, Karnaprayag, Mussoorie and Koti."

The five bombers stared at the map and their puzzlement grew. At last, Bahadur spoke for them all. "These targets don't make sense, Aali. They're all towns, rather than cities, and indeed, some of them are so small there can be nothing worthwhile in them."

"Do you question my judgment?"

"I'd be interested in knowing your reasons. We'll be risking our lives."

"In God's service, or do you question that too?"

"No," Hatim said. "We don't question your commitment, nor should you question ours, Aali. We've all made our peace with God and will do his work unflinchingly, even if it means our deaths for we'll find ourselves in Paradise."

Aali looked around at each of his men, and they looked back at him, all serious and fanatical except Saif, who wore his usual small smile below twinkling eyes. "I'll tell you, so you'll have no doubt that the choice of targets is a wise one." Aali tapped his finger on the map. "The Narad Temple in Rudraprayag – it's not the largest one or the most popular, but it serves my purpose most excellently. It's not in the main town but over the Alaknanda River on the spur of land where the Mandakini River joins it. Legend says the false god, Shiva, appeared to the sage Narad Muni on that spot, but there's also an ancient peepul tree that exists there. Both the temple and the tree have more significance in the eyes of Hindus than many other larger and more popular temples. A car can be parked close to the temple and the tree, and I'm sure that both will be destroyed. Bahadur, this is your target."

Aali looked at the map and tapped it again. "Karnaprayag – a little further up the Alaknanda River. Not in the town itself, but nearby across the river is a road that leads up into the hills. At the top of the ridge, among a stand of ancient Chir pines, stands an old cemetery and the hill shrine of Pihokri, dedicated to some hero or other. It's a tourist spot, but once more, its importance doesn't lie in the number of deaths caused or the amount of destruction – just that the shrine is demolished. Ghalib, this is your target."

Ghalib stirred uneasily. "Forgive me, Aali. I hear your command and obey, but it seems like a very small thing to risk my life over."

"When you return, I'll tell you exactly why it's important. Now, the next target's in Nainital, and once more the target's a shrine, this time dedicated to the Hindu gods of healing and of animals. Dhanvantari and Pashupati, I think. Yes, of itself it's not worth much, but its true value is limitless.

The shrine was once in the forest, but houses have spread up the hillsides and now many will die in the explosion. This target belongs to you, Saif.

"Mussoorie, or actually the town of Charangat that lies close to it. An easy target for you, Fadi. Drive into the Main Square and park near the temple of Vishnu. There's a sizeable Muslim population in Charangat, but don't let that worry you. They've developed friendships with the polytheists and must be reminded of the realities.

"And lastly, the town of Koti on the Koti River, a tributary of the Alaknanda. Again, it's a simple task, and Hatim will handle this one. In the town square is a temple to Shiva. You'll be able to park right outside it, and as a bonus, you'll find the community centre next door to it and a school a few doors down. There are no Muslims in Koti, but some years ago the inhabitants of the town made a decision that made things difficult for the faithful elsewhere. It's time to settle the score."

The men were silent for a time, each contemplating his own part in the upcoming strike against the infidel and each secretly appalled that the targets were such unimportant ones. They looked to Bahadur, who had been the first man recruited and was often in their leader's confidence, to say something, but he avoided their gaze and just stared at the map. In the end, it was Saif, the newest member, who spoke up.

"Don't take this amiss, Aali, but I say only what everyone's thinking. We've worked hard to strike a blow against the polytheists, yet on the eve of our success, you throw it away on blows that I'd expect of some uneducated fanatic, not someone who can manufacture and deliver powerful explosives. We have the fire power to demolish a hotel, to blow up a railway station, an army barracks or police station, yet you aim us at unimportant shrines and temples that no one has even heard of." He paused for a moment and then continued in a flat voice. "One might wonder if you're fully committed to the struggle."

Aali's colour rose as Saif spoke, and though he frowned and clenched his fists, he did not say anything until he had finished. "You want to withdraw from this enterprise?"

"No, I don't, nor, I believe, does anyone else. We just want to know where we stand."

Aali's hand strayed toward the pocket that held his gun, but he knew that killing Saif would not really solve anything. He turned away and stared out of the window at the ramshackle roofs and walls of Meerut's slums. "Won't you just obey?" he asked quietly.

"Yes, we'll obey," Saif replied, "But don't we have a right to know why our chance to strike a mighty blow for Islam is to be turned into a mere slap across the face of the infidel?"

Aali considered the demands and carefully weighed his options, debating whether to kill his team and start again with fresh men, perhaps younger and with more malleable minds. Regretfully, he decided the time lost would be more than he wished. *The truth then – or at least a measure of it.* He turned to face his men and put a solemn expression on his face.

"I belong to a secret Islamic organisation that was formed six hundred years ago shortly after the Moghul emperors first brought the Truth of God's Word to India. We spread Islam throughout northern India and up into the mountains now known as Uttarakhand. Here, our armies were driven back by a group of Hindu fighters who had taken a vow to stamp out Islam from all of India. They knew the truth of the Qur'an, but they fought against it, killing Muslims where they could, making life difficult for them where Islamic Law held sway or where Hindu Law gave them the advantage. Their original intent remains, however, and they won't rest until every single Muslim has been ejected from India."

"That's very interesting," Bahadur said cautiously, "but what has it to do with us?"

"Everything. The Islamic India Organisation was formed to counter this heathen group, and we've been moderately successful. We've maintained a Muslim presence in northern India."

"More than a presence," Saif said with a smile. "Muslims make up fifty per cent of Meerut and other cities similarly."

Aali fixed the smiling man with a sour stare. "On the other hand, Islam hasn't taken over all of India – yet. We have much yet to do, and this cell, my cell, was given a very important task. Unfortunately, it seems as if I'll have to report failure before we even try, if I cannot persuade you to perform this task."

"We didn't actually say we wouldn't do it," Hatim said. "We just wanted to know more."

“Yes,” Fadi agreed. “Like why those targets?”

“In the history of any organisation, particularly a religious one, there are holy places – places where God caused something to happen, where a miracle occurred or a great victory was won. In our own history, we acknowledge as meaningful the Kaaba, the Well of Zamzam, the site of the Battle of Badr. So too, we think, does this Hindu organisation hold certain places sacred – the shrines of Nainital and Pihokri, the temples of Vishnu, Shiva and Narad Muni. We believe that destroying these sites will demoralise the enemy, or at least draw it out into plain sight where we may destroy it.”

“What is it about those sites that make them so holy in the eyes of Hindus?” Saif asked. “Do you know?”

Aali shook his head. “All I know is that they mean something.” He looked at his team. “What’s your decision? Will you continue?”

The five men looked at each other and then nodded. “Yes, Aali,” Ghalib said.

“There was never any real doubt,” Hatim added.

Aali nodded curtly in return. “Good.” He opened a box and took out five mobile phones, sliding them across the table. “You’ll leave tomorrow for your destinations. Because it’ll take some of you longer to reach your target than others, detonation time is set for noon the day after tomorrow. You will, when you reach the town, scout out the position, looking for police or roadblocks and searching for the best place to park the car. You’ll call me on the mobile phone and tell me you're in position. I will acknowledge. On detonation day, at about half an hour before noon, you park your car in position and leave it unarmed. Walk about a hundred metres away and call me on the mobile phone. You'll say, 'Shall I deliver the goods?' and I'll answer yes, if everything looks good, or no, if I think we've been compromised. If I say yes, return to the car and plug in the system. You'll then have five minutes to get clear – about two hundred metres should be enough, but put some buildings between you and the blast site. Any questions?"

"The timers are set for five minutes, you say?" Fadi asked. "How accurate is that?"

"I've tested many wires of many thicknesses in the acid. There's a certain margin of error, but it's no more than thirty seconds each way." Aali spoke to Fadi but looked at Saif, wondering whether he would speak of the mechanic's assistant.

"And if it doesn't?" Saif asked softly.

"Then you'll die knowing you've waged war on God's enemies and your reward will be Paradise." Aali looked around the circle of men again. "It won't come to that however, for I value your skill and training too much to have made a mistake with the timers."

They were up before dawn, preparing themselves carefully for prayers and then assembled in the courtyard by the cars. Aali handed out the keys to each of them, and the men stood by their vehicles as Aali offered up a special prayer for their success.

As it finished, Saif walked over to Bahadur and took his keys, tossing his own to the man. "I'd rather drive a Hyundai than a Maruti Suzuki. You don't mind, do you, Bahadur?" Saif watched Aali's face as he spoke. *So you haven't singled me out. Does that mean all five cars are without timers or were you telling the truth*?

Bahadur shrugged. "I don't mind what I drive." He walked over to the car Aali had assigned to Saif.

Aali said nothing, nor attempted to interfere, and the men got into their vehicles and started up. One by one they drove out into the streets and followed a circuitous route out of Meerut. Saif guided his Hyundai onto Highway 119 to Najibabad. He had the most roundabout route, and in view of the explosives on board, Aali had ordered them to use the main highways and drive slowly, avoiding potholes and unpaved surfaces where possible. From Najibabad, Saif would run southeast along the line of the foothills on Highway 74 until he reached Udham Singh Nagar before turning north on Highway 87 to Nainital.

The other vehicles headed north on Highway 58 to Rishikesh, where Fadi turned off on Highway 72 to Dehradun and Mussoorie and thence to Charangat. The others continued on up the Alaknanda River Valley to Rudraprayag for Bahadur, Karnaprayag and the Pihokri shrine for Ghalib and lastly the town of Koti in the Koti Valley for Hatim.

For Aali, the next day and a half was one of waiting for news. He stayed in the house, completing the wiring of several caches of explosives with real timers that could be detonated should anything go wrong. If his men were discovered or prevented from blowing up their cars, then Aali would vanish in what would look like a simple accident, and he would start again somewhere else with another team. There was no great hurry, sooner or later he would provoke a response from this Hindu Defence organisation and his Master would then destroy it.

Sunset approached, and just before the muezzins started their calls to prayer, Aali received the first phone call. It was from Bahadur in Rudraprayag and said simply that he had arrived and was in position. The others called a little after sunset, and Saif woke him in the early hours of the morning to report in, adding he had had a puncture, which delayed him. Aali could hear the laughter in Saif's voice, and he ground his teeth. *I made a mistake with that one. I'll be well rid of him tomorrow.* Aloud, he acknowledged the information and hung up.

The day dawned hot in Meerut, and Aali turned on the news broadcasts on radio and television, waiting for news from five of the holy places of Uttarakhand. He had researched the area thoroughly before he ever assembled his team, and he knew the sites well, far better than he had ever let on to his team. *They don't need to know everything*.

The peepul tree in Rudraprayag was more important than the Narad Muni temple there, but Bahadur might have balked at destroying a mere tree. A large charge of hydrazine would almost certainly flatten the temple and kill anyone within a hundred metre radius, but it would also strip the foliage from the holy tree and perhaps even kill it. He knew the tree was holy, because a Buddhist monk, Sonaka, had taught under its limbs, but exactly why this monk was more important than a thousand others Aali had not been able to find out. *If this works, maybe I'll find out*.

The Pihokri shrine was another mystery. It was near Karnaprayag on the Alaknanda River, but it was famous only for an ancient hero who had fought off a gang of robbers, killing them all. Aali failed to see the significance of this action, but it meant something to the force that guarded the northern mountains. *Ghalib's bomb will destroy the shrine in just a few hours, and then we'll see. If nothing else, these bombs will provoke them ... him*?

The towns of Koti and Charangat were ordinary and as far as Aali could make out, had no reason to be remembered by anyone. Charangat had had an incident in the troubled times of Independence, but so had hundreds of other towns and villages. Nobody had even died there. As for Koti, it was a tiny farming and forestry town that had been the scene of a logging death thirty or forty years before. *Why are these towns important*? Today bombs delivered by Fadi and Hatim would strike at their hearts, eviscerating the town centres and provoking a reaction. *Surely*?

And then there's Saif in Nainital. I've never trusted him, but it's too late to worry now. Aali looked at his watch – *just after eleven o'clock. If he betrays me, it's just one bomb. He cannot touch the others now, and at noon, he'll either plug the timer in and find he's run out of time, or he'll not, in which case I'll track him down and kill him with my own hands.* Aali had made five working timers, all set for an hour, and they were connected to the bombs that sat ready to demolish the building in which he sat. The others in the five cars were just hollow tubes through which wires ran directly to the detonators. The instant they were plugged in, the explosives would rip the heart out of the town and all trace of the men and their vehicles.

The minutes counted slowly down to noon. The telephone buzzed, and Ghalib was on the other end. "Shall I deliver the goods?"

"Yes." He rang off, and Aali imagined him walking toward the Pihokri shrine on the crest of the ridge, set about by ancient Chir pines and an even older hill cemetery. He would open the car door, reach in and push the plug into the cigarette lighter socket…

The phone buzzed again, and Fadi asked the question, receiving the same answer and then Bahadur and Hatim. *Ten minutes to go, where's Saif*? The telephone sat silently on the table, while the watch next to it slowly closed its hands on the twelve … and then past it. Aali imagined he could hear the distant roar of destruction and felt sure his scheme would work. This blow to the holy places of Uttarakhand must surely be sufficient provocation, even if there were only four blasts. *God burn Saif in hell for all eternity. Well, I'll find him and …* The phone buzzed.

"Hello, Aali."

"Saif! I knew you were a coward. You couldn't go through with it."

"If you mean I've no intention of bringing death and destruction on these people for your amusement, you're right. I won't let you."

Aali swore for a moment and then caught himself and laughed. "Four or five bombs – it's all the same to me. I'll find you, you know. No man can hide from me."

Now Saif laughed. "Turn on the news, Aali. None of your bombs went off."

"What do you mean?"

"I'll call you again in an hour or so. Listen to the news." Saif broke the connection.

There was a delay, but by midafternoon, the first brief reports were coming in on radio, and shortly after, the first pictures on television. Aali stared at images of the cars – his cars – surrounded by police and army bomb squads and even a glimpse of Bahadur and Ghalib in custody. He swore fluently and long and then leaned forward to hear what was being said.

"… reports are in from three and possibly four towns in Uttarakhand State that police and army bomb disposal groups have succeeded in disarming sophisticated car bombs. No one has yet claimed responsibility for this attempted act of terrorism, but two Muslim men have been detained by police, and a third one shot dead as he attempted to escape. A police spokesman said short time ago that the explosive power of the bombs was potentially 'catastrophic' and that tragedy on a massive scale has been averted. No one knows for certain how the terror plot was discovered, but it is rumoured that one of the bombers confessed to police an hour before the deadline …"

"You son of a whore, Saif," Aali swore. "I'll hunt you down and eat your liver for this betrayal." He switched off the television and radio and went down into the basement to check that his bombs had not been tampered with. As far as he could make out, they were still lethal, so he prepared everything and was on the point of connecting the timers when he recalled that Saif had said he would call again. *I should wait. What for? He's probably betrayed me too. Still, he might give me a clue as to his whereabouts. If the police come, I can short circuit the connections and send them all to hell.* Aali waited, and an hour later, the phone buzzed again.

"You've seen the news reports?"

"Yes, curse you."

Saif laughed. "Four bombs disabled, only the Nainital one is still intact. Do you want it?"

"What do you mean?"

"I want to talk to you face to face. Come up to Nainital, and maybe, just maybe, I'll let you have this one."

"Why would you do that?"

"As I said, I want to talk to you, discuss something with you. As an inducement, I'm offering the sole remaining bomb."

The opportunity to kill you is all the inducement I need. Aloud, Aali said, "You want me to come to Nainital? Why? So the police can trap me?"

"No trap, no police. Just a talk. If you agree, drive up to Nainital and come to the target shrine.

The bomb's no longer there, but when you arrive, I'll tell you where to go." Without waiting for a reply, Saif cut the connection.

Aali controlled his anger and sat in the upstairs room for a few minutes, deciding what he would do. *Of course, I go, but how? He's expecting me to arrive by road. Do I go another way and surprise him*? A cruel smile grew on the man's lips as he contemplated the nature of the surprise. *On the other hand, I do want him and the bomb. Perhaps if he sees me arrive as he wants, it'll put him off his guard. He only thinks he knows me …*

Abruptly, Aali screamed and collapsed into unconsciousness. The air in the room shimmered and coalesced into a simulacrum of Aali. Ignoring the man on the floor, he left the room and carefully set the timers on the explosives secreted throughout the building. The simulacrum returned to the upstairs room and contemplated the man who was just stirring into consciousness.

"You have my thanks, Abdullah Nasib," said the simulacrum. "I will take over the role of Aali for a short while now. You will stay here and continue to serve my purpose."

The new Aali took the keys to the sole remaining vehicle, one that had not been adapted to harbour a bomb and after setting the timed detonators in the basement, drove north toward Nainital. He drove through the night and arrived with the dawn. This time, however, he ignored prayers and drove slowly toward the shrine on the upper road near the water reservoir. Below him through the trees, he could see the sprawling town and the bright lake, and for a moment, his mind wandered from the business at hand and took in the beauty of the scene.

A man stood by the side of the road, and if it had not been for the presence of passers-by, Aali might have run him down, for it was Saif. Instead, he pulled over and let the man slide into the passenger seat. Aali turned to look at his enemy, wanting to kill him, but also wanting the car bomb. Even one major explosion could tempt his greater enemy out of hiding.

"Where is it?"

"What? Oh, the car? It's safe enough. I've even left the detonators in place and the fake timer connected. It can be set off at a moment's notice."

"Why did you turn traitor, Saif?"

"I choose to think of it as common humanity, Aali. You wanted to kill thousands of people. I couldn't just stand by and watch it happen."

"But they're the enemy of Islam, and we're at war with the infidel. Do you side with the polytheists?"

"If the polytheists display God's love and mercy, then yes."

"Then why are you offering me the last car bomb, if you feel such love for the men of these hills. Aren't you concerned I'll blow it up and kill them?"

"No, for I won't let you. I've stopped you so far and will continue to do so."

Aali laughed. "You've failed. A city block or more of Meerut lies in smoking ruins, for I set off timed bombs when I left."

Saif frowned. "Most of the people in that sector of the city were Muslims. You'd kill your own so easily?"

"My own? Do you take me for their god or their caliph that they should be my own? I care nothing for these people. I welcome their deaths, if it will further my desires."

"Then there too I've stopped you, for the contents of those bottles is water. I changed them that last night before I left. I've anticipated you at every step, Aali, or whatever your name is. Now there's just you to deal with."

Aali took out his gun and trained it on Saif. "Where's the car?"

Saif smiled. "About a mile away in a deserted part of the hills."

"Take me there."

"And if I don't?"

"I'll kill you."

"You'll try and kill me anyway."

"Deliver the car to me intact, and I'll let you live."

"Now why don't I believe that?" Saif raised a hand and shook his head wearily. "I'll take you there, but will you drive or shall we walk?"

Aali glanced out at the road and noted there were few people around and most of them were heading down into the town. "We walk. Out of the car, slowly, and keep your hands where I can see them." He slid out his own side quickly and joined Saif. He patted him down quickly, but he carried nothing in his pockets except a set of keys for the Hyundai.

Saif walked in front, his hands straight by his sides and Aali a few paces behind, his hand holding the gun in the pocket of his kurta. The road was bituminised and in good condition, rising steeply at first and then at a lesser gradient. The pines near the shrine gave way to mixed forest of banj oak, deodar pine and rhododendron, though grasses and introduced weeds grew along the road edges. The morning was still, but in the depths of the forest, unseen, a Streaked Laughing Thrush uttered its distinctive call. Small yellow butterflies danced in the verges, and occasionally, a larger black or brown butterfly with flashes of white and blue would dip down toward the two walking men as if investigating them. They saw no one after the first couple of minutes, and the only sounds were the tread of their feet, the call of birds and the sighing of the light wind in the trees.

"It's a beautiful day, isn't it?" Saif asked. "Even one such as you must appreciate beauty."

"Just keep walking."

Saif shrugged. "Well, I'm enjoying myself anyway."

A few minutes more brought them to the Hyundai parked on the grass verge. Aali told Saif to open the door and take off one of the door panels. While he bent to the job, Aali stepped back and kept a look out up and down the road. They were not disturbed, and within a short time, the inside door panel was off on the driver's side. He told Saif to lie down on the road and with his enemy rendered harmless for the moment, quickly checked all the circuit connections. They were all in place and had not been tampered with.

"Alright, you can get up now. Get into the car; stay on the driver's side." When Saif had done so, Aali got in behind him, his gun out again and pointed at the back of his head. He handed him the keys. "Start up and drive back into town. I'll tell you where to go."

"No."

"What do you mean, no? I'll shoot you if you don't."

"But if I do, then you'll explode it in town, killing many people."

"You have a choice. Your life or those of strangers."

"Don't you mean my life or my life *and* those of strangers? This car has no timer. As soon as the connection is made, it'll blow up. I scarcely imagine you'll let me get clear before you commit suicide. Oh, and I understand that suicide isn't a favoured action in Islam. How do you reconcile that with your intended actions?"

"It isn't technically suicide. I'm carrying justifiable war to the enemy. If I die in the process, I die as a martyr and will go straight to Paradise."

"I wonder if you really believe that."

"Enough of this talk. Either start the car or die." Aali cocked his gun.

"Well, when you put it like that …" Saif turned the ignition and put the car in gear, stamping hard on the accelerator. The car leapt forward and then screeched to a halt as Saif slammed on the brakes. Aali was thrown back and then forward, disoriented for a moment, and as he struggled to bring his gun up, his finger already tightening on the trigger, Saif grabbed for the timer connector and rammed it into the cigarette lighter socket, stopping it millimetres from the terminals. Aali saw the action and reacted to it, jerking the gun up as he fired. The bullet slammed into the roof and punched through with a metallic clap.

Aali lowered the gun and laughed. "Why do you hesitate?"

"You can drop the pretence, Aali, or whoever … no, let's say, whatever you are. Why are you here?"

"I sought a raksha, but instead I found you." Aali put the gun back in his kurta and opened his door. "Never mind, I'll try again. So, if you're going to blow us both up, do it; otherwise, I'll try again until I find what I'm looking for. He cannot hide forever."

"Oh, I'm not hiding." Saif pushed the connector home, and the car erupted in a cataclysm of white heat.

***

My name is Abdullah Nasib, but they tell me my name is Aali. I have never heard of this man, and the crime they accuse me of is horrifying, indecent even. It is not something I would ever contemplate. They tell me I masterminded a plot to kill thousands of innocent people, but I am a good Muslim and would never contemplate such an act of terrorism. Killing innocent people is expressly forbidden in the Qur'an, and in God's Name, I swear I am innocent of such heinous acts.

I found myself in a house in the Muslim slums of Meerut without any idea how I got here. I remember Mumbai – I live there and work on the trains. I am a simple man, and I have a simple job at Wadala Road Station where I am responsible for making sure the rubbish bins are emptied in a timely manner. I was on the evening shift, and I clocked out at three in the morning. The streets of Mumbai are never deserted, but that morning, they were the quietest I hava ever seen them. I walked quickly, looking forward to a meal and my bed. A man accosted me near my home. I cannot remember what he looked like except to say his eyes were blue. No, that is not right, for it was night time and the street lamps were few and far between in that part of the city. His eyes were not blue as some European's eyes are blue; rather, his eyes seemed to shine with an inner blue light like a still flame that evokes terror.

"Come with me, and I'll make you famous," he said.

I cannot remember what I replied, but he left me immediately. I stood in the street and saw the night-darkened streets of Mumbai as if they were lit by the sun. I was afraid, and that was the last I remember until I found myself in this Meerut house with the police breaking down the door.

They confronted me with the evidence in the house. They told me my fingerprints were all over the equipment and the bombs in the cellar. They read to me the evidence of the two bombers they caught in Uttarakhand and said both had identified me as the mastermind behind the scheme. The other two bombers died, and as I am supposed to have commanded them, I am to be charged with their murder. If it is true, it would be just, but I honestly cannot remember.

I sit alone in my cell and rack my brain for a single memory of this lost time and there are only two vague ones. I can recall, as my mind entered the lost time, seeing the streets of Mumbai shine with an unnatural light, and I saw something else at the other end of this time. I was disoriented as I regained consciousness, and it is likely that what I saw was no more than a dream, but for a few moments I saw myself. You can see yourself in a mirror, but this was no mirror image I saw. The man – me – smiled and turned away, and I saw him leave the room. I moved to the window of the room and looked down into the courtyard where I saw myself, foreshortened, climb into a car and drive off.

If I am not convicted of murder and terrorism, I will likely be judged insane, I know. I am sure there is a disease that involves memory loss and seeing me in two places at once. I could live with this, I think, even in jail, if it were not for the dreams. I know they cannot be real for I am only twenty-seven years old, yet in my dreams, I have memories that span thousands of years. I see myself in places I have never been, meeting people I cannot ever have met and doing things that are so horrific I wake up screaming. Maybe my conscious self slept through these last few months also, and the things they said I did I really did as another personality. If so, I have gone mad, and if they do not sentence me to death, I will pray to God they lock me up somewhere and give me drugs to prevent me thinking. I pray to God not for forgiveness, for how can I be forgiven for sins I performed while dreaming, but rather for mercy.

"In the name of God, the Beneficent, the Merciful. All praise is due only to Allah, Lord of the worlds. The Beneficent, the Merciful. From you only do I seek help." I also use the words of the Prophet Moses. "Lord! Admit me into your mercy; you are the most merciful of those who have mercy." May God have mercy on me for I am in hell.

Chapter Twenty-Eight

My immediate reaction was one of shock as the car erupted into a white-hot fireball. My thought was Saif had opted for suicide by setting off the car bomb in the hope of taking me with him. The poor fool. I was well rid of him, and I would continue my search for the raksha demon who considered Uttarakhand his personal fief. My will-engendered body vanished in the white heat, leaving behind only my essence, the still blue-green flame that hung in the air unaffected by the heat, by the blast or anything physical. I hung there in the aftermath of the explosion, watching fragments of metal, globs of molten plastic and shards of glass rain down on the road and rip through the leaves of the forest trees. Fires started but only smouldered as the vegetation retained enough moisture to resist the conflagration. The sound of the explosion rolled like a thunderclap off the hills and died away into silence. Soon, the road would be swarming with people from the town and police would be searching the wreckage, but for now the forest road was completely silent and still without even an insect moving or a bird calling. Into the silence, a voice intruded.

"Why have you come here, Djinni?"

I looked round and saw … In case you have forgotten, I will remind you that, of course, being a still blue flame I do not 'look round.' Nor do I turn, see, smell, feel, shrug, utter words or hear them, at least not as a human would understand the terms. I have my own senses which are far keener than a man's, and I hear and talk by other means which I will not describe, as you could not comprehend them. Suffice it to say, I use everyday human terms so you will understand me. Now, as I was saying …

I looked round and saw a rich golden flame hovering a few feet from me. The glow that came from it was redolent of warmth, of comfort and of peace, and I hated it the moment I saw it.

"Who are you?" I asked.

"You knew me as Saif, but I'm as much Saif as you are Aali. I know you're a djinni, so answer me. Why have you come here?"

The command in his voice gripped me with a compulsion so strong it could not be denied. "I came to find a raksha and destroy it." I watched the golden flame and saw that, unlike me, it was not completely motionless. Tongues of fire flickered subtly, yet when I stared at any part of it, it was still. Looking past it, I could see its constant motion, and I knew this was a different order of being. "What are you?" I asked.

"What raksha do you seek? How do you know of raksha? You belong in the desert wastes of Arabia."

"Islam is everywhere and where it goes, I go. As to the raksha," I said, gaining in confidence, "I saw it in these hills six hundred years ago."

I felt the being's scrutiny. "You were with Bin Tughluq?"

"Who? Oh, you mean the Sultan of Delhi? No, I came along afterward quite peaceably with a human. I saw a raksha."

"And why do you want to destroy it?"

“That’s my own business,” I started to say, but the being’s will gripped me, and I found myself answering. “Life has become dull. I’ve decided I will rid the world of demons and become a god.”

Amusement flowed from the golden flame. “You think it that easy to kill demons or to become a god?”

I shrugged mentally. “I’ve killed demons before, and I’ve been a god.”

“Show me.”

A most unpleasant feeling came over me. I felt my mind opened, and every secret of my long life laid bare. Unwillingly, I revealed my exploits, my destruction of other djinn, my masquerading as a god, even as Allah of the Muslims.

The golden flame withdrew. “To call yourself a god is not the same as being a god. I don’t imagine you ever discussed the matter with Allah.”

“Men worshipped me,” I said sulkily.

“There are fools everywhere.”

“I’ve answered your questions. Answer mine. What are you?” I radiated coercion but to no effect. The being ignored attempts to force an answer.

“And why this bombing campaign? What did you hope to achieve? Was it really as you told us in Meerut – that you believe Uttarakhand has a spiritual defence force?”

“Yes, but the defender is the raksha. The places I targeted are somehow holy to this raksha, and I hoped by destroying them I could draw him out to his own destruction.”

“It didn’t concern you that thousands of people would die?”

"Why should it? They're only humans."

There was silence for a few minutes, and I looked around. People were starting to arrive at the blast site, and though I doubted men could see me easily in the bright sunlight, I thinned my flame almost to the point of invisibility.

"You see, Djinni," went on the golden flame, "This is what troubles me – you desire to rid the world of demons, yet you're prepared to sacrifice human life to do so. I'm not sure that you aren't worse than the demons you seek to destroy."

"Who are you?" I asked again.

"I am Lord Pandalis, Destroyer of Demons."

I laughed. "A grand title. And what are you? A god?"

"Yes."

"You're not as I imagined a god."

"Oh, and how did you imagine one?"

"Grander, more imposing perhaps. I always had the impression that Allah, the real Allah, was immensely powerful, omnipotent. Not just a little flame."

"You should know that size is unimportant. And I'm not Allah, nor Jehovah, nor Brahma, nor any of the truly powerful aspects of God. As I said, I'm Pandalis, a very minor aspect of the All-Knowing. However, my function is to rid India of demons. It's a duty I take seriously."

I was worried. I had come looking for a demon and found a god. Mistakes like that could prove fatal. "I take it then you've already destroyed the demon I looked for here in Uttarakhand. You've even taken his name."

Answering with amusement again but with a tinge of self-deprecation, "Actually, I am that raksha."

"And you became a god? How does that work?"

"It's unimportant."

I felt the god's will grip me and his power grow. "Wait. If you became a god, tell me how. Maybe I can do the same."

"Examine yourself, Djinni. Your spirit reeks of the blood of men. Are you suitable god material?"

"What of yourself? A raksha is also bloodthirsty. You managed it."

The pressure on me eased a fraction. "I gave up killing many years ago, and I atoned for my past sins."

"How did you atone?"

"I started to save lives instead of taking them."

"Incredible. And you were actually a raksha? You really killed people?"

"Yes. My atonement did not come easily, but I fought against my nature and overcame it."

"You offer me hope," I said. "If you could overcome your demonic nature, then so can I. I've saved people. I can save more."

"You won't have the opportunity. I am Destroyer of Demons." I felt his power grow, a killing power if I could not prevent him.

"I throw myself on your mercy, Pandalis."

"I'll show you the same mercy you showed your victims."

"Your justice then."

"The same."

"The gods showed you mercy after six hundred years. What if they'd destroyed you when you first started to seek a better way? There'd be no Pandalis now." My mind was racing as I sought a way out of this situation. "I'm like you six hundred years ago. I seek a way out, but I don't know the way, so I make mistakes. Help me, Pandalis. Be merciful, be just."

The power around my life force was very great, but it grew no greater. "I cannot trust you," Pandalis said. "Djinn lie, especially to save their lives."

"I'm totally in your grip, Pandalis. You know you're far more powerful than I. What danger can I possibly be to you? What danger can I be to humans if I'm trying to convince you of my change of heart?"

"An hour ago, you sought to kill humans by the thousand."

"In a good cause … in what I thought was a good cause … the destruction of a raksha. I admit I was mistaken. Is there no forgiveness in you? No mercy for an honest mistake?" I waited, trying to appear suitably penitent.

After what seemed like an aeon, I felt his stranglehold ease. "I will show mercy. I won't kill you today," Pandalis said, "but there are conditions. You won't kill another human from this day forward. You'll come to me when I call you, and you won't attempt to hide from me. You'll be completely honest with me. If I catch you in a lie, I'll kill you on the spot."

I carefully hid my elation and contempt, and after a period of what looked like thoughtful consideration, I agreed to his terms. Truly this god was a neophyte if he would accept my word so readily. He had shown me mercy and in keeping with his concept of honour, would not now probe my mind to find out if I was sincere. The fool. I drifted away several metres, expecting his coercion to lash me anew, but it did not.

"I'm free to go?" I asked.

"Yes, but remember that I know the pattern of your flame, and I can find you when I want. Put aside your demonic nature, and I'll let you live. Return to it, and you'll die."

I leapt, rejoicing into the thin mountain air, up through the clouds to the eternal sunshine of the upper atmosphere, my thoughts still guarded, but my mind scarcely containing my triumph. I sped south, faster than any bird, away from this god's presence, until I found a secluded spot in the hot southern plains. I folded myself into the guise of Aali once more and set myself about with walls and warnings, attempting to hide myself. Then I cautiously put a feeler out to see if I could detect this Pandalis.

There was no trace of him in Nainital, though there seemed to be a faint shine of his flame to the north on the mountain massif of Nanda Devi. It was enough. If I could only just detect his massive energies, it was hardly likely he could detect my lesser ones. I dropped my thought guards and considered the problem that lay before me.

I had come to India to find and destroy a raksha but had encountered a god bent on my own destruction. I had evaded him for the moment by spinning a veil of lies, but unless I gave up my way of life, he would hunt me down and destroy me. I needed a plan that involved the elimination of Pandalis and anyone else who might get in my way. But how do you kill a god? Is it even possible? I sat and thought, and the thinking made me hungry. I found a farmer in a field and approached him as Aali, wondering how I could feed without alerting Pandalis.

I dared not risk a slow, painful, terror-filled death, though those deaths are the sweetest. If I gave the farmer the opportunity of prayer, Pandalis might hear of it and that would bring me to the final struggle before I was ready. So I paralysed him and snuffed out his life in an instant. I fed on the farmer's cooling body and the unconscious flaring of his dying nervous system, hating the god that had driven me to this.

It was time to use my mind to solve a problem. I am unused to being balked in my desires, but all I can do is curse the god and get on with finding a way. I will research the problem of killing a god, and I may indeed find it in India. With their hundreds of gods, surely one of them must have died at some point in their long history. I will find the way, and I will carry the battle to Pandalis; I will destroy him utterly and set myself up in his place, for I am Aali – a djinni, most powerful of the flames of Arabia, and I bow to no god, demon or man.

THE END

www.ingramcontent.com/pod-product-compliance
Lightning Source LLC
Chambersburg PA
CBHW011359010726
47495CB00009B/2693

* 9 7 8 1 7 8 6 9 5 5 9 9 9 *